# BACK TO BERKELEY

COPYRIGHT © 2025
TXu2-499-535

**Irene Scalise**



**Published By:**
Woodstock Mountain Press

**Printed in the United States of America**

**First Printing Edition, 2025**

ISBN 979-8-9996563-0-8

**Cover Concept:** Irene Scalise
**Cover Design:** Outskirts Press

# Dedication

*I would like to dedicate this book to my husband Frank, my children Gloria, Renee and Frank, my sisters Pamela, Bonnie, Laura and Amy, grandchildren Ana, Vivienne, Johnny and Isaac, my in-laws, my high school chums, Nina, Julie, Diane and Michelle, and my childhood friend, Christine.*

*-Irene Santagata Scalise*

# Table of Contents



## 2003



## 1971

# *PROLOGUE*

## January 2002

Prince Ali sat at his desk at the National Gallery of Art in Washington, DC. As a well-respected dealer in arts and antiquities, he always had much on his plate and today was no exception. Bequests, acquisitions, and preservation were his specialties, currently in the process of securing Middle Eastern treasures in danger of being looted or destroyed. Things had become unstable in his part of the world, and he wanted to protect its ancient history.

He'd gotten back to his office the day before, after celebrating the new year at his residence in Zatari, the oil-rich Middle Eastern country of his birth, with his family. His dual citizenship with the United States made it easier for him to travel back and forth, but after the events of 9/11, going through TSA became an ordeal.

He asked his long-time assistant to hold all calls today as he needed to put a dent in the paperwork built up over his absence. He muted his office phone, however the incessant blinking light of incoming calls kept distracting him so he put the phone in a drawer.

His assistant knocked at his door. Ali responded, "I've told you I needed one day of no distractions. It can wait."

"I'm sorry, Ali, but he's insistent on speaking with you immediately."

"Who is it?"

"Harold Morgan."

Under his breath, he muttered some choice words. "Tell him to call back tomorrow."

"I've told him three times and he's called right back."

Ali knew Harold wouldn't let up. He didn't respond to excuses. Ali sat back in the chair, removed his glasses and rubbed his eyes. He thought to himself, "What now?"

His assistant peeked his head through the door. "What do I tell him?"

Ali removed the phone from the drawer and said, "I'll talk to him, but no one else. I've too much to do." He looked at the phone, took a deep breath, and pushed the button on the lit line.

"Harold! It's been too long. Happy New Year. I hope your holidays were joyful."

"Hey, Princey. How've y'all been?"

"Very well, but quite busy as you can imagine. And we agreed, I don't call you Butch and you don't call me Princey.

"Still so touchy. Lighten up, Man."

"What can I do for you, Harold?"

"I've got some great news, Roomie." Whenever Harold used "Roomie," harkening back to their semester in 1971 as roommates at UC Berkeley, he wanted money.

"Wonderful! What is it?"

"Well, Roomie, I've been approached by the Republican Party to seek the presidential nomination for the 2004 election, and their polling says I can win. Y'all know what that means, right?"

Ali was shocked. How can this great country even think about electing Harold Morgan to run its government? His heart suddenly quickened, and he thought…this is it. He took a deep breath to hold his voice steady.

"So, I'm assuming you're looking for a financial donation."

"Sure am, Roomie, though we have to keep it on the Q.T., seeing how y'all are an A-rab and the good old US of A doesn't feel too kindly towards your sort at the moment. You know, attacking us on 9/11."

"Zatari is a friend to the United States and its greatest Middle Eastern ally. We're doing all we can to help root out those responsible for that horrible day. That's public knowledge."

"Yeah, but I don't want any questions about my loyalty. The Party made that clear. So, I'll expect triple my usual stipend from y'all this year. Right, Princey?"

"Right, *Butch*." Ali's tone had become icy. "I'll put my assistant right on it."

"I knew I could always count on my little buddy Ali. Make sure it's untraceable, like always."

"Anything else, Harold? I'm swamped with paperwork."

"Y'all could wish me luck."

"Of course. Good luck. I'll be following it closely."

"Thanks, little buddy. I can always count on you. G'bye."

Before Ali had a chance to respond, Harold hung up. Ali buzzed his assistant. "Could you come in here for a minute, please?"

His assistant entered the room and could tell Ali was troubled by the call. Ali looked at him for a moment, not saying a word. "Harold would like the amount of money transferred tripled. It seems he's running for president."

The two exchanged knowing looks, and Ali nodded his head and said, "Now it all begins."

# CHAPTER 1

*April 2003*

Martin Cater was in a fog. He looked around but didn't know where he was. He's unable to move and felt enclosed in something. He thought he was paralyzed until he realized he could move his hands and then his arms. He was in a tight place and felt the air quickly leaving the space he was in. He was able to see out a small window where he saw wooden beams. He seemed to be moving on what may have been an assembly line.

"Where the hell am I?" he said aloud to no one as he was alone. He kept trying to kick or punch his way out of whatever he was squashed into but didn't have enough room. "Hey!" he yelled out. "Is anyone there?" Panic started to set in and he tried to reason his mind out of it. The assembly line he was on was beginning to move at a slightly faster pace, and he didn't know where it was leading. He tried to remember where he was before being in this unyielding space, but his mind was blank.

As he moved along, he passed a sign overhead that read "Crematorium". He could no longer reason his panic away. "Help! Somebody! Help! I'm alive! Get me out of here!" He screamed and fretfully tried to punch and kick his way out of the box, which he realized was a coffin. "Get me out of here. Somebody help me!" Alarms began to go off, and Martin continued to punch and kick to get out. He was in a complete frenzy, screaming, punching, kicking, doing whatever he could to get someone's attention.

The assembly line stopped but the alarms and noise continued. He heard footsteps approaching. "Thank God! Help me!" A shadow appeared over the window. "Help me get out of here!" he screamed. "I'm alive!" There was no movement. "I'm a rich man! I'll pay you! I'm Deputy Chief of the CIA. You'll be well compensated for your assistance." The shadow moved closer.

He knew money or fear of the CIA would get whoever was out there to move to his aid. The alarms and noises continued, which was a relief as it should alert someone to this huge mistake. When he finds out how he ended up in this box, someone will pay. The shadow came closer. One more step and he'll see his savior. "Thank God you're here. Get me out of here."

A face appeared in the window. A sound of terror came out of Martin. John Pucci was looking directly into his eyes. "I told you before, Marty, I'd see you burn in hell before I'd let you use my wife for your dirty little game. Now you're going to burn in hell!" Pucci laughed, and the sound of his amusement echoed throughout the room, filling the hollow space with his darkness.

Martin screamed, "You can't stop me from using your wife! You're dead, Pucci! I killed you! Get me out of here!" Pucci continued his vengeful laughter. "My wife isn't one of your little puppets that you can pull the strings and put her life in danger for your schemes! I won't let you use her, making her Prince Ali's plaything! Goodbye Marty. Hell is waiting for you!"

He saw Pucci push a red button and Martin's death trap started moving again. He saw huge red, orange, and yellow flames up ahead getting closer and closer. He went into full-blown panic and began to cry, kick, and scream, trying to thrash his way out of the coffin. The alarms were blaring while he forcefully pounded his deathtrap, screaming and crying for someone to help him amid the sound of John Pucci's laughter.

And then he was violently shaken. "Marteen! Marteen! Wake up!"

"Deputy Cater! Wake up!" His driver/assistant Charles VanEtten and René Barrineau, the French agent specifically selected for his newest mission, were in his bedroom, shaking him awake. Martin slept with his room locked, so they broke down the door to get in. Wood was scattered throughout the room from their forced entry, with Martin's alarm clock giving off a piercing sound. His phone was beeping as there were calls from Charles, René, and his secretary trying to reach him. It took him a moment before he realized it was a dream. He was disoriented but relieved to be back in reality.

"Marteen, are you quite alright?" René asked.

"We were worried about you, Boss." Charles added, "We've been trying to reach you for a couple of hours. The office insisted we come to investigate."

"It's most unlike you, Marteen, to be late, given your intolerance for tardiness. We had the utmost concern for your welfare. When we arrived, we heard you screaming."

Hoping to lessen Martin's anger, Charles said, "I hope you don't mind, but I used the spare key you gave me to get into the apartment. We've been knocking and pounding on your bedroom door, and when the commotion continued, we thought the worst."

"I insisted we break the door down, Marteen. It sounded as though you were being tortured."

It took a few minutes for Martin to regain his bearings. What did they hear? Was he screaming out loud? Anger was building up in his chest. The last thing he wanted was to show them or anyone weakness on his part. "Charles, call Maintenance and have them pick up this mess and replace my door immediately," he barked. "That means now!" he screamed, his voice quavering.

Charles instantly left to find the Super. "Marteen, no need to treat him in such a fashion. He was concerned for your welfare."

Damn fucking Percocet, Martin thought to himself. I won't take those again! I'd rather be in pain than relive something like that! "What time is it?"

"Well, Marti, it is now 11:25 and we are quite late."

"SHIT!" Martin punched the bed. The day Martin needed to be alert and on time was the one day he overslept and was groggy from the mixture of scotch and Percocet. On top of that, Martin realized he had soiled himself and the bed linens.

Martin snapped at René, "Go turn on my coffee maker. I have to shower. When the coffee's done, I expect it to be waiting for me when I get out. I take it black." When René didn't move, Martin screamed, "What the fuck are you waiting for? Get your ass in gear and do as you're told!"

René was incredulous that Martin was speaking to him in that fashion. "First of all, I'm not your servant, your driver, your employee, or even your friend, so don't think for even the tiniest millisecond that you can speak to me in such a way. I'm certainly not to blame that you overslept, are extremely late, had a terrible nightmare, was screaming like a little girl, and pissed yourself. I'm not your whipping boy. If you want coffee, make it yourself, you miserable, worthless prick." René turned and angrily kicked some of the splintered wood out of his path, muttered something in a foreign language, and left the room.

"Fucking arrogant asshole!" Martin whispered to himself when René walked out of the room. It'll be such a pleasure to take care of him once this mission is completed, as he has his wife and daughter. Martin knew René would eventually figure out he was responsible for their deaths, so he'd have to be taken care of as soon as this mission was completed. René's expertise in Middle Eastern languages was needed for this assignment. Eliminating them was the only way to get him to agree to join the team. It's his fault they had to be removed; he got all sentimental, saying he wanted to enjoy a quiet life as a father and husband. Fuck him! As Martin struggled to get out of the wet bed linens, he smiled to himself knowing he still had the upper hand by taking the best part of René's life and removing them from this earth.

When he got to his feet, he realized his limbs were still shaking from the dream. John Pucci can't hurt me, he thought. He's dead, I saw to that. Martin tried to summon the usual feeling he'd get when he thought of a vanquished enemy, but the dream was too real and he was still shaken by it.

He hobbled to the bathroom on unsteady legs and turned the shower on. He peeled off his urine-soaked pajamas and got into the shower. His hip stung and ached, and when he looked at it, he could see the bruising was no better where Pucci shot him the night Martin killed him.

Martin had concocted a story about defusing an IED, but CIA chief Thomas Metzger was having it investigated and could find no evidence of it. Martin couldn't risk removing the bullet right now as it would confirm Metzger's suspicion that Martin's story was a lie. He and Metzger had a hate-hate relationship, so he took nothing Martin said at face value.

The hot water helped alleviate some of the trembling of his body and raw nerves, but he was still on edge. What bothered him now was René and Charles witnessed him not only screaming and crying in his sleep, but he did piss himself. He punched the shower with the side of his fist in anger. This day was getting off to a bad start.

When René heard the shower running, he went to the room farthest from Martin, making sure Charles and maintenance hadn't returned. He took a pen out of his pocket and clicked it. His pen was a sophisticated, untraceable recording device, and captured every conversation he was having with Martin including last night's briefing. It will eventually work to his advantage because knowledge is key. The US isn't the only country with innovative spying techniques and gadgets.

He listened to Martin's screams, recorded on the pen, along with everything he said during his dream. René listened carefully and was intensely attentive when Martin screamed, "You can't stop me from using your wife! You're dead, Pucci! I killed you! Get me out of here!"

Hearing Martin's words confirmed his suspicions of Cater's involvement in the deaths of his family. He killed John Pucci to get his wife for this unique mission, as he removed the obstacles stopping René. He had no proof, and the mumblings of a sleeping man would hold no water. He decided his only recourse was to garner the help of Pucci's widow. He'd have his revenge, there was no doubt. He needed the Pucci woman, but how to assure her agreement?

He looked around for some paper and used the pen for its usual purpose. He wrote something down, folded it up into a small piece, and put it in his pocket. He had a feeling he was going to need it later today when he meets the two women who've been chosen as his team.

He was irritated that Martin chose two unproven women, one who had been used by the CIA for simple tasks and the other an inexperienced, recently widowed housewife with no clandestine background. This isn't a mission for an amateur team. He's a senior field agent with a stellar record known for his success rate, not a tutor or babysitter, and it irritated him.

When Martin told him what this dangerous, relatively untried mission entailed, he thought to refuse it, but hearing "the confession of murder", he thought it might be worthwhile to meet this team before rejecting his participation. He learned some interesting things about them last evening and used his pen to refresh his memory before being picked up this morning.

He heard Charles coming with a maintenance team, so he rushed into the kitchen and sat at the table. Charles showed them the damage, gave them instructions, and left them to their work. He walked into the kitchen, looked at the coffee maker, and turned it on.

"Is that your usual duty, Charles?"

"Among many, yes."

"*C'est dommage.* Not particularly challenging for a promising young agent. I hope you're well compensated."

Charles shrugged and didn't answer. He was a junior agent, assigned as Martin's assistant. He continued his morning routine, poured a cup of coffee, and brought it into Martin's bedroom. Martin barked for his coffee and clothing to be put in the bathroom, so Charles did as instructed. Charles hated Martin, as everyone did, but was promised his help getting ahead in the Agency. Who knows if he'll keep his word?

Charles left the bedroom area and went into the kitchen with René to give Martin privacy as the bedroom door was in pieces. "I suspect we'll be leaving shortly. Thanks for your help this morning."

"Oui, Charles, the day has certainly been exciting so far, no? And it's only begun."

Martin limped into the kitchen, looking haggard. His clothes were crisp but his demeanor was shaky. He had his briefcase and was using a cane to take the weight off his hip. He announced they needed to get to the office immediately.

As they were leaving, Martin hooked René's arm with his cane and pulled him towards him, away from Charles. René recoiled from the grasp and shook the cane from his arm.

"Marteen, you're overstepping yourself again. I'm not afraid to use any of the means I have of knocking you out. Remember yourself and exactly who I am. My training was as extensive as yours, maybe more so and I'm not currently crippled. I could rip out your throat before you realize it's been done."

Martin replied, "I want you to give me your word you'll keep the events of this morning to yourself." René walked away.

As they got into the car, René started to get into the front seat with Charles. Martin snarled, "René, get in the back with me." He continued into the front seat. Martin thought how he hated the French. He swallowed hard and said, "René, please sit in the back with me. There are a few things to go over, which we'll have to do on the ride to the office. Charles, call and tell them we're on our way, and should be there shortly."

René reluctantly got into the back seat and said, "I thought we covered everything last night."

"Maybe if you weren't two fucking hours late, we would've had time to go over everything. Punctuality is paramount, and you know I insist upon it."

"Am I to control the flight from Paris and the traffic in New York City? We should have stayed later and finished last night. You're the one who cut it short. I should've followed my original instinct and told you to go fuck yourself."

"If you were on time, we would've had enough time, but you weren't."

"Maybe if you didn't oversleep, we would've had time before the meeting and not have to go over things in the car. Certainly not like the Martin Cater I know. You're slipping."

"Don't give me that shit. Your flight arrived early, and there was no traffic yesterday. I checked." That French fuck was deliberately late.

Martin was correct. René's tardiness was intentional because he knew of Martin's intense impatience and was determined to make things as difficult as possible, in the most innocent of ways. Being a Frenchman, he had ways of being charmingly annoying, and that's his plan.

He'd refused Martin three times before the accident took his wife and daughter. He'd retired from the Secret Service. He turned 50 three years ago and wanted to enjoy the life of a country gentleman with his beautiful wife Adele and sweet four-year-old daughter Mercedes. René never met anyone he wanted to spend his life with until he met Adele. Young, beautiful, intelligent, and kind, she stole his heart from the moment he set eyes on her. He wooed her and wouldn't take no for an answer because she kept refusing him, as she thought he was too old for her.

She finally relented after being deluged daily by flowers, fruit, wine, and whatever else he could discover that made her happy. After a whirlwind courtship, they started living together, and soon she became pregnant. They were overjoyed with the news and were married in a quiet ceremony, looking forward to having a family together. René couldn't believe his happiness, and before his daughter was born, he officially retired from the secret service. He now had bright sunshine in a life that had been spent in the shadows of espionage. His every waking moment was spent with "his girls", doing everything in his power to make them happy. Her doctor confirmed Adele was pregnant again. Their happiness couldn't be contained. That was all in the past. They were gone.

There was an "accident" which he never believed. Adele had driven on this road many times. It was in the countryside near Paris where they had a small country chalet, raising chickens, ducks, and goats, along with an extensive vegetable and herb garden. The gendarmes said she missed the curve. René didn't believe it. The damage to the vehicle wasn't extensive, and neither should have died. The investigation didn't find anything suspicious, but René knew there were ways to make covert actions look like an accident. His life was in shambles, and his grief and sorrow were overpowering.

Martin suggested he take the mission to take his mind off his loss; in fact, was insistent. That's when he suspected Martin killed his family for this mission and when he heard Martin admit to killing Pucci, albeit in his sleep, he was certain. Martin needed a master of Middle Eastern languages and René Barrineau was the best man suited for many reasons.

He was an extremely handsome man, tall in stature, with the inherited good looks of his Iranian/French mother and the coloring of his French/German father, who'd been an emissary to the Middle East. Having spent a good deal of his childhood bouncing back and forth between Europe and the Middle East, he learned the different languages of those parts of the world from his mother and the European languages from his father. He was fluent in eight languages. His Iranian grandfather was a professor of language at a school of higher learning for the rich and elite, and he taught his mother and uncles many different languages from birth.

René was their only child, and they had a home in Paris but traveled and lived throughout Europe and the Middle East on diplomatic assignments.

As a young man just out of college, he was recruited by the SDECE (*Service de documentation extérieure et de contre-espionnage* -External Documentation and Counter-Espionage Service) and spent many years on clandestine assignments throughout the world, using most of the languages that came naturally to him. He had collaborated with Martin in the field and found him to be exceptionally brutal and refused many assignments that included him. René knew everything there was to know about him, what pleased him, what annoyed him, and planned to use it to his advantage, starting with making him wait, his pet peeve.

His hatred towards Martin had to be masked by cordiality, and who would be better than a Frenchman to pull that off? He'd eventually throw him off his game and go in for the kill. He was certain Martin caused the accident. He removed the reasons René had continuously refused. He had no proof, but he's learned to rely on his gut feelings, which have never been wrong. Revenge would come, one way or another, and John Pucci's widow might be the key.

# CHAPTER 2

At last night's meeting, Martin started by showing René information on his team, which consisted of himself and two women, Christina Pucci and Zoe Janis. Unbeknownst to Martin, René knew Christina Pucci was wanted for this assignment but kept this to himself. He found neither woman had much experience in espionage, although one did the simple work of taking photos of certain areas and exchanging information. The other was a recently widowed housewife of an FBI agent. After looking them over, he asked, "So, Marti, please explain to me how you think two women with no field experience, plus me, can pull this off?"

Martin's irritation from waiting started to show. "First, let's get one thing straight. My name is Martin, not Marty. How many times do I have to tell you that? If you can't pronounce my name correctly, call me Deputy Chief Cater. Don't address me as Marty again, *ever!* Is that clear?" He didn't wait for a response and quickly got back to business. "I need you to be aware of all the aspects of the plan of action before tomorrow's meeting." A sharp pain struck Martin's hip, and he cried out, which irritated him as he felt it showed weakness. René moved to help him, and Martin growled, "Leave me alone! It's nothing." He took a deep breath and said, "Let's get to business."

The pain in his hip, coupled with his impatience at the two-hour delay, made him irritable and intolerant. René smiled to himself. He's getting under his skin, as planned. He intended to throw him off balance at every opportunity.

Martin started barking instructions. "Tomorrow morning, we'll meet here at 9:45 AM *sharp*! Agent Zoe Janis and Christina Pucci will be here at 10:00. They've been instructed to be prompt. I won't tolerate tardiness, and it's one of the easiest ways to get on the wrong foot with me." René immediately began to apologize again for being late, and Martin briskly brushed it off.

"Don't let it happen again," he snarled. "To ensure you're here on time, Charles will pick you up at 8:45 AM. Be ready!" He shot him a dirty look and said, "You never know when traffic will be snarled."

"Certainly, Mart*een,*" he replied, emphasizing the "n" at the end of his name.

Martin got up from his chair and winced in pain as he did. He limped to the bar and poured himself a scotch, drank it down quickly, and poured another. He asked René if he'd like something to drink, and René politely refused. It's obvious Martin was in a great deal of pain, and the scotch seemed to take off the edge, though he was trying his best to hide it.

"Did you injure yourself, Mart*een,* or is it an old battle wound?"

"It's nothing I care to discuss," he replied in a gruff voice.

"Well, you're in discomfort. I was only wondering what..."

Martin cut him off. "It's none of your business."

"You know, Mart*een,* there are excellent doctors in Paris. Come to Paris, take some time off, and let them have a look. They'll have you on your feet in no time."

René was waiting for the scotch to take effect and soften the edges and loosen the tongue. "An agent such as yourself, who has given so much for his country, with a record of success and so many years in the field, should have the best of care when he needs it, no?" He waited for an answer and got none, so he continued. "Did you have a skiing accident this past winter? The Alps are a wondrous place to ski. Do you ski, Mart*een?*"

"Enough!" he screamed and slammed his fist on the bar. "I don't ski and I didn't break my hip." He hobbled with the bottle and his glass and gently lowered himself into the seat at his desk and said, "It seems I vastly underestimated an adversary." This statement shocked René because he wasn't expecting a reply.

"An adversary? I thought you were out of the field."

"I am out of the field, but that doesn't mean I don't have enemies.

"Oui, Mart*een,* in our line of business, we've made many enemies through the years and probably continue to do so." The two men stared at each other.

Martin downed his scotch and poured another. He hated sympathy, but at least there was someone who recognized his worth. Too bad he hated the French.

The scotch settled in, and the pain in his hip started to subside. He downed his third and poured another. There were still things to discuss with René before the meeting tomorrow. He checked the time. He was expecting someone in half an hour, so their meeting got cut short.

René broke the silence. "How do you think this inexperienced duo will be able to do what needs to be accomplished? I'm not a tutor or babysitter."

Martin sneered, "It's a mission unlike any you've done before. I'll explain fully tomorrow. It's quite involved, and I don't intend to repeat myself. To answer your question, being French, you know the saying '*cherchez la femme*'?"

"Of course, but it's unlike you to employ women for your operations, being inferior in your thinking. What's different this time?"

Martin licked his lips, snickered, and opened a locked drawer in his desk. He pulled out a folder with photographs, opened it and presented it to René. "A little pussy to sweeten the pot. My ace in the hole, so to speak."

René opened the folder and saw several photographs of a girl, from the styling of the hair and clothing, looked like the late 60's/early 70's. A few photos were enlargements of a group at an art gallery with a familiar-looking Middle Eastern man, and the woman next to him was circled in red.

"Mart*een*, please explain." Martin laughed, and it sent a chill up René's spine.

"All these photos," he explained as he referred to one group of photos, "are of our little widowed housewife, Christina Pucci. These photos," pointing to the group shots, "are Princess Saadiya, wife of Prince Ali El-Machmud of Zatari. Photos of her are extremely rare. I've had her face enlarged. Even with my connections, these were the only ones I could procure. You know how those Arabs feel about photographs. Those two women could be twins."

"That's impossible! Are you sure it's not the same woman?" René looked at the photos and could hardly believe his eyes. There were several copies of the group photo in various stages of enlargement. He grabbed the magnifying glass off Martin's desk and used it to compare the two women. The wife of Prince Ali and Christina Pucci were nearly identical, with only very slight differences. Mrs. Pucci had a playful ease and innocence not evident in the princess, most likely from being an American, but the resemblance was uncanny.

"I'm positive. I learned the prince and his wife met after his semester at Berkeley. Pucci is his type. Prince Ali will be drawn to her.

She's the carrot we need to put under his nose and is the only option for this mission. This information is for your eyes and ears only and not to be shared with your fellow agents, especially the Pucci woman. Is that clear?"

René eyed Martin suspiciously, and things began to make sense. He needed them both to make this mission work, and he removed what stood in his way. He'll need Christina Pucci as an ally. "I must say, Marteen, it's most coincidental and advantageous for you that John Pucci is dead, for if he were alive, he'd never allow his wife to be put in such a situation. Exactly what were the circumstances of his death? An accident on a country road?" René took an intimidating step closer to Martin.

Martin shot him a filthy look, and René noted a fleeting image of fear on his face. "How would I know how he died? He's FBI. We don't get involved in each other's shit."

"I see. Don't you think it's perilous for a civilian? She's not trained, certainly not for a CIA mission." René didn't like where this was headed. "You said these women wouldn't be in danger, but Christina Pucci, with her striking resemblance to Princess Saadiya, will be put squarely in the prince's bullseye. Whatever you're planning, it's a waste of time. From what I know of Prince Ali, he's devoted to his wife. He's not going to have a dalliance with another woman, no matter how much she looks like his wife."

"When we all meet tomorrow, I'll explain the mission and you'll understand the plan."

"No, you'll explain now, or I'll go back to France tonight."

"I don't want to have to go over this twice. I'm not going to get into the specifics, but this mission involves time travel, and the three of you and a backup team will be going back to 1971, UC Berkeley in California. I'll give you the details tomorrow. This is a once-in-a-lifetime opportunity. It's a secret program developed by a wunderkind in his day. It's been tested, perfectly safe, and used by the CIA several times."

"Time travel? Are you out of your mind? Our mission is in 1971? No, I don't agree to this. It's too dangerous."

"You're not listening! I fucking told you, it's perfectly safe and has been used on several occasions." That part was untrue. It seemed safe, but it had only been used twice. Martin had no intention of telling

René everything. He needed him on this mission, and besides, he's got nothing to go home to.

"What equipment will we have to achieve success? It's too dangerous. Time travel? *A quoi tu penses, putain?*" René was pacing the floor with an angry expression on his face, muttering in French.

"Calm down! It's all taken care of. That's what your backup is for. They'll have what you need. I'll explain everything further tomorrow." Martin's irritability was showing. "I don't need to answer questions more than once and I'm sure those bitches will have a lot of them."

"But, surely you see the danger this presents. Members of Middle Eastern royal families have diplomatic immunity and are protected by the US government when they're in the US, not to mention their disregard for women. They won't be safe, especially in 1971. If they were more seasoned agents and knowledgeable in self-protection, they'd have a chance, but they'll be, how do you say… sitting ducks!"

"That's why you're needed to keep an eye on things and serve as their guides and protectors, along with listening to conversations Prince Ali has with his countrymen."

"And what happens if things go wrong in 1971? It's too dangerous."

"You'll have a top-notch back-up team. Factors come into play with time travel, and our window of opportunity for success is from August to December. After that, the situation is no longer viable, and we'd have to wait another year. The time is now. It has to be before Morgan gets the Republican nomination for president. That means this year."

"Is it that important that you must put two women in danger? What's the ultimate goal?"

Martin started to laugh that bone-chilling cackle that sickened René. He looked at the Frenchman and said, "Harold William Morgan is the front runner for the Republican nomination for president of the United States. He has enough money, power, influence, and the public's support to win in November. We need to begin the process of ending his political future by proving he's a draft dodging, treasonous, dim-witted rich boy who betrayed his country, exchanged secret documents with a foreign government, and prove, that's the important word here, *prove* all this is true.

"The prince and Morgan were roommates, so we need an in with them. The prince will be a teenage boy who won't be able to resist the scent of a woman, especially on his first time away from the constraints of his culture. I'm banking that a woman will be his weakness and Christina Pucci fits the bill.

"Morgan's family has gained power and money over the last few decades, and a large portion of it came because of their relationship with the Zatari Royal Family, starting immediately before Prince Ali and Harold were roommates for that one semester at Berkeley. Harold's father, Bradley Morgan, was a political powerhouse and headed a branch of the CIA at one time. It was pre-arranged for his son and the prince to be roommates."

"So, you think pillow talk with the prince will doom the Morgans?" asked René. "That's absurd!"

"Not necessarily pillow talk, but Christina Pucci and Zoe Janis will have access to their dorm, and every teenage boy is a skirt chaser. Pucci is the prince's type, and he'll home in on her immediately.

"With your placement as a foreign exchange student in the same suite of rooms, it'll make things that much easier. We'll have intelligence and surveillance materials available to all of you, and I believe we'll easily get the proof needed to bring down Harold Morgan."

A small buzzer went off, and Martin said, "Enough for tonight. My driver will bring you to your hotel and pick you up on the way tomorrow." It sounded to René like a dismissal. Martin picked up his cell phone and called Charles.

"Mr. Barrineau is ready to be taken to his hotel. He's coming down now. I'll call you when I'm ready to leave." Martin struggled to get up and held out his hand for René to shake. "We'll resume our briefing tomorrow with Janis and Pucci and go over some of the finer points and explain what's expected. No sense in doing it twice. This is a one-of-a-kind mission. Very few are given the opportunity this "Operation Berkeley" mission offers. Remember, my driver will pick you up at 8:45 AM sharp!"

"But time travel, Marteen? Are you sure it's safe?"

"Positive. Nothing for you to worry about. The success of this mission will ensure this country isn't led by a treasonous buffoon. We'll go over more of it tomorrow."

They shook hands, and he walked René to the door. René knew Martin was meeting someone else now; why else would he have been given the bum's rush? He thought about sticking around to find out what Martin was up to but decided to let it go for now. He got on the elevator, rode down to the ground floor, got into the waiting car, and was taken to his hotel. As soon as he sat in the car, he realized how tired he was and was looking forward to a good night's sleep.

Martin opened the back door, and a man walked into his office. He had a medical bag with him and, without talking, took out a vial and a syringe and gave Martin a shot in the hip. A look of relief came over Martin's face, and he thanked the man, who was a doctor the CIA used for certain situations, such as gunshot wounds, and wounds occurring during undercover activity. These doctors employed by the agency don't report such injuries to the authorities.

The two men were old acquaintances having served together in Vietnam in the Army Rangers. "How'd the briefing go?" asked the doctor.

"Better than expected. Things are moving in a successful direction."

"So, the puppet-master once again is quite adept at pulling the strings?" the doctor asked.

"Quite adept." The two of them laughed. "I'm feeling jubilant!"

The doctor handed Martin three bottles of pills. "One bottle is OxyContin, another is Percocet, and the third is an antibiotic. There's no weakness in taking these. We have to keep an eye on the bullet and fragments. As soon as they've moved to a place where we can access them, you need to have them removed and your hip replaced. You can't continue for very long with your hip in the shape it's in now."

Martin looked at him and said, "When this mission is over, I'm all yours. I can't do anything until they're back with the information I need."

"Take a Percocet now. You look haggard, worn, and in pain. This will help you get a good night's sleep tonight, and you'll be ready to chew everyone up in the morning." They laughed.

Martin swallowed a Percocet with the rest of his scotch. They talked for a few minutes, the sort of chit-chat of old friends discussing the Yankees' chances of making it to the playoffs, some politics, and the whereabouts of some of the old gang from the army. After twenty minutes or so, the doctor left, and Martin made a phone call.

"All set for tomorrow?"

"Yes. I've checked out the place and can easily disable the alarm. It will be done by three at the latest. "

"I'll be in touch tomorrow. Even if you find the pistol, lay the insects."

"Gotcha. Should be a piece of cake. Talk to you tomorrow."

Martin smiled. Everything was going exactly as planned. He put all the files into his briefcase and called for Charles, who had returned from dropping off René. He rode down the elevator, slipped into the back seat, and felt quite self-satisfied with the events of the day.

Yes, the puppet-master once again had the power to control all the strings. He masterfully manipulated all the players or puppets, as he liked to refer to them, and those who stood in the way of success were eliminated. What fools they were to think he wouldn't get exactly what he was after, and that included which puppets he'd be using. Sometimes collateral damage is necessary. Martin will sleep well tonight.

He must've slept too well because he overslept, and now they're late for their 10:00 appointment with the two women and the backup team. Charles called the office and told them they're on their way as instructed and Martin took out two folders from his briefcase and handed them to René. In the first folder were photos and intelligence regarding Zoe Janis. René instantly liked what he saw. "She's very well put together, no?" He looked over the information in the folder and flipped through the pictures, some recent and some from the early 70s. There were pictures of Zoe and Danny, her deceased husband. René felt a pang of sadness for her loss, for they were a beautiful couple. "No children?" René asked.

"None," replied Martin.

"A shame, such handsome people. Their child would've been stunning." Martin hated sentiment and groaned his distaste for it.

René opened another folder and recognized Christina Pucci from last night's briefing. The first few photos showed a very vibrant, happy, and beautiful woman, some with her husband, and some photos with her three children as they grew. Even as the years progressed, she remained quite lovely. It was obvious to René when the photos were more recent. Her eyes seemed empty, and deep sadness seemed to envelope her, and she looked like she'd aged.

"Ah, see what happens when your beloved is taken from you?" René said sadly.

"Yeah, that's life, René. That's what happens in this business. When you're careless, you die."

René stared at this unfeeling monster and said, "Marti, you're a mean and selfish prick. I'm starting to despise you."

"Like I care how you feel towards me. Our objective today is to get these two bitches to agree to this mission. And from the looks of Pucci, I can't see why she wouldn't want to relive some younger days. We can entice her with a semester of college, as she was never able to attend.

"She was Christina SantaLucia, and her father was a controlling Italian who didn't want to waste money on his children's education. Hell, he thought his daughters would get married anyway, so why spend the money on college, which is exactly what Pucci did." Martin leafed through the folder. "Too bad because she's extremely intelligent. A semester scholarship to Berkeley should be of great interest to her. We have her taking art courses, which will pique her interest immeasurably and serve our purpose. We know she's on the board of directors of her city's art museum."

Martin pulled out another photo, this time of a very handsome, dark young man. He handed the photo to René. "And of course, from our meeting last night, you know this is Prince Ali in the early 70s. The prince went to Berkeley for a semester to study art before studying in Europe. He went on to become a mover and shaker of the art world and procured many works of art and antiquities, helped with the formation of the D'Orsay Museum in Paris, and founded the Museum of Art in Zatari. He has been the Cultural Attaché for much of the Middle East. The art museum in their capital city holds a treasure trove of many works of art, especially historic Middle Eastern pieces. It also has a few paintings by Impressionists, Dutch Masters, Renaissance Era, along with some Byzantine art, a Picasso or two, along with a Jackson Pollack, all of which were purchased through Ali. I can't believe he bought some of that Modern crap. It's blotches and shapes, and they call that shit art.

"Prince Ali was very intellectual and appreciative of all aspects of art and his family had the money to purchase it. He tried to bring culture to those savage nomads." René shot him a dirty look after that remark which Martin ignored and went on. "Your knowledge of the Middle East and its languages will be invaluable to us, and Pucci's knowledge of art will be invaluable to Ali. They can be study buddies. I'm sure she'll enthusiastically sign on for this assignment. Look at her now! I'm sure she'd welcome a chance to see a better reflection in the mirror. Look at that face! She looks at least 70 years old."

"Have you been secretly photographing her in her grief? You're truly a repulsive man, and you sicken me. Why would you intrude on her mourning and invade her privacy in this manner?" René asked, but he knew the answer. Martin loved to see the suffering he caused.

"We needed a visual of what Pucci looks like now. She's our main target. Janis will go along with any assignment. Use your French charm on the old bag and get her to agree." Martin took the folders from René.

"And what if my French charm doesn't work?" asked René. Martin didn't answer.

They pulled up to the office, and Charles let them out at the front door and parked the car. As the two men walked in, the receptionist jumped out of her seat and announced that Deputy Cater and Agent Barrineau had arrived.

There was a woman with her back to them on the phone. Her sensuous silhouette caught René's eye immediately. She had beautifully shaped, well-defined legs, standing with them crossed at the ankles, a stance René found to be extremely erotic. When she turned around, he was taken aback. Agent Zoe Janis was incredibly beautiful with a European quality to her features. She was impeccably dressed in a navy Chanel suit and looked much younger than her age. The photos Martin showed him didn't do justice to the woman standing in front of him.

She quickly ended her phone conversation and waited for the two men. René walked ahead of Martin and went right up to her and introduced himself. "Bon jour, Madame. René Barrineau at your service." He took her hand and kissed it. "I believe if you accept this assignment, we'll be working together." Their eyes locked in on each other, and he was instantly reminded of Adele's. Was it the color, the shape, or the twinkle?

Martin hobbled over and held out his hand to shake. "Deputy Chief Cater. And I presume you're Agent Janis?"

"Yes," she said, shaking his hand. "But please, call me Zoe unless protocol demands more formality. It's a pleasure to meet you, Deputy Chief. I've been looking forward to our meeting."

Martin looked around. "Where are Pucci and Agents Needham and Holbrook?"

The receptionist quickly answered, "Mrs. Pucci is in the ladies' room and Holbrook and Needham couldn't wait any longer. They apologized but had an eleven o'clock appointment pertinent to this assignment that couldn't be changed. They left you the information you needed," and handed him a folder. "Would you like me to send Mrs. Pucci up to your office when she returns?"

"No, we'll wait a few minutes for her."

René took this time to get better acquainted with Zoe and was delighted she was fluent in French and three other languages. They had much in common, and their conversation seemed very much at ease. Martin disliked how effortlessly it was for René to mingle with anyone. Martin was never relaxed with people he'd just met, which was probably one of the reasons he was always gruff in his manner. It masked the insecurity he felt, especially around beautiful women.

He looked at his watch and was becoming visibly aggravated. "Where the hell is she? Did you tell her we were on our way?"

"Yes, sir, but she insisted I show her to the ladies' room."

Martin kept looking at his watch. After seven minutes, his anger was palpable. "She's being quite discourteous! Doesn't she know I'm a busy man?"

"Yes, sir. I tried to dissuade her but she was adamant."

Martin had had enough. "We're going up to my office. I've no intention of staying here waiting for her. Hold all my calls and absolutely no interruptions. When she finally decides to emerge, show her up to my office. Ms. Janis, René, follow me." This day started out badly for Martin and it was continuing a downhill spiral with every passing second. He was infuriated by this woman. How dare she?

Zoe was reluctant to leave her friend behind but felt obligated to follow. They rode the elevator to the second floor and entered Martin's office. Martin asked Zoe about some of her travels and the missions she'd done in the past. Martin and Zoe kept looking at their watches. After fifteen minutes, Martin picked up his phone and buzzed the receptionist downstairs.

"Did she leave the building?" After listening to her response, he said in a gruff manner, "Go and find that woman and bring her up immediately."

Zoe piped in, "I'm sorry, Deputy Cater, for this delay. I can't imagine what's keeping her." Zoe was lying through her teeth. She knew exactly what Christina had up her sleeve. She knew her like a book. After all, they've been close friends all their lives.

The phone rang and Martin picked it up. He listened to the receptionist and his face went from red to purple. While Zoe was feeling dread, René was enjoying the whole scenario completely. "*Jesus Christ Superstar*? Tell her I'm not waiting for the end of side two!" and Martin slammed down the phone.

Zoe jumped up. "She's not singing in there, is she?"

Martin exploded, "YES SHE IS! She's locked herself in and says she's not coming out until she gets to the end of side two!"

"I'll be right back," Zoe said as she rushed out of the room. René started to laugh.

"Well, let's hope they don't decide to sing a duet." René was thoroughly amused by this Pucci woman. He hadn't met her yet and knew he was going to enjoy collaborating with her. She was getting under Martin's skin and destroying his nerves with no effort. He couldn't wait to meet her. This was going to be an interesting day.

# CHAPTER 3

"Tee! Stop pacing and sit down! Can you be still for *one minute*?" Zoe Janis was on the phone with her staff at *La Fashionista,* a world-renowned fashion magazine based in New York City, where she was a layout editor and translator. This was the only magazine circulated in all the fashion capitals of the world with an in-house language expert. She kept getting distracted by Christina's endless fidgeting.

Christina stopped pacing, shot her a dirty look, and said, "One minute? Sure! Two hours, *HELL NO*! We're going to be waiting here all day. They have no idea where this Cater guy is!"

"How would you know that?"

She pointed to the receptionist and said, "I've been listening to calls she's making, and they can't reach him. He's not answering his phone."

Zoe smiled broadly. "Wow! Really? See? You're perfect for this sort of work. Look at you, using your powers of sneakiness to gather information." She started laughing. "All the spying you did on your old boyfriends is being put to good use. Be a good girl and sit down. You're embarrassing me." She patted the seat next to her like she was trying to entice an ill-behaved child.

"Up yours, Zee! I should've never called you after getting your ridiculous telegram. How stupid I was to fall into your trap." She whispered loudly, "CIA? Really? What the hell are you trying to get me into? Whatever it is, the answer is no. I should've never left Cheetaqua. I'm such an idiot! I swear, I could punch your face in!"

"How many times have I heard that before? Come and sit."

"I could've brought my book so I'd have something to do besides look at these ugly, blank walls!" she hissed, continuing to pace.

"Sorry, Tee. You can't bring 'The Key to Rebecca' to CIA headquarters. Not cool bringing a spy novel here."

"Why? It might give me pointers for whatever hairbrained scheme you're trying to get me into. I'm not feeling agreeable right now, so I have half a mind to march out that door."

"Yeah? And where would you go? You're such a hometown girl, with no clue how to get around in New York. I'd need the CIA to find you. Come and sit."

"Screw you, Zee! If you think I'm going to agree to do *anything* for the CIA, especially after this interminable wait, you're wrong. They're like the FBI, using people with no thought of their safety, family, or lives. I'm wasting my time here. I should've stayed home."

"Then you wouldn't have gotten your fabulous makeover. Look at how great you look. You were really looking like an old bag lady. Stop being disagreeable."

Christina flipped her the bird and resumed pacing, doing a slow burn, her anger and irritation increasing with each passing minute. They've been at the CIA New York office for over two and a half hours, waiting for the deputy chief to show up for their ten o'clock appointment. She had no idea why they were requested, and neither did Zoe. Her husband John, was recently killed while working for the FBI, so she had no warm feelings toward government law enforcement agencies. Now she's stuck here, and after more than two hours, she's losing her cool.

At Zoe's insistence, they arrived at nine-thirty, and it was well after noon. Christina was extra grouchy because she was awakened at the crack of dawn after spending a sleepless night because of Zoe's revelation that she works for the CIA. Not anything dangerous, she said, taking photos and exchanging information. With her job at the magazine, she wasn't suspicious and could get into places others couldn't.

Christina argued that Zoe had no idea if she'd done anything dangerous, which caused a minor disagreement. Christina wished she had ignored the telegram, but Zoe isn't someone to be ignored for long.

She'd been calling Christina incessantly for the last three weeks, but after John's death, Christina wasn't talking to anyone, including her best friend. She disconnected her answering machine and shut off her cell phone. She remained holed up with her trusty mini poodle, Sam, and would only open the door to her children. She crawled into a hole and stayed there for months. Her marriage was full of love, laughter, fun, and some great sex. She couldn't face the rest of her life without him. It was too much to bear, and nothing could bring her out of her deep, depressing mourning.

Zoe finally sent a telegram with the message "Ya wanna go on a trrrrrrip?" That was their secret code for some sort of mischief. It worked. She wondered what Zoe had up her sleeve and called her shortly after the telegram arrived.

Zoe insisted that she come to New York and would explain all about the adventure when Tee arrived. Christina agreed out of curiosity because Zoe dreamed up some fun and crazy shenanigans over the years and was being very mysterious about what was planned. Zoe insisted it would help her get out of her depression and bought her a train ticket for the next day. On the 4-hour train ride while watching the countryside of New York State pass by, she mused on how she had gotten to this point in her life and her friendship with Zoe over the years.

Zoe Janis and her family moved to the central New York town of Cheetaqua from Brooklyn, to a house two doors down from Christina in a newly built neighborhood in 1958. They were both five years old, and from their first meeting, the die was cast.

They became fast friends from the day the Janis family moved in, spent all their days and some of their nights together, and the fabric of their friendship grew stronger with each passing year. Christina, affectionately known as Tina, was "Tee," and Zoe was "Zee," and they were inseparable.

They went through school together, swooned over the Beatles, shared secrets, heartaches, and joys, found rock and roll, dabbled in pot and alcohol, survived supreme acts of stupidity, and dated the same boys. Both were big in personality and beautiful in different ways. Zoe looked European with green oval-shaped eyes and long light brown hair. Christina looked Italian with huge brown eyes, long dark brown curly hair, which she struggled to keep straight. Their first separation was when Zoe went to NYU while Christina, who was the class salutatorian with numerous awards and scholarships, was stuck in Cheetaqua, unable to convince her father to let her go away to college.

Her dad, an old-fashioned son of immigrant Italians, was blessed with five daughters and twin sons. He didn't graduate from high school, yet became extraordinarily successful, so he saw no need for his daughters to attend college. Her mom was a homemaker of Irish descent, busy raising seven children, never questioning her husband's decisions.

The unrest on college campuses, students protesting the Vietnam War, and the Kent State shootings reinforced her father's decision regarding college. Without parental supervision, she might get into trouble, drugs, or worse yet, teenage pregnancy. So, while Zee was going to NYU studying journalism and languages, Christina was stuck at home.

She dreamed of being an art historian. She discovered art when she saw a collection of paintings in the New Yorker Magazine as a young child. She was obsessed, studied them, concocted stories for each one, and taught herself to draw. Her "special pictures" opened her eyes to art and envisioned seeing them in person someday, giving birth to her great love of Impressionism. After an argument with one of her brothers, he destroyed the magazine.

Cheetaqua had an art museum with a school, and it became her refuge, taking all the art classes offered. Art opened doors for her imagination and eventually gave her a career.

As her high school senior honor society project, she developed a children's program for the museum and started the implementation of it during her senior year, starting in January 1971. It was an instant success. Christina would be up early on Saturdays, take the bus to the museum, and spend the morning teaching art to little ones.

During the second half of her senior year, she was burning the candle on both ends, with her children's art program, a part-time job at the library, term papers, and cramming for Regents exams. She had an active social life with her high school chums, along with helping to plan the events for graduating seniors. Her library paychecks and high school awards went into a savings account to pay for night classes at the local community college. If her parents wouldn't agree to college, she'd do it herself.

After graduation, she was diagnosed with mononucleosis and put on bed rest. It stymied her plan to attend the community college. Zoe, too, had to delay her first semester when she was in a car accident and suffered a severe concussion. She stayed with her auntie, who lived in Brooklyn, to convalesce. They wrote letters back and forth because long-distance calls were expensive.

Christina had a slow recovery and spent most of her time reading books on Impressionism from the library. She pored through those books and could find nothing on "her paintings". By Christmas, she was feeling more energized.

In late December, the president of the museum offered her a full-time position running the children's program she created, building a summer program, and becoming a docent for school field trips. She readily accepted, keeping her part-time job at the library. They were across the street from each other and could easily go from one to the other. She started in early 1972, putting college on hold as she needed to ease back slowly for fear of a relapse. It was at the library where she met John Pucci, and everything changed.

It was summer, 1972, one of the hottest days of the year. She left the climate-controlled museum and, walking across the street, the humidity instantly turned her long hair into a mass of curls. There was no air conditioning in the library, only free-standing fans. Few students needed research help in the summer, so her task was returning books to their shelves. On her way to the second floor, she stopped in front of one of the fans, closed her eyes, letting the breeze overtake her, lifting her shirt, moving her head, shaking her curls to cool off. A coworker joined her and thinking no one was in the library, they started to talk and giggle, cooling off, playing with the distortion of their voices.

John Pucci was interning at the local FBI office, enrolled in Cheetaqua University for his master's degree in criminal science in the fall. He was a gadget guy, fascinated by mediums of intelligence. He was researching new instruments of technology when he heard the playfulness of the girls, drawing his attention. One of their voices seemed uncannily familiar. Where did he hear it before? He was intrigued and had to see the face that went with that voice. He peeked over the balcony, watching them. It was the girl with the long curly hair blowing behind her. It was her voice catching his attention, and she was a knockout. He had to meet her.

The head librarian came rushing in, ordering them to stop the foolishness and get back to work. Christina headed up to the second floor to put away the books and straighten out the tables. As she turned into one of the aisles, she was startled when John Pucci popped his head out from the stacks and said, "Hi! How are you doing?"

Christina jumped and dropped the books, which he helped pick up, apologizing for startling her. She, in turn, apologized for disturbing his studies and was mortified he witnessed her shenanigans with the fan, explaining she thought the library was empty. He said they could make it up to each other by getting a burger after she leaves work. She sized him up, wondering if he had ulterior motives. In this time of free love, Christina had no intention of being a part of that. She thought he was a major hunk with a winning smile, looking awfully cute in his tight jeans and cropped shirt. She agreed, and he continued his research while she finished her shift. She insisted on walking to the White Castle restaurant a block from the library, not wanting to get into his car.

The bells from the oldest church in Cheetaqua started ringing, playing a song for the 5:00 pm hour. Christina told John she had a thing for church bells and always stopped to hear the tunes they played. As they walked, they told one another a little more about themselves. He told her she had a sexy voice and asked if anyone ever told her that. She laughed and replied that no one ever said that to her. He kept saying she seemed familiar to him and wondered if they'd met before and kept asking if he knew her through his roommate, Bobby. She was certain they'd never met, for she would've remembered him and didn't know anyone named Bobby Sanderson.

That first burger was the beginning of their great love story. They had a special song that came out soon after they started dating, and it became "their song." They danced to it on their wedding day and whenever John was away with work, he'd sing it to her over the phone before saying goodnight. On every anniversary, they'd re-enact their wedding dance, sway, and kiss to their special song.

They were a perfect match that complemented one another. Their relationship was full of love and mutual respect. They built a beautiful life together, had three children, two daughters and one son, and the romantic thrill never left them until the moment Christina opened the door to two police officers who came to tell her John had been shot and killed. She couldn't bear to hear their song anymore and turned the radio off if it came on.

She crawled into a hole, and going to see Zoe in New York was the first time she'd been out of the house for more than a grocery run or to walk the dog. She wondered if she was making a mistake venturing out to New York. Zee could be so bossy, and if Christina decided she didn't want to take part in her scheme, Zee could be worse than an annoying brat to get her own way.

As the train pulled into the city, she thought, "Curiosity killed the cat. I wonder what it's gonna do to me." She grabbed her bag, which held the clothes Zoe instructed her to bring. It was something she always did when Tee visited her.

"I'm a big shot in the fashion world! I can't be seen running around New York with a country bumpkin." Christina would reply with the usual, "I swear, Zee, I could punch your face in!"

True to form, as soon as Christina was greeted by her friend at the train station, the first words out of her mouth were, "Oh, Jesus, Tee! You look like shit! I can't be seen with you looking like that! It's much worse than I thought. It's a good thing I made an appointment for you with my hairdresser."

"Wow! Can you say hello first? Thanks Zee. Way to bolster my fragile ego."

"You know I love you. Come on, let's make you beautiful again."

Christina was treated to a full beauty treatment and didn't realize how much she needed a makeover. She had a feeling there was an ulterior motive for all this attention. She was thankful but kept asking what was going on. Zoe kept mum about it, saying she'd explain over dinner.

They had dinner delivered to Zoe's apartment. While eating, Zoe said very seriously, "Tee, I've something to tell you. Less than a handful of people know this, so it's in the strictest confidence. You have to swear to keep it to yourself."

Christina stopped chewing. "Zee, you're scaring me. If it's something bad, don't tell me. I can't take any more heartache right now, especially losing you."

"No, Tee, it's nothing like that, as I told you before, we have an opportunity for something fabulous."

"Gee, fabulous and a secret? You're no fun!"

Zoe blurted out, "For the last 15 or more years, I've been an undercover agent for the CIA."

As soon as the initial shock wore off, Christina burst into uncontrollable laughter. Zoe got irritated because she couldn't stop laughing. "Oh, Zee! You crack me up!"

"Tee, I'm serious, stop laughing and listen to me." That made Christina laugh harder with tears rolling down her cheeks. She tried to stop, but the thought kept coming back, and she couldn't contain herself. Zee? CIA? Ridiculous!

Zoe was getting irritated. "Ha, ha, very funny. You've had your laugh, now it's time to listen. Stop right now!" Christina managed to stop, but not for long. She made a motion of a spy opening his jacket to show a gun, badge, or whatever they have on the inside of their jackets, and said, "Zoe Janis, *Super Spy*!" and started laughing all over again.

Zoe sat there giving Christina that impatient look she'd give when Tee was annoying the hell out of her, which was often during their long friendship. Christina had a crazy sense of humor and was always playing around, which sometimes made Zoe impatient. "I'll wait until you can act like an adult." Christina started to get her composure, then "Zoe Janis, *Super Spy*!" would pop into her head, and laughter would begin anew.

The look on Zoe's face was a laugh killer, so Tee tried her best at being serious. "Ok. I'm under control." She sucked in her cheeks, took a deep breath, stifled a smile and a laugh, and with a serious look said, "Tell me what you need to say," and prayed for composure.

"Are you through?" Zoe's irritation was evident.

"I'm sorry, really, but…" She started to laugh again.

"I knew you were going to laugh like an idiot!"

"Zee, what did you expect when you threw something so insane at me? Really! CIA? Undercover agent? Zoe Janis, *Super Spy*? Come on!"

Zoe got serious. "You know I do a lot of traveling. I've traveled for the magazine to some very exotic locations, and Danny and I went everywhere. Before we went on our Moroccan, Turkish, and Middle Eastern trip in the nineties, I was approached at *La Fashionista* by a member of the CIA. He asked if I'd exchange documents with other agents who were acting as tourists and take photos of certain locations in specific areas of buildings and places of interest to the United States.

"I know it's hard to believe, but I've had assignments on almost every trip I've taken since my first contact with the CIA. And I'm well compensated for my efforts. As a tourist couple, when Danny and I traveled, or when representing the magazine, I'm not a suspicious person and my camera is expected. The contacts I have with document exchanges are either other tourist-like individuals or people within the fashion industry. I've helped gather intelligence to keep our country safe, and after 9/11, we need all the intelligence we can get."

Christina was shocked. "You're serious!"

"Very serious. What I've been doing so far is exactly what I mentioned. I haven't done anything dangerous or…"

"That you know of."

"Tee, I haven't done anything dangerous."

"You don't know that. From what I've seen with John, our government is flippant when it comes to people's lives. They don't care who's in danger, as long as they get what they're after."

"It's not like that with me."

"Don't kid yourself, they'd sell you out in a heartbeat."

Zoe looked pensive and replied, "No, I don't think so."

"You're being so naïve! People are expendable. Look at all the young men and women who are currently dying in Middle Eastern wars, and how the wounded soldiers are treated upon returning with horrific wounds, inside and out. Don't you remember the Gulf War? For God's sake, I've lost my husband for this country and let's not forget, even though it was over forty years ago, my brother George was killed in Vietnam, and nobody gave a shit."

Zoe changed the subject. "The reason I've asked you to come here is I've been contacted by the deputy chief of the New York office, and they want us, specifically you and me, for my next assignment." She took out the letter stating where and when to report and showed it to Christina.

"Nope! No frickin' way am I doing *anything* that would remotely be an assignment for our government. I'm living with the results of one right now. I can't believe you'd ask me to do something like this. Does this 'Martin Cater' know I lost my husband? I'm not going to put myself in danger when I'm the only parent my kids have."

"Tee, I was told there's no danger. We'll be going to a college and it's important. They said it'd be a way to relive our youth." She turned on the Zee charm. "Come on! Let's go tomorrow and hear what they have to say. What could it hurt?"

"Oh, now I understand your plan. That's what the big deal is tomorrow, and why I had to get this makeover. Were you told to do that, too? What, they don't want an old bag who's in mourning to remind them my husband was killed doing their dirty work?"

"This is the CIA. John worked for the FBI."

"Oh yeah, right! They're worse!"

"Let's go to the meeting and hear what it's about. We can have the chance to relive our youth. Doesn't that intrigue you? Aren't you the teeniest bit curious about what that could be?"

"Pick another one of your friends to go along with you. I'm not interested in reliving anything at this point."

"They don't want anyone else. They asked specifically for you."

"Who asked you? This Cater guy? Why me? Why'd they ask for me?"

"I spoke with my usual liaison. They didn't give particulars, they wanted me to have you come to New York for the meeting tomorrow, and they needed the two of us."

Christina looked at the letter on official stationery, stating the time and place for the two of them to report, addressed to them both, stressing tardiness was not tolerated.

Christina wasn't impressed. "Where's your brain? For real? I'm not doing anything for any government agency. I can't believe they'd be so insensitive to ask such a thing. They have some giant balls asking anything of me. And so do you!"

After Zoe's pleading and cajoling, Christina agreed to the meeting, but that was all. How dare they ask for something like that when they've taken the best part of her life? She'll walk into that meeting with chips on her shoulders and a skeptical attitude. They'd better be ready for her wrath.

She couldn't fall asleep that night with questions racing through her head. "Why me? I've nothing in my background that could prepare me for a CIA operation. Senseless. How do you relive your youth? At a college campus? At our age? Yeah, that's covert. Two middle-aged women going to college is normal? We'll stand out like sore thumbs." She tried pushing these thoughts away so she could sleep. There were too many questions and no answers. We'll find out tomorrow. Her last thought before falling asleep was, "Christina Pucci, *Super Spy!*"

After a sleepless night and waiting over two hours, Christina was in a foul mood. It didn't help that Zoe acted condescending and superior, treating her like a child. As the minutes ticked off, she devised a plan for this deputy chief who insisted on timeliness yet kept them waiting. She's going to make this meeting as uncomfortable as she can, waiting for the right moment to implement her plan. At last, the moment arrived.

The receptionist announced the deputy chief was on his way and instructed them to only address him as deputy chief. They'd be at the office within minutes. That was Christina's cue.

In her sweetest voice, she asked. "Where's the ladies' room?"

The receptionist started to panic. "You can't go now! He'll be here momentarily. Making him wait puts him in a disagreeable mood. You should have gone before. You've had enough time!"

Christina smiled. "Well, that's not how nature works. Shall I wait until he gets here, we start the meeting, and then ask *him* where the bathroom is? I'd rather it be done before he gets here."

She handed Christina a key, directed her to the hallway, and pointed out the bathroom door. Zoe instructed her to be quick about it. Christina headed into the hallway and unlocked the door. She chuckled to herself, muttering after she locked and bolted the door behind her, "So long, suckers." After using the bathroom, she started singing *"Jesus Christ, Superstar"*. This was going to be fun!

# CHAPTER 4

Christina had started singing "*Pilate's Dream*" when she heard pounding on the locked bathroom door. "Who is it?" she asked in a sing-song voice.

"Christina Teresa Santa Lucia! Open this door right now!" Zoe sounded upset. Time for more fun.

"Mom! What are you doing here?"

Zoe wasn't amused. "You're making a fool of yourself. Open the door!"

"Well, not until I get to the last song of side two."

"Open this door right now!"

She unlocked the door and said, "Yeee-eeees?"

"Tee, this isn't funny! Can you imagine how pissed Deputy Chief Cater is right now? Have some respect for his position."

"Screw him! I didn't ask to come here; he asked me, or did he demand it? Insists on punctuality and then he's almost three hours late! You know I *hate* waiting. The nerve of that guy! He's damn lucky I'm not singing '*Les Mis.*' I don't stop singing that one until the end."

Zoe rolled her eyes, grabbed Christina's arm, and pulled her out of the ladies' room. "Enough of this, Tee!"

"Would you rather I sang in the bathroom releasing my frustrations or go into the meeting pissed, start messing up his papers and throwing his folders all over the place? You know I'd do that."

"Grow up, Tee! This is serious business. This building is not a playground. People here are trying to keep our country safe. Have some respect for where you are."

"Honestly, Zee, I haven't had this much fun in months. Screw him!"

They reached the office door, and before she opened it, Zoe said, "Behave!"

Christina curtsied and said, "Yes, Mommy Dearest," completely enjoying herself.

Zoe opened the door, and Christina saw two men in the room. The one who looked like Adonis was standing, and the one who looked like a toad was sitting at the desk, looking at his watch. If there's a God, the toady-clock-watcher was the deputy chief. Toady stood up and held his hand out for her to shake as she walked towards him. Zoe handled the introductions.

"Deputy Chief Martin Cater, Christina Pucci."

He shook her hand, saying, "At last, Christina. We've been waiting quite a while for you. It's a pleasure to finally meet you."

"I wish I could say the same, Marty. Waiting around for almost three hours does nothing for my pleasant personality. And please, Marty, call me *Mrs. Pucci*." She turned to Adonis, who took her hand, kissed it, and said, "I am Agent René Barrineau, Madame Pucci."

"Well, Monsieur Barrineau," she replied, "it's certainly a pleasure to meet you. And please, call me… *anytime!*"

René laughed. "Madame Pucci, you're a pure delight! *Jesus Christ Superstar*, eh?" The chief looked ready to explode.

"Well, Monsieur, I figured it's perfect for the CIA: love, betrayal, capture, torture, and we know how it ends. Lucky for you, Marty, I didn't want to sing the entire album, especially after waiting almost three hours for you to show up." She threw eye daggers at him and sat down.

Martin cleared his throat and said in a negative tone, "We're certainly not getting off to a good start here. Is the small talk finished? Are you through, *Mrs. Pucci*? We've a lot of information to cover and are running behind. Let's get started. I do have other matters to address today!" That was the wrong way to start things off.

Christina gave him both barrels. "Marty…, honey…, Zoe and I have been here since nine thirty, per your instruction. *You're* the one who was late. Don't try to turn the tables here." Zoe tried to say something and was cut off. "I hate to wait even more than you do, and maybe *you* have gotten off to a bad start with *me!*" The room was silent.

"So, *Chiefy*, the way I see it, you owe Zoe and me an apology for your tardiness." Zoe started to say something and was cut off again. "No, Zee, if we were even a half hour late, we certainly would've apologized first thing. It seems to me, *sir*, you've no manners." She smiled sweetly and said, "I think an apology should be your first order of business."

Martin's fists were clenched. Christina's first mission at the CIA was an accomplished success!

"Agent Janis, *Mrs. Pucci*, I apologize for my tardiness today. Is that sufficient?"

She looked at Zoe, nodded her head, saying, "I guess so, but Marty, it didn't sound very sincere. I think you need to lighten up.

Well, I accept your apology anyway. Zoe? Apology accepted?" Zoe looked horrified, and René looked totally amused and stifled a laugh.

The unamused deputy chief said, "Right, let's get to business, shall we?" He reached into his briefcase and pulled out a folder. He opened it and showed the two women some photos. "Do you know who this man is?"

Zoe answered, "It's Harold Morgan, the front runner for the Republican presidential nomination. Not one of my favorite politicians."

He looked at Christina, "Mrs. Pucci, are you familiar with Harold Morgan?"

"As much as I can tolerate. He seems to be a spoiled, rich, middle-aged brat who's buying his way into the White House. I'd equate him to a village idiot, but that's insulting to village idiots around the world. The only difference is that Morgan has money and connections. God help us if he's nominated because the scary part is, he could win."

Martin took another two photographs out of the folder, repeating his question. By the style of the clothing, the first photo looked like it was from the 60s or 70s. It was of a dark, handsome young man who looked either Indian or Middle Eastern. The other photo was more recent of a man in Eastern clothing wearing the shemagh or keffiyeh, the traditional headdress worn by Middle Eastern men. Neither knew who this man was. Martin nodded his head and dug into the folder for subsequent photos.

In these, one was definitely a young Harold Morgan, with the same dark, handsome young man. They were dressed in clothes of the early seventies with a cigarette hanging out of Harold's mouth. The other pictures were of an older Morgan with that Middle Eastern looking man wearing regular clothing, traditional Arab garments, and some wearing suits, jeans, and other manner of clothing from America.

In one photo, they looked as if they were deep in a guarded conversation, and in another, it showed Morgan kissing the Arabian man on the cheek, as they do respectfully in Middle Eastern culture. They were both able to identify Morgan, but not the other man.

As they looked at the recent photos of Morgan and the Arab gentleman, Christina remarked, "My, my," in her ever-sarcastic tone, "doesn't Harold look quite kissy-face with this Middle Easterner? It seems a little too cozy for my comfort, especially since he's on his way to the White House." Then asked, "Um, Marty, not sure if you can answer this, but is this young hunky guy the same guy with Morgan in the latter pictures? If it is, he certainly aged well."

Martin stared a hole through her with hatred in his eyes. "Mrs. Pucci, my title is Deputy Chief. Do not address me as Marty."

"Sure, Marty, oops, I mean Deputy Chief. I'll try to remember that." She didn't like this sour, angry, and ugly guy one bit. As he spoke, she thought she didn't want to work for this ogre.

He began the briefing. "The Arab man in these photos is Prince Ali Tariq Al-Machmud, a member of the Royal Family of Zatari. He and Morgan were roommates at UC Berkeley for a semester in 1971." He took out more photos of them at Berkeley and passed them around. "It was pre-arranged by both families that the Prince and Morgan would be roommates. Normally, a member of royalty attending a school in the US would have a private room in an exclusive part of the campus. This was not the case with Ali and Morgan.

"We believe information changed hands during their time at Berkeley, and this information was vital to our national security, to the burgeoning fortunes of the Morgan family, and the Zatari Royal Family's leading place on OPEC." He stopped and stared at the women before adding, "Your country needs your assistance to find out exactly what information was exchanged and to bring back proof of this treasonous act by the Morgan family."

They were both confused. Zoe asked, "Excuse me for asking, but exactly how would we get this information? I hope you'll elaborate more on what you expect from us. If it's as serious as you claim, neither party would keep such damning information lying around for forty years. It's not like we can go back to 1971 and witness the whole exchange."

"Actually, Agent Janis, that's exactly what we're asking," Martin replied. The two looked at each other and must have had the same incredulous expression on their faces. "I know it sounds unbelievable, but our government has immeasurable amounts of diverse and progressive technology at their disposal that would overwhelm and astound you, and time travel is one of them. I assure you it's safe and has been done on numerous successful missions. Of course, you realize this information doesn't leave this room.

"We've tentatively enrolled you both for the first semester at UC Berkeley in California in August of 1971. Our monthly timetables are exact; it's the years we can modify. Timing is of the utmost importance to this mission, so we must know today if you're both up to this task. Preparations need to be done before embarking on the past."

Their confused expressions didn't change, but Martin continued. "Agent Janis, we've enrolled you in the creative writing/journalism program under the name of Athena Christos. Mrs. Pucci, you're enrolled under the name of Teresa Brendes, taking the same classes as Prince Ali – Fine Arts, History of Art and Architecture with concentration on Impressionism along with painting and drawing classes."

"Why were we selected for this mission?" Zoe asked. "I don't have field experience except for photography and information exchange. Don't get me wrong, this sounds extremely inviting. The chance to go back to the 70s and relive a fabulous time in our past is intriguing and tempting, but how are we qualified to perform this critical task? This sounds more than what we can manage, and the logistics of it don't make sense."

René answered, "Agent Janis, you're extraordinarily successful at your job at *La Fashionista* Magazine, which means you're of above average intelligence to achieve such stature in a cut-throat field. We've every confidence you'll be able to attain success in any mission you're given. You've never failed in the time you've worked here, and it feels like you can handle something more substantial.

"Mrs. Pucci, you've a vast amount of knowledge of Art. You know Impressionism as though you lived during that time. Your knowledge of architecture, artists, and the different periods of art will give you an in with the prince, and we need someone who'll be able to get close to him and help him with his studies. You both are perfect for this assignment and from what I've been told, are old friends who've shared much of your lives."

Christina felt violated. "How do you know so much about me? Have you had me investigated?" She looked at Martin. "How dare you!"

Zoe was intrigued and immediately changed the subject, asking, "Don't you think two women approaching their 50s are going to be alienated from the rest of the students, no matter what era we're in? How would the two of us, and if you're including Monsieur

Barrineau, the three of us, be able to mingle with any of the student body?" She looked at Martin and said, "I seem to recall the mantra of that era as being 'Don't trust anyone over 30.' How would we ever fit in and be accepted? Pardon me for saying this, but it doesn't seem like a successful plan at our age. We'd be looked upon as the enemy. I wouldn't have trusted someone my mother's age when I was 18 years old, and neither will they."

Martin began to explain things more. "This is the beauty of our technology. When you travel backwards in time, so does your outward appearance. Your mental capacity and knowledge stay at your current age, but your physical appearance will be exactly what it was when you entered the time into which you're traveling." He was getting excited, and Christina thought she saw a sneering smile. "When you enter 1971, your external manifestation will be as you were that year. You'll have no problem fitting in because outwardly you'll be teenagers."

Martin handed them a folder. "These will give you a better idea of what to expect. Please read them over. You'll be on opposite sides of the US from your original manifestation, so there wouldn't be a problem of running into 'yourself,' which would be the only problematic factor to go wrong.

"Our time-travel liaison is a professor at UC Berkeley who collaborated with us on previous forays into the past with some of our more seasoned agents. He'll be your link to the present, to the Agency, your families if necessary, and your guide when you get into the past."

"I have a question," Christina interjected. "What happens if we die on this mission?" Everyone looked at her. "Well, it could happen, couldn't it?" It was something she had to ask, thinking of her children. She needed to make sure their existence wasn't being played with, and if anything went wrong, their lives wouldn't be affected in any way.

"Glad you asked that question, Mrs. Pucci. If anything should happen in the past that would end your existence there, you'll immediately wake up in the present time, and your visit to the past will be done. There are no consequences in the present in case of a fatality occurring during your mission," Martin lied, then added, "which, we positively don't foresee."

That answer didn't sit well with Christina. "Of course you don't foresee it, and even if you did, you wouldn't tell us. What happens if we get caught and tortured? Are you saying we won't feel anything, that we'll wake up with a bad headache in the present day?" Martin was getting completely exasperated by this woman, and his voice reacted with an irritated tone.

"Mrs. Pucci, this method has been used on numerous occasions, and nothing has gone wrong. Read the reports and you'll see there are no adverse effects and that it's actually quite enjoyable."

She put on her glasses and opened the folder. The first sentence stated that the maximum amount of time spent in time travel is six months. "It says here we can only spend six months in the past. What happens if something happens and our time, for whatever reason, is extended longer than six months?" He rolled his eyes at her. She thought to herself that she might have to start singing again.

"Mrs. Pucci, you'll be monitored and protected by Professor O'Connell at Berkeley and the very capable Agent Barrineau. Your time in 1971 will be from the beginning of August until mid-December. By my count, that's slightly more than four months. Do you come up with a different number, or do you find counting to be above your comprehension?"

She felt her anger intensifying. "You didn't answer my question. What if something happens and we overstay six months? I'm sure one cannot sustain two existences indefinitely. Will one overrule the other? What would happen to Christina Pucci if Teresa Whoever gets trapped in 1971?"

She could tell he was infuriated with her, and that played right into her plan. She continued on that track. "So tell me, how is this time travel achieved? Do you have Doc Emmett Brown with a plutonium-laden flux capacitor in a DeLorean in a garage somewhere? You know, 1.21 jigawatts, 88 miles per hour? Or maybe you have H.G. Wells' time machine hidden in a secret place?"

She got out of her chair and threw the folder on the desk. "You aren't very forthcoming with answers, and I think this whole thing is too risky. I have children to think about and I don't want them to disappear because you want to end the political career of someone who probably pissed you off because he forgot your name or even worse...*called you Marty*!"

He wanted to slap her and once again his fists were twitching and he spoke through clenched teeth. "Mrs. Pucci, you don't know who or what you're dealing with, and I don't appreciate you making a mockery out of everything we're doing here. We aren't here today for your amusement. The assignment you've been selected to execute for your country is of the utmost importance. I'd find it most desirous if you'd remember your place and keep your inane comments to yourself!"

"Screw you, Marty! As I recall, you asked me to come here. I was quite content staying in my little cocoon up north. I don't need this crap from you, the CIA, or the FBI. I've sacrificed enough for this country with the life of my husband and the future we were to have together. I don't need you to tell me my country needs me. My country has taken enough from me."

Zoe tried to smooth things over and calm her down, but the entire day from the minute Christina entered these offices to this moment grated on her nerves and her impatience was palpable. And then Martin, for whatever reason, opened his sarcastic mouth and inserted his foot.

"Mrs. Pucci, by the looks of things, this trip to New York and the prospect of something exciting has been good for you. You seem to have come to life and are certainly looking much better."

That hit her like a slap in the face. Better? Better? What the hell does that mean? "Really, Marty? Better? Better than what?" He moved in his chair and compiled the files and photos on his desk, not looking at her, ignoring her question. "Better than what, Marty?" she repeated. He made no reply. "Answer me! Better than what?" There was no response. He wouldn't even look at her while straightening the dossiers. She decided to speak louder and in his face.

"*Marty...better than what?*" Still no reply or eye contact. She could no longer hold her temper. With her left hand in one fell swoop, she shoved all the folders and his briefcase across the room, sending all the file materials and photos flying everywhere. The hatred for this woman was written all over Martin's face. He started to think of how he was going to kill her from that moment on. If she doesn't know how dangerous he is, she will as soon as she gets back from this mission. Nobody treats him with this kind of disrespect and gets away with it.

Zoe was horrified and she and René scrambled to pick up the papers and photos that were strewn around the room. Neither Martin nor Christina moved an inch, their intense stare-down in a deadlock. She asked again, "Better than what, Marty?"

He still didn't answer but averted his gaze to a pile of photos picked up by Zoe, which made her look in that direction. He quickly tried to hide them, which made her spring into action because she noticed a picture of herself in that pile. She moved more quickly than he did and was able to grab the pile of photos he was trying to hide.

"Geez, Marty, you didn't show me the file you had on me." She wasn't surprised. She knew how these agencies operated, especially with a husband in the FBI. It's common to investigate people for all sorts of reasons, including mission inclusion. They have to know if the person being considered is up to the task. She saw a recent picture of her walking the dog. She held it up and asked, "Better than this? Is this what you're referring to?"

Zoe was trying to shut her up and kept apologizing to Martin. Christina found another sad photo, looking so despondent with hollow eyes and cheeks. She held that one up, "Or maybe you're referring to this? Am I looking better than this?" Her eyes were drawn to her other pictures, some much younger, maybe when she was in her late teens or early twenties, and some of them threw her for a loop. She didn't remember ever being dressed in this sort of clothing. And who were these people in the group pictures? The man standing next to her looked like that prince. What the hell? Where was this? She looked more closely at the photo and was able to read part of a caption and then looked at Martin.

"You fucking snake!" she said as she flipped through the photos, thinking, this isn't me. The resemblance was unbelievable, but the closer she looked, she noticed subtle differences in appearance. The noses were similar but different. Her eyes were more exotic than Christina's and her hair seemed darker, thicker, and straighter. Upon reading the names on the captions, she realized this was the wife of the Zatarian Prince he wanted her to take classes with in 1971. Now she understood why she was wanted for this assignment.

"Marty, you're a filthy snake! You want me on this mission because I look like the prince's wife. You're trying to set me up with this Arab guy! You'd better not have it in your mind that I'm going to sleep with him, royalty or not. I never slept around, not even during that whole 'free love' time I grew up in, and I'm not going to start now! If that's what you have in mind, you'd better start thinking of another plan! Asshole!" She took the recent photos of herself, crumpled them up, threw them in his face while still holding on to the file materials and photos of the Arab woman.

Martin sat like a statue, trying to stare a hole through her, but she didn't scare easily nor let anyone intimidate her, having more balls than brains, as she always said of herself. After living with twin brothers, this guy is a piece of cake loaded with whipped cream frosting.

She leaned over with her face almost nose to nose with his and said, "My answer to your invitation to attend Berkeley and accept this assignment is most definitely *no*. I have no intention of working for an inconsiderate, lying slimy piece of shit like you."

Zoe stood up and started to protest. "Tee, think about it! 1971! We're back to our teens. We grew up in the best time of so many things – civil rights, peace, love, young people finding their voice through sit-ins and protests, not to mention the great music in California at that time. We'll be in the center of where the Haight-Ashbury movement took place. How can you turn your back on that? It's a chance to live some of the history of our time and help our country simultaneously. And you can go to college, like you always wanted."

René gently took the photos and file materials from her hands. "Mrs. Pucci, you and Agent Janis are vital to this mission. It cannot be done without you." He put the files back down on the desk. "You'll be able to manage the prince with no trouble. You're fearless. Look how you've stood toe to toe with Deputy Cater, one of the most feared men in the CIA."

She looked the French agent squarely in the eyes, searching for some sort of truth in them. "Without the two of you, there's no mission. It's of the utmost importance that you and Agent Janis travel with me to 1971 and obtain the proof needed to bring this mission to completion. It's in the best interest of this country that Harold Morgan's quest for the presidency be stopped at all costs."

She looked at him, then at Zoe and said, "Well, I'm not ready to cover those costs. I'm sorry, but I have to say no. I feel like I'm being set up with this Prince, and I don't trust any government agency to look out for me. I'm an expendable life, like my husband's. I've no desire to return to my youth or those times. My answer is no."

Martin started to say, "We have ways of getting you to..." and René cut him off.

"Are you threatening me, Marty? You miserable fucking prick! How dare you!"

René needed to diffuse the situation and stepped in between them, looking directly at Christina. "Marteen, where is the powder room? I think maybe Mrs. Pucci needs a few minutes to compose herself and think things through quietly, with no one giving her their opinion." He looked at her and said, "Would you do that, please? Take a few minutes, open your mind to the job, and know I'll protect you with my life."

"Ok, but it's not going to change anything. I guarantee I'll come back to this room with my same answer, which is a most definite and resounding no."

"Please let me escort you to the ladies' room. One thing you must promise me, though," he said as they walked out the door into the hallway, "no singing." They laughed and walked towards the restroom. René took her hand, and as he did, she felt him put something into it. It felt like a small, folded piece of paper. He opened the door for her, kissed the hand that held his note, looked at her hand, then into her eyes before looking back at her hand. "Please," he said as he gently squeezed her hand, "think about doing me the honor of accompanying me on this journey. You and I have much to accomplish."

She went into the bathroom, entered a stall, and locked the door. She opened the folded paper, reading it over at least four times. She sat on the toilet, letting the contents of his note sink in. She read it again, tore it into tiny pieces, put them in the toilet, and watched as the papers swirled around and then disappeared down the drain. To make sure all the papers were completely disposed of, she flushed the toilet a second time. She unlocked the door, went to the sink, washed her hands, and stared at her reflection in the mirror. "Oh, John! I won't let you die in vain. If this motherfucker had anything to do with your death, I'll make sure he pays. And you know how I get when I make up my mind. Protect me, please."

She made her way back to Deputy Chief Cater's office. When she walked into the office, the conversation stopped. She looked at the three of them and said, "I'm in."

# CHAPTER 5

Shortly after Christina returned announcing she'd take the assignment, Martin excused himself to an inner room to make a phone call. When the call was answered, he said, "Operation Berkeley (OB) is on with those we discussed."

There were questions on the other end, and Martin answered, "Yes, I've every confidence we'll have success, especially with this team." More conversation ensued. Martin replied, "Notify all interested parties. We're on schedule, and they'll return with proof in December. I'll apprise you as things progress. Pass on to the president that I worked hard to put together a team that will ensure success." After they hung up, Martin made another call.

"Find anything?" The answer was negative. "Did you look everywhere we discussed?" The answer was affirmative. "I know you're the best, but make sure your visit can't be detected. Clear?" The conversation continued, then Martin asked, "Observation equipment in place?" A sick smile came over his face. "Excellent. I expect to see you in my office for a full report." He hung up, putting his phone in his jacket pocket.

He returned to his office and found them huddled around the dossiers of Morgan and Ali. They all accepted the mission and spent the next half hour going over instructions and expectations. Martin's intercom began ringing, which he ignored. When the incessant ringing wouldn't stop, he picked up the phone, screaming, "I told you not to bother me until this meeting is over!" and slammed the phone.

He resumed the instructions, and the intercom rang again. He didn't know how this day could get any worse. He was infuriated by Christina strewing files from his desk and her disregard for his position grated on his nerves. If she weren't vital to OB, he would've bitch-slapped her for disrespecting him from the moment they met. She'll regret her actions, and he'll get his retribution once she's back with the needed proof. Every time he looked at her, he imagined himself choking her, watching life recede from her eyes.

Except she refused to look at him. He tried to shake hands when she returned, accepting the mission; commonplace practice when closing a deal. She looked at his hand and said, "Don't even think about it, Marty. I wouldn't touch you with a stick. Let's get one thing clear. I will not have sexual relations with Prince Ali. If you're expecting me to be your prostitute you can kiss my ass goodbye! I'll go back to my quiet little life. Understood?"

No response was warranted, and he gave none, wondering how René got her to agree. He'll insist on being told everything spoken in that hallway. To make sure René tells the truth, he'll view the surveillance tapes and hear for himself what was said in the hallway. Fucking French and their phony charisma.

René already had these two women eating out of the palm of his hand. How shallow women are, Martin thought. Agent Janis was inquisitive and highly intelligent. Martin was as pleased as his miserable personality would allow that she was in on this mission, even though she's a woman. He had confidence she'd be able to manage the trickier aspects they were to perform. They were the nation's last hope of preventing a traitor from reaching the White House. If they failed, Morgan would be on his way to the White House, and that cannot happen. That Pucci whore better be worth the trouble he had to get her.

The ringing intercom sent pyrotechnics to his brain. He picked up the phone and, without a word, slammed the receiver down. His secretary will be sorry when this meeting is over. She'll wish she had stayed home today. It started ringing again, and he did the same thing again.

René asked, "Don't you think you should see what's so important?" Martin ignored him, giving him an annoyed look, and continued with what would be expected when they got to Berkeley. "Orientation for incoming freshmen is August 12$^{th}$, and classes begin on the 15$^{th}$. You three need to be there by August 1$^{st}$, and by that, I mean in California, 1971. I'll arrange with O'Connell for your arrival on August 1$^{st}$. Agreed?"

Martin looked at everyone and Agent Janis and René nodded but that whore refused to look at him. She kept looking down at the papers, nodding her head. He suppressed the urge to backhand her face. "Anything you bring with you must be approved and be of the time you're entering, nothing from our current time. Is that clear?" They answered yes. Zoe started to ask something when there was a knock on the door.

Martin insisted it be ignored, but René said, "Marteen, we cannot continue until your secretary relays whatever is so vital that she'd risk your wrath at the interruption. It'll only take a minute and then it's done."

Martin started to protest but René had already walked to the door and opened it to find Martin's secretary in a complete tizzy.

"I'm so sorry to have interrupted you, but it's very important!" she blurted out.

Martin got red-faced and started to shriek at her, "I told you I was not to be disturbed!"

René stepped in, "Let's hear what's so important before you fly off the handle."

The girl was shaking. "Chief Metzger has been trying to reach you for the last fifteen minutes! He wants you in his office in Washington right away. He's sent a car to pick you up and take you to the airport. Your ticket is at the main counter. His office booked you on the next flight to Washington. He must see you today, no excuses. No need to pack a bag because you'll be back in New York tonight. He'll have a car waiting for you in Washington to bring you directly to Langley." She looked scared to death. "The car for you is here now. It's been here for about ten minutes and Chief Metzger's assistant keeps calling for status reports on why you're not on your way." She waited a few seconds and asked, "What shall I tell him?"

Martin screamed, with spittle flying, "I'm in the middle of an important briefing and a trip to Washington is out of the question! Tell Metzger he has to wait."

René, with all the tact he could muster asked, "Marteen, when your superior summons you, you shouldn't refuse. It must be of great importance. We've finished here, and I can wrap things up on this end for the time being." René wondered if Martin being summoned to Washington had anything to do with OB. "Please let us know if anything changes regarding the mission. No sense making arrangements if it's called off."

Martin snapped, "This mission will NOT be called off." Martin's rage was at volcanic levels, but he knew he had to fly to Washington. He never relished taking commands from anyone, but that was the biggest lesson learned in the military: a soldier follows orders.

He told his secretary to send files 184 – 188 to his laptop, and he'd review them in transit. He grabbed his cane, briefcase, laptop, and coat and ushered the three of them out of his office and locked the door. Charles will take them wherever they need to go.

The trio got into Martin's car, and Charles drove off. Martin would insist that Charles tell him where they went. Martin kept the carrot of career opportunities dangling in front of Charles but had no intention of letting his little lap dog get a promotion. Fright and bullying, that's how you get people to do as they're told, and those tactics worked absolutely on Charles. He knew Martin was ruthless; he'd seen it firsthand and knew from experience that he was not immune to Martin's cruelty. Martin thought of Charles more as an indentured servant than a CIA employee and treated him as such. Charles was promised advancement, but in the three years he'd been working for him, things hadn't improved. Nothing Charles did was right or appreciated. Charles wanted a field assignment, something promised but never given.

Martin got into the waiting vehicle and was taken to JFK. He had an inkling of the reason for this impromptu meeting but didn't want to jump to conclusions. He wasn't surprised; in fact, he expected it, but not so soon. Good news travels fast in Washington. Martin was ready for whatever reason he was being whisked off in such a hurry. He didn't have good feelings about this, but he could handle Tommy Metzger.

He loathed the current Head of the CIA, Director Thomas Metzger. He detested the fact that Tom was now his superior and had to take orders from him. Through backdoor politics, Metzger was instrumental in getting Martin out of the field, releasing Martin's torture techniques when being considered for the position of Director. That bastard beat him out of the position, and Martin bore a deep grudge. Martin was called a "loose cannon" during the initial phase of the interview process and never made it to the confirmation hearings.

He and Metzger were at odds on everything and rarely agreed. He doesn't know how to get things done, thought Martin. When would they realize that sometimes heads have to roll and body counts have to rise? Fear, pain, and intimidation are the ways to get people to give you what you need from them. Now that bastard is flexing his muscles, demanding Martin jump on a plane and head to Washington. He couldn't possibly know everything this soon.

Once in the air, Martin settled into his business class seat with his Dewars on the rocks. He opened his laptop and downloaded the files sent by his secretary. He put in his earphones and watched and listened to René and Christina Pucci in the hallway. Kissing her hand! What a fucking phony! "And women fall for this shit!," he said under his breath to himself. He looked at their exchange from four different angles and found nothing that looked suspicious, nor heard anything to sway her to accept. He wished they had surveillance cameras in the bathrooms. How the hell did he get her to agree?

The plane ride was a little more than an hour, and when Martin arrived in Washington, a car was there to pick him up. He was driven to Langley, and Director Metzger's assistant was waiting at the entrance. Martin was ushered into the Director's office and told to have a seat. Chief Metzger would be with him directly.

Martin sat for almost an hour and was seething. Metzger knew of his impatience, and Martin felt he was purposely left to sit and wait. How disrespectful he was to one of his higher echelon deputies. If Tom didn't walk through that door within five minutes, Martin was leaving, even if he had to limp back to New York.

Thomas Metzger looked at his watch and decided Martin had waited long enough. In truth, Thomas needed time to cool down as he was infuriated with the absolute balls Martin had. This wasn't going to be a good meeting, and he needed his anger to subside before entering the room. He wanted to be composed and relaxed, while Martin was agitated. Thomas had no idea Martin's whole day had already been thrust into total distress by none other than the woman Thomas was trying to safeguard. Now was as good a time as any for this showdown.

Thomas walked into his office, saying nothing. He strode to his desk, sat down, and stared at Martin. "Do you know why I've asked you here today?"

Martin curtly replied, "I didn't know you asked. I was under the impression you insisted I come immediately. Maybe that's why I've been sitting here for so long, you didn't know I arrived so quickly. Maybe you're finding the job of Chief too much for you and need my help."

"Sarcasm is unwarranted and won't be tolerated. You've seriously breached protocol." Thomas sat with his elbows on the desk, his fingertips touching. He got up and started to walk around Martin's chair as he spoke.

"Imagine my surprise when I'm called by the White House Chief of Staff, who tells me to please hold for the President. And when the President and I are connected, I'm thanked for the green light on Operation Berkeley and how pleased he is that it's a go and to personally convey his thanks to Agent René Barrineau, Agent Zoe Janis, and Christina Pucci." Martin didn't move or blink. It was as though he was in the room by himself, with no one speaking to him.

"I thought I made it perfectly clear to you that this mission was dead in the water. I told you specifically there would be NO Operation Berkeley. The information and proof that the President is interested in obtaining is impossible to get and this time travel business is too risky. I know it's been used in the past, but it's too dangerous, especially for the women, one of whom is a civilian."

Martin replied flippantly, "Well that's because we need females to pull this off for those two pussy chasers and with the two bitches I've lined up, it cannot fail."

Metzger flew into a rage. "You're putting the lives of an inexperienced agent and a civilian woman, a recent widow of an FBI agent thought to have been killed in the line of duty, in grave danger!" Metzger was furious. "How dare you break the chain of command and go directly to the President? You knew he wouldn't be able to resist this mission! He wants to be re-elected and would probably sell his own mother for the kind of information you're promising to bring back on Morgan!"

He stared at Martin, trying to control his anger. "I tried to talk sense into the President, but he's been assured by you that it's fail-proof and perfectly safe. Are you fucking insane to give that sort of guarantee to a sitting president? He's informed me we're to go full speed ahead with your proposed action, no questions asked. If I could, I'd have you terminated and your military pension revoked."

The pension was the only thing Martin coveted and worked towards. He earned every cent of it with his blood, sweat, and tears, and the thought of losing his financial security momentarily terrified him. But now Martin knew the President was insisting on going ahead with Operation Berkeley. It not only gave him pleasure, but it increased his bravado a hundredfold. If there hadn't been this push from the White House, then his position at the CIA would've been very precarious for not following the chain of command. For the first time that day, Martin felt he finally had the cards in his hand. What could've been a meeting bordering on his termination, the puppetmaster was once again holding the strings. Martin sat very smugly, knowing Metzger was pissed because his hands were tied. The mission was a go and there was no turning back now that the Commander in Chief gave it the green light.

"Does Christina Pucci know the dangers and risks involved in this time travel mission?"

Martin lied and said, "Yes, in fact, she does. This escapade to 1971 has given her something to focus on and bring her out of mourning."

"Does she know the risks to her children? I've discovered in my investigation of this method of travel, rule number one is there must be no spouse and absolutely no children!" Thomas shouted. "How can you jeopardize all the lives of John Pucci's family? This is a fellow agent and we watch out for each other, not set the widow and children up for possible annihilation! You're a liar, Martin. She has no idea the dangers involved with time travel, especially if their time in the past is extended. You told her all the possible scenarios of disaster?"

Martin nodded his head. "Of course I did. She's looking for an adventure."

"Liar!" Thomas shrieked. "She'd never put the lives of her children in harm's way, no matter how depressed she is over the death of her husband."

Martin didn't give a shit what would happen to the Pucci whore or the three brats she spawned. He needed that information brought back. And if she cannot do it, then it will be up to the other two. Martin started to get up and said, "All of this is moot as the President has given this mission his blessing. Is there anything else? I need to get back to New York to get things moving. I only have two months to get things in line for Operation Berkeley."

Thomas couldn't believe how blatantly disrespectful Martin was being towards a superior. "Martin, I could have you fired right now."

Martin laughed. "No, you couldn't. I have the President on speed dial, his Chief of Staff and I speak daily. I got you this time, Tommy."

"When this mission is over, you're done with the CIA. I'll make sure of that, Marty."

Martin laughed again. "When this mission's over, I'll have a Cabinet post so you can shove the CIA right up your ass. I'll probably end up being your boss, and then we'll see who gets fired and who loses a pension." Martin snickered, "Haven't you learned that nobody fucks me over and gets away with it, including you, Tommy?"

"We'll see, Marty," Thomas replied. "If anything happens to any of the people on this mission, I'm going to make sure you're criminally charged. You're too cock-sure of yourself, and that's when you make mistakes.

"By the way, Marty, the midnight visits by Dr. Slaven are over. No more shots to your hip, no more portable X-rays. He's reassigned in Europe."

Martin looked surprised. He didn't think anyone knew of the treatments he'd been given. "Rest assured, Marty, I'm going to find out exactly what happened to you and why you're using a cane and needing clandestine visits from one of our doctors for an injury that wasn't reported."

Martin clenched his teeth, and his jaw line became visibly taut. Thomas continued, "If you think for one second that I believe the bullshit story of you thwarting an IED explosion and getting hit in the crossfire, then you're a bigger fool than I thought." They were nose to nose. "You're under orders, which I've insisted upon because of the perilous nature of this mission with inexperienced agents, and the President agrees wholeheartedly. You're to be available to the President and me twenty-four-seven. That means no surgery on that injury until this mission is over and these people are home safely. I don't give a shit if your leg is falling off, and neither does the President. Understood?"

"And the reasoning behind this order?" Martin asked. "I was injured in the line of duty."

Thomas backed Martin into the wall, "Bullshit! You would've reported it if things were on the up and up. You're known for doing things underhandedly, and I'm going to find out exactly how this injury occurred. You wanted this mission, proposed it to the President, and now you're responsible for briefings to the White House and my office. Those are orders from your President. And as for me, I want to know every time anyone from 2003 takes a shit in 1971."

Thomas kicked the cane out of Martin's hand and said, "I'm going to be so far up your ass until those women are home that every time you look in the mirror, you're going to see my face. You've made a huge mistake this time, Marty, and you'll regret Operation Berkeley, disrespecting this office, breaking the chain of command, and playing with innocent lives."

Thomas walked back to his desk and said, "You'll have to find your way back to the airport and get yourself back to New York. I only made plans to get you here. Now get the fuck out of my sight before I end up beating up a cripple with his cane."

# CHAPTER 6

"What an *ASSHOLE!*" Christina said as she got into the back seat with Zoe. René climbed into the front seat with Charles, who was introduced to the women by René. Christina thought he seemed like a nice guy but didn't know how anyone could work for that jerk on a daily basis.

"Charlie, is it okay if I call you Charlie?" she asked, not waiting for an answer. "How can you stand him?"

He shrugged. René told him of her bad girl temper tantrum with the flying files and the bathroom serenade. Charles was shocked, amused and then worried.

"Ma'am, you should be careful with Deputy Chief Cater. He doesn't respond well to that sort of behavior."

"Oh yeah? I don't respond well to bullying from a filthy, disgusting, slimy snake! And they took my picture! Recently! How dare he spy on me! He's lucky I'm going ahead with this creepy assignment."

She looked at René. "Can I say that? Is this on the Q.T.? I've never been a spy before. Not sure of the code of behavior, not that I follow any sort of etiquette, as I've demonstrated."

René looked at Zoe and asked, "Is she always like this?"

"Always!" Zoe replied. "That's why I love her and want to choke her at the same time."

"Well, ladies, and gentlemen," said René, "I say we all go out for a bite to eat if that's agreeable. Charles, that means you, too. Martin's away and we'd love your company."

Christina looked at Zoe, who was the "cruise director" of her time in New York and didn't know if she had something planned or had to get to work. "That sounds like a wonderful idea. Merci, Monsieur," replied Zoe.

"Please ladies, call me René." He turned to Charles and said, "Right around here is a nice little restaurant called *5 Napkin Burger.* I usually stop there when I'm in New York because there's nothing to compare with an American hamburger. Is that acceptable?" They all agreed and found the restaurant close by.

They settled into a booth by the window and watched the hustle and bustle of New Yorkers and tourists go by as they got more familiar with each other. René insisted on a bottle of wine and toasted their newfound friendship, which included Charlie, and to the success of their venture into the past.

While they were waiting for their food, Zoe asked, "So, Tee, why did you finally agree to the assignment? I thought for sure you were dead set against it, especially after you threw the files all over the room. I thought Deputy Cater was going to kill you with his bare hands! Why'd you do something like that? Are you crazy? You could've cut the tension in that room with a knife. You know, Tee, that was really inappropriate. You need to control your temper."

"He's a jerk and deserved a slap in the head, which I didn't give him. That was controlling my temper," she replied. "Spying on me and taking my picture? Don't get me all riled up again with this crap. How dare he? And then he wants me to screw a chauvinistic, disgusting Arabian prince who might not even be circumcised? Gross!"

Zoe laughed and said, "I think they are, so you don't have to worry about that."

"Oh really? Speaking from experience?" She gave Tee the finger.

Charlie was shaking his head and laughing at the two of them, and Christina decided to bring him into conversation. She pointed her finger at him and asked in a half-serious, half-kidding way, "By the way, Charlie, were you the one taking my picture? You could've at least let me comb my hair! Come on now...fess up!"

He laughed and put his hands up and said, "I'm staying out of this. From what I've heard, I don't want to mess with you! And for the record, I'm circumcised!"

They were all laughing, and Christina hoped Zoe forgot her question went unanswered. No such luck! She refused to let the subject change.

"Ok, Tee, now *you* fess up. What made you change your mind?"

She fingered the edge of the glass of wine and made sure not to look at René. She didn't want Zoe to think he had anything to do with her decision. "There are a couple of reasons. Once I had a moment to consider the whole thing without Marty's nasty, ugly presence in my face, I started to think quietly to myself." She paused to collect some thoughts and had to think of something plausible quickly. "I weighed the pros and cons. I knew how much it meant to you, and I wouldn't have to clear my busy schedule, so I decided to go with it."

"Oh, Tee, puh-leeze! That's the biggest line of bullshit I've ever heard from your mouth!" Zoe said laughingly. "I know you better than that. Once your mind's made up, you're too damn stubborn to change it. I thought for sure I was going to have to beg you. I think there's more to this story than you're telling us. If you don't want to talk about it now, that's ok. You can tell me later."

Shit! She's being relentless. Christina had to think of something fast. "Ok, I really didn't want to get into it, but my best friend is forcing me to come clean and tell the truth." She rubbed the inside corners of her eyes with her thumb and forefinger to give her a few more seconds to come up with something believable. Here goes!

"Honestly, I couldn't live through this Thanksgiving without John. The thought of that holiday without him was torturing me. It was always his favorite holiday, taking over the kitchen, cooking the turkey, and having everyone at our house. It was the one holiday I didn't have to do a thing. John did it all and loved it. He always said he had so much to be thankful for that he wanted to make this holiday extra special every year. And he always did."

Tears welled up in her eyes because she wasn't lying. She was dreading November. It was one of the first things she thought of when told of the time frame of this assignment. This Thanksgiving holiday was going to be hell. Her children all had other commitments, with her son having a gig for the week, her daughter's dance company in South Carolina was hired for the Thanksgiving holiday, and her local daughter and her husband were going to be with his family with her tagging along. The thought of Thanksgiving made her want to crawl into a hole.

"Now I can spend that time with my best friend in California, walking around with the body of a hot little eighteen-year-old hippie chick, surrounded by flower power, peace and love." She wiped away the tears and said, "It'll be groovy, man!" and flashed the peace sign with both hands.

René took her hand and said, "We're all thankful you shared your reason with us, Mrs. Pucci." By his eyes, it was obvious that he meant, thank you for not telling the real reason you agreed.

"And please," she said, "if you're not going to call me anytime, feel free to call me Christina. Better yet, call me Tee. All of my close friends do, and I think we're going to become incredibly good friends in the near future, or should I say the distant past? That way, when I become Teresa Whoever, you can still call me Tee."

"*Tres bien*," said René. Their food came shortly, and as they ate, they got to know one another. René and Zoe conversed in French, talking about Paris and what a wonderful city it is. Sparks seemed to be flying between the two of them, which made Christina happy for her. Maybe she shouldn't read too much into it. He could be being polite, but it seemed more interest than good manners.

During the meal, Christina's cell phone started ringing, and the caller ID was the FBI's main office. She excused herself and went into the foyer. It was John's local associate and a good friend of his, Lou Jenkins, on the other end. She wondered what he could want. He couldn't possibly have found out about this 1971 thing already.

"Christina, I hate to bother you."

"Lou, you're not a bother, you know that. Do you have news?"

He took a deep breath. Never a good sign. "I have some items for you that were on John the night he died, some personal items you should have, and a couple of questions that hopefully you can clear up. I stopped at your house yesterday and today, and there was no answer either day, and I was concerned." It warmed her to know John's coworkers were thinking of her and had been so caring and helpful.

"I'm in New York visiting a friend for a couple of days. I'll be back on Sunday, probably mid-afternoon, as I'm taking the early train home. I can't bear that two-hour wait in Albany on that later run. You know me." He laughed, actually quite hard. It seems my impatience is well known, she thought to herself.

"Would it be ok if I stop by the house around four o'clock on Sunday? If you'd rather put it off for a few days, I'll understand." He sighed again and went on. "You know how all of us at the Bureau felt about John, and we know how hard it's been for you and the kids. He was one of a kind." Enough, please, she thought, I can't hold myself together if I hear things like that.

"Thanks, Lou, I appreciate that more than you can know. Four o'clock on Sunday would be perfect." She almost asked what he was bringing but decided against it. No sense in working herself up to a crying jag right here in the restaurant. Better to find out in the comfort of her home. At least she knew some of what he'd be bringing of John's belongings. They said goodbye, and then she called her son.

He didn't answer, and it went to voicemail. They'll answer a text but won't answer a phone call! She hung up and sent him the text," *Will be home Sunday around 2. Beulah will be there on Sunday too, so make sure you're at the house by 2:30 at the latest, and please get Sam from Kenzie's house and bring him with you. NO EXCUSES! YOU CAN'T BE LATE! You have your instructions, and they need to be followed exactly. Love you. See ya Sunday.*" She knew the mere mention of Beulah was enough. He may even be early.

She returned to the table, and Zoe asked, "Was that one of the kids making sure you didn't get mugged here in the Big Apple?"

Before she could answer, Charlie asked, "You have children?" with noticeable surprise in his voice.

"Why Charlie, do I look too young to have kids? You're sweet!" she said playfully. "I have three children; except they aren't kids anymore. Two daughters, Mackenzie and Roxanne, a son, Johnny, and two sons-in-law: Paul, who's married to Roxanne, and Matt, who's married to Kenzie. Johnny's too busy being a lover boy and professional drummer, so I don't expect a daughter-in-law in the near future." She went on, "He's young yet with groupies all over him and certainly not ready for a wife. And no, it wasn't one of the kids; they never call, they text. It's positively maddening!"

"Oh," Charles said, "I didn't think you had children." Then he asked René and Zoe if they had children, and Zoe said no, and René took out his wallet and removed a photograph of a lovely exotic exotic-looking woman and a beautiful hazel-eyed little girl with dark blue bows in her hair.

He passed the photo around for all of see and said, "My wife and daughter. They both died a few months ago near our home outside of Paris." His whole demeanor changed, and a deep sadness overtook him. They all expressed their sympathy. It made the grief for her husband pale in comparison to losing one's cherished spouse and a beautiful child whose life was just beginning.

When Charlie looked at the picture, his jaw tightened. "Was she an agent, René?"

"No, and she didn't know of my involvement in clandestine activities. She thought I was a professor. Adele was a sweet and innocent young girl whose life ended much too soon. And my dear little Mercedes. We were expecting our second child. *Comme c'est tragique.*"

Charlie looked intently at the photo as if trying to memorize it and said, "If you don't mind me asking, René, what were the circumstances of the car accident, and where did it take place? Was there an explosion?"

René stared out the window for a few minutes, not answering, and then looked puzzlingly at Charles and replied, "No explosion. The reports are inconclusive as of right now, but I'm working on finding the truth. Thank you for your concern, all of you. As Mrs. Pucci knows, it's very soon after their deaths, and the open wound of the broken heart hasn't fully healed. I believe my sweet girls died shortly before your husband." He took the photo back, gently outlining their faces with his finger, and put it back into his wallet.

Feeling his pain and not wanting to cry, Christina looked away, and her eyes landed on Charlie. She must've been the only one to notice how visibly shaken he seemed from the photo. "Charlie," she whispered, "I didn't really take you for being such a softie, especially working for the CIA and Satan himself."

He said nothing for a few minutes and then responded. "It's tragic when there's the loss of life, especially a child. René, I wasn't aware of your circumstances, and that it was so recent. My deepest and sincerest condolences."

"Ah, Charles, how could you know? We've only just met, and I keep much of this to myself. Enough of all this sad talk," said René. "We three have all sustained the loss of our great love, and as Charles mentioned to me this morning, he recently lost his father. I say we have one more toast, to those who have gone, and then we can be on our way."

They lifted their glasses and toasted John, Danny, Adele, and Mercedes along with Charlie's dad. René paid the bill at his insistence, and they went back to the car. Zoe gave Charlie her address and they were dropped off first.

Charles pulled up to Zoe's building to let the two ladies off. Although he was young enough to be their son, he really had a good time with the three of them and couldn't remember the last time he laughed so hard and enjoyed this sort of fellowship. As they were getting out of the car, Christina kissed him on the cheek and a hug from the back seat. It caught him by surprise, but it was a pleasant one.

She said, "Charlie, it's been so great to meet you. If my daughters weren't already taken, I might take you home with me." She gave him a gentle slap on the shoulder and said, "And you're even circumcised!" He laughed and told her how great it was to meet her, too. "Take care of yourself, Charlie, be careful and don't stay with Marty too much longer, please. He's downright evil! Hopefully, we'll see you before the big adventure!."

Before the two left the car, the three Berkeley travelers exchanged cell phone numbers and email addresses so, if necessary, they'd be able to contact one another. In the meantime, René would meet with Martin for more instructions.

As soon as they got into Zoe's apartment, she asked again why Tee changed her mind. She had no intention of telling her the deciding factor. She told her what she said before was the truth and wanted to do something for her friend because they're always there for each other.

She knew how much Zoe would want to relive the best part of her life, even if it was only for four months. How many people get to go back and relive some of their youth with the knowledge of their experiences? The more Christina thought about it, the more she began to anticipate the adventure awaiting them. If there was no danger to her or her children, what's to lose?

They had a cup of coffee and rehashed the day laughing about Tee's bad girl antics but the conversation always seemed to steer back to René being a hunk and Marty being a toad. Truth be told, René was definitely a hunk.

"I think I saw a spark or two between the two of you," Tee said to Zoe.

"I thought the same thing about you," she answered in her dry way.

"No, I'm unquestionably not his type," Christina said. "He wouldn't be leaning towards the dowdy housewife with children. He's a man of the world, and the two of you have much in common. You're definitely not the small-town girl who grew up in upstate New York. The two of you have traveled everywhere, it seems. Besides, didn't you see his wife and daughter? You're definitely his type."

"Yeah," Zoe said, "the story of my life. I always come along too early, too late, or someone has a completely broken heart and can't bear to love again. *C'est la vie!"*

"Yeah, well, at least you don't look like the poor unfortunate wife of the evil prince. I'll be looking him up on the internet when I get home. I want to learn all I can before we go so I know who and what I'm dealing with. Maybe I'll find out if he's circumcised." That brought on hysterical laughter from both of them.

For the rest of the night they giggled over past adventures and tried to imagine a future-past adventure. Then Zoe started singing, *"California Dreaming"* and they laughed their asses off. She looked at Christina and said, "Oh Tee! The TeeZee gals are back together again, and the world and California had better watch out!"

<h1 align="center">CHAPTER 7</h1>

As the two women exited the car, Charles got a call from Cater. "Yes, sir," Charles answered. René could hear Martin barking orders to Charles and didn't give him a chance to respond before hanging up.

René asked, "Do you have to pick him up at the airport now?"

"No, not until 9:00 tonight. He wants me to go to his apartment and make sure things are back to normal and all the damage has been fixed."

René stared out the window for a few minutes with several thoughts running through his head. First and foremost, he never said a car accident killed his wife and child. How did Charles know it was a car accident? Did Martin tell him? If so, he wouldn't have been surprised to discover there was a child in the car. He hoped Charles wasn't involved in their deaths. He genuinely liked Charles and would take no pleasure in extracting revenge on him for their deaths if he were an accomplice. He had to find out what he's done or knows.

René said, "Charles, may I accompany you to Martin's apartment, and then can I beg a ride to the airport for my flight back to Paris this evening? My departure and Martin's return flight seem to coincide, and I'd much rather not be alone. Of course, only if it's agreeable to you."

Charles said he'd be happy to spend the rest of the day with him and take him to the airport. "After we check on Martin's apartment, we can go to my hotel and I'll gather my things. Is that agreeable, Charles?"

"Sure!" said Charles. Before René boards his flight to Paris, he'll learn everything he needs to know from Charles.

They got to Martin's apartment, and René asked, "Would you mind if I came up with you? I'd rather not wait in the car, but if you'd prefer, I'll stay here." Charles planned on going in alone so he could have a quick look at Martin's desk but couldn't think of a plausible reason to refuse.

"Sure, René, why not? I can always use a second set of eyes to make sure everything looks right and is fixed properly." René got out of the car and joined him. Charles had a key, and when he opened the door, they found the workmen were gone. Charles said, "You check the bedroom door and make sure it's in working condition, and I'll make sure all the rest is taken care of. Please don't tell Martin you came up. He can be a miserable prick."

"Really? Martin Cater a miserable prick? Ah, Charles, once again, you're being too kind." They laughed and went into the apartment."

They walked around the apartment, and René tried the bedroom door a few times to make sure it closed and locked properly, and all the splinters of wood were picked up. The workmen were very neat, and everything looked as though nothing had occurred in the apartment that morning.

Charles went into Martin's office situated on the other side of the bathroom. He picked the lock on Martin's desk and started rifling through the drawers. He shuffled through some papers, all the while checking to make sure René wasn't watching. He unhooked a hidden part of the desk and quickly scanned over papers concealed there.

René called from the bedroom saying everything looked perfect, so Charles quickly shut the drawers, locked the desk, went to the bathroom, and checked the laundry hamper. Neither the urine-soaked pajamas nor the sheets were in there. He walked around the room and checked the bed and found the sheets must have been changed by Martin's private cleaning service.

He checked the mattress to make sure the bed wasn't made over a wet spot. As he pulled the sheet on a top corner, he remembered Martin had recently purchased a new mattress and insisted on a plastic zippered cover over it because of the vermin in New York City.

The two men walked around the apartment a few times, making sure everything was neat and tidy, with all evidence of the morning's excitement removed. René said, "All looks in place to me, but you must be the judge of that, Charles." Charles walked around the rooms a few times, and all substantiation of the events of that morning was gone.

"Well," said Charles, "I think we can leave with a clear conscience. Everything looks as it was."

René replied, "Well, I'm not sure how it was before, but the workmen were quite fast and very neat. It's like it never happened." He put his arm around Charles' shoulder and said, "Onward to bigger and better things!"

They got into Martin's car, and René asked, "Could we go to my hotel now, and I'll collect my things and check out? We can possibly catch a bite to eat or at least finish my bottle of Pouilly Fumé wine.

"Sounds good to me," replied Charles, and they headed to René's hotel. René stopped at the front desk and told them he would be checking out shortly to catch his flight to Paris and to get his bill together. He loved this particular hotel in New York. It was pristinely clean, the service was excellent, the sheets were crisp and soft, and the mattress was exceedingly comfortable. He always slept well when he stayed here.

As the two men headed up to the fifth floor, Charles chatted away about how funny the two women were today, and René tried to follow the conversation, but in truth, all he could think of was what was going to happen in the next half hour. He hoped he wouldn't find out that Charles was the enemy, for in the short time he'd known him, he found him to be very likable. Although a serious young man, they scratched the surface and found his sense of humor and a friendly and pleasingly entertaining side to his personality.

They arrived at René's suite and the first thing he did was turn on the television. René had left the bottle of wine encased in ice which was now cool water. He dumped the water out of the ice bucket and told Charles to find whatever he'd like to watch and headed for the bedroom.

Charles immediately turned on the Yankees vs. Mets game. It was always great for New Yorkers when the two New York teams played against each other. The score was currently 5-2 with the Yankees winning. René stuck his head in the sitting room.

"Ah, yes. America's pastime. Are you a Yankees or Mets fan?"

Charles replied with a shake of his head, "Unfortunately, I root for the Mets and always have, ever since I was a kid. My dad was a Mets fan. We'd go to games together every year. It was a great time in my life. On the way home, we'd sing the theme song. My dad was a diehard fan right until the end. We even buried him in his Mets cap." Melancholy covered his face.

René was quick to notice and said, "Then our first toast will be to your father and the Mets. I'll get the glasses."

René went into the bedroom part of the suite and retrieved two things from his briefcase: a vial with a dropper and a zippered case. He went into the outer bathroom area and got two glasses. He took the vial and put one drop into one of the glasses. He put the zippered case down near the sink and carried the two glasses out to where the empty ice bucket was holding the wine, in the room where Charles was watching the game.

René uncorked the wine and poured it into the two glasses. He gave Charles the glass of wine containing the drop from the vial. He held up his glass for Charles to toast with him and said, "To the Mets and to fathers," and they drank from their glasses. René held up his glass for another toast and said, "To newly found friends," and they took another drink.

One more toast, thought René, and the glass of wine will be drained, and he can get to work. He held up his glass and said, "To love, for without it we're walking blindly through life."

Charles said, "I'll drink to that with the hopes we both find it." And with that, they drained their glasses and René filled them up again.

Charles put his glass on the table in front of him and started yelling at the television as the first baseman missed the throw and the Yankees scored again. René said, "Excuse me, Charles, I'm going to get my things together. I'll try to be as quick as possible."

"Take your time, René. I'll be making myself miserable watching the Mets get creamed." René went into the bedroom to pack.

He pulled his suitcase out and started to neatly pack his clothing. It wouldn't take long because he didn't bring much for this short trip. "Any change to the score?" René called out to Charles.

"Not yet," Charles replied, and René heard him yawn.

Shouldn't be much longer, René thought to himself. He put his extra shoes in the suitcase and looked out at Charles. His chin was down on his chest, and it looked like he was asleep. René walked to where Charles was watching the game and called his name. There was no reply. He called out once again, and again there was no reply. The rhythmic breathing told René the drug had taken effect. It was time to get busy.

René grabbed the zippered case from the bathroom, took out the paraphernalia, and swiftly got to work. With meticulous precision, he applied the tourniquet to Charles' arm and inserted an IV in his left hand. René would get the truth out of Charles whether he wanted to tell him or not. He checked his watch, and after he timed two minutes on his watch, he gave his pen a click to record and began his interrogation.

"What is your name?"

"Charles Andrew Van Etten."

"In what city do you reside?"

"Manhattan."

"Who do you work for?"

"Central Intelligence Agency."

"Who do you report to?"

Charles seemed to squirm and mumble something. René repeated the question. "Who do you report to?"

"Chief Thomas Metzger." René was surprised by that answer. He expected him to answer Martin Cater. He looked at his watch and the amount of drug left in the small bottle to gauge how long he'd be able to continue his questioning, because now he had additional questions.

"Who is Martin Cater?"

"A murdering fucking scumbag."

"Does Martin know you report to Chief Metzger?"

"No."

"Are you reporting Martin's actions to Metzger?"

"Yes."

"How are you gathering intelligence on Martin?"

"Undetectable phone trace on cell phone." That makes sense, thought René. Charles would have access to Martin's phone, but it still must be dangerous for him to execute.

"Does the information from Martin's phone go to you or directly to Metzger?"

"To me. Weed out immaterial calls. Report calls of interest. Account of all given at the end of the week."

"Did Martin Cater cause the death of a woman in France a few months ago?"

"I think so."

"Do you know for sure?"

"No."

"Is there any evidence?"

"No."

"Did you help Martin with this?"

"No. With my family, my dad died. Cater made his own arrangements. Went to France on the sly. No assignment." It surprised René how relieved he was to hear that.

"How do you know the French woman died in a car accident?"

"Thought I saw something this morning in Cater's apartment. Went back to confirm."

"What did you see?"

"Report. Woman killed. Mission accomplished. Berkeley. Think Cater did it. Said went to France for a terrorist plot. IED. Explosion. No evidence or record." Charles paused for a second and said, "Fucking liar."

"Does Metzger know about this accident?"

"Not yet, will report. No proof. Had to find out why France, gather intelligence."

"Did Martin tell you René Barrineau's wife died in a car accident?"

"No. Didn't know him until yesterday. It must have been his wife. All fits now." Charles started to moan. "Agent's wife! Berkeley. Get the agent on a mission. Kid in the car!" René could feel the anguish in Charles's voice. Charles started to whimper. "Little girl. His wife and child. Killed." René could feel the lump beginning to form in his throat. "Found out today. The photo. Berkeley. René,…good man."

"How did Martin get his injury?"

"Says IED in France. No evidence. Lies. All lies." Charles started to mumble something and then said, "Can't be. Timeline wrong. No injury on return from France. Something else."

René checked the amount of drug in the bottle and found only a drop or two left. Soon all that would be left would be what was in the tubing. He quickly continued.

"Who is John Pucci?"

"FBI. Cater contacted him. Wants something."

"What did he want from Pucci?"

"His wife. Take the assignment."

"How do you know about this?"

"Found evidence, Cater destroyed it."

"Does Martin know you're watching him?"

"No, I'd be dead."

"Have you ever met John Pucci?"

"No, but Mrs. is sweet. Calls me Charlie." Charles smiled and let out a small chuckle. René checked the bottle. It was empty. All that was left was what looked like a few drops in the short length of tubing. He had to finish up quickly and remove the IV.

"Did you report to Metzger his meetings with Pucci?"

"Yes."

René asked the next question even though he knew from Martin's dream admission what the answer would most likely be. "Did Martin kill Pucci?"

"Get Pucci out of the way. No proof. Get wife on mission. He thinks Pucci knows."

"What does he think he knows?"

No answer. Charles rolled his head back with his eyes fluttering and moaning. The serum was wearing off. René wouldn't be able to obtain the answer to that question.

The tubing was now completely empty. The interrogation had to end now. René quickly removed the IV, clicked his pen, gathered his equipment, and swiftly left the room. Charles would be awake in a matter of seconds, and he had to make sure he was nowhere near him when he awoke. It had to seem like Charles had dozed off for a few minutes. The effects of this particular truth serum were practically nil, so once Charles was awake, he would be in his pre-interrogative state.

René was in the bedroom of the suite, packing his clothes and yelled into the sitting room, "Charles, it's rather quiet out there. Has there been no scoring for either team?" He heard some movement and once again called out, "Charles?" He walked into the sitting room with a hand towel as if he had just left the bathroom. Charles was running his hands through his hair.

"Sorry, René, I must have dozed off. Maybe I should take it easy on the wine."

"Ah, no need to worry, Charles, it's been an extraordinarily long day. Shall I have room service bring us up some coffee?"

Charles took a deep breath, stood up, stretched, and unconsciously rubbed his hand where the IV was, although there was no outward evidence of it. "Sounds like a good idea, if you don't mind. Thanks, René."

"I'm happy to oblige," René answered. He went to the phone, called the front desk, and asked them to bring up two coffees. Within minutes there was a knock at the door and a young woman had a tray with a carafe of coffee, two cups, cream, and sugar. René took the tray, gave the woman a tip and set it in front of Charles. "Help yourself, my good man," and went back to packing.

Even though René had performed this sort of questioning many times before, he always felt a certain exhilaration when it was over. He got most of the answers he was looking for and was satisfied that Charles wasn't involved in the deaths of his family. He would've liked to have a few more minutes for interrogation, but he got most of the information he was searching for. But now there's a new question. What did John Pucci know? Did Pucci have incriminating information on Martin, or was he exterminated to get his wife on the mission, or both?

René finished packing and joined Charles for a cup of coffee, and they finished watching the game. The Yankees won, which Charles said wasn't a surprise. René did a final check on the room, made sure he had his passport and ticket, and they left.

They caught a bite to eat and drove out to the airport. René thanked Charles for all his help and for keeping him company that afternoon. Charles told René to make sure he contacts him whenever he comes to the States. "You know where to find me," he said. They shook hands and René turned and headed to the international concourse and Charles turned towards Delta's to wait for Martin.

# CHAPTER 8

Zoe and Christina were wound up with the excitement of the day and couldn't stop talking. Their bodies were exhausted, but their brains were over-stimulated. Christina couldn't stop bitching about Martin Cater spying and sneaking pictures of her and Zoe couldn't stop talking about René.

This came as no surprise. It's how Zoe always was. Once she's interested in someone, he became the all-consuming topic of her conversations. Christina was used to it and found this was Zoe's behavior whether in love or in lust. She took on a little girl's sweetness when she spoke of her new obsession and all her edges got all soft and mushy. For someone with such a tough exterior, she melted like butter when speaking of her newest obsession.

Now her preoccupation was René, and questions and statements about her new fascination began. "Isn't he gorgeous?" "What do you think he thinks of me?" "I'd love to get in that guy's pants." "Do you think he's a good lover or a selfish one?" "I think he's more interested in you than me." "Do you think he's got a big dick?" "French men are so sexy!" "I can't wait to get my hands on him when we get to 1971! He'll be all tight and young with smooth skin, and his balls will be close to his body. Not like…" and then she did her hysterical move of slapping the back of her fingers on the palm of her other hand, making this hard and slow rhythmical clapping noise, repeating it four or five times. They doubled over with hilarity as it represented the saggy balls of old men hitting your ass during sex.

They howled with amusement, barely able to catch their breath because of laughing so hard. It became a running gag and the words, "slap…slap…slap" or the slapping gesture took on new meaning and always brought peals of laughter.

Zoe was always funny, full of life and had a crazy way of bringing humor to everyday things. The only thing she didn't find humorous was aging, which was why Operation Berkeley was something she wouldn't want to pass up. The chance to be young again was deliciously tempting for her. Christina tried to ask questions about their undertaking and the conversation always veered back to René. Finally Christina gave up and let her go with it.

The next day, they stayed in Zoe's apartment, enjoying each other's company, talking, reminiscing, and most of all laughing, which helped Christina as she hadn't laughed in the months since John was killed. Christina almost told Zoe of the note René slipped into her hand but decided against it.

They agreed to tell her children they'd be going on a photographic Safari in Africa for the magazine. It was believable because they knew Zoe traveled the world and that she'd invite Christina to pull her out of her depression. The remoteness of Africa was perfect because there weren't many cell phone towers.

Zoe would have no problem with her job because the editor of her magazine was also on the CIA payroll. The travels of a fashion magazine editor don't seem to hold much suspicion, and magazine shoots take place all around the world. Her editor knew Zoe was being assigned to something, so leaving her position at the magazine for the four months she'd be gone was acceptable.

Talking about it made Christina's apprehension resurface. Thinking of the contents of the note from René made her trepidation lessen slightly. In the back of her mind, she kept seeing the pictures taken of her without her knowledge. She wished she could've gotten a closer look at them to see where she was at the time and if any were taken inside her home. Dirty, rotten, filthy snake. Every time she thought about the invasion of her privacy, it infuriated her. She hoped René could be trusted.

The day went by quickly as it usually did when they're together. Laughing and reminiscing about their days as teenagers and little hippies, which is what they thought they were. Christina had to be up early the next day because she was taking the morning train home, so they called it a night early. Now she was thinking about Lou and his visit tomorrow. She sent her son Johnny another text message reminding him to be at the house by 2:30 at the latest. If Beulah is with Lou, which she most likely will be, she and Johnny have lots to do. He needs to be on time.

The next morning, she was on her way to the train station by 7:15. By 8:00 AM, she was on the train, heading back to her home in the suburb outside of Cheetaqua, NY. The train ride went quickly, especially since her thoughts would give her brain no respite. She was being bombarded with doubt and started worrying about Operation Berkeley, those damn recent pictures taken of her and what may happen with this Arabian prince. What did they need to find out, and how were they to achieve the goals set forth by the CIA? She wondered why she was worrying about accomplishing any objective for success, for it was obvious she was only the bait. The more she thought about it, the more her anxiety became overpowering. She started having misgivings about entering the world of spying and intrigue.

The train pulled into the Cheetaqua station at about 12:30. She gathered her bag, headed to her car, and drove home. Usually, when she walked through the door, her dog Sammy went bonkers, but he's with her daughter Mackenzie for the weekend. It'll be nice to get home, she thought. She pulled into the driveway and noticed the rhododendron was beginning to bloom, as were the azaleas. Spring is such a beautiful time of year. She made a mental note to check the apple trees in the backyard to see if the robins came back to nest as they always seem to.

She unlocked the door, walked in, and put her bag and purse down. With the quiet of being alone without the energized pawing of the dog, she was able to cross the entry in peace. She looked straight ahead. Oh no, something's wrong! She looked to her right…and then to her left. What the hell? She entered the dining room, stood in a certain spot, and looked at the photos on the hutch. Although nothing seemed out of place, she knew something was amiss. Someone had been in her house!

John installed a security system when they built the house and kept updating it as technology advanced. He was away so often and worried about his family, especially in his line of work. He set up a portion of the system so that photos arranged in a certain way will look directly at anyone standing in certain spots. When Christina walked through the door and stood on the threshold, everyone should be looking at her. When all are aligned as they should be and were when she left, the photo of John should look straight at her as she walked in the door. To the right is the photo of her parents, to the left, John's family is supposed to be smiling at her, and none of the photos were positioned correctly. Not one of them looked her in the eye.

Johnny wasn't here this weekend, and he wouldn't have moved any photographs even if he were. Lou said he stopped by twice, but no one was home. Did maybe Lou get in somehow? She grabbed her keys, entered the kitchen, walked to a very well-hidden corner closet, unlocked it, and entered, shutting the door behind her. In this secreted space, John had installed monitors and a high-tech security system. It was triggered by motion, so if someone was in the house in her absence, they would be on video. This was also where her pistol and ammunition were concealed. She got her revolver out of a locked drawer and unlocked another drawer for the ammunition and loaded it. "God bless you, John for being so damn smart!" she said aloud.

She pushed the correct sequence of buttons in the security system and the monitors came alive. Sure enough, on Friday morning, a man with a Cable TV uniform entered the house. He picked up almost every picture and seemed to study the faces of her family. She felt violated and extremely pissed off but glad he touched the things he did because it alerted her to his presence in her absence. When John set up this system, she questioned him about using the photos as points of disturbance.

"Christina, people want to know their subjects, the people they're spying on. It's a morbid curiosity, but I know what I'm doing. Hopefully, we'll never find out if I'm right or not." He was right.

She watched the intruder on the monitors and noted the rooms he went into, what he did and the time he left. This was definitely an undercover, clandestine activity. He was quite obviously looking for something, going through drawers and searching behind wall pictures, she surmised, looking for a safe. After his futile search in which he came up completely empty-handed, he began the business of bugging the house. He was the only person who entered her home in her absence.

Was this the work of that filthy, slimy fucking bastard Martin Cater? Could it be the FBI was trying to find something out? The only other people recorded were the mailman and Lou, and they were both outside. No one outside her immediate family knew of this security system.

She flicked a blue switch and looked at the monitors. As soon as the detection light was a steady blue, she walked out of the safe room and closed the door behind her, trying to seem as nonchalant as possible, acting as though she'd been looking for a grocery item. Her pistol was securely tucked into the back of her pants, hidden by her sweater. She looked up in the kitchen, and there was a steady blue light telling her where the surveillance device was placed in this room. She tried not to look directly at it, not wanting to give away that she was on to them, whoever "they" were.

She grabbed her bag and wove her way through the house, looking for the steady blue light that was undetectable by the surveillance equipment. As she walked through the house, she started to get angry. The "bugs" were in the kitchen, dining room, living room, master bedroom and what pissed her off the most, the master bathroom. Fucking perverts! This had to be Martin Cater. But what if it wasn't?

She went out the back door and walked through the garden, trying to decide what to do. She had to keep a cool head. What do they want? And who are "they"? John put in a scrambling device for this sort of thing. With the flick of a switch, their best-laid plans will be put to waste. She wondered if she should scramble the signal or let them think she's unaware they're watching and listening to every move she makes. She saw the intruder leave on their cameras, so she felt her home was safe.

She hatched a plan and decided to play their game. If they want to watch, she'll give them a show. She went inside, took her bag to her bedroom, hamming it up, dramatically looking around the room, throwing herself on the bed, "crying."

Okay, folks, it's showtime.

She started punching the bed, "John, how could you leave me?" throwing in a few staged gestures. "We had so much to look forward to! How did this happen?" She "sobbed" heavily and started taking her things out of the room. "I decided on the way home that I can't stand to be in this room without you. There's too much pain being in the room we shared. It's too much to bear!" (Sob, sob). "Please forgive me, but I can't spend another night in here with nothing but memories. I have to move out of here, John, I'm so sorry." (Sob, sob).

She went into their bathroom and, while "sobbing," removed all her toiletries from the closet and medicine cabinet and put them in a plastic tub and moved them into the girls' bathroom. Their shared bathroom was in between their bedrooms and was going to work out fine. Drawer by drawer, she moved her clothing into her new camera-less bedroom that was her oldest daughter's room and put the pistol in the bedside table drawer. She took clothes from her closet and moved everything into her new room. Within half an hour, she was completely moved into rooms with no watching eyes.

She went back into her bedroom with a large picture of her and John. It was her favorite from when they were younger. She lay on the bed, hugging the picture, staring at the ceiling, noting where the spy device was located. She kissed John and said, "I'll love you forever, but these memories are too hard to handle right now."

She situated their picture on his side of the bed and placed it so that John was looking straight at the surveillance, hoping to unnerve whoever thought it was a good idea to spy on a poor defenseless widow. She walked to the door, turned and looked around one last time and said, "Goodbye, my love," shut off the light and left the room.

She went into the kitchen and headed back to the security room. With its secluded position, it was impossible for it to be in view of the watchful eye of the spying intruder, so she felt secure going in there. Besides, it would've looked as though she was going into a pantry. There she procured a set of keys for a locked door accessible only from this security room and opened it.

This was John's office, and she hadn't been in there in months. She was safe from prying eyes in here. She hit the wall at a certain point with the ball of her hand and part of the paneling popped out, revealing a safe. She entered the combination and took out a sealed envelope with her son Johnny's name on it, with the instructions his father had left for him. John asked her not to open the envelope, so she didn't. It was between father and son.

She sat at the desk with paper and pen and thought about what to say and how to say it. She hadn't expected this, but her situation changed with the watchful eye of unknown individuals. After some thought, she hurriedly scribbled her message and sealed it in an envelope. She had to work quickly so the "blue light special" was turned off before Johnny got there. She didn't want him to know about this yet.

She left John's office, locked the door, secured the keys, and shut off the blue lights. She finished as his truck pulled into the driveway with her dog Sammy, who was wild with excitement. Christina wanted to give Johnny the envelope outside. He was expecting it, but she didn't want whoever was watching to know about it.

She went outside to greet them. Johnny let the dog out who bolted to her, jumping, pawing, and crying excitedly saying hello. Johnny got out and sauntered over to his mother. He was a laid-back kind of guy, looking very much like his dad, never in a hurry, always with an easy gait to his step even if he's late, which he wasn't today. She was sure the thought of Beulah gave him added incitement.

"Wow, Mom, you look fantastic!" he said giving her a hug and kiss. "Glad to see Zoe got you to do something with your hair. You've been looking pretty sad lately. I was hoping you'd come home a little spruced up."

"Yeah, the first thing she made me do was get my hair done. She didn't want to be seen with an old bag."

"Have a good time?"

"Yeah, you know how things are when we get together. We had lots of laughs. It was an interesting trip, to say the least."

"Really? How so?"

"I'll tell you about it later. I think I'm going on an African Safari with her in August for a few months. I'll talk about it more when Mackenzie is around."

He started walking towards the house, and she called him back. "Take this and read it now." She handed him the envelope from his father with his name on it. "I know you two discussed much of what's in there. Dad said it was between the two of you, and I respect that. I don't want to know what you two agreed on, especially since it was your father's wish." She locked eyes with him and said, "Your father trusted you to honor his wishes, and so do I. Please read this now, and don't let anyone else see it. It probably involves Beulah, and you'd better follow his instructions to the letter."

She gave him the envelope and the note with Lou's name on it. "This is for Lou Jenkins. When he comes, give it to him before he gets to the house. Tell him to read it immediately. He's going to ask what's going on and if I'm serious. Tell him I said to humor me and go with it. It's what Dad would've wanted."

"Ok, Mom but what…"

She cut him off. "Please do as I ask. One more thing, I don't want to see Beulah, so if she's with him, you tell him that, take her and leave. She is not to enter my home, understood?"

He looked at her questioningly. "Mom, what's going on? You're acting weird. Did the hair dye get to your brain or something?"

She took a deep breath and answered, "For the first time in months I'm thinking clearly. Let's go inside and get a cup of coffee. No more talk of this inside, okay?" Johnny looked at her strangely.

"Okay, Mom. I won't argue with you."

They headed into the house, and she put on the coffee. They took their coffee outside so Johnny could smoke. The house phone was ringing, so she went in to answer it. It was Lou.

"Christina, I wanted to check if you were home yet and if I could stop by earlier. Is now okay?"

"Sure, Lou, that's fine. I've put the coffee on, so it's perfect timing."

"Great, I'll see you in a few minutes." She went back outside and told Johnny that Lou was on his way. "Remember, make sure he reads my note and agrees to it before he comes to the door."

"Okay, Mom."

They heard Lou's car enter the driveway and went back into the house. Johnny kissed her goodbye because he'll be leaving with Beulah. He walked to the car and when Lou got out, they made small talk and Johnny handed him the envelope from Christina. It looked like he was asking Johnny what was going on. He opened it and read it. More words between them and Johnny shrugged and waved for Christina to come out.

"Hey, Lou! How's it going?" she asked, walking towards them.

"Christina, you look fabulous. New York agrees with you."

"Thanks, Lou, it was long overdue. Something wrong?" He looked puzzled.

"What's going on?"

"We're following directives left by John. Beulah may be the only witness to John's death, and she has to be kept safe. Johnny has his instructions, and I don't want her in my house. She'll be safe with him." Then she looked at Johnny and said, "Take her and get out of here." She was in the front seat.

"But…" Lou started to say something and was interrupted.

"Lou, don't piss me off. I've been through enough already. We all have our instructions from John. Let's do as we've been asked." Johnny and Beulah left, leaving Lou and Christina alone.

"I hope you know what you're doing, Christina." He grabbed a box and a briefcase out of the back seat, and they headed towards the house.

"Did you read the note from me?"

"Yes, but I don't understand."

"Play along with me, okay? What's the harm?"

"I learned a long time ago not to argue with you. I know how stubborn you can be."

"Smart man. Let's go in and I'll get you that cup of coffee."

They settled in the living room and sat across from each other. "This is hard for me, Christina. You know how close John and I were. I hate to be the one to bring these to you, but I wouldn't want anyone else to do it." He handed over the box, and in it were the personal items from John's office at the FBI. Framed photos of their family, books, knick-knacks, and things that make an office a homey place. She went through the box with tears flowing down her cheeks. Words can't describe her loss. She felt hollow and empty.

"Where's the gun?" she asked.

"Excuse me?"

"John's pistol. It's not in the box. Is it in the briefcase?"

Lou looked uncomfortable. "We haven't finished the forensics on it."

"Bullshit, Lou, you've had it for months. I was expecting it back today. Where is it?"

"Christina, these things take time. It's in a secure place, and you'll get it back as soon as we've finished testing it. We want to know what happened to John almost as much as you do." She silently stared at him.

He handed her an envelope from his briefcase with her name on it in John's handwriting. In it were two handwritten pieces of paper. She opened the first one, which was a poem from John. A very small key fell out of the paper and onto the floor. She picked it up and held it in her fist as she read the poem.

*"Nestled deep within our heart*
*The two of us stand together*
*Confusing to all, but we know the truth*
*We've withstood all kinds of weather.*

*No reason to ever trust others*
*To give us what we need*
*We Cater to each other's souls*
*Our love will not recede.*

*The proof of what our heart does know*
*Now rests inside your hands*
*The key to our heart I give back to you*
*Our eternal love still stands."*

Through tears she opened the second paper which was a letter from John.

**My Dearest love Christina,**

If you're reading this, **I'm** no longer with you. My poem to you, as with all the others written over the years, **tell**s **you** the **things** I **may not have been able to say at the time.**

**We are two pieces of a puzzle that come together** to make a beautiful picture. Your safety **and** the safety of our children have always been of utmost importance to me. You **give** my life **meaning** and made me so incredibly happy.

My biggest regret is we never made it to **France. The City of Light** is for lovers, which is what you are to me. **On my last visit to that fair city,** I promised myself to take you there.

There are **no accident**s in life. Everything happens for a reason. If I'm gone – live your life and be happy. You have much love to give. I give you back the **key** to y**our heart. Find where it can be opened**. You'll know what to do with **the contents** when you do. Make sure he is worthy of the **apple** of my eye, the funny, beautiful, and cherished woman, my Christin**a**.

**All my love forever and longer,**

John

Christina sat for a few minutes, not saying anything, taking in the last words of her beloved husband. She read it a few times and looked at the key. Lou pulled her from her thoughts.

"Christina, I have a few questions if you don't mind."

"Huh?" She had a million thoughts going through her head. John was telling her something. This little key was important, but she had to keep cool. John always did things like this, getting her to figure things out and find things by clues in poems and letters. If he wanted Lou to know anything about this, he would've told him himself.

"Why are some of the words and sentences darker? Is John trying to tell you something?"

"John used his fountain pen, which you dip into the inkwell. The darker words are where he dipped the pen back in. He thought it was romantic when writing his poems and letters to me. He was like Robert Browning, and I was Elizabeth Barrett." Wow! She surprised herself with that answer. I might be good at this spy thing, she thought. "Do you know he used to call me whenever he was away and sing 'our song' to me every night we weren't together? He was such a romantic man. It's going to be hard getting used to not having him around."

"Christina, I don't think you're being honest with me. He's leaving you some sort of message and wants you to find where the key opens."

"If you think there's more to it, that's your problem. Stop trying to read into things that aren't."

"Alright. What about the key?"

"What about it?" she asked him right back. "It's the key to my heart. John carried it with him everywhere. It's obvious he wants me to find love again and give it to someone worthy of it."

"So, do you have the key to his heart?"

"Lou, where are you going with this?"

"I'd like to see the key you have that's supposed to be the key to John's heart."

"Go fuck yourself!" She didn't have a key to John's heart! For whatever reason, this key John left her was important, and he wants her to find where it opens. She had to think fast.

She looked down at the key and noticed scratches on it, and it dawned on her. "You read my letter and poem and have been trying to find out what this key opens, didn't you? Lou, how could you?"

"We're trying to find out what happened. That key may hold the answers to what John was working on when he was killed." He paused for a minute and then added, "So can I see the key you have to John's heart?"

"*Fuck you*, Lou. You've got huge balls coming here and asking me that after you invaded my privacy, reading the final letter from my husband to me and taken the key to my heart and scratched the shit out of it trying it on who knows what locks. Is that why it's taken so long for me to get these things?"

"If you'd show me the key you have..."

"I wouldn't even if I still had it. I put it in his cold, dead hand before they closed the casket. Sorry, but I'm sure it melted during cremation." She was livid. "Thanks for dropping off John's things. I appreciate it, but it's time you left."

"Christina, please, we're trying to help."

"Save it, Lou, I'm not buying your story. I'm crushed that you opened my letter and read the private thoughts my husband meant for me alone. How could you invade our lives like that? You should be ashamed of yourself."

"I'm sorry, Christina."

She laughed bitterly. "No, you're not. You're sorry you didn't get the answers you wanted. You Bureau people are all alike. It's not enough that my husband gave his life in the line of duty. You felt it necessary to invade the privacy of his widow. Do I have to worry that you're going to bug my house?"

"Of course not, Christina, we'd never do that. I'm sorry I upset you. That wasn't my intention."

"Thanks for bringing John's things. Sorry, you have to leave so soon. Come again when you can't stay so long." She stood, walked to the door, and opened it, letting Lou know she wanted him to leave.

"I'll be talking to you soon, Christina. I promised John I'd watch over you if anything ever happened to him."

"Yeah, sure, Lou. I gotta tell ya, you're doing a bang-up job so far." She closed the door after him and watched him walk to his car. As he pulled out of the driveway, she looked at the key in her hand. She went to the living room where the cameras could see her. She put the key near her heart and made a noise as though a door was being closed, turned the key as if locking her heart, and said, "John, my heart was open for you forever. Now I've locked the door until I find someone worthy enough to open it."

She chuckled to herself and wondered if she should prepare a speech for the Academy Awards or try to figure out where this key fits.

# CHAPTER 9

For the first time that day, Martin sat comfortably in his business class seat on his flight home with scotch in hand. What a bitch of a day it'd been! Metzger will regret what occurred in his office today. Martin will make sure of that when he's in charge after the success of Operation Berkeley.

He thought about which cabinet position would be the one he coveted the most. I'll write my own ticket in Washington once the President gets the information from 1971, he thought. He felt quite pleased with himself, even though Tommy was breathing down his neck. "Who cares how often I have to report to that twat of a man? I'll have the President beholden to me, owing me, Martin Cater, and then my revenge on Tom Metzger will begin." These thoughts put Martin in a giddy mood. He didn't think anything could spoil the end events of this day.

He had the privacy and time to check the surveillance cameras from his apartment. He trusted no one, especially those working for him. His apartment was his sanctuary, and he always wanted to know what was going on there when he wasn't home. How else could he know if his cleaning service was doing as requested or if they snooped or stole from him? It'll be interesting to see how they cleaned up from this morning.

The flight attendant brought him another scotch, and he was ready to view the surveillance from his apartment today. He was interested in what Charles did while alone in his residence. Giving Charles a key was a ploy to see if he could be trusted. Thus far, he hadn't done anything underhanded, but one couldn't be completely trusted. Charles wasn't CIA material, being too soft and easily bullied. He's become the perfect shit-upon under his tutelage, so eager to please it was nauseating, which wasn't a characteristic Martin admired.

He turned on his laptop and opened the file for his apartment surveillance. He put the earphones in and waited for the file to upload. He always insisted on the last row window seat of business class, so no one was sitting behind him, eavesdropping on what he was working on.

He opened the file and started it at 9:30 AM this morning. He watched as he was sleeping, and the alarms going off. He must've been out cold if he couldn't hear the alarm clock blaring right next to him. He shifted in his seat as his hip began to ache. He fast-forwarded until he saw Charles and René at his apartment door. He watched them knock and wait. The monitor of his computer was quartered with Martin's bedroom, the outside hallway, the office, and the threshold to his bedroom visible. The two men stayed outside in the hallway for five minutes, knocking and waiting until Charles decided to use his key.

Martin watched as they entered the apartment slowly, and it looked as though René was ready to draw his weapon. He heard his own voice screaming and crying. He uncomfortably watched himself as he thrashed in bed, kicking his feet, arms flaying amid his agonizing dream. When he screamed for help, that was when the two agents took matters into their own hands. Although he'd never admit it, Martin was warmed by how quickly they rose to action when he called for help.

He watched as they kicked in the door with amazing force. As soon as the door was down, the screen went blank. Martin tried to reboot the file, but the result was the same. He realized when they broke the door in, the connection to the equipment was lost. Martin set it up himself with infinitesimal wires attached to the door frame, so thin they were unable to sustain the breakdown of the door.

His mood instantly soured and went from jubilant to irritable truculence. He tried the other rooms, but nothing was visible from the time of the break-in to his bedroom. He was looking forward to watching what Charles did in his apartment when he wasn't there. Fixing his security system will be the first thing he'll do when he gets home.

Maybe it'll be the second. The first thing is to get the zip drive from his man in the field, who set up the surveillance at Pucci's house. He wants to see what goes on there when she gets back from New York. She has no idea what he's capable of. No one gets away with the shit she pulled today with no consequence. I've killed many worthless women for much less, he thought.

After the evidence is back from 1971, he'll personally take care of her. Since he'll undoubtedly be a member of the presidential cabinet, no one would suspect him of being involved in her death or disappearance. They'll be looking at the Morgans, who'll be ruined, or the Zatari Royal Family, who would also be suspects. Whoever is blamed, that Pucci whore will be dead within a year.

The flight from Washington went quickly, and he was soon back in New York with Charles waiting for him. He limped over to him and tossed his briefcase. He was surly now that he was unable to view the goings on at his apartment. Charles took the briefcase and asked, "How was your trip, sir?"

"Fine," Martin answered. He had no baggage, so they headed for the car.

When they got into the car, Charles said, "All has been taken care of at your apartment. It looks as though nothing happened there." When Martin didn't answer or comment, Charles added, "I apologize for busting in and destroying your doorway. We were concerned for your safety, sir." Martin grunted.

They rode in silence for the next few minutes until Martin realized Charles was driving to his apartment. "I need to go to the office. Go there first and wait for me in the car."

"Yes, sir," Charles answered, hiding his irritation. Why couldn't he have stated that when they got into the car? What an asshole he is.

When they got to the office, Martin grabbed his laptop and got out. "I don't know how long I'll be. Wait here until I'm done."

"Yes, sir." As the door to CIA headquarters was opened for Martin by the security guard, a man walked towards him. Charles got the minuscule camera out and zoomed in for a picture of the man Martin was meeting. His camera took five pictures in rapid succession. He checked out the pictures to make sure they were clear. The phone calls Charles monitored from Martin's phone today revealed the man he was meeting was the same person he spoke to earlier, immediately after phoning the White House.

He sent the photos, information, and phone conversations to Metzger as instructed. No one at the Agency was aware of the informational exchanges taking place between Charles and the Chief. Martin was looking for something, and it seemed he'd stop at nothing to find whatever it was. Charles hoped the data he sent would help to get rid of this evil man.

Once the two men were in the privacy of Martin's office, he was handed a component for his laptop. Martin told the agent to install it as he watched. After a few minutes, the computer monitor was divided again, this time into five sections. He showed Martin how to access the surveillance in Christina Pucci's home. They looked at the screen and Martin remarked, "Nice touch. I'll see some interesting things, especially in the bathroom. You're a sick fuck, you know that? I'm going to have some fun with this one."

The man replied, "I put one in the bathroom because that seems to be a place people tend to hide things. Knowing you as I do, I didn't think you'd object to some inappropriate viewing." The two men laughed heartily. Martin was virtually drooling over the prospect of such a presentation. He was feeling jubilant over the expectation of the potential vistas he'd soon be experiencing.

"I take it you didn't find any of the items I'm interested in."

"No," he answered, "I looked all through the house and couldn't find any folders or safes of any kind."

Martin grunted. "Well, over the next month or two, she'll show me exactly where the things I'm looking for are located. When she does, I'll contact you immediately, and you're to drop everything and deal with it. It's of the utmost importance."

"I'm always at your disposal, Chief."

"Disposal," Martin laughed, "that's an appropriate way of putting it."

They had a drink, and the equipment was further explained to Martin. He'll thoroughly enjoy watching that bitch go through her day, from sunup to sundown. He didn't doubt she'd lead him to what he was looking for. People have the tendency to revisit things and he was confident that dumb bitch will lead him directly to his quarry.

They left CIA Headquarters, shook hands, and went their different ways. Charles sat patiently in the car for Martin's return. The back door opened, Martin got in, and Charles drove to Martin's apartment. He didn't question Martin about any events of the day, not wanting to seem too anxious to find out what Martin was up to. He knew the best way to deal with him was to stay as close to the periphery as possible.

Martin told Charles to pick him up Monday morning at eight and didn't want to be disturbed over the weekend unless it was an emergency. He got out of the car, and Charles drove off.

Martin had a busy weekend ahead of him. Tomorrow he'll be rewiring his apartment, and Sunday has been set aside for the big show. He couldn't wait until the Pucci whore got home. Not only was he looking forward to her leading him to his target, but it would be interesting to see what she had under those clothes. Things were working out to his liking.

He unlocked his apartment door and did a walk-through. He inspected the new doorway and the new door. The workmen did a superb job, although he'd never admit it to anyone. He'll repair the wiring in the morning. He went into his bedroom and inspected the bed and the laundry hamper. Everything was washed and put away, including the pajamas he'd been wearing and the sheets that were on his bed. He took the pajamas and sheets, put them into a garbage bag, and walked into the hallway to the incinerator. He watched as the bag dropped down the long chute. He had no intention of using them again.

He went back into the apartment, poured himself a scotch, and went into his office. He put the laptop on the desk along with his briefcase and sat down to peruse the Operation Berkeley files again. He was quite pleased with himself, especially because he was able to assemble what he considered the dream team.

René was a seasoned agent who knew how to procure needed intelligence, and his proficiency in Middle Eastern languages will be invaluable in listening to conversations between the prince and his family. Pucci was exactly what the prince looked for in a woman. She'd better cooperate and use whatever charms she has to attract the prince and get into his inner circle. She'll spread those legs for him, whore that she is. Janis is the icing on the cake. Beautiful and beguiling, she knows enough to help René in any of the clandestine activities they'll have to perform.

He put their files on the desk and looked them over a few more times, congratulating himself on procuring these three. It didn't bother him in the least that he sacrificed the lives of their loved ones to achieve his goal. Collateral damage is expected. Feeling pleased with himself, he had another scotch and went to bed.

To his relief, there were no dreams about John Pucci. After his coffee, he started fixing his surveillance system. It was more difficult this time because of his hip injury. It was cumbersome climbing the ladder, and what had taken him a few short hours when first installing the equipment, now took him most of the day to get things into working order.

He was overly anxious about her arrival home tomorrow. He had the laptop set up so he could view her home most of the day. He momentarily switched to his own system after the wiring was completed to make sure it was in working order. He looked forward to his new favorite pastime and couldn't wait until she walked through the door, and he'd be able to watch how she spent her days.

His hip was on fire, most likely from climbing up and down the ladder rewiring his equipment. He swallowed one of Doc Slaven's pills and before bed, took a hot shower and inspected his wound. It looked worse than it did this morning. Fucking bullet. If he'd been able to get it removed immediately after Pucci shot him, he wouldn't be in this position. He could wait another few months. After all, he'll have the best doctors once he's in a cabinet position. He was a hero; he detonated an IED with only himself as the casualty. He was sticking to that story, and there was no one alive to disprove it.

He slept well and awoke in a euphoric state with the expectation of watching Christina Pucci in her private moments. Not only would he be able to find Pucci's pistol, but he'd be able to watch her bathe, dress, and undress and watch her sleep if he so desired. He could not only watch her in real time, but the equipment recorded any movement in the rooms, so he'd be able to view the tapes at his leisure.

In mid-afternoon, he heard what sounded like a key entering a lock. He sat down in front of his laptop and watched. She opened the door, putting her bags down. She stood in the doorway looking one way and then another. She walked into the dining room and looked around. What's she looking at? Was this her normal behavior? He watched as she entered the kitchen and moved into an area not visible on the surveillance equipment. He became impatient saying, "Come out, come out wherever you are, you stupid bitch."

She was out of view for about ten minutes. When she was visible again, she walked through the house, looking around but doing nothing. She went out the back door of the kitchen and was once again out of sight. "Come on, Sweetie, let's see some action." He'd soon regret those words.

She reentered the house, grabbed her bag, and proceeded to the master bedroom. "Ok, time to change out of those traveling clothes and give us a show." In her bedroom, she started to cry, fell on the bed, punching it. Martin got closer to the monitor to get a better look, watching with no emotion.

"Cut the drama, bitch and give your buddy Martin something worthwhile to see." She went to the closet, removing clothes and taking them out of the room. Were those his clothes? While crying, she emptied drawers, moving everything, and he watched her leave the bedroom she shared with her husband.

"No, you can't move out of this room!" he screamed at the monitor. "You fucking bitch! Stop!" This wasn't going as planned. This bitch was ruining everything!

He watched as she went into the bathroom and started removing things, putting them in a plastic tub. Maybe she got new shampoos from her makeover. He watched as his plan went down the drain. "What the fuck are you doing?" he continued yelling at the monitor. "You stupid fucking slut. You can't do this!" He started throwing things.

Everything she's done since he met her has put him on edge. Never has a woman tormented him in such a way, and he couldn't do anything about it which angered him further. He despised her at this moment, more than when she threw the files in his office, wanting to choke her with his bare hands.

She went back into the bedroom holding something in a frame that he was unable to see. She kissed whatever it was, saying maudlin bullshit. She placed it on the bed and left the room. That's when Martin saw that it was a photo the two of them. Martin looked away because John Pucci was staring at him. It was haunting the way she set the photo on the pillow, with him looking directly at the "bug," mocking him. It reminded him of his nightmare and wished he could block out that room. Now whenever he looked at the monitor, John Pucci was staring at him.

She walked into the kitchen and disappeared. Where the hell did she go? He wished his man had taken photos of the interior of the house. He'll ask him if he recalls what was off the kitchen. She remained out of sight and when visible again, she walked to the front door and exited. Martin couldn't see outside but could hear the excited barking of a dog.

She returned with her son and went to the kitchen. He couldn't hear their conversation because that damn dog wouldn't shut up. He hated animals! They took their coffee outside. Couldn't they stay in the kitchen like everyone else? The phone rang, and Martin regretted not putting a bug in the phone, talked out of by the field agent. He reasoned that most people use cell phones nowadays, and bugging the house phone would be senseless. Why did he listen to dumb assholes?

She came in to answer the phone. Some guy Lou was stopping by. He looked for the FBI roster of employees and found the name of Louis Jenkins listed in the office where Pucci had worked. Hopefully, this would lead to the whereabouts of the pistol.

Her son came back into the house, put his cup in the dishwasher, and kissed his mother goodbye. She watched him leave, then walked out. "No!" Martin screeched. "Can't you stay in the fucking house?" She walked in with a man who was carrying a briefcase and a box. He sat in her living room, while she got him a cup of coffee.

When she returned, he gave her the box. She went through it without taking things out. Martin couldn't see what was in there but assumed it contained items from his office. She put the box aside and asked where the gun was. "Yes, my friend," Martin said, listening closely, "exactly what I want to know. We're finally getting somewhere!"

Lou says they're still doing forensics on it. "Fuck! They still have it! What can they still be testing on it? I need that gun!"

The man pulled an envelope from his briefcase and handed it to her. She opened it and read the contents. He noticed something fall out of the envelope, which she picked up. She seemed to read the contents over and over. Then he asked her about what was written.

Martin listened intently to their conversation. When she remarked on Browning and Barrett, his cynicism rose to the surface, and he yelled out, "Good Lord! I could puke! What a sap Pucci was! All that bullshit to get laid." Listening to the conversation, Martin learned that a key had fallen out of the envelope. Maybe that key will lead to the gun. He continued eavesdropping to find out more about this key. He leaned in closer, even though he was as close as he could get. He turned up the volume as high as it could go.

They argued about the key, with her insisting it's the key to her heart. Then things got nasty between the two of them. That feisty little bitch doesn't frighten easily and has quite a temper which Martin could attest to. He could tell by the man's behavior that he wasn't enjoying this visit. They argued about the key, with Lou not believing her story about keys to each other's hearts.

*"I'd like to see the key you have to John's heart."*

*"Lou, go fuck yourself!"* Martin didn't see that coming. After the man said he wanted to see her key the shit hit the fan and things got ugly. She was pissed, he could see it in her eyes, even on the surveillance it was obvious. This guy hit a sore spot.

She bitched him out for reading her private letter and trying the key on various locks. Most interesting. Martin loved a good fight.

She swore at him a few times and told him to leave. The man said he'd keep an eye on her. Shit! She's bitching about an invasion of privacy. Honey, you have no idea. Then she asked if he's going to bug the house. Does she know her house is bugged? Is that why she moved everything out of her bedroom? She couldn't possibly know. If the FBI decides to go in and install surveillance equipment, they'll discover what's already there. Fuck! Why does she make everything so complicated? What a pain in the ass she's turning out to be.

When she was alone, she motioned locking her heart with the key. Martin didn't believe her syrupy performance, but why do it if no one was watching? He didn't believe that bullshit about keys to their hearts. He needs to know what Pucci wrote to her, wondering how to get his hands on it. Was it schmaltzy crap or was there more to it, like this guy suggested? If Martin can't get his hands on it before she goes to Berkeley, he'll have time to search the house while she's gone. One way or another, he'll get his hands on the key and the letter from Pucci. For him, it was a matter of life and death.

And for the entire time Martin was eavesdropping on Christina Pucci, her husband's eyes had not moved and uncomfortably stared a hole through the center of Martin Cater's soul.

# CHAPTER 10

Christina sat in her living room in full view of the surveillance, purposely staying in there to not raise suspicions that she knows she's being watched. She went through the box with John's belongings with her secret observer looking over her shoulder.

She missed him terribly and couldn't hold back the tears. His possessions still carried his scent. She buried her face in a handkerchief to smell him again. What else in this box was going to break her heart?

There were books, photos, miscellaneous office items, and a clock given to him for 25 years of service. She sneered at the irony of something from the FBI to calculate time when they took the very gift it was made to measure. Time is something to contemplate and treasure. She wished she could go back to when John was alive, get one last look into his eyes, when his spirit would be looking back at her. After delving into that thought, it reminded her of the agreement into which she'd entered, most likely with the devil himself.

She picked up the box and decided to deal with this another time. She took it to their bedroom, put it on the floor, walked to John's wardrobe, and opened it. She opened a few of his drawers, looking for something locked. To confuse her observer, she removed clothes and smelled them as she did the handkerchief. She'd done it quite often before, only this time she was looking for something her key would open. After not finding anything, she closed the wardrobe. She didn't want the appearance of looking for anything this key could open. She got her jewelry box and left the room.

In the privacy of her new bedroom, she opened the jewelry box and found a chain that was of a strong design and linkage. Until she discovered what this key opened, it would remain around her neck. When she held it in her hands, John felt near. She needed to discover what he's trying to tell her.

She went into her room and turned on the television for some noise. She opened the poem and letter from John and grabbed a notebook and pen. John's been doing little coded message games with her since he sent her on a search for her engagement ring. He's never been able to stump her, and that's what he's banking on. She set out in her usual way of figuring out John's cryptic messages, sentence by sentence, writing her thoughts on his clues, starting with his usual hints, the darker words.

**Nestled deep within our heart, the two of us stand together**

**Confusing to all, but we know the truth. We've withstood all kinds of weather.**

*It's a heart-should've written* our hearts, *not our heart. Doesn't make mistakes when giving clues, everything is specific. Singular heart belonging to us. Heart locket? Don't have one. This clue is deep. Maybe I'll find something as I go along.*

**No reason to ever trust**

**Cater**

What? *Didn't realize the word "cater" had significance! How would John know? It's capitalized, so it's a name. Why write that unless he knew something? Did he find out I was being considered for an assignment? Why warn me unless our paths might cross? Disturbing. Should I back out? René's note explains the consequences. I'm stuck if I want to remain safe. What was I thinking- the safety of my children?* "Well, John," she said aloud, "I don't trust him, and you're right about that slimy snake." She continued.

**The proof of what our heart does know now rests inside your hands**

**The key to our heart I give to you.**

*Same heart, our heart, no idea where, but holds proof of something I need to find.*

She unconsciously clutched the key in her closed hand. She hoped he didn't die because of the proof he's referring to. Giving it to her and not to Lou, it's personal.

**My Dearest Love, Christina,**

**I tell you things**

**may not have been able to say at the time.**

**We are two pieces of a puzzle that come together,**

**and give meaning**

*Stumped! Two puzzle pieces. No, two pieces of a puzzle that come together. He's specific. What does he mean?*

**France. The City of Light, on my last visit to that fair city,**

*Why France reference? Was he there before he was killed? Can't check passport - would've used an alias. Paris? No, if he meant Paris, he would've written Paris. Maybe somewhere in the vicinity of Paris, an area nearby.*

**no accident**

*Accident is darkened but not the "s" at the end, so maybe an incident made to look like an accident? City of light, last visit, no accident; whatever he's referring to, it happened in France.*

**Key/our heart. Find where it can be opened/the contents**

*Our hearts again. The proof I need to find is in a heart, which has to do with this non-accident in France. Key opens the heart. Hopefully not in France! Wouldn't have left it there for me to find.*

**apple**

*Apple? What does an apple have to do with any of this? Not NYC. Would've called it the Big Apple. Maybe there's a city near Paris with the name of an apple.*

**Cia**

*Did he really darken those letters in my name? Must have something to do with the CIA.*

She thought of René and wondered if the non-accident John was referring to was the accident that took the lives of his wife and child. He's her only link to France and the CIA. But only met two days ago! Am I trying to make it easier on myself? Where do I begin to delve into finding the answers, let alone the proof? "John," she said aloud, "you usually give me more to go on than this!" And then his final line:

**All my love forever and longer.**

That's for me; no clue, not part of any puzzle. We had a great marriage, one half of the other. Always said, "*Love you forever and longer.*" Reading it brought heartbreaking tears, realizing she'd never hear those words from him again.

She assumed the FBI made copies and sent them to be analyzed by code breakers or cryptographers. Lou insisted he's sending a message, and the key opens something because she's sure he's right. It was left for her to find its secret, not the FBI, so it's personal, not business.

Her eyes kept going over the words he'd written, leaving her confused, which is what usually happens when she first gets the clues. Once she's figured it out, the clues make perfect sense, but where to begin?

She wrote the words of the note René slipped into her hand. This France reference made her think about emailing René and running some of this past him, including the bugging of her house. She wasn't sure if she could trust him but didn't trust anyone. She wanted to follow her instincts, hoping they would lead her in the right direction. For the next month or two, it's going to have to be life as usual.

It was time to walk the dog, and she felt uneasy knowing she was clandestinely photographed on their nightly walk and her home was invaded by an invisible interloper. She put her pistol in the back of her jeans and the writings from John and her scribblings in the safe of their security room. Maybe whoever's watching wants them and thinks that while she's walking the dog is the opportune time to obtain them.

When they returned from their walk, she checked the security room to make sure there was no illegal entry during her absence. That's going to become a regular part of her days. When all was clear, she double bolted the locks and made her way to bed. Sam wanted to go to the old bedroom and stared at her like she was crazy. "We've got to get used to new stuff, buddy, and this is our new room." He happily followed her in and jumped on the bed.

The next morning, she sat down at the computer in her little nook in the kitchen, ready to check her emails and send one off to René when she realized that "someone" was looking over her shoulder. They could easily get her email if they wanted, but she wasn't going to make it easy for them. She swore under her breath, went online to read the news on a few sites, all while thinking, "How can I do this without being seen?" and then got a brilliant idea.

She got dressed, retrieved her scribbling of the writings from John from the safe, and the paperwork from the meeting with Martin Cater, and left the house. She went to one of her favorite places, where she had a different email address and complete privacy, the library.

She had resumed her job voluntarily and helped with research and read to preschoolers on Friday mornings. When she walked in, everyone complimented her on her new look. She said her computer was on the blink and came to catch up on some internet searches and check her email. She sat at her usual computer and used the email address from the library. No one knew this address, so she felt her privacy was protected. She sent an email to René and put in the subject: *It's 'T' time*. Seeing how he's in the spy business, he should figure it out.

She cut right to the chase. "René, something about my house is 'bugging' me since I arrived home. Got a puzzling message, would like to discuss. I don't trust anyone and don't know where to turn. Hate to bother you, but not sure how to proceed. Can't talk at home and don't trust cell phones. Please advise how we can speak privately. Email me at this address asap. Prying eyes are on my home computer, so I'm using the library. Looking forward to hearing from you soon. T." She hit the send button and hoped for an answer soon. She calculated the time in France, and it was late afternoon there. Hopefully, he'll get it soon.

While waiting for a reply, she googled *"Prince Ali Al-Machmud."* Most of what came up was in Arabic, but she found some information in English. From what she read, he seemed to be more interested in Art than oil or foreign intrigue. She thought it best to read this at home, so she printed up whatever she could find.

As the articles were printing, she got the little "ding" telling her she had a new email. She waited until the print job was finished before checking the email. She didn't want to leave the printer while printing materials on a Zatarian prince. It may draw unwanted attention.

The email was from René. He wrote: *"Dearest T, I find your message disturbing. Go immediately and procure a disposable cell phone for international calls, or if not available, a phone card you can use to phone abroad. Don't use your current cell phone. Email me your new phone number to the address listed in this email, and I'll call you immediately. We definitely need to speak. René"*

She was on her first solo mission. Disposable cell phones were readily available and easy to activate. She went back to the library and emailed the new number as instructed. She went out to the library garden gazebo and waited. The gardens were beautiful with all the spring perennials coming up. Pink, purple, and white flowers, coupled with the smell of some of the flowering trees, made her feel as though she could be somewhere tropical. She closed her eyes and let the warmth of the sun and the floral aromas send her off to a peaceful place. She was brought back to reality by the sharp ring of the new phone.

"Bonjour," she said as she answered.

"Bonjour. Madame Pucci?"

"Please, call me Christina or Tee."

"Very well, Christina. What did I give you in the hallway?"

"A note, which you wrote to destroy and did."

"Making sure it's you. It seems things have been exciting since arriving home, no? Can you speak safely where you are?"

"Yes." She proceeded to tell him about the bugs, the writings from John, what she could decipher from them, the key that opens something vital for her to find, and most importantly, the no-accident-France reference. "Do you think John may be referencing the non-accident of your family?"

"Yes, I believe he's referring to it."

"How could he know about that?"

"He may have been in France when the accident occurred."

"Oh God, René, please tell me you don't think he's responsible."

"I don't. Martin Cater is responsible. Your husband may have been following Martin and perhaps witnessed the staging of the accident."

"Are we looking for a scapegoat for our grief and pointing the finger at that vile excuse for a human?"

"No. As I stated in my note, we can help one another find the truth about the deaths of our loved ones."

"The warning John gave me about Cater makes me feel I should back out of this assignment. I'm so confused as to whom I can trust, and I'm sorry to say that includes you." There was silence. "René, are you there?"

"Ah, Madame, I cannot blame you for doubting me. After all, I'm a member of an organization in the business of schemes, deception, and trickery. But I give you my word, I'll protect you and make sure you're unharmed and return home safely. We must be allies against this common enemy. We need time and privacy to talk and plan freely, and we can achieve that in 1971. There's safety for us there. If we back out now, we're useless to Martin, and we'll be in danger, and that includes your children, and the lovely Ms. Janis. With the surveillance in your home, you must realize Martin will go to great lengths to attain what he desires."

He paused. "We both lost loved ones because we were required for this mission. I'd hate for their deaths to be for naught and lose our leverage to avenge their deaths, for there's nothing else we can do for them."

"Yeah, I didn't think of that." She let what he said sink in and asked, "Should I scramble the signal or leave it and let them watch?"

"I think it would be wise to leave it, as long as you know they're watching.

"Do you think it's the FBI?"

"No, I think they have more respect for you as the widow of one of their own. As you said, they're probably trying to make sense of what your husband wrote to you. They wouldn't invade your home. It's more in the spirit of Martin Cater."

As their conversation continued, she dictated the clues John gave her. She was apprehensive, but maybe he could figure something out that she couldn't. She relayed to him some of what she thought his clues might mean. She asked him if he could figure out what the "apple" reference meant, and he said he'd work on it from the French perspective. When she got to the end and told him of the three letters darkened in her name, he assured her they were on the right track.

"Ah, Madame, I wish I could have known your husband. He must have been a person of great worth and wisdom. Now I can honestly say I'm sorry for your loss."

"Thanks, René."

"These phones we should use only for communication between us, no? Let me know if you find where your key belongs. I have a feeling that whatever it opens, we'll both find satisfaction. Please don't hesitate to call me if you need to. I'm at your service."

"*Merci, René. Au revoir.*"

"*Au revoir, Madame. Bon chance!*"

Now she had no choice but to go ahead with that bastard's plan. If she backed out, he'd take revenge on her and her children. No wonder John said not to trust him. If she'd only gotten his message a week earlier. She would've never agreed to any of it, including going to New York. But then would he take revenge on them all?

One thing was certain: she was being underestimated. She had no intention of looking over her shoulder at every turn. René was right. She's on the right track. She's still apprehensive about this mission, but now her disdain for Cater deepened to intense hatred. She wouldn't let John die for nothing, and he was right about Martin, but now that she jumped in, it's either do or die, literally. She had some planning to do.

That night, Christina went to Mackenzie's house. Johnny was there, and they Skyped with her daughter in South Carolina. She told them all at the same time about the trip to Africa with Zoe and the times she'd be gone. There were the usual protests, but eventually they started to think it was a good idea to get away, especially for Thanksgiving.

She asked Mackenzie and her hubby, Matt, if they'd consider moving into her house to take care of Sam. It's hard enough for the dog, waiting for John to come home, but with her gone for four months, Christina wanted him at home and didn't want her house left empty. "Whoever" was able to bypass the alarm system, but if they knew her son-in-law Matt, a New York State Trooper, and one supreme badass was there, one would wisely stay away.

She thought of telling Zoe about what was going on but decided against it. She wasn't keeping things from her but didn't feel safe speaking on the phone. She could email her from the library but didn't know if they were monitoring Zoe's emails. She has enough on her plate right now with her job and this upcoming adventure and didn't want to add more stress to her life. When they get together, she'll fill her in on everything.

For the time being, she'll research the prince and his relationship with Morgan to ensure she knows all there is to know about him before meeting him, while trying to find out as much as she can about Martin Cater. Best to arm oneself with knowledge, which can be stronger than steel. One thing is for certain, Cater has no idea who he's dealing with and has vastly underestimated the adversary he has created. One way or another, she was going to get retaliation for John.

# CHAPTER 11

Martin kept a close eye on Pucci's house, which was in his sights with a click on his laptop, but the bitch was never there, which infuriated him. She was seldom in any room under surveillance. She was visible in the morning when she had her coffee, in the evening when fixing her dinner, or when she was on the computer, which she didn't seem to use very often. She was never in any of the other rooms set up for observation. Where does she hide herself in that house? He needed to get his hands on the house layout that his field agent possessed.

Martin was trying to contact him because he wanted the house outline and wanted him to go back, remove the bathroom camera, and place it in whatever bedroom she's using and move the one in the kitchen. Martin was calling the usual number to reach him and kept getting his voicemail and no return call.

Martin was aggravated, in pain, and increasingly annoyed because he'd learned nothing about her daily routine or where things he's interested in are located in that house. His biggest provocation was that the FBI hadn't returned Pucci's pistol. What could they be testing on it? They've had it for months, and it doesn't take that long to do the necessary forensic tests. Are they expecting the fucking thing to start speaking to them? It's the FBI, nothing but a pack of morons. He anticipated it would've been returned by now. He needed to get that gun in his possession and destroy it.

The day Martin started viewing Christina, he called his field agent to see if he could recollect what was in the area of the kitchen where she kept disappearing. There was nothing his accomplice could remember that stood out, such as a room or nook of any sort. The only thing in that space was a pantry and a door leading to the backyard. He assured Martin he checked it out thoroughly and there was nothing there. Martin questioned the placement of the equipment.

He told Martin there was nothing in that particular area of the kitchen, and more important to view it as a whole with a view to the backyard. It was an ordinary pantry, filled with canned goods and foodstuffs. He searched for hidden rooms in every part of the house, including the kitchen, and there were none to be found. There was prickliness in his voice as he answered Martin's questions. He was a pro; this was his area of expertise, and he was damn good at it. The pantry was investigated, as was the whole residence, for what Martin was interested in.

Except now, there's a key.

This key gave Martin a new fixation, and he needed to get his hands on it. It didn't matter if he knew what it opened. If it's in his possession and not hers, that's all he needs. The important thing is she won't be able to find the contents of whatever this key is hiding, if in fact that's its purpose. He didn't believe the bullshit story she gave the FBI. They're nowhere near as smart as CIA agents who would never believe a fable of those proportions. Give me a break! Key to her heart! Christ Almighty!

Martin needed someone to acquire that key for him, and assignments of this nature are this particular agent's forte. He didn't trust anyone else to handle something of this type and didn't want to use any of his other contacts. The fewer people who knew the underhanded things he was up to, the better.

The last thing he wanted was for Metzger to catch wind that he had the Pucci household under surveillance. He needed to stay under the radar as much as possible. Once the President is in the palm of his hand, he'll write his own ticket. But he not only needed the items that didn't turn up from the original search, but now he had to get his hands on that key.

He didn't know where she put it, and it could be anywhere. If someone had to go through the whole house again, it would have to be while she's away. Maybe he'd wait for her to leave for OB and have someone do a thorough check throughout the house, except he didn't want to wait that long. He was impatient with this situation and wanted to keep the upper hand. He had to figure out a way to get into that house. The ideal time is when she's at Berkeley. His agent wasn't returning any phone calls, so he must be out of the country. Martin needed to make contact, so he emailed him at a secure and private address. Agents were never far from communication via the internet, so it should reach him.

Short, sweet, to the point: "*Urgent! Need help regarding the recent assignment. Certain areas were questioned. Assistance is required for further investigation. Matters are unfolding, necessitating your expertise. Reply immediately.*" Martin waited impatiently for a reply.

Within an hour, a response came back. Charles was with Martin, going over travel plans and instructions regarding OB. Martin told Charles to leave his office, giving no reason. Charles did as ordered, replying with a sappy "yes, sir." What a weakling, Martin thought, and wondered how he made it into the CIA. At least he knew how to take orders.

He opened the email addressed to "de Sade," the nickname Martin was given by his platoon while serving in Vietnam. They were the only members of their unit along with Doc Slaven who left that country alive. They shared camaraderie and the inner scars and demons of that war.

"Sorry, no can do. Assigned to Malaysia - rest of the year or EOM. Needed on counter terrorism task force, sleeper cells investigation, planning something big. For further assistance on the QT, suggest a rogue member of the British SIS, kicked out for violent methods, codename '*Caveman.*' Fitting name - man of few words with tactics like ours: strike first, questions later. Done work together, be warned, he's a loose cannon, dangerous and excellent at what we do, keeping a low profile. Demands a high price - worth it. If interested, contact you through this email address, as I know it's secure. Phones are too dangerous. JTR"

Martin didn't want to hear that and thought about how to proceed. He didn't know Caveman and wasn't sure whether to contact or not. He trusted J with his life, but if Caveman is as dangerous as he claims, he may scare the whore off before the mission starts and then OB gets scrubbed. All his plans would be up in smoke with Metzger doing exactly as he'd threatened. That can't happen.

JTR, which stood for Jack the Ripper, wouldn't steer him wrong. Recommendations from him were high praise. After much thought, Martin wrote back that he'd like to get Caveman on board. Not being affiliated with the CIA made him an ideal choice. He'd be paid well to wait until Martin knew how to proceed, thinking it best to hold off until the house was empty before going back to search for the key and Pucci's pistol. If the gun is returned before they leave, he'll use him within twenty-four hours. He sent the email and will wait for Caveman's answer.

René headed to his office on the Right Bank, walking leisurely, watching the beautiful people pass him by. He loved Paris, but it wasn't the same without his girls. The pain of loss cannot be described, and the absence of their laughter was torturous. They had a country house outside of Paris, where the accident took place. He thought about the clues John Pucci left for his wife. "Not in Paris, but near Paris."

He'd written down the clues she gave him and went to his office to see if any of them coincided with the file on the accident. He entered his building and took the stairs up three flights. Upon entering, he walked to the window and looked out at the streets of Paris. Spring is such a beautiful time of year in this extraordinary city. He had looked forward to planting flowers with Mercedes this Spring. He pushed that thought away. He had work to do and couldn't let the thoughts of what could have been get in the way.

He unlocked his desk and leafed through some files until he found what he was looking for. After the accident, when he came out of his haze of grief, it was replaced with rage and a determination to find out what happened. The reports said Adele missed the curve. Impossible! He refused to believe that. She was a careful driver, especially cautious when Mercedes was with her. To find the truth, he had to do it on his own.

He opened the file and there were photos of John Pucci with a sophisticated looking camera around his neck. He looked very much like a tourist in the lobby of one of the quaint little hostels dotting the area near where the accident took place. It was a bucolic and peaceful setting away from Paris. Those looking to get away from the busyness of city life usually patronize this particular inn. Because of terrorism and recent robberies, security cameras were installed.

As a member of the DCRI (*Direction Centrale du Renseignement Intérieur),* it was strongly requested of the local gendarmes to humor René and allow him to investigate the registry records, photocopies of passports, and view the security videos. René went to all the country inns, making copies of needed information. After using his agency's facial recognition program, he found only one person wasn't who he said he was; an American by the name of Richard Randall, later identified as John Pucci, of the FBI.

René initially suspected him of causing the accident; at the time, he was sure of it. Why would an FBI agent be in this exact area at the time of his family's supposed accidental death? He had no contact with the American FBI, so that piece of the puzzle didn't fit. Then Pucci turns up dead shortly after the accident, and René discovers he and Pucci's wife are wanted for the same mission. The more he researched John Pucci, the more he proved an unlikely suspect of guilt. He and René had a common link; people standing in the way of Martin's plan. The information he retrieved from drugging Charles confirmed that Pucci was not a part of the death of his family.

René believes Pucci was tailing Cater and either had photos of Martin causing the accident or proof of his guilt, and that's what he wants his wife to find. If he had proof of Martin causing the accident, why wasn't it brought forward immediately? Charles said Martin went to France on the sly, but Martin wasn't in any of the passport photos. He was either disguised or didn't stay in the local inn. He got out his pen, replaying the interview with the drugged Charles to be sure he wasn't missing something.

He spent the next few hours making notations, comparisons, and trying to figure out some of the clues John Pucci left for his wife. He tried to find the apple reference in everything and could find nothing. He thought he should take a drive out to the scene and see if there were any apple trees or apple-named streets near the site of the accident or near the hostel where John Pucci stayed. But first he had things to attend to in his office.

He removed a framed Renoir print of *"La Grenovillere"* from the wall, revealing a faded outline from around the painting. His keys opened a safe practically invisible to the naked eye hidden in the wall. He pulled out three small, zippered cases, much like the one containing the equipment used on Charles.

These cases held some of the tools of his trade. He had a number of pens that record audio with a click, minute cameras disguised as every-day items, video recorders the size of small coins looking like buttons, aspirin tablets that could render one paralyzed for certain lengths of time, small syringes and tubing, vials containing an assortment of drugs, a cigarette lighter that when activated became a pistol releasing BBs coated with a drug to knock out someone for a few minutes and a variety of other items necessary for someone in his line of work.

Martin said they could bring nothing from the present with them, but René wasn't going to depend on the 70s technology to keep them safe and retrieve the desired information. He'll argue that a foreign exchange student would have things from their home country. He'll bring whatever he needs and will cleverly disguise them as items of the 70s. He felt Martin wouldn't argue with him, especially since René has the option to walk away and the ability to rip out Martin's heart in one move, except for the fact that he has none.

He put the zippered bags and the files containing the information on Pucci and the accident into his backpack and went home. They'll be leaving for California at the end of July, which is only weeks away. Martin requested that René be back in the United States by the second week of July. As he walked back to his apartment on the Left Bank, his mind was swimming with thoughts coming in all directions. He needed to concentrate on one thing at a time.

Today, he'll drive back to the scene of the accident and question people with a photograph of Martin Cater. Surely someone would remember him. His coldness came through immediately and that wasn't easily forgotten by people who encounter it. He'll look for the apple reference but the accident was in late fall, so how would a stranger distinguish an apple tree from the others?

He got in his car and headed out of Paris. If John Pucci had hidden anything in France or if there was an apple reference to be noted, it would be there. As an agent, René didn't think John would've left something lying around pointing guilt at a particular person, but he wanted to eliminate the apple clue from that area.

On the drive into the countryside, he had the chance to clear his head and formulate some plans for how he was going to bring his equipment with him and how he'd disguise it. He'll make sure he's as sharp as a tack with a plan of action in several different scenarios. Above all, he'll have all the means to succeed and get them home safely, with a few weeks to get things in order. He thought with confidence that he had enough time to make his preparations. The trio had a lot to accomplish in one semester.

After a week, Martin received an email from Caveman. He's available for any services Martin needs. He didn't disclose his location but could be wherever he was needed within hours of notification. His price was a thousand a week to be "on call" and once given the specifics of a job, he'd name his price, which was non-negotiable. Caveman was open to any sort of job and made it clear he didn't shy away from breaking and entering, torture, brutal beatings, or assassinations. He was seasoned enough to never get caught. He was, in his own words, the best money could buy and worth every cent.

He left instructions on how to transfer funds and stated if the funds weren't there every Monday, he'd not only become unavailable, but he'd find Martin and make sure he got paid. The payments were to begin on the first of July or sooner if Martin had an immediate assignment. He instructed Martin to email him at this address when he wanted to contact him. Caveman insisted there be no personal contact and no face-to-face meeting. Their only contact will be by email. "I have bloody good safeguards in place to ensure the anonymity of all my mates." He gave Martin forty-eight hours to back out with no monetary loss. Once the terms were agreed, there would be no turning back.

Martin gave it twenty-four hours to think it through. He tried to find out information through his European contacts but could find nothing. He was told there were many rogue agents, which was why they use aliases. Without his real identity, they couldn't help but would put feelers out if needed. Martin declined, not wanting to call attention to what was going on.

Martin admired the Caveman's balls and "take no prisoners" attitude. Like Martin, he wasn't a man to be underestimated. With JTR unavailable, he needed someone to act on his behalf if necessary. Caveman seemed like the perfect person for what Martin needed; someone with no regard for the life and safety of individuals in the way. He wrote back to Caveman that it was going to be a pleasure doing business with him and he'll contact him when his services were needed.

Martin was satisfied with how things were falling into place. He clicked on the Pucci household and checked the tapes of the events of the day. The surveillance seemed a complete waste. The only good thing was he was able to view any visitors, and he'll know the minute Pucci's gun is returned and if she finds what Martin knows that John Pucci possessed. He looked at the photo the whore placed in their bedroom that mocked him every time he viewed the surveillance.

Looking right into the eyes of the photo he snickered and said, "Well, well, well, Johnny, my friend. I think Caveman and I are going to have the last laugh," and cackled to the face of the man whose life he snuffed out when he tried to stand in his way.

# CHAPTER 12

Time was flying, with a little more than a week before heading to New York for a few days of briefing and then to California. Christina felt she wasn't going to get everything done before leaving. She didn't have to pack much but kept the appearance of going on a safari.

She spent very little time in the house and being early summer, she spent her days doing yardwork and nights doing research on those she'll meet in 1971. She wasn't surprised to find little on Cater but found information on the Prince and the Morgans.

She used the back door when entering the house to sneak into the security room unseen. After finding it all clear, she'd sneak out the back and enter through the front.

She decided to tell her son-in-law, Matt, what was going on in the house since he and Mackenzie would be staying there during her absence. Christina was concerned about the dangers if she wasn't honest, at least about the bugging of the house.

She devised a plan and asked Matt to come to the house after work in his State Police uniform, text her when he arrives, and she'll meet him at the back door. His shift ended at 6:00 pm, and he was at the house shortly afterwards. She wanted them to slip undetected through the back door and directly into the security room.

"Mom, what's going on?"

"I've some things to show you. I'll explain everything when we get into the house. Dad has an elaborate security system in place, and I want you to know how everything works. And there's something I want you to do for me, but I can't explain yet." As they were about to enter the back door, she looked at him and said, "If you decide after today that you don't want to stay here, I'll completely understand."

He looked at her very strangely. "Mom, why wouldn't we want to stay here, and why aren't we going in the front door? You're being weird." She didn't answer.

"Stay as far to the left as you can when you get in the house. Do you see the pantry? That's where we're going." For some levity, she added in her best Elmer Fudd imitation, *"And we must be vewy, vewy quiet!"* She put her finger to her lips and opened the back door, stepped into the pantry, and he followed. She unlocked the hidden door, and they stepped into the security room.

"Holy shit!" he said softly. He looked around at all the monitors, controls, and switches John had installed. "Wow! He's added a lot since the last time I was in here. When did he add all this?"

She sat at the controls and said, "It's been a work in progress, upgrading as technology changed. You know what a techno guy he was. He always had to have the latest and greatest."

She showed him how some newer things worked, how to turn the controls on and off and how to use the alarms. She told him whenever he comes home, he can come in here to check and see if anything happened and who came here while he was gone. He was overwhelmed by all of it and truthfully it was quite an extraordinary set up. John knew his stuff.

"Okay Matt, pull up a chair and sit next to me. I've something to show you and don't say anything until the tape is finished."

He took off his gun belt and sat down. Christina played the tape of the entry of the "cable guy" and watched as he walked through the house, picked up the photographs, searched the premises and set up the surveillance. The look on his face showed anger.

"Mom, what the hell is going on? Do you know what he's doing? Did you notify the police?"

"Sit tight and watch."

"Mom, this guy is bugging your house! When did this happen, and why didn't you tell me or the police right away?"

"It happened while I was in New York visiting Zoe."

"And you've known about it that long?"

She explained how she noticed it as soon as she arrived home, with the tip off being John's set up of the family photos that had been moved and her actions after that.

"Mom, who'd want to spy on you?"

"Matt, you know Dad was FBI. I have reason to believe he was in contact with an agent from the CIA and possibly Dad had information or proof of something. I can't be sure, but I think this unknown agent is responsible for putting the surveillance on the house."

He started to yell about her being irresponsible and stupid to have kept this to herself and the danger she put herself in, especially if it was the CIA. She didn't tell him she felt safe as long as she was of use to them or of the insane mission she agreed to.

"Matt, stop it right now and calm down. I don't want them to hear you carrying on like this!" He was pacing around the room, mumbling about safety and insanity and what was she thinking by not telling anyone. "Get back here and sit down!" He gave her a dirty look and sat down. He started in again and was stopped immediately. "Matt, shut up and listen to me!" He quieted down enough for her to start her explanation.

"John put in a scrambler so I could've scrambled their signal immediately. There's also a detector that shines a blue light where these surveillance devices were installed. My first impulse was to flick the switch and ruin their plans to watch the house. Then I thought I may have more fun playing their game, only I have the ball and I've changed the rules. I've given them incorrect information, moved out of the master bedroom and bathroom. They only see what I choose for them to see."

He seemed to calm down a little. "If I scrambled their signal, how do I know they wouldn't be back? I've always kept my pistol with me and I'm not afraid. I wanted to make sure I was upfront with you about this before you agreed to stay here. I need you to do exactly as I ask. I've thought this through, and my plan will work. We're going to turn on the blue lights which they can't detect, so we can see where they are. I'm going to ask you to change the light bulb for me in the kitchen and you're going to "find" the bug that's placed there. While changing the light bulb, I want you to ask me if I've heard anything yet from the FBI about John's pistol."

"Why?"

"Humor me," she said with a smile. "I want whoever's watching to know for certain it's not here. After you find the "bug," act as angry as you like. You'll go to your trooper car and come back with this," and she handed him a small device John had in one of his drawers used to detect surveillance bugs.

"It's obsolete and doesn't work, but they don't know that. You'll sweep all the rooms in this house and disconnect all five of them. You'll make them think you're taking them with you for analysis, but you're going to give them all to me.

"I'm going to be acting shocked, pissed and start accusing the FBI of bugging the house, calling them all kinds of names. I want to make sure I throw off those who're watching and let them think I believe the FBI is behind this because they think I'm hiding information from them. From what they've seen, they'll believe it."

He was staring at her. "Matt, are you still with me here?"

"Yeah, I'm here, but shocked you're so calm and that you've thought up this elaborate plan."

"Yeah, well, I'm not done yet," she went on. "I don't care when you do it, but when you disconnect one or all, please be as menacing as possible, look directly into the bug and threaten whoever has been spying on me that they'd better stay away from this house. Say you'll have it protected by fellow troopers 24/7 and that you'll have someone here tomorrow to install a foolproof security system so that this can't happen again.

"One other thing, don't tell Mackenzie about any of this. She knows about the room, but only how to check out who visited in our absence and how to turn on the alarm. They were somehow able to bypass it to get in to do their dirty work. She doesn't know about any of the other equipment in here, and I don't want her to. Understood? Most of all, I don't want her to know the house was bugged. You know how dramatic she gets, and the last thing I want before I leave is drama."

"Mom, I don't like keeping things from her. Our relationship is built on trust, and she'll kick the shit out of me if she finds out."

"And how will she find out unless you tell her? Look, if I could've thought of a way to disable these without your help or knowledge, I would have. I didn't want you two to be in danger while I'm gone or to have your every move watched. If you don't want to stay here, I'll understand. I'll make other arrangements for Sam."

Matt sighed. "One thing I've learned since joining this family is I don't argue with you. For someone so tiny, you're absolutely fearless. You're like a little stick of dynamite, posing no danger until you light the fuse, and then all hell breaks loose. I've no intention of putting a match anywhere near you. After our little show for the cameras, no one will be coming back to reset the surveillance, especially if I do my most menacing impression of a Trooper. We're pretty bad ass, you know."

He said he had no problem staying at the house. "I couldn't tell Kenzie we changed our plans. She loves this house and what's not to love with the pool, the yard, the hot tub, and the koi pond, which we'll take good care of."

"Ok, so now we creep out the back door, and I'll head for the garden, and you beep the horn. I'll come in the back door, walk through the house, and let you in the front. Before we disconnect anything, I want you to say that you guys decided to stay here while I'm gone. I want them to know the house won't be empty and someone from law enforcement will be living here."

"You've thought of everything, haven't you?"

She laughed and answered, "Matt, you've no idea, and neither do they." They laughed, and they slipped out the back door. She grabbed her trowel and a potted plant and crossed over in full view of the kitchen surveillance into the garden.

Okay, folks, it's Showtime!

Her plan went off without a hitch. He came in the front door in full view of the camera and said he and Mackenzie are happy to house-sit while she's gone. They did some small talk and she asked if he would please change a light bulb in the kitchen because it was too hard to reach, even with the ladder. As soon as he got up on the ladder to change the light bulb it was like the director called "Action!"

"So, Mom, have you heard anything yet from the FBI about Dad's gun? Have they finished the testing on it?"

"No idea. They still have it, and I haven't heard a word about it. Douchebags! My last encounter with Lou when I came home from visiting Zoe didn't go well. I hope they're able to find out what happened." She wiped her eyes and turned away as if crying.

"Sorry to bring that up, Mom. I didn't mean to upset you. I was wonder....," and then he stopped mid-sentence. "What the hell is this?" he asked.

"What? Don't tell me there's something alive up there. Is that why the bulb burnt out? Is it a dead mouse?"

Matt started to stammer. "Um, it's um, ah, it's, it's...nothing," in a nonchalant voice.

"Matt, you're lying to me. What is it? I can call an exterminator if I need to."

"Well, Mom, I don't want to scare you, but it looks like a bug."

Feigning ignorance, she got the phone book. "I'll call one right now. It's not a cockroach, is it?" she asked, flipping through the yellow pages.

"Mom, it's not that kind of bug, it's the other kind."

She stopped in her tracks. "What other kind of bug is a bug? Is this a trooper joke?"

"No, Mom." He held up the device. "This kind of bug."

"What is that? I hope you're joking. You don't mean a spying bug, do you?"

"That's exactly what it looks like," he answered. That was her cue to go off on a tirade.

"*Mother fucking* FBI. How dare they? Those sons of bitches! I *knew* they thought I was hiding something from them! I even asked Lou if they were going to bug my house! Do they actually think I'd hide something that could help find out what happened to John? Matt, come down off that ladder and let me see that thing."

He climbed down and put the tiny device in her hand. "Are you sure that's what it is?"

"It sure looks like it to me."

"Those fucking FBI bastards. How dare they?"

He gently took hold of her arm and asked, "Mom, what if it's not the FBI?"

She looked at him questioningly. That wasn't part of the script, but she ran with it. "Well," she asked, "who else could it…" and didn't finish the sentence, and acted as if a thought came into her head.

"Mom, do you know of anyone else who'd want to see what's going on here?"

"Um, no,…No, I don't."

"You sure, Mom?" She didn't answer but kept examining the device in her hand.

Matt went to the door. "I'll be right back. I need to get something from the car to see if there are any more of these babies in the house."

As he was walking out the door, she asked, "Can I step on this one?"

"No," he replied, "I want to take it for analysis." He went outside and returned with the gizmo Christina gave him to use. They went through the house, and he removed all the surveillance equipment, threatening whoever was watching that if they try to do this again, he'll be waiting with his service pistol and blow their brains out and someone from the State Troopers will be here tomorrow to install an alarm that can't be deactivated by outsiders.

He was quite menacing, and Christina was sure he wasn't acting the whole time. It was obvious he was angry, especially with the bathroom one. Looked right into it and called whoever was watching a disgusting, perverted sick fuck.

While Matt was removing the bugs, Christina went into the security room and got a small steel box she'll put the little buggers in and then into the safe. Maybe she'll take them to New York next week and see what René has to say about them. They may be useful in Berkeley, but they can't ask permission from the person who most likely put them in her home.

Matt put them all on the kitchen table, and Christina got a magnifying glass and examined them over a cup of coffee. He found the activating mechanisms and turned them all off. He asked if he could take one with him to have it analyzed and see what its capabilities are. She agreed but wanted to be sure she got it back before she left on her adventure. He said he was going to take it immediately to their surveillance department and would have information on it within a day or so.

She walked him out to the car and thanked him for all his help. "And remember, say nothing of this to Mackenzie." He assured her his lips were sealed and said he'd be back tomorrow or the next day. He got into his big, bad State Trooper car and left.

On her nightly walk with Sam, she was feeling self-satisfied and laughed to herself at how clever she was. There was a lilt to her step that had been previously missing. She wished she could see the face of the person watching her when they viewed her discovery of the bugs. She didn't know if she was pissing anyone off with her plan of action, but she certainly hoped so.

The next day they celebrated Christina's 50th birthday coupling it with a going away party. Mackenzie brought her laptop and they Skyped with Roxanne and Paul in South Carolina. She had her family with her, and everyone sang Happy Birthday, ate a Japanese dinner, and had her favorite cake from the local Italian pastry shop.

There was a lot of laughter. It was so good to be together, even if some were only on a screen. As she looked at them all, she silently prayed for their safety, that she wasn't harming them by participating in this crazy assignment. Her children were the most important things in her life.

As Johnny was getting ready to leave Christina pulled him aside. "How are things going with Beulah? Anything yet?"

"You know how stubborn she is, Mom. I haven't been able to get anything out of her. I've tried everything I know to get her to open up, but she's keeping quiet. Sorry, Mom."

"That's okay, keep trying and if by chance you find anything while I'm gone, I want you to keep quiet about it until I get back. I want to hear for myself what she has to say and then I'll figure out what to do next. Okay?"

"Is that what Dad would want?"

"I dunno," she answered pensively, "but it's what I want. If you have to tell anyone you can tell Matt but that's as far as it can go. Do NOT under any circumstances call Lou or the Agency with anything. It can wait until December when I get back."

He gave her a tight hug and said, "I'm going to miss you, Mom. Please be careful in Africa. Nasty things are going on over there, not to mention all the wild animals. We need you even more now that Dad's gone. It's so far away and we can't reach you. What if something were to happen to you over there? How would we find out or even be able to get to you, being so far away? I'm worried and wish you weren't going."

She told him everything was going to be fine. None of them were happy she would be out of cell phone range and kidded them that it was like going back to the last century by going to Africa. They didn't know how truthful she was being.

Over the next few days, Christina packed, and Matt and Mackenzie moved some things in from their apartment. She left a notebook of things they could refer to with the names and phone numbers of those who are used for different things at the house. They went over the security room, given instructions on how and when to cover the pond and who to call to close the pool. It was only for four months, but things had to be ready for winter before she returned.

The night before she was to leave for New York, which would be her last night home, Matt came over and explained the bugs which was remarkably interesting. She looked forward to sharing this information with René with the hope that these could be used to their advantage. They were completely self-contained, and each can record up to six months.

She told Matt if Johnny was able to find out anything from Beulah, they were not to divulge it to anyone until she hears it first, no matter what they find out. She gently fondled the key around her neck, which she noticed she did quite often but never in view of the surveillance. She didn't want them to know where it was, so she cautiously kept it concealed while in any of the rooms being watched. She was now free to caress it whenever she spoke of or thought of John, which was often. She knew he was with her, and it was comforting.

The day of her departure for New York had arrived and as she was going over her checklist and making sure she had everything, there was a knock at the door. "Now who the hell could that be?" she thought. Everyone knew she was leaving today. Hopefully, it was someone she could get rid of in a hurry because there was no time for chit chat. Johnny would be arriving in a few minutes to take her to the train station, and she still had things to do.

She opened the door, and Lou Jenkins was standing there. "Hey, Lou, what's up?" What could he possibly want? Maybe they found something out about John's death. He couldn't have come at a worse time.

"Hello, Christina. How are you?"

"I'm okay, Lou, how are you? What brings you here?"

He barely made eye contact with her. She didn't have a good feeling about this visit. "Can I come in for a few minutes? I have something to tell you."

"Is it about John? Have you found out about his death?"

"I don't want to talk in the doorway. Can we go in and sit down?"

"Sure," she said, "come on in."

He saw the suitcase in the hallway and asked if she was going somewhere.

"I've been invited to accompany my buddy Zoe to Africa. I should be gone for about four months."

"Sounds like a wonderful adventure for you. I hope you have a good time. Be careful over there. Things can be dangerous."

"Thanks. Have you found out what happened to John?"

"Christina, I don't know how to tell you this."

Oh my God, why today, why now! Her heart started pounding and she could hear it beating in her ears and her palms immediately started to sweat. "Lou, spit it out. I'm going to have a heart attack waiting to hear what you have to say."

"It's not good news, Christina." He took a deep breath and exhaled. "Christina," another deep breath, and he continued, "the Agency has been unable to find out what John was working on or the circumstances of his death. We can't find a link with any of the cases we've been working on."

"So, you don't know what happened, is that what you're telling me?"

Johnny pulled into the driveway, and they turned to look out the door. "I know you're getting ready to leave, so I'll be as brief as possible." Another deep breath. "The Agency can't find a link to any case, so we can't give you the benefits for a widow whose spouse was killed in the line of duty."

"What? You've got to be kidding me!"

"Christina, we've tried! We've gone over everything, and we can't figure out what he was working on, if he was working on anything that had to do with the Agency, or if he happened to be at the wrong place and the wrong time."

She buried her face in her hands and could feel the tears of bitterness sting her cheeks as they fell from her eyes.

"You'll still get the regular benefits, not the double indemnity or things that would be entitled to you if he died in the line of duty." Johnny walked in and saw her crying and asked what was going on and if the Agency had found out what happened to his father.

"Yeah, Johnny, I'll tell you what happened. The FBI took Dad's almost 30 years giving them his blood, sweat and tears and pissed on his work, his memory, his widow, and family."

"Christina, please, this isn't easy for me."

"Well then please, Lou, let me make it easier for you. I'm getting ready to leave and I really hate to give you the bums rush, but you need to get the fuck out of my sight."

He started to apologize and was cut off. "You can relay to whoever has made this decision that they haven't heard the last of this yet, rest assured. As soon as I get back, I'll be in contact with my lawyer, and if I have to, I'll also go to the head of the FBI and then the press."

"Christina, I'm really very sorry…"

"Lou, if you say that one more time, I'm going to punch you right in the face." She opened the door. "Thanks for the good news. John would be so happy you're taking such good care of me. I can only imagine how pleased he'd be."

Lou was standing at the threshold of the door, turned and started to say something when she ushered him out the door and said, "You're such a harbinger of good news, aren't you? So long, Lou, and do me a favor. Next time you think of stopping by to visit, *don't*." She slammed the door so hard behind him that a photo fell off the wall.

She was livid and started throwing things around and yelling nonsensical gibberish in a rant against the FBI. It was too much to handle this news on top of all the other things cluttering her mind. She was ready to throw the suitcase into the pool and go immediately up into her bedroom and revert to cocoon mode. The tears came in a wave like a waterfall, and she couldn't turn them off. Everything had been taken from her, her husband, and the future they were to have, and now they were taking away the benefits she deserved.

Johnny stood there, not knowing what to say or do. Meanwhile, Christina was slamming drawers and doors and bordering on total hysteria.

"Mom, I'm sorry. Is there anything I can do for you? I'll work harder on Beulah while you're gone. I'll make her tell us what we need to know to get this whole thing straightened out. Please don't cry."

The tears wouldn't stop. She was unable to think about anything else, but in the back of her mind, she knew she had to get herself together to make it to the train station on time.

"Mom, don't think about it now. Go and have a good time and enjoy yourself in Africa with Zoe. Get lost in the beauty of your surroundings, and we'll think of something, or we'll find the truth. When Beulah decides to talk, we'll know exactly what happened that night, what Dad was working on, and we'll take it from there." And then he added, "Who knows, maybe Dad wasn't working on an FBI mission. Maybe it was something else."

That sentence hit like a slap in the face and brought her back to her senses and ended the histrionics. Johnny's words brought reality back to the forefront of her mind. He was right, of course. It *was* something else. John wasn't working on an FBI case. That's the reason he left the clues for her and didn't involve anyone from the agency about what was going on. Her anger was completely misdirected. It belonged on the shoulders of one person, Martin Cater.

Johnny noticed how she stopped in her tracks like a deer caught in the headlights. She could vaguely hear him in the background saying, "Mom…Mom…what is it?"

"Nothing," she answered. "You're right. It makes no sense to get all worked up, especially since I'm leaving the country. I can't call off the trip or do anything about it now, so I guess I'll have to let it go until I get back." She picked up a few of the items she had sent flying in anger, looked at her son, and said, "I'm sorry about my tantrum. We'll think of something, but I'll need you to really push Beulah for some answers."

She tried to act as though she had calmed down, but her insides were in turmoil with thoughts jumbling together. Did John think the scenario currently being played out was a possibility, and that's why he left her the clues? She had to throw all this into the background, she had a train to catch. She'd have the next four or five hours to think about what happened. Looking at the clock made her move into high gear. The only thing in her favor today was that the train was always late.

She grabbed the checklist to be certain everything was accounted for and made sure that she had her notes and research on the Morgan family and the prince and left the writings from John in the safe. She had hoped to find the secret the key held but had no luck with that or the apple clue, which she thought must be essential to the puzzle.

Johnny grabbed her things, and they did a final walk through the house. She had a feeling in her gut that things would never be the same after her return. Was it foreboding, dread, fear, or a melodramatic imagination running rampant? She couldn't say for sure, but knew she was looking down a road with life-changing events ready to greet her. She kissed a picture of John and asked him to please watch over all of them, no matter where they are. She walked out the front door and closed it behind her. No turning back now.

Johnny drove her to the train station. He once again expressed his concern about this trip. Could he feel the nervousness coming from her or maybe the butterflies in her stomach were flying out of her mouth with every word spoken.

The train pulled into the station, and she hugged and kissed her son goodbye. She didn't want to let go of him. The train was ready to depart, and she was told she had to board immediately. She got on the train and grabbed a window seat right where her son was standing. She wanted to get off the train and stay in her safe, mundane life, and couldn't stop the tears running down her cheeks as the train started to move out of the station. She waved and watched as Johnny grew smaller and smaller and then disappeared as she rode off into an adventure she knew she wasn't prepared for. Things were moving too fast, and she felt overwhelmed.

# CHAPTER 13

July was flying by with Martin going back and forth to Washington. He tried to find out about events in Malaysia, but either people weren't aware or it was on a need-to-know basis. He hated being out of the loop with goings on within the CIA. He may head this organization in a few months if he so chooses, or maybe the Secretary of Defense. Time will tell.

Martin regularly spoke with the White House Chief of Staff, relaying progress, objectives, and preparations for the upcoming mission. The President was anxious to render his fiercest opponent impotent and out of the race. The polls showed Morgan was the only Republican who could win the next presidential election. Although the Republican primary was yet to take place and the debates and individual state primaries were in the process, with the candidate not yet decided, Morgan was a favorite, even with some Democrats. His family had money, pull, and connections. It was vital to the reelection of the current president that Morgan wasn't his opponent.

Martin promised success and by God, he's going to make sure the whore and the other two did as expected. He didn't care what they did or how they did it to ensure a triumphant end to their time in 1971. If the women had to use their feminine wiles, it's what they'll have to do. If Prince Ali wants to bang her, she'd better do whatever she has to, including spreading her legs to gain an in with the prince, which will lead to Morgan and the needed treasonous information being brought back. She needed to remember the outcome was for the betterment of our country. Morgan's relationship with Zatari has the potential to put the whole world at risk of annihilation.

Martin wasn't afforded the privacy to regularly check the live feed or the tapes of the Pucci home. But no matter how busy he was, he made certain one thousand dollars was sent every week to Caveman. As soon as she's in California, he'll send him to Eastbumfuck New York to search her house again.

Martin got the impression Caveman was willing to do whatever it took to achieve success, no matter the outcome. Being a free agent, not affiliated with any agency, he could break rules with no consequence. From their exchanged emails, it was clear failure was not an option for him. Martin looked forward to using him in dealings with Christina Pucci.

René was back in New York and given files, instructions, and objectives for OB. The meeting with Martin got off to a rocky start when René started the meeting by asking how he'd been sleeping. Martin was not amused.

After that sarcastic jab, Martin wanted as little to do with René as possible and put Charles in charge of him while in New York, reporting back to him. From Charles' reports, he, René, and Ms. Janis got together a few times, going over certain information. Martin insisted that Charles be with them whenever they met so Martin would find out what was discussed. Charles wanted to be an active agent, and this is his first covert assignment. Martin laughed to himself. That was all Charles was good for; that and as his chauffeur.

It was a Sunday afternoon and Martin had some down time. The three OB agents were meeting with him tomorrow morning at his office and off to California soon after. He thought it's a good time to catch up on what's been going on at Pucci's home. He clicked the icon for her house and the screen was blank. He rebooted and tried the live feed again with the same result. Perplexed, he went to the tapes and started with his last viewing.

Nothing was happening, every day the same: coffee in the morning, a quick look at the computer, outside doing yard work, in and out throughout the day and then inside for dinner. After dinner she disappeared and wasn't seen again until leaving to walk the dog. The scene repeated every day. Martin could only observe the five rooms on the divided screen. The only time this equipment taped activity was when there was movement or the sensors detected body heat.

Many times before she entered the house, the sensor started recording in the kitchen for a few seconds, stop and then repeat a few minutes later. The equipment was too sophisticated and tested to have glitches. It reinforced Martin's feeling that something was suspicious in the area of the kitchen that couldn't be seen.

This scenario repeated daily with the kitchen surveillance going on and off with no motion visible. He rewound it, looking to see if there was any movement. It once again went on momentarily and then he saw her walking across the yard with gardening tools in her hand. She entered the back door, walked through to the foyer, activating the unit by the front door. Looks like she's got company.

A broad-shouldered cop came walking through the door. By the conversation, he surmised it was her son-in-law. Did he say they're going to house-sit while she's gone? He rewound the tape, and sure enough, that's what he said. "Fuck!" Martin said aloud. How will he be able to get Caveman in? Their conversation continued, consisting of family bullshit.

She asked him to change the light bulb in the kitchen. Martin held his breath as he watched him climb the ladder. This could be bad. The cop asked if Pucci's gun had been returned or if they had learned anything. Martin leaned forward to listen to her reply and was slightly relieved to hear the gun was still with the FBI. Martin agreed with her assessment of the FBI, laughing at her response because he agreed they were douchebags. Then the shit hit the fan.

"What the hell is this?" the cop asked. Martin stopped breathing. The view in the kitchen changed from seeing the man's face to seeing his thumb and forefinger picking up the device. The cop eyed it and eventually ended up in the whore's hand. Fuck! They found one! She started bitching about the FBI and pointing the accusation towards them which was a relief to Martin as she didn't mention the possibility of it being the CIA.

The screen was dark as it lay closed in her hand. She wanted to step on it. "No!" he screamed at the screen. "Do you know how much those fucking things cost?" The cop came back with something looking like a bug detector and proceeded to go through the house, found and removed every surveillance apparatus installed. He menacingly threatened whoever was watching and assured the anonymous viewer that an alarm would be installed, and the house would be under the protection of New York State Troopers. Fuck! Son of a motherfucking bitch!

The cop had choice words when disconnecting the bathroom, but Martin was unfazed by his remarks. He was too furious they'd been found and couldn't reenter the house to reinstall them. He started to throw things and almost heaved the laptop before he regained control of himself. He called Christina Pucci every vile name he could think of and dented the wall of his home office where he punched it.

The next thing he saw was the ceiling in the kitchen with the cop holding a magnifying glass and the two of them looking down into the devices. One by one, they were shut down, and the screen on his laptop went blank.

Nothing regarding this bitch of a woman goes according to plan. If he didn't need her so much for the success of OB, he'd kill her with his bare hands, but not before torturing her and making her beg for mercy, which he'll never show her.

He can't send Caveman in there at this point if there's a police presence in the house. If he says they'll be watching the house, there's no doubt it's the truth. He knows enough about law enforcement personnel to be cognizant that when one of their own is threatened, they're a force to be reckoned with. It's a brotherhood with ties stronger than the links of a steel chain, and only a fool would go up against them when they're linked together for the protection of a fellow officer and his or her family.

Martin was livid. That woman has been nothing but trouble from before he ever laid eyes on her. And now he was going to have to sit in the same room with her tomorrow! His state-of-the-art equipment is now in the hands of the New York State Troopers. It won't be long before they find out exactly where this technology came from. He was infuriated! He can't get them back because he'd have to admit he had them installed, and that he can't do that.

How is it possible this woman bests him at every turn? She's a nobody, a housewife with no training, so how is she able to keep undermining his plans? He despised her more than ever and was still in the same predicament as he was the night he killed her husband. He thought back to that night and wished he were able to retrieve Pucci's pistol. Pucci must have known how things were going to go down at their meeting because he came prepared for more than a chit-chat.

Martin contacted John Pucci again, shortly after returning from obliterating René's family, getting them permanently out of the way. Now he's ready to do the same to Pucci if he refused once again to cooperate. His wife was necessary to the success of this mission, and he'll get her on his team with or without Pucci's consent. He gets one more chance to agree to his plan or he'll be joining René's wife and child.

Martin never expected Pucci to have a plan of his own. When they met, Martin asked him one last time if he'd agree to his wife joining the Operation Berkeley team. Pucci laughed and told Martin it'd be in his best interest to drop the idea of going anywhere near his wife. Then the bastard blackmailed him.

He told Martin he saw some interesting sights on a recent visit to France and took some wonderful photographs of a winding country road. The photographs not only captured the beautiful countryside, but caught the image of Martin staging an accident, from start to finish, with the car overturning and tumbling down a hill. He was able to photograph him running down to the car and holding the nose and mouth closed of the woman who was driving and then performing the same procedure on the child.

"As vile, horrific, and obviously criminal as this exploit of yours was, I could remain quiet and extend to you the professional courtesy of being a veteran and a fellow agent by holding on to these photos as long as you stay away from my wife and family. They're hidden where only I know, and they'll stay there unless you continue to harass me about my wife. I've told you twice before, stay away from her. Don't make me go to your superiors." Those were the last words John Pucci uttered.

They seemed to simultaneously draw their weapons, with Martin being faster and able to shoot Pucci first, so the bullet meant for Martin's heart made contact with his hip instead. Martin searched Pucci and found his cell phone, which he put in his pocket to be destroyed later. He quickly seized Pucci's gun for the same purpose of removing evidence, but that bastard had the gun chained-locked to his wrist. He wasted so much time trying to release it from Pucci, he barely had enough time to wipe his fingerprints off the weapon before the sirens started heading towards the scene.

He ran to his car and took off undetected. He didn't notice he was shot until he got home and felt a sticky wetness on his leg. He showered and threw his clothes and Pucci's phone down the incinerator. He bandaged himself up and called Doc Slaven, who arrived at Martin's apartment within the hour. Slaven brought some equipment with him, but the bullet seemed to be in a position requiring extensive surgery to remove. Martin wanted him to perform the procedure immediately in his home, but Slaven refused as it was too risky without the proper medical tools and the sterility of a hospital.

He cleaned the wound, no questions asked. He gave Martin two shots: one antibiotic and one of Demerol for the pain. He handed

Martin two pill bottles and instructed him to take one every four hours. He and Martin concocted the story of the shrapnel from the IED he'd claimed to have encountered in Europe. Martin honestly didn't care if anyone believed this story or not.

He made sure Charles was out of the picture before he went to France and for the Pucci caper by making a surreptitious visit to his father's hospital room after visiting hours. He snuck into his room and injected digitalis into the IV of Charles' father. The man was already in the hospital because of a heart attack, so it was easy to give him another one with no suspicions and no autopsy. The death of his father would keep Charles busy with his family and out of his hair while his plan played itself out.

It'd worked like a well-oiled machine until the night he killed Pucci. It added another problem, knowing there was proof of him killing René's family. How would he find those photographs? Pucci could have hidden them anywhere. That they haven't surfaced thus far gave him some consolation. His man searched the house when laying the bugs but found nothing. Martin saw on the surveillance video that Pucci left her a key. Martin was certain he had left it for his wife to search out where the key opened, and the photographs would be the prize she would find.

In a way, he'd have preferred never seeing her image as a teenager and her remarkable resemblance to Prince Ali's wife. As soon as that bitch came into the picture, things seemed to fall apart. He wished he didn't need her and dreaded their meeting tomorrow. He'll put on his fiercest face and stare her down if she tried to pull any of her shit. He wasn't sure where she got the impression that she's in control, but he'll make it known exactly who the superior manager of OB is.

His intuition was telling him he's being backed into a corner, taking him off his A-game, making him susceptible to foolish mistakes. Confident in what he'd gain after the mission's success, he started to get the feeling that more was at stake.

One thing was certain: Christina Pucci had better enjoy herself for the next four months. Once she returns and the treasonous evidence is in the proper hands with credit given to Martin, she'll be exterminated, with great pain and great pleasure. He may even fuck her a few times before ending her life. Better yet, Caveman can have his fun, and then Martin will take sloppy seconds and personally finish the job.

For the first time that day, a smile passed over Martin's face. He'll have four months to ruminate on the plan for her end. Soon she'll be off to 1971, and it'll give Martin time to think of how to secretly put an end to her while throwing the blame towards the Morgans and get Pucci's gun and those photos into his hands.

# CHAPTER 14

When René arrived back in the US, he called Christina to tell her he was in New York and the progress he had made in France, which was very little. He'd gone over a lot of data and looked around the accident scene but was unsuccessful in finding anything pertinent to the apple clue. He thought there may have been some apple trees near the accident site, but that avenue proved to be fruitless, pardon the pun. He was able to find some people who may have recalled seeing Martin Cater in the area, but they couldn't be sure as to exactly when it was or if it was at the time of the accident.

He said Charles was assigned as his constant companion, who was in the men's room, which was why René took advantage of an opportunity to contact her without his shadow. He told her he hadn't forgotten about their conversations and would see her soon. He won't be able to call again. Hopefully, they'll have enough privacy to resume their discussions once Christina gets to New York.

Before they had to abruptly hang up because of Charles' return, she started to tell him about the incident with Matt and the surveillance devices but didn't get too far. She wanted him to know about it, but there will be time to discuss it in the future, or will it be the past? She didn't want a situation where Charles would suspect something was amiss. She liked him, but he was the eyes and ears of Cater and didn't want him to know any more than he already did.

Christina was lucky to be able to get everything ready and completed for her departure. She had some ideas she would've liked to discuss with René but would have to keep them to herself for now. She should be there soon as they were pulling into Penn Station shortly.

Since her last visit to New York, she'd hardly spoken to Zoe. She tried a few times, but it always went to voicemail. Christina knew she was engrossed with work, especially as she'd be gone for four months. Zoe missed calling her on her birthday, which is the one day, no matter where she is, she always manages to call.

She returned Christina's call while out to lunch with René and Charles. It was a wasted call because her attention was on René. It's impossible to talk to her when she's with him. Throughout their conversation, she was giggling, speaking in French, being her coy, coquettish self. After asking the same question four times with no reply, she lost her tolerance for listening to Zoe's playful flirtations.

She'd been through this so many times in the past but didn't have the patience she usually did. Zoe called her, but she's only talking to those she's with. Christina was becoming increasingly annoyed. She needed five minutes of Zoe's time but couldn't get her attention. She hung up on her, and when Zoe called back, Christina wouldn't answer. Zoe left a voicemail apologizing, saying she's a terrible friend, and they'd talk soon. She asked Christina to call back, but Christina wasn't in the mood for games. Zoe could be exasperating, and it usually involved a man.

On her voicemail message to Christina, Zoe said they're required to stay at a CIA apartment before leaving for California. "It's like a pajama party, Tee!" Christina said into the phone, "Zee, I could punch your face in!"

René had been there since his arrival, and Zoe joined him three days ago. Christina wouldn't feel safe talking freely as she's sure they're being watched and listened to by someone. Can she go anywhere without someone watching her?

The train pulled into Penn Station, and she gathered her things and headed for the exit. Most of the ride was spent going over the history between the Morgans and the Zatarian Royal Family. It was very interesting. There's a connection between the two families going back a number of decades. She wouldn't feel comfortable having a president with such close business ties with a Middle Eastern conglomerate like the Royal Family, especially after 9/11, and wondered why this wasn't made public by some rogue reporter.

She stepped off the platform, looked around, and didn't see Zoe anywhere. There's always a moment of panic when getting off the train in New York. Being alone in this city is frightening to this small-town girl. She walked on, looking around and seeing no familiar faces. Her bags were cumbersome, giving her trouble navigating the crowd.

She felt a tap on her shoulder, and Charlie was standing behind her. "Can I help you with your bags, Mrs. Pucci?"

"Charlie!" She put her bags down and hugged him. "Are you the welcoming committee? Where's Zoe?"

"René and Ms. Janis are at the apartment. We'll head there now for you to drop off your bags and then out for dinner. Zoe thought you'd want some time to wind down and freshen up before going out to eat."

She handed over her bag and followed him to the car. "So, you got nominated to pick me up?"

"Well, no, not really, I offered. I kind of missed you. To be honest, I had a lot of fun when you were last here. I hadn't laughed that hard in a long time. You're quite funny, you know, and I enjoy your company. Picking you up was my idea, Besides, I'm the one with the car. I hope you don't mind."

"Aw, Charlie, thanks! You're really sweet! How could I possibly mind when a handsome young man like you is being so chivalrous?" Then she asked, "Are you sure Zoe didn't suggest it so she could have some time alone with our dashing French agent?" They laughed.

"You may be right, Mrs. P. She does seem interested in him."

"Oh, Charlie, you have no idea, but I won't give away her secrets."

He opened the door to the back seat, and Christina asked if she could sit with him in the front. "There's no reason to be so formal. It's within protocol, isn't it?"

"Sure, Mrs. P., hop in." They exchanged small talk as he maneuvered his way through the crazy New York City traffic. She was in awe of those who could weave in and out in this city where everything moved at a feverish pace.

When they got to the building where they're staying, Charlie parked the car and opened the door for her. He said he'll be staying with them until the three of them leave for 1971. Not being one who holds back, she asked, "Charlie, are you staying to spy on us and report back to your vile boss?" He laughed as he got her bags out of the trunk.

"You know, Mrs. P., I knew you'd think that, and you're partially right. He does want me to report back to him, but I'm here mostly to make sure things stay on track and nothing endangers the mission."

"Like what?" Christina asked.

"Oh, I don't know, maybe singing *Jesus Christ Superstar* until the end of side two."

Christina chuckled. "Good one, Charlie! Yeah, keep me away from those double albums, or I should say those two-disc sets."

Christina promised not to cause any trouble, at least by singing. He led the way up to the apartment, and the first thing she saw was the breathtaking view of Central Park and the city that never sleeps. She yelled out, "Honey, I'm home," after which Charlie echoed, "Me, too."

Zoe and René came out to greet them. Zoe hugged Christina and apologized again for the phone call. Christina gave Zoe one of the looks she'd given her a zillion times over the years. Zoe was aware that Christina knew that she was besotted with René. Christina understood Zoe's infatuation; René was a handsome man, with dark blue eyes, great body and looking so distinguished with the touch of gray around his temples.

René addressed Christina, kissed her hand, and said it was a pleasure to see her again. They acted like they hadn't been in contact since their first meeting, as they agreed it would be kept secret. Charlie can't know they'd spoken, and neither can Zoe for the time being. In a few days, they'll come clean to Zoe about what's going on. For now, they had to keep up appearances.

Zoe showed Christina to her room. When the door closed, Christina asked if there'd been any action yet between her and René.

"No, unfortunately. I wish! I think he's still in mourning for his wife. Out of respect for her, I'll take it slow." Then she gave Christina one of her sheepish looks and said, "And you know how much I like to initiate things," and licked her lips.

Christina chuckled, "Well, there's time for that when we're sweet young things again, and I'm sure you'll take advantage of our newfound youthfulness."

"I can't wait!" she replied, licking her lips once again. Christina laughed, thinking she'll never change.

"Did you bring anything with you to take to 1971?" Zoe asked.

"Yeah," she answered, "but not much. She changed the subject quickly as she didn't want to get into a disagreement because of what she was bringing. "When do we meet with Mr. Evil?"

"Tomorrow afternoon and Tee, please, don't act like an ass with him. Try to be respectful, okay?"

Christina wanted to tell Zoe everything she'd found out about him and John's warning not to trust him but knew their conversation wouldn't be private. "Yeah, well, he'd better be respectful to me. That's all I have to say."

"Please, Tee, be good!"

Christina unpacked a few things and put them in the bathroom. "I've got a lot to tell you." She sighed heavily. "Things have been pretty shitty since my last visit. I'll tell you everything over dinner."

"Then let's leave now!" Zoe replied anxiously. As soon as Christina was settled, they left. When they sat down, the three of them ordered wine, and Christina had a cup of coffee. Zoe started as soon as the waiter left earshot.

"Tee, I'm dying. What's been going on?"

Christina gave Charlie a stern look. "I'd prefer if this didn't go beyond this table, but I know Charlie has a job to do." He started to say something, but she stopped him and told him not to worry about it, it's his job.

She told them about her widow's benefits being reduced because they couldn't find any FBI case John was working on at the time of his murder. She told them about the visit from Lou, the box of personal items from John's office, and the beautiful poem and note he left for her. The FBI thought there was more to his writings, and they're clues to something he wanted her to find.

"Of course, they're nothing except beautiful words from a man to his wife, whom he loved very much. These spy agencies always need to read more into things that aren't there. I can't understand why the FBI can't believe that?"

"What did he say, Tee? Did you bring it so I could read it?"

"No, Zee, I didn't want it getting lost in the shuffle between this century and the last. It's too precious to chance losing it. I put the letter, poem, and a keepsake he gave me in our safe at home."

She gave René a look and tried to send him a message with her eyes but wasn't sure if it got through. The key wasn't in a safe. It's where it'd been since it came into her possession, around her neck. She had no intention of going anywhere without it, and that included 1971, and she won't be telling Cater about the key coming along with her. If he finds out and refuses to let her bring it, she'll cross that bridge when she comes to it. She wasn't going anywhere without it. Then she told them her house had been bugged.

"Tee, I think becoming involved with our little caper has given you an overactive imagination. Don't you think maybe you're being a little paranoid? Who'd want to bug your house and why?"

She shared the story about the changing of the light bulb and how Matt found them all, telling them there was even one in the bathroom which everyone thought was disgusting.

"Are you sure, Tee? It sounds far-fetched to me."

"Why would I make that up, Zee?" She looked at everyone at the table and said, "Matt took them to the State Troopers, and they're using their resources to find out more about them. I hadn't heard anything more before I left."

"Are you saying the authorities have them in their possession? All of them?" René asked.

"I wanted them out of my house. Who knows how long they'd been there or what they'd seen?" She could tell by the look on his face that he was disenchanted with her answer. "I'll be filing charges against the FBI for not only reducing my widow's benefits but for invading my privacy. Now it'll have to wait until I get back in December. I haven't had a chance to talk to my lawyer yet."

"Oh my God, Tee! You're not kidding!" Zoe was shocked. "You think the FBI's bugging your house?"

"Well, I think it's obvious. Who else could it have been? They think I'm hiding something, and this would be how to find out. Dirty bastards! I've no secrets and John didn't leave me any messages from the grave."

Christina noticed Charlie seemed to take it all in, which is exactly what she wanted. Hopefully, he'll go back to his boss and relay her sad story. She wanted to throw Martin off track, so he felt at ease that her suspicions didn't include him. They ate and went back to the apartment.

Their appointment with Martin was at one o'clock, so they had to be there at noon. Christina brought a book in case they had to wait. For shits and giggles, she asked the receptionist where the bathroom was. The girl went completely white and started to stutter. Christina laughed to herself thinking, "I'm so damn funny." When she said she was kidding, her color returned, and the look of panic was replaced by one of relief.

When his majesty was ready to receive his minions, they were ushered into Martin's office. Zoe and René shook hands and exchanged pleasantries, but Christina walked in with her nose in the air and ignored his outstretched hand. How dare he think for even one second that she'd afford him any courtesy? He rudely dismissed Charlie and told him this meeting didn't include him. As he walked towards the door, Christina said to him, "I'll fill you in on all the details later, Charlie." Martin shot a look of hatred towards her, which she answered with a fake smile.

Martin cleared his throat and said, "Let's get started, shall we?" He proceeded to convey the main objectives and arrangements of the mission. Zoe and Christina would be roommates and René will room with a British student by the name of Adam Wallingford. Adam was from the aristocracy of British society and will be in his second year. He failed most of his courses last year because of too much socialization which meant too much indulgence in "sex, drugs and rock & roll."

"Adam is a musician and is at UC Berkeley for Music and Arts. Mrs. Pucci, he'll be in some of the classes shared by you and Prince Ali, if he decides to go to class this year. We put him with you René, because past practice illustrates he's not usually present at the dorm."

Morgan and the Prince's room will be between René and Adam's room and the two women. There will be two other girls in another room on that floor next to Zoe and Christina's room, but Martin felt it immaterial to get their names at this point. On the opposite side of the dorm rooms were the Common Rooms and the bathrooms. Morgan and the Prince had the biggest room offered at Berkeley at the time because of the status of the prince and Morgan. The Common Rooms included a kitchen. This suite of rooms was the only one to have this luxury, which once again was attributed to the presence of the prince and Morgan.

He went over the main objectives and obligations of what was expected of them. René's main objectives were to keep the two women safe, listen in on conversations between the prince and anyone he may converse with in his native tongue, and find and photograph the evidence that will quash Morgan's political career. Under no circumstances should the prince be made aware that René was fluent in Arabic. Zoe was to lend support to René in whatever way she could and ingratiate herself with Morgan and the prince, which was the mission for the three of them. Christina's mission was to befriend Prince Ali, do whatever she could to gain his trust, help with his studies and discover more about the two family's relationship.

"I know you're averse to this, but sexual favors are unequivocally encouraged. It's a tactic used by many female agents to garner trust and information and it's expected of you."

For the first time that day she looked straight into his evil eyes. "You talking to me?" she asked in her best *"Taxi Driver"* imitation. As she received no reply, she repeated the question. "Are you talking to me?"

"Well, Mrs. Pucci, who else would I be talking to?"

"Marty, if I could slap you across the face without having to touch you, it would've already happened." She tried to hold her fiery temper in check, but she was never good at that.

She walked over to his desk and leaned over to get closer to his ugly visage, only mere inches from his face. "That'll only happen when hell freezes over, pigs fly and monkeys come out of your ass! For your information, *Marty*, in the year 1971, Zoe and I were still pure as the fallen snow. Neither of us had any sexual experience. It means nothing to you, but the first sexual encounter for a girl is precious and not to be given up lightly. I've no intention of giving that sort of gift to a repugnant Arab prince and I don't care what you say, suggest or even demand. That was given to my husband and that ain't…gonna…change, you miserable fuckface!"

Their eyes were locked, and they were thinking similar thoughts. Christina wasn't going to blink or look away and it seemed neither was he. The muscles in his jaw were tensing up while she kept her facial muscles relaxed. They were locked in this tempestuous embrace of intense aversion.

Out of the corner of her eye Christina saw René rise from his seat and approach the desk. He broke the tension by saying, "Now that we've settled that, let's move on, no?" Their gaze broke at the same time to look at René and the situation was momentarily diffused. Christina sat down and shot a daggered look at the loathsome man on the other side of the desk who mirrored the look back at her.

"I agree, René." Martin said. "Before we go any further, I'd like to see what each of you brought to make sure it's time appropriate." René pulled out a pouch and emptied it onto Martin's desk. There were a few pens with engraving on them, buttons, a cigarette lighter, a couple of over-the-counter pill bottles, a few medals on chains and some coins which were no longer being used as currency in France.

Martin checked them all thoroughly. René said the pens were given to him by his parents and grandparents upon his graduation from school and were dated appropriately. Martin made two piles and put the pens, a lighter, a bottle of aspirin, one of the medals on a chain, and two of the coins in one pile and everything else in another pile.

He told René he could only take the pile containing the pens, and the other pile would go into a safe until his return. René started arguing with him, intermixing English and French. Martin sat expressionless, telling him his decision wasn't open for discussion. "I know exactly what these items are, and they cannot be brought with you to 1971."

René protested that he needed them, and no one would know what they were. "How do you expect us to succeed if you tie my hands on the equipment I'm allowed to bring? Don't punish me or this mission because this woman has dared to challenge you and put you in a pissy mood! What purpose does it serve to deny us the proper tools?"

Martin said nothing, sat with his fingers together like a spider on a mirror, and a smug expression on his face. "If you prefer, René, you can go empty-handed. The pens are allowed because they're dated and inscribed in French, as is the lighter. They're exactly what they seem to be: pens and a lighter. You're lucky your name isn't on any of them, or they'd be out. The medal I'm allowing is just that, a medal. The others are surveillance devices, as are the buttons and most of the coins. Do you think I can't recognize equipment when I see it?" René became agitated and threatened to back out of the mission if the CIA wasn't going to allow his equipment.

Martin sat there waiting for René to finish his diatribe. "Are you through, René?" He paused as if to give René a chance to answer but had no intention of listening to what he had to say. "They cannot be brought under any circumstances because they're recent technology. The ramifications of someone getting their hands on advanced technology could be disastrous. You'll have a Middle Eastern Prince in the room next to yours. We can't take the chance that he could identify that any of these items aren't what they seem and bring them home for their scientists to examine and use against us.

We're not going to give them our technology. You can take what's in this pile, and the other goes in the safe. Or you can take nothing."

"Or I can back out, and the whole thing will be scrapped! Marteen, I need these. How are we supposed to do what you ask if I can't bring what's necessary? What sort of apparatus will be available to us?"

"You'll have disguised cameras to photograph the evidence on the communications between the families, and I'm sure there are other tools you'll find useful."

They got into an intense argument in French. A few times, René pointed at Christina, and she wondered what was being said. As the disagreement wound down, it was obvious from the angry look and demeanor of René that he had lost the dispute.

"Agreed, René?"

"*Nous ne sommes pas d'accord*!" René replied. He snatched the approved pile and walked out the door, slamming it on his way out.

"Will he be back?" asked Zoe.

"Yes," Martin replied, "after he lets off some steam. You know the French; they hate to lose an argument." Martin mumbled something, then asked, "Do either of you have anything you're planning on bringing?"

Zoe shook her head, and Christina replied, "Yes, I do. It's something very precious to me." He straightened up in his seat and watched eagerly as she leaned down to get the item out of her bag. Christina thought he was expecting her to produce a key.

Before she pulled her item out, she said in a louder voice, "Ladies and gentlemen, for one night only!"

Zoe stood up and yelled. "Oh no! No!" She looked at Martin and said, "You can't let her bring that!"

Christina started to laugh. "After a long hiatus, back by popular demand…"

"No, Tee, you're not bringing him!" Zoe yelled. "I swear to God, you're not bringing him."

"Oh yes, I am! You know, wherever I go, he goes."

Martin sat there with a quizzical look on his face and asked, "What the hell is it?"

"It's the world-famous 'Theodore Edward Dashingest Daredevil *In* Entertainment Bear!" As she brought her time-worn teddy bear out of her bag, she started humming his theme song, "*Entry of the Gladiators*."

She announced in a ringmaster's voice. "Theodore Edward has traveled the world with his beautiful assistant Christina, playing for heads of state worldwide and the Royals of Europe."

While Christina was doing her "act," Zoe was yelling, "You're not bringing him to Berkeley. I'm not living through your foolish circus acts again!"

"Ladies and gentlemen, watch as Theodore Edward does his death-defying act." She threw him in the air, caught him, and did it again, twirling him in the air, this time missing her catch. "Oops! As you can see, we're kinda rusty. We'll try again, and this time his lovely assistant will catch him with one hand!" Christina proceeded to "perform" their act, while Zoe voiced her protest.

"Tee, I'm going to kill you if you make me live through another night of your asinine circus acts with that stupid bear!"

Martin wasn't amused. "What the hell is that?"

"Marty," she said, "are you so deprived that you don't know a Teddy bear when you see one?" He gave her a dirty look. "I admit he's on the worn side. I've had him since I was a baby, and he's coming with me. A teenage girl would bring her favorite stuffed animal, especially if she's far from home. I'd think it'd be suspicious if we didn't have one. Zoe's going to have to buy one when we get to Berkeley."

They both sat there saying nothing. "Go into any dorm room of a girl and you're going to find a number of stuffed animals, some that've been around for most of their lives. Girls have attachments to them, and he's coming with me. End of story!"

Martin held out his hand and told her to hand him over. She didn't want his slimy hands all over her precious possession, but had to get him approved, so she reluctantly handed him over.

He checked out his sweet little chipped button eyes and tried to pull them off. He did the same to the battered buttons on his cute green jacket, worn but still connected to his body. Try as he might to get the buttons off, they were sewn on too tightly. His fur was gone in many areas, and his nose was almost completely squashed in. Martin roughly squeezed him, pulled his arms and legs, turned him over a few times, pulled at the jacket to take it off and violently shook him, which pissed her off.

"Hey, cut that out! Go easy on him! He's over 45 years old."
She looked at Zoe and said, "But he can still perform all of his tricks!
Isn't that great?"

"For Chrissake, Tee! Do you have to bring him?"

"Yes, Zee, I do."

Martin brutally checked him over and asked if there was
anything else she was bringing.

"Nope, just the bear."

"Well, Mrs. Pucci, if he's that important to you, we should be
able to strike a bargain, that's if you really want to bring him."

"Kiss my ass, Marty. He fits the criteria, and I'm bringing him.
Try to remember I'm not one of your employees, so you've no power
over me. What're you going to do? Fire me? You need me more than
I need you. I'm bringing my bear."

She snatched the bear from him and checked him over to make
sure he wasn't missing an arm or leg with the rough handling he
endured. She asked Theodore if he was okay. She replied for him in
his voice, both were looking at Marty, "He's a mean man." She
snapped his head to look at her, they both nodded, looked back at
Marty, and smiled.

Martin said nothing, trying to intimidate her with his evil stare.
It didn't work. She didn't scare easily, especially when she was
enjoying herself, knowing she was annoying him. He buzzed his
secretary to find René and get him back in there.

René came back into the room and sat in the chair like a
petulant child. For someone who seemed so calm and cool, he was in
direct opposition to his usual disposition. He angrily stated they were
doomed to fail and why bother going ahead with the mission.

Then he asked, "Where's our backup? We need others there for
our protection. I hope you're not sending us there with no one to help
if something happens. You do understand we don't have modern
technology, and we need another team there. It's standard procedure,
Marteen, and I won't accept this mission unless I know we're not
alone, like sitting ducks. We should meet with them and know who
they are and what they'll be doing."

"You worry about what you need to take care of and let me
worry about taking care of the backup. There'll be agents around to
assist you, and they'll make themselves known if necessary. They

know you three are primary and they're secondary. They know you're the primary head of the mission. Does that make you any happier?" His sarcasm was obvious and not appreciated.

Martin pulled out three folders and gave one to each of them. "These are reports and information regarding the two families. Mrs. Pucci, I expect you to memorize what's in these before you go." She looked them over and threw them back on his desk.

"Nothing in there I don't already know," she said. His fists were clenching, and she was enjoying his irritation.

"Really, Mrs. Pucci? What do you already know?"

She proceeded to tell him all she knew of the relationship between the two families, their finances and fortunes connected for many years by oil, suspected shady deals, defaulted loans, and outright fraud. Morgan's father, through his vast political power, was instrumental in getting key members of the Zatari Royal Family into powerful positions on OPEC and the World Bank.

A large portion of Harold Morgan's fortune began to accumulate shortly after 1971, which he was exceptionally good at pissing away on frivolous undertakings such as a losing basketball team and a restaurant franchise that couldn't pass board of health inspections, even with bribery. As the Morgans were powerful in Louisiana politics, Gulf oil drilling figured heavily in the relationship between the two families. And that was just the tip of the iceberg.

Martin stared at her, saying nothing. "I'd appreciate it if you'd all take the file and look it over." They went over a few more things regarding the mission and wrapped up the meeting. As they walked out the door, Martin wished them good luck and told them they must report to the liaison, Professor O'Connell, on a weekly basis so reports could be sent back to him. "Your country's interested in your weekly progress, so I expect a full report every Friday. Understood?"

René's foul mood hadn't brightened in the least. As he got to the door he said, "Fuck you, *Marti*! Sleep well while we're gone. Pleasant dreams, you contemptible, loathsome prick! I do *not* look forward to our meetings when we return." He slammed the door so hard that the glass broke and shattered all over the floor. Martin started to yell, but René turned and gestured, hitting the inside of his elbow with his hand, turned back, and kept walking. Zoe and Christina could tell he was furious. Christina wanted to tell him everything was going to be fine, but now wasn't the time.

Charles was waiting for them in the reception area and René walked past him saying, "Get me the fuck out of here before I kill someone." Charles looked at them quizzically, but no one responded. The intercom for the receptionist was buzzing furiously and Martin's booming voice could be heard demanding someone get to his office immediately to pick up the broken glass and for it to be replaced ***TODAY!***

Martin was about to explode and needed to get out of his office. He hobbled over to his briefcase and retrieved his phone from its pocketed space. He went to his contact list and found who he was looking for. He waited impatiently for an answer. "Come on, you fucking whore! Answer your phone!"

"Hello, lover," she answered. "Are you looking for some special time with me?" Martin wanted no small talk.

"I need to see you now!" he answered. She's always available for Martin and never refuses him. He wasn't sure which one of them enjoyed their encounters more.

"Well, lover, I need a few minutes to freshen up."

"No need for that. You'll need to do that after I leave. I'll meet you at the usual place in half an hour. Don't fucking be late or make me wait." Martin hung up before waiting for a reply.

He limped over to his safe, put his briefcase in, and opened an envelope full of cash, which he kept for these occasions. He counted out $10,000, which should be enough for his session today. He put the rest of the cash back into the safe and the envelope with the cash in the breast pocket of his jacket. He grabbed his cell phone and left his office.

His feet crunched over the broken glass and with every sound of it under his feet, his anger at René and that son of a bitching whore Christina Pucci swelled to a fevered pitch. It'd taken every ounce of self-control not to have backhanded her face when she dared to confront him *in his own office!* He silently wished the prince would rape the shit out of her and leave her bloodied and beaten just as he'll be doing to that fucking whore, whose name will be Christina today. He couldn't wait to fuck and beat the shit out of her as he does on all their sadistic encounters. He hailed a cab and thought how much he needed this today.

# CHAPTER 15

Charles drove the trio back to the apartment. The mood in the car was tense, and no one spoke the entire ride. When they arrived, before getting out of the car, René apologized for his outburst and for making them feel uncomfortable and he's committed to the mission. They shouldn't be concerned about what occurred in Martin's office and they'll work together for success.

Feeling the tension and apprehension of the two women, he kissed their hands and said in a much calmer voice, "Onward to 1971 and to hell with Martin Cater. At least we won't see him until December. Now, where shall we go for dinner on our last night in the 21$^{st}$ Century?"

He wanted to tell them his actions were meant to throw Martin off and make him think he's upset about not being able to bring the equipment he desired, but Charles was always around. He felt quite smug that he was able to fool the Deputy Chief. Although he wanted to bring the buttons which were video recording devices, he was content with what was allowed.

It'll be harder with the absence of visual recordings, but he'll make it work. They'll be getting there at least a week or two ahead of the rest of the student body so it'll give them time to plan and set things up if necessary. He wished he'd been able to sneak in at least one video recorder but was thankful for what he slid through.

It was a bonus when the glass of Martin's door shattered. He knew the fastidious man would be incensed that an underling dared be so disrespectful. He chuckled to himself but kept the stern, unhappy look on his face so as not to give away his true feelings.

He didn't like being so ungracious in the company of women, but he'll explain once they're out from under Charles' watchful eye. He hoped they'd be able to discuss things on the plane to California, but Charles informed them he's to be their constant companion until entry into the time-travel chamber. He wondered if Charles knew how intrusive his presence was to their communications.

Their every move and conversations were being monitored by the CIA, with video and listening devices in the apartment, the car, and on Charles. René knew of it and was fairly certain Christina did too. The lovely Ms. Janis didn't seem to have a clue or didn't care because she had nothing to hide. He wondered if they were monitoring her private life.

He looked at the two women across the table from him at dinner and marveled at them. So different, yet so alike, and both stunning to the eye. Ms. Janis was exotic-looking, extraordinarily intelligent, more reticent, secure in who she was, and carried herself like royalty. Christina held things closer to herself, unassuming, and then pulled out the big guns. René was surprised by her cleverness, quick wit, unassuming wisdom, and her sheer fearlessness, especially regarding Martin. As different as these two women were, there was a similarity between them he couldn't quite grasp.

They went to bed early, but none slept, with thoughts of what was on the horizon for them. People aren't given the opportunity to relive their youth with the knowledge of their years. Hopefully, they'll be successful in attaining the information that's the purpose of this mission. If Harold Morgan isn't fit to rule as the leading world power, they need to find that information and bring it back. Although René wasn't a citizen of the United States, only a fool would think what happens in the US doesn't affect the world. One careless man can wreak havoc and destroy the planet and humanity. There's a global need to find out if Morgan is that sort of careless man.

The next day, the four of them flew by private plane to Oakland, California. They all seemed to sleep through most of the flight. When the plane landed, they were met on the tarmac by a limousine and taken directly to the University of Berkeley, which was a relatively short distance away. California is a beautiful state, and the vista of the Bay was breathtaking on the ride to the college. There were a few "oohs" and "aahs" taking in the scenery, but overall, none of them said much as they were feeling the apprehension of what was to come.

They pulled into the college campus and headed directly to the Science & Technology Building. A gentleman was waiting for them and opened the door to the limousine when it pulled up. "Welcome to UC Berkeley!" René was the first to exit and shook hands with the man who introduced himself as Professor Glenn O'Connell. He was very distinguished, probably in his early 60s, and looked very professorial. He sported a moustache and goatee, which, along with his receding hairline, were graying. Everyone exited the vehicle, and the driver was told by the professor to be back in two hours. He graciously opened the door and the group walked into the building.

O'Connell led the way and while they walked, he gave the group some history on the University, wondering if anyone was listening. The professor loved the college like it was family and spoke proudly as he imparted the knowledge he seemed eager to share.

"The word Berkeley comes from the Old English *beorce léah* meaning birch meadow. Berkeley is the site of the University of California and the oldest of the University of California system. The city of Berkeley is noted as one of the most politically liberal in the nation, with one study placing it the third most liberal city in the United States," he confirmed proudly.

"According to the *Centennial Record of the University of California*, in 1866, a group of College of California men watched two ships standing out to sea while standing at Founders' Rock. One of them, Frederick Billings, thought of the lines of the Anglo-Irish Anglican Bishop George Berkeley, '*westward the course of empire takes its way*,' and suggested the town and college site be named for the eighteenth-century Anglo-Irish philosopher." The four of them nodded their heads as he spoke.

"UC Berkeley is identified with the rapid social changes, civic unrest, and political upheaval characterized in the late 1960s. During that period, Telegraph Avenue became a focal point for the hippie movement, which spilled over the Bay from our neighbor, San Francisco. Many of the hippies were apolitical dropouts, rather than students of the college, but in the stimulating atmosphere of UC Berkeley in 67–69 there was considerable overlap of the hippie movement and the fundamental left, as I'm sure you all remember."

The professor continued as though he were conducting a lecture. "An iconic event in the UC Berkeley Sixties scene, *Bloody Thursday, May 15, 1969,* a conflict over a parcel of university property south of the adjoining campus site that came to be called 'People's Park'. Governor Reagan had been publicly critical of university administrators for tolerating student demonstrations at the UC Berkeley campus.

"He had received enormous popular support for his campaign promise to crack down on what the public perceived as a negligent attitude at California's public universities. Governor Reagan had called the UC Berkeley campus '*a haven for communist sympathizers, protesters and sex deviants.*' Reagan considered the creation of the park a direct leftist challenge to the property rights of the university, and he found in it an opportunity to fulfill his campaign promise."

Professor O'Connell looked at his audience and knew he'd lost them except for one of the women and it pleased him immensely that it was Ms. Janis who's following his narrative. She seemed to hang onto every word he'd spoken. He became irritated by the inattentiveness of the others, and felt since they'll be attending this University, they should be aware of some of its history.

Once again, he found it hard to take his eyes off Zoe Janis. She was still so beautiful and hardly looked a day over 35. She still had that same effect on him, even though he was happily married now. The memories of her in 1971 flooded back to him, however, nothing can be revealed to them of what happened in those short four months. Playing with time has its consequences, so one must be extremely careful. He was going to go into a dissertation on the Campanile but decided to let things play out as they had. Christina Pucci, whom he remembered loved their bell tower, will learn about it soon enough.

Their minds were obviously on what the future, or more correctly, the past would hold for them. "I won't get into the whole ordeal as I'm certain it'll be something you'll become aware of when you're back in 1971. Today, People's Park is a free public park. Although it's currently open to all, it's now mainly a daytime sanctuary for Berkeley's large homeless population. Such a rich history for such a small parcel of land."

Ms. Janis spoke up, "Thank you, Professor. I recall much of what you'd been speaking of from accounts in the news when in high school. I eagerly followed all the news on what was happening with all the unrest and protests on college campuses while in my teens. It's thrilling to be able to be here at this college, in the heart of Telegraph Ave, and the People's Park, only two short years after *'Bloody Thursday.'* I can hardly believe I'm here!"

She was ecstatic, barely containing her enthusiasm. "Those protests taking place on campuses gave young people a voice, and they brought about much change to this country. Thank you for sharing this exciting history of this wonderful and electrifying period in Berkeley's past. I look forward to finding out more once we're attending classes here."

The friendship between the two women showed itself immediately when Christina said to Zoe in a very good-natured and playful manner, "What a suck-up you are! You're not even in class yet and you're already bucking for an 'A'." It seemed to lighten the atmosphere as there seemed an overt tenseness had overcome the group.

O'Connell laughed and said, "If she continues in that fashion, she'll definitely get that A." The group walked until they reached an odd-looking elevator, and O'Connell used a key to summon it. Before its arrival, he said to them, "What you're going to see is top secret, a fact which I'm sure you're well aware of. Where this elevator drops us off is one room off the time chamber. I hope the three of you are prepared and have all you need with you, as once we exit the elevator, you're minutes away from being a member of a small elite group of people who've actually experienced time travel."

The elevator doors opened, and the five of them entered. No one spoke as the elevator began its descent. There were no buttons to push, no knobs labeled "close door" or "alarm," knowing exactly which direction to go. The doors opened slowly, and the passengers exited. The doors didn't shut; they remained open and stayed that way until the two who weren't traveling back in time returned to the first floor.

The Professor led the way toward a closed door. "I'm not going to try to explain the science of how this works, as it's complicated and unnecessary to go into. All you need to know is that it works. The CIA and the Science and Technology Department of UC Berkeley have worked together for many years to achieve time travel. Please, follow me."

He used the same key attached to his wrist that summoned the elevator to open the door. He motioned the four of them to enter the room.

Charles spoke first saying, "I'm the witness today and I'll be reporting back to Deputy Chief Cater that the sendoff was successful."

"Very well," O'Connell replied. "It's time for us to get started. First, I need to make sure what you're bringing is on the list of items sanctioned by the Agency. Please set the items here on this table, and I'll check them off with the list sent to me. After we take care of this, you'll go into the changing room and remove all your clothing and put on the robes provided. All your personal items, cell phone, chargers, laptops, etc., will be kept safe. They will be sent to your homes during your stay in 1971.”

René removed his pouch from his pocket and emptied the contents onto the table. Christina opened her bag, took her well-worn teddy bear, and put it on the table. As René was not in the room when she’d shown her item to Martin, he was surprised by its appearance.

“Madame, is that what you’re bringing with you? A teddy bear?”

“Wherever I go, Theodore Edward goes with me.”

He laughed to himself and thought it odd for a 50-year-old woman to still be attached to a teddy bear. Women cannot be understood. Zoe said she wasn’t bringing anything.

The professor looked everything over, checked off the list, put René’s items back into his pouch, and gave the teddy bear to Christina. “Well, now all you have to do is go into the changing rooms, and then we’ll secure your items.” The three of them went into the rooms and came out wearing robes. Each in turn handed their personal items to the professor, who put everything into the safe. He closed the door and turned toward the three of them. “Well, I believe the next step is to go into the chamber.”

As they walked past him, he noticed something. “Mrs. Pucci?”
“Yes?”

He looked over the list. “I don’t see your necklace on the list of items.”

“Oh, you mean this?” and she held out the key on the chain around her neck. “Well, I didn’t even think about it. My brother George gave it to me before he went to Vietnam, so it’s time appropriate. I wanted to keep him with me. He died over there, and his twin gave me the box the key opened, which held those springy snakes that fly out when you open the can. It’s the last practical joke George played on me, and I’ve had it since 1969. It didn’t occur to me to have it okayed by the CIA. I’ve no intention of leaving it here.”

Zoe obviously didn’t recall it and thankfully didn’t remark about it. René smiled to himself. He knew the key was left to her by her husband. He marveled at her gumption and the way she’s playing out this scenario.

O’Connell wasn’t happy. “I can’t let you bring it unless the Agency clears it.”

"Well," she said, "Charlie's from the CIA, he can clear it."

"I don't think you understand the ramifications of time travel and keeping things time appropriate."

"I told you it was given to me in 1969. Don't you believe me?"

"It's not a question of belief, it's a question of protocol that must be followed precisely. I'll have to contact Deputy Cater immediately."

"Okay, Professor, I understand your position. While you're speaking with him, mention that if the key around my neck doesn't go, I don't either." René looked at her, smiling, and very slightly shook his head. What an amazingly cunning woman!

O'Connell went to the phone on the desk and dialed. He identified himself, asking to speak with Deputy Chief Cater. A few moments later, he was explaining the situation to Martin. From the look on his face, the conversation wasn't going well.

"She states the key was given to her in 1969 by her brother before he went to war." Everyone was watching the professor except Christina, who was ignoring the ensuing drama, focusing on her teddy bear.

O'Connell was trying to talk privately, but the phone was a college phone and not portable, so he used the long cord to enter a changing room. As soon as Christina saw him leave the room, she walked to the phone and hit the button to put it on speaker. Martin Cater's screaming voice filled the room.

"...a fucking lying conniving slut! That key wasn't given to her by her brother, and I know that for a goddamn motherfucking fact! That bitch had this whole thing planned! Under no circumstances is that key to go with her! She's to leave that key with..."

She interrupted the conversation between the two men, saying into the speaker, "Oh really, Marty? And how would you know any facts about the key around my neck? Huh? What makes you so damn sure you know anything about my key? You want to explain yourself? So now I'm a lying conniving slut and bitch? Marty, sweetie, I don't go without my key! No key, no me, no mission. Ball's in your court, you miserable pri.."

She's unable to finish her sentence as O'Connell rushed into the room and took the phone off speaker. He apologized to Cater, telling him it never crossed his mind that anyone would pull a stunt like that. They continued their conversation with as much privacy as the small space allowed. René wanted to rush over and kiss Christina. She's got quite a few tricks up her sleeve, knowing that without her, there's no Operation Berkeley. She has Martin in an awkward position, and it's a beautiful thing to witness.

The conversation ended, and O'Connell walked over to Christina. "That was an embarrassment to me and disrespectful to the Agency and Deputy Chief."

"I apologize for your embarrassment, and I meant no disrespect. I'm not employed by the CIA, and Martin Cater has no jurisdiction over me. I'm a recent widow and mother, thrown into this sea of espionage with no life jacket. I accepted this mission to assist my country and owe no loyalty to the CIA or Martin Cater. Excuse me if I feel the need to flex my muscles once in a while to assure I'm not being bowled over."

He looked at her and said, "The fact that you have children is not in my report."

"Well, I do," she answered, "Three of them, and why do people keep asking me that? It's unnerving!" O'Connell didn't answer. "So, what's next? Are my key and I going or not?"

"Although you've vastly overstepped the bounds of propriety and protocol, Deputy Chief Cater is making an exception and has reluctantly given the okay to the chain and key. The mission is still a go."

"Well," she said, "let's break out the band for good old big-hearted Marty." René and Charles chuckled, finding her remark amusing, but it was lost on the other two. Zoe began scolding her friend, but Christina waved her off with a quick flick of her hand and said, "Zee, give me a break! You'll understand once we get out of this century."

She turned to O'Connell, "Let's get this show on the road. If I start thinking about helping that asshole with this mission, I may change my mind." The three of them were led into the chamber and told to lie down. There were spaces for four people. The women took the chambers on the right, and René took one on the left. Before closing the chamber and sending them off, O'Connell told them what to expect.

"You'll feel a sensation of light-headedness and then fall asleep. The process will take approximately one hour. You'll be awakened by a much younger and hipper manifestation of the man standing before you, and from there, you'll be re-acclimated to 1971. You'll each be given an expense account as you'll have to purchase clothing, toiletries, and sundries. We have your sizes and have assembled some clothing for you to wear on your arrival. I'll be your guide and give whatever help I can in 1971 and be your liaison to this century. Your weekly reports will be given to the younger me and then sent through the chamber to reach this century."

He paused for a moment and asked, "Are there any questions?"

"Yeah," Christina said. "Do we succeed? You'd know because you lived through it already, right?

"I can't answer that, Mrs. Pucci. Time travel has to be respected, and I can say nothing about what's happened. Things must play out without any of you having previous knowledge of past events. Now, onward to 1971."

Charles and O'Connell wished them good luck and success and exited the room. Christina said a silent prayer, "God, please, let me come home safely after successfully fulfilling this mission and may my children not be affected by the foolishness of their mother."

O'Connell went to a panel, pressed a few buttons, uttered "God Speed," and hit the last button, which made a loud whooshing noise. He looked at Charles and said, "That was quite a departure! I'm astounded at what she did! She certainly caught me by surprise! The Deputy Chief deserved what happened because of the way he spoke to her. I don't shock easily, but I found his language toward her quite disturbing. How would he know for a fact anything about her necklace?"

Charles shrugged. "She's really a good egg. In the short time I've known her, I've found her to be an extremely likable woman who's been thrown into an improbable situation. I hope Agent Barrineau takes good care of her."

"We shall see, won't we?" O'Connell answered. "Time travel is very tricky and must be respected. Having children puts a different slant on things. Cater's aware that the consequences can be life-shattering, and he's purposely kept that information from me. If something goes wrong, the existence of her family could be completely wiped out. Care must be taken to ensure she makes it back. Hopefully, everything is in place to make sure of that."

Charles thanked him and they shook hands. "Well, my good man," said O'Connell, "we have an hour or so, I say we have lunch and raise a glass to the travelers."

"Sounds like a great idea." The two men walked to the waiting elevator. As they ascended, the next chapter in the lives of the time travelers was beginning.

# 1971
## *UC Berkeley, California*

# CHAPTER 16

Christina heard someone calling her name in the far-off distance. She moved towards it but the strength of the voice didn't increase. It wasn't a voice she recognized and being surrounded by thick fog, wasn't sure which way to go.

She tried to answer, but nothing came from her mouth. She listened for the direction of the voice, but something held her back. She was stuck, unable to move, feeling like she was in one of those dreams when you're trying to run but can't. She looked around, seeing nothing because of the fog. She looked behind her.

Through the fog, she saw her three children, only they were all little. With their age differences, she thought it odd. She tried to run to them but was frozen to the spot. The voice kept calling her in one direction, but her children were in the other. She felt dizzy and nauseous. Then she heard Zoe's voice.

"Tee! Wake up!" She was sobbing, calling her name. "Tee! Come on! Wake up!"

Christina wondered what was going on and why Zee was crying.

She looked towards her children, and they started to fade. "No, guys," she said, "don't go! Please stay." Their images faded and Zoe's voice got louder.

"Oh my God! She's not waking up! Tee! Wake up!" Then Christina heard two male voices along with Zoe's, calling to her with an urgent tone. She looked where her children were, but they disappeared into the murky fog. Looking ahead, the fog was starting to dissipate. She was able to move forward, toward the sound of Zoe's voice.

Zoe kept pleading with her to wake up. Christina was feeling confused but kept moving toward Zoe's voice until the fog disappeared. She opened her eyes to a blur of faces, unable to focus. One was a very young and glowing Zoe with a couple hippies. Where am I?

Zoe had a look of horror on her face. "Oh, my God, Tee! Are you alright?"

Christina felt very lightheaded, like she was drunk. The sound of bells chiming was loudly filling the air. "Zee? Is that you? Did we die and go to heaven? Are those the heavenly bells?" She was totally confused, and the bells continued to sound. She couldn't focus on their faces, but one of the hippies answered her.

"No, Mrs. Pucci, you're not in heaven, just the University of Berkeley, California, and those are the bells from the Sather Tower, our Campanile, ringing the hour of ten. It's the symbol of the University, and it's quite impressive."

"Oh, yeah? For real? I love bells."

"It plays a song at **the end of the** semester before finals. Mrs. Pucci, do you know where you are?"

"Heaven?"

"No, Tee. Remember? We're at Berkeley! We made it! Tee, you look amazing. Can you get up?"

"Berkeley? In California?" Still confused, one of the guys helped her sit up. When her hair fell over her shoulders, she ran her fingers through it and was immediately aware of the difference in its texture: soft, vibrantly shiny, and very long. She looked at her hands and was shocked. They belonged to a child. She put them to her face and felt the youthful smoothness of her complexion. They traveled down her neck, and it had a youthful feel with no sagging. She felt the key still firmly attached and sighed with relief. The bells of the Campanile continued to peal as if to welcome them to Berkeley.

She was able to focus and saw Zoe, "Holy shit Zee! It's your teenage self! You're gorgeous! And your hair! It's so long and shiny! Are you sure we're not dead?" Then she noticed Zoe was crying and asked, "Why are you crying? We're dead, aren't we?" Zoe assured her they were alive.

"*Merde*, Christina, you gave us quite a fright!" It was one of the hippie guys with an accent. When Zoe addressed him, it jarred Christina's memory.

"Reneeeé! I remember you. Wow! You're cute! Am I drunk?" She felt high.

The guy who seemed in charge said, "I had to give you more of the mix of oxygen and other gases to help you come around. It's nothing to worry about. You'll feel yourself soon enough." The bells stopped chiming.

She focused on everyone and thought René was some hunk of ooo-la-la! He was handsome in his middle-aged incarnation, but he's a freaking teenage dream, with his cute little moustache and light brown hair with soft curls not quite to his shoulders. As Christina came out of her stupor, she found it easier to find the face she remembered through his eyes. The two men helped her out of the chamber, and Zoe grabbed the teddy bear.

O'Connell introduced himself and said they were getting worried. "We couldn't awaken you, and it's never happened before. You gave us quite a scare. How are you feeling now?"

"Pretty good, I think. I heard my name but didn't know which direction to go. I couldn't see anything because of the fog. I thought I was dead or something, especially when I looked behind me, my three kids were off in the distance, but they were all toddlers. I didn't know where to go. When I heard Zee crying, I needed to find her, so I followed her voice. With the bells chiming, I thought I was in heaven."

"Three kids? Please don't tell me you have children." O'Connell looked horrified.

"Again? I have three children. Why do I keep getting asked that question? There has to be a reason, and you're going to tell me right now. I discussed this a little while ago with your older self."

"Well, that explains why we had a difficult time awakening you. Ideally, people who travel through time are supposed to have nothing to hold them to their present. You have three particularly good reasons to want to cling to your present existence and not let go. That's why you saw your children behind you. This is unprecedented and adds an unexpected twist."

"How so?"

"I'm not going to worry you about things that most likely won't happen."

"Too late. I'm already worried. My kids are in danger, aren't they? That douchebag Marty lied to me and so did you. Why didn't your 21st-century-self tell you I have kids? I feel like I'm in a Twilight Zone episode!"

"I honestly don't know the reason, Mrs. Pucci. You'll have to ask me when you return."

She was feeling set up. "Martin Cater never mentioned anything of that nature to me or that my children could be harmed by this, and *neither did you*. You know now because I told you, so how did your older self not remember such a thing? I'm being completely bamboozled by everyone! I don't care how young I look here in 1971,

I'm going back to the 21st century right now, so get this contraption ready!"

O'Connell shook his head. "It doesn't work that way, Mrs. Pucci. Now that you're here, you have to stay for the time agreed. The only things to be sent through the chamber until December are the paper reports. I'm sorry the CIA wasn't honest with you or me. You've no alternative but to stay here in 1971. We need to make sure you get back as planned, and everything should be fine."

She started crying. She didn't know if it was out of frustrated anger, sadness, anxiety about her children, or that she'd been duped. She was now a teenager and who knows, it could've been those damn hormones!

"I'm going to get that filthy motherfucker if it's the last thing I do. And believe me, Professor, I'll have a few choice words for *you* when I get back to the 21st century. Marty may have thought I was trouble to him in the past or future or whenever it is or was, but when I get back, I'm out for blood!"

"Okay, sounds cool. Well, now that everyone is awake and alert, let's get out of the chamber house. I'll take you to your temporary quarters, where you can change into the clothes we've purchased for you. Tomorrow we'll go shopping to purchase everything you'll need. After that, you'll be able to get settled in the dorms with full access to Ali and Morgan's room. I'll go over with René the tools available for your use in the next day or two."

Zoe tried to reassure Christina that things would be okay, and René said he's committed to their safety and safe return. All Zoe wanted was to find a mirror, curious to see her reflection.

They rode the same elevator that brought them down in the 21st century. The doors opened on the main floor, they walked to a different elevator and rode to the fourth floor. They were led to a suite used for visiting faculty which was beautiful, but different.

Everything was, of course, in the style of the late 60s, early 70s, so it looked like they stepped into the family living room of her parents' house. The colors were burnt umber and a funny color blue, with a boxy-shaped couch with accompanying rounded chairs that had buttons in rows. The coffee tables were of dark mahogany, and it felt strange walking into this room of the past. The bedrooms had square and functional furnishings. Everything was beautiful, but different.

O'Connell showed them their rooms and clothing picked out for them. Christina put Theodore Edward on her bed and picked up the flowing skirt and peasant top lying across the bed. There was a wide-brimmed floppy hat, a couple of scarves, along with some underwear, pajamas, and a pair of sandals. Like Zoe, she was anxious to find a mirror. She walked into the bathroom and as soon as she saw her reflection, her heart stopped. She walked up to it, dumbfounded. She was beautiful and so young!

She closed the door, opened the robe, and inspected her naked body. There wasn't an ounce of fat on her! Her breasts were small and perky, and everything was tight, soft, and youthful. She thought, Is this what I looked like? Why didn't I know it back then? Her hair was long and so beautifully shiny. At eighteen, her hair was almost down to her waist, but because of her natural curls, it never looked that long. She thought how youth was wasted on the young.

She yelled out to Zoe, "Zee, have you seen yourself yet?" Zoe came running into Christina's bathroom.

"Tee! We're beautiful! Look at us." They stood side by side in the mirror and started to giggle. They grabbed hands and started jumping around together, acting silly, marveling at how they looked, remarking about every nuance of their new (or was it old?) selves. O'Connell yelled to them that it's time to get dressed, as there was much to be done.

Zoe giggled and skipped back to her room. Christina stared at herself in the mirror. The reflection was a welcome shock. She pulled herself away and walked over to where the clothes were and dressed. Everyone's clothes fit perfectly.

O'Connell left to get food and snacks, saying he'd be back in about an hour. They were finally alone with no one watching or listening. They went out on the balcony, taking in the beauty of the campus.

Looking over the grounds, Christina's attention went directly to the clock tower as it began to chime the hour of eleven. She closed her eyes, listening to the chimes which she found enchanting. Everyone knew she had a thing about chimes, finding them soothing and reassuring, ticking off the hours. One church in Cheetaqua chimes a song at noon and again at five to alert those of lunchtime or quitting time. It's a slice of small-town Americana. She'll have to find out more about this treasure in her midst.

They sat quietly listening to the chimes, taking in the scenery of their current present. Christina asked René if it was safe to bring Zoe up to speed on the events since their initial meeting. Zoe looked at them quizzically.

"What are you talking about?" she asked.

Christina started to tell Zoe everything that happened from the time she walked in her door and noticed the photos out of place. She told her about John's secret room, and it wasn't the FBI bugging her house, watching her every move. She and René concluded it's the CIA. Zoe didn't believe it until René told her of their conversations with their private phones and the messages left for Christina from John in his final letter and the truth about her key.

"Oh, I see. You two have been having secret conversations on private phones. How terribly sweet!" Zoe uttered with the venom of a cobra. Christina stared at her with her mouth open.

"Is that all you can say after everything you heard? That René and I were speaking to each other and you weren't included?" That was so Zoe. It always has to be about her.

"My dear Madame Zoe, you're in the CIA. You know how they operate. Didn't it occur to you that you were being monitored?" René asked.

"No, it didn't," answering in an unpleasant tone, "and if I was being monitored and spied on, I would've appreciated it if you had contacted me with a private phone and told me so."

"Well," Christina said, the level of her voice rising, "maybe if you answered your fucking phone instead of letting it go to voicemail, I would've been able to tell you."

Christina knew Zoe's attitude was because of her obsession with René, reverting to insecure Zoe. Zoe was probably thinking René was interested in her friend and she's making a play for him. That sent Christina over the edge and the war of words began. Both were screaming at the other with René in the middle. Suddenly René stood between them, held his hands up and yelled, "*Arrêtez!*"

Christina wasn't sure what that meant, but Zoe did, and they started exchanging words back and forth in French. Zoe was shouting, and Christina could tell by his tone that he was trying to be soothing. She heard Zoe mention her name, and that's when Christina joined in.

"English! Stop this French shit and speak English if you're going to talk about me." That caused the argument to escalate until René had had enough.

"You're both acting like immature little children, and I'm not here to babysit!" He went to his room and slammed the door.

They were both shocked by his actions and it brought them out of their anger. They looked at each other, not saying anything. Finally, Christina broke the ice with one of their teenage sayings.

"Uh oh! We're in big trouble now!" Zoe burst out laughing, and they hugged.

"Oh, Tee, I'm sorry."

"Me too, Zee. I was panicking when this happened, and didn't know what to do, and couldn't think straight. I couldn't trust anyone or any of the phones. I wasn't sure I could even trust him. I used my library email to contact René and see if he had any advice. He told me to get a disposable cell phone. He listened to my plight, and we talked over my options."

"What made you think of René?"

"Who else could I confide in? He gave me a note while we were at CIA Headquarters that convinced me to agree to the mission and say nothing about it. I destroyed it as he asked by flushing it down the toilet. Marty, we believe, is the reason his family and John are dead, sacrificed for this mission. We need to make a plan to get that fuckface when we go back. We couldn't tell you anything because René was sure all our communications were being monitored by the evil one. Even the CIA apartment we were staying in had ears everywhere, not to mention Charlie being up all of our asses. I couldn't let Marty find out I'm on to his schemes."

Christina looked into her friend's eyes, that young, beautiful face to whom she told all her secrets from the time they were children. She didn't want Zoe to think for one second, she would ever betray their friendship. "I'm not interested in René or any other man, for that matter. But he's freaking gorgeous."

"Oh my God, Tee, he really is!"

"We're going to be roomies for the next few months, so we'll have lots of time for me to tell you everything. I really don't want to start off with an argument over a guy! We never did that ever, so why start now?"

Zoe agreed, and they put this disagreement behind them, as they had done with all their little tiffs over the last 45 years. They hugged and reverted back to their teens and "pinky swore" they'd never argue over a guy. They left the balcony and went back into the suite. Christina felt hungry and went to check out what there was to munch on in the kitchen. Zoe knocked on René's door, to which he replied, "*Va t'en.*"

She replied, "*Ouvrir la porte s'il te plait.*"

Christina yelled from the kitchen, "Come on, guys! English, *s'il vous plait!*"

She found some pretzels, soda and some cheese and gathered it all together and went to where Zoe was standing outside René's closed door. Zoe knocked again and Christina said, "René, please open the door. We can't be like this. Besides, I come bearing gifts of food and drink. Please, can we start over?"

He opened the door, and once again, Christina was struck by how gorgeous he was. He stood in the doorway, with one arm above his head, leaning against the door jamb with the other on his hip. She wondered if she was currently drooling.

"Before we go any further, we need to have some ground rules," he said very seriously. "I don't care what you two do when you're in your dorm room without me. You can beat each other senselessly and exchange heated words all night if you desire. I won't tolerate your bickering in my presence. I'm not here to babysit adolescent girls. I was under the impression I was working with intellectual and mature women. We've serious matters to attend to and highly sensitive covert intelligence to procure. We cannot be diverted from the seriousness of what we've been engaged to do, no? Do we agree?" They both nodded. Christina thought about doing another pinky swear but didn't think it was good timing.

"I, too, have a proposal," Christina said. "No speaking French unless the two of you are alone. I don't care what the two of you do when you're in a dorm room without me, but when I'm around, I ask that English be the language of choice. Agreed?"

They agreed, and René motioned for them to come into his room, where there were several items on the bed. "I was looking over my instruments, making sure they made the trip intact. Come see what I've brought."

They sat on the bed, and he explained each item and how it could be used to their advantage. The pen and pencil sets, in addition to being writing utensils, were also audio recording devices, able to record up to 250 hours each. He had two of each, all with the same capability.

The lighter could be used as a weapon, although not lethal, it could certainly do damage. The St. Remigius medal was a camera with the capability to take up to 500 images. Some of René's equipment would need the technology of the 21st century to obtain its secrets so it won't be known what was captured until their return. The recordings of the pens and pencils could be listened to immediately.

"Christina, once the prince is here, I'll give you one of the pens for you to record your conversations with him. It's vital I know what's going on with him, and it's for your protection. Agreed?"

She nodded. "You're the boss."

"Good!" he replied.

Zoe asked, "What do you think you're going to need the lighter gun for?"

"It's insurance. I won't be put in a position where I've nothing for protection. Not just for you young ladies, but also for myself. We don't know what'll happen in the next few months, and I'll be ready for the worst."

They heard some shuffling by the door, and René quickly put his things back into the pouch and said, "Mention none of these items to O'Connell or anyone else. No one knows I've brought anything to be used in a clandestine manner, and it must stay that way. They need to believe they're what they look like and nothing more. It's important."

O'Connell entered the apartment with some Chinese food from a restaurant in Chinatown, which was across the Bay.

Christina put away the snacks, and they sat down to eat. The food was delicious, authentic Chinese cuisine, and they were all hungry. The conversation during their meal centered on the plan for tomorrow. O'Connell will accompany them to shop for clothes and essentials. When they return, they'll be going directly to the dorms instead of the apartment they're currently in.

"We've supplied the linens and towels, and because a kitchen is in your suite, you won't need dorm refrigerators. Your Common

Room will have a television, and each of the rooms has an AM/FM clock radio. We'll supply the books for your classes and any school supplies you'll need. The only things you'll need to purchase are clothing and personal items. Remember, Zoe- you're now Athena Christos. Christina, your name is Terry Brendes, and René, you're Jean-René Soulliere."

After eating, they discussed more about the college, their courses of study, and the time they'll be going shopping. As they were talking, Christina felt an uncomfortable feeling in her lower abdomen. She excused herself and went into the bathroom. "No! I've only been 18 for a few hours." She groaned and thought what a cruel joke this was, only she wasn't laughing because she didn't think it was at all funny.

She walked out of the bathroom. "Professor, I hate to ask this, but where can a girl get a box of tampons?" Zoe looked at her with her mouth open and burst into peals of laughter. "Zee, can you believe this? It's not funny!" O'Connell turned various shades of red, got up, and said he'd be right back.

# CHAPTER 17

To the casual observer, one couldn't discern the turmoil swirling in the head of Glenn O'Connell upon leaving the newly arrived time travelers to get food. He was relieved to get out of there. Outwardly he remained calm and composed but inwardly he was a mess. He needed to get to the chamber and send a scathing message to his future self.

The first rule of time travel was that there must be no ties, especially no children, for those using his chamber. The consequences are insurmountable if something goes wrong in the past. Although he's currently in his 20s, he's worked on the time chamber most of his short life and didn't want his work obliterated by his future incarnation.

Glenn O'Connell was a genius with a photographic memory. In the 21$^{st}$ century, he'd probably be diagnosed as a savant in the fields of Science and Mathematics. His parents, who were of normal intellect, had no idea how to deal with such a brilliant child. They were, after all, a salesman and a housewife.

Glenn was a cold, unfeeling child who desired no interaction with other children, having no patience for their lack of understanding, interested only in mundane childish games. He had no interest in participating in sports, preferring his head tucked in a book.

*Popular Mechanics* was one of his favorite magazines, pouring over every monthly issue. After viewing the diagrams for projects, he had every step in the procedure of construction memorized. He could take everyday objects and turn them into something completely different. He was continuously constructing something using mathematics, science, and physics to accomplish success, always thirsting for a new project or challenge.

He eagerly left home to attend a boarding school for brilliantly gifted children. He reveled in the mental stimulation and excelled in math and science as expected. He felt at home surrounded by others who, somewhat, but not quite, shared his mental abilities.

At this school he found the book *The Time Machine* by H.G. Wells. After reading it, time travel became an obsession. His mathematical and scientific mind could fathom no reason why it wasn't possible. He researched physical matter and anti-matter, studying the works and hypothesis of Nikola Tesla. Using electromagnetic power and Tesla's theories, he devised the beginnings of his own time machine.

His teachers, amazed by his intellect and inventiveness, sent letters to Harvard University about this remarkable boy, and he became the youngest person to attend that storied academy. It wasn't long before the US government became interested in the boy with PhDs in Physics, Mathematics, Electrical Engineering, Chemistry, Kinetics, Applied Sciences, and Human Biology.

At thirteen, he was approached by the US government and commissioned to put his theories to the test, creating a usable time machine. His country required his expertise for the various spy agencies as a means of procuring information. After much thought and advisement from his learned Harvard professors, Glenn agreed on the stipulation that if triumphant in achieving time travel, it must be used with the utmost respect and never used to change history. For example, one couldn't go back in time and kill Hitler, as it would change too much of the present.

Glenn, aided by Harvard lawyers, drew an elaborate contract with the government as to how his machine would be used and set the criteria before it was built. He had no doubt it'd be realized and wanted to maintain complete control of his technology. He'd be the master of his invention or there'd be no invention.

He had an unlimited budget and although quite frugal, certain items had to be of the utmost quality, confident of accomplishing his lofty goals. By the age of sixteen, he'd transported five mice into the past through his time chamber and brought them back to the present with no physical damage. He'd lost many mice in the process of finding the right equations and controls, but knew it was only a matter of time.

There were controlled experiments using convicts currently awaiting their punishment on death row. At first, there were some fatalities, but Glenn reasoned they were to die anyway, so at least they gave their lives in a more noble way, giving them to science and their country. It wasn't long before the bugs were worked out, and his top-secret weapon for the US spy agency became a reality.

One major discovery using prisoners was that if a death occurred during a time travel adventure, the death could occur for each incarnation, both happening in the year the death occurred. One incarcerated prisoner died in the past, and it was discovered that his "present self" also died in the same year and time he traveled to. This only occurred in one death during the initial trials, but it was enough for O'Connell to insist there be no spouse or children of those who time travel in his machine. This was why he was so troubled by Christina having children. Another discovery was a certain amount of time must pass before the human body and its organs can withstand the return trip back to the present. That's why Christina couldn't return to the 21st century immediately as she'd requested. She'd have been nothing but a pile of flesh, bones, and blood.

He should've been nominated for the Nobel Prize for this amazing contraption, but it had to be kept top secret, and he saw no reason for the acclaim. It was enough that he succeeded in such an astounding capacity. Someday the world would know of his greatness, and that could wait.

The government decided on UC Berkeley as the home of this amazing invention. Dr. Glenn O'Connell was appointed Head of the Science & Technology Department, becoming the youngest in the history of any college in the world. Many professors were miffed when this teenager became the head of their department, but upon meeting him, all were astounded by his knowledge and expertise in the many fields of science. Intellectually, he was a genius; socially, he was totally inept.

As he made his way to the elevator to the time chamber, he thought of the women who had come from the 21st century, disturbed in more ways than one. He wished neither had come and believed they'd bring nothing but trouble. If he could've sent them back immediately, he would have.

The first and obviously troublesome problem was the woman with children. It placed his life's work in jeopardy and could have devastating effects on time and space. They were the first women to come through, and it made him uncomfortable. The mother would have to be watched and protected, and that angered him. He was an intellect, not a fucking babysitter! For the next four months, they had to make sure nothing happened to her.

The other woman posed a different problem to him. She was the first to be awakened, and her robe had fallen open, exposing full frontal nudity. He'd never seen an unclothed woman in the flesh and was shocked by his reaction. He knew about biology and sex but never found an interest in it. Science was his love and his life, never desiring the company of a woman. Her sleeping face and nakedness stirred him, and he couldn't look away.

He gently closed her robe and began the process of awakening her. While standing over her, she opened her eyes and smiled at him, giving him a foreign feeling in his stomach. She took his hand to be helped out of the chamber, and his knees weakened. He made himself snap out of it and chose not to look directly at her. The two of them set out to awaken the man. After he was alert, the three of them set out to rouse the second woman, and when she wouldn't regain consciousness, he felt panic setting in.

For the first time in his life, he felt two very foreign emotions; fear and attraction and didn't like either. The college president and O'Connell were the only people who knew the true circumstances and method of travel for these three students. He was unfortunately tasked with taking them shopping and wished there was a female professor he could've asked, but no one else can know their place of origin. He'd rather stand in front of a train with spikes in both eyes.

He needs to speak with the French agent privately to relay the information they weren't given regarding the perils of time travel and the utmost importance of keeping the women safe. He felt the man could remain composed with these revelations and didn't want to deal with hysterical females. That one woman has quite a temper.

He got to his office, which led to the travel chambers. He wrote a long critique on the dangers on his end and voiced his frustration with his older self for being foolhardy and careless, breaking the cardinal rule of time travel. After putting it into the chamber and sending it off, he opened his safe, pulled out a baggie containing a large Thai stick and some rolling papers, and proceeded to roll a fat joint. He needed to calm down and think. Nothing helped him more than a good marijuana buzz.

After his "attitude adjustment," he felt better. He called his favorite Chinese restaurant in Chinatown and placed a take-out order.

Before he left, he checked, but there was no answer from the 21st Century. Normally, this would've upset him, but pot always calmed him, so he shrugged it off. He left the chambers and set off for San Francisco.

The next day Glenn accompanied the trio on the shopping expedition. His anxiety heightened around Zoe. He found her overt flirtations unnerving. Zoe loved clothes shopping and was overly playful with their uptight chaperone. She linked arms with him whenever they left a store. She knew the effect she had on him as his discomfort was obvious. Christina told René she'd address it with Zoe when he and O'Connell were going over the available equipment.

The women were getting settled, putting everything away. Christina's things were in order, which was odd because she's less organized and sloppier than Zoe, who had her purchases all over the room, matching things up and reliving the whole shopping experience. Zoe was ecstatic and Christina was exhausted from the whole ordeal. Shopping isn't something she enjoyed, another big difference between the two friends.

Christina sat on her bed, waiting for the right moment to address Zoe on her behavior towards O'Connell. She played with Theodore Edward, thinking how much she'd love a cigarette, but kept telling herself she wasn't going to start up again. Her heightened craving was right at the surface, and everyone she saw today had a cigarette in their mouth.

Another thing coming back to haunt her was her hair. Upon arrival, her hair looked great, soft, straight, and smooth. She had to work ridiculously hard to keep the curls under control including ironing it on occasion and setting it with lemonade and soup cans. She had to be innovative back then because there weren't many of the products of the twenty-first century to keep those curls in check.

It wasn't a losing battle, it was a losing war. Now, with the ocean breeze flowing through her unruly locks, she said goodbye to the straight hair for the duration of her time at Berkeley. As the day wore on, it kept getting curlier. It wouldn't be long before her waist-long hair became the biggest afro this side of the Rockies. Everything today made her feel cranky, not to mention her monthly visitor.

At one of the stores, she saw a cute blue and gold UC Berkeley Golden Bear baseball cap, which made her remember her trick to control the curls. She bought it, flipped her head upside down, and maneuvered her hair to tuck it into it. She had a denim cap in her original go-round at this age and forgot how much she depended on it. If her hair even smelled moisture, it became a mass of curls. The cap was the school mascot, so along with her UC Berkeley sweatshirt, she felt school spirit shining through. She bought only things she knew she would need: underwear, jeans, a jacket, a coat, and a sweater, two dresses, a couple of pairs of pants and shorts with tops to match, shoes, a short skirt, and a long one. Let's not forget those damn tampons. The joys of womanhood.

Her one extravagance was scarves. They were hanging outside a boutique, blowing in the wind, and she bought a lot of them in all sorts of colors and materials. She'll use them to accentuate her outfits. When she was younger, she didn't have the self-confidence to wear them. But being a middle-aged teenager, she didn't care what anyone thought, so she couldn't resist. Finding the scarves boutique gave her a small attitude adjustment and took her mind off the cigarette she was craving.

Zoe dragged them to every store, and Christina was exhausted. Zoe *had* to try on something hanging in every window. She was a clothes hound, and went hog-wild buying clothes and accessories, spending all her personal allowance, and borrowing from Christina to get everything she wanted, which was more than the dorm closet and dressers could hold.

Her overt flirtations with O'Connell made the shopping trip uncomfortable. The poor man looked terrified. Zoe was euphoric while shopping and overly playful with their uptight chaperone. Christina decided now was a good time to address this with Zoe.

"You know, Zee, you're playing with fire, and you probably went a little too far today."

"How so? Isn't this blouse adorable? I need more hangers. You mean with Glenn-boy? Oh, Tee, I'm only goofing with him." She looked at Christina through the mirror while admiring one of her new outfits. "You're blowing things way out of proportion and making a big deal of nothing. Okay, be honest, do my legs look big in these pants?"

"A big deal out of nothing?! Really? How about 'Oh, Professor, does my ass look fat in this?' sticking your ass almost right up into his face, or 'Do you think I need to wear a bra with this shirt' or 'Would you mind zipping this up for me?' Oh yeah, and here's the best of all, 'Is this skirt too short? Can you see my underwear when I bend over?' Zee, what the hell were you thinking? I know you realize he's attracted to you, and flirting like this with him isn't funny. You can't treat him like one of your playthings. What if he doesn't know you're playing with him? He might think you're sending a message that you're attracted to him. Don't mess with something as sensitive as sexuality and attraction. It's too dangerous, not to mention it's cruel."

"Oh, Tee, I was having some fun. Did you forget we're teenagers again? We don't have to act maturely. Don't start acting like a parent."

"We're not teenagers. We may look it, but we aren't. Try to remember that. You could make a small effort to act closer to your true age?" She was irritated with Zoe acting so irresponsibly. She should've known Zoe would revel in their new physical state. She loved being a teenager, and this trip back in time was like the Blue Fairy coming along to grant her fondest wish.

"Tee, you don't get it, do you?"

"Get what? That you've no intention of acting your age?"

"No! Tee, you're such an old lady! We have a second chance to be eighteen again! All the things we wanted to do when we were younger but were too afraid, we can do now with no consequences!"

"How can you think there'll be no consequences? We're accountable for our actions and even more so the second time around because we're supposed to know better."

"Get out of your middle-aged mindset and think about it for a minute. This is our chance to live it up during the best times in our lives. Make love, not war, and all that! It will be groovy, man! I don't know about you, but I've every intention of taking advantage of this incredible chance to be a teenager again. We can be kids again! We can smoke pot, hash, take LSD, go to fabulous rock concerts, and see all the great bands we couldn't when we were this age. We can have sex, and I'm guessing it'll be great because now we know what we're doing. There's going to be some hot guys, starting with René and I'd love to fuck them all! It's too irresistible with the chance to do all those crazy things our Catholic-guilt upbringing and our fearful little girl goody-two-shoes attitudes wouldn't let us do when we were teenagers!"

"Can you hear yourself? We're here for a few months and have a lot to accomplish! What're you thinking? I think your brain got scrambled in the travel chamber. You need to snap out of it! You're not in some fairyland where you're the newly appointed queen. You're here for a reason, not to relive being a teenager. With you being a CIA agent, you should know this trip isn't meant to be all fun and games. Have you forgotten we're here for a reason and an important one?"

She wasn't paying any attention, kept holding up her new clothes, and looking at herself in the mirror. "You've got to stop acting like my mother, Tee. It's unattractive and annoying. You can be an old lady if you like, but I'm going to have fun and enjoy being young again. I really don't give a shit what you think."

"Zee, sometimes I want to punch your face in. I should've ignored that stupid telegram. I've risked everything, and all you want to do is smoke pot, drop acid, have sex with anything that moves, and play games with guys. What the fuck, Zee? Are you going to be too busy having fun or too spaced out on your drug choice to pay attention to what we're here to do?"

"Lighten up, Tee. It's all in good fun. We have to take full advantage of this opportunity while we can. Ok, tell me, do I look better in the navy-blue midriff shirt or the light blue one? I like the navy because it makes my eyes stand out more and shows my tight abs. I love having a hot body and not having to live in the gym to get it."

Christina groaned, forgetting how Zoe could sometimes make her crazy. "Don't come crying to me when the professor makes a move because I'll tell you to lighten up and that you're blowing things out of proportion. Zee, sometimes you're a real asshole!"

"I know! And you love it, Tee, admit it!"

"I must. I've stuck around you all these years." Zoe kept humming and trying on clothes. Christina ignored her for the time being and turned her attention to Theodore Edward, deciding to spruce him up. Anything to take her mind off the cigarette calling her name. She took out the scissors, needle, thread, and buttons she purchased to make him look dapper. He was in need of some surgical procedures, so it was a welcome distraction.

There was a knock on their door, which made them both jump. Zoe opened the door and it was René. His face looked strained.

Christina asked, "How was the meeting with the professor? Did he give you the equipment?" He shrugged his shoulders. It was obvious, something wasn't right. "What's the matter? You're worried. Are we in danger?" Selfishly, she was thinking of her children.

"We're not in danger, at least for now. Even if we wanted to return to our present, we couldn't. O'Connell was quite candid with me today and I should relay to you both some of what I was told."

Christina felt dread seeping through her. She wanted to hear what he had to say but also wanted to run away and hide so she wouldn't have to hear anything at all, wishing she was sleeping and could wake up from this nightmare that was now her life.

"He's already explained that our vital organs can't sustain the changes again so quickly so we must stay here until the predetermined time to depart this century."

"Okay, understood. What else? From the look on your face, I can tell there's more."

"We were deceived by Martin as to the equipment available to us. What they're offering us is ineffective and useless. Martin said we'd have video devices, and we don't. The surveillance materials I brought are much more sophisticated than anything we're being offered. It'll be very difficult to procure any information on a clandestine level with the mechanisms at our disposal."

"What about your pen and pencils?" Zoe asked. "Won't they be able to capture the conversations between the prince and Morgan?"

"They only work when activated, and I can't leave them in their room. They need to stay in our possession. It'd be disastrous if it's discovered that it's a listening device, especially when using it on a person with diplomatic immunity. Not only would the consequences be disastrous if we're caught, but our technology would become available to our subject from Zatari at a time when it doesn't exist."

"Wouldn't the CIA and our government back us if we're caught?" Christina asked without really wanting an answer.

"The CIA in 1971 knows nothing of us and our mission. We are, as you say, up the creek with no paddles. Martin assured me we'd have full cooperation from the CIA and video equipment. Neither is true. Without the proper surveillance materials, it'll be extremely hard to prove anything we've been sent here to find and bring back proof. We've no way of finding out what they talk about, what sensitive information is exchanged, or what they do in their room. I should've known better than to put any sort of faith in that bastard."

"So, are you saying that basically, we're on our own?"

"Basically, yes, Christina. I'll try to devise some sort of plan, but I need to figure out exactly what we can do. I apologize to you both for encouraging you to take this assignment."

"What if we could get our hands on some kind of video equipment?"

"Christina, there's nothing available. I've spent a good deal of today with the good professor trying to find something that would work to our advantage and have come up with nothing. The only alternative is for me to see if I can create something with the materials I've brought with me, although even that feels futile."

"Cheer up, René, and don't worry about that now. I know! I think right now we could all use some cheering up, and I know exactly how to do that." She picked up her teddy bear and started to hum his theme song, "*Entry of the Gladiators.*"

Zoe started to flip out. "Tee, I can't believe you'd think it's an appropriate time for this bullshit with your fucking bear! I'm sure René isn't in the mood for this, and you know how I hate it when you start doing your circus act. Stop it right now or I'm going to rip him to shreds."

Ignoring her, Christina continued. "Ladies and gentlemen, right before your very eyes, Theodore Edward will do a trick never before seen, in this century or the next." Zoe tried to grab him out of her hands, but Christina grabbed her scissors and menacingly pointed them at her. "You keep your filthy, shitty-ass hands off my bear or I'll rip *you* to shreds. Look, I had to go to every store that exists in the city of Berkeley today so you could satisfy your clothes addiction. Theodore Edward and I have been working on this new trick for almost a month, and I want to see if it works. The least you could do is give me the two minutes it'll take to see if we can pull it off. Geez!"

Neither of them said a word, so she continued. "We'll need the assistance of a member of the audience. Theodore originally wanted to ask the lovely young lady if she'd help, but since she threatened him, we've chosen the handsome young Frenchman to help us instead. Monsieur, can you come and stand beside me? I promise there's no danger to you at all."

"Christina, honestly, I'm not in the mood for this right now. This isn't the time for frivolity when there's much to be done before the arrival of our subjects. We don't have time to waste."

"Monsieur, I ask your indulgence for only a moment or two. You've never witnessed one of his performances, and Theodore is anxious to show you how talented he is. Please?" She made the bear do a little dance in his direction.

René got up and stood next to her. He sighed and said, "Very well, Christina, if it'll please you." It's obvious from the look on his face that this wasn't something he wanted to do.

"Watch very carefully, ladies and gentlemen." With the scissors still in her hand, she had Theodore do a few flips to throw them off track. Then, as quickly as she could, she turned the scissors on her lovable furry circus performer and started to cut the seam down his back, all the while singing his theme song. They both were looking on in disbelief. Her teddy bear truly is the Dashingest Daredevil In Entertainment Bear!

"Lady and gentleman, for our main trick of the evening, Theodore Edward will prove beyond a shadow of a doubt that he's not only the best performing bear in the world, but he has hidden talents in the world of espionage." She put her hand into the open seam and, one by one, snipped off his three buttons on his jacket and his two button eyes.

"I will now ask my handsome French assistant to hold out his hand, please."

She put the snipped buttons into René's hand. "You see, ordinary, everyday buttons. Now with a few turns of our hero bear and..." She pulled out the devices Martin Cater had planted in her home. "Voila, Mademoiselle et Monsieur. Count them aloud as I drop them into the hand of my handsome French assistant. One, two, three, four, and five! Five very sophisticated video recording devices, courtesy of our brave hero Theodore Edward, the all-encompassing evil Martin Cater, the twenty-first-century CIA technologists, and the very cunning Christina Pucci."

René's eyes looked like they were about to pop out of his head. "Christina, are you telling me these are the devices Martin placed in your home? I thought your son-in-law brought them to the authorities."

"I lied, and I never had an opportunity to mention anything about them before now because I never felt safe speaking freely with no one listening. I know how to turn them on and activate them."

René picked Christina up, twirled her around a few times, and then gave her a big kiss. He put her down and said, "Christina, you're a marvel! At every turn, you amaze me with your cunning and incredible ideas. I find it hard to believe you haven't been trained as an agent. I'm going to love working with you on this assignment. You're a lifesaver and have single-handedly saved this mission. Come with me to my room, and you can show me how they work. Zoe, you can join us after you've put all your things away, and then we can go somewhere to celebrate with dinner and plot our next plan of action. *C'est une très bonne nouvelle!*"

"Yeah," Christina said as she turned to Zoe. "Whatever that means," and the two of them were off to his room to check out the equipment.

René stuck his head back in to say to Zoe, "Please don't take too long, Madame Zoe, *parce que j'ai tres faim.*

# CHAPTER 18

Prince Ali was summoned to his father's office and walked nervously to his side of the palace. His heart was pounding so loudly he could hear it in his ears, which along with the sound of footsteps, blocked out the instructions he was being given on route to the meeting. One-on-one encounters with his father made him feel inadequate and insignificant, and he's quite thankful there had only been a few of them. He wondered if he'd ever be able to live up to the expectations put upon him. He took his position in life very seriously but wasn't sure how to accomplish anything that would live up to his father's expectations.

The King, his father, was the youngest of his family and had no living brothers. Ali was born eighteen years ago, the second child of King Machmud's third wife. Ali was the ruler's seventh son, so he knew that unless there was a family massacre, he'd never be king, which suited him fine. He wasn't interested in the politics of running a country, especially at this time when oil and the possession of it seemed to be the real sovereign of countries and men.

Having grown up in the shadow of his older brothers, he wasn't outgoing or ambitious. He didn't excel at anything deemed important by Arab society, mostly because he was surpassed in every endeavor by one or more of his brothers. He found his only solace was in books. Once he learned to read and speak English, he discovered there were many books from the western part of the world at his disposal in the royal library. He immersed himself in the classics from the great authors of the world. Because of his love of the written word and being a bookish sort of boy, he was shunned by his brothers, who were more interested in physical activities.

To make matters worse and much to his father's chagrin, Ali was captivated by works of art and taught himself the nuances of sketching, painting, and sculpting by studying the works of some of the great artists. He perfected the knack of shadowing to give his drawings dimension and life. These talents were frowned upon as not being of value or serious enough for a male member of the royal family and a frivolous waste of time. His father felt he should be spending more time doing constructive activities. Nothing he did pleased his father, which made him feel isolated and worthless.

While alone, which was often, he'd pull out his sketch pad and get lost in his world. He'd done some impressive landscapes, still life drawings, and portraits of his mother and older sister Taja, two women with whom he had a special relationship full of love and respect. Drawing people was frowned upon by his religion, so the portraits were kept hidden from everyone but them. He was one in a sea of children and one with no outstanding attributes.

As he walked the long corridor to his father's quarters, he knew this meeting was a briefing of what was expected of him in the coming months. Last year, he was summoned to his father and his advisors and told to perfect his English within a year and given a duty to fulfill. Outwardly, he was going to an American college. Secretly, he was to exchange papers, information, and contracts through the son of a powerful senator in American politics who was currently the head of the US Energy Commission. He'll be sharing quarters with the son of this senator, and through him, illegal secret documents will be exchanged.

As they reached the door to the King's quarters, the aide asked Ali if he understood. He was too ashamed to tell the man he hadn't heard a word because the pounding of his heart and thoughts of terror drowned out all outside noise. He couldn't bring himself to admit his fear, so he nodded. The aide opened the door and bowed for Ali to enter.

Ali entered the room, and his father was sitting at his desk. The young man bowed deeply to his father and gave the customary salutation of greeting to him in their native tongue. He looked up at his son and immediately rose from his seat, walked over to the aide, and thrashed him. "Farooh, did I not tell you to inform the prince that from now on we will converse in English?" The man kept his head bowed and answered his sovereign, gazing angrily at the young man. Ali felt ashamed and wanted to tell his father he didn't hear the instructions given to him because of his fright but didn't dare to do so.

"Leave us!" the King ordered. All those in the room bowed and left except Ali. When they were alone, he walked up to his son and gave him the same slap across the face. "Do you not listen to instructions?"

"A thousand pardons, sire. I regret I didn't hear what Farooh was saying on the walk to your quarters. I'm the one at fault, and I beg forgiveness." His father slapped him again, this time harder.

"You're the son of a king! Princes don't beg! And more importantly, they *never* take the blame for an underling. They serve you! You're royalty! Act like royalty!"

He turned and walked back to his desk. "You disgust me! You're as soft as a woman! Be a man! Act like a man! I wonder if you'll be able to handle what's expected of you. This is of great importance to our country, our way of life, and our people. You must always be alert and listen with both your ears and your eyes! Americans are filthy thieves and trying to steal the oil out from under us! I need Senator Morgan to assure that our country and oil don't get stolen by these infidels."

"I won't fail you, my father. I'll do whatever you ask of me. I only ask for the chance to serve my king, my country, and its people." Ali felt that no matter what he said or did, he'd never be able to please his father.

"In three days, you leave for America. You will first stay with Honorable Khalid, who'll be your guardian while in America. When papers or information need to be exchanged, you'll give them to him. Have you read all the materials given to you on American customs and the Morgan family?"

"Yes, Father."

"Good. America is going through many changes, both politically and in the thinking of its population. Much unrest is occurring, so you must be careful not to get involved in any of the instability of their current events, especially at the school you'll be attending. A great deal of student misadventure has gone on there, and I'd rather you were attending a more stable university, but it seems Harold Morgan cannot get into the more prestigious universities because of his troublesome ways and failing grades.

"Your roommate, who as you should know from the reports you were to have read, is commonly known as 'Butch.' Our intelligence reports he is well known as a rogue, drug dealer, and all-encompassing troublemaker. Senator Morgan was able to buy his son's way into UC Berkeley along with excellent grades for the first semester, so he'll be able to transfer to a more prestigious school at its end."

Ali listened carefully to his father, but knew it from reading the reports, and from what he's read, he already formed his opinion of

Butch Morgan. He wasn't looking forward to living in the same room with such a disrespectful and abhorrent young man. He already disliked him and would've preferred that this assignment wouldn't necessitate that they share a room. He wanted to ask why it was essential for him to share a room with this repugnant young man, but two thrashings from his father were enough for one day. He didn't wish to anger him further with questions not relatable to the task at hand. The one thing he looked forward to was he'd get to see America.

"Khalid Al-Dossari will travel with you and get you settled into the college and be your contact. A college representative will meet with you both upon your arrival. I expect you to act like a member of the royal family and not give any college officials a reason to contact me or Khalid with complaints or reports of unseemly behavior. I also expect you to receive high grades. If you can achieve success at this university, I'll consider allowing you to attend any school of higher learning you wish. That includes the Ivy League institutions in the United States and universities in Europe. Your future rests in your hands, Ali, so take advantage of the circumstances allowing you such opportunities."

"I won't fail you or my country, my father, and I'll do nothing to disappoint or cause you to regret the responsibility you've put upon me. I'll study hard and always remember I'm a prince and conduct myself according to protocol and your wishes."

"Khalid will give you the particulars of what's expected of you and how to contact him once in America. The future of our sovereignty is dependent on your success, and it's of the utmost importance that you be very circumspect and discreet. I only hope Morgan's imbecile of a son will retain the same propriety I'm demanding of you."

He walked over to Ali, grabbed his shoulders, looked into his eyes, and said, "Allah be with you, my son. May He watch over you and guide you. Don't forget to honor Him with your daily prayers. As you know, your mother is greatly worried. I've assured her of your safety, but it's quite tiresome listening to her lament. Goodbye."

Ali replied appropriately. He knew he was being dismissed, and it was time to leave. He felt relief as he walked back down the hallway to the other side of the palace. In a few days, he'll be in a new country where he'll be able to be himself. He anticipated the next few months with excitement but also with great trepidation. What does

America have in store for him? He couldn't have imagined how life-changing it would be.

Butch Morgan cackled as he turned up the radio as Creedence Clearwater Revival's *Fortunate Son* came on. He looked in the rearview mirror of his midnight blue Jaguar and noticed a couple more police cars had joined the chase to stop him as he sped around Lake Pontchartrain heading home on Interstate 10 to Baton Rouge. He wasn't worried there'd be any consequences because he's a Morgan, son of the senior Senator from the great state of Louisiana, who was also its former governor.

His family led this state politically for generations and law enforcement agencies were beholden to them for a shitload of reasons. He wasn't worried they'd be able to catch him because his little blue devil was the fastest vehicle on the road. Butch shifted into overdrive and left them in the dust. They knew whose car it was and who was driving. It's the same old story. The chief of the Baton Rouge police would be waiting at his house on LSU Ave when he got home. His father would be rabid, which meant nothing to Butch. Fuck him!

Butch went to New Orleans for his latest supply of pot, hash, Quaaludes, Black Beauties, speed, and heroin to sell to a new set of customers he's sure to find at Berkeley. He had an undetectable compartment built in his car for transporting his wares. He also picked up a supply of chloral hydrate for his personal use so he could have some nasty fun. He knew circumstances would arise to put it to use. His mind was always working on devious plans, ways to make gains for himself sexually and monetarily, and a good supply of that drug would come in handy. A little bit in a drink, and someone's out for the night with no memory. It's commonly called being "slipped a mickie."

He had spiked a few drinks before and had some wild, unusual sexual fun. He enjoyed himself so much that he made sure he had enough to last the semester at Berkeley. He'll make a small fortune selling the drugs purchased from his supplier. His regular customers were going to have to make do without him. He cackled again. Fuck them. Who needs them?

He should be more careful in California, but he knew his father would get him out of trouble before it made news or the courts. Daddy was eying the White House and getting Butch out of Louisiana was part of the plan to keep him out of the way. He told Butch he wouldn't help him get out of the draft and maybe the best thing for him was to go fight in Vietnam and become a man. They came out with the birthday lottery and his number was 358. Not much chance of being drafted with that number. He cackled again. His daddy's a dumb fuck.

The only good thing about Vietnam was they have some dynamite drugs over there. He'll try to find someone in that hippie Berkeley college to score some Asian shit. He cackled again. He hated his parents, always on his back about something. It was like this for as long as he could remember. Nothing was ever good enough so why bust his ass? Didn't they realize he doesn't give a shit about them or what they think? He didn't care about himself or anyone for that matter. The only people he ever loved, Violet and Odelia, were both gone.

Violet Blue was his sister, who was 4 years older than him, and Odelia was his African American nanny. They were the only people he ever loved and felt loved by. Maybe at one time he felt some affection for his mother, but not since the accident. Now he couldn't stand to be in the same room with that bitch. After the accident, Odelia was the only one who showed him any love and once she was gone, he was a ship out to sea with no one at the helm. He was completely lost, mentally and morally, without the maternal-like love and guidance of Odelia.

Odelia hailed from generations of black slaves working the Morgan family plantation. After the Civil War, Horatio Morgan begrudgingly offered wages to the slaves he formerly owned. Horatio was fairly kind, but he was first and foremost a businessman and knew keeping his slaves was paramount to a successful plantation. They knew their jobs and he treated them better than most. Many of the newly freed stayed on and Odelia descended from those who remained. She was a housemaid, and when Master Bradley married Rachel Dawson, she went to work for them. When their first child, Violet Blue was born in 1949, she was entrusted with the care of the newest Morgan.

Violet Blue, or Vi as the family called her, was full of beauty, vitality, stubbornness, and a fearlessness her father admired, and her mother feared. Her eyes were the color of violet blue with long, lush lashes surrounding them. The dark curls surrounding her face contrasting with her eyes gave promise to a rare beauty when she would become a woman. She was a vivacious child who lit up the room with her presence. Cherished children have a certain confidence that manifests in their personalities, an assurance inherent with the knowledge they are deeply loved. Anyone who met Violet had an immediate affection for her. She had two large dimples and soon found how irresistible they were to everyone. Everyone except Odelia.

Odelia had her hands full when it came to Violet, always trying to escape her watchful eyes. One couldn't turn your back on her for a second because she'd be off like a shot. Vi wasn't trying to be bad; she was determined to do whatever bit of adventure popped into her head.

Odelia told Mr. Morgan that she was worried about Missy Violet, saying she had too much life in her for a four-year-old. Bradley Morgan would laugh, but Odelia didn't think it funny. She never bothered Missy Rachel with it because that would cause more worry, and with a new baby on the way, Odelia was instructed not to trouble her. Rachel was a loving and attentive mother, but with her husband running for Governor of Louisiana, she had a lot of responsibilities, mostly on the social level, and had to oversee all the fundraising and parties along with accompanying her husband on the campaign trail throughout the state.

Rachel was always available for her daughter, spending part of every afternoon with her, doing puzzles, reading stories, or sitting in the big rocking chair, swing, or hammock, talking, dreaming about the future, and napping together. Violet was a vibrant and loving child, and Rachel worried she wouldn't love this new baby with the same fervor and devotion as she felt for Vi.

Before the election, Rachel went into labor and gave birth to a boy, who was named Harold William. Violet didn't like that name, so she called him Butch or Butchie-boy from the start and the name stuck. The birth of the newest member of the Morgan family gave a boost to the candidate's popularity, and Bradley Morgan won the Governor's seat by a landslide. Now Rachel had the duties of First Lady, so Odelia was given the task of taking care of Harold in addition to her duties with Violet.

Truthfully, Rachel was glad to be relieved of feeding and diapering duties. She was suffering from postpartum depression, called the "baby blues" back then, and wanted little to do with her new son, who was a colicky baby and cried constantly. Odelia rocked and cooed him, sang him lullabies, doing her best to soothe him. Miss Rachel had love for one child, and that was her daughter. She barely paid any attention to Harold, but Violet was still the bright light of her life and always made time for her. Vi was the only person to always put a smile on her mother's face, and the joy Rachel received from her daughter was undeniable.

Violet adored Butchie-Boy, and as they grew, he became her accomplice to all sorts of adventures at their vast estate with sprawling grounds and places to explore. Odelia put boundaries in place but knew Violet would do as she pleased. She knew the meaning of the word "no," but she ignored it.

Vi and Butch had built a tree-fort in the woods behind their home with the help of the groundskeeper, and would spend many hours there, playing and pretending, being kids and doing what kids do. Vi's vivid imagination would send them on adventures. Over the years, they were cowboys, pirates, orphans, runaways, Indians, superheroes, and anything else Vi thought up.

One of their favorite spots was the water hole that was on the grounds of their estate and depending on the amount of rainfall each year it varied from ten feet deep in its center to two feet. On hot days they would sneak off as soon as Odelia turned her back and cooled off in the waters in what they called "the forbidden zone." Odelia was aware and kept a watchful eye at a distance.

The year Butch turned eight was the driest and hottest summer on record, with little rain. During Vi's twelfth birthday celebration, her mother announced she's to stop this tomboy playing with Butch and start behaving like a proper Southern lady. Rachel planned for Vi to attend a prestigious girls' school with only six years until her "coming out." She needed to learn the appropriate lessons for girls her age. Vi would politely say she wasn't going, and her mother couldn't force her. Angry words would follow but Vi would worm her way around her mother and head off with Butch for some fun.

Rachel was pregnant again and thought that as soon as the baby is born, she'll put her foot down regarding Vi's training. Bradley was running for Governor again, and she's campaigning throughout the state at his side. Jeremiah James was born four years after Harold, and she was due with her fourth in the middle of October. Every four years, like the election. She was beginning to think Bradley planned it so he'd be able to garner more votes, especially from the women. Rachel hadn't enjoyed her last three pregnancies and didn't care what he was running for in four years, there would be no more children.

With Odelia as the sole caretaker of the Morgan children, and with Vi's penchant for mischief, it made matters difficult. She had to watch over Jeremiah, called J.J. and keep her eye on Vi and Butch. With a new baby coming, she wondered how she could handle four of them, and Missy Violet coming into the age of womanhood. Then there was poor Master Butch. She worried because there was no love coming for that child from anyone except herself and Violet. Rachel tolerated him, and Mr. Bradley was busy running the government.

Butch idolized Vi, and they were inseparable even though they were complete opposites. She's headstrong, he's fearful; she's outgoing, he's meek; she's smart as a whip, and he has trouble learning. He thought she was the smartest and bravest person who ever lived. Vi was afraid of nothing and Butch was afraid of everything.

On this particularly hot summer day, the two of them tried sneaking into the "forbidden zone." Odelia, while giving J.J. his lunch, ordered them to stay away from the water hole. There hadn't been enough rain, and the water was too shallow. If they jumped in, they'd get hurt.

They kept on walking, although Butch turned and waved goodbye to Odelia. Violet saw her chance for a head start and started running. Butch tried to keep up, but she was too fast. She had this one favorite thrill at the water hole where she'd get a running start, swing on a kudzu vine, and splash into the water. Butch thought that was what she was planning to do. He tried to catch up to her, yelling, "Vi, don't swing into the water. Odelia says you're going to get hurt. Don't swing in the water, Vi." She didn't answer, kept on running, like a graceful deer frolicking through the forest, giggling, and yelling that he couldn't catch her.

She reached the water hole before Butch. She ran to her kudzu vine, grabbed on, and swung. Butch came into view, yelling for her to stop. She yelled out "Yahoo" and let go of the vine as she was over the water. Butch couldn't see her but heard a horrible thud. He ran to the edge of their cliff over the water hole, and there was Vi, head and limbs in awkward positions, and the water around her turning red. Butch kept screaming, "Vi! Vi! Answer me!" but she didn't move, didn't blink, didn't respond and the water kept getting redder. He was terrified and didn't know what to do. Vi was the one who always took control of things. He needed help.

He ran back to the house screaming and crying. "Help! Somebody help Vi! She's hurt real bad." He was hard to understand because he was crying so hard. Finally, Moose, the family groundskeeper, understood and ran to the "forbidden zone." Odelia tried to calm Butch down. He buried his head in Odelia's shoulder and kept saying between sobs, "I told her not to jump. I told her what y'all said, Odelia, but she wouldn't stop. She's hurt real bad."

Odelia caught sight of Moose, a big, muscular black man, walking out of the woods carrying what looked like a life-sized rag doll. Moose was crying and all it took was a glimpse of him for Odelia to know she had to get Butch into the house so he wouldn't see his sister like this. She quickly picked him up, grabbed J.J.'s hand, and brought them away from the horrible scene.

The commotion woke Rachel from her nap, and she went outside to see what was happening. One look at Moose carrying her bloodied, limp daughter, her body and mind couldn't take it and she fainted. The household servants tended to Miss Rachel while Moose brought the lifeless body of Violet into the house, putting her on a settee in the children's playroom.

The butler called Governor Morgan at the office and told him to come home immediately, as something horrible had happened to Miss Vi. Another servant got warm water and tried to wash the blood off Vi's face. Everyone was crying and scurrying around, trying to do something. The future of that family changed in one split second. Vi's beautiful eyes, where a moment ago the light of her essence was vibrantly shining in those violet-blue orbs, were now open in a lifeless stare.

The state of Louisiana went into mourning and just like the light was snuffed out of Violet's eyes, Rachel and Butch suffered the same fate, only they were still alive. Neither was ever the same. Rachel blamed Butch and Odelia and treated both with icy coldness.

A month after the accident Odelia approached Rachel regarding Butch. Due to deliver her next child soon, she spent her days sitting in her usual spot, the same rocking chair she shared with her daughter. Only now, instead of stroking Vi's dark curls, she was stroking her cat, staring off into space, not speaking, staring out the window.

Odelia was very worried about Butch, who was carrying the blame for the accident. In almost a whisper, she tried to talk to Rachel. She turned her icy stare to Odelia and didn't say a word. Odelia tried to reach her saying that it's too heavy a load for young Butch to carry and he's too little for this sort of burden. It was weighing him down so deep that when he finally crawls out, he's going to be a different boy, and he needs his mama to tell him it's alright.

Rachel turned her stare away from Odelia, stroked the cat, and looked off into space. Odelia apologized for disturbing her and turned to walk away. As she reached the doorway, Rachel started speaking in a voice with a hushed, menacing monotone, still petting her cat, and staring out the window.

"Do *not* call him Butch. His name is Harold. He should've stopped her, and it's his fault she's dead. But he isn't the only one to blame. I recall the children were under your care and supervision at that time. You're lucky I haven't had you horsewhipped or hung from a tree by now, and your insolence coming to me, telling me what to do with my own child is beyond impertinence. The only reason you're still alive is that my husband seems to have a fondness for you. I find the presence of you and Harold intolerable. It's time for you to pack whatever you have in this house that's yours and leave. I don't ever want to see you again, and you're never to speak to me or any of this family again, especially the boys. You're to leave immediately."

Odelia was in shock. She had nowhere to go, all her family worked for the Morgans. "As you say, Ma'am." Tears streamed down her face, with her mind spinning in a million directions. How could she leave her boys? The Morgan children were her life. What would she do, where could she go? What's going to happen to her poor little man? She went to her quarters and packed the few belongings she had. Rachel had one of the servants accompany Odelia to make sure she didn't steal anything and that she didn't say goodbye to the boys.

That's the last she ever saw of the Morgans or anyone else, for that matter. Odelia's body was found in a small ravine. The death of an elderly black woman in the South back in the early 60s didn't even make a blip on the radar. Her cause of death was never discovered, but Governor Morgan suspected Rachel had a hand in it.

Within the next month, Harold was shipped off to a boarding school for the next ten years. He was allowed home only for the holidays, and summers were spent at a camp. Odelia was right in her assessment of her little man. The weight put upon him was too heavy, and it buried that sweet little boy as sure as death buried Violet. And when he did crawl out, he was changed. He was mean, spiteful, and sadistic with a deep-seated hatred for his parents. He vowed to do whatever he could to embarrass them and make their lives as miserable as they made his. He spent the next ten years doing just that. And he was incredibly good at it.

Butch, which is what he insisted on being called, pulled his Jaguar into the family garage which was accessible from a back entrance to their estate. He checked his compartment and all his purchases from New Orleans were safe and intact. He locked it back up, swung his jacket over his shoulder, locked the car and headed to the house. He only had to stay there for a couple more days before leaving for Berkeley.

He saw the two police cars and cackled. He entered the house and saw four policemen, one being the Chief. His father came into view, walked up to him, and backhanded him across the face. The large ring on Senator Morgan's hand cut across his son's face with a gash, and it started to bleed.

"Geez, Daddy, is that the best y'all could do? Y'all are slipping! Are y'all getting too old or am I getting too big?" and he cackled again.

The Chief pulled him aside, away from his father, twisting his arm behind him.

"Boy, this-a-here bullshit a yours all ends right here, right now, tonight. No one wants to see y'all go to jail, 'cept maybe me and your mama. This reckless driving is going to get y'all or someone else killed. Out of respect for your family, we've overlooked much of what y'all have done in the past. Y'all are getting too old to be behaving like a hooligan, and the next time, I swear to the Lord Sweet Baby Jesus, we're goin' to lock y'all up and confiscate that car of yours."

"OOOOOWEEE! That would sure make Mama feel like she died and went straight up to heaven, right, Daddy?"

The Chief twisted Butch's arm a little tighter saying, "Boy, don't y'all be usin' that tone 'cause at this point, I don't care whose son y'are. And don't y'all go temptin' law enforcement with a repeat of tonight. Y'all had your last joyride in this here state of Louisiana. We can lock y'all up, real hush-like, so nobody would know, and the newspapers wouldn't find out. We got places here in Louisiana, gonna make y'all pray for death to come. Y'all hear me? We clear on this, Boy?" He let go of his arm and pushed Butch away from him.

Butch didn't reply, kept doing his evil cackle. The Chief got his nightstick and whacked the back of Butch's knees which brought him to the ground.

"I'm right glad y'all think this is funny. Gonna be me who is laughin' when I see y'all behind bars or on a chain gang somewhere. Now, once again, I said, are we clear on this, Boy?"

Butch nodded, got up to leave but his father told him to stay put. Senator Morgan thanked the police and led them to the door. Butch could hear the whispered tones and strained to hear what they were saying but couldn't make out any of the conversation.

Senator Morgan came back to his son and looked at him. He thought he should've insisted he not go to boarding school after the death of Violet, but he was too broken to argue with Rachel. He felt responsible for the way his son turned out, and this was a chance for redemption for them both.

"Harold, y'all have to understand, we want what's best for you."

"Please, Daddy, that's bullshit."

"I'm entrusting y'all with a big job here and setting y'all up to get into an Ivy League college in January. I'm giving y'all the responsibility to help your country, your state, and make a connection with a prince from Zatari. Y'all know oil and gasoline run this world right now, and this is a chance for y'all to get in on that. If we pull this off, y'all will be set for life. Not only with the Morgan name, but we've had the chance to make a fortune on oil. I'm trusting y'all, Son. Think ahead for once. Do this for yourself and y'all may not have to work a day in your life."

That gave a new interest to Butch in this relationship with this A-Rab prince. For the next hour, Senator Morgan explained the Zatarian customs and culture, their plan for the future and what was expected of him. Little did Senator Morgan know, with the information he gave him, Butch began to hatch a devious plan of his own.

# CHAPTER 19

"René, please buy me that snow globe with the Empire State Building. I miss my New York." She's begged René for that silly snow globe ever since she saw it in the window of the shop near the diner they've been frequenting.

"Zoe, I've told you we can't make any frivolous purchases until we're sure we've enough money to eat until the dining hall opens. Why don't you ask your secret admirer, the Professor?"

She did a pretend pout. "Because I don't want him to buy it for me, I want you to."

"I'm sorry, *chéri*, not today."

"Okay. I won't ask again until tomorrow."

They walked into the Berkeley Diner, located near the college, and headed to their favorite booth. The dining hall wasn't operational until next week when the freshmen began to arrive for orientation. They found the Diner on one of their strolls around the college, trying to acclimate themselves to the area. The food was good and relatively inexpensive. It seemed to be a favorite place for the locals, which is a sign that it's a good place to eat.

Their mood was very playful. After Theodore gave up his secret stash of equipment, the atmosphere became euphoric. René's mood changed in an instant and kept getting better. He worried that they weren't able to acquire the materials needed. Fortunately, Marty didn't discover the devices when inspecting Christina's bear.

After revealing Theodore's treasures, Christina showed him what she knew about them. As sophisticated as these recorders were, they're relatively simple to operate and virtually undetectable unless you know exactly what you're looking for, and even then, they're hard to see.

They're set up to record whenever movement is detected, and three were put in the dorm room occupied by the Prince and Morgan, in places to ensure every angle of the room was covered. The size of the bedrooms in their suite was bigger than the others in the college, but still relatively easy to set them up to overlap one another, which is exactly what René wanted. He bought a peace sign pin and attached it to it for Christina. He put the last one on a cross he purchased for himself. Zoe felt left out, but René teased her, saying if he didn't have to buy her meals, he'd have extra money to get her something too. She pouted and dropped the subject. They discussed more of the plan at the Diner.

"Christina, when you and the prince are in class or studying, use the pen for recording. Try to wear and activate the pin whenever you're with the Prince and Morgan if he's with you. It's a good idea to video the conversations occurring in your presence. It'll be helpful to read the faces while words are spoken. I hope you agree."

"Sure. I've nothing to hide."

"Now, Tee, you never know. There's a possibility you'll fall head over heels for Prince Charming."

"Not likely. Unlike you, I'm not here for love or adventure. I'm here to do this thing and get my ass back home safe and sound."

"Okay, but life has a way of throwing curveballs. Be ready when it happens."

"Zoe," René asked, "is that why you're here, for love and adventure?"

Her face reddened, and she gave Tee one of her sheepish Zoe looks. "I'm ready for anything that comes my way and willing to go along with whatever happens. *Que será, sera.*"

The sparks between René and Zoe over the past week were flying fast and furious. It's a wonder they haven't gotten burned with the heat coming from the two of them. They're very flirtatious with each other, with an obvious mutual attraction. Zoe had this cowlick that always got in her eyes. When it got in her face, René would gently push the hair away. It's so cute to watch. Christina tried to give them space, but there wasn't much opportunity for them to be alone.

Now with everything in place, they're able to relax and spend their days walking around Berkeley, taking in the local color. Christina found the clock tower and the Sather Bells enchanting. Every day, she'd go outside and position herself to hear the noon chimes. She was able to finagle a private tour by begging the curator, a sweet guy named Stan Cook. O'Connell was right. The Campanile was impressive. She looked forward to hearing the "Deever Song" at the end of the semester. She begged Stan to play it for her, but her charms didn't work, telling her she'd have to wait. They became buddies over her bell infatuation.

Many days, he'd let her climb to the top of the tower and look out over the Bay at the Golden Gate Bridge, with Alcatraz Island and a good deal of San Francisco visible. It became her little refuge. She had to make sure she wasn't up there when the bells started to chime.

After dinner, they seemed to end up in René's room listening to the radio and eventually fall asleep together. They're always laughing at something and use this time alone in the dorm to get to know each other better.

They left the diner and headed back toward the dorms, with René in the middle and the girls on either side of him, arms linked. When Christina caught their reflection in a store window or mirror, she marveled at how young they were. So full of life and promise. She thought to herself, enjoy it while you can. This opportunity to relive youth was unbelievable.

As they passed the little novelty store, Zoe made her usual plea to René about the snow globe.

"You said you weren't going to ask again until tomorrow, Madame Zoe. I think you should ask O'Connell to buy it for you. I'm sure he'd be eager to buy you anything to attain an advantage. He's quite smitten with you."

"Tell me why you keep saying that. What did he say about me?"

"Ah, a man can tell. I've told you before, it's not what he's said, it's what he hasn't said. He sputters like a little boy when I mention your name. Would you like me to set you up?"

He loved teasing her but it's obvious he wasn't too pleased about O'Connell's infatuation with Zoe, obvious by the way he says his name, with a hint of distaste. He's uncomfortable with someone having feelings for "our Zoe."

She did a pretend pout. "No, I don't want you to set me up with him," giving him one of her Zoe looks.

René continued to tease her about the effect she has on O'Connell. She ate it up like candy. They kept flirting until she relented.

"Okay. I won't ask you for it again until tomorrow, and I mean it this time."

They got back to the dorms, and their books and supplies were in the Common Room in boxes with their names on them. They checked out the boxes and René carried them to the girls' room. Christina couldn't wait to open her new Art book, looking for paintings from "her collection." She flipped through it, thrilled that this semester of art history was on the Impressionists and the American artists of roughly the same time frame. Thomas Cole was one of the artists she'll study this semester, always quite taken with his works, especially his series paintings "*The Voyage of Life*" and "*The Course of Empire*." She's looking forward to this class.

They made coffee, brought it into René's room, and turned on the radio, enjoying the music of that time. They're laughing up a storm, René, and Zoe kept flirting with each other.

Christina noticed and said, "If you two want to be alone, I'll take my coffee and my art book to my room."

Zoe immediately answered, "Okay!"

René answered, "No, of course not."

Christina stood to leave, and René grabbed her arm, asking her to stay. She wasn't sure what to do. She knew Zoe wanted to make out with him because it's all she talks about when he's not with them, and Christina kept feeling that she was in the way.

"No, I think I'll leave you two alone for a while."

"Please, Christina, we only have a few more nights to have this place to ourselves. I want us to spend it together. We're a team, sharing a unique experience, and I really want you to stay."

She walked to the door, but René once again asked her to stay. Maybe he's afraid of getting hot and heavy too soon. If things started to go badly, they'd still have to work together. Whatever the reason, he wanted them to remain together.

Christina noticed Zoe had a disheartened look, trying not to show disappointment, and René must've noticed. Christina looked at her when René turned away, shrugged her shoulders, and mouthed, "I'm sorry! I tried!"

When René turned back to them, he had a package in his hand, wrapped in blue paper with a blue bow. He walked over to Zoe and handed it to her.

"For me? Really?"

"Open it, please."

Zoe carefully undid the bow and opened the seams of the wrapping paper to reveal a box. She opened the box, and in it was the snow globe of New York City.

"Oh, René! I can't believe you got this for me! How did you know I wanted it? You're the sweetest man I've ever met! Thank you so much." She hugged him and gave him a quick kiss.

"I told you I'd make it up to you when Christina got her pin and I got my cross. See the tiny man and woman standing on the Empire State Building? They're you and me. Someday, when all of this is behind us, we'll go there together, like in this snow globe."

Christina wondered what's in store for them after this was all over. She looked at them and the snow globe and got an idea.

"I've got to get something in my room. Can I leave you two alone for a minute, or are you both going to spontaneously combust if someone isn't here to make sure the fire doesn't burn out of control?"

She turned when she got to the door and asked, "Should I knock before coming back in?"

"No, *chéri,* leave the door open. We'll behave."

"I'll be right back."

She went into her room, took off her clothes, and quickly got the scarves out. She wanted to achieve the look of a fortune-telling gypsy, so she tied them to her bikini underwear and draped them so it looked like she was wearing a handkerchief dress using almost all her scarves. She wrapped one around her bra, her wrists, fingers, ankles, over her head, and put one around her face so only her eyes were visible. She put on huge hoop earrings and grabbed Zoe's bangle bracelets and hippie beads, and voila, the mysterious Madame Fortune, seer of the future.

When she got back into René's room, the two of them were on the bed. René had his arm around Zoe and they're looking at the snow globe. Christina walked into the room and they started laughing.

Christina tried to look and act as enigmatically as she could, using big hand movements and a gypsy accent. "How dare you laugh at the mysterious Madame Fortune? I have the gift of being all-knowing and can delve deep into people's lives and see the future. My powers are all-encompassing. I've come very far to look into the crystal ball of New York City snow to tell you what's yet to come in your lives."

"What's your name?" René asked. "Madame Fortune? Where'd you come up with this alter ego?"

"I'm the gypsy who sees the future. Enough questions! I've come to tell you about your future. May I have the crystal ball, young lady?"

Zee handed Christina the ball, saying, "Don't drop it!"

Christina shook the snow globe, waited until the snow settled, and then began. "Ah, I see clothes; lots of clothes, shoes, handbags, and coats. I see airplanes, skyscrapers, and more clothes. I see great happiness and great sorrow, and more clothes. I see a kind, considerate, patient best friend who's shared your mischief. You and this friend will travel very far and share an adventure with a handsome, hunky Frenchman who'll make you both feel like teenagers again.

"Now let's see what the future holds for the handsome Frenchman." She shook the globe, letting the snow fall over the New York skyline. When it settled, she did a little hocus pocus over the globe. "Ah, I see the Eiffel Tower."

"Of course you do, he's French!"

"Don't interrupt the great Madame Fortune, young lady. I see many adventures in the world of intrigue. As with the young lady, I see happiness and sorrow. You'll meet two incredibly special women, one of whom rudely interrupts people. You'll share an adventure in a faraway place. I see a college in America for one semester, and great success in all you do. I see a middle-aged teenager who's obsessed with you."

Zoe got up and took the globe from Christina. "Okay, Christina, that's enough!"

"Uh oh, she called me Christina. I must be in trouble. Did Madame Fortune give away a known secret?"

The DJ cut short the conversation by mentioning something about Jim Morrison and the Doors. Zoe jumped to turn it up. "It's been a little over a month since Jim Morrison was found dead in an apartment in Paris. In memory of Morrison, station KBRK/FM will play tunes by the Doors for the next hour with no commercial interruption. We're going to start with one of my favorites, *Roadhouse Blues.* Crank up the volume, hipsters, because it doesn't get better than this! RIP Jim!"

Zoe and Christina looked at each other, and as those first chords of the song started, they reverted to teenage mode. They spent hours in Christina's bedroom listening to the music of their time, and this song was one of their favorites. They made up a dance, sticking in their own words. Any time it came on, they'd do their thing. Because lyrics are repeated twice for much of the song, Christina did the first line and Zoe the second, with both of them screaming out the chorus with suggestive motions.

They remembered the whole thing with their own words. René was quite amused by their antics, especially when they sang, *"I shoulda laid her, lift up your blouse. Taste our titty,"* all the while doing innocently obscene motions, singing at the top of their lungs. By the time the song ended, they were rolling with laughter on the floor.

"You two must've been a lot of fun in your teens. Did you do this sort of thing often?"

"All the time," Zoe said. "We were such good girls. This sort of thing was really the worst we did. God, Tee, didn't we have fun? Nobody had as much fun as we did."

And it was true. They had a blast! That song brought back so much of their teen years and here they were again, teenagers reliving moments that were gone forever. Christina decided it was time to get out of her fortune telling costume since she was only in her underwear with scarves and shawls added for effect.

"Madame Fortune will be changing back into Christina. I'll be right back."

She walked out the door, talking to Zoe and René, not watching where she was going because no one was in the dorm but them. "Turn it up a little more so I can hear it while I'm changing."

Christina scampered out of the room and ran right into someone, knocking him down with her falling directly on top of him. Hitting the ground brought her back to reality, and she looked up, and two men were standing, one in a very expensive suit and the other in what looked like Arab clothing. She looked at the person she knocked down and saw an extremely handsome, dark young man with a huge smile on his face. She immediately noticed his warm eyes and felt her stomach do a flip. Oh my God! What have I done? From the photos she'd seen, she recognized the prince.

Ali could see nothing but her huge brown eyes as the rest of her face was covered with scarves. When their eyes met, with the two of them lying on the floor with the weight of her body on his, he felt a tingling throughout his body. He wasn't prepared for this feeling, which was foreign to him. He knew he'd play this moment over in his head for the rest of his life.

"Oh my God! I'm so sorry! I guess I wasn't paying attention. Are you okay?"

The man in the suit grabbed her arm and helped her up, and she could tell by his rough manner that he wasn't at all pleased. Christina kept apologizing. Zoe and René came into the hall to see what had happened. When they saw they weren't alone, René shut off the radio.

The man in the Arab attire helped up the felled victim who couldn't stop laughing. Neither of the men seemed amused at what happened. Even after Ali was helped up, his legs felt unsteady over his feet.

The Arab man angrily asked Christina, "Is this your normal attire, young lady, or is this in some way mocking our culture?"

René spoke up, "Please, sir, no disrespect was intended. We don't know of any of the other students in our dorm or their cultures. Terry was entertaining us by playing a fortune teller and decided to dress the part. We're having some innocent fun. Please accept our deepest apologies if you've been offended by anything you saw or heard."

Ali was unable to stop laughing as Christina tried to recover and kept apologizing for her clumsiness, which Ali found to be endearing. He wasn't sure if he were laughing out of nervousness or because of the collision but couldn't take his eyes off her. She looked bewitching in her scant gypsy attire and wondered what she looked like under the scarves. Khalid, his guardian, was insulted by her demeanor and found it disrespectful to the Arabian culture. Ali was mesmerized.

Khalid wanted Berkeley to take action against them because of the ridicule of their country. Ali asked to speak privately with Khalid, and they stepped aside and argued in their native tongue. René secretly turned on the recording pen in his pocket.

Ali kept insisting the whole episode was completely innocent. How would they've known a prince from Zatari would be living on the same floor and would be coming at this particular time to view the accommodations? Khalid responded that they didn't know of their presence, and that wasn't the point. They're making a mockery of their culture, and it isn't to be tolerated.

Ali argued that what they saw had nothing to do with them and the whole incident should be dropped. Khalid didn't want to budge an inch in his assessment of the scene, but Ali kept insisting it was quite innocent. Didn't he know they're young adults having fun, and in America things aren't as strict as in Zatari?

While arguing with Khalid, Ali kept trying to maintain a serious demeanor but was having difficulty because every time he thought about their collision and her eyes, he couldn't stop smiling, which led to giggling. That angered Khalid further, but Ali couldn't help himself and the more he tried to regain composure, the more he lost it. Khalid ended their communication and told the Dean he wanted to discuss this further in the privacy of his office. Disrespect won't be tolerated. Ali selfishly didn't want anything to happen to this girl because of him, and, for the first time in his life, he used the weight of his position and ordered Khalid to drop the matter.

"I'm not disturbed by any of this; in fact, I find it to be a welcome way to have met some of the people with whom I'll be sharing my living quarters. I'm not going to start my university semester by causing trouble for anyone. I want to be like any other student in this school. No one needs to know my position. If you act on this and cause them any difficulty, you'll be sealing both our fates as untrustworthy. As a son of your king, you're bound to do as I command. I've told you I'm not offended by anything that occurred, and it ends right now. This goes no further. Is that understood?"

Khalid was taken aback by the authority in Ali's voice. "With all due respect, Prince Ali, I'm here as a representative of the king and your guardian. In my judgment, this was disrespect of the greatest degree. I insist we investigate these students, especially as you'll be living in such close proximity. Your father would agree. I must act in your best interests and that of our country. You giggling like a schoolgirl wouldn't please your father, seeing his house represented so reprehensibly in light of what's occurred."

Ali was getting angry. "Honorable Khalid, as we can see, my father isn't here. I believe he'd wisely put this behind him and move forward. You are making much out of nothing. I'm sorry, Khalid, but I won't have it! I order you to drop this and consider the incident forgotten! I'm sure you don't wish me to contact my father and tell him you're trying to sabotage the mission I've been sent here to do. It ends now, and I'll have no further discussion on this!"

"As you wish," he replied.

"It's not as I wish; it's as I command." Ali surprised himself with the way he's speaking to Khalid but was quite serious. He told the Dean no matter what Khalid insisted on, it'll be against his wishes if there is any trouble for his dormmates and his father will be notified which will mean the large donation to the college will be rescinded.

"Are we all of the same understanding?" They nodded and Khalid's face reddened in anger.

"Very well, thank you," Ali said to the two of them.

René extended his hand to the young man in greeting. "*Bon jour*. My name is Jean-René Soulliere, but please call me René. I believe you've already met Terry Brendes and this young lady is Athena Christos."

Ali's guardian started to say exactly who the young man was but Ali interrupted.

"My name is Ali, I'm from Zatari, a country in the Middle East. It's a pleasure to meet all of you. I believe my room for the next few months is next to yours and we're to be neighbors. We were being shown my accommodations. We're sorry to have intruded on all of you."

Christina (Terry) was feeling extremely uncomfortable in her scarved underclothes. "Please excuse me while I change into more normal attire." She addressed the Arab man, "Sir, my deepest apologies if you were offended in any way." Then addressed the Dean, "I'm very sorry if I've embarrassed you or Berkeley University. It certainly wasn't my intent." She ran into her room followed by Zoe, saw her reflection in the mirror, and wanted to crawl into a hole. Way to make an impression! She ripped the scarves from her face and started to cry.

Jean-René asked Ali if he'd like to stay with them and get better acquainted and Ali jumped at the chance. He agreed, much to the chagrin of Khalid who vehemently differed with Ali's decision to remain with the three co-eds. Ali wanted to learn what it was like in America, out from under the constraints of his customs and palace convention, but in truth he was intrigued by this girl.

"I think it's a splendid idea to remain here and acclimatize myself to the university and the outlying areas. Thank you, Jean-René, for the invitation. I'd like to formally meet the beautiful young lady who knocked me over, without the scarves covering her face." He started laughing again. "I hope I'll not be too much of a bother. Would it be possible for you to show me around before the orientation for new students takes place?"

"It'd be our pleasure. In fact, why don't you stay in my room until our roommates arrive? There's no sense in being alone, especially in a new country. When I arrived from France, I admit I was lonely until the arrival of Athena and Terry. We'd be more than pleased to have you join us."

"Then it's decided. Khalid, have my things sent over, I'll need them immediately." He addressed the Dean, "I'll take the key to my room now and begin settling in once my belongings arrive." He turned to Jean-René and said, "Shall we go? I've much to learn about America and look forward to getting to know the three of you. What's her name again?"

"Teresa, Teresa Brendes, but everyone calls her Terry or Tee."

"Ah yes, Taraysa, the girl who knocked me off my feet." He chuckled, reliving the thrill of their meeting.

As he walked away, he turned to the two older gentlemen and bowed. "Thank you both very much. Khalid, we'll speak soon." The men began walking away and Athena was trying to coax Terry out of her room. As soon as the men were out of earshot, Khalid told the Dean he wanted the names and any information the college has on those three students.

Jean-René knocked on Tee's door and told her they'd be waiting for her in his room. Zoe answered, "Terry will be out in a minute or two. She's fixing herself up." Zoe tried to console her.

"It's okay Tee. Don't cry. Everything's fine."

"Oh yeah, sure it is! It's the prince, isn't it? I know it! He's much cuter than I expected. Oh God! I knocked over the prince, landing on top of him, and showed my whole crotch area to the Dean and possibly the King of Zatari. I've probably started an international incident and there's going to be a jihad on me for what happened."

"Tee, you can't talk like you know anything about their culture and jihads. That vernacular isn't part of this century, at least that we know of in the US."

Christina continued crying and Zoe said, "Well, you made a good impression on him. He's been laughing over the whole thing. That's a good start, right?"

Christina sat on the bed untying the scarves, crying. "How can I face him? I'm so stupid! My father always yelled at me to watch where I'm going because I was never paying attention. And now my ass was hanging out for the world to see! Oh my God, kill me now!"

Zoe helped undo the scarves and Christina stalled as long as she could. She wanted to make sure the three of them were gone before she emerged from her room.

"I'm going to be kicked out before I even get started."

René knocked on the door asking if she was decent. Zoe answered not yet. Christina yelled back, "If I were decent, I wouldn't have caused an international incident against a foreign exchange student!"

"All's well, Terry. Hurry and come out. Ali would like to formally meet you."

"Shit!" She whispered to Zoe. "He's still here! I can't face him now! And I definitely don't want to look into the faces of those two men. I think they would've killed me on the spot if they could. I can't face him. I'm too embarrassed!"

"Tee, get changed and come out. You're making too much out of it. He seems very cool and not at all upset. What better way could you've met him? If you think about it, it plays perfectly into our assignment. Get dressed, comb your hair and for God's sake fix your make-up. We'll be waiting for you in René's room. If you don't hurry, I'm going to send Ali in to get you," and she left the room.

Christina reluctantly changed into jeans and a clean shirt and fixed her make-up which had smeared around her eyes from crying, making her look like a horrific raccoon. Her hair was a long mass of unruly curls that wouldn't be tamed. She gently combed it which did nothing to alleviate the curl. Time to face the music.

She peered into the hallway and was relieved there were no official men with their frowns of discontent so she walked to René's room. She could hear their voices and wanted to run away. She peeked in the doorway and Ali saw her first.

"Ah! Here she is!"

Christina entered the room. Ali was taken by her beauty with the scarves off her face. Not only were her eyes large and tantalizing, but the total package was stunning, leaving him captivated.

"I'm so, so sorry! I apologize if the way I dressed offended you. I was pretending to be a fortune teller and decided to play dress up. It wasn't meant to insult your culture if it is your culture. Is it your culture? I don't even know what your culture is only that I pissed off the guy with the Arabian clothing. Was he your father? He won't have me expelled, will he?"

Ali laughed. "Of course not. No, he's not my father, just one of my family's associates. Let me introduce myself. My name is Ali Tariq Al-Machmud, but please, call me Ali. I come from a small but prosperous country in the Middle East called Zatari. I'll be here at Berkeley for one semester studying Art. Hopefully, if my marks are good enough, I'll be able to transfer to any school of my choosing."

"You must be pretty important for the Dean to be showing you around. Oh God, I can't believe I embarrassed myself in front of the Dean! This is awful!"

"I find the circumstances of our meeting to be straight out of a great novel. Not many people meet in such a dynamic way. And I'm not important, my father is, but please don't treat me as such. I'm a regular student as the three of you are."

"Terry, I've invited Ali to stay with me until our roommates arrive so we can show him around over the next few days. I hope you don't mind." At first Christina wasn't sure who René was talking to, but remembered Terry was her Berkeley name.

"I'll never forget this day as long as I live!" she said as she slumped on the bed. She studied his face and thought to herself that he's a very handsome young man, with beautiful dark eyes and a winning smile.

Ali smiled and said, "It's not every day that I'm swept off my feet by a beautiful young woman and I too, will never, ever forget this day either."

# CHAPTER 20

While together in René's room, they got to know each other, asking Ali about his country and what he's planning to study. Ali didn't want to tell anyone he's a prince, so he'd be treated like any other student.

He told them as little as he could without sounding evasive. He was captivated by Terry and found her more beautiful than he could have imagined. Whenever he looked at her, he got that tingling in his stomach again. She kept apologizing, which he thought was endearing. He couldn't take his eyes off her or stop smiling. He hoped his nervousness wasn't obvious.

The four of them made small talk and Athena asked if Ali would like some coffee. Jean-René said they needed milk, and he'd go to the store and pick some up. As he started for the door, Athena offered to go with him, and he accepted. Before they left, he went over to the desk and wrote out a list of items. No one saw him pick up one pen and put it in his pocket and then write with another.

"Why don't the two of you get better acquainted? Athena and I will be back shortly." As soon as they left, "Terry" opened the door to check the hallway to see if either of the men returned. She left the door open in case they did so they wouldn't think she was corrupting his morals.

They talked about themselves, art, their upcoming classes, and some of their interests. Ali noticed the key around her neck and asked what it was for. Her hand immediately fondled it and then kissed it. She told him the fable about her brother and the springy snakes that jump out at you. Talking about the key seemed to make her sad so Ali tried to lighten the conversation. He told her he'd never seen those fake snakes but had definitely seen some real ones. She seemed to cheer up with his stab at humor. While they were talking, Ali couldn't stop thinking how he wanted to feel the softness of her skin and wondered how her lips would feel if he kissed her. He'd never felt this before.

The bells began to chime the hour of four and she revealed her love of the clock tower and told him all she'd learned from the curator. She became more vibrant and spoke about it in a way that was so animated, he could feel her passion.

Meanwhile, as René and Zoe were walking to the store, they passed an empty doorway. René suddenly whisked her into it, pulled her to him, and kissed her. It completely threw her off guard, but she responded with ardor. They stayed there for a few minutes, locked in a passionate embrace and kiss. Once they started, they didn't want to stop. René pulled slightly away, looking at her.

"I've wanted to do this since I first saw you standing in Martin Cater's office. You're bewitching me, Zoe, completely and totally, mind, body, and soul. I kept telling myself not to start because I wouldn't want to stop, which I don't. I never mixed business with pleasure, and now I've broken my own rule. You're too hard to resist and try as I may, I find I can't control myself. That's why I didn't want to be left alone with you. I cannot behave myself. Please accept my apology."

"Apology? You gotta be kidding!" Zoe pulled him to her, and they were once again locked in a passionate kiss. They stayed there in the doorway for a few more minutes connected to each other in the excitement of a first kiss.

"As much as I'd love to stay here all night, we've things to do. Please don't mention this to Christina. I don't want her to think I'm not present in our mission and her protection."

He took her hand and as they walked together, there was a difference in their steps than before they shared their first kiss. They no longer looked like friends walking together, but a couple, especially when they looked at each other. Before they went to the store, they took a detour to the People's Park and sat on a bench. At that time, René took out the pen and clicked a button and they could hear the conversation between Ali and Khalid in Arabic.

"Can you understand what they're saying?"

"Yes, they're coming in very clearly. I set the volume for recording on high so that it could be picked up at a good distance away."

"René, when did you get the pen to record this conversation?"

"When I went in to shut off the radio. I wanted to make sure I recorded any discussions taking place between Ali and the two men, especially after what happened."

"What are they saying? Was that the king?"

"No, the king wouldn't have accompanied his son, especially as he's from a secondary wife. That duty would fall to an Aide or one of the higher subjects in his administration. It seems the Arab gentleman wants the Dean to take action against Christina. Ali insisted that nothing be done and used his position as prince to throw some weight around. Did you notice he doesn't want us to know he's a prince? I find that quite interesting and a pleasant surprise. Between you and me, and if you can believe in love at first sight, I think he's already quite smitten with Christina. After hearing some of the conversation in the hallway, I decided to ask him if he wanted to stay with us. I thought it a good idea to become acquainted without Morgan or any of the others who'll be living on our floor, even though it'll only be for a few days."

He listened to the conversation twice and then said, "Hmmm. We may have a problem."

"What?"

"The Arab wants to know all there is to know about the three of us. After we get the groceries, we'll have to pay a visit to your sweet professor and find out exactly what will be told about us. I didn't think we'd have this problem straight away. As far as I know, we really don't exist, so we need to know our precise backgrounds. Hopefully, O'Connell has already fabricated our history, but we need to let him know immediately what happened and that the Dean of Students will most likely be making inquiries about us."

They left the park and headed to the little grocery store near the campus. After making their purchases, they took the detour to see O'Connell. Before they knocked on the door, they could tell by the acrid smell coming from his living quarters that he was smoking a joint. When he opened the door, he was surprised to see Zoe standing there with René.

"Sorry to bother you, Glenn, but we may have a slight problem. Can we come in for a minute?"

He didn't answer, opened the door for them, and motioned them in. The apartment reeked of marijuana. He offered them to join him, but René declined for them both.

"We have the prince with us, and I want the two of us to be alert but thank you."

O'Connell continued to talk and asked them to have a seat. The apartment was unkempt but clean. His glassy eyes kept darting to Zoe, and the memory of his surreptitious viewing of her body while she slept wouldn't leave his thoughts. He could feel himself getting hard and found it very difficult to stop it with her being so close to him. She'd become his object of desire, and thinking of her usually led to self-gratification. He was so lost in his thoughts that he wasn't listening to what René was saying.

"Glenn, did you hear me? Are you listening to me? Glenn? Goddamn it! Put that damn joint out and listen to me! It's important!"

"I'm listening," he said, taking another hit off the joint. He tried to focus on what René was saying, but his attention kept reverting to Zoe.

Finally, René had had enough. He grabbed O'Connell by the arm and dragged him into the kitchen. "Zoe, please stay here."

"Glenn, I know she's irresistible, but I need your attention! Look me in the eyes while I'm talking to you so I can see if you understand what I'm saying. For God's sake, man, you're a genius! Why are you spending your time zoning out on pot?"

"It helps me think."

"I think it helps you not to think. Please listen. We may need your help." René told him the whole story of what had occurred, and the Dean of Students would be looking into their backgrounds. "I need to know exactly what'll be told to the Dean and to the representative from Zatari who accompanied the prince. I need this information *yesterday*! Do you understand? Get your head out of that bag of pot and join planet earth!"

René turned and walked out to the living room where Zoe was sitting. He grabbed her hand and they walked to the door. René turned and said, "It's important, and we're depending on you. You're the only one who knows the truth about us and our only ally here. Don't fuck this up!" They walked out the door.

All O'Connell could concentrate on was her ass as she walked away. He sat down, noticed his "man in the middle" was standing at attention. He relit his doobie, put his hand down his pants, and pleasured himself. Afterwards he tried to remember what they came here for but all he could think of was her ass.

They headed back to the dorm, not really saying anything. Before they got to their building, René put down their bag of groceries and pushed Zoe up against a tree, kissing her again. They stayed there a few minutes, locked in each other's arms. They eventually pulled away from their embrace and walked to the dorm.

When they arrived back, Tee was telling Ali about her "collection" from the New Yorker magazine, describing each one in great detail while searching the textbook for any reference to them.

Athena (Zoe) said to Ali, "By the time she finishes, you'll know all about her collection, as she calls it."

Ali smiled, looking at Tee, and said, "She's very good at describing them. I wish I could see them."

René put on the coffee, and the four of them spent the rest of the night helping Ali put his room together while listening to music on the radio. That night, they stayed in the same room and were up almost until dawn talking. One thing Ali found odd was that the three of them didn't smoke cigarettes. He thought everyone in America smoked, because almost everyone did. These three are nothing like what he thought American college students would be. He was enjoying his new friendships in America.

For the next three days, the four of them were inseparable. The trio showed Ali around campus, the People's Park and they ate together at the Berkeley Diner with Christina making a big deal out of the clock tower. They went into San Francisco, rode the cable cars, and viewed the harbor from the hills. They listened to music, laughed a lot, and walked around the city.

Ali was in culture shock. He had to adjust to weaker coffee, different attitudes, and American diner food. It amazed him how there was so much life going on right on campus with jugglers, mimes, people playing instruments and singing, people hawking merchandise and illegal drugs, protestors voicing their displeasure about a number of issues, disciples of the Unification Church evangelizing about Rev. Moon, and "Jesus Freaks" as they were called, evangelizing about Jesus. There was so much to view and take in. He found himself in awe of the freedoms of the citizens of the United States. This sort of behavior would never be tolerated in his country.

While walking around, Terry would link arms with Ali, and it thrilled him to feel her touch. He wondered what she thought of him and if his desire for her was obvious. During one of their late-night rap sessions, the girls admitted they hadn't had any sexual encounters. This shocked Ali because he thought all women in America lost their virginity in their early teens. They looked upon their chasteness as something to be proud of and a gift they'd give to someone they love and didn't view sex as something taken lightly. This made Terry more attractive to him because in his culture, it was required that women remain virgins until marriage. Sex in his country was not discussed. Here in America, "free love" was a slogan and a way of life for the young. He found himself not only enjoying their company but also the more he got to know them, the more respect he had for them both.

Ali had been staying with Jean-René the past few days and wasn't looking forward to having a new roommate. He knew it was his duty to share quarters with Butch Morgan, but he felt a kinship with his three new friends and wished things could stay as they were. He'd had few friends his age, and being with them made him happy. He was always laughing in their company, and every day he seemed to fall deeper in love with Terry, a feeling foreign to him. She dominated his thoughts, and he looked forward to each new day because she would be in it.

When they were together, he'd brush up against her arm or turn his head towards her as they walked so he could smell her hair, which had a very heady scent, and feel its softness on his face. He was thrilled they were in most of the same classes together, and that meant he'd be able to see her almost all the time. He sometimes got a slight feeling of aloofness from her, so he was mindful to take it slow. He had all semester to win her over. He'll woo her and be attentive to her, content for the time being to be near her. Hopefully, she'll come to feel the same way towards him.

Everything was going so well, and then Butch Morgan arrived.

# CHAPTER 21

Classes would be starting soon, and everyone from their suite arrived except for René's roommate. His things turned up, but there was no sign of him yet. Ali didn't want to leave René's room but felt it rude and inhospitable to Morgan if he didn't go to his assigned room. On the morning of Butch's expected arrival, Ali moved into his room.

The first to appear was Butch, who came the day before orientation in the late morning. He was alone, which was surprising. Freshmen are usually accompanied by a parent or guardian. They greeted him and Ali introduced himself as his roommate. Butch immediately got off on the wrong foot with them, especially Ali. He was trying to be funny but everything he did and said seemed vulgar and insulting.

He made offensive remarks about the "fucking French," the "A-rabs" of the Middle East and Ali's short hair, asking him how he expects to get laid looking so uncool. His remarks for "the bitches," quickly established him as the resident asshole with his lewd and suggestive behavior. Zoe and Christina tried to be nice, but he made it very difficult. Living on the same floor as him was going to be a challenge. He was rude, crude, and a chauvinistic pig. It's hard to believe he and Ali will become good friends because they're night and day.

The next person arrived a few hours later and caused quite a stir on campus. Her name was Sarah Richardson, a sweet and humorous girl who was kind of chubby with a weakness for chocolate, a face like sunshine, and a disposition to match. The mood on the floor lightened up when she arrived, especially after the negativity of Butch. She had a contagious laugh and upbeat outlook on everything. She came with her father, and he's who caused the commotion. Robbie Richardson was the Academy Award winner for Best Supporting Actor in 1970. People from other dorms were crowding around him to get his autograph. He wanted to slip through unnoticed so he could get his little girl settled.

Sarah came to UC Berkeley to study performing arts, directing, voice, and elocution with aspirations to become an actress. Christina and Zoe were star-struck meeting the person who would become an award-winning actress, surpassing her father in fame, awards, and public adoration, the highest paid and in-demand female star of her era. Her greatest achievement, in her own eventual words, is philanthropy.

She'll become a champion to those with AIDS as well as its top fundraiser. Zoe and Christina could hardly contain their excitement upon meeting her. They tried not to act out of the ordinary, having a tremendous amount of respect for how she was the first to come to the defense of those who were HIV positive and afflicted with AIDS, a disease that affected everyone in one way or another. She worked tirelessly educating the public regarding its facts. Millions of dollars were raised by her Foundation, and all monies were used for research and to make sure drugs were available to all those afflicted. She used her fame and fortune to help victims and families of this incurable disease.

Upon meeting her, one would never guess she'd become this huge star. She's someone who's great to be around. Even without knowing the impressive achievements she's to make, one couldn't help but like and respect her immediately. Unfortunately for her, her roommate was the female side of the coin housing Butch Morgan.

Regina Whitfield was the daughter of Congressman Lindsey Whitfield, the senior representative from South Carolina. She arrived a few hours after Sarah and acted like she was gracing everyone with her presence. It's obvious this southern belle was extremely spoiled. As she unpacked her designer hippie-chic clothes, her parents doted on her. While there, she was disrespectful to them both, yelling at them as if they were her servants. And they tolerated it.

Nothing made her happy. She wanted the bed, closet, and dresser Sarah had chosen. Sarah said no, things stay where they are. When Regina started to move Sarah's clothes from one closet to the other, Sarah jumped into action.

"Oh no, you don't! Back off, Sweetheart! What do you think you're doing? Leave my stuff alone!" Sarah took her clothes from Regina and hung them back in her closet.

"But I want this closet. It would be so cool and friendly-like if y'all would let me have it." She spoke with a thick southern accent that sounded so pseudo-friendly.

"Yeah, and it'd be even cooler and more friendly-like if you left my stuff alone. Sorry, you snooze, you lose. If it was that important to you, you should've come earlier. If I catch you touching my stuff, I may have to break your fingers. Ha ha." Sarah wasn't a pushover and couldn't be bullied.

Once everyone was settled, they met in the Common Room to get acquainted. Zoe and Christina hadn't met Regina, although they heard her big mouth yapping away at her parents and arguing with Sarah. Regina immediately went up to René and put the make on him with her sickening southern charm, acting like the sweetest peach on the tree. When she heard his French accent, she started to lay it on thick. Zoe didn't seem too happy, and neither was Christina.

Butch was trying to get Regina's attention and said, "We got a lot in common. My daddy's the former governor of the great state of Louisiana and is now its senator. Isn't your daddy a congressman, Reggie?"

"Why, yes, he is, and bless your heart, it's pronounced Regina, not Reggie. My letter from Berkeley said that because of my father's status, I'd be living among the elite. Butch is from the prestigious Morgan family and obviously Jean-René is a foreign exchange student. Sarah, how did you get here?"

Butch jumped right in. "Her daddy is Robbie Robertson, the famous actor." Sarah shot him a dirty look.

"My, my, Hollywood royalty right in the next bed. Why, it's absolutely thrilling."

"Yeah, well, I got real royalty for my roommate. Did y'all know Ali here is a bona-fide A-rab prince?"

Ali immediately piped in. "Well, Butch, not really. I'm a secondary son from…"

"Yup, Ali here is the son of the king of Zatari. Don't judge him by his short hair." He ruffled Ali's head. "He can't help it. Princes gotta have short hair, right, buddy?" Ali swatted Butch's hand away from him but that didn't stop him. "He's here to learn how to be cool like us civilized folks. You know, sex, drugs, and rock and roll. Maybe he's here to learn about running water, toilets, showers, stuff like that, eh, Ali? Betcha he's here for a chance to grow some hair!" He slapped Ali on the back and laughed his sickening snicker, they'd all come to despise.

Christina, wanting to make it seemed they'd no idea he was royalty said, "Ali, you didn't tell us you were a prince. Oh my God, is the king angry I knocked you over? Am I in trouble?"

"Please don't think like that. I'm still the same person I was before you knew my lineage. Don't treat me differently, please, any of you." Zoe and René also acted surprised. It's obvious Butch's disclosure made Ali uncomfortable.

"I didn't see any reason to mention it. I'm here, as all of you are, to learn. I wish to be treated as any other student would be treated. I'm a regular teenager in my first year at a university away from home, as all of you are. I'll be disappointed if any of you act differently towards me. I didn't see any reason to make it known, but Butch decided differently."

"Hey man, don't get all bummed out and bent out of shape. It's a sure way to score with chicks, am I right? I'm sure they'd love to bang a prince or at least shine your knob, eh, roomie, even with that short hair!"

"Please, everyone, I'm the same as the rest of you."

René said, "Ali, we'll honor your wishes and won't tell others if that's what you want, right Butch?"

"Chill out! I didn't know it was top secret, heh, heh, know what I mean, Princey? Get it? Top secret." He gave Ali a wink and an elbow in the ribs. Ali gave him a dirty look and walked to the other side of the room.

Regina looked at Zoe and Christina. "So, we have a dreamy French student, a senator's son, a prince, a movie star's daughter, and everyone knows who I am. What about you two? How did you two get on the elite floor?"

Zoe and Christina looked at each other. "Are you talking about Athena and me?"

"Well, bless your hearts, I don't see anyone else here, do you?

Christina answered. "Gee, Reggie, I guess Athena and I didn't need our fathers or a fancy bloodline to be assigned the elite floor. We didn't even apply to Berkeley, we were sought out by the College and given a full scholarship for a semester before we moved on to an Ivy League school. So, it must've been our superior intellect, our near-perfect SAT scores, and our above-average IQ. Some of us receive benefits because of our own merits and not by bribing with a large donation or being the spoiled child of a politician. No offense intended to any of you."

Regina frowned. "It sounds pretty jive to me. I think y'all are total bullshitters." She went close to Zoe's face and said, "I think we'd all like to see for ourselves how smart y'all are."

Christina said, "Sorry, Reggie. Don't have to prove anything to a Scarlet O'Hara wannabe who needed her daddy to get into a college. We're here on our merit, and if you don't believe it? Who cares? Do you care, Athena?"

"No, Terry. I could give less than a fuck. And you'd better get out of my face, bitch, because, in the first place, *Reggie*, I don't do parlor tricks and don't have to prove anything to anyone. I don't know who the hell you think you are, *sugar*, but if you're thinking for one second that you're better than any of us, you'd better think again. I know, too bad Terry and I got here on our own merit, and poor little you, only accepted because of your father's position. We won't hold it against you. And one other thing, don't you ever call either Terry or me a liar again, which is exactly what you did when you called us bullshitters."

Zoe stormed out of the room and started bitching up a storm in Greek. René excused himself and ran after her, which burst Regina's bubble. They started speaking to each other in French and went into her room, where he calmed her down.

From that moment on, there was no love lost between Regina and the other girls in their suite. Sarah tolerated her but spent as much time out of her room when Regina was around. She and Butch made quite a pair. He's always looking for someone to get high with or to sell some pot to, and Regina liked being connected with the Senator's son, who always had a joint to share or a nickel bag to sell.

Butch's remarks about Ali's hair made him insecure about it. On one of their walks before classes started, Christina noticed he pulled up his collar when passing a group of hipsters in the Peoples Park who heckled him about it. She yelled, "Fuck off, douchebags! You think long hair makes you cool? None of you hairbags look cool to me, just a bunch of dirty slobs." She could tell Ali was self-conscious and had an idea. "I know exactly what you need," and she took the Berkeley cap off her head and put it on his.

"There. Perfect! You can wear it with the visor in front when you're trying to be mysterious, or in the back, or on the sides to be hip. It's a UC Berkeley cap, so having it on your head makes you cool right off the bat. Only groovy kids go to Berkeley. It looks really good on you, Ali. It was made for you."

"I cannot take your cap, Taraysa."

"You're not taking it, I'm giving it to you. I bought it to control the curls, but it isn't working, see?" She flipped her hair, and the curls were obvious. "I want you to have it. As a gift from me. Your first gift from an American girl. And look, doesn't the bear look a little like Theodore Edward? Please take it. I'll feel bad if you don't. You look really cute in it, not that you need a cap to make you look cute. You do that all on your own."

"Do you think so? I don't look foolish?"

"How can you look foolish wearing a Berkeley cap? We're at the coolest school in the country. Just being a student here makes you cool. I insist you keep it. It looks better on you, anyway."

"Thank you, Taraysa. You're very kind." He looked in the window at his reflection and said, "I'm glad to have a friend like you. Now I can be cool." A big smile crossed his lips. "I'll treasure it always." From that day on, Ali wore the cap all the time, and no one made fun of his hair.

Every Friday, the trio met with O'Connell for a progress report to be sent to the $21^{st}$ century. It was also the day Ali had dinner with Khalid, so they never had to explain their absence as Ali became Christina's constant companion, as Martin Cater surmised.

After their Friday meetings, Christina would often visit Stanley Cook, the Sather Tower curator, who happily filled her in on the history of her newest obsession. She'd climb the tower, take in the view, and enjoy the needed alone time, looking out at the beautiful San Francisco Bay and Golden Gate Bridge. It also gave Zoe and René some time alone.

Her first time up, Stan climbed with her to point out landmarks and what to look for. She enjoyed Stan's company who, every week, would say it's Friday night, and she should be spending it with her peers, not an old man. She wanted to tell him they were closer in age than he would've ever thought. A sweet guy who was a fountain of knowledge about anything Berkeley. Christina looked forward to visits with him and learned something new every week.

Classes began and their first assignment for their drawing class, which was held outside, was to draw something inspiring at Berkeley. It was a warm Friday afternoon and Ali and Christina sat on a small hill to better take in the scenery and the vibrant life of the campus.

As they parked themselves, Christina's thoughts turned to Ali and, much to her surprise, she was beginning to like Ali a lot and looked forward to seeing him each day. He brightened her spirits in a way that surprised her and took a heavy load off her heart. Being that they had almost the same schedule of classes, they were always together and found humor in the same things. There was a lightness to their friendship and a certain kindness in everything Ali did. Christina found the stories of his life in Zatari remarkably interesting and was intrigued by their way of life. And it was exciting to see her world in a new light, through the eyes of someone who knew little of America.

Christina held the pencil René gave her to record their conversations in her hand. She argued that it was unfair to record Ali. It made her feel like she was entrapping and betraying him. René reminded her they were here for a certain reason, and it was necessary. He made her promise she'd continue as planned. She reluctantly agreed.

She was ready to start drawing, so she put her hair into a high ponytail to stay out of her face. She started sketching her inspiration, which of course, was the Sather Tower. It pulled her to it and felt peaceful whenever the chimes rang. It gave her an old-world feeling, of simpler times in the lives of the citizens of the world.

Sitting there, she noticed a girl with a guitar singing *"Blowin' in the Wind,"* a few feet from her was a young man singing *"Day by Day"* from *"Godspell,"* and another playing a mandolin. A crowd was protesting the Vietnam War, a kid played the spoons, a mime, a juggler, someone playing the harmonica and a co-ed selling tie-dyed t-shirts.

Wherever one looked, someone was doing something. Young life and vitality were everywhere. It felt good to be part of this time, this place, with these people, surrounded by the magic that comes with being young. She did a rough drawing to be fine-tuned later. She added some of the details from the clock tower, and because it was the first hour she heard it ring, she set the time in the drawing for ten o'clock. With all this activity on campus, she decided to include some in the sketch around the base of the tower as well.

It was a hot day with the sun beating down. A delicious breeze kicked up and the smells of Berkeley, floral mixed with patchouli oil, floated through the air. She stood up, closed her eyes, and released her curls to cool off, lifting her face into the wind, basking in the moment, the breeze blowing her cares away sending her off somewhere wonderfully peaceful.

She heard the unmistakable rumble of a Harley-Davidson motorcycle pulling up near her. She and John rode his Sportster all over New York State in search of waterfalls, which made the sound of a Harley music to her ears. It joined the peaceful assaults on her senses, with memories of their many motorcycle adventures.

Then, putting the icing on the cake, the three o'clock chimes started to peal. She whispered to herself, "Ah, yes!" smiling, her eyes still closed, listening to hours tick off, with her curls being taken on a wild ride in the wind.

When she opened her eyes, her peace was broken by the person on the Harley. He was still sitting on the bike, holding his sunglasses, staring at her as if amused by her appreciation of her surroundings. As soon as their eyes met, he rubbed the back of his neck and then had the balls to blow her a kiss, like he was god's gift to womanhood. She sneered at him, put her hair back into a ponytail, and went back to drawing. She hated guys like that. Did he expect her to be impressed? It'd be a bruising blow to his ego if he knew her interest was in the Harley and not the driver. Pompous ass!

Ali noticed and asked if she knew him. "No, but I know his type. Probably thinks he's every girl's dream. If you ask me, he's more like a nightmare."

"Why do you say that Taraysa, if you don't know him?"

"Watch him for a few minutes. I've met a lot of guys like him. He'll show you exactly what a jerk looks like. He's way too sure of himself, which is so unattractive. Watch."

As if he knew people were watching him, this guy, who reminded her of Robert Plant from Led Zeppelin, got off the bike. He had a knapsack attached to the bike, which he unhooked, and a guitar swung around on his back. Of course! He's a musician. They all think that because they play the guitar, girls will flock to them, which they do. And if they're in a band, there's always a fairly good chance of getting laid. Girls can be so stupid and shallow. Christina continued drawing.

He took off his helmet, ran his fingers through his hair, shook it back into place, rubbed the back of his neck and surveyed his domain. He put on his sunglasses, yelled out to Christina, "Hey! Luv!" She looked up from her drawing and he lowered his sunglasses and winked at her. This time she gave him the finger.

He blew her another kiss and proceeded to strut off like a vain peacock. Ali watched him as he confidently pranced over to a group of girls, asking them, quite loudly, "Who are you, luv, and where have you been all my life?" with probably a fake British accent. He swaggered over to as many females as possible, asking them the same question, not intending to wait for an answer. He must've thought it was a great icebreaker or pickup line. After the first few times, it became annoying.

"Sickening, isn't it?" Christina stopped looking and went back to sketching.

"No, just interesting to watch. He seems to be making quite an impression on the ladies."

"Well, if you ask me, girls are nothing but trouble and too easily impressed, especially by a guitar player." Ali laughed, but Christina was serious.

After seemingly making his rounds to all those who were currently in the vicinity, he sat down cross-legged on the grass and started strumming some chords on his guitar. Girls came from everywhere to sit and listen to this handsome peacock as he apparently held court. They were close enough to Ali and Christina that they could hear his playing and asking his obnoxious question, "And who are you, luv, and where have you been all my life?" The girls seemed to eat up this artificial question, giggling and acting like star-struck teenyboppers. Maybe because that's what they are, Christina thought. She forgot she was once like that, too.

After strumming a few chords and tuning the guitar, he started playing a song. Christina recognized immediately from the first few notes he plucked. It was a song that always made her cry, and thoughts of John made it even worse. He was playing *"Comin' Back to Me"* by Jefferson Airplane from their *Surrealistic Pillow* album. She tried to turn her focus to any of the other surrounding activities but could only hear that song. She unknowingly caressed the key around her neck, and a lone tear trickled down her cheek.

Ali noticed immediately and asked what was wrong.

"Nothing. It's a sad song that always makes me cry."

"Why? Does it make you think of your brother? I see you're holding your key."

She felt the key in her hand and gave a soft laugh.

"I hadn't realized I was holding it. I wasn't thinking of anyone special. There are pieces of music that can reach into a person's soul. No explainable reason, and you never know what's going to give you that chill down your spine. Art affects me like that, too. Sometimes something grabs you and makes you feel something. Like my "collection" that I'm sure you're sick of hearing about. My girl with her dog. Her face, and my imagining her finding her love in the crowd. Certain things thrill me to no end. Music is one of those, art is another."

"And clock chimes are another. Taraysa, sometimes you remind me of the elders at home. You don't speak like an American teenager and appear too wise for one so young. You seem to be an old soul in a young woman's form. And you're teaching me so much about so many things."

"I hope it's not all terrible stuff because I don't want you going home and your guardian telling your parents that a silly American girl corrupted you while at Berkeley."

"Never, Taraysa."

She smiled and asked if she could see his drawing.

"I'll show you later. I want to finish it before anyone sees it. There are so many things to give me inspiration in America, where there's freedom to be whatever you desire. America gives her people that gift. To become who you're meant to be instead of what's expected of you. To be the captain of your own ship, deciding which direction to go. I wish there was some way to draw the feelings of freedom and friendship I'm experiencing."

They continued working on their sketches and watching the peacock show. Christina saw René and waved to him, so he walked over and joined them while waiting for Athena to get out of class. The clock started to chime the hour, which put a smile on Christina's face.

René remarked to Ali, "Don't you have your dinner meeting this evening?"

Ali looked at his watch. "Ah, yes. I almost forgot. Thank you, Jean-René. It wouldn't have been pleasing to Khalid for me to miss our weekly dinner. Excuse me, Taraysa. I'll see you when I return or in the morning."

Ali gathered his things and left to get ready for his weekly meeting. René and Christina waited for Zoe to get out of class. They're scheduled to meet with O'Connell in thirty minutes.

"Did you use the pencil out here to record?"

"Yes, but I don't like it, and I feel horrible doing it. He's so kind and trusting. I don't want to ever hurt him. He's such a good person, René."

"Christina, don't get in too deep. It could be dangerous for you. He's a diplomat from a foreign country. Maintain friendship and contact but keep things from getting serious. He seems quite taken with you, and I don't want to see you put in danger."

"You don't think he's going to kidnap me and take me home to meet the parents, do you? Ali wouldn't do anything to endanger me. He's so sweet. I'm not worried."

"Well, you should be cautious. Men in his culture have supreme dominance over women, and I have to protect you. I want to protect you. Not only because it's my assignment, but because I have a deep fondness for you and Zoe. Please keep things under control."

"It's so confusing, René. Sent here to do this thing, and all we seem to be accomplishing is playing with emotions." She sighed heavily. "Don't worry. I'll be careful, but I really like him. I really, really like him a lot. He's not what I expected." She changed the subject. "And speaking of deep fondness for me and Zoe, I think it's time for the two of you to stop trying to hide your budding love affair from me. Do you think I can't tell what's going on between the two of you? I've known Zoe for over forty-five years, and I know when things are going well romantically. It's time for the two of you to fess up. Every time I ask her, she changes the subject."

"What makes you think we're having a love affair?"

She laughed. "In the first place, I have eyes. In the second place, she stopped obsessing over wanting to kiss you. I've been listening to her since she first met you, and then all of a sudden it stops? And there have been times when she starts to say something and then stops midsentence. It's so obvious to me that I find it hilarious that the two of you think I don't know. The jig is up, Monsieur. Why keep it from me? Does she think I'd be jealous? She knows better than that."

"Actually, it was my idea. I didn't want you thinking I'm not protecting you while carrying on with her. I'm not one to mix business with pleasure, and I was feeling the guilt of breaking my own rule. Forgive me?"

"Don't be silly! You can't tell the heart who to love because it decides for itself who it wishes to belong to. You both deserve some happiness. It's safe to tell her I know. She keeps denying it, but she can't fool me. I see through her like she's a clean glass window."

René smiled. "She should be coming any minute now." He noticed the crowd surrounding the inquisitive guy with the guitar. "I see we have a new fan club setting up over here. Is he someone famous?"

"To himself, maybe. He's acting like a pompous ass. Guys are such suckers if they think women fall for their crap. He's been using the same line since he started to entertain the female population here. 'Who are you and where have you been all my life?' Nauseating!" She used an unattractive voice to drive her point home. René looked over to where the crowd had gathered, with a few more girls approaching to see what was going on.

"You see that group of girls coming this way? Watch the peacock in action. Ali and I were watching him since he got here, and he's such a horse's ass."

Sure enough, as soon as the girls got close enough, he motioned them over and asked his question. René laughed. "Well, it looks like he's charmed the fairer sex in the area, but not you, eh? Has he asked you the question yet?"

"No, and he'd better not. Look at what a conceited jerk he is. He had the balls to blow me a kiss. Not once but twice! Like I'd ever want to speak to someone as vain as he is. Someone should tell him how unattractive self-promotion is. I'm sure he'd never believe it."

They sat and watched. René laughed and commented on it while Christina worked on her sketch, having lost all amusement for his antics. How many times can he ask that stupid question? Girls can be such simpering idiots.

Zoe came walking towards them and had to pass the fan club. Mr. Peacock got up and went up to Zoe and gave her the line. "My God, you're stunning. Who are you, luv, and where have you been all my life?"

In true Zee fashion she said, "Obviously, avoiding you, not wanting to encounter another asshole like you who thinks he's Adonis or Romeo. Get the fuck away from me!"

He stood there in shock, having met his match. She kept walking and gave him the finger, calling him names in multiple languages. René and Christina laughed because that was typical of Zoe. They waved her over.

"Who was that? Can you believe that asshole? We don't know him, do we, Tee?"

"No, Zee, I think we'd remember a jerk like that."

"Yeah, you're right, but doesn't he look kind of familiar? At first, I thought he was Bernie DelGiorno. I was going to say hi, but knew it wasn't him as soon as he opened his mouth."

Christina took another look at him from afar. "Yeah, he does, kind of. Maybe it's the hair? Anyway, we've been watching him in action, and he's the self-proclaimed god's gift to womanhood. He's cute, but the narcissism ruins the whole picture."

Christina gathered her things, and they headed off to O'Connell's office to give their report. As they walked, Christina told Zoe she knew her relationship with René had left the friend zone. She tried to deny it, but René told her Christina couldn't be fooled. Zoe whispered in her ear, "Now I can tell you all the details. I've been dying!" Christina laughed and was happy for her best bud.

René asked Christina for the pen with the recording of today's conversations, and they listened on the way there. At one point, Ali said he had to make sure he remembered everything he was supposed to bring with him tonight.

"Christina, do you know what he was to bring this evening?"

"No, as you can tell, I asked, but he didn't give me an answer."

"Well," said René, "we don't have much to report this week. I haven't seen Ali and Butch together much. He seems to spend all his time with you. Maybe you can find out more about what goes on between him and his guardian on Fridays."

"I'll try."

They arrived at O'Connell's office and went through the usual briefing. As every week, he made sure he brushed up close to Zoe with René doing his best to sandwich himself between them. The meetings last about half an hour. When they left, Christina stopped at the clock tower as usual and then met the two of them in the cafeteria. They got something to eat and headed back to their suite.

As they exited the stairs, René held his arms out for them to stop. He whispered, "Lock yourselves in your room and stay there until I let you know it's safe."

"What is it?" Zoe looked worried.

René pointed to his room. "I locked my door and turned off the lights as always. Someone's in my room. Get into your rooms. Now!"

They went into their room and sat silently, listening by the door for any kind of commotion, and heard nothing. They heard voices talking, some laughing, and then, eventually, there was a knock on the door.

Christina opened the door, and René was standing there. "Everything's fine. My roommate has finally arrived. Would you like to meet him?"

"Sure!" Zoe walked over to the door.

"Athena, Terry, I'd like you to meet my roommate, Adam Wallingford."

A familiar face stepped into view and greeted them with, "Well, hello…" A look of recognition crossed his face along with a disarming smile. "Hel-lo luvs! Who are you lovely ladies, and where have you been all my life?"

Christina slammed the door in his face, saying, "Oh, puh-leeze! Spare me! Give me a break and get over yourself!"

Outside the door, they could hear René laughing hysterically.

# CHAPTER 22

Adam stared at the door slammed in his face and wondered why she did that. It was the girl he saw when he pulled in on his bike. He felt a chill go up his spine and the back of his neck tingled when he first saw her and couldn't pull his gaze away from her. The way the sun and wind were playing with her hair gave each curl a blend of different colors. Her face was so beautiful, so serene, her neck, which he found to be so sensual, was so long and inviting.

When she opened her eyes, he lost his breath. He'd never seen eyes like that in his life, so huge and dark, and they caught him staring at her. He was embarrassed and flustered, so instead of being a gentleman and waving an apology or shrugging his shoulders, he covered it up by blowing a kiss. That usually worked on American girls, but not her, and he couldn't stop looking her way. When he noticed her looking at him, it emboldened him to wink at her and blow another kiss. That usually never fails to get a bird's attention. He's never received this sort of reaction from an American girl.

"Well, I say, that was quite cheeky!" He looked at his roommate, who was laughing, and felt much the same as he did when he was twelve. "I don't find it funny. She's quite the brassy little bird. Was it something I said, or was it blowing her kisses?"

He just met his roommate and didn't like that he was having a good time at his expense. Why would the university put him with a frigging Frog? Must be payback for last year when he was blamed for corrupting his knobheaded roommate by turning him on to the fine art of getting totally pissed on booze, speed and stoned out on grass, among other things. He didn't turn him on to it, they happened to find them at the same time. Rather made their lives more exciting. Isn't that what going to university in the bloody States is for?

He wasn't sure which bothered him more: his roommate laughing or this mare who didn't have the decency to even say hello. Jean-René eventually apologized. "Sorry, Adam. She's really genuinely nice. A word of advice: don't ask her those questions again. It may sound put-on."

Adam felt old hurts return, and the defenses came up. He realized it bothered her and intended to use that line on her every time he saw her. Rude, impudent bitch! He did nothing to make her react so rudely. He wasn't going to let another girl make him feel like a fool. This git made an enemy so now his new life's mission was to bugger her up.

Since coming to America for his first year at UC Berkeley a year ago, he'd come into himself. Being away from Britain's upper-crust society and all the girls who've known him since childhood was the best thing for him. They found him unattractive, but American girls rather liked him, especially after shedding some weight and losing the conservative haircut and clothing. He found something he was lacking - a sense of self.

Girls loved that he played the guitar and sang, that he was a performer, and they all went crackers for his accent. The attention he received from girls in America gave him the boost in confidence he was sorely lacking in England. He wasn't unloved back home. In fact, it was the opposite.

Viscount Adam Wallingford was the only living child of Lord Edward William Henry Charles Wallingford and Lady Charlotte Elizabeth Mary Cavendish Wallingford, with Edward being the only living descendant of a 15th-century duke in England. The family had vast estates, railroads, factories, farms, coal mines, businesses, and textile firms throughout England. Lord Wallingford was a member of the House of Lords, the family, part of the upper echelon of British society.

Adam was born late in his parents' lives. His mother had problems with every pregnancy. Two miscarried, two were stillborn, one was born prematurely and died shortly after birth, and three babies made it home. Eventually, all died within the first three months. They seemed to have an inability to thrive, leaving them heartbroken.

She was forty-one and quite shocked when her physician told her she was with child, in her fourth month. She assumed she was beginning her change of life when she skipped her monthly flow. Neither had hope nor expectation of this child surviving. They were resigned to the fact that the Wallingford family line would end with Charlotte and Edward. The news of this pregnancy didn't bring joy, only uneasiness and apprehension.

Charlotte thought she was too old to have a child. Edward worried her mental health would suffer when this pregnancy ended as the others had. They thought they could break the cycle of childhood deaths that seemed to plague the Wallingford line.

Edward's family tree seemed to be cursed. With each generation since the 15th century, only one child, always a male child with a birthmark on the back of his neck, seemed to survive. What began as a large line from three families, nephews of the childless original Duke, whittled down to one family, the Wallingford line, which absorbed the losses and gains of the family.

This family's book of the dead was heavy with childhood fatalities. Edward and Charlotte's offspring were no exception. With a childless home, they filled the void with charity work.

They didn't discuss names or get a nursery ready, having had too many sorrowful days dismantling the nursery and giving the layette items to Goodwill. The only item kept was the cradle, believed to have been used for the heirs of the original Duke, passed down for hundreds of years. After the death of her last child, Charlotte demanded that the cradle be put out of her sight. It only reminded her of all she'd lost.

They told no one, and she stayed at Grace Point, their estate away from London's society. Edward visited and stayed there when business dealings allowed, but Charlotte kept quietly to herself. She declined her usual invitations, including fundraising and charity events, stating only that she was unable to attend, never giving a reason. The staff was sworn to secrecy, and if any visitors came, they were told Lady Wallingford was traveling. The employees of Grace Point hoped against hope this child would live, for their employers were beloved by them.

As her time approached, she secretly made her way to London and stayed at the hospital under the watchful eye of her team of doctors. They'd given her positive reports, but she knew the outcome, especially at her advanced age. She basked in the joy of feeling the movement of life inside her, trying valiantly to partially disconnect from any feeling of expectation. She prayed, read the Bible, and promised that if this child lived, she would name the baby either Adam or Eve, depending on which God deemed to give her, praying for a boy because they were the ones who survived.

She chose the name Adam for another reason. It was the name of the original Duke, and no subsequent descendants were given this name. She hoped this honor would make him smile upon this child and let him live. The other reason was obvious. Adam: the first to live.

Word came to Edward that his wife was "in town," their code for in labor. He excused himself from Parliament and hurried to the hospital. Entering her suite of rooms, he found it empty. He was met by a nurse who scurried him into a waiting room, saying things were progressing quickly and she should deliver within minutes.

He paced until the doctor came in, with a huge smile on his face, and shook Edward's hand. "Congratulations, Old Boy. Your wife has given you an heir. You have a strong, healthy baby boy with a set of lungs that will make sure everyone hears his voice."

"Does he have the birthmark?"

"Bright red! Very visible. A very good sign, Edward, very good, indeed. You can see your wife and child now."

Edward burst into tears. He stodgily tried to contain his emotions, but the joy, love, and relief he felt overtook him, and he couldn't stop. He walked into the room where his beautiful, radiant wife was holding their son to her breast, and at that moment, knelt and thanked God for this joyful event.

Charlotte said quite confidently, "He's going to make it, Edward. I can feel it. He's strong. Look at him! And his birthmark is so bright!" He unlatched himself from the breast as Edward came closer. "Oh, Edward, he's strong and feisty already. I see such a difference from the others. Give him your finger!" Edward put his pinkie in his son's hand and could feel the strength in his grasp. He started to howl for food, and the strength of his voice gave them hope.

They were ecstatic, to say the least. Edward agreed to the name Adam and felt it very fitting. He, too, thought it might appease the powers that be to name their son after the original head of the family. A hopeless couple has been replaced by a jubilant new family. Mother and child were given a clean bill of health, and news spread quickly of the newest member of the Wallingford family, with many well-wishers dropping off gifts and sending wires of congratulations. Edward passed out cigars to members in the House of Lords and his gentlemen's clubs. He gave hefty bonuses to employees of all of their households, with extra bonuses given to those at Grace Point for the excellent care given to Lady Wallingford. Many a glass was raised, toasting young Master Adam Mayhew Edward George Wallingford. Their joy could not be contained.

His parents were totally devoted to him. He wasn't spoiled but definitely adored. He grew to know his place in society and how to act accordingly, accompanying his mother to her fundraising or charity functions. A nanny was employed but rarely used. Charlotte nursed him herself, attended to his needs, and spent her days with him. As with most children of privilege, he had tutors at home with his mother in attendance. From the time he was a baby, she spoke to him in French and German, so even as a young lad, he could converse in three languages.

Lord Wallingford brought him to gentlemen's sporting events such as polo, fox hunts, horse racing, and golf. Adam caught on quickly to everything and especially loved the stables where he'd brush their horses and question the trainers endlessly. He was riding at an early age and could handle any horse who responded to his kind demeanor. He was a dry sponge eager to soak up all the knowledge he could.

At eight years old, he started complaining of pain in his left hip. His parents thought they were growing pains, but when he screamed out while mounting his horse, they took him to a physician. Tests pointed to hip dysplasia, which is a misalignment of the hip joint. His parents, consumed with worry, were told treatment was available and if Adam cooperated, he'd completely recover.

They set up a room at Grace Point, his favorite residence, and had the needed traction consisting of pulleys, strings, weights, and a metal frame attached to his bed. It stretched the soft tissues around the hip to allow the femoral head of the leg bone to move back into the hip socket.

The room was on the main floor with large windows so he'd be able to see the outside world. He continued his studies and had a full-time private nurse and a doctor who visited him weekly. Adam wasn't an idle child and resented being attached to his bed. He missed the stables and riding his horses. When his nurse was out of sight, he'd undo the traction and get out of bed. He was told not to walk but to scoot along on his bum. He was uncooperative and fought his treatment daily. His parents tried to reason with him, and he'd smile and promise to behave the next day, but when the next day came, frustrations came with it.

After six months with no improvement, his doctors agreed Adam should enter hospital, where he'd be monitored and unable to disconnect himself from the traction. There was a hospital in

Southampton that successfully treated this ailment. His parents rented a flat nearby, and Adam had no choice but to go.

Once in hospital, he became sullen and unhappy. His mother visited daily, doing her best to cheer him up, even bringing his favorite cousin William to visit, but he was inconsolable. He hated being connected to the bed with none of his familiar people around him. He was unable to charm those who cared for him, which was most unusual as he had a way with adults and could elicit a smile from the sternest of Britain's stiff upper-class. Not at Southampton Hospital. They were immune to his lively personality and quirky sense of humor. His only happiness came from sweets his mother brought, and he overindulged. With limited physical activity, he began to gain weight.

As a diversion, his mother brought him a radio, and one of the younger orderlies on Adam's floor changed the channel from classical music to rock and roll. Adam became immediately hooked on the music generated in the United States. Elvis Presley, Ray Charles, Buddy Holly, Richie Valens, and Jerry Lee Lewis brought him out of his doldrums. But when he heard the blending harmonies of the Everly Brothers' "*All I Have To Do Is Dream*," he felt himself come alive and needed to hear all their music.

They bought him a phonograph and some LPs from the list of records he asked for. The phonograph was at his bedside, and he spent many happy hours with his newfound love of music. Of them all, he still favored the Everly Brothers with their sweet sound and felt their guitars spoke to him when listening to their songs floating from his phonograph.

Seeing his enthusiasm for music, his father made a surprise visit carrying a big box. He watched as Adam opened it to find a Custom Gibson Acoustic Guitar, with the case, shoulder strap, picks, and books. Adam's joy was obvious, and he thanked his father through tears. A music tutor was hired to come twice a week for the rest of his stay at Southampton to instruct him on tuning, playing, reading music, etc. The guitar became Adam's best friend.

Adam needed surgery for a full recovery. His parents were frantic but kept their fears from him. The surgery was successful, but Adam had to spend more time in bed with light exercises and movements to keep the other leg and hip working properly. There was no walking.

Adam was kept in hospital to recuperate faster, as they'd ensure he stayed firm with his treatment. Although bedridden, he busied himself with his guitar and soon knew the complete catalog of the Everly Brothers. When his mother would visit, he would play a song and sing to her. His enthusiasm was contagious, and Lady Wallingford relished his performances, so relieved he was alive and happy. Every day, she continued to bring his favorite sweets.

Adam was becoming quite chubby. No, not chubby, rotund. With little physical activity and eating the sweets his mother brought daily, he was fifty pounds overweight by the time he left hospital. He needed to start activities slowly but found something more important than any other pursuit: Music.

He loved the music from America, but now his country was taking the world by storm. When he was eleven, the British Invasion took over America, and British musicians began to control the airwaves. The Beatles, Dave Clark Five, Gerry & the Pacemakers, Herman's Hermits, The Rolling Stones, and the Animals became popular at home and abroad. The States were overtaken by the British Invasion. Adam immersed himself, learning to play many of their songs.

He resumed regular activities and, on many occasions, found himself among children in his social circle. Being overweight, he was belittled and teased about it, especially by girls, and his best mate, his cousin William, was teased about being a "poof." Their peers were ruthless and derided them for their appearance and their sexual orientation. They were cruel, heartless, and wanted nothing to do with either of them. Adam also had a slight case of acne, which made him more self-conscious about his appearance. He'd talk incessantly about music, and they'd quickly tire of it and walk away. Except William.

They were cousins of the same age and spent many hours together at Grace Point and school. Their mothers were sisters, and when William's mother passed away, Charlotte stepped in as much as possible. Charlotte noticed they were ostracized and found it upsetting because she wanted her child and her nephew to be happy and accepted. Two things were indisputable: William *was* a poof, which in no way altered the love she felt for him, and Adam definitely was not.

With Adam's trouble relating to his peers, they stayed with their original plan for his education, and Adam and William went to Eton. There he'd be with youths his own age and making lasting friendships and future business associates. They were sad to see him go, and Adam was sad to leave, but excited about getting away. He and William always looked forward to going to Eton.

Adam enjoyed his years there. He made quite a few good friends and many fine acquaintances. He was still chubby and one of the few boys who had never had sex with a girl. He was stuck in the mold of a music-obsessed, acne-faced fat boy and couldn't get out.

Upon graduation, his parents told him he could pick any university to attend, anywhere in the world. Adam didn't have to think twice. He had his heart set on UC Berkeley in the US. He'd kept abreast of the music scene, and this part of California was where a lot was currently happening. He felt an unexplainable pull to this university and was sure it was because of the music. His parents hoped for something a little more prestigious, but he charmed them, getting them to agree to two years and then a more serious course of study at university.

California, USA, was where Adam felt he belonged from the moment he walked off the airplane. His parents accompanied him in his first year, touring the campus, getting him settled. His mother cried when saying goodbye and told him to be sure to write. He embraced them both and watched as they sadly walked away.

His first year at Berkeley was full of new experiences. He and his roommate found the pleasures of no adult supervision and living in an altered state via grass, hash, LSD, speed, and alcohol. They barely squeaked by and attended classes infrequently.

Adam was always looking for music and those who created it. Unbeknownst to his parents, he bought a Harley-Davidson motorcycle, which he found to be the closest thing to riding a horse. He could travel to gigs and landed a number of them in local college pubs, with one of them offering him a regular spot on Friday nights from eight to midnight. As a wealthy aristocrat, he wanted no payment. It wasn't about the money, just the music.

He loved performing, playing, and singing. He wrote a few original songs that his audiences liked. While at Berkeley, the pounds melted away, he grew his hair out, the acne disappeared, he grew four inches and was suddenly "a major hunk."

One night after a gig, he shared a joint with the bartender and downed a few shots of tequila. He was quite high when a pretty girl came up to the bar. Adam looked at her and asked, "Who are you, luv, and where have you been all my life?" Worked like a charm! He got laid that night for the first time and discovered that whenever he asked that question to an American girl, he got lucky. Except with this girl. All the rejection he'd previously received swelled to the surface, and this bird was the one who was going to pay. He's going to have some fun getting under her skin.

He was taking Art History classes as the family has many extraordinary works of art dating back hundreds of years. If he were to whittle away two years at UC Berkeley, Lord Wallingford wanted him to walk away with some appreciation for the treasures he's to inherit. When Adam walked into his Impressionist History class and saw the object of his revenge sitting there with Ali, who was also on his floor, he hit the jackpot.

"Who are you?" he asked when their eyes met, and they were intoxicating. She turned away, scratching the back of her head with her middle finger. He laughed to himself. Cheeky bird! He caught her eye again and mouthed, "Where have..." with the same reaction. This was more fun than he thought.

During class one day, she reported on a stupid collection. She described these Impressionist paintings, although she didn't know all the artists, and described them vividly from memory. While giving her report, he decided to have some fun. He wrote in big letters, "Who R U? Where have U been all my life?" and held it up whenever the professor wasn't looking. It threw off her concentration and screwed up her perfect report.

His coup de grace was when she mentioned the expression on the face of a woman in her favorite painting of this collection. It was as if she found the face of her love in the crowd. Adam yelled out, "You should know that look because it's how Ali looks at you all the time." This brought peals of laughter, and she shot him the dirtiest look she could muster. Ali looked embarrassed. Adam couldn't resist; it was delicious buggering her up.

After class she called him an asshole to which he asked, "Who are you, luv?" As she's walking away, giving him the finger high in the air, he yelled, "And where have you been all my life?"

She yelled back, "As far away from you as I could get."

In the library, she's always with the poor, pathetic git Ali. He'd sneak up behind her and whisper in her ear and run off laughing. She'd tell him to grow up and get lost. Ali asked him to stop, to which Adam simply said, "Sorry chap, no. I'm enjoying myself."

Adam had a regular Friday night gig at the pub, and occasionally Sarah would join him for a few songs. She was usually with Jerry, a theater major she was besotted with. She had a brilliant voice and was a sweet girl whom he rather liked. They always had a good laugh together. Even she asked him to ease up on Terry, but so sorry, it's too much fun.

His roommate and Athena were hot and heavy; that's obvious. He couldn't figure out the relationship between Ali and Terry. He knows they aren't shagging, maybe not even snogging! And she…well, he can't figure her out. She's a hot number, that's for sure, and those eyes of hers could charm a snake. And that neck? So delicious. She could have her pick of any bloke. So why this "do not touch" attitude? Is she a lesbian or just uptight? He knows that type. Lived with them all his life. She's just a bitch.

Adam was taking some of the same music courses as Sarah and one evening in early October, they were jamming with some of their fellow music students in the Common Room. Sarah was hitting on Jerry, who's also in the performing arts program. There were about seven of them hanging out and were soon joined by the "traveling trio." Butch and Reggie weren't there which was a relief as their presence changed the atmosphere of the dorm.

René brought a twelve-pack of beer, which caused them all to take a break. They started drinking, smoking, and getting silly, telling stories of some of the crazy things they'd done in the past. One of the guys thought it would be fun to go around the room and spill the beans about their first sexual experience. They all took turns relating their experiences, which were quite humorous, and they were all chuckling and having a good time. Ali laughingly passed when it was his turn, saying his culture frowned upon such things.

Adam told his story of the girl in the bar and how his "questions" worked like a charm. Terry sat as far from him as possible, not making eye contact. He's still able to get under her skin and ask his "questions" again. He smiled, and she gave him the finger, saying, "Give it a rest, buddy. It's getting old, don't you think?" Sarah diverted the conversation and started talking about her first sexual experience when Butch and Regina entered the Common Room, getting in on the conversation. When it was Terry's turn, she stated she had no story to tell.

Ali was touching Terry's hair, and she seemed uncomfortable with it. Adam watched Ali as he moved her curls away from her neck (Oh that neck!) and started to kiss the nape of her neck. She started to respond, her eyes closed, and her head rocked and then she seemed to snap back and asked him quietly to stop.

He continued and his hand started to move up her thigh. All this talk of sex must have set Ali's juices flowing. He watched as she thwarted his advances. What a cold fish! He heard her say softly, "Ali, we've talked about this and you know where I stand. I'm not going down that road with you or anyone else. I don't want to start something that'll leave us both frustrated." Ali grabbed her face and tried to kiss her. When she pulled away, she looked at him for a moment, got up and said she was going to her room. As she walked towards the door, Adam said something loud enough for all to hear and immediately regretted it.

"Gee, Terry, aren't you the uptight one. No wonder you haven't had sex yet. If one were to put a piece of coal up your twat, within seconds there'd be a bright and shining diamond in its place."

Everyone laughed and thought it was very funny. Christina ran to her room and as she passed Adam she hissed, "I hate you!" to which he replied, "Who are you, luv, and where have you been all my life?"

Butch and Regina loudly laughed at the remark and Ali said, "I can't believe you could think something so uncouth and hurtful is funny. You disgust me," and then to Adam, "You should be ashamed of yourself. You're nothing but a bully." Ali knocked on her door, begging her to open it but she wouldn't answer.

Butch Morgan was beginning to get pissed. According to his father, he and that A-Rab roommate were supposed to become best buds, but the jerk barely spoke to him. The "disgusting" comment got under his skin. He's asked him to go barhopping, get high or hang out together and he always refuses. He only wants to be with that bitch or Frenchy and his squeeze. Ali's such a loser! When he does talk to him it's usually about that stupid bitch. "Oh, she's so smart." "She's so beautiful." It's enough to make him puke! It grossed him out to think how pussy whipped Ali is. Whatever. He's a stupid ass.

At least he has Regina and the two of them are like two peas in a pod, both from Southern political families with Southern upbringing. She ain't too bad in the sack, either. She sometimes acts like she's the queen shit, but what the hell? She's an easy lay and has lots of sexual tricks up her sleeve, especially when she gets high, so he happily supplies her with whatever drug she wants. She's easy to please – a joint here and there, maybe some hash and it puts her in a sexually giving mood.

They go to Butch's room because Ali's never there. He walked in on her giving him a blow job and they got quite a laugh out of his reaction. Such an A-Rab Prissy Prude. Princey could have any girl who'd bang him or take care of his peter, but he insists on hanging out with Polly Purebred and letting the best years of his sexual life slip by. What a fucking jerk. He actually had the nerve to scold Butch after catching Regina polishing the old knob.

Butch told him, "Princey, this is the US of A, home of the sexually liberated gals. Get with it!" He even offered to help him find a girl who'd put out but he looked at him with disgust and walked away. Yeah, his dormmates all look down on him. Do they think they can treat Butch Morgan like he's dirt under their feet and get away with it? They'll be sorry. He'll end up richer and more powerful than all of them put together.

The packet his daddy told him would arrive came a few days ago and it's a crucial part of the plan that's going to make all of them rich – millionaires! When it arrived, Butch signed his name where indicated and then gave to Ali which he brought to his guardian on their Friday night dinner. It should take a week or two to get back from Zatari but once it's signed by all those concerned, Ali will bring it back to Butch who's to send it back to his father by certified mail. All this is top secret, and nobody is to know about it. He tried to figure out what it was about, but the language was pretty much gibberish to him. He didn't care what it was about, only that he was going to make a shitload of money.

Hopefully, this deal will allow him to flip them all the bird. But he had his agenda and ideas. He thought it was time to set into motion the plan he started to hatch when told a deal was to be made with the A-Rabs and he'd be rooming with this pain in the ass A-Rab prince.

Yes, soon it'll be time to set that plan in motion, but now he's decided he needs to take care of Little Miss Snow White, too. He had to be in the right place, at the right time, with the right intended victims. He'd show them exactly who Butch Morgan is and to never underestimate, disrespect or piss him off.

He couldn't wait to pull off his little devious schemes. His daddy isn't the only one who knows how to give a good screwing. He laughed that devious cackle at his own private joke.

# CHAPTER 23

College life was in full swing as October was winding down. Halloween was coming, and students were gearing up for the big weekend, with costume parties planned throughout the dorms.

Christina left early one morning, and when she returned, she rushed into the Common Room announcing to everyone there, "A performance of *Jesus Christ Superstar* is being performed by the American Conservatory at Geary Theater! I saw the poster in this little shop I went to. Who's going with me? The tickets are selling out quickly, and all that's left is this Friday, October 29th."

No one answered. Sarah was the first to say no. "I'd definitely go, but I have a theater workshop I have to attend that starts Friday. Sorry, Terry."

She looked at Zoe and René, and he laughed, shaking his head.

"Athena? Jean-René? What about the two of you? Please!"

"Tee, you know I'm not a fan because you drove me nuts with it, and I have a paper due. Schoolwork keeps butting in on my Berkeley experience. Besides, I think I have a date," Zoe said, smiling at René. He looked at Christina and shrugged.

Christina remembered René planned a romantic evening for the two of them that night. Zoe's chomping at the bit to get him in the sack, but he wants to make it special for her.

"I'll go with you," Ali said from the hallway.

"Ali, that's not a good idea. It's Friday night, and it would make trouble with your guardian. It's ok."

"I'll tell Khalid I can't meet with him that night."

"Thanks, Ali, but I'd better pass on the whole thing. Forget I mentioned it. It's sweet of you to offer." She gave him a peck on the cheek.

"Are you sure? I'd like to see it. I'll go with you if you change your mind."

"Thanks, but I'm already corrupting you, and this would send him over the edge. I'd have to start looking over my shoulders." She said with a laugh but was serious.

"Taraysa, I'd never let anyone harm you."

"I know. I'm kidding. But he wouldn't like it and it's not worth it."

"As you wish. On a different subject, what time do you want to go to the exhibition?"

Their drawing class was exhibiting everyone's inspiration drawings in a gallery on campus. The opening was that day and ran through the weekend.

"How about two o'clock? That gives me enough time to get ready."

"By the way," Zoe asked, "where'd you go this morning? I woke up and you were already gone."

"I had something to do and that's when I saw the poster for *Jesus Christ Superstar*. I'll tell you about it later. Gotta get ready to go." She had gone to the local head shop to make some purchases. She wasn't going to let asshole Adam have the last word.

He's the most annoying guy she'd ever met; rude, conceited, infuriating and a pain in the ass! Granted, he's cute and looks hot in those hip-hugger jeans and shirt he buttons only the three middle ones leaving the upper and lower ones undone. Not that she noticed. It gets ruined by his attitude.

If he doesn't stop with this "who are you?" bullshit, she's going to strangle him. He hit below the belt with that diamonds remark. Totally uncalled for and in front of everyone. It's none of his business what she does or doesn't do. But she'll have the last laugh.

She got ready and met Ali in the Common Room. She was starting to have strong feelings for him and knew she should be taking a step back. "Let's go check out all the inspirations."

The "Inspiration" works were in pencil only, no color. Christina's drawing had the Bell Tower at its center with protesters, a mime, musicians, and religious fanatics on the grounds beneath it. Musical notes signified the ringing of the chimes leaving no doubt that the Campanile was her inspiration.

Ali did a take on the freedoms he saw - speech, dress, to be whatever you desire, with the American flag in a sort of washout in the background. Freedom is different in his country and his drawing was impressive. It'll be interesting seeing what inspires others. As they got to the door of the gallery, Ali said he was nervous.

"Why be nervous? You're so talented, and your drawing's great."

"What if people don't like it?"

"Screw 'em!"

"What if *you* don't like it?"

"Ali, I've seen it and it's really good. It doesn't matter what people say. You've done your best and that's what's important."

They found the gallery with the, *"Inspirations"* banner and walked in. She was immediately floored. There, as big as life, were three portraits of her; one was her enjoying the wind, eyes closed and hair flying behind her with the Sather Tower lightly sketched in the background, one with a scarf on her head trying to control her curls and one of her laughing. She looked down to see who the artist was, and it was Ali.

"Do you like them, Taraysa?"

"Ali! What happened to the one you showed me? I'm like, in shock! When did you do these? They're wonderful! And you can definitely tell it's me. They're so lifelike. But what about all the freedoms that inspire you?"

"*You* are my inspiration, Taraysa, my inspiration for everything. I've told you and I'll tell you again. I've never met anyone like you. I've fallen in love with you and the thought of the end of this semester coming is like a death sentence for me. I don't want our friendship to end."

"Can we talk about this after? We have to see all the drawings for our class critique and then we'll go somewhere and talk. I'm flattered by the portraits you've done of me."

"There are many more. I have your face, your laugh, everything about you etched in my heart and mind."

"Let's check out the others so we can leave and talk."

Walking through the exhibit, people pointed to Christina, asking if she's the one in the portraits. Their professor told Ali his drawings had gotten the most attention and feedback from viewers. There's an offer to buy one if he's interested in selling it at the end of the semester. Although he was flattered, he said they weren't for sale. After they'd been through and taken notes, including Adam's, which was a guitar with musical notes surrounding it, they left as the clock chimed four. Christina had an idea.

"I know where we can talk. Race you to the clock tower." She started to run, laughing and Ali, a little surprised at first, hesitated and then did a full-on run, chasing after her. She reached the tower first with him close on her heels. They were both trying to catch their breath when Ali came up and kissed her for the first time, and she kissed him back. And it was good, incredibly good. It felt wonderful to feel the warm lips of another and the thrill of a first kiss. His lips felt warm and sweet, and it had been ages since she kissed anyone like that. She looked into his eyes and couldn't deny it. She has deep feelings for him and that can't be. Christina! Snap out of it!

"I was afraid you'd block my attempt to kiss you like you did at the dorm," Ali said as he moved a newly formed curl from her eyes.

"Our first kiss wasn't for the entire dorm to share, especially with all Sarah's chums there. It's special between you and me. And because of the conversations at the time, I was uncomfortable. I don't make out in public."

"I'm sorry, Taraysa."

"It's okay, and we had our first kiss at my inspirational tower."

She knocked on Stan's door and they exchanged their usual pleasantries. She asked if they could go up so she could show Ali her secret treasure. While climbing, she gave Ali a mini tutorial. When they got to the top, Ali gasped at the view.

"Isn't it magnificent? And when the chimes aren't ringing, it's so quiet and peaceful. I come here every Friday evening."

"I see why it's your secret treasure. Every direction gives a beautiful view, and more beautiful because you're in it." They kissed again, and he held her tightly. "I sketched those drawings from memory, except the one where you're enjoying the wind and the bells when we were sketching for our inspiration. You looked enchanting with your eyes closed and the wind flying through your curls. I took advantage of the moment to capture it. I hope you're not offended."

"Of course not. I'm flattered."

"Are you angry that I captured a moment of you?"

She smiled and put her head on his shoulder. "We all capture moments. That's what memories are: a way to relive something whenever we want. We'll have lots of those before December. And you're very talented, Ali, with a gift for art, and gifts need to be used and shared. If art isn't readily accepted in your culture, maybe you're meant to change that. Art lifts the spirits. All manner of the Arts."

She paused a moment, taking in the inspiring view. "Look at the vastness of the water. Up here, looking at this view, it's like the universe is saying you can be whatever you want to be." They stared at the Pacific Ocean. "Like the vastness of the ocean, the limits of the human soul are boundless with chances of greatness. Great things lie in store for you, Ali. And not just me, the great Madame Fortune sees it too."

They laughed, and he got serious. "Some people in my culture believe one shouldn't paint portraits because it steals their soul. I couldn't stop myself from drawing your face because I do want to possess you. Not only your soul, I want all of you…forever. I cannot help but draw your face because it's the only thing I see. It's all I want to see."

She faced him, "Ali, I have strong feelings for you. I could easily fall in love with you if I let myself, but I can't. Things can't work out for us."

"Why do you keep saying that?"

"Because it's true. You have to see all the obstacles that cannot be overcome, and you mentioned one. Your culture doesn't allow portraits. I've spent most of my life drawing people. There are too many differences we can't overcome, that *I* can't overcome."

"Such as?"

"Such as *everything*! I'm an Italian Irish middle-class Catholic girl from the Northeast United States. You're a Muslim prince from an oil-rich country in the Middle East. I've lived with freedoms that women in your country can only dream about. The equality of men and women is dawning here in America. I can't live by the rules and restrictions of your kingdom.

"Your original inspiration piece was about the freedoms so new to you that I've known my whole life. Do you think it's fair to send me backwards, control who I am, and what I can do? I won't give up my heritage or my religion. It's who I am, and in your country, the girl you love won't be the same person. I'll become bitter, and you'll despise me."

"I could never despise you." After a pause, he said, "We could live here."

"Your family expects you to live in your country. I'd never be accepted as your wife because of who I am and where I'm from. I'd probably be thrown into a harem or something like that. A prince has to marry a woman the king approves of, and it wouldn't be me. And my father would never approve of someone from the Middle East for his daughter. If he had the slightest inkling of your thoughts, I'd be back home under lock and key in record time."

Ali stared out silently at the Golden Gate Bridge. Without moving his gaze, he said, "But I love you. Doesn't that mean something?"

"Of course it does! It means a great deal." She started tearing up because of the hurt look on his face. "If we're allowed to marry, which I doubt, how long before you become tired of me and take a second wife and a third? I'd be shunned, and who knows what would happen to me in your country? I could never feel secure knowing I'm not accepted and that you can replace me with no consequences. Then where do I go? What do I do? If we have children, what happens to them? Women are property, and you know I couldn't tolerate that. I'm too stubborn and liberated. The sense of humor you love will be gone. I need stability and a safe haven, and I want my children to have the same freedoms I've been given, which can't happen in your country. I'd lose my rights as soon as my feet hit your soil."

He took out his hanky and wiped her tears. She squeezed his hand and held on to it. "Oh, Ali, if only things were different, but they aren't. My life and family are here, and this is where I belong. Let's make the most of the time we have left. Can't we continue to enjoy each other's company and not think of December?"

"I understand, but it doesn't make me happy. You've thought everything through and made the most logical decision. My heart is heavy, but I understand. You're right, I wouldn't want that for you. But the thought of living without you…"

"You're young. There'll be many women in your life. If I'm your first love, you won't forget me, and I promise I'll never forget you. You're my very own Prince Charming."

"Prince Charming?"

"And the differences between us continue. I'll tell you all about him on the walk home."

They climbed down and continued their conversation on the way back to the dorm, stopping at the cafeteria for something to eat. They went back to the Common Room and worked on the critique assignment while still fresh in their heads. Before they went to their rooms, they made plans for breakfast at eight the next morning, before class. They shared a kiss goodnight and parted. Christina thought to herself, oh God, what am I doing?

When Ali didn't show up for breakfast, she went to his room and knocked on the door. Butch answered stating Ali was still sleeping. She looked at the hall clock and it was nine-thirty. Ali was an early riser, so she became concerned.

"Is he ok? We're supposed to meet for breakfast. Is he in there?" She tried to get into the room, but Butch blocked the way.

"Sorry, honey bunch, y'all can't come in. He's fine, just tired. Maybe he'll see you later."

"He's still asleep? That's not like him. I'd like to see for myself if he's ok." She tried pushing her way into the room but was blocked at every angle.

"Hit the road bitch. He's sleeping and y'all ain't coming into my room."

"What did you do to him? You did something, Butch." He did his evil laugh. "Did you drug him or something? I know you have drugs that you're selling from this room. Let me in to see him."

"Sorry, girly, no dice. My room and y'all ain't getting in. Maybe Princey will see y'all later."

She started to yell Ali's name and got no response. "What've you done to him?" She kept trying to push into the room, but Butch kept blocking the way.

"I'm going to find the RA and get to the bottom of this."

Butch grabbed her arm and squeezed it hard with his nails digging into her skin and said through his teeth, "You mind your own fucking business, Miss Priss."

"Let go of me, you slimy shithead!" and when he wouldn't, she slapped him across the face with her free hand.

He laughed and squeezed tighter. "Don't y'all go forgetting that I'm his roommate, and Princey and me got business to do. Y'all go ahead and get the RA. He'll see him sleeping. Me and Princey gotta discuss some stuff and y'all need to stay the fuck out of it. Understand, Missy? I think this little love affair y'all have going with him is about to come to an end." He cackled and let go of her arm.

"You're loathsome, but you know that already. Don't think for one second that I won't find out what you're up to with Ali. Maybe not today, or tomorrow, but someday I'll know exactly what went on in this room and if you've done anything to hurt Ali in any way, you'll pay." She turned and walked away.

"Groovy! Can't wait! Here, sweetie, got this for you."

She turned around, and he gave her the finger, laughing his sick laugh.

"Keep laughing Butch. Someday the joke will be on you."

She didn't see Ali that day. She knocked on his door a few times but there was no answer the first time and Butch told her to get lost the next. She'll have to wait to see him in class tomorrow.

He didn't show up for class, and she was worried. She told Zoe and René about her encounter with Butch, and René became concerned.

"It sounds like Butch has a plan. Maybe they need to discuss their fathers' plan and don't want you distracting Ali. The relationship Ali has with you may be disrupting the friendship that's supposed to develop between these two. It's the end of October, and they only have a month and a half to forge the friendship that's meant to be. Maybe it's for the best."

"René! I can't believe what you're saying. They're like night and day…literally. One's evil and darkness, and the other's light and kindness."

"That may be, but you need to remember, we aren't here to change things from what's to be, only to find out and prove what was. Did you record your conversations with them?"

She handed him the pen that's always in her pocket but didn't mention she shut it off before they went into the Inspiration Gallery. It was against René's rules, but she wanted to keep personal conversations private. René took it and replaced it with another.

"I'll take this and listen carefully to everything. Make sure, especially now, that you have one of these at all times. I'm not prying into your life. I need to know what's going on. Understand? *Oui*?"

"*Oui*," she said unenthusiastically.

When Ali finally emerged, he looked terrible. His eyes were hollow, and his face was ashen. He brushed off Christina's concerns, saying he's fine. She knew he wasn't. He's expecting a phone call and then he and Butch had plans.

"What? Why?"

"Taraysa, it's complicated and something I must do. Please, no questions. I've no choice."

"Ok, if that's what you need, I guess I have to accept that."

"It's not what I need. You know what I need. Maybe I'll see you later. I wish I could carry you in my pocket."

"Ali, I have the next best thing." She went to her room and got the peace sign pin with the recording device and pinned it on his jacket.

"Now, along with your Berkeley cap, you're extra cool with a peace sign and have me with you at the same time. It's not for keeps, it's for when we aren't together. Ok?"

"Thank you." He hugged her and they kissed as Butch came out of his room.

"How sweet. Hey Princey, you kiss her with that mouth?"

"Drop dead, Butch." Christina knew he'd done something to Ali but didn't know what.

Everyone was in the Common Room except Adam, who was in his room playing his guitar, and Regina, who went home because of a "family emergency." Sarah told them Regina was pregnant with Butch's child and went somewhere for an abortion. They agreed it's a gene pool they wouldn't want for their future offspring.

Christina whispered to René that Ali was expecting a phone call, so René maneuvered himself closer to the phone with his pen ready. The phone rang and René answered it. Although he understood, he responded in French that he didn't. The operator switched to French, saying there was a person-to-person call for Prince Ali. René called Ali to the phone and clicked his pen to record Ali's side of the conversation. As soon as Ali hung up, he and Butch left. With the pin securely fastened to Ali's jacket, they'll eventually find out what's going on with the two of them.

According to the conversation, papers from Senator Morgan were signed by the King to be delivered to Ali through Khalid this Friday. Ali had to repeat the instructions to whoever was on the other end, enabling René to discover the gist of the call. Ali was to befriend Butch and stop this dalliance with the American girl. René nodded to Zoe and Christina, motioning them to their room, where he listened to the recorded conversation again.

"The papers we've been sent for will be delivered back to Butch this Friday. Zoe and I have plans immediately following our meeting with O'Connell. Christina, can you stick around and make sure Ali brought the papers back with him? Somehow, we'll need to get our hands on them and see if it's what we need. I'll make sure I'm wearing my St. Remigius medal from now on in case I need to photo anything. Zoe and I will return Friday night, probably by ten thirty. I wish I could reschedule, but everything's set. What time does Ali usually return?"

"I'm not sure. I know Khalid's trying to keep his corruption from me and the United States down to a minimum. Khalid's trying to keep him true to the practices of his religion."

"I'm relieved as I felt we weren't making progress, but I'll feel better when the evidence is in our hands."

"René, how can I get him to give me the papers? He won't if they're that important."

"Once they're here, we'll think of something. Don't worry about that part. That's my job. You need to find out if the papers are with him when he returns. Agreed?"

"Agreed."

They left the room and went back into the Common Room. Sarah was there with Jerry, working on lines for their workshop on Friday. Zoe and Christina were certain he was gay but hadn't come out yet. In the 1970s, homosexuality was still very much in the closet. She was head over heels for him. They knew it was inevitable that somewhere down the line, she's going to get hurt.

Zoe, René, and Christina played the audience for Sarah and Jerry. Adam came in to get something to drink and pulled his "who are you" on Christina. She gave him the look of steel and went into her room, gathered a handful of her recent purchases, and went back into the Common Room. It's showtime!

# CHAPTER 24

Christina walked past Adam and as he started to ask, "his questions," there was a "plink" on the floor diverting his attention enough to stop him mid "who are you...". The item rolled and stopped. As she walked, every few steps there'd be another "plink and roll." She walked to the sink, poured a glass of water, and there were three "plinks" in a row. Everyone looked at the sparkly little gems on the floor. Christina sat on the couch, dropped three more on the cushion, and got up. Adam was laughing so hard that tears were running down his face.

Christina asked, "What's so funny, Adam? I don't see anything funny. Do you see anything funny, Sarah?"

Sarah was howling with laughter, trying to explain to Jerry what it was about. Christina kept walking around the room "plinking," asking, "What's so funny?"

She stood in front of Adam who was trying to compose himself but unable to stop laughing and said to him, "You know, I took your advice. I got to thinking about what you said and thought Wow! Easy way to make a fortune! I got some coal, gave it a try and voila, you were right! I've got freaking diamonds dropping everywhere!"

She continued to drop quartz crystal "diamonds" she got from the head shop. They were from the Herkimer Diamond Mines in New York State. The Pucci family spent many a summer afternoon digging and mining for the treasures that, especially after a good rainfall, were plentiful. They're not real diamonds, but they're the closest thing to them.

"Touché, Terry." Adam was laughing so hard he could barely talk. "Caught me off guard with that bit of action. Very well played." He applauded, still laughing. "Brilliant, actually. I'm gob smacked!" Christina dropped twelve little crystals all over the Common Room.

"Oh, Terry, you're actually quite a nutter! Brilliant! I wave the white flag! I reckon you got me there! Honestly, I don't deserve a comical comeback after my horrid behavior, and actually quite out of character. Would you accept an apology from a contemptible chap?"

She picked some diamonds off the floor and said, "Only if you accept a few of my personal creations." She put the crystals in his hand, and they shook on it. Everyone was laughing.

"I have one condition: no more of those questions, ok? I'm sorry for slamming the door in your face. That was rude and unwelcoming and out of character for me, but you've been acting like an asshole. Peace?"

"Peace, Terry. Friends?"

"Friends. But not best friends because diamonds are a girl's best friend." The roaring laughter started all over again.

Still laughing, he said, "You're a lovely but strange bird. I'll miss buggering you up. I was having quite the jolly time of it. Sorry to say, but it was bloody fun."

"Honestly, Adam, it's something I would've done too."

"Must be we're both daft."

They laughed, agreeing it felt good to no longer have tension between them. They started talking, eventually discussing their assignment on the mediums of Degas. Adam asked if she'd read what he'd written so far.

"I need to pass this class. It's the one thing my father asked of me, and I don't want to let him down. As you can probably imagine, I'm using my time at Berkeley for play instead of study. My weakness is music, which eats away my free time. I'd be ever so grateful for some pointers."

"I'd be happy to. Watch out if you have to give a report. I may hold up a sign saying, 'Diamonds are a girl's best friend.'"

He laughed, went to his room, got the paper and Christina started to look it over.

"Terry, I have a fantastic idea. Instead of reading this boring paper, how'd you like to take a walk to a pub for a drink or take a ride on my Harley?"

She thought about it, trying to size him up. He seemed sincere, but he'd been driving her insane since he got here, so she was leery.

"Come on, luv. It'll be my way of making it up to you for being such a toad."

"Yeah, you've definitely been a toad. What the hell, why not? Let's walk if you don't mind. I'd love a ride on your Harley, but not today. Give me a minute to grab my jacket."

Zoe saw Tee get her jacket. "Where are you going?"

She looked at Adam, "Where are we going?"

"I thought Poorman's Pub, where I play on Fridays. Is that alright?"

"Fine with me." She answered Zoe, "We're going to Poorman's Pub. Anyone want to join us?"

There was a collective negative answer, so Adam and Christina left. As they walked by the Campanile, it chimed the hour of eight, and she gave a mini tutorial of what she'd learned about it and her love for it. The pub wasn't far, and it was a mild night with only a slight chill in the air. Being a weeknight it wasn't as crowded as on weekends. They got a booth and Adam got a beer and Christina got a ginger ale.

As he sat down he asked, "Would you like a fag?"

"What?"

"A fag, a cigarette. What did you think I said?"

"I wasn't sure. Truthfully, I'd love one, but I can't start that again. I quit a while ago."

"I don't smoke either, at least not fags. Everyone smokes, so I like to offer one as an ice breaker." He put the cigarettes back into his pocket. "So, you don't smoke, drink, or shag. What do you do?"

"Well…, I manufacture diamonds."

He started to laugh and shook his head. "Touché again! You're off your nut."

"Thanks, I think."

They sat for a while getting to know each other better. He told her about his parents, childhood, constant rejection (which Christina doubted), his hip problem, and how he came to love music. He apologized many times for the diamond remark and how ashamed he felt after he said it.

"It's actually quite refreshing in this day and age to meet someone with enough self-confidence to stick to their morals and not go in for all this bloody free love thing. Quite admirable. Though I'm sure there's a long line of broken hearts behind you."

"No, there aren't. With my father's strict parenting, you'd find it believable. Dating isn't for his daughters. Plus, we've got Catholic guilt. Oh, by the way, you owe Ali an apology for the remark in class while I was giving my report. It's hard enough for him being so far from home and in such a foreign atmosphere. You made him feel very self-conscious and uncomfortable. Not cool, Adam. That was worse than your diamond comment."

"Yeah, I regret that too. So unlike me. I don't know why I said that. No, I take that back. It was more to bugger you, I guess. So, if you don't mind me asking, what is the lowdown on you and Ali? Are you two dating or friends? If it's none of my business, just say so. I find it curious."

"Curious?"

"Well, from where I sit, you two seem to be a couple. He seems to be totally bonkers, while you seem to hold him off. You're always together, but are you together? See? Curious."

"Well, it's a situation and relationship that can go no further than this semester. I like him quite a bit, which I didn't think possible. I could like him more if there weren't such hopeless circumstances, but things are what they are. There can be no future in anything that occurs here in Berkeley. I'm leaving at the end of this semester. For me, it's a one-shot deal and then I'm gone."

"What makes it hopeless? Doesn't love conquer all?"

"Only in fairy stories. There's no happily ever after. Life is hard, sometimes ugly, and you can get knocked to your knees. Ali is royalty from Zatari, and I'm a small-town girl from America. I live where freedom is for everyone, and he lives where women can get beheaded for minor accusations. I'm Catholic, he's Muslim. Love can't conquer all that, and even if it did, I know my future. Ali isn't the one who holds my heart." She subconsciously reached for the key around her neck.

"The key to your heart?"

She looked at the key and let out a sad laugh. "Not really. It's complicated. I'm here until the end of this semester, and then I go home."

"Are you digging on that guy?"

"Ali?"

"No, the guy with the key to your heart?"

"Well, I haven't met him, yet I know everything about him. What can I say? I'm hopelessly romantic."

They walked back to the dorm, and Christina thanked him for a nice evening and said she was glad the tension was gone between them. Her first impression was way off, and he's nothing at all like her original opinion of him. She was surprised to find he was shy, blushed often, and totally unassuming, especially because he's a major hunk with eyes the most unbelievable shade of blue surrounded by long, lush lashes. She felt ashamed she'd misjudged him. But he acted like an asshole. They parted with a "see ya," and as Christina headed toward her room, he said, "Terry, wait a moment."

She turned, and he walked towards her. "I should explain myself now that we're on speaking terms because it's haunting me. That first day when I rode in on my motorbike, my eyes were drawn to this girl who seemed to be somewhere wonderful. The wind was blowing her hair, sending it flying behind her in lovely cascades of curls and colors. Her neck looked inviting and graceful, like a beautiful swan. You see, necks are my weakness. I was spellbound and couldn't take my eyes off you. When you caught me, I was mortified and covered up by being cheeky. Please accept my humble apology." He held out his hand. "Forgiven?"

She took his hand and looked into his eyes. At that moment, the clock started to chime the hour of ten. It changed the focus of her attention. She smiled, turning her head toward the sound and said while still holding his hand, "Ya know, there's something about the chimes of that clock tower. That day, I was enjoying it all, the smells, the breeze, the warmth of the sun, the hustle and bustle around me, the sweet sound of a Harley, and then the bells started to ring. Yeah, I was pretty close to heaven. When I opened my eyes, I was being stared at. It abruptly brought me back to reality from such a peaceful place with an unexpected audience and a disrespectful air kiss. Thank you for apologizing. It's appreciated."

They said goodnight and walked to their respective rooms as the chimes ended.

Zoe asked about her evening and said laughingly, "When those diamonds started dropping, I thought I was going to piss my pants. Tee, where do you get these ideas?"

"I guess I'm off my nutter," she said using her best British accent.

Ali wasn't happy about the new budding friendship. She told him about the diamonds, and he didn't think it was funny. He kept saying they went on a date.

"Ali, it was one soda and a get-to-know-you conversation, not a date. That's it, nothing more. Ali, I'm getting worried about you. You don't look well. What happened? I can tell something isn't right and it has to be something with Butch. What's he done to you? I'll kick his ass if he's hurt you."

"I'm stuck, Taraysa. I can't speak of it. He's shamed me in the worst way. I hate him. Before, I was sad to see this semester end, now I can't wait for it so I can get him out of my sight. I'm so sorry. I'd rather spend every second with you, but…"

"What's he done? Does this have to do with your phone call from home?"

"Partially, yes. I can't say any more. My heart is breaking for it wishes to be with you, and in the last few weeks I'll be here, I cannot. I'll treasure the moments we spend together in class, away from him. I fear we'll be unable to spend much time together."

Christina tried to get him to tell her more, but he clammed up and shut down. She assumed his father laid down the law.

Christina saw very little of Ali that week, except for their mutual classes. She realized that she'd spent all her free time with him and now found herself alone. Zoe and René were constantly together, and she wasn't going to butt in on them. Sarah was always with Jerry and with Regina gone, Butch had taken control of Ali's free time.

It relieved René to see the friendship between Ali and Butch beginning to blossom without Christina dominating Ali's time. He was looking forward to this night with Zoe to get his mind off everything. He'd been plagued by worries, but relieved that the proof they needed may soon be within their grasp. He was too distracted by Zoe and couldn't think things through. He felt helpless, futile, and wondered if the risks they'd taken to get here were worth it, especially with the losses he and Christina endured. He had a feeling of unease he couldn't shake.

He wanted to make sure everything was perfect for his date with Zoe on Friday. He knew it really wouldn't be her first sexual experience, but these are most unusual circumstances. It was all planned, and he skipped class to ensure everything was perfect.

He booked a suite at a hotel near the college and spent the day getting the room ready for their first romantic escapade with jasmine candles, bubble bath, and fresh flowers. He contacted the college radio station, asking them to play a certain song at a certain time. He'd thought of everything.

Zoe knew nothing about his plans, only that he had a surprise for her. He tried since meeting her to keep things on a professional level, but one cannot deny the heart to play the song when its strings are strumming for only one. He told Christina his plan, knowing she wouldn't divulge anything to Zoe.

Now, with the news that the proof they came for possibly within their grasp tonight, it added worry to an already full plate. If he hadn't spent most of his stipend for the last two months on this one evening, he would've changed the date, but with his limited resources, it was impossible. He couldn't wait another day to feel her body in the closeness lovers have. It had to be tonight. He could wait no longer and found it difficult to think straight about things because his ponderings always came back to her.

He's had many troublesome thoughts these past couple of months, one being their backup. Glenn continuously brushed off questions about them. Were they here? If so, could they assist Christina or at least observe Ali when he returns? He's uncomfortable not being there when this was the moment they'd been waiting for. He'll make sure they're back before Ali returns from his meeting with Khalid. He planned for them to spend the night together, waking up beside one another, but that had to change. It wouldn't have the same effect waking up together in a dorm room with either of their roommates in the next bed.

He was concerned the relationship between Butch and Ali wasn't developing. All their intelligence stated they became close, life-long friends during their semester at Berkeley. Since Ali's arrival he had eyes only for Christina and they were constant companions. They had become close too fast and that troubled him. He kept telling her to be careful and she kept brushing him off. She doesn't know how dangerous it can become with Ali's diplomatic status.

René knew Christina was the reason their friendship wasn't developing, but he couldn't fault her for doing what she was sent to do. Messing with time has ways of biting your ass. He hoped with the new turn of events, Butch and Ali will develop the friendship they're meant to have.

On Friday of the big Halloween weekend, the trio went to their weekly meeting with O'Connell, reporting the week's progress, which included Butch and Ali's budding friendship. Everyone was relieved except Christina. According to Ali's phone conversation, the papers will arrive back with him tonight and they'll hopefully have the weekend before Butch sends them off to his father, giving them time to discover if they're what they're looking for.

He asked Zoe to dress for dinner and met them at O'Connell's office at the usual time. René cut their meeting short, saying they're anticipating something this evening and after the discussion about Ali and Butch's new-found friendship, the three of them left. Before they parted ways, René went over with Christina what to look for and when they'd be back. He apologized for not being there tonight, but she raised her eyebrows and told them to have fun.

At the restaurant, they sat at a table with a fantastic view of San Francisco. They toasted each other with a glass of wine and Zoe kept asking what the big surprise was and René smiled and said, "You'll see."

After dinner, they walked to the hotel and went to the bar where a band played mostly music of a quieter nature than the music of the current day. They danced slowly and sensually together, with the heat of their bodies against each other. He held her close to his body and she could feel his longing. While dancing, he kissed her neck, whispered in French how much he desired her, and his hands explored her back. At the end of their dance, he cupped her face in his hands and kissed her with all the pent-up craving he was feeling to possess her.

Upon entering the room, Zoe saw a bottle of champagne on ice, candles, and flowers everywhere, and rose petals on and around the bed. René lit the candles and started the bubble bath. He popped the champagne and poured them each a glass. Zoe started to undress, and he stopped her. "No, *Chérie*, not so fast. That's my privilege tonight." He turned the radio to the college station. He had ten minutes until they played the song he requested.

They toasted "to us," and he sat her down on the couch and lifted her legs, taking off her shoes and massaging her feet, murmuring in French how much he needed her, desired her, wanted her, loved her, kissing her ankles, inching his way up her thighs. Zoe was whispering the same, begging him to make love to her.

At exactly seven on the dot, the DJ said, "This next song is for Zoe with the message, '*Je t'aime. Je veux être avec toi pour toujours.*' Hope I didn't butcher that too much. Not sure what it means, but somebody out there is digging this chick. For Zoe, with love, here are the Righteous Brothers singing one of the greatest love songs ever recorded, *Unchained Melody.*"

As the song began, René took her hands and lifted her off the couch. Throughout the song, he very slowly began to undress her, kissing and murmuring as he did. When her dress was off, he kissed every inch of her stomach, arms, neck, and inner thighs. He slowly undid her bra, revealed her youthful breasts, and kissed them both, using his tongue to taste every bit of her. She was moaning with desire and begging him to make love to her. He removed her panties and kissed around her heavenly triangle. He picked her up and brought her into the bathroom and gently laid her in the tub. He got the champagne, took off his clothes, and joined her in the bath. They continued their fondling of one another, with the smell of jasmine everywhere.

He lovingly dried her off and carried her to the bed covered with rose petals. He began kissing her everywhere, tasting her, feeling as though he was trying to memorize every inch of her. He kissed her neck and settled on her lips, and they kissed as if they were trying to become one with their tongues.

When they both could take no more, he opened her legs and tried to penetrate her. He was met with her virgin muscle trying to stop his passage. He didn't want to hurt her, so he gently pushed and released until he was granted access into her body. It felt unbelievable. It wasn't long until she was screaming in ecstasy, and when he was sure she had achieved an orgasm, he pulled back, they changed positions, and she reached the heights of passion again. Once she had her second orgasm, he allowed himself to succumb to the delight of her body and reached his sexual peak.

They lay together, their bodies spent and intertwined, a sea of arms and legs connected like a gnarled tree. Zoe said, "Thank you for this wonderful, romantic night. You're such a tender and passionate man, and you've made this a night I'll never forget. Please tell me it won't end. I wish we could stay here and live our lives from this moment, here in this time and this place. Don't leave me when we return to our lives."

"I'm afraid, Madame Zoe, you're stuck with me, now and forever. After the death of Adele and Mercedes, I felt empty. Then I walked into Martin's office and saw you standing there, and you breathed life back into me. I don't fall in love easily. It's not in my nature, but you've captured my heart. Please be careful with it. If it breaks again, there can be no repair. *Je t'aime. Je veux être avec toi pour toujours.*"

They kissed again and lay in each other's arms, falling into a deep, contented, and unplanned sleep.

# CHAPTER 25

After leaving their meeting, Christina watched Zoe and René walking hand in hand to their romantic rendezvous. She hated to admit it, but she was envious. She wiped away tears and told herself to suck it up and stop feeling sorry for yourself. But one can't change how you feel, and she felt sad and alone. She wished she'd gotten a ticket to *Jesus Christ Superstar* so she wouldn't have to spend tonight alone. She walked to the Sather Tower, which was locked because of Halloween pranksters, which made her go into a full-on cry.

She sat at the base of the Tower until she stopped crying. She decided to stop at the cafeteria and pick up some soup for supper. She missed being with Ali, which made her despise Butch even more. What has he done to him?

In the meantime, Butch scored some high-grade speed and headed to his room to cut it with baby powder. He stopped at a store and bought aluminum foil to separate it into ten, twenty, and, for the big spenders, fifty-dollar packets. Hopefully, Ali would be gone by the time he got there, so he could get an early start getting his product ready for the big Friday night sales. Friday seemed to be the night everyone was itching to party, and Halloween was an added excuse for revelry. In his few months at Berkeley, Butch achieved the dubious honor of being one of the top dope dealers. This weekend was going to be extra profitable because there were nonstop parties everywhere.

The dorm was empty, so he could do what he needed to and get out before any of the ass-wipes in his dorm came back. Regina was the only one he could tolerate, and that bitch was off unloading their kid into a garbage can. Bitching whore! On the one hand, the last thing he wanted was a kid, but on the other hand, it bothered him that she was so willing to throw his kid in the trash. That pissed him off in a big way. She wouldn't even discuss it with him. He hated it when fucking women ruled the roost. That bitch wouldn't give him a choice in this decision. He didn't want the kid or the responsibility, but it raised his hackles that she was so flippant about obliterating his potential offspring.

He sat at his desk and emptied the speed and baby powder and got ready to mix the two together and portion them out according to price. He left some of the speed in its pure state for himself and snorted a line before getting started. He measured and sorted the mixed powders, then put the foil-wrapped packets into three baggies. He got his pot, hash, Quaaludes, and Black Beauties and was getting ready to head out for the night. He decided before he left, he'd snort another line of the pure stuff and have it available for his own consumption throughout the night.

Everything was loaded into his jacket, ready for a night of big sales. He made a line of speed and snorted it. Immediately after inhaling the drug, he heard someone in the dorm, which made him paranoid. He made sure all the evidence of drug paraphernalia and his jacket were out of sight.

Christina dropped her soup off in the Common Room and thought she'd see if Ali was still there. She checked to make sure she didn't look like she'd been crying and knocked on his door. She was disappointed when Butch opened it.

When he saw it was Christina, he thought to himself, what the fuck does she want? She reminded him of Vi with her spunky attitude, huge eyes and dark curly hair and he hated to be reminded of her.

"Has Ali left yet?"

"Who wants to know?'

"Butch, go fuck yourself."

After their verbal exchange, he realized this was the perfect night for his BIG plan. Fell into his lap like his fairy godmother waved her wand. He'd taken Ali away from her, and now he's going to take from her the one thing she treasured. Her cherry!

He'd been mulling this over since he heard she was a virgin. Ali was so taken with her, always gushing over everything about her that Butch wouldn't be happy until he ruined her. But how could that be achieved when she's never alone? He was waiting for the chance and knew that with no one else in the dorm, it was now or never. He flew into action and, with the effects of the snorted speed, he moved like lightning.

He grabbed the chloral hydrate and waited. She went into her room, and he flew into action. What a dumb stupid bitch! Her soup was right out there, as if inviting him to spike it. He quickly poured some into her soup, not caring if it was enough or too much.

She went back into the Common Room with her art book, and he had enough time to make it to the sink and pour a glass of water.

As he swallowed the water, he could taste the speed he'd snorted minutes ago. Butchie's gonna have some fun tonight!

When she saw him, she asked, "Are you planning on being in here, because if you are, I'm going to my room."

"Just came in for a glass of water, honey bunch. I'm leaving. How sad. Poor little pseudo princess all alone on a Friday night and a big party weekend, too. Boo hoo for you."

"Eat shit and die, asshole."

He cackled and went back to his room to put the chloral hydrate in his drawer.

Christina sat down, opened her book, and started eating her soup.

Butch snuck into the hallway and watched through the crack in the doorway. It wouldn't take long for the drug to take effect. He impatiently waited for her to drop off. This was going to be his best night since coming to Berkeley. He'll wait until Ali gives him the signed papers to tell him of his escapade with his sweetie. He'll dump her in her room and lock the door, and no one will know. Princey won't say a word because he knows the consequences. Butch had Ali right where he wanted him. That part of his plan was taken care of very efficiently. Now it's time for the bitch.

Looking at Monet's *Waterlilies* was the last thing she remembered.

He watched her head begin to bob up and down, trying to stay awake. She tried to get up and walk, but fell to the floor, knocking the chair over. Butch sprang into action. With her eyes closed, she looked so much like Vi that it threw him off guard. How dare she? He ripped open her blouse and saw the key. He grabbed it, trying to tear it off her neck, but the chain was sturdy, so it took a few tries. He studied the key for a second and then threw it somewhere in the Common Room. He snickered as he took hold of her hair and dragged her into the hallway.

As he maneuvered her across the floor, her body was banging into walls and doorways, hindering his progress. He picked her up to carry her the rest of the way and was shocked at how light she was. When he got to his doorway, he fumbled with the doorknob and was unable to get it to turn. Frustrated, he threw her to the ground, with her landing on her side. He opened the door and used her hair to drag her into his room. He picked her up and threw her on the bed like she was a rag doll. He went to the doorway, looked both ways to make sure no one saw or heard what was going on, shut the door, and locked it. His erection was telling him it was cherry-popping time.

In his speed-induced frenzy, he unzipped her jeans and ripped them from her body. Her underpants came off at the same time. She was on her back, so he decided to get his Swiss army knife and slice the bra in the front and got the idea of tying her hands to the top of the bed using her bra. While executing his devious plan, he was talking to himself and laughing. He got her all trussed and roughly squeezed her breasts, remarking to himself how small they were. He unzipped his pants and released the monster that would do the desired damage. He was ready to break into her body when he decided he would like her to be aware of what he was doing. He wanted her awake.

He slapped her face a few times, roughly shook her, tried to open her eyes, but she was out cold. He became angry because he wanted to look in her eyes when he thrust himself into her. He backhanded her hard across the face, and his ring cut her lip. He kept yelling at her to wake up, and she wouldn't. Before he could stop himself, his anger took over, and he started pummeling her face. She moaned and moved her head from side to side, which was a momentary relief because he thought he might have killed her. He started telling her what he was going to do to her, laughing his sickening snicker. He spread her legs and was all set to impale her with his penis when the door opened.

"Honorable Khalid, I've explained why I cannot stay this evening. Please have the car take me back to the college. I've work to do for my classes." Ali was in Khalid's sitting room, which was where they convened before dinner.

"Your father is insistent that you honor his wishes and keep our weekly meetings. He needs to know what's going on and that you're not dishonoring your family."

At that remark, Ali lost his temper. "I've been doing what he's asked me to do! I'm living with the most loathsome, disgraceful person I've ever met to fulfill his wishes. Did he consider that before he threw me into this den of repugnancy? I've been made to endure much from Morgan, all at his behest. I hope whatever they've planned is worth it to him." He stood up and started to walk out of the room. Khalid stopped him.

"Ali! You cannot go! We've much to discuss and our evening prayers. Besides, the cook made some of your favorite dishes. You don't want to disappoint him."

"Give me the papers I'm to bring to Butch. I'm going back to my room now. If these papers are so important, I suggest you get them to me immediately because I'm leaving. If you won't call the car, I will. Make no mistake, Khalid, you're a subject and I'm a prince. You may suggest, but I'm not obligated to be obedient to your wishes; you're to be obedient to mine."

"Ali, I cannot believe how you're speaking! What's happening to you? I knew it wasn't a good idea for you to come to this country of no morals and infidels. You've been tainted by your current surroundings. Your father will be most displeased to hear of this!"

"I'm sure once my father has whatever it is I was sent for, he won't care about my welfare. If he did, he would've never put me in the position he has. Power and money are the only things that interest him. He doesn't give a second thought to me. Has he asked you once how I was, if I was well, or how my studies are progressing? I know exactly where I fit in the household of the royal family. All he's concerned about is the deal with the Morgans. We're all dealing with the devil, but I'm the one who has to walk through hell. Now give me the papers and call for the car. That's not a request, it's an order. I'm leaving now."

Khalid opened a safe and took out a large envelope. Before handing it to Ali, he said, "I don't know what's happened, but I believe it's this girl, this Taraysa, who's putting strange ideas into your head. You must stop this relationship with her at once."

Ali laughed sarcastically. "How would you know anything about her? You've found it so convenient to blame her for anything you find fault with. I'm weary of your constant denunciation of her. She's the only good thing that's happened this whole time I've been in America. Don't pretend to know what's going on in my life. I order you, keep out of it. Give me the papers so I can leave. I've much to do and it doesn't include dinner or evening prayers with you."

He snatched the envelope out of Khalid's hand and stormed out of the room, slamming the door behind him, yelling for the driver to take him back to the college.

The car doors slammed and Khalid watched as it pulled away. He went back to the safe and retrieved a small black book. He found what he was looking for, walked to the telephone, and dialed a number. When the call was answered, he said, "It's time for you to find out everything you can on that girl."

There was talk on the other end, and Khalid answered, "Ali is my responsibility, and I'll be accountable for any repercussions. I know what Ali's ordered. He's being childish and obstinate. I represent the king in my request. I want parents' names and occupations, family history, siblings, if there are any criminals in her family background, and where her ancestors came from. Understood? I'll send you what I've been given by the college. My driver will bring it over. I'm expecting results by Monday." He abruptly hung up the phone. He'll find out the truth about this American girl regardless of Ali's wishes.

On the ride back to the college, Ali's mind was spinning. He was avoiding a confrontation with Khalid, but when he mentioned dishonoring his family, it hit a nerve. Thinking about it, Ali pulled his cap over his eyes and kicked the back of the front seat, making the driver jump and ask if something was wrong. Ali didn't answer, turned his head, looking out the window. He took a small envelope out of his jacket pocket, looked at the contents, and smiled. It'll be a good night.

When they drove up to his dorm, Ali put the small envelope back into his pocket and grabbed the packet for Morgan. Damn his father for putting him in the middle of this vile family. He didn't know or care what the contents were and wanted no part of any of it. From knowing Butch, he knew this venture was corrupt. He thanked the driver and started towards his dorm.

He got to his floor, and it was eerily quiet. Although he's never here on Friday evenings, it felt too hushed for a college dorm. A radio was usually on in at least one of the rooms. He stopped by Terry's room. The door was ajar, but she wasn't in there, which was odd. He looked in the Common Room, and a chair was knocked over, and her art book was on the floor. He started calling out her name and getting no reply. The only noise was coming from his room. Ali's heart sank because he thought Butch would've been gone by now. Ali's plans for this evening would undoubtedly be ruined by Butch. He thought he could escape him tonight because he's with Khalid on Fridays.

Hopefully, the packet of papers will occupy him tonight and give him a break from the new "buddy rule."

He turned the knob to his room and it was locked. He knew Butch was in there because he could hear him. Maybe he's having sex with some co-ed. He thought about turning around and leaving but decided if Butch were having sex with someone, Ali would enjoy interrupting. He put his key in the lock and opened the door. For a moment, he was frozen where he stood. This can't be happening! The packet of papers fell from his hands onto the floor in the hallway outside his room.

"Hey, Princey! What're y'all doing here? Wasn't expecting y'all back for a few hours."

"What are you doing?" Ali screamed. "Is that Taraysa?" On Butch's bed, Christina was passed out, with her arms tied above her head to the headboard. Her shirt was ripped with her breasts exposed. She was naked from the waist down, and her jeans and underwear were thrown on the floor. Butch was poised with his penis out, straddling her, getting ready to rape her.

"Princey, if y'all know what's good for ya, y'all better turn around and forget what y'all are seeing here. Y'all know what'll happen if y'all don't do as I say. Besides, I'm only getting her ready for you, buddy, breaking her in, popping that cherry for ya. I'm doin' y'all a favor here. I'll let y'all have sloppy seconds."

Ali was momentarily paralyzed, petrified to do anything. He couldn't let anything happen to her, especially this! Whatever the consequences to himself, he has to get her out of this disgusting scenario. He couldn't let this animal steal her innocence. He ran to Butch, pushing him away from her, knocking him to the floor. "Leave her alone! Get away from her." He tried to untie her and Butch pounced on him, pushing him out of the way.

"Sorry, Princey, but y'all know the rules. I call the shots, remember? What I say goes and I say I'm gonna pop that cherry and then fuck her brains out. Wanna watch?"

"Get away from her!" he screamed. "Why would you do this? Her face is bleeding! Have you beaten her?" Ali shouted her name, over and over, with no response. "What've you done to her? You've drugged her!" They fought with each other, and any time Ali was free from Butch's grasp, he tried untying her. He kept calling her name, asking if she was all right, trying to cover her up. Butch kept up the onslaught by trying to push him out of the room. Ali pushed back with all his might and Butch fell into the hallway, slipping on the packet of papers, ripping the envelope, sending papers sailing into the Common Room, banging his head hard against the wall. Ali continued to try to untie Christina.

Butch went into a frenzy of anger which was exacerbated by the speed. He was like a mad, rabid dog. His common sense was thickly veiled by the drug and the pain from banging his head. He was going to get that A-Rab out of the way, even if he had to kill him. He rushed into the room while Ali was trying to free Terry and grabbed his throat from behind, trying to squeeze the life out of him. Butch was a madman in a drug induced fury and kept saying he was going to kill Ali and then ruin his precious little sweetheart. A small part of his brain kept telling him to stop, but his body wouldn't listen. He heard a loud crack and blacked out.

As Ali felt himself blacking out, a chair came down on Butch's head from behind, knocking him out. Ali fell to his knees, holding his throat and coughing. He turned around and Adam was standing there with the remnants of one of the dorm chairs. Adam took one look at the bed and immediately grabbed the blanket from the other bed and covered her up.

"What in bloody hell is going on here? Is this Butch's doing?" Ali nodded his head, still coughing.

Adam untied her arms and wrapped her in the blanket. He picked her up and carried her into his room, away from Butch who looked as though he was beginning to come around. He set her on his bed and tried to wake her by slapping her gently on the cheeks, but she was out like a light. He checked her breathing, and she seemed to be breathing regularly. He checked the pulse on her neck, and it was strong and steady.

Once Ali stopped coughing, he went to the doorway of Adam's room and watched as he tried to revive her. "Is she going to be ok? This is my fault." His voice was coarse and raspy from the attack.

Adam ignored the remark because all his attention was on Terry. He wondered whether they should bring her to the infirmary or maybe even hospital. He wasn't sure what to do. They have to keep a careful eye on her tonight and make sure she starts to respond.

As they were getting her settled, Butch came to, rubbed his head, and saw the remnants of the chair that rendered him unconscious. Who hit him from behind? Terry was no longer on his bed, so he went looking for her and to beat the shit out of that fucking A-Rab and whoever knocked him out.

He heard voices in Adam's room and found the three of them in there. Intense rage because of his foiled plan came back to the surface. He grabbed Ali and threw him out into the hallway. He held him up against the wall in a chokehold with his forearm across Ali's neck, spouting gibberish about his ruined plan and yelling threats.

"I was doing it for you, Princey. Breaking her in, your little Miss Purity. Y'all don't appreciate anything, do you? Now that y'all have found out my plan, I may be forced to tell everyone about you! Won't your daddy be proud?"

The next thing he knew, he was pulled away from Ali, and Adam got him with a right hook that knocked him off his feet and bloodied his nose. "You know, mate, I took boxing at Eton so if you want to continue, I'd be ever so happy to beat the living shit right out of you. Unfortunately, I'm more concerned about the girl you drugged and were going to rape and your roommate who you tried to strangle. You'd better get the fuck away from here because I'm trying to hold myself back."

Butch writhed on the ground. It was that fucking Limey! Where the hell did he come from anyway, and what was Ali doing back so soon? He touched his nose and saw the blood on his fingers.

"Don't think y'all won't pay for this, you Limey shithead. My father will hear of this."

The reality of the past five minutes hit Adam, and his anger rose. "On second thought, I *will* beat the shit out of you." He ran up to Butch, picked him up and threw some body punches. The reality of what he was caught doing by the two of them finally reached Butch's addled brain and had to get out of there before Adam landed any more punches.

Butch broke away, holding his stomach, running towards the stairs to get away from Adam. Adam chased after him and kicked him in the ass as he reached the stairs. Butch realized while running down the stairs, he didn't have his drug jacket and his pants were still unzipped. He ran blindly into the night, still feeling the effects of the speed, not sure where to go or what to do.

Adam yelled, "Don't forget to tell your father how I kicked your ass, literally! I'm sure he would be quite chuffed to hear what you've done this evening. If I were you, I'd bloody well think twice before coming anywhere near these rooms. I promise you'll be lucky to walk away with your life. Either that or I'll call a bobby and you can spend the night in the nick."

Adam shook his right hand and looked at his swollen knuckles, thinking it was worth it. He walked to Ali, who was sitting up against the wall, crying. Adam held his hand out to help him up, asking if he was hurt. Ali couldn't answer; he kept sobbing.

"Well, mate, I'd say you did a bloody fantastic job getting here when you did. You saved the day, mate." Ali was inconsolable and continued sobbing. "Why don't you go into my room and check on our girl while I get a washcloth and see if we can get the blood off her face."

Ali went into the room, still crying. He saw his small envelope on the floor and picked it up and peeked at its contents. This was supposed to be a wonderful night. He only wanted to make her happy, see her smile, hear her laugh. Instead, it was a nightmare. He flopped onto the other bed, looked at his beautiful Taraysa and cried.

Adam got the washcloth and gently wiped the blood off her face. She had a nasty cut on her lip, and her eyes were starting to get black and blue. He put the washcloth on her forehead and asked Ali to keep an eye on her, thinking that giving him something to do would help him stop crying. Adam was so angry looking at her. He felt like punching the wall but instead started picking up the disarray in the suite.

He went into Ali's room and picked up the remnants of the chair. He looked around the room and opened some of Butch's drawers and found a bottle of chloral hydrate among other drugs. That dirty bastard! The bottle looked half gone. He wondered how many girls he had drugged this year. He took the bottle, walked into the bathroom, and poured the contents into the toilet. Butch wasn't going to be able to do this to anyone else. He picked up Butch's jacket with all the drugs in the pockets and put it in his room making sure Butch couldn't get it.

He went into the Common Room and picked up Terry's art book and the chair she'd been sitting on. Something shiny caught his eye in a corner of the room. He walked over and picked up Terry's key, which she always wears. "Bloody bastard ripped it from her neck!" he said aloud to no one. He looked for the chain and found it in pieces. His anger was building, wondering what he had done to her while unconscious.

He picked up the papers scattered around the room. They looked like official documents or contracts with the Morgan name on them. Adam smiled. "Bloody fantastic! Karma's a bitch, eh Butchie Boy? I'll hold on to these for a while." He brought them into his room and surreptitiously put them inside his desk with his music books and papers. He'll let Butch sweat it out worrying about their whereabouts. Ali was still crying with his face in his hands, paying no attention to what Adam was doing at his desk. Adam walked over to him, trying to console him, saying he was the hero who saved the girl.

"Come on then. It's quite alright now. You were brilliant! She's safe with us, right, mate? We'll watch over her together. Stay in my room as long as you like. I don't think you should be in your room tonight, in case that dirty bugger returns. We shan't let her be alone tonight either. We'll stay here until Jean-René and Athena return. I wish we could dress her in something. It may put us in quite a pickle when she awakens."

Ali looked at Adam and said, "Thank you for all you've done tonight. I don't know what would've happened if you didn't show up when you did."

"I only did what a proper English gentleman would do. I say, it's a good thing I broke a string on my guitar and came back for extras. Once again, music saves the day."

Ali opened the small envelope and took out its contents. He looked at the two tickets to *"Jesus Christ Superstar"* and said, "We also must thank Jesus Christ Superstar, because if not for that, I'd still be at Khalid's. It was a surprise. She wanted to see it but couldn't find anyone to go with. I wanted to make her happy."

"And what you did tonight will make her happy." He rubbed the back of his neck and sighed. "It's been quite an exciting evening. We'll have to report this to the proper authorities. Can't let Butch get away with this. Not only what he's done to Terry, but he tried to kill you."

Panic overtook Ali's face, which Adam picked up immediately. "We'll talk about this tomorrow when Terry's awake, and we're thinking more clearly. No reason to fret over it now. I need to call the Pub to cancel my gig for tonight. Can I get you something to drink? Beer? Wine? I think I may need ice for my knuckles."

Ali shook his head. "Maybe a glass of water. I don't drink alcohol."

"Well, mate, if there ever was a night for it, this is it!"

"I've missed my evening prayers tonight and feel I shouldn't. Thank you, Adam, for being a friend. I'm going to need all the friends I can get."

"Keep an eye on our girl while I head out to call the Pub. I'll only be a minute. Lock the door. I'll get your glass of water, some ice, and a beer. I certainly could use one right about now." He rubbed the back of his neck and left.

Ali looked at Terry, who was still out cold, and felt tears welling up again in his eyes. He thanked Allah for letting him find Butch before he could take advantage of her drugged state. But now there are consequences to think of. Life just got even more complicated for Ali.

René awoke with a start. He jumped up and looked at the clock. *Merde*! It was 2:40 am. When he jumped it caused Zoe to awaken.

"What's the matter?'

"We've overslept. We should've been back to the dorm by ten thirty. We have to get back there immediately!"

"Why? There's nothing we can do now. Everyone will be sleeping, and we won't find anything out until morning. Please, let's enjoy this night completely. I want to wake up next to you, especially after the wonderful night we've had. There's no way to get our hands on those papers tonight, and we don't know if that's what Ali was bringing back."

"I don't feel right. Something's wrong. I've an uneasy feeling in my gut."

"Please, let's stay here tonight. Tee is a big girl and can handle this. If anyone can weasel something out of Ali, it's her. Put those thoughts out of your head and lie next to me. I don't want to cheapen our night by sneaking out like we've done something wrong. I've never felt anything so right in my life."

"Ah, Madame Zoe, you're bewitching! You're probably right. We can't do anything now, or can we?" He got back into bed and made love to her again before the two of them fell asleep until morning.

Butch stopped running somewhere off campus, sat under a tree and cried. While commiserating over the possible ramifications for his actions, he remembered the papers Ali was to give him, which made him cry harder.

They were important, the basis for the whole impending operation between the two families, the reason he's at Berkeley. Without these signed contracts, there's no deal. His father won't take failure lightly.

He had to get those papers, but how? He needed to stay out of sight for a few days and let things cool down. If Ali knows what's good for him, he'll make sure the authorities aren't notified about what transpired in their dorm this evening. If he does, Ali can kiss his ass goodbye.

Butch had no friends and nowhere to go. He'd see if he could crash one of the Halloween parties. Maybe with all the commotion and crowds everywhere, he could blend in with other passed-out co-eds who overindulged in drugs and alcohol. He wished he had grabbed his jacket. He won't be as welcome as usual without his drugs to dole out.

He hated them all, not just his dorm mates, but everyone.

# CHAPTER 26

Christina opened her eyes and was in a complete fog and had never felt so sick in her life. The left side of her face hurt, and her head felt like a freight train was trying to exit her forehead. She thought, "If I move, I'm going to puke. I can't get the kids to their after-school activities today. John is going to have to take over for me. I can't even open my eyes because my head hurts so badly, and I think my left eye is puffed shut."

"John?" Is that my voice? She thought. I sound like a feeble old lady. Is that me speaking? She tried to yell, but it only came out barely above a whisper. "John! Can you hear me? Please come here!" She hoped he was home. He's usually in the sitting room doing his paperwork. "John!" She had to keep calling until he answered. "John, please! Help!"

"What do you need, Terry?"

Terry? Who the hell is Terry? Did he say Christina or Terry? Whatever!

"John, I feel awful. If I move, I'm gonna puke. Please take the kids today. Dance is at four thirty. Kenzie - tap shoes, Roxie - pointe shoes, and a hairnet. Johnny – cleats. Soccer at four, town park, Johnny first, and then the girls. I can't eat, dinner's on you. Thanks, sweetie."

"What? Terry?"

"Who the hell is Terry? Please, John, no jokes today, I'm too sick. I'm going back to sleep. My head is splitting! Will you take the kids?"

"Um…yeah, of course, whatever you need. Anything else?"

"No, thanks. You're the best hubby in the world. Check me later to make sure I'm alive."

"Right-o."

As she fell back to sleep, praying for her head to stop pounding, she wondered why John was speaking with a British accent. She fell back into a deep sleep.

When she tried to open her eyes again, the room was too bright. She thought she'd feel better after sleeping, but her head still ached, and she was still nauseous. She turned away from the light and covered her face with a pillow, noticing she was naked. She never slept naked. Ever! What the hell's going on?

She wondered if she'd done something stupid. She tried to remember what happened, but her mind was blank. She wasn't sure where she was, and her face hurt. As she moved her hair out of her face, she wondered why it was long. She hasn't had long hair in ages. The left side of her lip, cheek, and eye were swollen and painful to the touch, with only her right eye able to open. She felt like she'd been in a boxing match. She squinted her one eye open and slightly moved the pillow so she could see her surroundings. Where the hell am I?

With one eye, she scanned the room, and things started to come back to her. Not how she got where she was, but she remembered where she was; in a dorm room, 1971, UC Berkeley, but not my room. She thought it might be René's room, but she wasn't sure. Her vision was blurred, and Ali was sleeping in the other bed. Is it his room? As soon as she lifted the pillow, she noticed Adam sitting in a chair by the bed. When he saw she was awake, he came to the bedside with a glass of water.

"Jesus Christ, Terry! Let me get some ice for your eye!" She noticed his jaw seemed to tighten in anger, and he was rubbing his neck. She hoped she didn't do something to piss him off because they just became friends.

He came back with some ice in a washcloth. "Can you hold this on your eye? If not, I'll hold it for you."

"Please, close the blinds. Too bright."

He did as she asked, and the darker room made it easier for her to open one eye.

"Thanks for the ice. I think I can hold it."

"How are you feeling? Please, take a spot of water. It'll help if you drink some. I can make you a cup of tea if you're feeling up to it." As he held the water up to her lips, he adjusted the blanket, wrapping her naked body so nothing private was visible. The water was deliciously cold, and she was so thirsty.

"Where am I? What are you doing here, and what the hell happened? Did I pass out and fall on my face or something?" She opened the blanket and looked down at her naked body. "What happened to my clothes?"

"Oh, Terry! I'm so relieved you're awake. You're in my room right now. It's been quite the night, but I assure you, Ali and I were perfect gentlemen. It is Terry, isn't it?"

"What?"

"Your name. It's Terry, isn't it?"

"Of course, it's Terry. Why'd you ask that? Have I turned into an old bag lady or something?" She was getting paranoid that she had reverted to her 21st-century self. She was relieved as she looked down again and saw she still had her teenage body. That's when she noticed her key was gone and started to panic.

"Oh no! Oh, God, please, no! My key! Where's my key? I have to find my key!" She groped at her neck, and it wasn't there. She padded around the bed and the blanket surrounding her and it wasn't there. She felt the back of her neck and could feel a long, thin cut going across the back of it, and became frantic. "My key! I have to find my key!" She tried to get out of bed, but as soon as she lifted herself, she became dizzy, and the pounding of her head intensified.

"Terry, please, don't worry. I have your key right here." He held it up to her open eye and put it in her hand. Relief ran through her entire body. "I found it in the Common Room. The chain is quite broken into some rather small pieces, so we'll have to get you a new one. Would you like me to hold on to it for you until you're feeling better? I swear to you, I'll keep it safe."

She had nowhere to put it at the moment, so she reluctantly handed it back to him. "Thank you for finding it. It's very precious and can't be replaced. Promise me you'll put it somewhere safe until I at least have a pocket to put it in."

Her crying awakened Ali. He opened his eyes, looked over at her, and started to cry.

"Oh Taraysa, I'm so sorry. Look at you! This is my fault! When I think of what could have happened, it makes me sick!"

"Ali, please shhhh! My head is splitting. I can't deal with this right now. And what happened to my face? Is it really bad? Do you have a mirror?"

Adam grabbed Ali and said they'd be right back. She could hear them in the hallway, Ali crying and Adam trying to calm him. She tried to hear what they were saying, but it was painful trying to think. She lay back down and put the pillow over her head with the ice up against her face.

Adam came back into the room and said, "If it's quite alright with you, we'll talk about this later when you're feeling better, but I assure you, you're safe now, maybe a tad worse for wear. Would you care to rest more? I'll check on you every hour or so to see if you need anything. Would you like that?"

She started to cry. "I'd like my clothes. I'd like my head to stop hurting. I'd like to know what the fuck happened to me last night and if I have to kill someone when I'm feeling better." Adam went to her bedside and held her as she cried. It was peculiar, but she felt safe with his arms around her. He rocked her, and for some reason, she believed him when he said everything was going to be fine.

She stopped crying and asked, "Where's Zoe?"

"Who?"

"Zoe!"

"Who?"

"Zoe! My roommate!" And then it hit her. Son…of…a…bitch! That's not her name! Can this situation get any worse?

"I mean Athena. Don't know where that came from. My brain is foggy and I'm not thinking straight. Sorry. Is she here?"

"No, she and Jean-René have been gone all night. I'm sure she'll be anxious to see you when she returns. Please try to drink more water. As my nurses would tell me when I was in hospital, 'You need to stay hydrated.' Take another sip then I'll freshen it for you."

As she took a few more gulps of water, he walked over to his dresser and pulled out a T-shirt from Eton and a pair of boxers and brought them over to the bed. "If you like, you can put these on if you don't mind wearing my skivvies. I promise they're clean. I don't feel comfortable rummaging through your things, and I locked your door last night. Will these do until Athena returns?"

"Yes, thank you, Adam. These are perfect. Thanks for everything. I'm sorry, but my head needs to find the pillow. I'm going to try to go back to sleep, which I don't think I'll have to try too hard."

He took the glass from her hands and said, "Have no worries, Terry, Ali and I are here. I'll be right back with your water. Please take a few more sips before going back to sleep." When he left the room, she put on his boxers and T-shirt. He brought the water in and gently closed the door behind him. She felt shaky picking up the glass, but did as he asked and took a few sips, adjusted the ice on her face, and the smell of Adam from his clothes filled her nostrils as she fell asleep.

René woke early and couldn't shake the feeling of unease in his gut. He woke Zoe at six thirty, but she wouldn't get up. He was tempted to leave her there but didn't feel right about that. He showered, making as much noise as he could, packing what he'd brought the day before and whatever items Zoe wasn't going to need into his backpack. She got up at 8:30, and he was pacing like a tiger. She needed to get moving. He'd become irritated with her, and it showed in his voice and attitude. He told her there wasn't time for her to shower. They had to leave now.

Zoe told him to stop worrying, saying they couldn't get the papers until later, so why leave now? She wanted to make love again, but René insisted they head to the dorms right away. She seemed sullen, but he couldn't give in. His sixth sense told him something wasn't right, and he insisted she hurry.

"René, it's Saturday morning. Everyone will still be sleeping when we get there. No one gets up before eleven on Saturday. What do you think you're going to be able to do at this hour? You won't even be able to ask Tee if the papers came because she'll still be sleeping, too. Let's make love again, have a nice breakfast, and then head back."

"We're leaving now! Get dressed. I've packed everything so we can leave quickly. I'll get us some coffee and be right back." He left the room and went to the lobby for two coffees to go. When he returned to the room, Zoe was naked, in bed, waiting for him. René became furious.

"Don't think I'm playing games. You're ruining the memory of last night with selfish behavior." He walked to the door. "I don't care what you do, but I'm leaving. Something's wrong. You'd better dress quickly because I'm checking out and turning in the key. If you're ready, we'll walk back together. If not, perhaps I'll see you later. You'd better hurry, as it doesn't take long to settle a hotel bill." He walked out and slammed the door.

Zoe was shocked and hurt by his rejection and sudden outburst. She'd never met a man who'd leave a horny woman in bed alone. She wanted to cry. Part of her wanted to hurry and dress to get down to the lobby, and another part of her wanted to stay put and make him come back and apologize for being so curt with her. From what she knew of René, he wouldn't come back for her. She jumped out of bed, dressed as quickly as she could, and headed for the lobby.

When she got there, he was gone, walking towards the college. He didn't have much of a head start so she ran to catch up with him. She couldn't believe she's running after a guy who just rejected her. That went against the grain of who she is and her view of men. In truth, she had a rather negative view of them. She thought they were heartbreakers, using women and throwing them aside.

Under her 21st century outlook on men, she would've told him to go fuck himself and reinforce her protective armor that shields her from a broken heart. René shattered that armor into tiny pieces, and she neither could nor wanted to put it back together. Although her pride was injured, she had no intention of letting him slip away. She hated to admit it, but she was crazy about him.

He was a gift to her heart that she couldn't keep unwrapped, tossed aside, and never opened. And he felt the same towards her. He told her so last night and gave her the most romantic evening of her life. Her breakfast that morning was a full stomach of swallowed pride, and for once, she didn't care. She ran after him, calling for him to wait for her. As she neared him, she could see the tense muscles in his face begin to relax.

As they briskly walked toward the college she said, "I'm sorry, René. I wasn't listening. Please don't be angry with me. I was selfish. Try to understand, I've never done anything for the CIA that was life endangering or as important as what we're here to do. From now on, I promise I won't question your reasons or feelings on what we do regarding our goal here. Forgive me?"

"Of course, Madame Zoe." He took her hand and kissed it. *"Merci.* We need to hurry because I know something's wrong. My sixth sense is screaming at me. Let's go!"

They rushed to the dorm and when they got there, they were greeted by Adam with the leg of the broken chair being held like a baseball bat, followed by Ali. René knew his gut feeling was right and became furious with himself. He asked, not realizing he was speaking French, *"Qu'est-ce qui se passe?"*

Zoe raced to her room, unlocked the door, and found it empty. She whirled around and faced Adam. "Where's Tee? And why are you carrying that like a weapon? What's going on? Where the hell is she?" She looked at Ali, and the expression on his face told her things weren't right. "Ali, where is she?"

Adam motioned to the Common Room. "Let's sit down in here, and I'll give you the lowdown on what happened. At least what I know. She's in my room sleeping off the drug that Butch slipped her. I'm quite sure she didn't take the drug knowingly."

"Drug? *Mon Dieu!* What're you saying?" René felt sick. How could he have let this happen? He looked at Zoe with horror in his eyes. Adam began to tell them what happened, not getting far into the story before the two of them rushed towards the room where Christina was sleeping. Adam bolted to stand in front of it, stopping them.

"Get out of my way, Adam. I'm going in there."

"I don't want to fight you, mate, but no one is going in there now. She's had a rather fitful sleep throughout the night with what seemed like hallucinations. What she needs is rest and not two bloody, frantic friends upsetting her more. She doesn't remember what happened, and you two have only heard the beginning. Let's go back to the Common Room and I'll tell you the complete story. Believe it or not, it gets worse. You need to be prepared before you see her because it's not at all pretty."

"What do you mean prepared? Prepared for what? I need to see her, Adam. I'm going in there, so don't try to stop me." Zoe started to rush to the door, and Adam stopped her.

"Sorry, luv, but you can't go in there now. She needs to sleep off the drug as much as she can. You certainly won't be helping matters by acting like a hysterical git. Come on now, luv, sit down, and Ali and I will tell you what we know about what happened. By the way, Ali was fantastic and acted quite brilliantly. Actually, he's the hero of this whole mess." Adam ushered the two of them back into the Common Room and told them what had occurred.

"When I said you need to be prepared, well, by the look of things it would seem most likely Butch literally used her as a punching bag. We've put ice on it, so hopefully it will be better when she awakens." Ali sat there looking down at his hands, barely making eye contact with any of them. René couldn't stop thinking about how he failed in protecting her. Zoe sat on the couch crying, cradling her head like she was holding it together with her hands.

René couldn't stop pacing the room, feeling guilty and responsible. He should've been here to protect her. The muscles in his jaw began to hurt because of how tightly clenched it was. Outwardly he tried to keep his cool listening to Adam but inwardly he was furious and wanted to pound Butch within an inch of his life. How could he have let this happen under his watch?

He knew he should've cancelled his plans when things started to fall into place. He'd regret it for the rest of his life. How could he make such a stupid and senseless mistake, leaving the one person he was assigned to protect in a situation where this could occur? In addition to this unsettling news, there was no mention of a packet of papers, and saw no feasible way to bring it up. It only compounded René's feeling of failure.

"Have you reported any of this to the police or the college?" René silently prayed the answer to that question was no.

"Um, no, actually, we haven't. Ali and I are on opposite ends regarding that. I agreed we'd hold off until you two were back and Terry was awake. Ali wants it all kept hush-hush and I think it would be quite lovely to see Butch shackled and dragged off and sent to the nick. So, now you partially know what happened. Have I left anything out, Ali?"

Ali sat there and shook his head. He should've felt relieved she was safe, and Butch was unable to finish what he started, but thoughts of what Butch would do next in retaliation to him clouded whatever good feelings he had about his actions the night before. "No, Adam, I think you covered everything."

Adam nodded but didn't tell them everything. He purposely left out what Terry had been saying in her drug-induced sleep. As he sat up with her for the night, he heard a lot of puzzling babble. He's going to keep that to himself and mull it over for a while. She had a number of conversations with "John," whom she referred to as her "hubby". Kenzie, Roxie, and Johnny sounded like they were her children, and then there was Zoe, who was obviously Athena. Those five names were spoken many times throughout the night. Who are they? Something's going on with his roommate and these two girls, and he wanted to sort this out in his head before mentioning any of it to them. Terry's only eighteen years old. How can she have a husband and three children? It's perplexing because those names were repeated throughout the night.

After hearing Adam tell the story, René whispered to Zoe in French, "I need to see O'Connell right away. This fiasco puts our mission and lives in a sticky situation. We need advice on how to proceed. There's no record of Morgan assaulting Ali and certainly no charges of attempted rape during his time at Berkeley. And there was no mention of the packet of papers we need to copy before they get into Morgan's hands. I'll be back as soon as I can. Please make sure nothing is reported to the authorities until I return."

René started to leave, and Adam stopped him and asked, "Where the hell are you going?"

"I've got some errands to do and want to make sure I'm back when Terry is awake. I'll be back shortly."

Ali looked panicked. "You're not going to the college authorities, are you? Please, we agreed we'd wait for Taraysa to awaken. I beg of you, if you consider me a friend, you won't report this."

"No, Ali, I'm not going to report this to college security. I have an appointment with a professor and I must attend. I'll be back as quickly as I can."

René headed off to O'Connell's quarters at a brisk run and pounded on the door. After a few minutes, a sleepy-eyed professor opened the door. "What are you doing here so early in the morning? What's happenin'? Do you have the papers already? Wow, man, you look bummed out. Is everything alright?"

"No, everything is not alright. The shit has hit the fan."

René told O'Connell the highlights of the events of the night before. O'Connell became extremely agitated. "Where in the hell were you when this was happening?"

"That's immaterial at the moment. We need to know how to proceed. We must contact the 21$^{st}$ century and get advice on what we should do. Butch Morgan beat, drugged and attempted to rape Christina and tried to choke Ali when he came to her defense. From what Ali and Adam have said, her face looks like he landed a few punches. She's still asleep, so I've been unable to speak with her. There were no witnesses to the beating, but Ali saw Butch standing over her, ready to rape her and Adam averted the attempt on Ali's life. Adam then, from what I've been told, proceeded to beat the living daylights out of Butch. None of this was in any reports we'd received before coming here. Ali's pleading we don't report it. Was this incident squashed by the Morgan family or was it never reported? We need to know how to proceed, and we need to know immediately, before Christina awakens."

"This debacle is all your fault! How could you let this happen? I thought you were a seasoned agent. Where the hell were you?"

"As I've said, it's immaterial."

"Bullshit it's immaterial! And where is the paperwork? Did you get it?"

"I believe we've more important things to take care of first, which is how to proceed."

"More important than the fucking reason you were sent here? You were with *her*, weren't you? Were you fucking her? You were! You mother-fucking son of a bitch! That's why she was all gussied up last night. You two were screwing each other's brains out while the one person who I told you over and over again needs to get back safely was left like a lamb to slaughter! You told me you keep business and pleasure separate. You're not only a failure, you're a liar!"

"Enough, Glenn! I'm fully aware of my shortcomings regarding this whole catastrophe."

"Do you have any idea of the ramifications if something happens to her and she doesn't get back to your present time? What part of that didn't you fucking understand? Do I have to say it in French for you to grasp the severity of the situation? And you gave me your word you'd keep your distance from Agent Janis and keep your head on this mission. What a mistake they made picking you. You're a lying, sneaky French fuck failure."

All this was too much for René to take. He threw O'Connell up against the wall. "I could kill you with one stroke of my hand. If I were you, I'd shut my mouth and send the message that needs to get to the 21st century."

Glenn laughed. "Go ahead. See if any of you get home. I know you aren't going to kill me by the mere fact that you're standing in front of me. Get your filthy hands off me, and don't you ever, ever think of threatening me again. In the scheme of things, I'm much more valuable to this country and the Agency than you could ever be."

René let go of him and Glenn proceeded to write something, entered the room where the chamber was and returned shortly. "It shouldn't take long for an answer. From what I know of your current time, communications are instantaneous. You'll have to sweat it out."

They both sat down, and Glenn kept goading René. "Was she worth it? Probably. Did she wrap her long legs around your back? I ever tell you I got a great look at her before I woke her up? Even copped a feel. Nice bod, great tits…oooh, I'm getting hard just thinking about her. I'm going to somehow get myself some of that before she leaves. Maybe I can get her before I send her off when she's put to sleep, or maybe before I awaken her when she goes back." This sort of talk was so unlike Glenn, but he was enjoying twisting the knife. He'll never let René forget this.

René sat in glum silence, trying to let everything being said go over his head. He knew his shortcomings in this mess and carried the guilt of his actions. The CIA, but mostly Martin Cater, was going to be livid with knowledge of these events. He won't feel comfortable letting Christina out of his sight again.

Within twenty minutes, a red light went on, and Glenn finally shut up and entered the chamber. He returned with a paper and a smile on his face. "You're in a shitty mess, man. The powers that be are super-pissed at you, and it seems there are no records, sealed or unsealed about the drugging and attempted rape of a co-ed or the assault on Prince Ali. Records were checked at the college, Berkeley police, and the FBI file on the Morgan family. If authorities are brought into it, they'll look into our victim, Teresa Brendes, and they'll find she doesn't exist. You have to keep this whole mess under wraps. And Martin Cater says he'll be looking into ways to sanction action against you for this breach of security and endangering the success of this mission. They're also quite upset that you were unable to procure the packet of papers. Seems you should've left your dick in your pants and taken care of business."

"I don't need you to tell me of my mistake. I'm well aware of the seriousness of what happened, which is why I turned to you for guidance. I'm going back to the dorm now that I have my answer. I'll keep you and the 21st century informed. Somehow, we'll get Butch back into the dorm and get our hands on that paperwork. From what Adam said, Butch left with only what he was wearing. If the papers came back with Ali, they have to be somewhere in the dorm. I'll find them, copy them, and make sure they get into Morgan's hands to deliver to his father. It's a small bump in the road, not failure. Many missions have glitches to overcome, but of course, you wouldn't know that because you're a scientist, not a field agent. If you were, you'd know there are many ways to accomplish success."

He walked to the door and slammed it. Glenn quickly got up, opened it, and yelled, "Say hello to Zoe for me. Tell her I look forward to seeing her, all of her!" René turned and gestured by hitting the inside of his elbow.

When he got back to the dorm, the atmosphere was bleak. Adam questioned where he went, and René responded curtly that it was none of his business. René was in no mood for any bullshit from anyone. His every remark was full of sarcasm, which heightened the mood to uncomfortable for everyone. Adam seemed to always be lurking nearby, so he pulled Zoe aside. In French he told her of what transpired with O'Connell. This ordeal must be kept under wraps, and the 21$^{st}$ century is upset by what the consequences could be. This event is not recorded anywhere, and the three of them technically don't exist at this time. Adam sat staring at him.

"What's your problem, Adam? You keep giving me the evil eye. Is my face upside down? What?" Adam kept staring at him, which pissed off René. "Do you have something you'd like to say? If so, get on with it, man! I've enough on my plate right now that I don't need any shit from you!"

"Tell me, mate, what do you have on your plate? You just entered this mess. It seems you were having a lovely time shagging your girl while Ali and I were saving Terry. You've no right to have any sort of attitude. You weren't here, so stop acting like you're the savior of the day."

This started an argument between the two of them, awakening Christina who needed to use the bathroom. She heard the chimes ring the hour of two and with the light coming in from the side of the blinds, she figured it was afternoon and René and Adam were arguing. On shaky legs she walked to the door, hoping Zoe was there.

She opened the door, and as soon as she stuck her head out of the room, the arguing stopped. The four of them looked at her as if she'd grown horns or something. René started to say something, but Zoe stopped him and went running over to her, asking if she was ok. Christina could tell by the look on Zoe's face that she wasn't.

"Would you come with me to the bathroom, please?"

"Oh my God, Tee! You're a mess!"

Christina looked at the three guys and said, "Please, enough of the arguing, ok?"

When they got into the bathroom, she saw her reflection in the mirror and was horrified. She could feel the tears ready to explode.

"What the fuck?! Holy shit and a half!! My poor face!" The left side was bruised and swollen, her lip was cut and puffed and had been bleeding as there was dried blood on it. Her left eye was bloodshot, with the whites of it completely red. The ice must have helped because she was able to open it more than earlier. Her cheek was discolored and painful to the touch. This didn't happen from a fall, of that she was sure. Tears started to fall, and she didn't know if they were from pain, anger, or sorrow.

"Tee, what can I do for you? Do you need more ice on your face?"

"Do you know what happened to me? Somebody did this to me, and what scares me is I don't remember a thing." She studied her bruises more closely in the mirror. "Zee, I need to use the bathroom, and then I'm going to take a shower. Would you please get me a towel and my shower stuff from our room? And I'd love it if someone could go to the cafeteria and get me some soup."

"Sure, Tee. Do you need some clothes?"

"No, I'm quite comfy in Adam's boxers and T-shirt. When I'm done, I want the complete story on what everyone knows about this. Someone beat the shit out of me, and I've a fairly good idea who it was."

"I'll be right back."

Zoe went to get the shower stuff, and Christina could hear her talking in a hushed tone. Voices rose again, and she shushed them. She came back in with Christina's toiletries, washcloth, and towel.

"Adam insisted that he get your soup, so he just left. He said he'd be back by the time you get out of the shower. From what we've heard, you have two knights in shining armor out there who came to your rescue while we were gone."

"Yeah?" She took the towel and toiletries and headed for the shower. "Thanks, Zee. After my head's on straight and learn what happened last night, I want to hear how your night went. René was so excited about it. I'm sure it was dreamy."

"It was, but this has put a damper on everything! I feel guilty having had such a wonderful night while all of this horrible stuff was happening to you. Oh, Tee, I'm so sorry! Call me if you need anything."

Zoe left the bathroom and Christina went into the shower. She stood under the shower, letting the hot water run over her. Being in water always helped her think. She tried to recall last night but the only thing she could remember was Butch was here. She didn't need anyone to tell her he probably did this, but why can't she remember? What else did he do and how did she end up in Adam and René's room with no clothes on?

She had a million thoughts going through her head. She felt the scratch along the back of her neck and knew he ripped the key from her neck. Dirty, filthy, scummy, sadistic bastard! Her genitals didn't hurt so she hoped she didn't get raped. Anger started to overcome her. There were bruises on her arms and one of her hips, and she noticed while washing her hair that she had tender bumps on her head.

She stayed in the shower longer than usual and wasn't sure if it was that she didn't want to face the reality of what occurred or was enjoying the water rushing over her. How foolish she was attempting this insane mission. She couldn't get the thought of her children out of her head, and John, the love of her life, who she knew would never have wanted her put in such a dangerous predicament, but this wasn't the danger she'd perceived contemplating this mission. She was thankful that in a month and a half, she'd be returning to her life.

She dried herself off and put Adam's T-shirt and boxers back on because they gave her a warm sense of protection. She didn't want to give them back to him yet, or maybe ever. She took one last look at her horrific reflection, wrapped herself in her blanket, and left the bathroom. Adam immediately came over, sweetly trying to take care of her. He brought her sunglasses and walked her to the table, where there were three different kinds of soup with a big glass of water. Christina noticed René had a sullen look on his face, and Ali barely made eye contact.

Adam thought she looked better, and Zoe and René were horrified. Tension in the Common Room was thick, and it seemed that any second, Adam and René would come to blows.

Christina sat down and ate the first bowl of soup and felt more of her strength returning. Sitting there, she started to remember - I did this exact thing last night. "Ok, it's kind of coming back to me now. Last night I knocked on Ali's door to say goodbye before he left for his usual Friday night and Butch was the only one in the room. In fact, he was the only one in the dorm. I put my soup here, where I'm sitting now, and went to get my art book. When I came back Butch was here. I think I said something like 'if you're going to be here, I'll go to my room.' That's the last thing I remember. Who can take it from there?"

"Taraysa, it's my fault that all of this happened to you."

Adam instantly spoke up. "Ali, you had nothing to do with what happened to Terry, so stop saying that. Actually, Ali was literally quite brilliant and heroic. He saved you."

"Saved me? From what?" She looked at Ali and Adam, and neither said anything. "What did he save me from? Look, I've already figured out Butch beat the crap out of me. I have bruises all over my body and head, and you can all see my face. I want to know!"

René spoke up. "Maybe you, Athena, and I should discuss this later privately."

Adam started to protest but stopped when Christina said, "No, I want to hear it from the two people who were here. There's no reason to wait until later or to talk privately. From what I can figure, these two guys were part of this story, and I want to hear it from them." René went and sulked in a corner.

Ali started to talk but began to stammer, his voice quivering. Adam took over telling the story of how Ali found her on Butch's bed with her clothing removed, unconscious, hands tied above her head with Butch hovering, ready to rape her. Ali pushed him away and while he and Butch were fighting, Adam came along, saw what was going on and stepped in to help Ali.

Christina listened to the story, how Butch tried to choke Ali for helping and Adam broke the chair over Butch's head and then beat the shit out of him and scared him off. Adam said he found the half-empty bottle of chloral hydrate, flushed it down the toilet, wrapped her in a blanket, and brought her into his room, where the two of them stayed with her.

"So, the scumbag slipped me a mickey! Filthy dirtbag! I don't know how to thank the two of you. So, neither of you saw him punch my face. He must've done that before you arrived. What an asshole he is! I'm not complaining, but why did you come back so soon, Ali? I'm grateful you did, but your meeting with your guardian is set in stone. What happened? Is everything ok?"

He set an envelope down in front of her. She opened it and pulled out two tickets to last night's performance of *Jesus Christ Superstar*. She could barely speak because of the huge lump in her throat that turned into tears. "Oh, Ali! How thoughtful and sweet of you!"

"I wanted to make you happy. I knew you wanted to go, so I bought the tickets and came back to surprise you. It was supposed to be a wonderful evening that turned out to be a nightmare."

"Oh, Ali, thank God you came back. Thank you! Not just for saving me, but for buying these tickets, and the thought that you did that for me does make me happy. What would I have done without you? Well, it's all over with and we can move on."

"But it's not over with, Taraysa. None of you understand. I cannot speak of it, but it's not over, at least not for me. I'm stuck with him until the end of this semester. I cannot report any of this to the university authorities. I'm honor-bound to continue as things currently are, acting as his friend, and there's nothing I can do about it."

Adam jumped up. "Ali, he tried to kill you! Look at the marks on your neck! Are you bonkers? You can't let him get away with that! He belongs in the bloody slammer! To hell with honor! We have him bang to rights! He's a bloody bumsucker and needs to answer for his actions! If we can't report his attempted murder of you, we have to report the attempted rape, beating and drugging of Terry!"

René spoke up and said, "I need to talk to Terry alone about that."

"Here we go again! What in bloody hell gives you the right to say that? You were off shagging your girl while that bloody scum was drugging, beating and raping *this* girl. I don't know who died and left you boss, or why you think you're the supreme protector of the chicks in this dorm. But after last night, I must say, you're doing a bloody brilliant job of it, aren't you? Frigging Frog!"

René started towards Adam, yelling "Les Rosbifs," and Zoe stepped in between them. "Enough! Ok everybody, calm the fuck down! Let's not get into a pissing match, you two. Cut the macho bullshit right now! The last thing we need is another fight on this floor. You're both letting Butch poison your friendships! Don't either of you dare give him that power! What do you say we all chill out for a while?

Tempers and emotions are a little high for all of us, and there's too much testosterone flying around this room. There are two victims here, and they aren't either of you, so you both need to back off and stop making it about you."

They both took steps backward. Zoe continued. "Adam, your feelings are completely understandable. You and Ali saw firsthand what went on here, and your heroics saved Terry, and we're all so thankful. It's logical that you're emotional about the whole ordeal. You need to understand that Jean-René has been with Terry and me since we got here at the beginning of August. We became close very quickly, kind of like family, and he's taken on the role of our protector. He's like Terry's big brother, and he's feeling as though he let her down."

"Athena, don't attempt to speak for me!"

"Shut the fuck up! Tell me, Jean-René, how many times on Friday nights did we go to the pub without Terry, or the library, or a walk, and not get back until well after ten? More than you can count, and it wasn't unusual for Terry to do things that didn't include us. Stop this bullshit and get real! None of this is anyone's fault but Butch Morgan's.

"All this shit stops now! Adam, lay off Jean-René's protective side, and Jean, you need to realize you can't be everywhere and protect us from everything. We're a family here, and we have to stick together. Stop tearing at each other and let's fucking chill!"

René started to leave the room, and Zoe blocked his way. "Where do you think you're going? You're not leaving here in a big huff, and not before all of this is in the past. You and Adam are roommates, and you both need to get over whatever it is that's standing between you. Stop feeling guilty that you weren't here! It's only going to stand in your way, and you have to let it go! We only have another month or so to be together. Let's enjoy the time we have left and climb over this hurdle together."

Adam walked over to René and held out his hand. "Sorry about the 'Frigging Frog' remark. Much of what I said was uncalled for. I'm taking out my anger on the wrong person. Friends, mate?"

René looked at the outstretched hand and grasped it firmly. "Sorry about the *Les Rosbifs*. Athena's right. I'm ashamed I wasn't here to protect Terry. I let my emotions take over, which I never do, and put my duty as secondary. *Je suis désolé mon ami.*"

"Ok, mates, now that that's settled, what do we do about Butch?" Adam asked.

Ali was the first to speak and seemed on the verge of panic. "Please, I beg all of you, can we do nothing? He'll retaliate against me in the most appalling manner, which will endanger my life. I'm not exaggerating my dilemma! My culture is vastly different from what's acceptable in the US. My life will be over if I do anything to avenge his actions. I don't care that he attempted to kill me. I feel anger and sorrow for what he's done to Taraysa, but I implore all of you not to contact the authorities."

Ali knelt down next to Christina and took her hand. He wouldn't meet her eyes, looking only at her hand. "Taraysa, you know how I feel about you, as I've told you many times. You hold my heart in this tiny hand that I now embrace. I'd do anything for you. Can you find it in your heart to do me this one favor? I helped you preserve your reputation, please help me preserve mine.

"I'm honor-bound to maintain a relationship with this vile and hateful young man. I cannot explain why, but I'm telling you the truth. Honor is everything to my family, and as a member of the Royal household, I have to sustain it. Butch, as degrading and evil as he is, is the reason I'm here with all of you now. Our families are united in certain ways, and I cannot let my King down. In my culture, the shame I'd put on them would mean certain death for me."

Christina asked him to look at her. He finally looked into her eyes, and she could see his anguish. "Ali, believe it or not, I understand more than you could ever realize. We all feel Butch should pay for what he's done to both of us, but I think the final decision should be made by you and me. I'd never do anything to you or against you that would endanger you in any way." She looked at everyone in the room. "As much as I want Butch to pay for what he's done, I agree with Ali. Karma is a bitch and will catch up with him sooner or later." She looked directly at Zoe and René and said, "It may take 30 years for it to happen, but at some point, Butchie's going down!"

Adam became visibly upset, trying to argue the point. "Adam, I don't have the strength to argue about it right now, but my decision is to let it go. Thank you so, so much for being there and saving me from horrible circumstances and for taking such good care of me. I can't let Ali be put in danger and don't think Butch will get off scot-free. He'll be watching his back for the rest of the semester, and he'd better watch his balls because the next time I see him, I'm going to knee him so hard that they're going to end up in his mouth. He's seriously underestimated me, and he'll pay for what happened. Are we agreed?"

Everyone said yes except Adam. "Terry, look at your face! If you could've seen what he was going to do to you and what he did to Ali, you'd think differently."

"Adam, please don't be upset with this decision. Someday in the future, you'll understand there's a time and place for everything, and these events will be more useful against him in another time and another place. Rest assured, he's not getting away with anything. All the bad things he's done in the few months he's here will come back to bite him in the ass. And at that time, we'll all get together and celebrate. Please, Adam, it means a lot to me that you aren't harboring any anger about my decision. I believe this information will do more damage to him in the future than the consequences will be now. Trust me, ok?"

"I don't know why I believe you, Terry, but I do. We'll play it by your rules for now, but if he ever does anything to harm you again, I'll no longer honor your wishes. You know the Chinese proverb: '*He who saves a life is responsible for it.*' I'm responsible for both you and Ali, and I plan to make sure that bastard behaves himself. I advise you all to make sure he stays away from me because it would be brilliant if I could kick the shit out of him again."

Christina ate another bowl of soup and started to feel better but still groggy. Adam got more ice for her face, and they hung out together in the Common Room for the rest of the night. Adam cancelled his playing gig, and they had pizza and sodas, smoked a few joints Adam rolled while Christina refrained from anything stronger than soup.

René asked to speak privately with Christina, so they went into her room. No one noticed the two of them except Adam, who stood by the door to listen.

"Christina, I'm sorry I let you down and wasn't here to protect you. I promised I'd keep you safe and the one time I put pleasure before business it's with catastrophic results. I'll never let it happen again."

"René, as Zoe said, it's not your fault. I'm not upset you weren't here, and I don't want you to be either."

"But this wouldn't have happened if I were doing my job. I'm in hot water with O'Connell and the CIA in the 21st Century. I failed in my mission. I was relieved you decided not to press charges because that would've caused an investigation. We know there's no charge of attempted rape or murder on his record. We must be careful not to change the past. The authorities would have looked into you, and that would've been disastrous."

"René, we need to look at this as one more thing to be used against him when we get home. It must've happened in his room because I guess that's where I ended up, so we'll be able to see the whole thing when we get back. Don't beat yourself up over this, my face is bad enough! And don't be upset with Adam. He's been amazing to both me and Ali. He doesn't deserve it."

"Well, Christina, nothing like this will happen again. I'm going to keep my distance from Zoe until we're safely back home. I cannot let my duty take a back seat to my passion."

"Please, she'll be impossible to live with. Keep things as they are. Don't fight what you're feeling. You two are obviously crazy about each other. I have two champions who'll make sure I'm safe. Enjoy this while you can because once we get back, we'll have a ton of shit to do and figure out a plan to take Marty down. I'll keep my eye on my drinks, and as long as I'm not drugged, I can handle myself. I have a slight indiscretion to tell you. While in my drug-induced fog, I kept asking Adam if Zoe was here."

"That's not an indiscretion? Of course, you'd want to see your friend."

"I kept calling her Zoe, not Athena. That's one of the reasons I don't like to drink or smoke anything. It takes me off my game. I hope it doesn't raise any eyebrows or cause suspicions."

"Hopefully, he'll think you were confused from the drug. With all that was going on, it probably went right over his head."

"I hope so. So please, no guilty feelings."

"It's hard not to feel guilty when I look at your face. I, too, will have the joy of inflicting physical pain on him when I see him. He needs to watch his step and behave himself. I'm sure we'll see many repulsive things when we view the tapes. Thank goodness for your teddy bear. By the way, did you happen to see if Ali brought home any papers with him last night?"

"No, sorry. I was out cold when Ali returned. I can't ask him about it without sounding suspicious. What do we do now?"

"We'll think of something." They walked out of the room, and Adam was standing by the door, listening to their entire conversation. Now he has more pieces of this confusing puzzle. He was surprised René didn't question him about lurking at the door, probably thinking he was being protective.

Adam was completely confused by this overheard conversation. Now it was added to the babblings of Terry in her drug-induced state, and all the conversations between Jean-René and Athena in French. He thought everyone, or at least all Europeans, knew that every upper-class Englishman was taught French right along with English. Could it be that René didn't realize that while he thought he was speaking privately? Adam understood every word he said to Athena. 21$^{st}$ century? What? That's thirty years into the future, the same amount of time Terry said it may take for retribution. What are they talking about? He had a lot of information to try to make sense of. But how can one make sense of such nonsense?

# CHAPTER 27

It was almost a week since the Halloween encounter with Butch. No one on their floor had seen hide nor hair of him since leaving the dorm six days ago. It was a smart move on his part because everyone there wanted to kick his ass. Adam was keeping Christina's key safe, at her request. She felt he would keep better track of it, because if it wasn't around her neck, she might lose it.

Christina got out of the shower, and with her hair wrapped in a towel, she inspected her rainbow-colored face. The white of her left eye was still red, although not as bright as it was previously. Everyone said she looked better, but she couldn't see it. She sported a black eye with a green and yellow blend on her left cheek. Her lip was finally back to its normal size, but the split from his ring was still visible. The bruises on her body were still evident and tender. Every time she saw or felt one of them, her anger towards Butch increased. She hoped they'd get the evidence needed to ruin his life forever. It will bring such satisfaction to knock him down. She was bitter, but who could blame her?

She dried her hair and put on some eye makeup. Sarah had given her some stage foundation to see if it would cover some of the discoloration around the eye and cheek, but it only made it look like it was covering up bruises, which is what she's trying to do.

Sarah was horrified when she returned from her weekend workshop and heard what happened. She'd been so sweet and sympathetic, but so excited when she came back to the dorm. She couldn't wait to tell everyone she landed the part of Kim MacAfee in *Bye Bye Birdie,* and Jerry, the object of her affection, got the part of her sweetheart, Hugo Peabody. She told them later that night about her excitement. "Now I'll finally get to kiss him!"

"Wait, you and Jerry haven't kissed yet?" Zoe asked, feigning surprise.

"Nope, not really. We've had little pecks and quick smooches but nothing juicy yet," she said, sadly shaking her head. "He's so shy, really. I know he's digging on me because he said so, but he wants to take things slow. I think he got his heart broken back home and is scared it'll happen again. It's hard to believe he likes me because he's so freaking gorgeous and groovy and I'm kind of like the tomboy girl next door. However he wants it, I'll go along with it."

Zoe and Christina exchanged knowing glances. It was obvious Sarah was crazy about Jerry and they were concerned Sarah was going to get her heart broken. Ah, such is love! Their "gay-dar" was blaring in regard to Jerry, but neither was going to say anything. She'll find out soon enough on her own and it wasn't cool to "out" anyone.

Jerry and Sarah spent a lot of time in her room going over their lines and singing their songs working on their harmonies. She told them so many times that she was "so into Jerry she could die." Throughout the last week, she was the one who was able to elevate the mood of everyone in the dorm and brightened up the place with her contagious laughter and insanely funny sense of humor. Sarah was human sunshine wherever she went, and laughter seemed to always surround her.

Jerry gave Christina pointers on how to cover up the facial bruising with regular makeup, which worked better than the stage makeup Sarah had suggested. Still, Christina thought she looked pasty with it on and made up her mind she wouldn't go anywhere until the discoloration got better.

Christina hadn't been out of the dorm since last Friday. She didn't want the stares, questions, or having to lie with the answers. Adam wanted her to get her face x-rayed, but there would be too many questions she wouldn't know how to answer. She knew she'd have to go out soon but felt overly self-conscious. Maybe next week. She'd use the story of falling down the stairs as her cover story.

Ali and Adam decided because Christina refused to leave the dorm, Adam would stay with her, and Ali and Sarah would bring notes and assignments from their mutual classes. René agreed she shouldn't be alone in the dorm so the three of them worked out a schedule. Ali still seemed uncomfortable around Christina, but at least he stopped apologizing every time he saw her and was able to look her in the eyes again.

"Although I'd much rather stay with you than leave Adam here, you're better protected if Butch decides to return when he thinks we're all in class. I'm no match for Butch and Adam's shown he's to be feared." Christina was relieved to see Ali more upbeat, most likely because they all had a break from Butch. It's only a matter of time before he shows his ugly face back at the dorm.

Truthfully, Christina was glad she wasn't alone. She hated to admit it, but for the first time in her life, she was uncomfortable being alone. Adam stayed during the day, and they'd work on their art class assignments together, and René would take over in the late afternoons or evenings so Adam could go to his gigs or work on his music assignments. Christina felt like a pain in the ass but was thankful to have a male presence with her.

She dressed and found Adam in the Common Room. Adam insisted they use his room in case Butch returned, so he'd be able to lock the door and keep her safely tucked away. Christina sat at his desk, and he sat on his bed.

"Did you get the books from the library?" Christina asked.

"I went straight away last evening. Here are the ones you asked for, luv."

He handed over two books on Toulouse Lautrec. "Thanks, Adam. Who've you been assigned to do your paper on?"

"Mary Cassatt. And actually, it's rather disappointing and frankly unbelievable. With all the bloody brilliant Impressionists, I end up with one of two or three chicks of that era and one who is an American to boot! I'd have preferred one of the blokes like Van Gogh, Monet, or Renoir. Very disheartening! Would you be interested in making a trade?"

"Excuse me, what's wrong with an American chick? And no, I don't want to trade." She got up and walked over to him. "Come on, Adam, are you kidding? She's a great subject. She had a stubborn determination to get accepted in a field that was like a 'good old boys club.' When I was a kid, I'd look at some of her paintings in our encyclopedia. I became interested in her because of her paintings in that New Yorker Magazine that I gave my report on. If you'd been paying attention instead of breaking my balls with your signs, you would've learned this already. 'Who are you, luv?'," she said in a British accent.

"Sorry."

"Ah, it's okay."

"No, really, luv. I'm sorry. But it was giddy fun."

"I'm sure! No harm done. You've redeemed yourself." They were looking at one another, and she could feel his eyes on her. At that moment, she felt something pass between them, though she wasn't sure what. She couldn't stop thinking about how incredibly good-looking he was and how dreamy his eyes were. Christina, get back to work! She pulled herself from his gaze.

"Anyway, Adam, back to Mary. After I learned her name, I tried to find more of her paintings. I found a lot, but not the one I was looking for. I haven't been able to find any of the artwork from that magazine article. I wish I still had it. In fact, I can't find any information on them. Haven't been able to find those paintings again in all my years of research."

"And how many years has that been, luv?"

Shit! Change the subject. "Come on! Look at her paintings. They're so cool, especially those with children." She opened his book on Cassatt and found one of her favorites, *Little Girl in Blue Armchair.* "Look at this painting! The expression on the girl's face is one I always thought was that she just wanted to get up and go play. Look at the plaid on her sash and the detail on her socks! And what about the uniformity of the design on all the chairs? And the dog? Look at that cute little dog. I love little dogs in paintings."

She turned the pages and found more photos of her paintings. "Now look at these, full of life with mothers and their children, families together, with themes of familial and maternal love. There's so much you could write about her. Get over the fact that she's an American woman and concentrate on the works of art."

Adam looked at her and laughed. "I must admit, luv, I genuinely like American women, especially those interested in art. Do you know you become alive when you talk about art? You're actually rather passionate about it. Quite attractive, I must say. Would you care to write my paper for me?"

"Thanks, but no. I have my own to do."

Adam looked through a few of the paintings by Mary Cassatt and stopped on *Five O'clock Tea.* He flipped the book over so Christina could see it. "These two ladies look quite cheeky. Probably because they had to wait until five to enjoy their cup of tea."

"Oh, I love that painting, too. Look at how she painted the wallpaper. And the tea service really looks like silver, doesn't it? I actually have this print in my office at the libra…ry." A nervous laugh escaped her lips. Shit! Why did I say that?

"You have an office at the libra…ry? I wasn't aware that libra…ries in the States gave offices to teenagers. What do you do in your office?"

"Um…I um…I…um," think fast! She decided to go with the truth. "I…I read to children, help students with research, and put books away. And it's not really my office, it's the room I use. I call it my office, you know, like I'm a big shot."

"Hmmm. I see." He looked at her like he didn't believe her, or maybe she was just being paranoid over her slip of the tongue.

"This paper is due by Tuesday, so we'd better get down to business."

"Right-o."

He didn't move or start writing, just kept staring at her. Without looking up from her work she said, "Adam, is there a reason why you're looking at me like that?"

"Like what, luv? Just thinking, is all."

"About what?"

"Well, I was thinking there's so much more to you than meets the eye, and you're quite the complicated little bird. Quite confusing, actually."

"There's nothing complicated about me. I'm a small-town girl at a big-time college. Just little old me. You should start working on your paper and stop trying to read into something that isn't."

"Hmmm. I see."

"What do you see?"

"I see a lovely girl with a veil of mysterious intrigue surrounding her."

"Really? Like what?"

"Well, if I had the answer to that, then it wouldn't be a mystery, now would it?"

She looked up at him and couldn't stop the smile from taking over her face. "Adam, I'm not at all complicated. What you see is what you get."

"Oh, luv! I beg to differ with you on that. You're quite the opposite, actually. I can't figure it out as yet, but I'm working on it."

"Well, let me know when you have it all figured out. But remember, one does need a hint of mystery."

"Hmmm. I see."

Christina thought it best to let it go, but her insides were in turmoil. Had she been discovered? If so, how could he know anything? He can't know anything. She needed to pretend there was nothing to hide and do her paper. Except now she couldn't concentrate on anything except what he just said.

They spent the rest of the morning working on their assignment. Christina was immersing herself in the task of writing about Lautrec and decided to feature the Jane Avril angle and concentrate a portion of the paper on the paintings and posters of her. Every so often, Adam would ask her opinion on an aspect of one of Cassatt's paintings, which would send her off on what Adam called "an art history lecture."

The ten o'clock bells rang out which made Christina put her pen down and close her eyes to listen to them. Adam noticed.

"Are you feeling well? What is it?" He had a worried look on his face.

"I'm fine. I love those chimes, and the ten o'clock bells are special to me because it was the first thing I heard upon my arrival here, like it was welcoming me. So, the ten o'clock bells are mine."

René stopped in shortly after his class with some lunch from the cafeteria. He asked how it was going and if anyone had stopped by, meaning Butch. They chatted and then went into the Common Room and had lunch.

"Well, I'm heading out. Any plans for the afternoon? Do you need to go anywhere today, Adam?"

"No, Terry and I will be working on our papers. I think we have all we need for now. Thanks, mate."

"Terry, aren't you anxious to get outside? Maybe you two could take a walk or sit outside and get some sunshine. It'd be good for you. Give it some thought. You could always wear sunglasses. In any case, I'll be back shortly. I'm going to meet Athena. *Au revoir, mes amis.*"

Christina knew what René meant behind the suggestion. He wants to look for the packet of papers that hopefully came back with Ali last Friday. Now that the dorm was never empty with Christina always there with a "bodyguard", it put a crimp in René's search for them. If they're here, he needed to get his hands on them before they got into Butch's possession.

When they went back to Adam's room to continue their reports, Christina noticed Adam wasn't working on his, instead staring out the window. He picked up his guitar, sat back on the bed, and started strumming. He was far off somewhere with no intention of doing a report.

"Do you have writer's block? Can I help?"

"No, thank you."

He put the guitar down, got up, and walked over to the desk. He took the pen out of her hand and, taking both hands, he stood her up and interlocked their fingers. Christina felt her stomach flip. His smell, his face, and the presence of him so close made her knees feel weak. The Noon chimes began to ring.

"There go your bells. It's a sign, luv. They're beckoning you. I'm weary of all this paperwork, aren't you? It's so very dull, and the weather is beautiful today. Your chimes are calling us to go outside." His expression changed to an excited little boy. "I know! I've got a brilliant idea! Why don't we hop on the Harley and go to San Francisco? We can do some shopping and get the chain for your key that I've so valiantly carried in my wallet for the last week. Honestly, Terry, it really belongs around your neck. Sound good?"

"I don't know, Adam. I still look like the loser of a twelve-round boxing match."

"Your vanity is showing, sweetheart. And why should you worry about what people think? You're still fantastically beautiful, just more colorful at the moment. And with the way people are nowadays, no one will notice. You can wear your big sunglasses and leave our cares and this frightful assignment behind us for the rest of the day. The fresh air will do you good, and there's nothing more freeing than galloping through the streets on a Harley. What do you say, luv? Please?"

"I don't know. I…"

"You can't hide in this dorm forever. Eventually, you'll have to venture out, and what's better than riding a Harley through the hills of San Francisco? We'll have a lovely time. We'll ride, get the chain for your key, have a bite to eat, and then maybe see that new flick. I hear it's quite brilliant and got fantastic reviews. It stars that American cowboy from the Italian westerns, Tank Yeastgood."

"Tank Yeastgood? You mean Clint Eastwood?"

"Yes, most likely. I sometimes have trouble remembering names. The flick is called *Play Misty for Me,* like the brilliant song by Johnny Mathis, one of my favorites. Come on, luv, what do you say? Please say yes."

"I don't know, Adam."

"Are you afraid to ride with me? I assure you, I'm a safe driver, and it's not at all difficult as a passenger once you get the hang of it. You can trust me."

She wanted to tell him she's spent more years on the back of a Harley than he's been alive, but of course, she couldn't.

"Don't say no yet, luv. Think on it awhile. You need to have some fun, especially after what happened. Your chimes are calling!"

They were standing so close, looking at each other, their fingers interlocked. As he moved in closer to kiss her, there was a knock on the door.

"Bloody miserable timing." He muttered and opened the door. Ali was standing there, looking visibly shaken.

"What's the matter, mate? You're looking quite frightful."

"Excuse us, please, Taraysa, but I must speak with Adam privately."

"Sure, Ali. Is everything okay?"

"Hopefully yes. But I need to speak to Adam. Please don't be offended that I've asked to speak to him alone."

"Of course not, Ali. Why would that offend me? Let me get my stuff together." Before she left the room, she gathered her papers and put them in one of the reference books. She picked up the pen and clicked it shut and turned the recorder on. She wanted to know what this private conversation was all about.

"Go into your room, luv, and lock the door. We'll get you when we're through."

"Okay." She walked to the door, turned to Adam, and said, "Now, who is the one with mysterious intrigue surrounding him, hmm?" They both watched her walk into her room and shut the door.

She lay on the bed and did some tricks with Theodore Edward. It's amazing how quickly she reverted to a little girl with her teddy bear. They were in the middle of some fantastic flips when she heard a key in the lock, and the door opened with Zoe and René standing there. Both looked surprised that she was in the room.

"Is everything alright? Why are you locked in here by yourself, and where's Adam?" René looked concerned.

"Ali came by and wanted to speak with Adam, so they asked me to go to my room and lock the door so they could talk privately. I'm starting to feel like an ill-behaved child."

René looked concerned. "I think I'll go in there and see what the conversation is all about. We're running out of time and have to find those papers quickly. I believe they're crucial."

"No need to butt in on their little tete-a-tete. I turned the pen on before leaving the room, so we'll get to hear the whole thing. They should be winding down shortly. They've been in there awhile."

"Why, Christina! Very smooth move! You're really becoming quite the agent." René was smiling, standing next to Zoe, holding her hand.

"Are you feeling better today, Tee? You look better, more like yourself. Want to come with us? I need to grab something to eat. Afterwards, I want to go be with the protesters."

Zoe will never change, always wanting to be in the middle of the excitement. "What are they protesting?"

"Don't know, don't care. We're at fucking Berkeley, Tee! You have to join in and enjoy the times we're living in. Come on, Tee! Let's go burn our bras. Don't stay in here. We need to enjoy being at Berkeley. René can bring the matches. What do you say?" Zoe and René looked so happy standing there holding hands.

She didn't want to be the third wheel again. "Nah, Adam asked me if I wanted to take a ride on the bike and go shopping for a chain for my key, grab something to eat, and then go to a movie."

René immediately responded. "That sounds like a great idea. I'd suggest you go and enjoy yourself."

"I agree, Tee. You really should get out. This staying in all the time isn't you. You can't let Butch steal your spunk. And if anyone says anything to you about your face, tell them to go fuck themselves, like you'd normally do."

There was a knock on the door, which René opened, and Ali was standing there. "We're through, Taraysa. You can go back to working on your paper if you like." He began to walk to the stairs.

"Thanks, Ali. Hey! Where are you going? You heading out somewhere?" They had all stayed very close together for the last week, and it was odd that Ali was not sticking around with them.

"Yes, I've some errands to attend to. Perhaps I'll see all of you later." Ali put his cap on with the visor over his face and walked towards the stairs. He once again had the demeanor of one with the weight of the world on his shoulders.

Christina went into Adam's room, and he was standing, looking out the window. She could feel a change in the atmosphere. "Gee, Adam, what's up with Ali? He was his old self for a while there, and now he's back to having a rain cloud surrounding him. Is everything okay?"

"Maybe, we'll see. So, tell me, have you given any thought to my suggestion for this evening?"

She breathed in a heavy sigh. "Can you give me a few minutes to think about it? Let me grab my stuff and put it back into my room. I promise I'll be back in five minutes with my answer."

She went back into her room with her books, papers, and pen. She handed René the pen, and he went outside to listen to the recorded conversation in private. Christina wanted to hear it too, but he said he didn't want to draw any attention to the fact that they were all huddled around a pen. She made him promise that she'd be able to hear the conversation later, and he agreed.

He came back shortly with an excited urgency in his voice. "Christina, you need to tell Adam that you'll be happy to take him up on his offer tonight. We've got to get him out of here so we can find those papers because tomorrow the packet will be turned over to Butch. Adam has them hidden somewhere, and Ali explained he couldn't meet with his guardian at his usual Friday evening appointment and tell him the papers aren't in the possession of the Morgan family. Questions will arise as to why they aren't, and Ali doesn't want to tell his guardian any of what happened. He kept saying over and over that his honor is at stake. Zoe and I will have to search both rooms until we find them, although I'm fairly certain they're somewhere in my room if Ali is asking Adam for them. We can't do that unless Adam and Ali are gone, and we're free to look everywhere. Can you do that, Christina? It's crucial to our mission."

Christina let out a groan. "But I look like Rocky Balboa after his first ass kicking. I really don't want to go out looking like this."

"Tee, if we don't find those papers, Butch wins. I know you don't want that. This is our chance to bring him down at the exact time he thinks he's going to waltz into the freaking White House! We can't let that happen, especially now that we know his true nature."

Christina thought about it for a minute, got up and walked out of her room, went into Adam's room, and found him sitting on his bed, playing the guitar. "Do you have a helmet for me?"

"Really? The answer is yes? Bloody brilliant! I do have an extra helmet. And I promise I'll knock out any bugger who says anything about your black eye. When can we leave? Are you ready now?"

"I have to change into something warmer and grab my jacket. I'll be right back." She walked into her room and told René and Zoe that she and Adam would be leaving shortly. They left the room so she could change her clothes. She grabbed her jacket and her Berkeley sweatshirt out of the closet and looked at the pairs of sunglasses she had. She wondered if the helmet had a visor on it, so she walked back to Adam's room to ask about that, and he was locking up his guitar case. She found that odd because she's never seen him lock it with a padlock. When he saw her in the doorway, he asked if she'd changed her mind.

"No, of course not. I wondered if the helmet I was going to use had a visor, so I know which glasses to bring."

"Oh. No, it doesn't have one. Is that quite alright?"

"Sure, it's fine. Now I know which glasses to wear." She hesitated for a moment and then asked, "Do you always lock up your guitar? No one here would steal it."

"It's not the guitar I'm worried about, luv, it's my papers, music, and original songs. I've got quite a few written and I want to protect them. Maybe if you're a good girl, I'll play them for you sometime. Go on luv, finish getting ready. We need to take advantage of the daylight left, and I want you to see the sunset on the bay."

"Oh, Adam, that sounds so cool. I'll be right back." She scribbled a quick note, got her things, and went to say goodbye to Zoe and René. She handed René the note in the same manner as he did at CIA headquarters. She suggested looking in Adam's guitar case first, as she thought Adam would've felt the papers were safe with his music. She hoped she was right.

"Let's go, luv!" He handed her the helmet and grabbed her hand, and they were off. His bike was a beautiful navy-blue Harley-Davidson Sportster. He took her extra sweatshirt and put it in his bag, and they were ready to roll. He started to give Christina the lesson on how to be a passenger, and she told him she knew how to ride on the back of the bike. "If I do anything wrong, let me know."

He kick-started that baby up, she hopped on, and off they went, headed to San Francisco. Christina felt great being on the back of a Harley again. It's very liberating, traipsing the hills with the wind at your face. Thoughts can be clearer when you think them on the back of a Harley surrounded by the beauty of Mother Nature and now, the Pacific Ocean.

It's a stunningly beautiful ride from Berkeley, as Adam zips his way to the Bay Bridge. As they go over the water, they are gifted with a breathtaking view, passing islands along the way, with Alcatraz visible off in the distance. When she saw the Golden Gate Bridge, she became overcome with the emotion of seeing two of the most iconic images in this area of California. She took a mental picture of it all, from the vantage point of a Harley, as it looks quite different from the perch on the Sather Tower. It felt good to feel the fresh sea air in her face, all the while knowing it was wreaking havoc on her hair, but for the first time in a long time, she enjoyed being alive again.

When they got into San Francisco, Christina was overwhelmed with the colors, the streetcars, and hills with views of the ocean. She thought of the television show, "The Streets of San Francisco" with Karl Malden and a very young Michael Douglas. She was soaking in all the local color of this beautiful city by the bay with its endless hills. Her head was whipping from side to side so as not to miss anything.

They pulled up on one of the streets with shops lining both sides. Adam pulled over and parked the bike. "Come on luv, let's get that chain for your key."

"Will we have enough time to get it before the sun sets? I don't want to miss that."

"We won't miss it, I promise! I've already picked out a chain for you. It needs your approval." She thought how sweet he was and felt guilty for how she had misjudged him in the beginning. He was nothing like she'd originally thought.

They walked into the jewelry store, and the salespeople seemed to know him by name. He asked them to get the chain he selected, and a salesgirl went into the back room and came out with a small brown envelope. She emptied the contents onto a black velvet square.

"Well, what do you think, luv? It's the strongest lady's chain they have, although I think it may be shorter than the one we're replacing." He got out his wallet and removed the key from one of its compartments. He gave the key to the salesgirl and asked her to firmly attach it to the chain. "So, luv, what's the verdict?"

"It's perfect! Thank you so much, Adam, for everything. I can't let you pay for this. You aren't the one who broke it. I insist on paying for it." She asked the salesgirl, "How much is it?" Adam held it up to her neck and had her look in the mirror.

"It's all cool, luv. It's a gift. The only payment I want is to see it back around your neck. Besides, my family is quite well off, and I'm their only heir. I have to spend my inheritance on something. It looks perfect. The length of the chain is shorter, but it complements your neck beautifully. Look how the key lies under your collarbone. It looks quite lovely. If you don't mind, I'd like to put it on you where we'll watch the sunset." Adam told the salesgirl he'd take it and to wrap it up. She gave him the package and they headed out.

"Are you ready to ride out to the sunset? Isn't that what they say in the cowboy movies?" He tucked the package in his inside jacket pocket, and they were off again.

He pulled up on a rocky area with a sensational view of the bay. They got off the bike and climbed down the rocks until they came to a place where Adam suggested they sit to watch the sunset. It was magnificent looking out at the water with the setting sun shimmering over it like a thousand blinking lights, with the sky taking on a pinkish-blueish-purple hue among the white clouds. They sat there silently for a moment, taking in the vista and the natural beauty surrounding them.

"Isn't it beautiful here, luv? I come here quite often to watch the sunset. It helps me to think. The water is so lovely and the breeze is fantastic."

"Do you bring all the girls up here?"

"What girls?"

"All the girls who you want to know 'where they've been all your life'." They both laughed, and he gave Christina a little push. "Go on! You're so naughty!"

"I'm naughty? I'm not the one flirting with anything that moves. But you're right. I'm sorry. That wasn't cool, and you've been so sweet to me. I shouldn't have said that, but I couldn't resist."

"Actually, luv, you're the only girl I've wanted to share my secret place here on the bay. It's quite peaceful and seems like the world stops turning while sitting here, doesn't it?"

"It does. That's how I feel looking out from the Sather Tower. With a view like this, it makes you think you can take on the world and actually win."

They sat watching the sun set over the water. When the sun was almost fully set, and the colors of the sky were a radiant purple, Adam reached into his pocket and took the jewelry box out and removed the chain with the key attached. "Turn around so I can put this key back where it belongs."

She turned her back to him, and he moved her hair out of the way. "I have to say, luv, you have one of the most beautiful necks I've ever seen." After the chain was clasped and secure, Christina felt a shiver go down her spine, and a warmth enveloped her. Adam ran his fingers down her neck and started kissing it.

"You see, I knew I wouldn't be able to resist kissing it, and I couldn't very well do it in front of the salesgirl. That's why I wanted to put it on you here. Mmmmm. So beautiful."

Christina closed her eyes, and her other senses took over. His touch, his smell, his lips caressing her neck, the sound and feel of his breath, all of it sent stirrings of desire all through her. She turned to face him, and he kissed her so softly, so sensuously, so passionately that she wanted to melt into him. This kiss was nothing like kissing Ali. She felt it all through her body and wanted more where that came from. This was so dangerous. For the first time since she got to 1971, she wanted to stay.

"I'm getting quite hung up on you, Terry. I know the key is important to you, and most likely from someone who's in love with you. I wanted to get you the chain because now, in a sense, I'm chained to you. I'm quite a chap of symbolism in case you hadn't noticed, and I wanted you to have this remembrance of me to go along with whoever it is who gave you that key."

"Oh, Adam!" They stayed there for a while, looking out over the water, holding hands, with her head on his shoulder. When the sun was fully set, they walked back to the bike, hopped on, and went to eat.

While riding, she held him close to her, with her arms around his waist. This was not supposed to happen. She thought she was falling for Ali, but Adam's kiss was like an electric shock, awakening a heart that was only going through the motions of life, beating for the sake of existing. But it's awakened and feels alive again, beating for a purpose. The last thing she intended was to fall for anyone. She felt euphoric happiness again, a feeling she hadn't felt since before John died. It's all wrong, but she didn't care.

At dinner, she could barely eat. Now, having felt the warmth and tenderness of his lips, she wanted it to continue. After dinner, when they were having coffee, he got serious. "Terry, I don't want to upset you, and please know that I'll be there to make sure everything goes well and hopefully everyone on our floor will be there, too."

"Uh oh, sounds like trouble. Does this have anything to do with your talk with Ali?"

"Yes, luv, it does. It seems that fateful night, Ali was given some papers from his family in Zatari to be given to Butch for his father. In all the excitement, Ali forgot about them and Butch left in quite the hurry without them. Needless to say, they've been in my possession ever since.

"It seems Senator Morgan is quite anxious about them and terribly agitated that Butch doesn't have them yet. In turn Butch is threatening Ali if he doesn't get them. It's quite important to Ali's family honor that these papers are given to Butch by tomorrow before his scheduled meeting with his guardian. Ali wanted me to give them to him today, but I refused. If Butch wants them, he needs to have the balls to get them himself."

"At our dorm?"

"Yes, luv. My condition for the return of the papers is that he is to apologize to you and to every one of us. It's up to you whether you want to accept his apology or not, but I want to see him squirm and quite possibly shit his pants. Are you okay with that, luv? If not, I'll make other arrangements."

"I guess I'm okay with it. Will you be there as my bodyguard?"

"I would prefer the title of 'personal protector'. The term bodyguard sounds so urban. At any rate, Ali and I will arrange a time, most likely at noon, so we'll all be there. At least we'll have the power of numbers. Hopefully, it'll make Butch feel extremely uncomfortable to have all of us giving him the hairy eyeball. Is it a go?"

"Sure. I guess I have to face the music at some point, even though I know I'll be uncomfortable, but I can't keep hiding forever. No sense in delaying the inevitable."

"I wanted to run it by you to make sure you didn't feel I was setting you up or some such thing. You know I'd never let anyone hurt you, don't you, luv?"

"I do." She interlocked their fingers.

He kissed her hand and got up. "Let's head off to the flick, luv." The theater was around the corner, so they walked over and stood in line to get their tickets. While in line, much to their surprise, Jerry came out of a bar and started making out in the doorway with the guy he was with. Both recognized him but said nothing until they walked away, with their arms around each other. Adam spoke first.

"Wasn't that Sarah's Jerry? Well, that was bonkers! You know, I thought that bloke might be a poof, and what do you know? Not that there's anything wrong with it. One of my dearest mates swings that way. People can't help how they're born. But it's quite unfair to our sweet Sarah. We shan't tell her. She'll find out soon enough."

"You're right, but poor Sarah. They're performing together in a few weeks, and finding out now could ruin their performance. Sarah has her heart set on the role of Sheila in *Hair* next semester. Getting that part is all she talks about, and Jerry is helping her with it. This scene has to play out on its own." She was pleasantly surprised by his attitude towards gay people. She would've thought he'd be the opposite and be homophobic.

"I'm sad for Sarah. So bloody unfair for such a good egg." They were silent for a while with their own thoughts. They got the tickets and headed into the theater. Christina had seen this movie a few times and knew when to close her eyes at certain parts but still jumped when the villainous woman jumped out at Clint Eastwood. At the end of the movie, people applauded and cheered when the hero saved the day.

When they left the theater, Adam asked if they could stop and get a drink before heading home. Christina agreed, and they walked to a bar not far from where they parked. All of the booths had a jukebox in them, which was normal for the times. The song "*Spooky*" by the Classics Four started playing. Their waitress came over, and Adam addressed her as "luv," which is how he addresses all girls. He looked at Christina and asked, "What would you like, luv?" She replied with ginger ale.

He turned back to her and while flipping through the play list he asked, "Any requests, luv?"

"I *do* have a request, and I hope you don't find it rude or snobbish."

"Well, luv, I've lived most of my life with the English aristocracy, so I'm quite sure it won't be snobbish. I hope I haven't offended you in some way."

"Oh my God, no. I've noticed that you call every female 'luv'. Can you please not use that on me? If you don't want to call me Terry, there's Tee. Or pain in the ass or anything, except 'luv'."

"I apologize, luv. Oops! There I go again. Sorry. It's become a habit. It's sometimes hard for me to remember names, so 'luv' seems to always work, and the girls seem to like it. So, what shall I call you? Not Terry or any version of it."

"Why?"

"I have my reasons. I need something all my own." They sat and drank their sodas, and she started singing along with the song, moving in her seat in a dancingly animated way to the music. One of the lines in the song makes reference to a spooky little girl.

"That's exactly what *you* are. A spooky little girl. I'm going to call you 'Spooky'."

"Spooky? Why? I'm not spooky, am I? Is it because of the black eye? Please, not Spooky. That makes me feel ghoulish."

"Well, you are mysterious, that's what I was thinking when I said spooky."

"It makes me sound creepy. Got something else?"

"How about Pookie?"

"Pookie? Really?"

"What's wrong with it, Pookie? See, it fits you perfectly." His smile was so disarming. She felt she was being charmed.

She repeated it a few times. "I guess I can live with that. Pookie, it is. Only use it when we're alone, okay? Neither of us will hear the end of it and I don't need anyone's bullshit."

"Agreed, and especially around Ali. He's quite taken with you."

"Yeah." She nodded her head and smiled. "That's sweet of you."

"Okay, 'Pookie', do you have any requests from the juke box?" He pulled out a quarter and flipped through the song list. She said in her best Jessica Walters voice, "Play *Misty* for me."

"Excellent choice. As you wish." The song came on, and she started moving to the music in the booth.

"Will you dance with me?" Adam took her hand and interlocked their fingers as he led her to the dance floor. While they were dancing, he sang softly in her ear, holding her close against his body. He murmured, "Your hair smells heavenly, like purple." Christina could feel his heart beating, and she was sure he could feel hers. The song ended, and he cradled her face in his hands and kissed her.

When they sat back down at the booth, he took her hand and said, "That's our song, Pookie. It will always remind me of today: your new name, our first date, our first kiss, our first sunset, our first movie, our first dance, and the first time I sang to you. Phew! We accomplished a lot today!" They sat in the booth until Adam looked at his watch and said, "I don't want this night to end, but unfortunately, it's time to head back."

As they were walking to the bike, he asked Christina not to mention any details of the evening to Ali or anyone. When asked why, he said, "Because today Ali begged me not to get involved with you romantically. He's crazy about you, and honestly, I don't want to hurt the bloke or make him feel I've betrayed him, which I'm such a cad, I have. I couldn't help myself, Pookie. I've wanted to kiss you since I first saw you when I intruded on your thoughts on my first day here. And even more so after you slammed the door in my face. Anyway, let's agree to keep Jerry and what happened between us tonight as our little secrets. Agreed? Not even Athena, okay?"

"Agreed. Thank you so much for the chain, Adam, but mostly thanks for a great night. I feel like a new woman."

"I'm going to kiss you goodnight right now instead of when we actually say goodnight because right now I have you all to myself." He kissed her and they could hear in the distance a clock striking eleven. Then he kissed her again, and again. Then Christina kissed him again and again, holding him close. She didn't want it to end.

Eventually, they hopped on the bike and headed home. Christina held on to him very tightly and rested her head on his back. She had that "in love" tingle all through her body and felt so alive. Falling in love is so magical. I must be insane! What am I doing? She threw her common sense out somewhere on the ride home between San Francisco and Berkeley and didn't care.

They got back to the dorm and walked up to their floor. Zoe and René were in the Common Room.

They all said goodnight and headed to their rooms. Christina thanked Adam again for the chain and the great evening and closed the door. As soon as Christina shut the door, she started to tell Zoe about her night but was immediately interrupted.

"Sorry, Tee, me first. Oh my God, Tee, you were right. The papers were right where you said they might be. And wait until you hear what these papers are! You're not going to believe what these two conniving, thieving families did to the American public and the world. Payback will be such a bitch! Butch Morgan will be going down for this when we get home! He can kiss the White House goodbye!"

# CHAPTER 28

Butch was on the lam. He was able to blend into the crowds at the frat houses for the Halloween party weekend, but after that, when all the passed-out partygoers came out of their stupors and went back to their living quarters, he found that without his money or illegal wares, he wasn't welcome anywhere. He wished he'd grabbed his jacket before running out of the dorm. Without his wad of cash and illegal drugs, he was like a lone man on a deserted island. And he really wanted to get high.

He tried to sneak back into the dorm but realized he didn't have his keys. He tried another time when he thought Ali may be there but when he did, that damn Limey was there, and he didn't dare show his face while Adam was there. He could've easily taken care of any of the bitches, especially Little Miss Priss, the cause of his current predicament.

He felt that after last Friday, she wouldn't be a problem for him if she were alone or with Ali. He was sure she was scared shitless of him, which gave him a good deal of satisfaction. He would've felt more empowered if things had gone off without a hitch. Now, every time he thought about how it turned out, there was a level of anger he had for himself and all those involved. It was the perfect plan, but it all went wrong and put him in a bad situation with his dormmates. He wasn't sure if they'd gone to the authorities or college officials, so he was reluctant to go to class for fear they were looking for him. He needed to lie low for a few days and see if he could find out anything through hearsay.

He was desperate for clean clothes and thought about going back to the dorm in the middle of the night and quietly knocking until Ali let him in. That didn't happen because as soon as he opened the door to their floor, he could hear that Limey asshole in the Common Room playing his guitar. Doesn't he ever sleep? With the little money he had with him, he got a room at a cheap motel and used the student cafeteria for his meals when he saw the coast was clear and no one from his floor was in there.

After almost a week of living on the run, he was getting anxious to get back into his room and to his drugs. He needed to catch Ali when he was alone to see if he could run interference for him and set a time and day to get back into the dorm and get his hands on those contracts and his drugs. He needed to get high.

He went to the Student Center and told them he lost his keys, which included the key to his dorm room and his mailbox. The woman there gave him the speech on being responsible and keeping track of your things. He wanted to tell her to shut her trap and give him the keys. He hated women. They were all sluts. He gave her his name and room number, and she said she'd be back shortly. After what seemed like an eternity, she returned and gave him replacement keys. He went to his mailbox and opened it up.

The only new items in there were four messages from the main office, each saying his father called and needed to speak with him immediately. Butch was supposed to contact him as soon as he got the contracts. He can't blow this chance for the easy life, even though his own personal plan is going to work out fine thanks to his manipulation of Ali. Such a dumb A-Rab. He had to find a way to get his ass back into the dorm, but he knew he couldn't saunter back in as if nothing happened. Ali was his ticket back in.

He looked at the clock and figured he'd try to catch Ali coming out of one of his classes or maybe intercept him before he entered their building. If he hid outside, he might be able to catch him before going in. He turned right as he walked out of the mail room and felt someone grab him by the back collar.

"Where do you think you're going, Mr. Morgan?" Butch turned and saw the Dean of Students standing there, holding onto his collar. Sons of bitches turned him in! Ali is going to pay for this! Butch didn't reply to his question, waiting for the axe to fall.

"Where in God's name have you been? We've been trying to find you since Sunday afternoon. Do you have any idea how much I despise having my Sundays ruined by a parent who is trying to contact his child? And not only that, but you disappeared completely! This puts our college in an unbelievably bad light, young man! You haven't been to any of your classes this week. We left messages with all your professors to have you report to me immediately as soon as you got the message. They've all reported you haven't been to class all week."

He was leading Butch by the scruff of his neck somewhere, and Butch started to panic. There was no proof of him doing anything to that bitch and if Ali reported him for trying to choke him, he'll pay dearly when he gets back to the Middle East. Butch would see to that.

It's their word against his and he was the son of Senator Bradley Morgan who gave a hefty sum to the college so that Butch could come for this semester. He was guaranteed passing grades regardless of his performance, so he could transfer to an Ivy League school. They'll all pay if they screw that up for him.

The Dean brought him to his office and sat him down on the opposite side of the desk. "What's going on with you, Mr. Morgan? You're a mess, and you stink to high heaven. When was the last time you showered or changed your clothes?" He paused, waited for an answer which did not come. "Are you involved with drugs, young man? I'd hate to have to tell your father that. We can get you help if you are, and we would do it quietly. You had us very worried about you with your disappearance. Where have you been?"

Butch sat there and shrugged his shoulders. He was ready to burst into tears. So much had gone wrong over the past few days, and he felt trapped in a corner with no way out. He thought for a split second about admitting to taking drugs, using that as an excuse for what he did to Miss Priss and Ali, but instead, sat there silently.

"Don't sit there like an idiot! I want an answer! What have you been up to?"

Butch burst into tears. It wasn't a ploy for sympathy or to think. He couldn't hold them back any longer, mainly because he wasn't sure if things were reported or not. He was a boy with no one to turn to. He couldn't face his father if what happened last Friday were found out. He sat there blubbering like a baby. It seemed nothing would ever go right for him. All at once, everything came exploding back at him. Vi, his childhood, his mother's distaste towards him, Odelia being sent away, boarding school, no friends, came back in the form of self-pity. Later, he thought how smart he'd been because it immediately changed the mood of the Dean. It took him off the offense, and he became the sympathetic elder. Though he'd never admit it, his tears were real, and he had a hard time stopping.

The Dean came over to the other side of the desk and pulled a chair close to him. "What's troubling you, son? Is there anything you need to tell me? It will stay strictly between us. I won't tell your parents. That's what we're here for. We're here to help you with anything you need."

Through his sobbing Butch managed to talk. "I was supposed to call my daddy last week, but I've been sick, real sick. I think it was the flu. I was at a Halloween party at one of the frat houses, and I started to get the chills. They let me stay there until I felt better. I lost my keys, so I couldn't get mail or into my room. I was in the office getting extra keys to my room and mailbox. I'm really scared because my daddy is going to kill me." He felt more at ease because nothing was mentioned about the events of last Friday night. If they had reported him, it would've been the first thing the Dean would've brought up.

"Calm down, Mr. Morgan. Everything will be fine. Your father will be relieved to know you're safe. He's been worried sick about you. We'll call him right now to let him know you're well, and you can speak to him yourself and explain where you've been." He picked up the phone and called the operator. "I'd like to make a person-to-person call to Senator Bradley Morgan in Baton Rouge, Louisiana, from Daniel McMillan of UC Berkeley."

They waited for Senator Morgan to answer. "Dean McMillan! I declare I'm right glad to finally hear from y'all. I sure do hope y'all are calling to tell me my boy has finally turned up. He's not in some kind of trouble, is he?"

"No, Senator, no trouble at all. From what I've been told, he had been sick and convalescing at one of the frat houses. I'll let you speak to him." Butch was handed the phone. He dreaded talking to his father.

"Hi, Daddy. I'm really sorry I didn't call sooner, but I've been sick with the flu bug or somethin'. I was feeling right poorly, Pop. Today is the first day I felt better, but I lost my keys and couldn't get into my mailbox for y'all's messages until I got a new set."

"Harold, do y'all have the contracts? You best be saying y'all have them in your possession!"

"Well, Daddy, not really because I haven't been to my room since Friday, so I haven't seen Ali since he got them. By the way, I'm feeling much better now, thanks for asking."

Senator Morgan was livid. "Cut the bullshit, Harold. Don't y'all realize how important those contracts are? Y'all want to tell me exactly where they are?"

He dreaded giving his father his answer. "Probably still with Ali."

"Are y'all telling me y'all don't know where they are? Son of a bitch, Harold! Can't y'all do anything right? Y'all better hope they're with Ali because if y'all fuck this up I swear to the little Lord baby Jesus, I'm going to personally strangle y'all with my own two hands. Then, by God, I'm going to turn y'all over to the Louisiana police and let them do whatever they want!"

"Daddy, listen to me. I was sick, real sick!"

"Do y'all really expect me to believe that with your track record? Y'all were either too drunk or too high. Are y'all ever going to grow up, boy? I told y'all this is important and not to screw it up! I should've listened to your mama when she said y'all couldn't be trusted to handle something like this! I put my faith in you and gave y'all this chance to prove yourself and the only thing y'all proved is that you're a fuck-up! Y'all have really done it this time, Harold."

"But Daddy, I…", his father curtly cut him off.

"Don't you dare say one more thing, do you hear me, boy? I don't want to hear another word out of your damn mouth until y'all call me to tell me y'all have the contracts. I expect to hear from y'all as soon as you have your hands on them. If y'all blow this deal, Harold, I swear, y'all will be out on the street, on your own. This is the last straw. I'll disown your ass if this deal falls apart, y'all can guarantee that! Now let me talk to the Dean."

Butch handed the phone over to the Dean. There were a lot of yeses on the side of the conversation Butch was hearing with stern looks being thrown his way. The Dean hung up and told Butch to come back when he needs to use the phone to call his father. "He told me you'll need to call him sometime today. I'll leave word with the main office that you're to use the phone whenever you return."

Dean McMillan looked at this crumbled young man and felt such pity for him. Although he couldn't hear what was being said by Senator Morgan to his son, he could hear the tone in which it was delivered, and it sounded like young Harold was ripped a new asshole.

"Are you sure you're okay, son? You seem troubled. I'm here to help if you need it. As I said before, it would be between us and no one else. Would you like to talk about it?"

"No thanks. I'm fine. I knew he was going to be mad at me. He's always mad at me, so I'm used to it." He got up and walked to the door. "Well, I guess I'd better go and do what my daddy asked."

"Your father told me that everything was fine. Is that true, Harold?"

"Why yes, sir! Would a senator lie to y'all?" He turned and walked out. He had to get his hands on those contracts. The first order of business was to find his little slave boy, Ali. He checked some of his classes and the library with no luck. He finally caught a glimpse of him leaving the cafeteria. He snuck up behind him, grabbed his elbow, and ushered him under a tree. Ali was startled by him as he grabbed him from behind. Butch wasted no time getting to the point.

"I need those contracts and I need them now!" Ali stared at him for a minute. He unbuttoned the top button on his crisp white shirt and the marks on his neck were still evident from Butch's attack. "Fuck you, Ali!"

"Is that all you have to say for yourself? You're even worse than I thought, and after what I know of you, you're lower than the lowest."

"Yeah sure, ok. Look, I need them contracts. Y'all need to give them to me today, ya hear? Like right now. They're important to our families and I'm sure both of us have a lot riding on them, so neither of us can fuck this up. Go get them right now and bring them to me."

"I can't."

"Yes, y'all can and y'all will, or suffer the consequences. Don't fuck with me on this, Ali because I ain't in the mood for any of your A-Rab bullshit!"

"I don't have them."

"What?"

"I don't have them. I've hardly even thought of them. I don't know what happened to them. If anything, I'd guess Adam has them. If he doesn't, I don't know where they are."

"Son of a motherfucking bitch, Ali! Don't y'all know how important they are? The first thing y'all should have done is make sure they were safe! Y'all are such a fucking asshole!"

"First of all, I don't know how important they are because I haven't even looked at them. My only involvement is as the delivery boy. This whole mess is because of you. If you didn't drug and beat Taraysa and try to rape her then you'd have your important papers. Maybe if you didn't try to kill me when I tried to stop you, then we would both know where they are. You're an evil beast! How could you do that to someone, especially a girl? You could have killed her! What would you have done if she had died? As it is, you may have broken some bones in her face."

"It was the drugs, Ali. I snorted a lot of speed."

"You're such a liar! It wasn't the drugs, it was you. You're malicious, mean, vindictive, and pitiful. Luckily for us both, after begging, she agreed not to call in the authorities about what happened. Don't think I've forgotten your promise of revenge if I don't cooperate with all your evil schemes. And now I see exactly how 'the file' you have on me came about. I despise you, and all this trouble with the contracts or wherever they are will remain your fault. You put this on yourself, and I won't share the blame with you. My only worry at that time was making sure Taraysa would make it through the night."

"How fucking sweet. Y'all make me want to puke. Well, Princey, all I can say is y'all better start worrying about it now because I believe both sides know I don't have the contracts and y'all were the last ones to have them. My dad is super pissed about it and y'all know I love to share misery. Y'all better hightail your ass to the dorm and tell that fucking Limey that I need those contracts and he'd better give them up. And I need to get back into the dorm. It's my room and my daddy's paying for it, and I intend to move back in tonight. Y'all get that all squared away for me. Understand? Y'all make those two guys give their word they won't try to beat the shit out of me when I come back. If they do, it will only be trouble for you, if y'all know what I mean, Princey."

"I'll do what I can. I have to say it's been so comfortable in the dorm without you."

"I'm sure it has. And I bet y'all tore our room apart looking for my special file on y'all." He snickered his horrible, evil laugh. "Do you think I'd leave it anywhere y'all could find it? If y'all did, then y'all are stupider than I thought."

"I wish I'd never agreed to come to this college and perform these duties for my father."

"Yeah, yeah, yeah. Boo hoo for Princey. I'll be waiting here for you. Y'all better get your ass up there and get my contracts. And bring me some clean clothes along with my jacket, with my drug stash and money in it. And don't take too long, asshole."

"I have a class now. I'll go as soon as my class is over."

Butch knocked his cap off, grabbed his arm and said, "You'll go now!"

Ali shook his arm free, picked up the cap and stared at Butch. Ali wanted to slap him across the face. Butch was caught off guard by the defiance Ali showed and he didn't like it.

"Don't you ever touch me again, you disgusting pig! I'm going to class now. I'll meet you back here in two hours and not one second before. That should give me enough time. I'm not your servant boy. You can get your own clothes when you're allowed back into the dorm."

Ali didn't wait for a response and walked away. Every day since last Friday, Ali was beginning to change from a sweet and kind naïve young man to one who was learning about the ugliness that can be in this world, and his soft exterior was hardening. He even entertained the thought of letting Butch exact his revenge on him and welcome the death that would be certain upon his return to his country because of the dishonor to his family.

The only bright spot in his life was Taraysa. He loved her more than words could express. The sight of her beaten, battered, and bruised sickened him and made him feel anger and shame. Adam kept saying Ali was the hero, but he knew in his heart that wasn't true. For that split second, he let his fear of Butch's retribution stand in the way of what was right. He thought for a fleeting moment to turn around and walk away so he wouldn't have any consequences. But he loved her more than his own safety and looking at what Butch was poised to do to her tore at his heart and riled him to the point of action.

Ever since he had to become Butch's constant companion in his free time, it left Taraysa alone and lately she has been in the company of Adam. He felt very secure when she despised him, but he was getting the feeling they were becoming closer, and it was eating away at him. He knew Adam was protective of her, and when he looked at her…well, Ali knew what that look meant because he looked at her the same way.

Having to be with Butch all the time meant the time they spent together out of class was gone. He lived for those moments, eating, walking, laughing, studying, watching how she flipped her hair and how it bounced as she walked, the smell of her shampoo, and the softness of her skin when he touched her. When she smiled at him, it lit up his world. Now those occasions are gone, and it seems by necessity he was replaced by Adam. He would still be able to share their classes together, but their whole dynamic changed because of Butch. And now he had to go to his dorm mates and advocate for the person he hated most in this world.

After class, he headed to the dorm and found Adam and Taraysa in Adam's room working on the art assignment. At least that's what he hoped they were doing. He asked to speak to Adam alone, and Taraysa made an odd remark and left. Ali walked over to the desk to check the progress of her report and was satisfied with the number of pages she'd written and that she was busy for most of the time. It made him uneasy to see Adam's guitar on the bed. Was he serenading her?

"So, Ali, what's up?"

"This is very difficult for me, Adam. I have to ask you something about that Friday night."

"Sure, mate. Is something wrong? You're looking quite miffed. Hope I can help."

"I do too." He took a deep breath and continued. "When I came back from Khalid's that night, I had a packet of papers with me. Those papers were to be given to the Morgan family. Amid that horrible night, I completely forgot about them. My only concern was for Taraysa." He covered his face with his hands as if trying to blot out the image ingrained in his memory. "I was so afraid she was going to die." As he spoke those words, his voice cracked, and he fought back tears. He hesitated for a moment, getting his thoughts back on track. "Well, it seems Senator Morgan is very anxious to get them. Since I don't remember what happened to them, I'm hopeful you have them in your possession and they weren't discarded, because that will be troublesome for me. Do you have them?"

"And if I do?"

"If you do, I'll be most indebted to you. I ask that you give them to me so I can give them to Butch who will in turn make sure they get to his father."

"What are these papers, Ali?"

"I don't know, and I don't care. All I know is I was given the responsibility to get them to Butch and I failed. My honor is at stake."

"You keep talking about your honor and the honor of your family. Does your family know what a dishonorable person Butch Morgan is? That he's a drug dealing, woman beating lowlife would-be rapist? If honor is so important to them, why would they align you with such a bloody turd? No disrespect intended."

"I'm duty-bound to serve my king as are all the subjects of my country, regardless of station or relation to our ruler. If I fail, I'll shame my king and country. I've only a handful of people whom I'd call a friend, and you're one of them. If I could, I'd let Butch fail in this task he was also given, but it's a double-edged sword that will injure me much more than it will harm him. Please, Adam, tell me you have them and that you'll give them to me. I also need your word and the word of Jean-René that you won't greet him with violence and retaliation for last Friday. As much as I'd prefer not, he needs to come back to our dorm. Questions will arise from college officials if he's not allowed back, and I fear the consequences."

"So, we have to let the bugger get off scott-free? Ali, have you looked at your neck? Have you seen Terry's face? Have you seen the bruises on her arms and legs?"

"Stop it, Adam. You know I have! I can barely look her in the eye, thinking about what he did to her. I feel ashamed that I wasn't able to do more to help her. My feelings for her are well known to every person who knows me. I'd die for her!"

"So, explain to me how you can ask us to let him back in and act like nothing has happened? I'm sorry, mate. It looks like we may be in a pickle here because I can't let it be that easy for him."

"This is the position I've been put in, and I have no choice but to follow through on the plans of my king. I'm no happier about this than you or anyone else in our dorm. I'm duty-bound to my country."

Adam took a deep breath, walked over, and sat on the bed. He ran his fingers through his hair, looking down at the floor, thinking of a solution. He rubbed the back of his neck and, after a few minutes, got up and walked over to Ali. "I tell you what, mate, I do have the papers and they're securely locked away. If Butch wants them, he needs to come and ask for them himself. Tomorrow around noon will be fine because everyone should be here then. He needs to apologize to each of us individually, with a personal apology to you and Terry. If he does that, I'll give you the papers. What you do with them is your concern. I'll speak with Jean-René, and you have our word that there won't be an assault on him by us. But you'd better warn him that all he has to do is put one toe out of line with any person from our dorm and I'll beat the bloody hell out of him, understood? And he can no longer sell drugs from his room. I'm bloody tired of all the riffraff coming around here."

"You won't give them to me now?"

"If he wants them, that's the only way he's going to get them. You've heard my terms. Besides, I thought the papers were yours, and honestly, I was flummoxed that you never mentioned them."

"Did you read them, Adam?"

"No, mate," he lied. "They aren't mine, so they were none of my business. I put them into a folder, and that was that, waiting for you to ask for them. If I had known they belonged to Butch I would've made a bonfire with them. Can I ask you something?"

"Of course."

"What does this bugger have on you to give him such power over you? Why do you let him bully you?"

"I cannot speak of it. He's a wicked person who lives to hurt. I'm stuck and there's nothing to be done. Thank you, Adam, for your concern. I'll relay your terms to Butch. He was hoping to get back into the dorm tonight, but I guess he'll have to wait one more night. Thank you for keeping the papers safe. You're truly a good friend. May I ask one more favor?"

"Sure, Ali. Whatever you need."

Ali walked over to the desk where Terry's reference book housed her report on Toulouse Lautrec. He sat down, opened the book, and stared down at the report, concentrating on her handwriting. He smiled to himself because he knew that when it got a little sloppy, she was on a roll and wrote quickly so she wouldn't forget her train of thought. Over the last few months, they'd spent a lot of time working together on projects and assignments. He picked up her pen and held it in his hand and nervously fiddled with it.

"I know you're spending a lot of time with our Taraysa. I beg of you, please don't get involved with her romantically. I know she looks to you for protection, and you do it so magnificently, whereas I'm so cowardly." Adam started to interrupt, but Ali cut him off. "If you knew the whole truth about everything, you'd know what I say is true. What is also true is… I love her. I've asked her many times to think about coming to my country to meet my family, but she sees our cultures as too different, and she's most likely correct. That doesn't change the fact that I'd do anything to have her in my life forever. I've even thought of forsaking my king and country and adapting to her way of life here. I've loved her from the moment she knocked me down right outside this room. And the people on this floor, with the exception of Butch have been my first real friendships.

"I know you feel protective of her, but I implore you to keep your relationship with her on a friend-only basis. We only have a little more than a month together before we all go our separate ways unless I can think of a way to stay with her. I can't let the rest of my time here be watching the two of you other than as friends. Please, Adam, promise me you won't take it any further than that." At that point, Ali put the pen down and stood up to face Adam. When he put the pen down, he unknowingly shut off the recorder.

"Sure, mate. You know me! I'm a lady's man, and the last thing I want is to get into a relationship. Especially being a musician. Chicks throw themselves at us all the time. Terry is a friend, just like all the mates here in this dorm are. I want to make sure she's safe, the same as I'd do for any girl, as an Englishman and a gentleman."

"Not even a kiss, ok?"

"Sure, mate. No kissing allowed. Besides, don't you remember, she really isn't too fond of me? She did slam the door in my face upon meeting me, remember? You've got nothing to worry about. All it is, mate, is friendship. Besides, I have my eye on this one particular girl."

"Someone you met here, or is she from England?"

"Honestly, I haven't the foggiest idea where she's from. Not even sure of her name, although I think her first name is Christina." Well, Adam thought to himself, at least that part's not a lie.

"Thank you, Adam. I'll tell Butch your terms. We'll be back at noon tomorrow. See you later."

Ali walked out and knocked on Terry's door to tell her they were done speaking and she could resume work on her paper. It warmed his heart when she asked where he was going. He knew she cared for him, but did she love him? He was always trying to think of a way for them to spend their lives together but could never come up with a sound idea. He couldn't bear to think of December when they would go their separate ways.

He found Butch in the same spot and told him of Adam's stipulations. He became outraged.

"Who does he think he is, God? Why do I have to apologize to everyone? That mother-fucking Limey asshole! He can't tell me what to do in my room and keep me from my shit! I'm not waiting until tomorrow to get into my room. Do y'all hear me? I'm not! And where's my jacket?"

Ali shrugged his shoulders. "I'm sorry Butch, those were his conditions. If you don't like it, maybe you should tell him yourself. But, seeing that he's the only one who knows where your precious papers are, it seems you have no choice."

"Oh yeah? Well, I do have a choice! I can choose to go to the Dean and tell him that Adam has something of my father's that he won't give me, and he won't let me back into my room!"

"If you do that, do you think Adam is going to remain quiet about what you did last Friday night, and that you sell drugs from your room, among other things? All the Dean would have to do is look at Taraysa's face and my neck, and he'd know Adam was telling the truth. I'd tread lightly around him. He's the only one who wants to turn you in and see you punished. If you were wise, you'd agree to his terms and wait until tomorrow. Maybe the next time you're given an important task from your father you won't let drugs, beating girls, attempted rape and attempted murder get in the way of your success."

"Are y'all forgetting, Princey, what your consequences are in all this?"

"How can I when you keep reminding me of it?' Ali began walking away.

Butch yelled to him, "I'm supposed to call my daddy as soon as I get those contracts! There's gonna be trouble if I don't call him today! And where are my clean clothes and my jacket, huh? And where am I supposed to stay tonight? Hey! I'm talking to you! Y'all get back here! Ali! Get back here! Y'all are gonna pay for this, Princey!" Butch thought about running after him but with all the people around campus right now, he thought he'd better not. He's already in enough hot water and didn't need to call attention to himself by getting into a fistfight with his roommate in front of everyone.

Panic started pulsing through his body. His father's going to kill him. Should he call him and lie and say he has the contracts? He could feel the tears once again rising up.

He called out again to Ali but was ignored. Ali had to get to the library for the paper due on Tuesday. Usually, he did this sort of work with Taraysa but because she wouldn't leave the dorm and needed to be shielded from any violence Butch may decide to rain on her, he stayed away from her. It still hurt him to look at her discolored face, and he felt deep shame and guilt for what happened to her. Although he's a prince, he felt completely unworthy of her.

At 10:30 that night, the phone rang at Dean McMillan's home. "What now?" he said to himself as he headed for the phone. It never rang this late unless something was wrong. He picked it up, and the operator stated there was a person-to-person phone call for Daniel McMillan from Senator Bradley Morgan. "Shit!" he thought to himself. He didn't know what was going on between father and son, but it wasn't good.

"Evenin', Dan."

"Good evening, Senator. Is something wrong? What can I do for you?"

"I've been waiting all day for that bastard son of mine to call, and I haven't heard a word from him."

"Well, Senator, he did seem shaken when he left my office this afternoon."

"I was supposed to hear from him today, and as of right now, I still haven't. I've booked a flight tomorrow and will be arriving in San Francisco at around noon. If y'all can't have a car pick me up, I'll rent a vehicle, but one way or another, I'll be seeing my son tomorrow. I insist he not be told of my arrival. There is a possibility I may be taking him out of Berkeley and bringing him home. I'll make my final decision tomorrow. Regardless of whether he stays or not, I'm counting on Berkeley to keep its part of the deal and give him glowing recommendations to the Ivy League schools y'all and I discussed earlier this year. There will be a hefty bonus for the school if he's accepted. Will there be a car waiting for me?"

"Certainly, Senator, even if I have to pick you up myself."

"Excellent! Then I'll see y'all tomorrow at around noon." Senator Morgan didn't wait for a response and hung up before Dan McMillan was able to say another word. Dan slammed the phone on the receiver when he realized the Senator had rudely ended the conversation. For the next hour all he could say over and over as he walked around his house slamming drawers was "Shit!"

# CHAPTER 29

Christina dreamt of John last night. The details of the dream became unclear so quickly, but they were young, in their yard, walking hand in hand towards the back of the property where the apple trees grow. Did she dream of him because of the awakening of her heart again? Maybe she felt guilty over the fact that she couldn't suppress the tingle she felt and the warm feeling overtaking her when she thought of last night. She was bursting to tell Zoe all about it but prides herself on keeping promises. There will be time later on when they return to their present lives to fill Zoe in on her first date in thirty-something years.

Oh, John, my poor, doomed, sweet, loving husband, she thought. As much as she wants it to be so, nothing could change what happened to him. She asked O'Connell if she could go back to the time right before John left the house the night he was killed and stop him from leaving. He told her if she did that, it would change too many factors, including being a part of this mission. "It's vitally important to let what's already occurred be allowed to happen. Time travel is very tricky and somewhat dangerous. You can't change events preceding your travel date. I'm sorry, but you can't save your husband. His fate has already been determined, and there's nothing you can do to change it."

That weighed heavily on her for a while because it was a restless idea that formed in 1971. Unfortunately, what's done is done, and when she gets back, she'll be going back to the same sad sack life alone. At least this year, she won't have to live through Thanksgiving looking at his empty seat at the table. She doesn't think she'll ever eat turkey again.

She lay in bed for a while, going over the whole wonderful evening she had last night. She tried to talk herself out of feeling so euphoric, especially because they only have one more month here. She started to feel a vastly different feeling for Adam as opposed to her feelings for Ali. Lying there thinking, she felt like Ali led her out of the dark forest, but Adam is the one leading her to the field of amazing wildflowers. Her brain knew this life here was going to end soon, but her heart wasn't listening. It had its path it was going to pursue, no matter what her common sense was telling her.

And now…it's like a light has been turned on. A bright hot light, and with that first kiss by the bay, she felt the pieces of her heart lift themselves up out of the darkness and fuse themselves back together to become alive once again, pulsing, vibrant, and beckoning this wonderful feeling. She wondered if the "other" Christina living on the East Coast felt this euphoria.

Last night, shortly after Adam and Christina got back, René went to the girl's room and played the recorded conversation of Adam and Ali from the pen and explained to Christina more fully what was in the contracts. Their plan deceived not only the citizens of the US but what Senator Morgan planned and eventually carried out, had a long-lasting effect on the global economy, and made the movers and shakers of this deal exceedingly rich, including Butch Morgan. The more René told Christina, the angrier she became. They had to play dumb and act as though they knew nothing. René mapped out his plan for tomorrow. The three of them agreed on how to play it out.

Christina got up and dressed and headed to the Common Room. Adam and René were talking, actually sort of arguing about Butch coming today. It abruptly stopped when Christina walked into the room. René was putting on the act, making it seem he knew nothing about what was going on, and Christina went along with it, following his lead.

René stopped arguing with Adam and asked, "Is this agreeable to you, Terry?"

"I have to face him at some point, why not today? Everyone will be here and now is a good a time as any, I suppose."

"Adam, how could you agree to this? I don't know if I can sit back and do nothing after what he did to Terry and Ali. He deserves to be beaten senseless."

"Well, mate, if you had Ali standing in front of you, asking his friend to do this one favor for him, I'd hope you would've also agreed. I'm a man of my word." He looked at Christina and gave her a wink. They both knew what it meant, and she felt the thrill run through her. Man, he's so damn cute. What am I doing? she thought.

"It's okay, Jean-René. Everything will be fine. What can he do with all of us here?"

They argued more until René reluctantly agreed and left the room, saying he'd be back at eleven-thirty. As soon as they heard the door to the stairwell close, Adam quickly moved in and whirled her around and kissed her. She wondered if she had ever kissed lips so soft and sensuous. He made her knees weak.

"Good morning, Pookie. I hope you slept well. I know I did. The best I've slept in an exceptionally long time, and I usually don't sleep well. You're looking rather lovely today, as always." He gently stroked the bruised left side of her face. "It's looking better. Are you feeling quite well? I hope you're not frightened or nervous about today. You need to remember that Jean-René and I will be here." He interlocked their fingers, which sent a tingle through her while staring into her eyes. "Thank you ever so much for such a brilliant evening last night. I didn't want it to end. I think you've put a spell on me and captured my heart. Whatever am I going to do with you, Pookie?"

"I don't know, maybe kiss me?"

"If you insist." He started kissing her neck, working his way up to her lips.

They heard someone enter the floor, which made them break their embrace, and Adam quickly sat at the table while Christina headed to the sink. She poured herself a cup of coffee from their electric percolator and turned to see Ali coming into the Common Room.

"Ah, good morning Taraysa, Adam. I hope you both slept well. Has Adam told you about today?"

"Yes, Ali, he has."

"I apologize for putting you in such an uncomfortable position. Too many questions would arise if Butch weren't allowed back into his dorm. I feel so much of a coward to be unable to stand up to him, but hopefully you won't hate me for what I've asked."

"I could never hate you, Ali, and I'm sure you know that. It'll be fine. Butch may have shaken me up, but I'm far from broken." She walked up to Ali and kissed him on the cheek.

"Adam, have I your word and the word of Jean-René that no harm will come to Butch? He asked me to come up here and make sure he won't be ambushed."

"You have our word that we'll control ourselves."

"He asked me to find out about his jacket. Have you seen it?"

"Hmmm, his jacket." He put his hand to his face in a thinking position. "Maybe he should ask about it when he comes to apologize and get his papers."

"You have the papers here in the dorm? Will they be here when he comes at noon?

"They will."

"He'll be here before noon so he can shower and change his clothes. He's been in the same clothing for the last week."

"That means he probably smells as rotten as his heart." Ali laughed, and it diffused some of the tension.

"Taraysa, can I speak to you privately for a moment, please?"

"Sure." Adam excused himself and left the room. "What is it, Ali?"

"Please don't hold it against me for acting in favor of Butch. I've no choice, and I'm put in a position where I'm helpless but to do as he asks."

"And why is that, Ali? I don't understand. He tried to kill you. The marks are still on your neck. What will stop him from doing that again? Why do you put up with his crap?"

"I'm a coward."

"Stop saying that! You upset me when you keep saying that! I don't know what's happened to you. You've changed so much in the last few weeks from the Ali I first met. The spark of life you had living here in America is gone, along with the joy in your heart. The twinkle in your eye is gone, along with your infectious laugh. Butch has killed all that. We used to be inseparable, and now I barely see you. I'm worried about you, Ali. I don't want him to ruin the person you are."

"Come home with me, Taraysa. Please! We can be far away from all the ugliness here and be able to be together and be happy. We can never be happy here."

"And we can never be happy there. We've talked about this so many times before, and you know my answer. My life will be over as soon as I set foot in your country. I know what would happen to me there."

"I'd protect you, I swear."

"You'd protect me? How would you do that? Your family honor would always dictate what you'd be able to do, and I'm sure protecting me would end up at the bottom of the list."

"See, you do think me a coward."

"No, I don't! I'm being realistic. You're an honorable and obedient young man and will always do as your king commands. That's not cowardly, that's integrity. Besides, I'd die in your country.

As I've told you before, my life is here. I'm a true red-white-and blue American girl. The future that lies ahead of me is here, not in the Middle East. Let's take pleasure in the friendship we've made with each other and enjoy the month or so we have left here at Berkeley."

"Is that all it is to you, Taraysa, friendship?"

"Ali, with all the differences we have culturally and spiritually, not to mention the freedoms so restrictive against women in your country, it can't go any further than friendship. As much as I'd love to see you in my future, friendship is all I can offer. Our backgrounds are vastly apart. It has nothing to do with my feelings for you or your feelings for me. Our worlds don't blend, at least not at this time. Please don't ask me again. Besides, I'm just a kid! I'm only eighteen years old and I don't even have a passport."

"You don't need a passport, you can come on my private plane. I'm a member of the royal family. We don't stop at customs, so that would be no problem."

"And that makes it worse and it honestly scares the shit out of me! I've a family who I love, parents who'd be worried sick for my safety if they knew you wanted me to come home with you and that I didn't need a passport. My father is a strict Italian Catholic. He'd be on the first flight out here and drag me home by my hair if he caught wind of what you've said. I had to fight to come to Berkeley for one semester, and you think he's going to be okay with me going to your country in the Middle East?"

"They don't have to know. You could come for a quick visit, meet my family, and be home before they knew you were away."

"So, let me get this straight. Lying to my family is okay? Honor and respect for my family doesn't matter as much as it does to yours? Can you hear yourself, Ali? My family deserves from me the same honor you give to yours. It's no different. What you're saying is like a slap in the face to me and my parents. I'm not going to keep going over this with you, Ali. Don't make it harder for me than it already is. My life is enriched by knowing you, but you and I cannot be." She waited for his response, and when there was none, she said, "This is the last time we're going to talk about this, okay?"

"Very well. Then will you at least promise me one thing?"

"What is it?"

"Please don't get involved with Adam. Please promise me you won't let things get past friendship."

"What!?"

"Please, you know what I'm asking. Promise me you won't get involved with Adam."

That hit a nerve with her. "I'll promise you no such thing! What makes you think you have the right to ask that? I'm in charge of my own destiny, and I'll do exactly as I see fit for me to do. By asking that, it tells me the kind of life you want for me in your country. My life belongs to me, and I'll pick who'll be in it."

"Don't get angry with me, please. I don't want to see you with someone else. It would hurt me if you and Adam became lovers."

"Lovers? Are you kidding? Don't you know anything about me yet? I'm a little hurt, Ali. You think I'm that easy? It seems like you're trying to control me, and I'm my own person who can think for herself. I'll never be the personal property of some man. My life is mine to live, and I can't have someone giving me orders and ultimatums. At this time, the only man who would have that right is my father, and he's not the one asking."

"I'm sorry, Taraysa. I can't help myself. You know how I feel about you. I couldn't bear to see you with someone else."

"Ali, in a month or so, some of us will be leaving here. I'm fairly certain I won't be seeing anyone whom I've met at Berkeley, with the exception of Athena, for a very long time. Don't worry about it. I'm not here to find love or romance, I'm here because I got a scholarship for a semester, and I'm making the most of it. I came here to learn more about art. You, Jean-René, Sarah, and Adam, are the icing on the cake. It's made the whole thing that much sweeter."

She remained calm as if he had said nothing to upset her. She took his hand and looked at him. He really had such sad eyes lately. It broke her heart, especially after how close they'd become. "No more talk of what happens after this semester, okay? You have a place in my heart, and no one or nothing can change that. Our whole lives are ahead of us. One never knows what the future holds. Our paths will hopefully meet again in our future."

He looked down at the floor and sighed. "Very well. I'm sure you're right. I'm sorry if I acted improperly." He turned away and started walking towards the door. "I'm going to find Butch. We'll be back sometime after 11:30. Please don't be afraid. I'll see you then."

Ali left, and Adam came out to the Common Room. "Everything alright?"

"Yeah, I suppose. I guess I'm frustrated with this whole situation. I'd love to know how Butch can manipulate him. I can't imagine what it could be, but it must be bad. I feel so sorry for him."

"Are you digging on him, Pookie?"

"Ali?"

"Yes, Ali. You two were together quite often, and forgive me, but I needed to ask."

"Honestly, I do love him, but I'm not *in* love with him. There's a big difference. Love is a very unusual emotion with so many layers." She grabbed his hands, interlocking their fingers, like he does to her. "I'd hope you already knew the answer." She kissed him to show him exactly where her feelings lie. The sensation of his lips sent thrills through her body.

They broke away and Adam said, "Let's head into my room and finish the art report, and then we'll be free to have a brilliant weekend. Would you come to the Pub tonight and hear me play? Sarah will be there too. It'd be lovely to have you come. Think about it."

"Okay, I'll think about it. Let's get cracking." Christina got her reference books and draft of her report and headed to his room and started to organize and rewrite it. She was using René's desk and Adam was using his. Time flew while they were working, and Adam looked at his watch and said it was getting close to the time Ali and Butch would be coming.

"I have to use the loo. I'll be right back."

She sat at the desk, totally engrossed in her paper, and didn't notice someone had entered the room. She looked up and jumped when she saw Butch standing next to her.

"My, my, sweetie pie. What happened to your face? Y'all fall down some stairs? Can I get y'all some soup?" He winked and cackled that horrible laugh of his. He hurriedly walked out of the room and into his.

His remark about the soup made her so angry that she was surprised steam wasn't coming out of every orifice in her head. She'd been thinking of how to handle this whole apology thing and wondered how she was going to ever get revenge. Now she was pissed. He lit the fuse of this little stick of dynamite. She looked down at her book and had her answer. She was going to keep this little encounter with Butch to herself for now. He set himself up for some big-time painful payback, and it's coming today and it's coming in spades.

Adam came back into the room, and Christina made herself look busy, but her brain was racing. Adam said Butch was here and was going to take a shower, get dressed and then they would meet in the Common Room.

"Are you alright, Pookie? I'll be here to protect you."

"Thanks, Adam. I'm fine." She knew exactly what to do and it was going to be so satisfying to get supreme payback.

As everyone arrived, they all went into the Common Room. Sarah stopped in quickly and told them to give him hell. She couldn't stay because of the play rehearsal, so it would only be the five of them. Christina sat between Zoe and René on the couch, and Adam sat in a chair. Christina had her art book, the same book she had been reading last Friday night. It was thick enough to act as a shield and she held it close to her chest.

Butch and Ali came into the room. Christina immediately pulled her knees up to her chest in an apparent act of protection. The cocky look on Butch's face made her want to punch him out. She thought to herself, we'll see how long that cocky look lasts.

"Well, I want to apologize to y'all for what happened last week. There, it's done. I said I was sorry. Can I have my papers now?" They sat there with none of them saying anything in response. Christina made it look like she was trying to hide behind René. She wanted to throw him off, let him think she was afraid of him, which she was until a few minutes ago. She didn't think that lame apology he threw at them was going to be acceptable; at least it wasn't to her. Adam thought the same thing.

"That was hardly an apology, mate, it was bloody pathetic. And no, you can't have your papers until I'm satisfied."

"I need my jacket, too. Y'all got that somewhere? It was here last week."

"Jacket? Hmmmmm. Ah, yes, the jacket. I remember now. I did find one with pockets full of pot, hash, pills and cash. That was yours? Oh my, I wasn't aware. So sorry, but it's gone. I played Father Christmas with the pot and hash. I gave it to some chaps around campus. They thought I was quite brilliant. The pills were flushed down the loo along with the contents of a small bottle. The cash, well the cash went to the soup kitchen, and they were ever so thrilled with it. Said they could feed everyone for weeks. Quite thankful, actually. The jacket I gave to a homeless man in Peoples Park. Looked quite good on him too. He was ever so grateful."

Butch turned multiple shades of color ranging from bright red to deep purple. His fists were clenching, and he started to breathe heavily. He was pissed and unfortunately for him, there wasn't a sympathetic soul in the room. He started to scream at him, "You had no right to do that. Those were my things! Do you know how much money I had in that jacket? I could have you arrested."

"An excellent idea. Let's find a phone right now and call the Bobbies. You can tell them how I disposed of your drugs and gave away your drug money. While they're here we can mention Terry's multiple bruises and Ali's neck." Butch took a step towards Adam which made Adam rise and stand nose to nose with him.

"You're such a wretched git! I took such pleasure in disposing your goods. If you'd like to take this matter outside, I'd be more than happy to show you my boxing skills. I'd find it fantastic to give you the beating you deserve, promise or no." Butch backed off. "If you want your papers, I suggest you start groveling. First, apologize to Ali."

"I'm not apologizing to him!"

"Fine with me, mate. No apology, no papers."

Butch gave Adam a filthy look, turned to Ali, and told him he was sorry for what he did to him.

"Now apologize to the rest of us." Butch proceeded to do as Adam instructed. "Now I want to hear a sincere apology to Terry. It is up to her to accept it or not." Butch stood in front of her with his eyes down, not wanting to look her in the eye. "Terry, I'm real sorry for what I did to y'all last Friday. I was so high on drugs and didn't know what I was doing. I'm sorry about your face." He looked at her with that cocky look and his evil grin. "Do y'all accept my apology?"

She slowly stood up, using her book as a shield, looking scared. She too, kept her eyes lowered so she could watch the lower half of Butch's body, waiting for his hands and body to relax before her next move. She inched closer to him until standing right in front of him. She saw him hold out his hand for her to shake.

"Friends, Terry?"

She looked up at him and then at his hand. Her posture went from being slightly slumped to full height, looking straight into his eyes. She started to move her right hand as if to shake his outstretched one and, in a lightning-fast move, she kneed him so hard in the balls that she was shocked they didn't knock out his eyes and replace them. A high-pitched squeaky groan came out of him as he doubled over in pain. Then she quickly struck again, using her book as a baseball bat, she swung it as hard as she could and bashed his face with it, hitting him squarely in the nose. The force of the blow reeled him around in almost a complete circle. Blood came running out of his nose. He lay on the ground moaning, cradling his groin area. Christina knelt down and used his words back at him.

"My, my, sweetie pie. What happened to your face? Fall down some stairs? Awww, can I get you some soup?" Then she mimicked his evil laugh. As he writhed on the ground she continued, "After our 'special night', I swore the next time I saw you I'd kick you in the balls so hard they would end up in your mouth. Since you're unable to speak and can only make foolish sounds, it looks like I succeeded. Oh, by the way, I do not accept your apology, you disgusting, filthy scum of the earth and I'll *ne*-ver, *e*-ver be your friend. The next time you come anywhere near me, I swear to God I'll cut your balls off and shove them down your throat. And you were worried about Adam and Jean-René beating up on you? You made the mistake of not making me promise the same." She stood up and kicked him in the gut causing him to groan again. As she looked down at him, she felt satisfying revenge.

The three guys seemed to be in shock. Zoe stood up and said, "Whoa!! Tee! Where the fuck did that come from? Slap me five, sister! Great move!! Now there's the Tee I know and love!" She looked down at Butch and said, "I'll bet you're sorry you messed with her. Watch out for us New York girls. We don't take shit from anybody!" She went up to Tee and slapped her five.

"Tee, that was far out! Why didn't you tell me you were going to do this?"

"Because I decided five minutes ago when that piece of shit snuck up on me while I was in Adam's room and tried to intimidate me. Man! That felt so good! I can't believe I let myself be afraid of such a worthless bully who can only get the upper hand when he drugs his victims. I realized that compared to my twin brothers, he's like little Bo Peep."

Butch was still on the ground moaning, cradling his groin area with blood coming out of his nose which looked crooked. René went to the kitchen and wrapped some ice in a towel and put it on his nose. Christina couldn't understand why he was being so nice to him because she would've let him rot there. René and Ali got him to stand up and helped him walk to his room because he wasn't able to walk on his own. They asked Zoe to grab the towel with the ice and follow them. Christina started to move in for another good kick and Adam grabbed her by the arm and moved her away from them.

"I'm not done with him yet. Let me go!"

"Terry, I think you've made your point and got in some great licks. It's not sporting to kick a man when he's down."

"Oh, and it's sporting to beat and try to rape someone who's unconscious?"

"Touché. As much as I'd love to let you loose on him and beat him to a bloody pulp, I think it best to let it end right now. Besides, you may break your foot kicking him and we don't want that to happen."

"When you were in the bathroom he came into your room and had the balls to sneak up on me, ask me what happened to my face and if I wanted some soup!"

"He never did!"

"Yeah, how about that? He's damn lucky that's all I did to him. I wish I had steel knee pads and steel toed shoes on for those kicks."

"Why that dirty bugger! You'd think he would've been on his best behavior today. Well, Pook, I'd say he deserved what you gave him and more. Between you and me, I thought you were brilliant! When you did that, I wanted to jump up and cheer! Surprised the hell out of me, but you did what Jean-René and I would have loved to do. I must say, you're quite the spunky little bird, and I'll think twice about getting you angry with me."

He laughed and pulled her into a secluded corner of the Common Room kitchen where they couldn't be seen. "You are, without a doubt, the most fantastic girl I've ever met. Beauty and brawn in the same lovely package. I find you so very sexy! Can we go snog somewhere?"

He moved in to kiss her right when René walked into the kitchen area. They instantly broke apart and looked like the cat who swallowed the canary.

"Sorry to interrupt, but we need more ice and a bucket or something because I think Butch is going to vomit." He looked around the kitchen, but all he could find was a large bowl. "Well, I guess this will have to do. Adam, Ali is asking about the papers. Do you have them here? Do you think you can get them?" René was anxious for them to get into Butch's hands so that things mentioned in the contracts could begin to take place.

"I'll get them straight away. I'll be right back." Adam went into his room and René went to Christina and whispered, "What are you doing?"

"I know, it's crazy but I'm going to enjoy it while I can."

"You're going to get hurt, Christina. Getting involved with him could be a recipe for disaster. For both of you! It'll be that much harder when we have to leave. You do realize you'll have no contact with him once you're home again. I'm not going to tell you what to do because you're a big girl, but tread carefully."

"I want a little happiness, even if it's only for a month. You have Zoe and will have her when we go back. Please don't tell Zoe, let me be the one to tell her. Adam asked me not to tell anyone, which I haven't. We don't want Ali to find out we've gone beyond the 'friend zone.' Adam feels bad enough to have broken his promise to him. It started last night and I don't care what you or anyone else says, I'm going to take advantage of every second."

"You do realize he's a musician, and they're notorious heartbreakers."

"Yeah, I do. But it's only a month. I'm loving this exhilarating feeling too much to walk away from it, especially after all the sorrow I've endured over the last year."

"Please be careful. I don't want to see you hurt. Forgive me if I'm over-protective but you're like my little sister." He started to walk out of the kitchen area with the ice and bowl when he turned back again. "By the way, I have to commend you on your sneak attack. You're full of surprises and more like an agent every day. It was completely unexpected but great to watch! I think you may have broken his nose. His eyes are blackening already. We'll see after he's iced it. And with that knee to the groin, he may not be able to walk for a while. Good work!"

Butch could be heard retching, so René quickly ran with the bowl and the ice. Christina looked in the room, and Adam was giving the packet of papers to Ali. She watched Butch as he puked into the bowl, his nose swollen and bleeding and two black eyes forming on his ugly face. Once Butch had started vomiting Zoe left the room. René made a couple of trips to the bathroom to dump the contents of the bowl. Ali and René were doing their best to take care of him. Christina and Zoe would've let him lie in his own puke.

The stairwell door opened, and Dean McMillan and Senator Morgan entered their floor. Zoe and Christina went to greet them. Zoe took the lead and did a great job of keeping her cool.

"Good afternoon, Dean McMillan. This must be Senator Morgan. I recognize you from the news. Your timing is perfect because I'm afraid Butch has had an accident, but we think he's okay. He was carrying some things and fell down the stairs. He's right this way."

She led them to Butch's room where Ali and René were icing his nose. "We think he may have broken his nose." Dean McMillan walked into the room and Butch began vomiting into the bowl again with some landing on Dean McMillan's shoes. He inched his way out of the room and asked Zoe for a towel while the senator looked in from the doorway.

"Where are the papers, Harold?" They were all flabbergasted! There was no greeting of hello, no compassion or concern for his son who was obviously in pain. He asked again, "Harold! Where are the papers?"

Dean McMillan interjected, "Senator, your son is obviously in pain and your only concern is the papers? I think he needs to go to the infirmary."

Senator Morgan ignored the Dean and asked again raising his voice, "Where are my papers, Harold? I want them now!"

Ali, who was tending to Butch said, "I have them, Senator Morgan. I'll give them to you as soon as I've washed my hands." Ali left Butch, went into the bathroom, and came out a moment later. He walked back into his room and grabbed the packet of papers and handed them to Senator Morgan. Morgan took the papers and went into Adam and René's room and closed the door. He came out and said, "Well, everything seems to be in order. Give my regards to the king, will ya, boy? I guess I'm done here. Dan, can I trouble y'all for a ride back to the airport? I need to get back to Louisiana as soon as possible."

"But Senator, what about your son? You've hardly spoken to him. You don't even know if he's okay! After traveling all this way, don't you want to spend a few minutes with him?"

"I can take a taxi back if y'all can't bring me. I got what I came for. Y'all will be happy to know that I've decided he can stay and finish out the semester. His mama made it clear she doesn't want him home."

He turned to Zoe and Christina and said, "Nice meeting the two of you." He looked at Christina and said, "By the way, little lady, what happened to y'all? Did y'all sass your boyfriend so he had to put y'all in line?" All she could think was how the apple doesn't fall far from the tree.

"No, Senator. I got into a fight, but you should see the other guy." She laughed to herself at the irony. Dean McMillan looked horrified, and then she told him she had fallen down the stairs but was fine.

"I must say, y'all have some dangerous stairs here. Y'all better get them checked. Are y'all taking me back or do I call a cab?"

Dean McMillan looked totally defeated. "Get that boy to the infirmary. I'll be back to check on him as soon as I drop off the Senator."

They watched them walk down the hall and out the door. Christina stood at the window and watched in disbelief as Senator Morgan rushed off with Dean McMillan. She thought, "What did I witness?" She was astounded by Senator Morgan's greed and lack of compassion for his son. How can contracts mean more than your own kid? Maybe there was nothing unusual for Senator Morgan to find his son in such a state, but still, not one kind word. Not even hello or goodbye.

For the first time since meeting Butch, Christina felt sorry for him and understood where all his meanness came from. There's nothing worse than being unloved, especially by your parents. She didn't know his history but understood every horrid thing he does, is done out of pain. She didn't regret what she did to him because he deserved it. What he didn't deserve was the treatment he received from his father. She was sure that hurt him more than anything she did to him today.

She was lost in thought about Butch and his father when Ali came out of his room with his backpack, and Butch's low moaning could be heard before he shut the door behind him.

Adam asked his dormmates, "Can you all come to the Pub this evening? Sarah will be joining me at my gig, and you're all invited. It would be fabulous if you could join us tonight. Ali, how about it, mate?"

"Unfortunately, no, but thank you. I have my weekly meeting with my guardian, and I cannot put him off again." He turned to René, "Do you think he'll be well? Shouldn't someone stay here to make sure, not that he deserves it? I'm sorry I'm unable to be here this evening. Because I missed last week's meeting, I have to meet with Khalid this afternoon." Khalid appeared and motioned impatiently. "Someone will stay here tonight?"

"Don't be concerned, Ali. Athena and I will stay here tonight, won't we?" René looked at Zoe and blew her a kiss.

"Yeah, sure, Ali. Jean-René can babysit the disgusting filth, and I'll babysit him." It was obvious from the look on her face, she had plans for the evening.

"Thank you, Jean-René, Athena. I'll see you all later. Good-bye Taraysa. Adam, thank you for the invitation," and Ali left with Khalid.

As soon as the door closed behind him, Adam came up behind Christina and pulled her from her thoughts of Butch.

"So, Pookie, what do you say? Will you come with me to my gig this evening? Please? Then Athena and Jean-René can have the entire dorm to themselves. You don't want to butt in on their plans, do you? Please say yes. And dinner, too? It's the least I could do for you since you're helping me finish my first semester after a year of complete failure."

She remembered her colorful face and thought, do I really want to go out to a bar? Do I want to stay here and have to see Butch when he emerges? Do I want to be here while Zoe and René make out and have loud sex all night?

She looked at Adam, and he had the cutest expression on his face, his eyes dancing, luring her to agree. All she could see was a little boy, and she thought about how young he was and how old she was. And then she thought, what the hell, so she smiled and said, "I'd love to. I'll be right back." She quickly changed into some warmer clothes, grabbed her Berkeley sweatshirt in case she needed it, put essentials into a big, fringed purse, threw it over her shoulders as a backpack, and headed back to the Common Room.

He turned to the others, "I hope you don't mind, but we're going to split for a while. It's been quite a day and time for some fresh air. It would be cool if we could all meet later at The Pub. You all know where it is. Our gig is from eight to eleven thirty if you'd like to join us." With his guitar case in his hands, he turned to Christina and asked, "Ready, then?"

"Ready. Let's go. See you guys later." As soon as they were out of view of the dorm window, he grabbed her hand. As he was strapping the guitar on his bike, she asked, "Before we go, will you be honest with me? Please don't try to shield my feelings. Ok, how bad is my face? Really. Do I look like a rainbow gone bad? Should I go out in public like this?" She thought to herself, if I was really eighteen right now, I'd never have even thought of leaving the house. I shouldn't care now, but vanity never takes a holiday.

# CHAPTER 30

René watched with triumphant relief as the packet of papers passed from Ali's hands into the hands of Senator Morgan. He was caught off guard, as they all were, when Senator Morgan and Dean McMillan came walking onto their floor. It was especially unnerving as it was moments after Christina gave Butch her surprise attack. Although quite deserved, René worried that if Senator Morgan and Dean McMillan discovered what happened, Christina would be held accountable. Although unlikely, she could possibly be charged with assault for her actions. That would open a whole can of worms that everyone on this floor, except Adam, wanted to keep closed. The reason for her retaliation could obviously not be made known.

Much to the shock of them all, Senator Morgan paid no heed to his retching son as he writhed in pain with blood spewing from his nose and his eyes blackening more as the moments ticked on. Zoe did a superb job once again of calming the situation with her quick thinking and unruffled demeanor. Neither gentleman would suspect that Butch got the shit kicked out of him by the smallest girl in the room.

René never thought Christina was going to attack Butch. She seemed so frightened moments before. She was an enigma wrapped in the mystery of a very confusing puzzle. One never knew what to expect from her. He was glad to see her fearlessness return. He didn't like her secluding herself in the dorm, afraid to venture out in case she met up with her assailant. He was sure the brutal assault and attempted rape had wounded her well-being along with the painful physical injuries. It seemed he destroyed her plucky disposition, but happily, she fooled them all. It was good to have her back, but it was better to see those papers fall into the hands of Senator Morgan.

The night before, shortly after Christina and Adam left for their evening out, Zoe and René watched to make sure they were gone before starting to search the dorm room looking for the hidden contracts. With Zoe keeping watch, René looked through Adam's closet for the guitar case. When not finding it there, he checked the entire room, including his own closet. He eventually found it under Adam's bed, hidden underneath piles of clothes. It was padlocked with a regular lock that opened with a key. René got his lock-picking tools and, within seconds, he had the case opened. He took the guitar out and looked for papers in some of the compartments and only found what looked like original musical compositions.

He handed the papers to Zoe and asked her to look through them while he looked for secret compartments in the case. Zoe deftly skimmed through the papers. Years in the magazine business were advantageous to her speedy manipulation of the papers. "René! I found them!"

René hurried over to her and took the complete pile of papers from her. He had to make sure he put them back exactly as they were in case Adam had put them in a specific spot within his music sheets. He set them on his bed and went to his dresser and got the cross housing one of the recording devices and took off his St. Remigius medal, which was a camera. He gave the medal to Zoe and showed her how to use it, and together, one page at a time, they photographed each page. René used both devices to ensure that when they returned, they not only had one copy of the proof they were there to obtain, but two. Unfortunately, neither would be accessible until they returned to the 21st century.

After they copied all of the documents, they read them all and found it incredulous that the culprits of the events that took place in the early 1970s regarding oil and oil shortages were Ali's oil-rich country and the Morgans. It was vitally important to make sure these papers got back into the hands of the Morgans. The worldwide effect of this plan changed the global oil market, and what they put in place was still affecting the oil-producing Middle East and the oil-purchasing Western world. Proof that Butch had a hand in this would most surely ruin any chance he had for becoming President of the United States.

There were deeds to oil rigs in the Gulf of Mexico under the name of LA-TEX Oil Co. and Refinery. They were secretly owned by the Morgan family but outwardly there was no proof as ownership was fronted by dummy corporations. Proof of the clandestine ownership by the Morgan family was now sitting in Rene's hands. The signed contracts in essence, were "loaning" one half of this company's shares to King Machmud for three years.

In addition to these shares, King Machmud or one of the representatives of his choosing would be guaranteed a place on the newly formed OPEC Board of Governors that would control the oil in the Middle East. Monetary profits would take place through accounts controlled by the World Bank, of which the Royal Families of Middle Eastern countries were heavily represented. In addition, there were to be deposits from the ill-gained profits for all parties involved, including Senator Morgan and his son Harold, in offshore, untraceable bank accounts. Millions of dollars, which would equate to billions in the 21$^{st}$ century, will be made while their plan is being carried out.

Senator Morgan, who in 1971 was the head of the US Energy Commission, which oversees the legislation and decisions regarding energy, and most importantly, US oil production and importation from foreign countries. These documents, signed by King Machmud, his representatives, and advisors, along with the Morgan family and some of his cronies, detail an elaborate plan for all those involved to make millions of dollars in profits.

All the oil-rich countries have to do for their part of this devious bargain is to proclaim an oil shortage and limit the number of barrels to be imported to the US. Anyone living in the early 1970s will recall the long lines at the gas stations and the "odd and even" days that allowed the purchase of gasoline, with no sales taking place on Sundays. If your license plate ended with an odd number, you were only able to purchase gasoline on odd-numbered days, with the same holding true for even numbers. Oil production was stepped up in the United States to accommodate the limited number of barrels available for import, and LA-TEX Oil Company and Refinery was the number one US supplier of domestic oil. The plan cooked up by Senator Morgan worked perfectly. The duped public had no choice but to take the word of those in power that oil was becoming scarce.

Their plan ensured massive profits would be made by bilking the global public and causing panic because of the supposed oil shortage. In turn, they were able to raise the price of oil because of supply and demand.

They now had photos of all this paperwork, the signed contracts, details of the plan, and offshore account information. Butch Morgan, being a key player in this plan by being the go-between for the untraceable clandestine exchange of information would also be given a large percentage of the profits. It seemed to René that the only person involved in this scheme who wasn't going to profit was Ali. Nowhere was he mentioned, and René wondered if he had any idea of what he helped accomplish.

Shared leases would last for three years. After which they would revert back to complete control by LA-TEX, who would be the heroes of the oil shortage, being able to supply the needed oil to the gas-guzzling cars on the road in the early 1970s. After three years, the Middle East would reopen its oil lines and resume sales to the United States, but now at a greater price than before the "shortage." During the three-year plan, gas prices almost quadrupled at the pump. No one questioned the price per barrel after their plan was through. During the three years, the price of oil went up all over the world, including Europe and parts of Asia. The Middle Eastern oil companies were able to make massive profits from this deal of a manipulated and manufactured shortage.

In hindsight, the plan was brilliant and worked even better than anticipated. US Government subsidies were given to LA-TEX and other American oil companies to help defray the cost of increased production. René estimated they were all still reaping profits from this scheme. And here it is, in black and white, Senator Morgan ensuring his worthless son was part of the scheme and profits; signed, sealed, and delivered.

René felt a huge sense of relief. This was the evidence needed to take Butch down as a presidential candidate. They had physical proof showing he did not have the best interest of the United States or its citizens in mind when agreeing to take part in this financial scheme. His signature on the contract was bigger than all the rest. Hopefully, this will seal his fate.

René and Zoe then reassembled the papers neatly and put them back in the exact place where they had been hidden. They arranged the music papers in the exact order as they originally were and put them back in the place where they were found. René put the guitar back into the case, locked it back up, piled the clothes back on and slipped it under Adam's bed where he had found it.

Neither could believe the oil shortage of the 1970's was manufactured by a US senator. Zoe was fuming because her family had been impacted by the effects of the increased price of gasoline and oil. The city of Cheetaqua's working class citizens couldn't afford to pay the higher prices of gasoline and heating oil and still maintain the social aspect of dining out.

The restaurant business in their city started to decline because dining out was one of the first things people cut back on when money needed to be stretched. It was during this time that her father's restaurant was demolished for urban renewal, and starting a new business at this time of fiscal uncertainty proved to be difficult. He was unable to find a new suitable location, which threw his family into economic turmoil. Although he was able to establish a restaurant closer to his roots in Brooklyn, the city they had grown to love and call home became only a sweet memory as they picked up stakes and moved to where they could flourish.

The city of Cheetaqua was caught in an economic downslide continuing for many years. It was common knowledge that the spark starting the fire of its decline was the increased price of oil. Winters are long and cold in Cheetaqua which meant the cost to heat homes and businesses during most of the year also quadrupled. This manufactured oil shortage and economic windfall for those involved caused the economy of the working middle class of most of America to suffer.

Zoe was melancholy for the rest of the night. Her whole life changed because of the actions of this plan and couldn't wait to tell Christina what those bastards did. She became more determined to make sure Butch never gets to the White House.

After the dean and senator left, René offered to stick around and make sure Butch was okay, much to Zoe's disappointment. This wasn't how she wanted to spend her Friday night. She had no intention of giving comfort to this creep who was instrumental in changing the lives of her family. The three of them were scheduled to go to their usual Friday meeting with Professor O'Connell but René didn't feel comfortable leaving Butch alone in the state he was in. He felt even less comfortable letting the two women go without him. O'Connell was waiting for the moment he could get Zoe alone and René didn't want to hand him that opportunity. For all his brilliance, O'Connell lacked social skills and René worried about how he'd conduct himself alone with the two women.

If they missed the meeting today, especially after last Friday's fiasco, it wouldn't bode well with the 21st century. But on the other hand, he couldn't reveal they had secreted unsanctioned clandestine materials when they were specifically told they couldn't bring such items with them to the past. He decided to tell them they had made definite progress, and it was looking positive for success. He'd give no details as to what they found. He learned long ago, especially dealing with the CIA, that you need to keep your ace in the hole hidden until the very last minute and thereby controlling the game.

He decided to go there quickly after Ali left for his weekly meeting with his guardian to tell Glenn they couldn't make it today. He was going alone to ensure the meeting was short and sweet. He didn't care if the three of them were supposed to be there every Friday. What were they going to do to them at this point? Once they get back and see the evidence they brought home, all will be well.

Zoe wanted to accompany him, but he told her to stay at the dorm in case something happened. The dean might return after dropping the senator off at the airport and wanted her to use her charm on him if he did. As he headed off to O'Connell's office, he thought how each one of them was vital to this mission, with none more important than another. The three of them each had their own strengths essential to their success.

Shortly before Khalid was to pick up Ali for their weekly Friday soiree, he received a call from one of the King's subjects with the message, "The bird has flown home". This message was to have come last weekend and Khalid waited all week and heard nothing regarding "the bird." He would have to wait until his meeting with Ali to discover what caused the delay. He ultimately suspected it had something to do with that girl. Ali had been so unlike himself the last time he was here, and Khalid wondered if the contracts had been delivered at all.

After last Friday Khalid was concerned about Ali's disrespectful actions because it was so unlike him. Khalid was responsible for him as well as the transfer of the written agreements between the King and the senator. He noticed definite changes in him and was disturbed the King had sent Ali to this country of no morals, rampant drug use, student uprisings and riots, with no concern for the well-being of his son. Ali was an obedient young man who knew his position, but Khalid thought it unwise to drop him at a learning institution with such a radical reputation and not think something would rub off on him. American teens were in a rebellious stage in this country's history and Khalid didn't like Ali being pushed into the center of it.

In conversations with his King, Khalid would hint about the environment Ali was in, but it was obvious the only concern of his sovereign was the communications from Morgan. He also relayed the scarred and unsavory reputation of the young man who was Ali's roommate, but the King would only respond that he trusted Khalid to keep Ali safe. The contractual business dealings with this senator were his only interest. When Khalid mentioned the girl, there was no concern from the King and he voiced his opinion to Khalid. "Women in the United States are immoral pigs. They have no sense of decorum, acting like prostitutes, having sex with multiple partners. This will show Ali the value of sexual restraint. And if not, then he'll have the chance to experience the sordid side of sex and appreciate our laws on female behavior. The women he'll ultimately have in his life will be pure and chaste."

The more Khalid tried to discuss this girl with the King, the more he was brushed off. He thought that secretly the King was pleased Ali had shown an interest in a woman. At least that meant he did not have an attraction to men. Khalid was told to be watchful because the Royal Family advisors had a concern about Ali because his interests seemed to gravitate towards things of a softer nature, such as art. Even if Khalid did find out something pointing to Ali being, in the views of his country, a sexual deviant, he wouldn't reveal it to anyone. In their culture and religion, that was a grievous sin punishable by death. In truth, he cared for the boy, probably more than his father did. He didn't want him to come to any harm.

But that girl is a growing problem as time goes on. And it got bigger when the investigation he'd ordered on her came up empty. As far as his investigator was concerned, this girl doesn't exist.

"What do you mean she doesn't exist? I've seen her with my own eyes! She most definitely does exist, and Ali is quite taken with her. There should be no reason you're unable to find out anything about her or her family. Are you that incompetent that you cannot handle a simple inquiry regarding an American teenage girl?"

"I've checked all the usual ways to locate her family, but I can find nothing on a family named Brendes in the city you say she is from."

"The information I gave you came from the college. I'm quite sure their information must be correct. She was given a scholarship.

There must be some records from her previous school. Did you check all the schools in her city including the private religious ones? Didn't you check the school listed from the college information?"

"Yes, honorable Khalid, I've checked all the ways I know how and can find nothing on her or her family. When I was unable to locate her, I began looking for Athena Christos and came up with the same answer. They don't exist."

"That's impossible! Keep looking. You have to come up with something on them somewhere. They're teenagers! They couldn't have fallen out of thin air!"

"Maybe, honorable Khalid, they haven't given their true names."

"I find it hard to believe two teenage girls would have the means or the connections to get into a university with a scholarship and not be who they say they are!"

"Maybe they're not teenage girls. It could be they're not who they say they are. Maybe they're spies sent to watch Ali and report to the senator or the American government."

"That is preposterous! I've met them. I've seen their immaturity when they thought they were alone. Their actions are not those of one who is older. Keep looking and report back to me in one week. I expect you to have success in finding out more."

He hung up the phone and said aloud how ridiculous those ideas were. But still, as unrealistic as they sounded, it planted a seed in Khalid's head that only needed some fertile ground in which to grow. Ali always says she seems so wise for one so young. This idea was very troubling. He had to find out about this girl!

Senator Morgan sat quite contentedly in his first-class seat on the return trip to Baton Rouge, sipping his Jim Beam. He was in such good humor, he grabbed the ass of that pretty little stewardess who served him his drinks and copped a good feel. "Ahhh," he thought to himself, "life is good!"

As soon as he dismissed that obnoxious Dean McMillan, he called his attorney to tell him the contracts were in his hands and the plan was a go and to get things rolling. He very smugly thought how brilliant he was to have thought of this plan. The American public he has served for so many years was going to put him on easy street for the rest of his life. It's the least they could do for all his years as a public servant. There wasn't one iota of his conscience that thought this was a betrayal of trust for the people he was elected to serve.

He thought about Butch. "Now I won't have to worry about that worthless piece of shit. If he can't live on what he's going to make out of this deal he certainly won't be getting any more help from me. My obligation to him ends with this deal. It's the last time I'll do anything for him and if he squanders this fortune, he'll need to find other means to live his life."

When he walked into Butch's dorm room earlier that day and saw him retching and bloody it saved him from having to beat the living daylights out of him, which is exactly what he had planned to do as soon as he saw him. He was furious with his son. This business of his mishandling the contracts was the last straw. The only thing he could be depended on is to fuck things up. His other sons were brilliant young men who were polite and trustworthy. Butch was the black sheep and there's no way to change that. He thought of Violet and immediately pushed that aside. After all this time, when he thought of her all he could think was the promise of what could have been. The burden of her loss still weighed heavily on his heart.

But now, his alliance with Zatari was going to pay off with unbelievably huge dividends. He'll not only gain financially, but politically he could go all the way to the White House. The thought of the power he would be able to obtain with his money and association with foreign dignitaries gave him an inner thrill. Nothing can hold him back now.

He put on his light to call the stewardess for another drink. This time when she came by, he put his hand up her skirt. She gently pushed his hand away saying nothing. He almost made it to the top of her leg but got the chance to feel the flesh of her leg at the end of her stocking. When she put his drink down on his tray, he grabbed her hand and put it on his hardening penis. She quickly pulled her hand away saying nothing and changed places with one of the other girls and for the rest of the flight she worked economy class.

He laughed to himself and thought, "Life is good, very good."

# CHAPTER 31

Adam chuckled. "A rainbow gone bad. That's a jolly good one. Where do you come up with these little gems? You're really quite funny, you know, and lovely. Well," he finished securing the guitar to the bike and looked her squarely in the eyes, "actually, you're bloody well the most beautiful girl I've ever seen. If you feel uncomfortable Pookie, leave your glasses on. But then I won't be able to see those intoxicating eyes of yours." He cupped her face in his hands and gave her an Eskimo kiss. Suddenly his eyes widened and he said with great enthusiasm, "I know! Let's eat in Chinatown." He quickly looked down at his watch. "We've got loads of time. I hope you like Chinese food. I have a favorite place on Grant Avenue. You'll love it. There's nothing like it anywhere in the world. Well, maybe except China." They laughed at his little joke. *He's so damn cute.*

"That sounds fabulous! And we get to go over the bridge again?"

"Sure do, luv." He started the bike, she hopped on, grabbed his waist and off they went. Once again, she felt an exhilarating thrill riding over the Bay Bridge and found herself looking forward to seeing San Francisco's Chinatown. Her only point of reference was the movie, "*Flower Drum Song*", so the song "*Hundred Million Miracles*" kept running through her head as they rode. When she saw the sign for Grant Avenue her mental song switched to the song of the same name from the same movie. *Cultural overload, here it comes.*

Not even in her most fantastical dreams could she have imagined the sights, smells, colors, and sheer delights to the senses of Chinatown. They could see the lights and colors before they got there but as soon as they turned onto the street, her mouth hit the floor. They entered the street through a pagoda with Chinese lions on both sides and dragons on the roof. Christina's head was on a swivel with assaults on her senses everywhere. It was like stepping into a magical world and she was enthralled by all of it.

The streetlamps were beautifully ornate; oblong Chinese lanterns shining like gold with tassels flowing in the breeze. People in all manner of cultural dress were part of the busy hustle and bustle in this part of town. As they traveled further there were different lanterns zigzagging lazily above the street, hovering little red balloon-like lanterns, looking like an airport with hundreds hovering overhead.

Beautiful pagoda buildings graced both sides of the street with vibrant greens, reds and gold being the dominating colors.

Banners of Chinese characters were intermingled with English. As they drove down Grant Avenue, Christina's senses were heightened by noises and visuals, but most captivating were the smells surrounding them; delectable, sensuous, and full of spice, leaving her spell bound. She understood why people say they left their heart in San Francisco because there was so much to love here. As Adam pulled into a parking space, her sense of awe was written all over her face. "First time in Chinatown?"

"Yes, and it's thrilling! I'm on architectural and cultural overload and loving it. Do you see why I love art so much? Look around you! It's everywhere! Every dragon, every lantern, every building, beauty and art everywhere! Thank you so much for bringing me here."

"My pleasure, Pookie. We'll ride through on our way home." He led the way into a restaurant, a small pagoda building sandwiched between two much larger buildings. They walked in and were shown a table with a superb view. They ordered dumplings, fried rice and won ton soup. While Christina was pouring the tea she noticed Adam staring at her.

"What?" She asked.

"Excuse me?"

"You're looking at me weirdly. It's my hair, right? It must be a complete mess with the ocean breeze frizzing out my ends and the top flat from the helmet. I'm going to the girls room to take a look. I'll be right back." Adam stopped her. He moved a curl away from her eyes.

"No please, Pookie, your hair is fine, and your curls look lovely around your face. I'm quite sorry if I was staring. You're such a puzzle. I've never encountered anyone like you."

"Well, that's because I'm one of a kind. So are you. We're all unique unto ourselves."

"No luv, you're different. When I think I have a small handle on you, you bloody well surprise me. Like, where did all that come from today? You were unbelievable. Bloody motherfucking brilliant! Honestly! And watching you…, you're so small, and Butch was as shocked as the rest of us. Did you see the look on his face?" He was smiling broadly.

"I did. But now I feel kind of bad for him."

"What? After what he did to you? Well, you shouldn't, and I can attest to that. His apology was bogus and quite obvious it was to get his stash back. He's a scoundrel."

"I know, but did you see how his father acted towards him? His child was hurt, puking and bleeding and not one word of concern or even a hello. I thought I was going to get in trouble for bashing him, but his dad didn't seem to be interested in what happened. That's sad. I wish I'd never seen his father today and how selfishly uncaring he was. He's more vile than Butch, if that's possible and he obviously passed it down to his son.

"The damn rich, always feeling entitled to behave in certain ways because they have power and money. And they leave their 'so called' most precious possession, their children, to be raised by nannies or au pairs, sitters, or anyone so they won't have to be bothered and can hobnob and jet set all over the world. It's sickening."

"Not all rich families are like that, most but not all. My family is what you'd probably consider not just 'old money' but 'veddy, veddy old money', and I did have a nanny, but she was more like a mother's helper who also helped my mum with my lessons. There were very few evenings my mum didn't read me a bedtime story, sing me a lullaby and tuck me into bed. My mother and father weren't going to leave my upbringing to someone else.

"I was overly cherished for they waited far too long for a child. The only times my mum was away from me were if she had no choice. My father was the same. I consider myself quite the lucky duck, actually. I was fortunate to have the love and devotion of parents who made me the center of their world. So you see, not all rich people behave so poorly in raising their brood. Now regarding Butch, it seems whatever the Senator came for was far more important than his own flesh and blood. Alright now, that's enough of that. Let's not let the bloody Morgans ruin our night out."

They ate dinner with Adam trying to teach Christina how to use chopsticks which she could never master and the rice kept missing her mouth. They laughed a lot, discovering they basically had the same weird sense of humor. He looked at his watch and said, "I think it's time to start back. One never knows how traffic will be." He signaled for the check and before leaving he spoke to all the wait staff with deep bows and impeccable manners. As he helped with her jacket he said, "I'm so glad you came tonight."

While walking to the bike he took her hand and interlocked their fingers. "I'll never forget what you did today. You were lightning fast...one, two and he's down. I've seen many bouts in my day, but nothing like that. My esteem has multiplied a hundredfold," and he did a fancy bow like one of the Three Musketeers. "Seriously, I was so proud of you when you bashed his smug face in, I could bloody burst, and I know that sounds awful, but you gave him what he deserved with the book! That was bloody brilliant. And I thought you were afraid."

"I was, and it wasn't planned, it just happened. I had a pit in my stomach thinking I had to face him, but when he intimidated me, making a joke of it, like it was okay and I'm some insignificant garbage under his feet, I got pissed. That was his big mistake because he empowered me to do what I said I'd do the next time I saw him." She let out an involuntary chuckle. "And he was afraid of you and René!"

"Are you ready? I don't want to be late because it's my last night." He got on the bike, and she followed.

"I thought you're booked for the semester. Why is it your last night? Isn't it what you love to do?"

"Maybe I've found something I love to do more." He started the bike which ended the conversation. They headed back towards Berkeley and the ride was exhilarating. Going over the bridge there was a cold breeze and she braced herself against Adam's body for warmth. She looked up at the stars and blessed the gods for where she was at this moment in time.

She could see Berkeley's clock tower, so she knew they were getting close. When they got to The Pub, Sarah was there at a table with easy access to the microphone. They joined her and the first thing she asked was how it went with Butch. They barely had enough time to tell her the whole story and finished up as they put their stools in place.

Adam sat at the microphone and did one of his "warm up the crowd" numbers, starting off with Herman's Hermits "*Can't You Hear My Heartbeat?*" He said it revs everyone up and he's right. The crowd responded enthusiastically, and the evening was off to a great start.

Christina wasn't a big bar person, but she liked this pub because it's quite eclectic, with tables and chairs made up of what seemed like old kitchen and sofa sets, put together with none of the sets matching, with complimentary popcorn and peanuts. She looked around and found she felt at home there because it reminded her of where she spent many evenings listening and dancing to live music. Being at Berkeley, getting to relive some of the carefree years of pre-adulthood, made her smile to herself, look around and take mental pictures of this moment in time.

The Pub was big enough for all types to patronize, which made it a great place for people watching. True to Berkeley form, aromas of pot, hash, cigarettes, hookah, and patchouli oil filled the air amid the sounds of different animated conversations regarding everything from Vietnam, race relations, women's rights, oil, religion to Washington and all things in between. There was usually a stoner or two in a corner, eyes closed, bopping their heads to either an imaginary song playing in their head or music from the stage.

Live performances took place in the back portion of the bar. Anyone could book time at The Pub's Stage which hosts all sorts of comics, poets, singers, musicians; jugglers, ventriloquists; anyone can play at The Pub Stage if they reserve their time. Near the stage on a makeshift dance floor, people grooved to the music; bodies grinding, playful flirting and joyful movement. Life in its youthful exuberance was everywhere and in the middle of all this, every time she looked at Adam and saw his smile, she knew she was falling in love.

A few drunken people made remarks about her face which made her feel self-conscious, so she wore sunglasses on and off. Guys came up and asked her to dance, but she'd rather watch Adam as he played, watching the movements of his fingers, the bounce of his hair, and every little nuance she could catch. Whenever their eyes met, he gave her a wink.

With enough time for one more song, Adam asked if there were any requests. Someone yelled out, "Anything by Jefferson Airplane!"

"Jefferson Airplane, eh? One of my favorite American bands. Hard to do without a bass player and drummer." Sarah grabbed a tambourine and the two of them were in quiet conversation over which song they both would know. Sarah said to Adam, "What about *Today*'? I know it, do you? We can pull that one off, the two of us, don't you think?" He nodded and pulled out a capo and tuned the guitar. They looked at each other and nodded.

As soon as he played the first few notes, the crowd started whooping it up in recognition of the song. He said the first word, "*Today…*," stopped and looked at Christina with a very puzzling look on his face. The light shining in his eyes made them look an intense deep blue, searching for hers. As their eyes locked, something exchanged between them and neither seemed to be breathing. Sarah looked at him, wondering what's going on. He paused for a few moments, tilted his head, shrugged his shoulders, smiled and then continued with the beautiful words to this song.

Christina's face felt hot and chills ran down her spine. She knew the words to this beautiful love song, off their "*Surrealistic Pillow*" album. He purposely made eye contact with her at certain points in the song, so she'd know he meant those words for her. They were wrapped in a spell, getting lost in the song. By the time it ended, Christina was wiping away tears. There was wild applause and Christina heard Sarah ask, "What the fuck happened? Did you forget the words? I was gonna start singing without you."

"No, I started to think of today and…"

"That's right! I forgot! Holy shit, man! I wish I was there! If I had known it would be so fucking crazy I'd have stayed." She looked at Christina and said, "Ya know, Terry, you're one far out, cool chick. Give me some skin." They slid their palms over each other's. "I can only imagine the look on his face when you kneed him in the nuts. Hah! He deserved it, the douchebag. Damn! I miss all the excitement, Damn theater rehearsals!"

She picked up her backpack and slipped it over her shoulder. "Speaking of theater rehearsals, I'm off to my leading man at 11:30. Who knows? Maybe I'll get laid tonight."

They laughed, and she left. Adam went to the bar and got a beer and a ginger ale. He got his stuff together and they sat with their drinks.

"That was a great set tonight. Your voices blend beautifully."

He smiled weakly. "Thank you, Pookie."

"What's wrong?"

"Terry, I…, oh Pookie, I…I…about that song, …it…it…so sor…" Before he finish, she grabbed his face and kissed him, which is what she wanted to do when he was singing that song.

He searched her eyes intensely. "I meant every word of that song. I haven't spoiled things, then?" He was looking at her with a troubled look on his face.

"No! Of course not. How could you've spoiled anything?"

"I thought I …Are you quite sure?"

"You've given me one of the best nights I've had at Berkeley. The only thing you're spoiling is me, buying my chain, taking me to the movies, to dinner, to Chinatown not to mention giving me rides on your bike. And you sang the most beautiful love song to me. If you'd like to spoil me a little bit more, we can do one more cruise over the bridge and back tonight."

"Your wish is my command, m'lady." They got back on the bike and went over the bridge and back with the wind blowing their cares away.

There was no more trouble with Butch Morgan. He made the mistake of lighting Christina's fuse, never expecting her reaction to his failed intimidation. He avoided her and whenever they saw one another, she'd stare him down until he looked away. His face was sporting two black eyes along with greens, yellows and purples accompanying the bruising. His plan backfired in a very big way.

Thanksgiving week was here and Ali and Khalid were invited to spend the holiday with the Morgans. Khalid respectfully declined but strongly encouraged Ali to spend the week in Louisiana with the Morgans. Christina tried to hide her elation because his absence freed her to spend time with Adam without worrying of being caught. They kept their budding relationship quiet because neither wanted to hurt Ali. Adam and Christina secretly met every night at ten at the Sather Tower for a goodnight kiss.

The Monday before Thanksgiving was the last day of class. Zoe, Adam, and René were still in class, so Ali and Christina walked back to the dorm together. Their relationship remained much the same except that Ali's free time was spent with Butch.

They got back to the dorm and Ali went to his room where Butch was packing and got his things together. Khalid arrived to take Butch and Ali to the airport. Christina was alone in the Common Room when he arrived and snuck up on her while she was reading. Her ability to block out everything while reading proved a disadvantage.

"Good afternoon, Miss Brendes," Khalid said loudly but with stiff politeness. "May I ask when you're leaving to spend the holiday with your family?"

Being startled, she jumped and let out a little squeal. "Oh, I'm sorry. I didn't hear you come in. I'll be staying here for Thanksgiving. No sense going home now as I'll be leaving at the end of this semester. I'll be catching up on my studies for the finals. Thank you for asking."

"If you like, as a gesture of appreciation for your kindness to Ali, allow me to procure an airplane ticket so you could be with your family. I need to know which airport you'd be flying into."

"That's truly kind of you, Sir, but I couldn't possibly accept, though it's appreciated. I'll be home soon and the college holds a dinner here for those who can't make it home. Thank you for the offer and your kindness."

He kept insisting and she kept politely refusing. She felt uncomfortable as he pressed on, asking questions about her family, her father's occupation, number of siblings she had, where she was born, how she injured her face and where she went to school. Christina felt like she was under cross examination and wasn't sure how to answer his questions. She was as truthful as she could be but not having a complete back-story on the life of Teresa Brendes, she used as much as she could from her life.

She was relieved when they were leaving. Khalid noticed the warm goodbye to Ali and the cold, icy stare given to Butch. She felt uneasy about their conversation and wished Zoe was there using her wiles to charm him. She had no doubt that he was sizing her up and wondered where this was coming from and why.

René came in as they were leaving and said his goodbyes. When they had gone, Christina told him of the exchange she had with Khalid, and he seemed as disturbed by it as she was. He had that distressed look on his face that she never liked seeing. "Well, at this point I see no reason to worry about it. There's nothing we can do. We'll be leaving in a couple of weeks, so don't give it a second thought."

"René, you aren't fooling me for one second. I can tell when things put you on edge and this is one of them. Trying to shield me from what could be troublesome really doesn't help at all. I'm not stupid and I know this conversation with Khalid could mean danger for all of us."

Right then Adam came strolling in and she got that flutter in her stomach when she saw him. He came right up to her, swept her in his arms, and gave her a kiss she felt all the way down to her toes.

"I saw Butch and Ali leave so I knew the coast was clear. I've got a fantastic idea! Why don't you change into some warmer clothes, grab a sweater and your heaviest jacket and we can have a lovely adventure on the Harley? We'll go to our secret spot and watch the sunset. The week is ours, Pook, and I intend for us to make the most of it. I don't think I'll let you out of my sight until our dorm mates return. Sounds quite brilliant, doesn't it?"

"It does! I'll be right back!" She floated into her room and changed into some heavier clothing with her Berkeley sweatshirt and a thick denim jacket. She could hear Adam and René arguing. She stopped what she was doing and listened by the door.

René said, "Don't you think the two of you should be cooling it down instead of heating it up? You do realize that in a couple of weeks she'll have gone home, and it will be over. She's going back to her life and you'll most likely continue your music career with the groupies who constantly throw themselves at your feet."

"Oh bloody hell! Are we going to go over this again? I think it would be bloody fantastic of you to start minding your own business, mate, and stay out of mine and Terry's. You can stop trying to protect her! I've no plans to harm her in any way. Unless you can't tell, I'm totally besotted with her. Get over it, mate, we care for each other."

"It's more complicated than that, Adam."

"I'm so bloody sick of you saying that every time we talk about her! If it's so damn complicated, explain it to me for I honestly don't understand why you feel the need to keep trying to keep us apart. You have your Athena, why deny us? And what in bloody hell gives you the right? Stay out of it, mate. It's none of your concern."

"It is my concern. Once this semester is over, she'll be gone and out of your life. You have to accept that."

"I don't have to accept anything. I think I'll leave that up to her."

"It's not up to her, Adam. She has no say in it. It would be best for both of you to cool things down. When we leave in December that will be the end of any contact you'll have with her. She'll be unreachable. Mark my words."

"Well, mate, we'll see."

"No, Adam, you'll see."

Christina came out of her room and the argument stopped. She was concerned by what she heard. She didn't want the questions to come from Adam and secretly wanted to wring René's neck. She knew he meant well, but wished he would stay out of it. "Fighting again you two? You fight more than two girls who want to wear the same outfit to the same party! Enough, already! Geez! I don't understand why the two of you can't get along! Well, Adam, I guess I'm ready. Do you think I'm dressed warm enough?"

Adam whispered in her ear, "Not to worry, Pookie, I'll keep you warm."

She giggled and he interlocked their fingers and off they went. Adam brought a thermos, and they were to stop for some hot chocolate for their sunset viewing on the Bay. As they headed out, Christina noticed René walking towards what looked like the Science building which meant he was going to see O'Connell. She wondered if it concerned her conversation with Khalid.

René dreaded the conversation he was to have with Glenn. He told him of the conversation between Christina and Khalid and asked his thoughts.

"The best and most logical course of action is for the three of you to go back right away." Glenn said. "You say you have the information you came to get, although I haven't seen it so I don't know if it's true and at this point I don't care. You three need to leave, the sooner the better. Why wait until December if you have what you came for? It's getting too dangerous for the three of you, which is making it dangerous for me and my work, which honestly is more important than all three of your lives put together!"

René started to protest but Glenn was on a rant. "With Ali's guardian questioning Christina in that manner in conjunction with him hiring this insidious private investigator who has been snooping around here asking questions about the three of you, it's putting everything I've worked for in danger. Curiosity about what goes on here is unacceptable! I won't let you or anyone else endanger my work! The government and I insist this facility and its purpose be kept classified. If it was discovered we've achieved time travel, the ramifications would be devastating, not to mention in no uncertain terms, my life wouldn't be worth shit! My life and my life's work would be in peril because of others wanting my technology. The 21st century will most likely insist your exit plan be implemented immediately, while everyone is away for Thanksgiving. The three of you can leave with no one knowing until they return from vacation. It makes perfect sense."

René thought about it for a few minutes. "We aren't ready yet. We need more time." He had no intention of telling him they have to remove all the recording devices they'd planted. The CIA doesn't know about them at this point and he has no intention of telling them. When they return, he can deal with any sort of fallout because of it, but not right now.

"Your exit plan should be implemented on Thanksgiving Day. That should give you enough time to do whatever it is you need to do before you can leave. You have two to three days to finish things up.

And don't be mistaken, René. I'm not asking you; I'm telling you. You three will return on Thursday."

René thought about Adam and how he is basically glued to Christina. How could they get him away from her long enough to get her here? He told her he won't let her out of his sight until everyone returns. That's a problem for an exit plan and he knows Christina will put up a fight about leaving beforehand. Zoe won't like it, but she'll cooperate. It's Christina who will balk at this.

"It's not as easy as you think, Glenn. I'll try but we may have to stick to the original plan."

"No, René, you figure out how to get everything completed and be ready to leave with the two girls on Thursday. It's getting too dangerous, for all of us."

"You forget, Glenn, we came from the 21st Century using your technology. Nothing must have happened to your machine, or we wouldn't be here. I think you're overreacting."

"Overreacting? Really? You're dealing with a Middle Eastern Royal family, which as you know, is a completely different culture. They don't play by the same rules as we do. If they are the least bit suspicious, which they are, it puts all of you in danger. Don't forget they have diplomatic immunity along with private airplanes. If they decide to hijack the three of you to Zatari, you're all screwed. You need to get your shit together and be back here on Thursday ready to go back to the 21st century."

"I'll do my best, Glenn." René left and headed back to the dorm. When he arrived, Zoe had returned from class and he told her of his visit with the professor.

"Oh René, do we really have to leave so soon? Isn't there some way we can stay until our original time to leave? I know for a fact that Tee is not going to like this at all! She's going to go all 'Christina' on me if I tell her we have to leave on Thursday."

"Well, Chérie, we have what we came for and it seems the dangers outweigh staying as planned. We should leave while everyone is away for Thanksgiving. At some point we'll have to talk with Christina about it."

"Well, we'll have to find a time when Adam is not attached to her hip."

354

After they stopped for hot chocolate, they headed to their secret place on the Bay. They got there in plenty of time for the sunset. Adam poured the drinks, and they sat there silently taking in the peace of their surroundings. Adam broke the silence.

"Terry, if you don't mind me asking, why does Jean-René think he is lord and master over you and your life?"

"I've told you before. He's protective of Athena and me. It's nothing more than that."

"Sorry, but I do believe it definitely is more than that. And you know, I still haven't figured out the big mystery surrounding you. I think I'm getting close, but either way, I don't think I'm going to be happy with how it plays out in the end."

She didn't know what to say, so she said nothing. The reality of her soon-to-end stay in 1971 rose to the surface. He's absolutely right. It's not going to end happily; it's going to end in heartbreak. The reality of it hit her and tears started forming in her eyes. Couple that with it being Thanksgiving, and she couldn't stop them. She tried to hide them, but he noticed immediately.

"Oh no, Pookie! Why the tears? Please don't cry. Was it something I said? How very boorish of me. I can be such a loutish cad! Forgive me, luv. I don't want this semester to end and Jean-René keeps telling me once it's done, you'll be gone forever. I'm so sorry. I don't want to hear that or even try to face it." He held her close, and she was able to talk herself out of full-blown waterworks.

"Ok, Pookie, we won't talk of what's to be. We'll take the rest of the semester as ours. We have almost an entire week to spend together and I plan on not letting you out of my sight for a second. I want to spend every waking minute with you and even throughout the night. It's my fondest wish that your face is the last thing I see before I fall asleep each night and the first when I awaken."

He must have seen the look on her face and he added, "No shagging, just cuddling, snogging, and sleeping. I'd never compromise your honor, Terry. I know your feelings about all that, my sweet little diamond maker."

That made them laugh and Christina was able to stop the tide of tears.

"Will you promise to stay with me all day on Thanksgiving, please? It's a difficult day for me and if you're with me, I know I'll make it through."

"Wild horses couldn't keep me from spending it with you. Besides, being that I'm not American, I don't really understand the whole turkey business."

They sat together with her head on his shoulder and his arm cradling her, watching the sunset over the shimmering waters of San Francisco Bay. It's a sight she'll never forget no matter how many lifetimes she lives.

They rode around San Francisco and went back to the same restaurant in Chinatown. He told her what he wanted to do with his life, which mostly entailed music. He has a few "mates" back in England who whenever they're together, they play the local pubs. "Hopefully I'll have enough original songs written so we can start some serious performing, possibly get a record deal and then maybe come to the States." He got serious for a minute. "I'm trying to make as many connections as I can while I'm here. Seeing how you'll be gone after December, maybe I'll be able to concentrate on my music. While you're near, I can only think of you, you bewitching little vixen." He paused and then asked, "Do you have any plans after this semester?"

"Plans? No, I guess I'm going home. Please, let's not talk about that. I can't bear thinking I won't be able to see you every day. I'm caught between that rock and a hard place and you're the only soft place I have. This wasn't supposed to happen, but I'm so glad it did. Nothing and no one can take away what's happened between us these past few weeks. It's the happiest I've been in an exceptionally long time." She took his hand, and they searched one another's eyes, seeing the feelings they have for the other.

After dinner they went back to the dorm and played backgammon until they were both exhausted. Zoe and René were in his room, so they went to Christina's room. Her side of the room was a mess with stuff everywhere, so she quickly opened a drawer and shoved in the contents that were on her bed. Adam laughed and helped her pick up. "How are you two friends when you're so different?"

"Karma, I guess. Our friendship goes way back. She's my best friend, always has been and always will be." Adam got on Zoe's bed. "So, shall I sleep here?"

"No, you're gonna sleep here with me. It took all this time to clean off my bed." She kidded him. "But if you'd like to sleep over there, I have my teddy bear to keep me company." She picked up Theodore and cuddled him on her bed.

Adam came over and tapped Theodore on the shoulder. "Say, mate, I'd like to cut in if I may." He gently took Theodore out of Christina's arms and set him gently on Zoe's bed. He crawled on the bed and straddled her. "Now exactly how were you holding your bear? I'm cutting in so I hope to be in the same position." He laid down and Christina rested her head on his shoulder, his arm wrapped around her, her leg between his. It was a perfect fit. They nestled in each other's arms and fell asleep. It was wonderful to have a warm body to snuggle with.

The next day they both slept late. Adam was lying next to her, and it seemed they opened their eyes at the same time. "Good morning, Pookie. Did you sleep well? I slept amazingly well and that never happens. Curious. But then again, what more can a bloke ask for than to wake up and see the most beautiful girl sleeping peacefully next to him?"

"I slept well, too. In fact, it's the best I've slept in ages. It's good to see your face first thing. I wish I could do that forever." He kissed her good morning, and they stayed in bed a little longer, cuddling and holding each other. Neither wanted to move.

When they got up, they went to the student center and had breakfast. There was a skeleton crew working as most of the students had gone home for the holiday. After breakfast they took a walk around campus. It was unusually quiet in comparison to the norm. It seemed so much less of the frantic campus at Berkeley and felt odd to not have the usual activity surrounding them; no protestors, musicians, jugglers, Hari Krishnas, people dancing to the beat of their own drum, passing joints and pipes, flowers and ribbons flowing from unkempt locks. Those were the times they were currently in and Christina was happy to be able to see all of this firsthand. So much to try to take in.

They came upon some of the homeless in Peoples Park. Many of them seemed to be veterans. Sad to see the United States did not treat her veterans fairly. Adam started to talk to them, asked them their stories. When they were finished, he gave each of them some money so they could get a meal or whatever they wanted. Christina was struck by how respectful he was to each person he spoke with and was moved by his kindness and consideration.

They neared the Sather Tower and she said, "Now it's my turn to show you my special place." She knocked on Stan's door and asked if she could show Adam the view. He started to tease her, "Another suitor?"

Christina laughed. "Well, Stan, you see, we have this little bet going. He says the view he showed me of the bay has to be better than my view. So, I want to show him that the view from up there can't be compared." He opened the doors and said to Adam as they started their ascent, "Pay attention. I'm sure before you get to the top, she'll have told you everything there is to know about our beautiful tower. She's its biggest fan."

They climbed to the top with Christina imparting all the knowledge Stan had shared about this fascinating structure.

"Isn't it magnificent?" They looked out and it was awe inspiring.

"I can see why you love it so much, Pookie. It's astounding and I agree, this view *is* magnificent. So much history and beauty." They stayed up there a few minutes, grabbed a quick kiss and scooted down before the next ringing of the chimes.

They strolled over to the movie theater that was close to campus and caught the matinee of *"The Last Picture Show"*. She remembered it had gotten some awards and rave reviews but had never seen it and now she knew why. It was sad and only made their mood melancholy.

"Well, that was quite the bummer, wasn't it? Why must flicks nowadays have to be so bloody realistic? Don't they know we go to them to escape from the sadness of our lives? We don't need them to make us feel worse. My God, that movie should have come with a box of razor blades!" They laughed at his remark.

They went back to the dorm and Zoe and René were in the Common Room. They decided to have dinner together and were in the process of figuring out where to go. The only vehicle available was Adam's Harley, so they needed to find somewhere within walking distance.

While they discussed their options, Christina got a hair band and put her hair into a high ponytail. Her curls had become very unruly, and she needed to get them out of her face. When she sat back down, Adam changed the conversation.

"Do you know what's my biggest weakness regarding a woman's body? It's her neck. When I see a neck like the one sitting next to me right now, exposed for all to see, it fairly drives me bonkers! I need to kiss it immediately!"

He attacked Christina's neck so suddenly it threw her off the chair. They were wrestling on the floor laughing, with him kissing her neck which tickled. He's making "yummy" sounds while she's laughing, trying to hide her neck with her shoulders but failing. They're rolling all over the floor, knocking things over, laughing, when all of a sudden they hear, "Adam, my dear, is that you?"

They both looked up and a very distinguished older couple was standing in the doorway of the Common Room. Christina could see the woman was still quite beautiful, with a serene grace, dressed very conservatively in a pale pink suit with a mink stole, gloves, handbag and her hair swept up into a hat with one of those nets on it. The gentleman was a very handsome man, with a neat moustache, wearing a suit with a raincoat, hat and walking stick.

"Oh my gosh! Mum! Papa! What are you doing here! I didn't expect you! What a pleasant surprise! Why didn't you tell me of your arrival?" He quickly jumped up, helped Christina up and went over and hugged his mother and father.

His father held him at arm's length looking at him. "So good to see you, Son. Of course, you know we've missed you terribly. We've gotten no letters as I recall. You promised your mother you'd write."

"Sorry, Mum. It's been a terribly busy semester. I promise to make it up to you."

His father had a warm, but stern look on his face and try as he may, he couldn't help the smile overtaking his face looking at his son. "Is this what you're learning at this school, Adam? I'm quite certain there must be a better way to use your time than wrestling with co-eds."

Adam laughed. "The school is on holiday, so we are allowed to slack off."

Adam grabbed Christina's hand and led her to his parents. "Mum, Papa, I'd like to introduce you to Terry Brendes. Terry is the reason I have such fantastic marks this year. She has been most helpful with my studies this semester. You'll be pleased to know I may be making the Dean's List. Brilliant, isn't it?" René and Zoe came over and Adam introduced them.

Christina shook hands with both of them but got the feeling they didn't approve. His father said, "Well, Miss Brendes, lovely to meet you. Thank you for helping our son with his studies. Dean's List, eh? Quite surprising, actually. I say, last year I do believe you never attended any of your classes. It's most gratifying, Adam, to see you're finally taking advantage of this learning establishment, although we'd like to see you go to university in England, not so far from home."

His mother took his hand and said, "Let me look at you, dear. You look so very thin. Why, there is hardly anything left of you. Are you eating well? And your hair! How can you see with all that hair in your face?" She moved it out of his face, and he moved it back where it was, giving her a devilish grin. "Oh Adam, I do wish you'd cut it. You look so shabby and lowly with your hair so shaggy. And you dress like a pauper. I don't understand this generation at all. You're such a handsome young man. It would be quite lovely if we could see your face without all that hair."

He gave her a peck on the cheek and whispered something in her ear which put a huge smile on her face. "Oh, Adam, I do love you so, even when you're so terribly naughty."

"We do love our naughty bits, don't we Mum?" She smiled broadly and laughed while his father smiled and shook his head at the two of them. Their relationship seemed remarkably close and unstuffy for who they are.

"Well, if you two are done being naughty, we stopped by to take you to dinner. Why don't you change into something more suitable, and we can go?"

"Well, you see Papa, we were deciding where to go to dinner before you and Mum arrived. Would it be agreeable to you if we all went out to dinner together? That way you can get to know the people who have become my Berkeley family." His father frowned slightly.

"We had hoped to have a family dinner, but you're quite right. It would be dismally rude of us to not open the invitation to your friends. Please excuse my ill-mannered behavior. Of course, we would love to take all of you out for dinner. If you'd all be so good to change into something a little more formal, we can leave."

Zoe and René tried to beg off, but Mr. Wallingford wouldn't hear of it. They all went into their rooms to change. Christina couldn't decide what to wear and was quite nervous.

"Really Tee, any of your dresses would be fine. That navy blue one looks great on you."

"I want to make a good impression. I don't want them to think I'm an uncouth, ugly American. I want them to like me."

"Tee, you do realize you'll probably never see them again after tonight. While I can understand you want to make a good impression, you need to remember exactly who you are. It doesn't matter what they think of you. In a couple of weeks, you'll be gone."

Christina wanted to punch her. The last thing she wanted to hear was that none of this mattered. It was an unexpected and hurtful remark and it upset her, especially coming from Zoe.

"Why thanks, Zee. It's so sweet of you to hit below the belt. Remind me to be supportive next time you need it."

"Tee, get real! Things are getting dangerous for us. You need to face facts and from what René says, we may have to leave sooner than we thought."

"What? Oh no we aren't." She walked over to her and continued her diatribe in a whispered tone between clenched teeth.

"I'm not leaving one second before our originally scheduled date of departure and I don't give a flying fuck what you, René, O'Connell, or anyone else wants or says. I've been through enough since coming to Berkeley. I've been forced into a situation I wasn't trained for. I've played by all the rules regarding what I was supposed to do including playing with the feelings of Ali. I've been beaten, drugged, nearly raped and now that I'm finding a few weeks of joy all of you want to pull the rug out from under me and take away the few precious days I have left to be with Adam. I can tell you right now and you can relay my message to your boyfriend who, lucky for you, gets to come home with you. I'm not leaving until the second week of December as originally planned. End of fucking story and don't you or René dare say one more word to me about it!"

"Tee, please. Listen for one minute."

"No! I expected more understanding from you. I don't want to hear another word out of your mouth." She grabbed the dressiest coat she had and the silk scarf that went with the navy-blue dress and left the room. Zoe followed and the tension between the two friends was obvious. Adam offered one arm to Christina and the other to his mother. "I've got the two most fabulous women on my arms. What could be better, eh Mum?" She gave Christina a wary look and they all left.

Throughout dinner there were great conversations going on at all ends of the table. Christina hit it off well with Mrs. Wallingford who was quite impressed with her knowledge of English history and some of the art pieces Adam's family owned. As they were speaking to one another, she could see Adam's face in hers. He had her eyes and the shape of her face.

The subject turned to religion when they were talking about Ali and Mrs. Wallingford asked what religion Christina practiced. She visibly frowned when told she was an Irish Italian Catholic with some German and English thrown in. She responded with a terse "I see." Christina momentarily forgot about the Protestant and Catholic problems in Ireland.

"Mrs. Wallingford, with all due respect, you must remember, America was founded on religious freedom and the differences between Catholics and Protestant faiths are not problems for us here, not like they are in the British Isles. We all basically believe in the same God, so there's no hatred for those of different faiths. At least not at this time in our history. All faiths live relatively at peace with each other. Our problem in this country is more racial than religious. Hopefully, we can overcome that prejudice."

They discussed many topics over dinner with Mr. Wallingford conversing in French with Zoe and René. When Adam piped into their conversation, René asked, *"parlez-vous Francais?"* None of them knew Adam could speak French. Now Christina was lost in a sea of unintelligible conversation. Adam seemed to notice and held her hand under the table. He whispered in her ear that he was happy she met his parents and couldn't wait to cuddle tonight. She looked into his eyes and felt that thrill she got whenever he looked at her in that way. How was she ever going to leave?

When dinner was over, Adam helped his mother with her stole and Christina with her coat. His father asked to speak to Adam privately and they went into the restaurant lobby. Christina could tell by the body language that what they were talking about was not good. His father held his arm and Adam took a step back, looked at all of them and ran his fingers through his hair and rubbed the back of his neck. In the short time she's known him, she's noticed he did that when he's troubled. Something was going on and it's not good.

He walked up to his mother, and she put her fingers on his lips as if to stop him from saying what he was going to say. He looked ready to cry, which made Christina want to cry. "Don't worry, my heart's love, everything will be fine. We'll speak of this later."

On the way back to the dorm Adam was noticeably quiet. He held Christina's hand so tightly and looked out the window. Everyone else in the car was talking and laughing but Christina knew something wasn't right.

When they got to the dorm, the four of them got out and thanked Mr. & Mrs. Wallingford for the wonderful dinner and how nice it was to meet them. They walked ahead and Adam stayed back for a minute. He caught up with them as they entered their building.

"Is everything ok? It's not, is it?

"No, Terry, it's not." When they got to their floor, Zoe and René went into their rooms to change while Adam and Christina stayed in the hallway. He waited until they were alone before he spoke.

"My mum is not well. The doctors think she may have cancer. She's having tests tomorrow at Cedars-Sinai hospital in Los Angeles with possibly surgery to follow. I'm so very sorry, Pookie, but I have to leave now and go with them. I hope you understand. I know I said wild horses couldn't keep me from spending Thanksgiving with you, but it's my Mum." He had tears in his eyes which made Christina tear up.

"Adam, please don't give it a second thought. The medical staff at Cedars is top notch. She's in good hands. I'll keep her in my prayers and see you when you get back."

He went into his room to change and packed a few things. He came out, said goodbye, and held her so tightly and kissed her so sweetly. She could tell he seemed to have the weight of the world on his shoulders.

"I'll be back as soon as I can. I'll see you when I return." When he got to the door, he turned around, rubbed the back of his neck, and said, "Goodbye, Christina," and blew her a kiss.

She said, "Goodbye Adam," and blew him one back. The door closed and as she turned into her room it hit her.

He called her Christina.

# CHAPTER 33

She stood there in shock, staring at the door and felt a chill run through her and a jumble of thoughts ran through her mind. "He called me Christina, didn't he? Did I imagine it? No, he said 'Goodbye, Christina.' Did he notice I didn't act surprised or put out when he called me a different girl's name? Shit! How does he know my name?"

She knew she should be concerned but it felt good if in fact he did know her real name. Have we been careless? René says we're in danger. She wondered if that was the reason. She had no intention of adding fuel to the fire by telling either of them Adam called her Christina. A million thoughts were going through her head along with a million questions. She'll pretend she didn't notice he called her a different name. She'll have to think of a comeback should it come up in future conversations with him.

To say she was disappointed Adam had to leave was an understatement. She was looking forward to days and nights with him, falling asleep next to him and waking up to a new day together with nothing but free time. Now she had to face Thanksgiving alone, which was the last thing she wanted. Tears were on the surface, waiting to burst. She hoped Adam's mother would be fine so the remainder of their time together wouldn't have a black cloud over it. It was totally selfish, but she couldn't help herself.

Zoe walked out of their room as Christina entered, and said, "Tee, I know you don't want to hear it, but René needs to talk to you as soon as possible. Things have gotten dangerous for us, and we're scheduled to leave on Thanksgiving. O'Connell wants us gone before everyone gets back from Thanksgiving holiday. Why don't you change, and we'll meet in the Common Room."

"Why don't you and your asshole boyfriend kiss my ass? I've already told you! I'm not leaving early and I'm not going to discuss anything with either of you. Leave me alone!" She slammed the door and locked it. For added measure, she got a chair from the desk and jammed it up against the door so no one could get in. Then moved one of the dressers up against the chair to ensure the only way in was either because she allowed it or with a battering ram.

She plopped herself on her bed and started crying, holding on to her beloved Teddy Bear, telling him over and over she wasn't going to leave now.

René knocked on the door and tried to talk to her, but she turned the radio on and cranked up the volume. She didn't want to hear a word he had to say. She was tired of being bossed and pushed into situations where she had no control. Her stubborn streak was bright red with no intentions of budging. She wouldn't leave Adam now, with no goodbye or explanation, especially after the circumstances surrounding his mother, thinking it heartless and cruel. She wasn't going to disappear and didn't care about danger or consequences. She had until December 14th and was not leaving one day sooner.

René thought the surprise visit from Adam's family couldn't have come at a better time. What made it even more opportune was Adam had to leave with his parents for a few days. René knocked on Christina's door and asked her to join him and Zoe in the Common Room. She told him to go fuck himself and she's not leaving early.

He tried to reason with her, but she was adamant in her decision. He tried to explain to her through the door the reasons why they needed to leave now but she turned the radio up even louder and ignored him. Even with the radio blasting, he could hear her crying. Zoe tried to get into the room, but the door was blocked.

René took Zoe's hand and led her away from the door. "Let's leave her alone and let it sink in. We can talk about all this tomorrow. It's been a very full day today and I have a headache. I know an incredibly good remedy to get rid of one and it involves a beautiful naked woman. Do you know where I may find one?"

"I think I may be able to find you one." They went into his room and after making love, they both fell into a deep sleep.

When Christina woke up the next morning, she listened for activity outside her door. She wasn't going to open it while those two turncoats were there. She moved the dresser out of the way and noticed a note slipped under the door. She picked it up and read it. It was mostly "blah, blah, blah, you have to remember who you are, blah, blah, blah, we have to leave right away, blah, blah, blah, getting too dangerous, blah, blah, blah, won't be able to protect you, blah, blah, blah." She wanted to rip it up but decided on writing a reply and leaving it for them.

She looked at the note again and reread it. "You have to remember who you are." Up yours!! Both of you! I know exactly who I am! Assholes! Then she read the part about "won't be able to protect you" and that statement struck a nerve. She grabbed Zoe's red pen and wrote in reply on the same note next to that sentence in big letters, "Why start now? Where were you when I needed protection? Oh yeah, I remember! Fucking your girlfriend! I'M NOT LEAVING NOW!" She knew it was hitting below the belt because it was eating away at him and felt he'd failed her by putting pleasure before business. She knew it was hurtful but didn't care.

She opened the door and the dorm was empty. They must have gone somewhere for breakfast. She went back to her room and found a stick of Zoe's gum. She chewed it for a few minutes and then used it to stick the note on René's door. There's no way he's not going to see it as soon as they get back. She needed to think of a way to be able to stay here until the originally scheduled date. How was she going to be able to finagle this? What would be a good enough reason to not leave immediately? There has to be something. Think, Christina…think!

She walked around the Common Room, wringing her hands, trying to come up with something. What could keep them here? There must be some way to make it so they can't leave right now. What could it be? She walked up and down the hall a couple of times, hoping they wouldn't return yet, wracking her brain for a solution.

She stopped in front of Ali and Butch's door, staring at it, and then it came to her! Of course! She should have thought of that sooner, thinking how deviously brilliant she was. She quickly went back into her room and opened her makeshift jewelry box and searched for a particular item. She was relieved when she found it. This was her ticket for an extended stay in 1971. She got her denim jacket and turned one of the sleeves inside-out and hooked the item on the inner part of the sleeve so it was below the inside of the elbow. She turned the sleeve right-side-out and tried it on. Perfect!

She had to disappear, at least until Thanksgiving night. Once she dropped her little bomb, the trip back home will definitely be postponed. A little white lie will get them to stay, hopefully until the original date of departure. Once everyone is back from Thanksgiving, they won't be able to disappear. Besides, they promised Sarah they would see her performance in *Bye, Bye Birdie*. It looks like they may be able to keep that promise.

She quickly went into her room and grabbed the biggest bag she had and threw some clothes, her teddy bear, and toiletries into it. She took Theodore Edward in case they decided to remove the bugs from Ali and Butch's room and put them back into her bear for the trip home. Where she goes, Theodore goes.

She put together all the money she had, which was a little over a hundred fifty dollars and took off. She felt like a super spy, peeking around corners to see if the coast was clear, hiding behind trees and running into doorways to avoid being seen. She was having fun in her own sick-humor sort of way.

Khalid sat comfortably for the long plane ride back to Zatari. Although it was only for a few days, he felt it necessary to speak with his King in person. Considering some of his recent discoveries, he was very wary of the telephone. He wasn't sure if he was being suspicious or if there was any basis for his apprehension. Ever since those contracts left his hands and given to Ali, he was worried this oil manipulation plan would be discovered. Why King Machmud and Senator Morgan thought it a good idea to let teenagers handle the delicate transfer of information, he would never understand.

He was in the private jet used for the Royal family, so his flight was luxurious with all the amenities fit for a king. He opened the cigar case located next to his seat and picked one out, sniffed it, rolled it between his fingers and thumb, snipped the tip, and looked around for a match or lighter which he was unable to find. He called the steward who came and gave him a light. These were the finest Cohiba Cigars from Cuba. Because they were illegal in the United States, he always looked forward to one whenever flying on the Royal jet. Although smoking is frowned upon by his religion, rules were only made for the common people, not for a man such as he who was in the upper echelon of Zatarian society. He was a distant cousin to the King and had been in the employ of the Royal Family for many years. That position set him high above the common citizenry of the Zatari population.

After he dropped off Ali and Butch for their flight to Louisiana, his driver took him to the restricted airfield housing where the private jet was waiting for him. Khalid felt it important enough to take the arduous trip home to meet with his King and personally show him the files and explain his concern over the findings of the investigation he had acquired on the girl whom Ali has become obsessed with and the rest of those who live with the prince.

Khalid had been given charge of the boy and if something were to go awry, it would be his head on the chopping block. He was to be rewarded with a portion of the profits if this oil deal between his King and Senator Morgan was successful. He currently enjoyed an extremely comfortable lifestyle and wanted nothing to disrupt his wellbeing and future profits. He felt certain this girl was there because of this deal and was somehow involved. His first allegiance was to his king and although Ali had ordered him not to investigate her, something didn't ring true about her and he was afraid his instincts were proving correct.

His first investigator suggested this Teresa may not be who she claims but could find nothing further. It was suggested he hire a particular local and much seedier investigator by the name of Pete See to possibly dig deeper, follow her, and find out more information.

Pete See was a small, thin man with an everyday face and a distinct laugh punctuating many of his sentences. He was a man who would not attract attention, which was as he liked it. He was a high school dropout who learned the ins and outs of private investigation from the streets. He was able to make a lucrative living at it, so it didn't matter what he was hired for. He was game for anything. Being nondescript, he blended well into crowds. As a native of the San Francisco area, he forged many connections over the years, helping him garner information and gained him the reputation for being able to get the job done.

He was constantly whistling between his teeth which he found would unnerve those he encountered. He used that and any other means possible to throw people off balance to get the information he was looking for. He was doggedly determined and never gave up. His caseload was usually catching cheating spouses, finding missing persons and runaway teens who wanted to be part of the "hippie craze" or knee deep in some fanatical religious cult. His specialty was following and photographing his subjects. His motto, which was imprinted on his business card was "Everybody's got a story, I'll find out what it is." It wasn't long before Pete was at Khalid's door with information.

Khalid's servant opened the door and found a rather disheveled looking man with a dirty wrinkled raincoat matching his dirty wrinkled trousers and rumpled fedora on his head. As Pete stretched out his right hand to shake hands with the man who opened the door it was immediately apparent the fingers on his right hand were permanently stained by nicotine from chain smoking his Lucky Strikes. His breath carried the stench of too many cigarettes.

"Pete See, here. Pleased to meet you. I'm lookin' for a guy named Mr. Calley or somethin' like that. This here the right place?" The servant looked at his outstretched hand and refrained from touching it. He told him to stay right there and left. He was back seconds later with Khalid.

"Thank you," Khalid said to his servant, "I'll take it from here."

Pete was shown into the privacy of Khalid's office and offered a seat. "So, am I to understand you have something new on this girl?" Khalid tried to keep his distance from the man. He reeked of cigarettes and clothes that had not been properly washed. His hair was greasy under his hat and there was dirt under his fingernails enhanced by the color of the permanent nicotine stains.

"Yeah, the chick and her amigos, but we gotta talk payment first, like we said." His annoying laugh ended every sentence which irritated Khalid more than his disheveled appearance. Khalid opened a drawer with a key and took out an envelope with cash in it.

"Now, my friend, you're talking my language." Pete hungrily eyed the envelope seemingly loaded with one-hundred-dollar bills.

"Let me see what you have and then we can negotiate the price."

The private eye took out an envelope with photos. They were of Teresa Brendes and Ali, her roommate, the French student, and the son of Lord Edward Wallingford. Several of them were the three in question. Khalid flipped through the pictures. He wondered why there were none with Butch Morgan. There were photos of Ali and the girl walking with their books looking very happy, the French student with her roommate with a few photos of them locked in a passionate embrace. Public display of affection was forbidden by his culture and for good reason. No one wants to see this. He felt lustful stirrings and quickly flipped to the next picture.

There were photos of the girl with Lord Edward's son who, if one were to surmise anything from them, it would be thought they were involved with one another. There were pictures of them on his motorbike and of them walking holding hands. In one photograph, they were kissing at the Sather tower. Women are such whores, Khalid thought. How dare she carry on with this boy and play with the affections of Ali! There were a number of photographs of all of them but what sort of evidence did they provide? He threw the photos on his desk towards the man. "Why would you think I should pay for these? I see nothing giving me any information I'm interested in."

"Well, my friend, you need to look closer." He took out a cigarette, offered one to Khalid who refused but before he could light it, Khalid told him he could not smoke in his house.

"You for real, man?"

"I insist you refrain from smoking in my home."

"If you say so." It caught him off guard. He was never told he couldn't smoke. That might raise his price. He put his cigarette back in the pack and then picked up the photos to point out what was worth a few bucks. "Well for one, your little girly here seems to be carrying on with this biker guy. Now, ya gotta look here, over at the edges of these here pitchers and you'll see times and dates. Lookie here at the building these three are going into. Your little sweetheart, her roommate and the French guy make regular Friday visits to the Science building. I asked around and found out they have been doing that since they got to Berkeley way back in August. They meet with this guy, Professor Glenn O'Connell, who I'm told is a certified genius when it comes to science. No kiddin'! A real genius!" Pete's enthusiasm was high while explaining what Khalid had in his hands.

"And this is what might interest you, my friend. None of these little teenyboppers are taking any science classes. So, I gotta ask myself, what's the connection with this O'Connell guy? Why these regular visits? Which brings me to this interesting little tidbit; every time I get close to finding out what this professor does in his science building, I get shut out with 'government classified information'. Imagine that! It seems the feds have given lots of cash to this cat for whatever it is he does. I couldn't find out what's going on no matter how hard I tried. I've worked my ass off 'cause I know it's important to you, but as soon as I get close, I'm stopped by good old Uncle Sam."

"Do you have any speculation on what it could be?"

"Any what?"

Khalid sighed. "Any ideas or guesses as to what's going on with this professor and those three?"

"Nope, and I had to pull strings and call-in markers to get these." He opened another folder and handed it to Khalid. "I got my hands on their official files from the college. Used to date one of the gals in admissions. She's still sweet on me so I can get her to break the rules once in a while. Gonna cost me dinner eventually."

He pointed out some things to Khalid. "There ain't much in each file. None of the usual stuff like background, admission essay, records from their high school or where they came from. Usual files have all kinds of stuff in them. Their files are almost empty. All three of them have this little gem." He pulls a piece of paper from the small pile in Teresa Brendes' file which is a memo stating all inquiries on her are to be directed to Professor Glenn O'Connell.

Khalid looked at it, found the exact memo in the other two files and then looked back at Pete. His mind was processing this, and it was quite disturbing to him. Pete watched the expression overtaking Khalid's face as he read the memo. He could see the wheels turning in his client's head as he took the memo from Khalid's hand and put it back in the file. These memos are going to be his big payoff. "Kinda shady is what I'm thinking." He pulled a cigarette from his pack, put it to his mouth, and then remembered he couldn't smoke here and shoved it back into the pack. He liked having a smoke while revealing his findings. It seemed to give him a boost. He continued his report without it.

"So, I go over to see that professor guy, but he gives me the bum's rush. It smelled like he was getting high on the old 'mary jane', if you know what I mean. I asked him why they all meet every Friday and got no answer. He told me to mind my own business and if I know what's good for me, I'll keep my nose out of it. Then he slammed the door in my face. Never did like to get threatened, kinda pisses me off, but I figure what can a bookworm pothead science freak pussy like him do to me, right?" He let out a dirty snicker.

Khalid gave him a malicious look and went back to looking at the photographs. Pete continued, "I tell ya, from what I've been able to find out, it's like the three of them fell from the sky outta nowheres. Seems like they didn't exist before they came to Berkeley. Mark my words my friend, they're gonna vanish into thin air after this semester because my gal told me that none of those three are registered for anything at Berkeley or anywhere else after December. None of those transcript things are going anywheres."

Khalid let all this sink in. "So, we don't know if they are who they say they are. Could they be currently working for the FBI or other government agencies? Were you able to find any direct connection between them, especially this Teresa Brendes and Senator Morgan?"

"No direct connection with the government except this professor guy and not sure about Senator Morgan. Still working on that angle but so far, it's comin' up a big zero. I got a buddy who I used to work with who moved to Louisiana, doin' private dick work out there. I had him put a tap on the Senator's office phone. It pays to have friends in low places, ya know what I mean? So far there has been no talk about this girl."

"If you were to come to some sort of conclusion about these three, what would be your best idea?"

"Honestly my friend, I'm stumped. Can't make heads or tails out of any of it. For some reason, my gut's telling me the feds have some angle. Why else would the three of them be going to see a guy who seems to get all his dough from the feds? There must be a connection with this cat or why would his work be classified? Believe me, my friend, it's killin' me that I can't find out more about these three or where they came from. If they're working for good old Uncle Sam, I'm stumped as to why they'd want to use teenagers. Teenagers are fuckups who want to get wasted on whatever they can get their hands on and fuck each other's brains out, singing about free love and peace."

"Do you really think they're teenagers?"

"Well, Mr. Calley, I had the photos analyzed and all my pros say they're the age they claim. The facial and physical features are what a teenager's would be. They all said these three ain't in their twenties yet." He started to explain using the photos to illustrate what his experts were looking at but Khalid wasn't interested in his explanations.

"So, Mr. See, you haven't given me any solid information. Why should I pay you?"

"Well, my friend, you know a helluva lot more than you did before I walked in. You know your little sweety here has probably been cheating. You know the three of them meet with a G-man professor every week and this particular pot smoking whiz kid is knee deep in money from the feds. And most importantly, you have in your hands their official Berkeley records which is almost no records at all, not to mention that sweet memo. You know they came from nowhere, with no birth or school records, no family, no social security numbers on record and they'll be leaving in a few short weeks to who knows where. I'd say all that was worth at least a few C-notes, don't you? Plus, ya know, I gotta pay my guy in Louisiana."

Khalid thought about it for a few minutes and let everything sink in. After what he's heard it seems the US government has to be involved somehow. There really wasn't time to discover all he felt he needed to know. One thing was certain, he couldn't shake the feeling that this girl and her friends are spying on Ali. The government may have gotten some information about the oil deal between his King and Senator Morgan and will use it against them. The US always has an underhanded angle for everything. Is the Senator behind this? It doesn't seem plausible, but one can never trust a politician. He may have a twist in this plan to come out on top. After all, Morgan is the one who came up with the oil plan. Khalid's priority is to protect his King and country which, in turn, will protect his own interests.

He paid Pete See seven hundred dollars and kept all the photographs and reports. He then made arrangements to return home and meet with his King and tell him his concerns and show him his findings. If they're spying on Ali, then they're probably also spying on him, which is why he decided to take the journey home and not use the telephone. It worked out perfectly that the Morgans invited Ali for the Thanksgiving vacation. The timing is ideal for him to return to his homeland.

Khalid sat in his office for the next few hours trying to formulate some sort of plan. The only solution he could produce was to try to get that girl alone, question her using their methods and get to the bottom of all this. It could get sticky so he needed to discuss with his King how this should be handled. He needs permission to go any further and feels King Machmud needed to see the findings of this investigation for himself. They have to move quickly because they'll be gone soon, and the wheels of this oil manipulation plan are already turning.

Khalid planned on recommending she be brought to Zatari. If in fact Teresa Brendes does not exist, which according to all sources he's used, she doesn't, it could be disastrous for them all. There are no parents, no school, no records of her birth or family. If she's a spy, it'd be interesting to see if and how the United States would be able to go through diplomatic channels to get her back. To do this, they'd have to reveal her true identity and the truth of what she and her friends were doing in Berkeley. They'll have to admit they're spying on a member of the Royal Family of Zatari and that would get very sticky diplomatically, especially with the oil market as it currently is. To proceed in his plan, he needs the permission of the king.

Maybe Ali will be able to bring this girl he is so love-struck with home with him after all. If it's discovered that she's a spy it won't bode well for her, especially if she doesn't exist and no family members are pressuring the US to get her back home. Punishment for women is severe in their country, which means most likely before either the final punishment of stoning or beheading, all the men of the Royal family will be able to get a little taste of this American girl. It's almost certain that once King Machmud feasts his eyes on her she'll most definitely become one of his little playthings and then passed down. He loves young girls, and truth be told, she may even be too old for his tastes. One thing is certain, by the time she'd get passed down to a lesser son such as Ali, if she is still alive, she'll have been a sex slave for months.

It all depends on how his King would like him to proceed.

# CHAPTER 34

Adam was sure of it now. She answered him when he said, "Goodbye Christina." She even blew him a kiss! He couldn't get that out of his head. It made him smile for some unknown reason. She didn't question him calling her another girl's name, she didn't blink an eye or skip a beat. It was as if it was nothing out of the ordinary. Now he was certain. The girl he was hopelessly in love with is named Christina.

On the flight to Los Angeles with his parents, he sat behind them in First Class. They thought he was studying for his finals, but he was studying something else, something much more important to him than any of his college courses. He had a small notebook he kept in his backpack that was always with him. He wrote down Terry's ramblings on the night she was drugged. He also wrote down the conversations he overheard in French between Athena and Jean-René and some conversations between Terry and Jean-René.

This was the perfect time to go over everything, categorize, organize, and try to put this puzzle together. He kept coming to the same conclusion, but it was so far-fetched he couldn't possibly be right.

*John* – kept calling him her hubby. Over the course of that night, she called out his name many times. A few times she sobbed and begged him not to leave her. Divorce? Death? Business trip? Where'd he go? Is he still in the picture? Hope not!

*Children* - Three children – Kenzie, Roxie and Johnny. Old enough to be taking dancing lessons and playing sports. If Terry's only eighteen, how is she married with three children who are old enough for those activities? She spoke with them all at different times during that night, always speaking to them as a mother. Mother??

*Names* – Why the name changes? "Who the hell is Terry?" My question exactly! Asked me that when I addressed her while she was drugged. Heard Jean-René call her Christina while eavesdropping on their conversations and once or twice from Athena. Question: if her name is Christina, why does Athena call her Tee? Wouldn't that be for Terry? Terry (Christina) asking "where's Zoe", "my roommate", asking more than once. Athena – real name Zoe, Terry is Christina, Jean-René? Bloody bumsucker! Don't like him and don't care a fig what that bugger's name is!

*The Key* – VERY important to her. John gave her the key? Symbolic or real – opens something? She's not engaged (or married) right now or is she? – not the cheating sort. How is this possible? Don't like John either!!!

*21st Century* – overheard conversations - Athena (Zoe) mentions it and also a MISSION (?), CIA (?) talk of 30 years in the future (??) Jean-René in hot water with CIA after what happened to Terry (Christina). GOOD, frigging frog! but why? Why is he so bloody overprotective of Terry (Christina)? Is it his mission? TOTALLY CRACKERS!!

*Butch Morgan* – More reasons than Ali begging not to notify police of drugging, beating and attempted rape. Should have been sent to the nick! Talking about taking 30 years to take him down. Using these events in the future?

*Oil deal* – read the contracts, mostly legalese, but able to understand what's planned and how to control the oil business and trade. Heard "packet of papers needs to be copied" and again 30 years into the future. Are these oil contracts what they're referring to? Is this the mission? How will they copy them when they've been in my possession until I gave them to Ali? How to copy anyway???

*Terry-Christina-Pookie* – Brilliant, fantastic, fearless, lovely, enchanting! Completely won over Mum, no small feat. No doubts…I love her! Absolutely and totally! So bloody confusing…office in a library…at 18? Jean-René - "it's complicated" (heard too many bloody times!), after this semester she'll be gone, unreachable, no contact possible. Why? Why? Why? She cares for me…I know it! Unreachable…Why? No plans, going home. Where is home? Husband and three children there? How? How can I let her go? Can one live without their heart? Will I be able to find her?

*Preliminary conclusion* – BLOODY INSANE!! Could they be from the future? Impossible!! Bloody confusing!

No matter how many times he went over all of this, he came to that same conclusion. Why else would she be gone with no contact possible? Could it be because she's going back to her life sometime in the future where she is married (?) and has three children(??)? How else can she know all that she knows? Is she a government agent? Why else would they have let Butch go unpunished? Would a report of what he did to her change the future if it became known now? Are they going to use all this against him in the future and if there is no record of it, how will they prove it? And why change their names? One semester scholarship? That's bloody unrealistic.

He needed to find out the truth about her. If he's going to lose her forever, he needed to know the reason why she had to leave him. Losing her after this semester is eating away at him and he must find a logical explanation. But most of all he's looking for a glimmer of hope. She refuses to talk about it so what else could it be? It must be true. Is there any way she can stay here with him? How can he live without her after finding the one person who makes him feel whole?

Only one thing seemed to give him pleasure at this point; he knew her name, her real name. *Christina*. When he looks in her eyes and tells her he loves her for the first time, he needs to tell her, not Terry but Christina.

Christina headed towards the library to hide out there for a while. Once it gets closer to dusk, she'll head to one of the motels within walking distance. She'll have to think of an alias for the register.

When she got to the library it was locked. Most offices and buildings were closed and locked, so she decided the best thing to do right now was get off campus. It was the day before Thanksgiving and things should be fairly quiet around town because most students are gone for the week.

She had breakfast at a diner and ordered a sandwich to go for later, while keeping watch for her would-be captors. She spent the afternoon going in and out of the open shops, making her way to the motel. She was going to register under the name of Rebecca Wittman, one of her co-workers at the library. Neither Zoe nor René would recognize that name, so she felt safe.

When she got to the motel she registered and gave them a story that she was visiting a friend at Berkeley and let her brother borrow her car. He's having car trouble and can't pick her up until tomorrow. She explained her license and ID were in the car. They believed her bullshit story and she paid cash for the room. Check out was at 12:30 PM which was good for her. It gave her less time to kill before going back to the dorm.

When she got to her room, she blocked the door in the same way she blocked her dorm room. She turned on the television and settled in for the evening. As the night wore on, she felt the loneliness of her self-imposed isolation. Every channel (all four of them) had Thanksgiving specials on, which made her feel worse. Her thoughts were dominated by John and all the wonderful Thanksgiving dinners he'd prepared over the years. He made it special for all of them. She realized how much she missed him, the kids, and the life they used to have. She thought about going back to the dorm and leaving for the 21st century as everyone seemed to want. Then she thought of Adam, his face, and his adorable smile, and thought, I can't go. Emptiness was the only thing awaiting her back home. None of her children would be around this weekend as they all had plans. Tears came again.

The reality of her life in the 21st century was she's a lonely, depressed widow with nothing to look forward to. Her children are grown with their own lives. And now she has a fierce enemy in Martin Cater which is something she hadn't thought about much. She and René were supposed to think of a way to prove his involvement in the destruction of both of their lives and that hadn't happened. That was how he got her to agree to this mission in the first place. Did we let ourselves become side-tracked? Will she be safe once they hand over the proof they want? Her life on both sides of the country in both centuries is shit! She thought how much she would love to be able to stay here with Adam. Then she started to try and talk some sense into her head.

"Don't be ridiculous, Christina, you *know* you can't stay! You're thinking like a crazy person! Can't have two lives at once, remember? You can get that out of your head right now. Besides, with your luck, Adam would leave you for some blonde with big boobs. And then where are you? You can't stay here with Adam! Nothing will change that. You'll be dead in a few months if you stay, and your children might never be born. Stop thinking crazy." With all these nonsensical thoughts she had running through her head, she tossed and turned most of the night before finally falling asleep.

When she awoke on Thanksgiving morning she was in a surly mood. She turned on the television and the Macy's Thanksgiving Parade was on every channel. John loved to watch the parade and even took the family a few times to see it in person. This time of year always brought out the little kid in him. This was not going to be a good day. She hated Thanksgiving and shut off the television.

She showered and took her time getting ready. Ready for what? Absolutely nothing. While doing her make up, she stared at herself in the mirror and said, "Who are you, anyway? You have to remember who you are!" She said it with a voice dripping with sarcasm while trying to imitate Zoe. Screw her! Bitch! She kept asking herself that question and never got an answer. Living two lives causes an identity crisis.

It was now a little past noon, and time to leave. She gathered her things, went to the main desk, and checked out. She started to walk out the door and then noticed a phone booth. Funny, since most people have cell phones, one doesn't see many phone booths in the 21st century with those old rotary dials. She walked back to the desk and took out five dollars and asked for change – quarters, dimes, and nickels. Christina, what are you doing? This is not a good idea! She tried to talk herself out of it as she walked to the phone booth, but ultimately, knew it was something she had to do. Screw the rules! Everyone wanted her to remember who she was and this was the best way to jar her memory.

She sat down in the phone booth with the phone in her hand, noticing she had started to shake. What can it hurt? It's a little after three o'clock on the east coast. She knew he'd be there. She rummaged through her bag and took out René's pen. She turned it on and put it close to her ear so it would record the conversation.

She dialed the number, and the operator told her to deposit $3.35 for the first three minutes. She could barely breathe at this point. She bowed her head and closed her eyes waiting for the person she knew would answer the phone. She wasn't prepared when she heard his voice.

"Gobble, gobble, gobble! Time to talk turkey! Happy Thanksgiving from the Pucci's. Johnny speaking."

The sound of his voice took her breath away. She was sure he could hear her trying to breathe. She tried to talk but the shock and sheer joy of hearing his voice, knowing he was alive, brought her to a place she hadn't been since before his death.

"Is this an obscene phone call? I can hear you breathing. Frankie, is this you? I'll get you for this, man! No pranking on holidays!"

"Um…, hello…I mean, hi John! Happy Thanksgiving." She tried to steady her voice but wasn't doing a good job of it.

"Helll-lllo and a Happy Thanksgiving to you, too. Can I ask who's calling?"

"Um…I'm, um… I'm a friend of your roommate. He's told me a lot about you and told me how much you love Thanksgiving, so I thought I'd give you a call and wish you a Happy Thanksgiving."

"That's cool! Thanks! Same to you.  Um…do I know you? Have we ever met?"

"No, but he's told me a lot about you, so I feel like I've known you for years."

"Really? I didn't think Bobby knew any girls. Well, what's your name, schweety-pie? I gotta say you have a really sexy voice."

Silent tears started to roll down her cheeks. He always told her that. Whenever she answered the phone when he called, he would say, "Hey, sexy lady".

"Well, why don't you call me sexy lady?" Her voice was cracking, and she could hear his mother in the background telling him to get off the phone and get back to the table.

"Hey, are you crying? Is everything okay? Please don't cry. Nobody should cry on Thanksgiving. Is there anything I can do? Are you with Bobby? Is he being a jerk again?

"No, John, I'm fine. I'm not crying. I'm shivering because I'm cold." That was the only thing she could think of saying.

"Well, Miss Sexy Lady, I'd be quite happy to help keep you warm. By the way, am I in some kind of trouble? I'm only called John when I'm in trouble. Did Bobby tell you to call me John?"

"No, I mean yes. Yes, he did, and he also told me you're a lot of fun and a prankster with a very crazy sense of humor, kind of like me. He says we'd get along great. He's told me lots about you."

"Really? Like what else? Did he tell you I'm cool, handsome, and debonair? Hmmm, probably not. Geez, I think because it's Bobby, I should probably be worried about what he's told you. He's a bigger ballbuster than I am. I hope he didn't give you a bad impression of me because I'm really a nice guy."

"I know you are and no, he didn't say anything bad about you. I don't know how anyone could have a bad impression of you."

"I guess you don't know everything about me then." He laughed that mischievous chuckle he had that she always thought was so damn cute. She closed her eyes and listened to that sweet sound.

"Well now you've got my curiosity up. Bobby has told you all about me, but he hasn't told me anything about you. I'm going to have to short sheet his bed for that. Roommates aren't supposed to keep secrets from each other, especially about intriguing girls with sexy voices. We'll have to find time to meet each other. Tell me, are you from around here and what do you look like?"

In the background his mother was still yelling for him to get off the phone and get back to the table.

"I'm from central New York, petite in size and stature with boring brown eyes and long dark brown curly hair. My dad says I'm a pain in the ass and too pretty for my own good but I think all father's think their daughters are beautiful. I'm a regular girl." She didn't think of what she was saying, she wanted him to stay on the phone to keep listening to his voice.

"Hmmm. I think I'm going to go with your dad. Not about the pain in the ass part, though. He's probably biased but that's okay. This is all so intriguing! And what's wrong with brown eyes? I love brown eyes. They're so much warmer than light colored eyes. It's like you're able to see the soul of people with them. They're so full of depth and truth. I could never trust a girl with blue eyes. That's not my type. So, tell me, how do you know crazy Bobby? Like I said, I didn't think he knew any girls."

"Let's not talk about him. Let's talk about you."

"Me? What about me? You probably know all there is to know if I know big-mouth Bobby. What would you like to know? I'm pretty boring, a fourth-year college kid trying to make it through to graduation."

"What are you studying?"

"I'm going into Criminal Justice. I want to be able to get the bad guys before they can get us. My goal is the FBI, but I'm sure Bobby must have told you that."

The operator cut in and said she had to deposit another seventy-five cents for the next minute. She fumbled with the change and put three quarters into the phone.

"Are you calling long distance? Where are you calling from? You're not only a sexy lady, you're a mysterious one! This must be my lucky day."

His mother's voice in the background was getting louder. "Johnny, you have one minute to get off that phone and get back to this table. If you make me get up, I'll hang it up for you."

"Well, Miss Sexy Lady, I hate to cut this exciting conversation short, but as you can hear, my mom is demanding my attendance at the dinner table. Thanksgiving is serious business in this house. I can't wait to talk to Bobby and find out more about you and see when I can meet you. I don't know…for some reason I think you're jazzing me! Are you sure he didn't put you up to this as a joke?"

"I swear to God John, I'm for real. We'll meet soon, I've no doubts about that. And John, …oh geez, I know I shouldn't say this but I…I…I really needed to hear your voice." The tears started to stream from her eyes. She tried to keep her voice steady. She took a deep breath. "I…um, John, I…uh, I want you to know that you and I are going to have such a wonderful life together. We're going to have the best marriage in the world, with deep love for each other, great kids and happiness will be ours, John, for as long as we live. Real happiness and there won't be one day of our life together that we won't feel the love we have for each other. You're the best husband and best friend a girl could ever want, and you and I will be like one heart joined together." That was something John always said about them.

"Huh? What did you say? I don't know if I heard you right. Can you say that again?"

"The only thing you need to know right now is that I love you, John. Nothing can and will ever change that, ever. With all my heart and soul! I have to hang up now because I've said more than I should, but I had to talk to you and hear your voice. I'm going to say goodbye now. And John, I promise we'll be meeting soon. Goodbye."

"Hey, don't hang up! Please! I don't even know your name! Hello? You still there? Hello?"

The operator cut in again asking for more money. She didn't put any more in and hung up the phone, keeping the receiver in her ear even though the line was dead. She sat there with the phone in her hand, staring at the good old rotary dial. At that moment she felt like a zombie, not dead but not alive, in a haze composed of a bittersweet fog of memories. She clicked the pen and listened to the conversation again…and again…and again. She was finally able to answer her question. She's Christina Pucci.

She sat there in the phone booth and then it hit her. When she first met him in the library, he told her she had a sexy voice and kept asking if she knew Bobby. Now she understood why. They had this conversation on Thanksgiving in 1971 and he remembered it. "Oh John!"

She was lost in thought until some guy started knocking on the door yelling, "Hey girlie, are you going to make a call or what? You can't sit there thinking! I gotta make an important call. If you're not going to use the phone, get the hell out and let somebody else use it!"

She opened the door and apologized to the guy who pushed her out of the way and made a rude remark about "sonofabitchin' kids these days have no respect". She thought about bashing his head up against the phone booth wall which made her feel better. She gave him the peace sign with her fingers (not the bird like she wanted to) and left.

She walked around with the pen to her ear, listening over and over to the sound of John's voice. She wished she could somehow do something to change the fact that when she gets home, he'll still be gone. She knew nothing could be done to change John's life, most importantly, the end of it. She was so glad she was able to talk to him again, even if he had no clue who she was. And it's recorded. René was going to totally flip out when he hears this conversation with her past, but she didn't care. What's he going to do?

She passed by the same movie theater she and Adam went to the other day. Today they're showing a double feature for the kids of *Pinocchio* and *Old Yeller*. She decided it was a good way to pass the time until she felt she could go back to the dorm. *Pinocchio* was one of her favorites, so she bought a ticket and went in. There were a lot of kids with their parents or older siblings. She was the only one who was alone.

She sat through *Pinocchio,* marveling at the animation. She was always amazed by the work of the Disney animators. Thankfully, it took her mind off everything else. She stayed for most of *Old Yeller* but left before the ending. Couldn't deal with that today, that's for sure.

It was starting to get dark, so she started walking back to the dorm. She wondered how pissed off the two of them were going to be, not that she cared. She's done being pushed around. She's played by the rules and did what was asked of her and now it's time for her to decide things for herself.

# CHAPTER 35

When René and Zoe returned from breakfast, they noticed Christina was gone. While Zoe went into her room to see if there was any hint as to where she went, René noticed the note on his door. As he read it, he could feel the anger building up. The funny thing was, he wasn't angry at her, he was angry at himself. Those big red letters glared at him. It was a thought that had been in the back of his mind and here it was, the truth in bright red ink.

Zoe came out of her room and said, "She must have gone somewhere because her makeup and toiletries are missing along with some of her clothes and her teddy bear." She noticed the note in René's hand. He handed it to her and after she read it, she got pissed.

"What a bitch! Why would she write down something so hurtful? You're not going to let this bother you, are you?"

"Of course, it bothers me! The truth hurts and it's the truth." For the rest of the morning, he was quiet and sullen. Every time Zoe suggested they do something, he sat there with no reply. She hated when he got moody. Tee was ruining her last day in 1971. She was hoping they could enjoy the last days here, but it wasn't going to happen with René in such a foul mood.

As the late afternoon shadows began to descend upon them, Christina still hadn't shown up. René became worried and suggested they go look for her. Zoe was willing to do anything to get his mind off that note. They looked all over campus, went around all the buildings, the Sather Tower and couldn't find her anywhere. They went off campus to look and went to the diner for dinner and had a quiet meal.

"Where could she be? I hope and pray that whoever is snooping around about us didn't find her first."

"René, I'm sure that didn't happen so don't worry about her. She took her teddy bear with her. If something had happened to her, she wouldn't have had the time or the sense of mind to take him with her before leaving. She probably took him so we couldn't sew the bugs back into him. Knowing her, she'll show up tomorrow when she thinks it will be too late to leave for home. She's proven she can take care of herself."

"She can't take care of herself if she's in the wrong hands. We shouldn't have left this morning. We should've waited for her to leave her room and stayed together. Now we have no way of knowing where she is and if she's safe. Once again, I've let you distract me from what I should be doing."

"Me? Oh, please, René! Don't throw this on me! I didn't drag you off to breakfast this morning. And Tee is acting like a spoiled childish brat who isn't getting her way! Believe me, I've known her much longer than you and she can be so stubborn to the point of wanting to slap the shit out of her. She's fine!"

"You don't know that for a fact, Madame Zoe, and for once I should have put her safety first."

"For once? René, you've been protecting her since we got here."

"No, *Chérie*, I haven't. I've been so enamored with you that you've been all I could think of. And she's right. Where was I when she needed me the most? We both know the answer. This failure weighs heavily on me."

"Well, snap out of it, René. It's not helping our situation." She hesitated for a moment because she wasn't sure if she should bring it up now or let it be. She decided it was best to toss it out there for him to think over.

"I hate to put another wrench in the works, but have you thought of the consequences of leaving early, especially with Adam gone? Maybe it's not such a good idea to leave tomorrow."

"Zoe, I know you want to stay but our safety may be compromised." He paused for a moment and sat back with a puzzled look on his face. "But now I'm curious. Why do you say that?

"Have you given any thought to what Adam will do when he returns, and Tee is gone?"

"Adam? No, I haven't. I have enough worries on my mind. What can he do at that point? She'll be gone."

"Oh my God, you men! No offense, but men are so stupid when it comes to the feelings of others and anything involving love. Can you ever stand back and see the big picture?"

"Zoe, what do you mean? I'm not in the mood for guessing games. What's going on right now is very serious, especially now with this disappearing act. We're supposed to leave tomorrow and here we sit, like we have all the time in the world. We should be looking for her and then start packing up what we need to bring back."

Zoe grabbed his face with both her hands and forced him to look her straight in the eyes. "René, think! Stop this self-pity, get out of this funk you're in and think! Okay, say the three of us leave tomorrow. We're gone with no way for anyone to find us, obviously. Even if Tee leaves him a note, Adam knows she would never go without saying goodbye to him in person, especially after what's transpired between them these past few weeks. They care very much for each other, and he's going to immediately think something bad has happened to her in his absence. Any note Tee would leave him would be suspect. Don't think for one second that he wouldn't call the police to investigate and inform them of what Butch did to her and why he should be the main suspect in her disappearance."

She could see the wheels turning in René's head. "Don't you see? After what happened between Tee and Butch, he'll immediately think Butch is in some way responsible for her disappearance because it's a completely logical assumption. Everything we kept quiet will be brought out into the open and there will be an investigation into Butch Morgan. That can't happen. There will be no one here to stop Adam from telling the authorities everything because Tee was the one holding him back. Leaving before our scheduled time could put the whole shebang at risk."

"*Merde*! You're right! Ah, Zoe, what would I do without your insight and your brilliance? You're always able to assess situations so keenly. Once again, I see how each member of this team has been necessary for our success."

He sighed very deeply, interlocked his fingers, and rested his face on his hands. "Now that you've brought that to my attention, I agree. It could be disastrous if we leave tomorrow. Adam would most definitely blame Butch, even though he's in Louisiana. We cannot have Butch implicated in the disappearance of a coed he has clashed with more than once. Adam would immediately think Butch did something to retaliate for the shellacking he received at her hands. That would leave a whole new set of problems with no one around who would know how to solve them. The possibility of it altering the path of Butch's life is too great a risk. You're right, we must stay." He sat back in the booth, looked at her and asked, "What made you come to this conclusion, *Chérie*?"

"Sweetie, men are from Mars and women are from Venus. It's from living as a woman in a man's world. Take it from me, I know for a fact the male ego can't accept a woman up and leaving when he knows or even has the slightest inkling she feels the same way he does. Adam could never accept that she would leave him after all they'd been through together without a goodbye. Couple that with the fact that the three of us will disappear without a trace, it makes the question of what happened to us even more pertinent." She paused to let it all sink in.

"Let me ask you, what would you do if I disappeared with no goodbye? You'd better think before you answer because the wrong answer will get the shit kicked out of you, especially since I've had to put up with your pissy mood all day."

"Sorry, Chérie. I'd be lost without you and would use any means possible to find you if you disappeared." He reached across the table, took her hand, and kissed it. "Ah, Madame Zoe, you're an amazing woman. We make a wonderful team, no?" He didn't need an answer. They both knew it was true. "If you're through eating, we should be heading back. Maybe she has returned while we were out."

They made their way back to the dorm and Zoe hopped into the shower. René went into his room and closed the door. He opened one of his desk drawers and took out a box and opened a secret compartment. He took out a lighter and went outside to make sure it was operational, which to his relief it was. When Christina returned, he was going to have to arm her with something to help her get out of a sticky situation should she find herself in one and alone. Once he was sure the lighter was working properly, he went back to his room and secreted it back in its original hiding place. He decided no one, including Zoe, would know of this secret weapon he was giving to Christina. Zoe could be so jealous and unreasonable at times, and he didn't want her to question why he would arm Christina and not her.

They spent the rest of the night in the Common Room, waiting for Christina to return. They both fell asleep on the couch and when they woke the next morning, they were still the only ones in the dorm. They had coffee and around ten o'clock O'Connell arrived, ready to send them back to the 21$^{st}$ century. He was not at all pleased Christina had flown the coop.

"This is unacceptable! You have to find her! It's vital the three of you leave immediately! What if something happened to her?

Couldn't you keep your eyes on her for one day? Oh Christ! I can't believe this. This is a super bummer! I've got some shit to do but I'll be back later this afternoon. Pack your bags, all three of you! Make no mistake, you're all leaving today." The entire time he was talking, his eyes kept darting towards Zoe. She always made him feel discombobulated. He was mumbling as he left the dorm.

René and Zoe looked around for Christina with no luck. In their travels they found a restaurant close by that was having a Thanksgiving buffet. The two of them sat at a small table and had their first Thanksgiving dinner together. They headed back to the dorm and there was still no sign of Christina. René was worried and Zoe was pissed. Tee was being a selfish bitch! She was sure Tee didn't care what her disappearance was doing to them.

When Christina finally walked into the dorm on Thanksgiving night, René was relieved beyond words. Zoe on the other hand was livid that Tee could have been so insensitive to the worry her disappearance caused and her words and attitude towards her friend showed her anger.

"Well, look who's decided to grace us with her presence. Tee, what the fuck are you thinking? Do you realize…", and that's when Christina cut her off.

"Hey, Zoe, fuck you and anyone who looks like you! If I wanted any crap from you, I'd squeeze your head, you shithead!" She started to walk into her room when René came forward and said very quietly, "Christina, I'd like to talk to you alone for a minute. Please. I know how you're feeling right now, but there are a few things I want to go over with you. It has nothing to do with us leaving now. I need to speak with you. Would you please come into my room?"

"We can't go back now anyway, René. We don't have all the recording equipment we came with. I don't know if you've removed all the devices from Ali and Butch's room, but if you have, I'm sure you noticed one is missing. The one on the peace sign pin you suggested I give to Ali, is with him in Louisiana. He had it on when he left. We can't go back and leave that with Ali." She crossed her arms and could feel the pin on the inside of her jacket.

Zoe piped in, "Really, Tee? Are you sure about that?" Christina ignored her and kept looking at René.

"As I've told you, what I have to say has nothing to do with us leaving now. Would you please come into my room?" She became a little nervous. He couldn't possibly know she called John, could he?

The door at the end of the hallway opened and she was sure it was going to be Adam. Even though she'd been through an emotional roller coaster talking with John that afternoon, she still felt that tingle in the expectation of seeing him. She turned, ready to run to greet him, and was disappointed when it was O'Connell who came rushing through the door running up the hallway.

"Christina, at last! Where in the hell have you been? I've been waiting all day for you so we can conclude this with your departure. What you've done is unacceptable on so many levels. How dare you defy my orders! This mission terminates today! None of you realize how dangerous it is for you to remain here. To make matters worse, all three of your student files are missing! I went to the main office to retrieve them and they're gone! Your immediate exodus is required! Gather your proof and whatever other objects you need and let's be off."

René took a few steps towards O'Connell. "What do you mean our files are missing? Why should that make any difference? Whatever is in them can be verified, can it not?"

There was no answer to his question. "This is all quite serious. The implications of what this means are of the utmost significance. You all need to get whatever you're bringing back with you right now so I can return you to the safety of the 21$^{st}$ century."

"Glenn, what is in our files, or should I ask what is not in our files? You did put all the necessary information required by the CIA in them, did you not?"

"Oh Christ!" O'Connell started pacing. "Your departure needs to be imminent! The situation and safety for the three of you is precarious at best. The disappearance of your files makes it quite perilous for all of you. The time to leave is now, the sooner the better! By my calculations, you can be back to your own time in a little more than a few hours."

"Glenn, you did have all the necessary and usual information in our files with corroborating information regarding our family, transcripts from previous schools, where we were from as required, did you not?"

"When will all of you retain the knowledge that I'm not a spy, but a scientist? What do I know of policies for clandestine activity? Who the fuck would've thought that someone,… *anyone,* would desire access to your files? The list from the 21$^{st}$ century of what to put in the files seemed inane and superfluous. I surmised no need to go through that entire nuisance when you were only going to be here for a few months. And besides, who was going to have access to them anyway? The only items in there were your application, a bogus letter of acceptance from Berkeley and a memo that all inquiries should be addressed to me."

René flew across the hall and pinned him up against the wall with his forearm across his chest. "It seems someone must have had access to them. Are you telling me there is nothing in our files to substantiate the story of our aliases?"

O'Connell could barely breathe. "Yes, that's what I'm saying. You're hurting me. Let go!"

Through gritted teeth René asked, "So you're telling us that as far as whoever has those files knows, we appeared out of nowhere?"

"Release me! I can't breathe!" René stared into his eyes and pushed his chest harder. Panic started to set into O'Connell, and he started flailing his arms and kicking his legs, trying to release himself from the arm cutting off his air supply.

"René, let go! You're going to kill him! René!" Zoe ran up to René and hit his knees from behind with hers which set him off balance and pushed him off O'Connell. The hate coming from René's eyes was torpedoed straight to the man who was now sitting on the floor, coughing and rubbing his chest.

René got up and stood over him. "The first rule in this sort of assignment is to make sure the cover of those in the field is secure with no holes. Did you think the CIA wanted to give you something to do to get you out of the fucking haze of marijuana you've been using to dumb yourself down with? How dare *you* defy *their* orders? If we didn't need you to get us back home upon completion of this mission, I'd kill you right where you sit, you worthless piece of shit."

He walked over to Christina and took her hand. "Christina, we must speak alone. Let's go into my room." He looked at the crumpled man on the floor and said, "We are not leaving now. You cannot dictate how we carry out our mission because as you so adroitly pointed out, you're not a spy but a scientist. Vast understatement! You may be a genius, but you're brainless when it comes to living life. You hide behind your gadgets in a drug induced stupor to veil the fact that you don't know how to be among the living."

He let go of her hand and walked over to O'Connell. "Your indolence has put our safety in jeopardy. We cannot disappear. Questions will be raised and most certainly if you knew anything about human nature, you'd know Adam Wallingford would stop at nothing to find out what happened to Terry if he returns, and she is gone. He needs very little prodding to go to the authorities and with what has happened between Butch and Terry, Butch would be the first suspect in her disappearance. Everything we worked so hard to conceal from the police would be revealed by Adam in his quest to find out what happened to her. That is what happens when people are in love, but those feelings are unknown to you.

"We'll remain until our originally scheduled date of departure. That's a judgment call from the lead field operator of this mission. If the 21st century isn't in agreement, they can either take it up with me when we return which will be in December after everyone has left for the Christmas holiday or they can send someone to force us back now, which I do not recommend." He turned to Christina and said, "We must talk."

Zoe started to follow them and as they got to the door of his room, he blocked her from entering. "This is to be a private conversation. Please tend to O'Connell and show him the door. I suggest you be on guard. He may try to 'cop a feel'. I'm sure you know he has a desire for you."

"But René, I'm part of this team. I should hear what's going on."

"Sorry. This is between Christina and me. Behave like a big girl and don't pout."

René closed the door behind him, and they could hear Zoe bitching. Now more than ever René had to arm Christina with something to protect herself from whatever dangers there may be. Of the three of them, she was the one who must get back. René promised to protect her, which would also protect her three children. If anything happens to her, her children's existence could be in danger. Since he had been remiss in this duty so far, he had to act now to ensure her safety.

Zoe was fuming over the actions of her friend over the last few days, but to make matters worse, she got shut out by the man she loved. She began spouting threats of retaliation against the two of them in Greek.

Now there were two people in the dorm screaming and yelling. O'Connell was in near hysterics, raving like a lunatic. He was rambling in a raised voice, flailing his arms going on about how they had to go back, and it wasn't his fault. Zoe kept telling him to shut up, but he was beyond the point of understanding. He was a hair's breadth from complete hysteria. It was as if he couldn't see or hear her or anything else for that matter.

Zoe thought about slapping him across the face but then knew exactly how to bring him back to earth and was angry enough at René to do it. She rushed him, pinned him up against the wall, grabbed his face and planted a very serious kiss on his lips. She kept it long and passionate, knowing it would snap him out of his histrionic drama and become putty in her hands. After the kiss, she whispered in his ear while stroking his head and rubbing her leg between his. "There now. Calm down." She kissed him again.

In a voice barely above a whisper she put her lips to his ear and began speaking, hesitating after each sentence. "Feeling better now? Shhhh. Relax. Yes, relax and don't worry about it, Glenn. No one is blaming you. Everything will be fine. We know you're a scientist and not an agent. And such a brilliant one at that. No one else has come near your achievements." She let that stroke of his ego sink in, looking at him while pressing her breasts into his chest. He stood there frozen, completely mesmerized, and unable to do anything but listen to the soft words being spoken in his ear.

"We really can't leave yet, okay? If we leave now, it will leave you and this whole mission in a big mess, and we wouldn't want to do that to you. It would raise questions with no one here to answer them. With what has transpired between Tee and Butch it would put him in the bullseye of blame for her disappearance. We wouldn't be here to steer things in the right direction. Understand, sweetie? We don't want to leave you here all alone to pick up the pieces. That wouldn't be fair, now would it? You've already done so much for us. If we up and leave, there would be too many unanswered questions that could cause trouble for you, your time machine and our mission."

She grabbed his hand and walked him towards the stairwell. "Now, promise me you won't worry about any of this. We'll take care of everything. Why don't you go back to your office, light up a big doobie and let the 21st century know we have to stay put until our originally scheduled date of departure. You're such a brilliant man! I knew you'd be able to understand the implications. What would we do without you?"

She walked him out, and he was like a little puppy dog. Zoe had a way with men. She knew exactly how to stroke the egos and then do as she pleases. As soon as he left, she set about finding that pin.

When they got into his room, René asked Christina to have a seat. He walked over to his desk and picked up the note she had stuck to his door with gum. He held it up for her to see it, with her reply glaring in red ink. Christina felt awful about it now and wished she could take it back. She started to apologize but he stopped her.

"You're quite correct, Christina. I ask you not to interrupt me and let me speak my piece before you say anything. What you wrote here is the truth, so an apology is unwarranted. In truth, I cleverly manipulated you to get you to agree to this mission. I coerced you to come here, selfishly, I might add. I saw the connection with you, me, your husband, and my wife and daughter. I knew Martin Cater was behind it and my desire to avenge the destruction of my life was all I could focus on. I thought through your husband you could provide the proof I need as it seems he is the invisible thread sewing us all together. I felt through you I'd be able to procure physical evidence to the manipulations and deaths of my sweet daughter and wife."

"René, please it's…"

"Please don't interrupt. After the death of my family, I became very dark and unhappy, though the life of one in secret service is already dark and unhappy. When this mission came my way, my only thought was it would get me closer to those I felt responsible or knew something about their deaths. I thought nothing of you Zoe, or your safety. The last thing I expected was to not only find someone I could love, but friends. These past months have shown me what my life could be. I've found camaraderie not only with Zoe, but with you, Ali and even my damned English roommate who I'm usually at odds with. I made a promise to protect you from all manner of danger and in that I've failed. I'm not sure I ever really tried."

He walked over to his dresser and started to go through one of the drawers. "Your bold, red response to my note made me reassess what's going on here. As much as my ego hates to admit it, without you this mission would've been dead in the water. Through your ingenuity you brought the equipment that's the only thing standing between success and failure. You've done exactly what has been asked of you and more while Zoe and I are basically doing nothing except enjoying our awakening romance in younger versions of ourselves."

"That's not true, René, we've all..."

"Christina, please. I need to continue. I never thought about the lives we're disrupting and possibly changing in the quest to gain information on the Morgans, most importantly, Ali and Adam. Both are quite infatuated with you and it's no wonder. It's what will happen next that has me worried. And now our files are missing. Both Edward Wallingford and King Machmud have the power and connections to gain access to our files. My fear is that it's King Machmud, or most likely Khalid in his stead."

He took a box out of his drawer and using a pocketknife, opened a secret compartment. "As I've dismally failed in my half-hearted attempt to keep you safe, I want to give you something. By giving you this, it doesn't mean I won't give two hundred percent from this moment on to keeping you safe but consider this an added safety measure. I've learned that you're your own woman and won't always listen to conventional wisdom. There are many times you're off with Ali or Adam, and they could be overtaken as they are schoolboys. I'm not saying they wouldn't do all they could to protect you. They've both shown they can and will do exactly that, but Ali is honor bound to obey elders and honestly, he is the one who has me the most concerned."

"René, Ali would never do anything to hurt me. You don't have to worry about him."

"Ali isn't my worry, it's his guardian Khalid. I'm almost sure he's been investigating us, mostly you, and if he's the one who has those files, then you can be a sitting duck. With this oil deal in the works, they may be on alert for anything that may reveal their plan to the unsuspecting public or inhibit its success. In any event, you need to have something to protect yourself and this little gadget will do the trick."

He pulled a cigarette lighter out of the hidden part of the box and asked her to come over to the desk where it was put under the light so she could see it better. He held it up for her to get a good look at it. "This lighter is one of the few things I was able to bring without Martin knowing what it was. Outwardly it looks like an ordinary cigarette lighter, and it does produce a flame enabling the person using it to light a smoke and thereby throw off suspicion. But it also is a very small caliber gun that won't kill but will give you enough time to remove yourself from imminent danger."

He showed her how to use it to protect herself should she find herself in a precarious situation. When using the flame, there was a small button on the bottom of the lighter that when pushed would release another small button on the side of it. As soon as the flame is extinguished, if you push the side button, three small BBs are projected out very quickly. Coated on these BBs is a drug disabling the assailant for ten to fifteen minutes.

"Christina, you need to make sure when you release the BBs, the lighter is aimed in the right direction. The BBs project out of the same hole the flame comes from. Once the flame is extinguished, aim it towards the danger and hit that button. It's meant to hit the face. It causes no permanent damage, and the drug is immediately absorbed into the skin. Within five seconds of release, your attacker is disabled. If you're still not safe after the fifteen minutes, use it again. It has multiple shots available so it can be used more than once. The button trigger will remain active until you deactivate it by closing the lighter."

He showed her the proper way to hold it and the easiest way to work it, so all the mechanics of the lighter/gun are worked with ease and no mistakes. She held it in her hand and went through the motions of activating it. She found it quite easy to handle and the buttons were in the right locations on the lighter, so they were right at her fingertips.

"Do you really think this is necessary, René?"

"If I didn't feel it necessary, I wouldn't give you this weapon. You're not to tell anyone about this. Do you understand? No one and that includes Adam and Zoe. You need to promise me you'll always carry this with you. I want you to make sure it's always within your reach, even during the night. Have it close by just in case. Things are looking more and more perilous for the three of us. It would be perfect if we could leave now, but circumstances as they are, we can't. Your lover-boy will most assuredly go to great lengths to find out what happened to you and the authorities can't get involved and find out about what has happened with Butch.

"The last thing we want right now is for Butch to be a suspect regarding a missing person. That will most assuredly change the path of his life and we can't let that happen. When we leave it must be that we've caused no shift in the course of Butch Morgan's life. Understood?"

"Yes, René, understood. So, we'll be staying until our originally scheduled date?"

"Yes. We don't have enough time to remove all the equipment from Ali and Butch's room and get them securely sewn into your bear. Besides, I think I'd like to keep them up until after they've left. It'll be interesting to see how the roommates end their semester and the last conversation they have with each other. I have a feeling we'll be shocked at the story we'll get from those devices."

There was a knock on the door and Zoe said, "Your majesty, you have a long-distance phone call in the Common Room." Christina could tell she was pissed.

She looked at René with a very puzzled look. "I do? Who would call me? I don't know anyone who would be calling me." She started to panic. John couldn't possibly have found her. There's no way. Oh God, she thought, why did I call him?

She walked out into the Common Room and noticed O'Connell was gone. The phone was dangling with no Zoe in sight. She picked it up with shaking hands. "Hello?"

"Hello, Pookie, Merry Thanksgiving!"

"Adam!" Relief flooded through her that it was him and not John. "Oh, it's so good to hear your voice!" That was the second time today she felt that emotion. "I couldn't imagine who was calling me! How is everything with your mother?"

"Mum is doing fantastic. They took out all the female parts and the doctors said she'll have a full recovery. She needs to take it easy for the next few days. They're going to stay in California until the end of our semester and then we'll go back home for Christmas together."

"Oh Adam! That's wonderful news."

"How are you holding up, my Pookie? I feel like such a lout leaving you and breaking my promise. Will you ever forgive me?"

"Hmmmm. That depends on how you kiss me when you get back. Do you know when that will be?"

"I think I'll be returning in the wee hours of the morning. Papa and I didn't realize Thanksgiving is the most traveled holiday here in the States. The only flight I could get leaves here at one in the morning. I should be back in the dorm by two-thirty or three. Can I sneak in and cuddle with you when I return or would you prefer I went into my own room?"

"I'd love it if you'd come and cuddle with me. I'll wait for you in the Common Room and if I'm not there, I'll be in my room. I think your room is being occupied."

"Fantastic! I can't wait to see you, Pookie, which should be quite soon. Got a kiss for me for the ride?"

She kissed into the phone and he kissed back. "I'll be waiting for you! Be safe!"

"See you in a few hours, Pook! Goodbye."

She hung up the phone and started to walk back towards her room when she heard John's voice coming from René's room. She ran to the room and stood in the doorway. Zoe was holding the pen and playing Christina's conversation with John for René. She rushed into the room, grabbed the pen out of Zoe's hands, and shut it off.

"We needed to know where you went today, Tee. What you do affects us all. I know you're lying about the pin because I saw it in your jewelry box the other day. I went looking for it to prove you're lying. And yes, I went through your purse and thought it might be in there. When I dumped its contents on the bed looking for the pin, I picked up the pen, and it accidentally turned on. I nearly jumped out of my skin when I heard John's voice. Admit it! You called John today. How dare you!"

"How dare I? How dare you go through my purse?" She grabbed it from Adam's bed and held it close to her. "You dirty, rotten son of a bitch! You're such a jealous fucking baby! You couldn't stand that I had a private conversation with your honey, so you felt you could invade my privacy and go through my purse?"

Christina wanted to smack her. René looked at the pen. "Christina, you didn't call your husband, did you?"

"With everyone telling me I need to remember who I am, yes, I did. And if you don't like it, you can all kiss my ass! No harm done.

Did you honestly think the thought wouldn't have crossed my mind, especially on Thanksgiving?"

"I need to hear the conversation." René held out his hand for the pen. Christina hooked it to her bra, securing its place out of reach.

"No, you don't and you're not going to. It has nothing to do with either of you, and it in no way puts us in danger. He didn't know who I was because we hadn't met yet. I needed to hear his voice, okay? What's done is done." Then she addressed Zoe. "What's with you lately? Is it your life's ambition to make my life miserable? What's your problem?"

"Oh, please, Tee. Like you're wearing a halo! And I know you're lying about the pin. I saw it in your jewelry box the other day. So, you can stop that line of bullshit. René, I really did see the pin the other day, so there, I've caught her in a lie. Doesn't it make you wonder what else she's lied to you about?"

"Christina, is this true?"

She looked at Zoe and was dumbfounded by this betrayal. "This is rich! You're worried about lies when our whole existence here in this dorm is exactly that, a lie! Sometimes you really amaze me, Zee. I can't believe what an asshole you can be sometimes. It always, *always* has to be about you, and if it's not, then you find a way to make it be about you or put yourself front and center. How very childish of you to try and make me look bad in your boyfriend's eyes to make yourself look better. And you're my oldest and dearest friend? You can go straight to hell! Asshole!"

She took her things, went into her room, and slammed the door so hard, the room shook. She locked the door, put the chair up against the doorknob and moved the dresser back over to block it. She turned the radio up full blast and started to cry. Some things don't change.

# CHAPTER 36

The soft knocking on the door woke Christina out of a very sound sleep. She tried to wait up for Adam as long as she could but must have dozed off sitting at her desk. She looked at the clock and it was 3:10 in the morning. Stumbling to the door she asked, "Who is it?"

"Why, it's me, of course! Are you expecting someone else? I dare say it's your knight in shining armor, and he's quite desperate to see his lady love. Hurry, Pookie, I can't wait another moment!"

"Adam?" She moved the dresser out of the way and then the chair that was up against the door. As soon as the door was clear, she anxiously opened it, so eager to see the object of her affection.

The moment the door opened, she felt his arms tightly wrapped around her waist as he pulled her towards him and kissed her. He held her face in his hands, and she looked into those extraordinarily blue eyes and watched them dart from one part of her face to another. "I've waited since the moment I walked out the door for this. I've missed you so very much. You haven't left my thoughts for one instant."

"Oh, Adam, I'm so glad you're back. It's been hell without you."

"Oh dear! Has something dreadful happened? Why is your room more disheveled than usual? Did Butch come back early? Did he do something to hurt or frighten you, for if he did, I swear, I'll give him the thrashing he truly deserves." He looked around the room with a confused look on his face. "I don't want to cause you any worry, but I don't think he's done with you yet, and it troubles me. He's completely untrustworthy, and I'm quite sure he's waiting for the right time to carry out a plan of revenge. You do know he thinks he's gotten away with everything he's done, which, of course, he has. I plan on keeping you in my sights."

"Oh, Adam, what would I do without you? You're the best! I'm so lucky you came into my life!" He put down his knapsack as she shut the door and locked it, putting the chair back up against the door and moving the dresser back in front of it.

"So then, what's all this about?"

"I barricaded the door earlier because I guess I was mad at the world and wanted to be alone until you got here. I did it now because I don't want us to be disturbed."

"You weren't angry with me, were you? I'm sorry I broke my promise. I really do feel such a lout to have gone back on my word. That's not the normal behavior of an English Gentleman." He took her hands and intertwined their fingers. It gave Christina a sense of comfort when she looked at their hands joined together. "You do forgive me, don't you?"

"Oh, Adam, family comes first, always! Your parents needed you, and that's where you belonged. I'm happy you were able to come back so soon because I really missed you. So tell me, how's your mother doing? I want to hear all about it."

"Mum came through it brilliantly! My father and I were quite troubled about the whole procedure, but she's doing splendidly. She'll be sore for a few days, but they took out everything that needed to be taken out and the doctors said that she'll be right as rain very soon. Quite a relief, actually. I hate to admit it so openly, but I have a rather soft spot for my mum. Because there are only the three of us, we are quite a close family, especially by English standards. Mum was completely involved in my upbringing and education. Growing up, I didn't have many friends, and then I was in hospital, so Mum was not only my mother but my best friend. I'd do anything for her. I do appreciate your concern for her. I'll tell her you were asking about her. You made a rather good impression on her, and that's quite a difficult task to perform."

"Did I really? Oh, I'm so glad! Please do send her my regards. I'm happy for the three of you that this turned out positively."

"We are, too. So, tell me, my sweet, what have you been doing while I was away, missing you terribly? Did you and Athena have a nice Thanksgiving celebration together?"

"No, we didn't. I spent Thanksgiving alone and by the way, she is at the top of my shit list but I don't want to get into that now. It's been a rough day, and I could use some TLC."

"Terry, please don't say you want drugs. I'd have thought after what happened with Butch that it would've cured you of any sort of nasty drug. Smoking pot or hash is one thing, but not drugs. Please, I won't let you do that!"

She couldn't help but let out a laugh. He's so damn cute! "I think you misunderstand me. TLC stands for Tender Loving Care.

That's what I need. I need to feel the way I feel when you hold me. You're the only drug I require. Can you hold me for a little while?"

"Well, that's a relief! You never have to ask that. Come into these arms that long to hold you forever."

He engulfed her in his arms and held her tightly with neither wanting to let go. After speaking with John, she was so confused as to her feelings, but here with Adam, feeling his strength surround her, she found herself in the warm sensation of enveloping love. She was going to hang on to this for as long as she could. Part of her felt she was betraying John, but her head kept telling her that although right now John's alive, when she gets back to her reality, he won't be there, and neither will Adam. He's the glue putting her back together again, making her whole.

"I don't know about you, Pookie, but I haven't really slept since our last night together. I'm utterly knackered. Let's snuggle up and get some sleep, and then we can have an adventure tomorrow."

"Sounds great." They cuddled together in her bed with Adam on his back, Christina on her side, with her head on his shoulder. His arm was wrapped around her, pulling her close to him, and her arm was around his chest. For a moment, he buried his head in her hair. "I've even missed the smell of your hair. It's so delicious, you know. Smells like purple." In less than a minute, he was asleep. His rhythmic breathing and the warmth of his body next to hers sent her off into a peaceful and restful sleep. Right before dozing off, she thought thankfully how on this Thanksgiving she was able to talk to her first love and fall asleep in the arms of her second.

They both woke up with a start to the sound of Zoe pounding on the door. Adam almost jumped out of his skin. Christina knew exactly who it was.

"Bloody hell! What is that?"

"It's my asshole roommate."

"Well, aren't you going to let her in?"

"No," she said quite nonchalantly, letting her keep pounding. After Zoe went through her purse and told on her like a kindergartener, Christina wasn't going to let her in. Since everyone was gone for Thanksgiving, she could keep knocking until tomorrow.

"Tee! Let me in right now! I have to get my shit. All my stuff is in there! I could kill you right now! Stop acting like such an asshole and open this door."

"Well, Pook, not exactly the way I'd have liked to have been awakened but seeing you first off makes it all quite lovely, actually." He leaned over and kissed her. "If you don't mind, I'm going to remove your barricade and let her in. If not, she's going to knock the entire building down around our ears."

"And if I do mind?"

"Oh, come on, Pookie! Don't be such a grumpy Grover." He walked over to the door, removed all the barriers and opened the door. Christina covered her head so she wouldn't have to see her and only had her arm with her middle finger standing up at attention to greet her.

"Finally! At least there's one human being in this room. Thanks for letting me in, Adam." She looked over at Christina's bed and saw her greeting. "Oh, Tee, you're so freaking immature sometimes. I'd love to slap you!" Christina could hear Zoe walk to her dresser to get what she needed. Her attention turned to Adam. "So, Adam, tell me, how's your mother?"

"Quite well, Zoe. Thanks for asking." Christina's eyes widened, and her body froze. Did he call her Zoe?

"We're so glad to hear it. Really. Good to have you back. It's great that your mom's doing well. You'll have to tell us about it later." After getting some of her things, she said, "Tell Tee I said screw you", and left.

Did she notice how Adam addressed her? Christina was motionless for a few seconds. What the hell is going on here? First, he calls me Christina, and now he addresses Zoe by her real name. How does he know our names? This is too weird! Is he part of this CIA team and we don't know about it? Could he be one of the two agents who are supposedly here but missing in action? No, he's too young, but then again, that's how she must seem. She didn't know how to react. Should she ask him why he called her Zoe, or ignore it? It obviously went right over Zoe's head because there was no reaction in her voice that she caught on to what Adam said.

He removed the covers from her head. "All's clear, luv. She's gone, at least for now. She asked me to give you a message. Did you hear it?"

Here's her chance to get out of this sticky situation. "No, I didn't. I was doing a low hum, so I couldn't hear anything that was said. And I don't care to get any messages from her. I've known her long enough to know exactly what she said. She's a stupid, ugly, stinky, miserable, smelly bitch!" Phew! She escaped that one, but it was going to bother her all day.

"What on earth happened while I was gone? You two are best mates!"

"It's a girl thing. They always blow over quickly. Things will be back to normal in a day or two. We have these little tiffs every so often. As soon as we can hash it out, we'll be fine."

"Well, now that we're up, let's make up for lost time. I'll leave you to get ready, and I'll do the same. We'll grab a quick breakfast and then head out. Dress warmly because it gets quite breezy on the Harley." He walked to the door and then unexpectedly turned around and looked at her. "Do you know you look even more beautiful first thing in the morning? What am I to do with you, or worse yet, what am I to do without you?" And then he left the room. She sat there for a minute, feeling the warmth of what he said, and found herself wondering the same thing about him.

Within five minutes they were on their way out the door. She caught their reflection in one of the windows they passed. They made such a cute couple; he with his shoulder length light brown hair falling in waves framing his vibrant blue eyes, surrounded by dark, thick lashes and her, a bundle of long dark curls with big dark eyes. Both of them, so young and alive.

They went to the cafeteria and grabbed a quick cup of coffee and some toast, and then they were off. Christina sat on the back of the Harley holding on to Adam's waist. She tried to memorize his smell, every curl in his hair as it stuck out of the helmet, the curve of his neck, and the lay of his shoulders. They rode off to the hills of San Francisco, went up and down the streets, enjoying the beautiful scenery with the rumble of the Harley filling their ears.

After a while, he pulled over and they got off to walk around. He immediately intertwined their fingers. She looked down at their hands united like the gnarled root of a tree and felt a wave of happiness overcome her. He saw her look and quickly put their hands up to his mouth and kissed the back of her hand. He pulled her to him and said, "I've got a much better idea." He gave her a long, sweet, passionate kiss. "Mmmmmmm. Thank you, Pook, I needed that."

"No, thank you because I needed it more."

"Well then, why didn't you ask? You know your wish is my command."

"Ok, then kiss me again!" They stood there on the busy street, with no one paying any attention to the two lovers locked in each other's embrace. That was one of the great things about San Francisco at this time: free love, no matter your gender or sexual orientation. It was great to be young, in love, and in San Francisco.

They walked around and went into a few stores, trying on big floppy hats, sunglasses, scarves, goofing around and acting silly. They stopped at a small diner for lunch where the conversation took on a somber tone.

"I've something to tell you, Pookie."

"Uh oh, sounds intense. Is everything ok?" He ran his fingers through his hair and rubbed the back of his neck, which meant everything was not ok. It's funny, she hadn't really known him that long but felt as if she'd known him forever.

"Well, yes…and no. Yes, everything is brilliant, but to me it's not, actually. It would be bloody fantastic if I could stay with you right here forever. I'm completely besotted by you. Since the moment I saw you on the hill on my first day back, I've been able to think of nothing but you. Do you realize how long it's been since I flirted or even cared to ask my 'special questions' to any bird? It's like I've found my other half, the glove that fits my hand so perfectly, the person who is all I could ever want, only to know that in a matter of days, we'll walk out of each other's lives. After this semester, I may never see you again, and it is torturing me."

"Adam, please, let's not talk about this."

"Well, unlike you, I want to be completely above board."

"Adam, please, I've told you before..."

"Yes, I remember, top secret, hush-hush, shan't speak of it and all that." He paused for a moment and took her hand from across the booth they were sitting in. "I'm sorry, luv. The last thing I want is to come off as priggish, which, of course, is exactly what I'm doing. I want to tell you that after this semester, I'll be leaving America.

"First off, my mum has asked me to come back to England. With this health scare, she wants me closer to home. I cannot refuse her. And secondly, I had struck an arrangement with my father when I first came here last year and had two years to fulfill my side of the bargain. As you know, I completely blew off my first year, so this year was my only opportunity to redeem myself. You know that music is my life, although my family would rather see me in a more civilized career, something more worthy of a Wallingford, if you will. We agreed that if I did well in my studies here at Berkeley, they'd give their blessing on my pursuing a music career and would arrange a meeting with George Martin, which is bloody brilliant. Do you know who he is?"

"Of course. He's the music producer who's worked with the Beatles."

"How is it you know everything? You're bloody amazing at times! Well, anyway, my father has arranged a meeting for me and my mates after the first of the year to discuss with Mr. Martin the possibility of helping us with our first recording. Musical success would be a dream come true for me, so I'll be leaving in December, sometime after exams.

"Much as I don't agree, it's been strongly suggested by the family solicitors and my father that if my music takes off, I should take a stage name to separate myself and my musical achievements from the family estates and businesses. I think they're worried I'll be careless and run amok everywhere, and my family will end up in the courts, I'll end up in the nick and the estate will have to pay for the band's foolish and reckless antics. I think they believe I may behave like a rocker, and my bad behavior could come to rest on my parents. One thing is certain. I must thank you for helping me get this golden opportunity my father is offering me."

"Me? How do you figure that?"

"If not for you, I'd have spent this whole semester doing exactly as I did last year, getting high, playing at pubs, chasing skirts, and certainly not going to any classes. You've been instrumental, pardon the pun, in helping to jump-start my music career with all the help you've given me in our art classes."

"I can't take credit for that, Adam."

"Whether you do, or don't, I know you're the only reason I went to class. And my paper on Mary Cassatt that you helped me with got one of my highest marks ever. The professor was quite impressed with it.

"My father made it perfectly clear, and he never changes his mind. This was my last shot at having a career in music. Before the start of this year's term, I was warned this was my last chance to show maturity and responsibility. He was quite serious about it. If I wanted this introduction to Mr. Martin, I'd have to show him I was worthy of his help and wouldn't disappoint or embarrass him with my behavior. And I wasn't holding up my part. I'd have thrown it all away because I had no intention of going to any classes. Then you had the balls to slam the door in my face. It was game on. I had to go to class to irritate you. So, you see, I'd have no hope of a future music career if not for you.

"First, I relished my ability to aggravate you. I loved to bugger you up and to my surprise, I started to enjoy seeing you, especially when you brought out the diamonds. Then, after the night of Butch, you completely dominated my thoughts and my heart. Your help on the reports and studying, along with the enthusiasm you have for art, helped me more than you know. You should become an art teacher, you know?"

She searched his eyes and became overwhelmed with feeling. She got up and walked to his side of the booth. "Stand up and kiss me. Kiss me like it's the last time."

"Here? Right now? Before we've paid the tab?"

"Yes, right here, right now."

"It wouldn't really be the last time, would it, luv?"

"No, it's definitely not the last time, but I want every kiss we share to be like the first and the last. With you going back to England and me going home, I want every moment to count because there isn't much time left." He stood and pulled her to him, and they kissed in exactly the manner she asked.

Patrons were remarking, some negatively, some hooting, and there was a whistle or two. When they stopped, she looked into his eyes and said, "Adam, what are you doing to me? This wasn't supposed to happen. I wish time could stop so that we could stay together." Time! That despicable word again! It's a friend, an enemy, a catalyst to happiness or disaster. And now it's something she's running out of too quickly.

"We could write, you know."

"Oh Adam! Kiss me again!" After that kiss Adam paid the bill and they left. Next to the diner was a five and dime store and in the window was one of those photo booths. Christina had an idea.

"Let's go in there and take a bunch of pictures of ourselves." She looked through her purse and still had change from when she called John. "Come on! I've got enough quarters for lots of pictures!"

They went into the store and got situated in the photo booth. There were four pictures on a strip so they decided the first would be normal, second would be crazy, third would be mean-faced and the fourth would be serious. Christina put the quarter in and they did their posing. After a few minutes, the picture strip would come out. It seemed like it was taking a long time and Christina was impatient.

"While we're waiting, we can play the game I'd play with my mum when I was younger. Time passed very slowly when I was hospitalized, so my mum made up this game. We take turns saying three things, and the other has to guess what they are."

"Three things? Like what?"

Ok, let's see. Alright, how about John, Paul, and George? What would you say?

"Ringo."

He laughed. "Right but not right. You'd have to say, 'the Beatles.' Or I could say red, white, and blue, and what would you say?"

"The American flag?"

"Right! It helps time go by more quickly, especially when the person you're with is bloody impatient!" He pulled her to him and kissed her forehead. "Do you want to give it a go?"

"Sure! Hmmm, let's see. Ok, I'll start with an easy one. Porthos, Athos, and Aramis."

"The Three Musketeers."

"Right. Your turn."

"Curly, Larry, and Moe."

"The Three Stooges."

The pictures came out and Adam set themselves up for the next series. "For the next pictures, I want us to start off looking at each other and then move in for a kiss. It would be bloody fantastic to have a photo of that." They did as Adam suggested and stayed in the booth a little longer, finishing the kiss. They started the waiting game again.

Their pictures came out, and after admiring them, they went back into the booth, put in a quarter, and posed. They kept playing the game while waiting for the photos to come out. They had ten strips of photos, and this was their last one. They got into the booth and sat waiting for the red light to flash, letting them know the camera was going to snap the picture. The red light went on. Adam turned her face to his, looked into her eyes, and said, "I love you, Christina." A picture was taken of that moment.

She looked back into those vibrant blue eyes and said to him, "And I love you, Adam." Another flash, and with it the photographic record of her declaring her love for him. The next two photos were of them looking at each other. And then it hit her. He called her Christina again. She couldn't let it slide and had to address it this time. They got out of the booth and stood in their usual waiting spot. She wasn't sure how to bring the subject up.

"Did you mean it, Pookie, what you said to me?"

"Yes, I did. Did you?"

"You know I did because I said it first."

"But you could have said that to see what I'd say. And by the way, what did you call me? Are you sure you were talking to me and not some other girl?"

"I called you Teresa. That is your name, isn't it?"

"Yes, but you never call me Teresa, it's always Terry."

"I wanted to say it with your proper name so you'd know I was quite serious. What did you think I said?"

"Something else."

"What else would I call you?" He acted so innocent that she let it go. At least she asked this time. She didn't want to spoil this wonderful moment. They went back to the guessing game, with it being his turn.

"I'm going to give you a hard one, luv. Here goes. Who are Pamela, Bonnie, and Michael?"

"That's a hard one. Can you give me a hint?"

"Sorry, no."

"Give me a minute." She racked her brain but couldn't come up with anything. "I hate to say it, but you win. You got me. I've no idea. Who are they?"

"They were my nurses when I was in hospital. Ha ha. Gotcha on that one!" He started to gloat that he stumped her.

"Adam, that's not fair! You have to do another one. Come on!" He looked at her and his smile seemed to slowly fade which made all manner of fun seem to slip from his face. She wondered if he regretted saying he loved her. Oh, the insecurities of being a teenager!

"Ok, here's one for you. Tell me, who are… Kenzie, Roxie, and Johnny?"

She felt all the air fly out of her lungs. Oh my God! What in the hell is going on? Her mouth opened, but no sound came out. And what would she say? She calmed down enough to make some unintelligible, staccato little noises. "I…um…uh…not too sure about this one. You stumped me again. I give up. Who are they?"

"I haven't the foggiest idea. I was hoping you could tell me."

"Me? How would I know?"

"Well, those were some of the names you kept repeating the night you were drugged by Butch. I sat up with you that entire night, and you quite fitfully mentioned them and spoke to them over and over. Sometimes it was Johnny, other times it was John."

She could feel her body start to shake. "Really? Um, I …um…I'm…um…uh…uh. I don't… know… who they are. I guess you win." He gave her a look that said he didn't believe a word of it.

"I'm not going to press you because you're looking rather upset right now. I'll let you keep this bit of mystery about you, but I believe you do know who they are."

"What else did I say that night?"

"You said quite a lot of things, actually, most of which really didn't make sense."

"Like what? Please tell me."

"Like, 'John, you're the best hubby,' which would make me think you're married and asking this John, who, by the way, I don't bloody well like at all, to pick up the kids for soccer, which I believe is really football and bring the girls to ballet and tap class. You also cried and begged John not to leave you. That was really quite sad, actually. Why anyone would leave you is beyond belief."

"Wow!" Ok, Christina, make it sound convincing! "Isn't that weird? I must have been having some crazy dreams, right?"

"I wouldn't call it weird. It was as if John was your husband and those three were your children, but how would that ever be possible? Bloody confusing to me, I must admit. How does a teenager have a husband and three children who are old enough to be taking dance lessons and playing sports? Another strange bit of business is that football is not really a big sport in this country, so why is little Johnny playing? I must say it's all rather bewildering."

She gave no response and felt like a deer caught in the headlights.

"Must be you were rambling about nonsense?"

"Yeah, that must be it." She tried to look nonchalant and calm, but the inner turmoil was showing on her face, or else Adam wouldn't have said she looked upset. God in heaven, what else did I say? Is that how he knows our real names? She wanted to ask him, but it was not a conversation she wanted to have. She could talk to René about it, but certainly not after last night and the stuff she had pulled. Then, for sure, he would recommend they leave right away, and she wasn't going to do that.

The photo came out which shifted the focus and there was no further conversation about her ramblings. She tried to hold on to some measure of composure but wasn't sure she was pulling it off. Have I given myself away? Different thoughts were darting through her head. She needed to calm down.

"You're upset, Pookie, I can tell, and I apologize. You see, I really do love you, you know. I've never said that to a girl before because I've never loved anyone before you. I didn't even bloody know what love was." He folded the pictures and tore them apart. "You take the one where I'm telling you, and I'll keep the one you're telling me. How bloody fantastic to have this photographic record of this brilliant moment." He handed her the picture and then asked, "Did you mean it?"

"Adam, I don't say anything I don't mean." She looked down at the picture. "I'll never forget this moment in my life." He lifted her face and kissed her.

"When we go to our spot on the Bay, we can sort out the photos."

Adam did his best to keep her mind occupied, and she tried her best to act like nothing was wrong. There were only a few more weeks until all this was over, so she couldn't let anything spoil the time they had left.

They walked around looking at all the Christmas decorations in the stores and went to see Santa. They sat on his lap together and had two pictures taken, one for each of them. They each asked Santa for more time to spend with each other, and Santa said if they were good, he'd see what he could do. Luckily for them, there were not many children in line, so Santa played along. Black Friday wouldn't become a phenomenon for another few decades.

They hopped back on the bike and headed off to their spot on the Bay to watch the sunset. They sat at their usual place and stared out over the water, both in their own thoughts.

He brought out the photo strips and they argued over who would get each picture and Christina suggested they keep them in the strips and divide them that way so there weren't small photos that could get lost. He agreed and then they playfully argued over who would get each strip. They laughed and kidded each other, and the lightheartedness was put back into the day.

They sat looking at the shimmering water with the setting sun, with his arm around her, holding her close with her head on his shoulder and his head lying upon hers. He spoke first, not looking at her, but speaking while staring at the water.

"I'm dreadfully sorry if I upset you today. I probably should've told you before that you were babbling on during that ghastly night. Truthfully, I didn't wish to remind you of it. It was all quite appalling, and I wanted you to forget it ever happened. I should've kept it to myself." He paused for a minute, possibly waiting for her to respond, but she didn't know what to say.

"I do believe, as unattractive as it is, I'm rather jealous of this fellow John, whoever he is. I was quite afraid you were going to tell me he's your dearest love back home, and you couldn't wait to get back to him. From what you were saying that night, it seemed he had exactly what I want and know I can't have. A lifetime with you."

He turned towards her with tears in his eyes. "You're so quiet, and that's not like you. Please tell me I haven't spoiled what we have by my priggish behavior today. I couldn't bear it if you were upset with me. I'm so sorry I mentioned those names. Tell me you forgive me."

"I'm not upset with you. What you've told me today is a lot to take in. I'm lost in my thoughts. You're the best part of my semester here at Berkeley. The rest of my life will never be the same. I'll never be whole again because a part of me will always be with you." They kissed and held each other close with the shimmering sun setting over the water.

"I suppose we should get back to the dorm. Shall we stop and pick up some burgers and fries to bring back and have dinner with Athena and Jean-René?"

"Screw 'em. Let them get their own dinner."

"Pookie! Come on! You have to get things ironed out. On Sunday Ali and Butch will return and our blissful days and nights together will end, and we'll have to go back to sneaking about. You'll have to at least let her into her room at some point. She can't spend the night with Jean-René while I'm in the room. Well, I suppose she could, but it could get rather awkward. What do you say?"

"Well, it's against my better judgment, but I guess if that's what you want to do."

He stood up and held out his hand and helped her up. As she stood up, he put his arms around her waist and looked into her eyes, searching in them. "I do love you so. I'm writing a song about you, you know. Before we part, I'll have it finished and sing it to you."

"I can't wait to hear it. And I love you too. Let's get dinner."

# CHAPTER 37

Zoe and René waited for Christina to come back from her day with Adam on the Friday after Thanksgiving to attend their weekly update with Professor O'Connell. When she didn't show up, they decided to go without her. This wouldn't be the best time to skip their meeting, especially after their encounter with him last night.

The two of them had a lengthy discussion about the missing pin and the phone call to John Pucci, but ultimately, there was nothing they could do. What was done was done and bitching about it wasn't going to change anything.

"But she lied to us, René. I know I saw that pin the other day. It did not go with Ali to Louisiana. This is a lying ploy so she can get her way. I know her better than you do. She knew rule number one was not to contact anyone from our past! What does she do? Call John! She blatantly disregarded all the rules and needs to be held accountable for her actions. If you or I did the same, there would be consequences, and you know it."

"*Chérie*, we need to remember Christina is not an agent and hasn't been trained as such, unlike you and me. She's a grieving, widowed housewife, unwittingly thrown into circumstances I could only term as 'dangerously unbelievable'. I'd think, as her oldest and dearest friend, you'd have more compassion for her."

"Screw her! You're always on her side! I'm sick of it always being about her throughout this whole trip. No one from either century gives a shit about us! I wish we were alone here."

"And where would we be if that were the case? She was the one who brilliantly snuck in the recording devices. Without her, we wouldn't have gotten the necessary proof, and we definitely wouldn't have been afforded the opportunities we have if she weren't here. Martin Cater was very smart in the recruitment for this team. He understood that without her, there'd be no success, and things happened as he predicted. Ali was immediately taken with her, which gave us the 'in' we required. He also knew the team needed you and me. He correctly surmised the only way to get me and Christina was to remove what was standing in his way: my family and John Pucci. I think the only one of us he undervalued is you. He had no clue of the invaluable gifts you bring to this team. The only thing he understood was that without you, there would be no conscription of Christina. He's like a fox, and I can only hope we outsmart him in the end."

"What about our meeting today with O'Connell? You know, Tee isn't going to be back in time to go. Should we go alone?"

"I think it's best even if she does return. Glenn will get over it, I'm sure, as long as you're there."

The more René thought about it, the more he felt Christina should not accompany them today. Tempers between Zoe and Christina were raging as evidenced by the blocking of the door and the one-finger greeting. He hoped it was teenage hormones causing these problems and nothing else. To make matters worse, she foolishly called her husband. There would be too much tension if Christina were with them today at this meeting. Things could escalate into a full-blown war regarding the exact things René had no intention of revealing to O'Connell or anyone else.

It would also only make Adam more suspicious of the three of them. He already seemed to know or suspect more than he's letting on. If the three of them left, he did not doubt that Adam would follow. He didn't want to have to go through a lengthy explanation that was composed of lies. It was best to go without her.

Truthfully, as much as he was enjoying life in this century, he couldn't wait to return. Things were starting to unravel, and he had a feeling of unease he couldn't shake. His sixth sense was screaming for him to pay attention.

When they walked in for their weekly meeting, it was obvious O'Connell was still angry and could barely look at them. "Where's Christina?"

"Well, *mon ami*, she's not here, obviously."

"She needs to be a part of this meeting. Go get her."

"Queen Christina is unavailable to hang with us peasants."

"Zoe, mind yourself, please."

"Whatever! The bitch isn't here."

"Zoe, please. She is off somewhere with Adam. They haven't returned, and we thought it best to attend the meeting without her rather than skip the meeting altogether. Yes? No?"

"Well, isn't that fucking groovy! Can things get any worse?" O'Connell threw his glass against the wall and watched the pieces scatter all over the floor. He was in hot water with the CIA because he didn't follow instructions with the back story for the three of them and then topped off by their refusal to leave at once as ordered. He tried to explain the reasons the time travelers felt it necessary to stay, but after failing to make them understand, he decided to let them explain themselves to the CIA. "You three are going to be the death of me yet!"

Zoe approached him, knowing full well the effect she had on him. "Oh, Professor. We've seen you in the 21$^{st}$ century, so we know that won't happen. And you're so handsome and distinguished in the future. Come on, admit it, you're going to miss us when we're gone, aren't you?" She linked arms with him, making his thoughts become jumbled.

He looked down at her, and their eyes met. "Well, I suppose maybe a little."

"We'll miss you, too." She looked at him for a second and smiled. She then quickly changed the subject. "Ok, boys, now that we have that settled, let's pick up this broken glass and get started." René was amazed at how easily she could diffuse a situation. He was quite sure she could charm the venom from a cobra with no problem.

René had written the complete explanation, of course, leaving out the self-imposed disappearance and phone call made by Christina. The present CIA concern, in light of the new information they'd received, was that Mrs. Pucci got home safely. René confirmed once again that they have the proof they came for in two forms and will be able to retrieve it once they're home with the 21st-century technology. Transmissions back and forth took half an hour to reach the other century.

Although the CIA was not pleased that the direct order for their immediate departure was ignored, their return correspondence revealed that the delay was approved due to the fact that Martin Cater, who unfortunately was head of this mission, was rushed to a hospital due to a massive infection from his hip. CIA Chief Thomas Metzger had reluctantly agreed to allow the surgery but only because his condition was life threatening. He'll be healed up enough by December 20$^{th}$ when they'll meet at Langley and go over the evidence.

The date for their return to the 21$^{st}$ century was as originally scheduled, December 14$^{th}$. It was agreed the date worked on all ends. It would give them enough time to be checked out by the doctors upon their immediate return, fly back to the East Coast on the 15$^{th}$, go over all the evidence at the New York office, and then meet in Washington on the 20th with their findings.

As they started to leave, O'Connell pulled René aside to speak to him privately. "We've learned there may be a plot underway to bring both girls to the Middle East. You have to remain diligent and watchful, so they're both kept safe. Although Ms. Janis doesn't have any children, it doesn't mean getting her safely back isn't of the utmost importance. The three of you must make it home safely. Do you understand?"

"I do. Do you know something we don't?"

"I believe Ali's guardian thinks Christina is a spy, and the King seems to fancy girls with green eyes."

"Glenn, where did this information come from?"

"Hey, man, I've got my ways of getting information. Do you think you're the only smart one here? You handle your part, and I'll handle mine. Keep the two of them in your sights at all times. Things are not cool, you know. You really should've gone back yesterday."

"Well, *mon ami*, we didn't so we have to take it from here." They both said goodbye to O'Connell and left the meeting with enough information to start a plan for their departure. Glenn watched Zoe as they crossed the dorm grounds. As soon as they joined hands he turned away.

As they walked back to the dorm, René was deep in thought, and Zoe noticed.

"So, what was that private little tete-a-tete you had with O'Connell?"

"He has some concerns for the safety of you and Christina."

"Wow! Concern for me, too? I thought our sweet little backstabbing heroine was the only important one on this team." There was an edge of sarcasm to her voice and rightly so, René thought. All this concern for Christina and none for either of them grated on René's sensibility. He hoped it was because of her children and not that the worth of their lives was less in any way.

"Ah, *mon Chérie*, I'm sure, much to Glenn's displeasure, he knows I'm almost always by your side, and I'd never let anything harm you. I've got plans for us when we get back. I've a personal stake in your safety. My future happiness depends on it."

He could see the warmth come over her with his words. She was like butter. A few warm words soften her, while cold, harsh words make her hard as a rock.

They were in the Common Room when Adam and Christina returned.

"We brought back dinner for all of us. Jean-René, will you help me set things up so that Athena and Terry can try to sort things out with each other?"

René and Adam went into the kitchen and Zoe and Christina went outside. They didn't want Adam or René to hear any of it. Zoe started talking as soon as they got outside.

"Tee, I'm sorry about everything. I was acting like an asshole, but you lied about the pin. I saw it the other day with your jewelry. What the hell, Tee? Talk to me!"

"And what were you doing in my jewelry box?"

"Tee, don't be a jerk. We've always shared stuff like that! I was looking for your purple earrings and saw it there. And you can thank me for convincing René that we have to stay. I was able to make him see that you couldn't leave because Adam would go to the cops if you disappeared, and he'd put the blame squarely on Butch. Everything we've done to keep what happened quiet would be out in the open."

Christina nodded her head. "Yeah, but I still wanted to smack you. You turned on me. I could take anything, Zee, but not that. We've been through too much together. I felt like you were both against me."

"Tee, we were so worried about you. We looked all over for you. You could have left a note or something. Especially when you know things are getting dangerous. René was an absolute wreck over your disappearance. He thought for sure something had happened to you. You have to admit, you were acting very childishly."

"I did leave a note, remember? And yeah, I was acting childishly, but I wasn't going to leave early. It's different for you because René is coming home with you. He'll be with you when we go back and be a part of the rest of your life. The next few weeks are all I'm going to be able to have with Adam. I'm in love with him. I was ready to do anything to stay."

"But, Tee, calling John? What's up with that! You know better than to pull a stupid stunt like that! It wasn't too smart."

"He doesn't know me yet, so no harm done." She took a few steps away from her and then turned back. "What do you want from me? I was feeling alone and bummed out on Thanksgiving. I passed a phone booth and suddenly got the idea that he was home for the holiday. I needed to hear his voice. It helped me remember who I am. Knowing that a living, breathing John was on the other end of the phone gave me a chance to have a connection to him. I don't regret it for one second. It was very bittersweet. We had such a great marriage. I wish I could change what happened to him, but I know I can't. I'm going back to my empty life, and I'm taking every advantage of the life I have right here, right now."

"You do know that it's getting more and more risky for us as long as we're here."

"Yeah, I do, but I don't care. I'm sure we can last another few weeks."

"I hope so, for all our sakes. So, Tee, did you fuck him yet?"

"Who, Adam? Oh my God, Zee! You never change! No, I haven't."

"What are you waiting for? It's great, especially with these teenage bodies. Everything is so tight and new. We don't have those middle-aged crotches as dry as the Sahara Desert. I can't get enough of René. Man, he is great in the sack! Best sex ever! Now we've got all the experience and sexual know-how with killer bodies that we know how to use! Tee, you gotta go for it."

"Oh Zee, that's why you're my best friend! You're the only one who would say something like that. I guess that's why I love you!"

"Love you too. So, we cool, Tee?"

"We cool." They hugged and went back upstairs. Both guys were happy to see things were back to normal with them. They had dinner and coffee and spent the rest of the night hanging out listening to music, smoking doobies, and shooting the shit.

Adam and Christina spent the rest of the Thanksgiving holiday off on the motorcycle, taking advantage of the absence of Ali. In the evening, they'd watch the sun set on the bay, walk to the Sather Tower for their 10 o'clock kiss, and Adam spent the next two nights with Christina, and Zoe stayed with René.

René decided to use this time to go over a few defensive moves with Zoe. They had a lot of fun playing around, along with the serious business of teaching her how to defend herself. She flipped him on one of the moves, got on top of him, and started making out with him.

"I think it's time to head upstairs while no one is here and make love in every room in our dorm."

"No, *mon Chérie*, we need to continue with your lesson. You need to be able to defend yourself."

"Well, I disagree. Right now, it's more important that you make passionate love to me as many times as possible while I'm still young, hot, and ripe for the picking." She started to rub herself against him, and he found himself, once again, desiring her body, completely under her spell. He couldn't argue with her once she had made her mind up, and truthfully, he couldn't get enough of her. She was able to excite him with a look or the lick of her lips. They made love at the very least once a day, sometimes more. She was very skillful sexually, which made their lovemaking unbelievable. Their bodies complemented each other, and they both always achieved intense orgasms.

As they walked back up to the dorm, he mused on how much he adored her, which he found so surprising. He didn't expect love to find him with Adele, and now he had this exquisite gift that was Zoe Janis in his life. To have the love of two women that he was able to love so deeply and purely is quite rare, and he knew how lucky he was. He had to keep her safe. He couldn't bear to lose this chance of happiness after living in such bleak darkness after the loss of his family.

Although he was determined to be with her at all times, he was realistic in knowing that it wouldn't always be possible. He was the only one of the three of them who opted out of taking the exams in order to keep his eye on everything happening with the key players of this game they were in.

It seemed everything was going along smoothly. He wondered if Ali and Butch were cementing their friendship in Louisiana.

# CHAPTER 38

Ali couldn't wait to get back to Berkeley. Every second he spent in Louisiana, he wished he had never accepted the invitation from the Morgans to spend the Thanksgiving holiday with them. He suspected their only reason for the invitation was so Butch's family wouldn't have to interact with him as much because he had a guest.

He felt awkward, even though Senator Morgan had been very hospitable to him during his uncomfortable stay in their home. As he sat at the Thanksgiving table with Butch's family, he couldn't mistake the lack of tension and lightheartedness of everyone without the presence of Butch. For the first time since his arrival in Louisiana, he felt the difference within the family without the negative energy radiating from Butch, or Harold as he is known in this house. Butch didn't make it to this holiday dinner. His father deemed it necessary for his son to remain in jail until they're ready to head back to Berkeley on Sunday. Seeing the family dynamic played out before him, he understood the feelings of aversion they all had for Butch and vice versa. Nonetheless, he felt out of place and ill at ease with them. He wished he had never come.

As soon as they arrived on Monday, the first thing Butch insisted they do was hop into his little sports car. Ali wanted to settle in first and meet his hosts as was decreed by propriety, but Butch had other plans. He had things to do, and Ali was coming with him. They hopped in the car, leaving their suitcases in the entryway. Every time Ali asked where they were going, Butch would laugh that evil cackle. Ali was impressed by the beauty and speed of the Jaguar but felt ill at ease with Butch's wild driving. When they stopped at a seedy looking apartment building, Ali wanted to remain in the car but Butch belittled him calling him a coward and insisted he join him. Butch was constantly reminding Ali he was still pulling the strings of his princely puppet.

Ali was horrified when he realized Butch was making a drug deal. All he could think of was the dishonor he'd cause his family if they were caught. Although he'd have diplomatic immunity, Khalid and his father wouldn't see it at all favorably, and things wouldn't bode well for him when he returned home.

Ali tried to reason with Butch but there was no compassion or empathy for the consequences to the prince. When Ali tried to remind him of his position and the morals of his country Butch would counter with, "All y'all need to worry about right now is doing as I say, right Princey? That's our deal. Y'all know what'll happen if y'all don't, right, Princey?" Ali's hatred for Butch which had waned after the visit from his father, began to intensify.

After the illegal purchases, Butch rolled a joint and lit up for the ride back to the Morgan mansion. All his purchases were put in the secret compartment in his car. Ali kept praying they wouldn't get caught.

When they arrived home, Butch's mother was there. She barely greeted her son and was coldly cordial to Ali, introducing herself. She took one look at Butch, grabbed his face and held it up to hers. She looked in his eyes and seemed to smell his breath. With the quickest of motions, she slapped him hard across the face, exactly where it was still bruised from the bashing he received from Terry. "How dare you come into my house under the influence of drugs! You're a disgrace as always, and you carry the odor of a drug addict! I do declare, from the look of your face, it tells me you can't get on with anyone, can you? To think that a member of this family is street fighting like a hooligan. I'm quite certain you got exactly what you deserved." She then looked at Ali and said, "I suppose you've also partaken the same substance as Harold." She walked over to Ali and sniffed him.

"No, Mrs. Morgan, it's against my religion to ingest any form of altering substances. We aren't allowed to drink or take drugs. I'd not put shame on you, my country, or your hospitality. Thank you for graciously inviting me into your home. I'm deeply honored by your kindness."

Butch countered with "Fucking suck up," to which his mother slapped him again, this time harder. "You will not use that language in my home, and especially in my presence! Can you ever be civil, Harold? I'm warning you right from this moment, you'd be wise not to do anything to spoil this holiday for us, like you've ruined every one of them in the past. I'm quite certain you know it was my wish to let you rot at Berkeley, but your father insisted on giving you another chance.

"The only thing you can be depended upon is to destroy everything. Why he needed to inflict your nasty persona on us, I can't fathom the reason! I hoped you'd be on your best behavior, seeing how we have a member of the Zatari Royal Family as a guest in our humble home, but that is beyond the realm of possibility for you, isn't it?"

"And I love y'all, too, Mother. Always so good to see y'all." He moved in to kiss her, and she recoiled from him.

"Snide and unpleasant as always. And stop saying 'y'all'. You know how I despise that. You sound illiterate." Then she looked at Ali and asked, "Has Harold shown you where you'll be staying?"

"Not yet, ma'am."

"Of course he hasn't. He has the manners of a swine and not a semblance of a Southern gentleman. Albert will show you to your room." Mrs. Morgan left and returned a few seconds later with a black manservant in formal attire. "Albert, please show Prince Ali the room we've prepared for him." She turned to Ali and said, "I hope you'll be comfortable in our home. So pleased you're spending the holiday with us. If you need anything, Albert will assist you." She turned and walked away.

Butch went up ahead into his room, swearing under his breath and Albert showed Ali to his room. At the top of the staircase was a portrait of a beautiful little girl with curly dark hair and vibrant purple-blue eyes. "Is this Mrs. Morgan when she was a child?" Ali asked.

"No, sir. That's Missy Violet, the oldest child of the Morgans. Done passed quite a few years now. Put a hole in this family as big as heaven itself."

"Oh, so sorry. I didn't know. Butch never mentioned her. May I ask how she died?"

"Wasn't working here then, but folks say it was a terrible accident. They say she was a wild child, full of spunk and fearless. Swung a vine into a watering hole that was pretty much dried up. Masser Harold saw it happen. He juss a young-un at the time, maybe seven or so. Got the blame for it fixed right on him. Took the life right out of this house. 'Specially Miss Rachel. She can't look at Master Harold without feeling he shoulda stopped Missy Vi. Horrible what done happened to this family and to Master Harold. Carryin' that load a-might heavy for a child. Seem to get heavier with every passing day." He turned away from the portrait and walked toward the room prepared for Ali. "Here you go, Sir, this here is your room. If you need anything, you just let old Albert know." As he turned to leave, he said,

"Now, you're better off not sayin' a word a what I told you. That be one scar ain't never gonna heal."

Ali settled into his room, which had a magnificent view of the grounds. He stood by the window looking out but not seeing the view. "So that's why Butch is the way he is," he thought to himself. He felt sorry for him, but one can never have those feelings for Butch for very long because he has a way of destroying good will with his presence.

At Butch's insistence, they stayed at the house as little as possible. On the Wednesday night before Thanksgiving, Butch and Ali left early. It was typically a big night at the bars because college students were out catching up with old friends. Butch and Ali bar hopped with Butch selling his wares. He kept embarrassing Ali by making fun of his Berkeley cap, inappropriately trying to get girls to have sex with him, telling them Ali was a prince and wouldn't they like to have a go with royalty. It became obvious by the way people reacted to Butch that there weren't too many people who liked him at all.

As they were headed home, Butch, who was high and drunk, started recklessly speeding through the streets of Baton Rouge. It wasn't long before they had a police car behind them with sirens screeching and lights flashing. Butch laughed, drove faster, running red lights, stop signs and nearly running over a couple walking to their car.

Ali begged him to stop but Butch cackled and said, "I've missed these pigs trying to outrun my Jag. A guy's gotta have some fun." By the time they cut his car off and he finally stopped, five police cruisers were chasing them, and three were blocking his progress.

They were roughly pulled out of the Jaguar, placed under arrest, cuffed, put into a police car, and hauled off to the stationhouse. Butch kept laughing, spitting at them and bad mouthing them. Ali kept saying that he did nothing, but the officers wouldn't listen. "Well, buddy, sometimes it's the company you keep. Y'all can tell your story to the judge when the time comes."

They were photographed, fingerprinted, and thrown in a cell. The officers did sobriety tests on them both with Butch failing miserably and Ali was proving to be sober. Butch was antagonizing Ali with now being arrested and how proud his daddy will be to hear it. He kept laughing at Ali's predicament. Ali was ready to cry.

Senator Morgan showed up with the police chief and asked to see the boys and was taken to where they were being held. The Chief instructed his men to release Ali and assured them this young man did nothing but have the misfortune of being a guest of the Morgans for Thanksgiving.

"This young man here is a prince from Zatari, and as y'all can imagine, it would be right embarrassin' for the Senator, the great state of Louisiana, and the United States of America if word got out that an innocent member of a royal family was in a Baton Rouge jail. That kind of trouble we don't need. He's under the care of the Morgans. Shit will hit the fan if this gets out. I hope you boys didn't do anything that y'all might regret to this young man. All evidence of his arrest must be destroyed, y'all understand me?"

They opened the door, and Ali was let out. Butch started to walk out but his father stopped him. "Y'all aren't going anywhere, boy. Y'all are staying here until Sunday."

"But Daddy, it's Thanksgiving!"

"Y'all should have thought about that before getting yourself arrested. I'll pick you up on Sunday in time for y'all to go home, put your things together, and head to the airport. Your mama doesn't want to see you, and I've no intention of listening to her complain about you for the next three days. When are y'all going to learn and grow up?"

When Senator Morgan and Ali got into the car, he asked Ali what had gone on that night. Ali didn't know what to say. He couldn't tell the senator the truth, but he didn't want to lie, so all he said was, "Our cultures are so vastly different. All this freedom, drinking of alcohol, promiscuous women, and drug use is very foreign to me and not allowed." He started to cry. "Forgive me for my weakness, but I've never experienced anything near to being arrested, and my father and my guardian will be furious. This will most likely ruin my chances to study in Paris, as was my plan after Berkeley. I've shamed my country, my father, and myself."

"Son, the way I look at it, y'all did none of that, and I see no reason to tell your father or guardian any of this. Y'all had the bad luck of being with that devil son of mine. I'm sorry if putting y'all up with Harold at Berkeley has made your life miserable. The more I try to straighten him out, the more he coils up like a snake. We'll have some peace for the next few days without Harold around, and my family and

I will show y'all an all-American Southern Thanksgiving. Now y'all forget about what happened tonight. This will stay between us. No one is going to find out."

The next day, the family was overly pleasant to Ali. Before dinner, Senator Morgan showed Ali the grounds, and as they walked, he explained the holiday and the symbolism of what they'd be eating. The family did everything they could to make Ali's short visit as enjoyable as possible. On the day after Thanksgiving, Senator Morgan and his sons took Ali to his club and taught him how to golf. On Saturday, they visited the Morgan stables and rode horses for most of the afternoon. Although they were kind, he still couldn't wait to leave.

On Sunday Butch was picked up, packed his things, and went to the garage to get his drugs to bring back with him. His car was gone. His father had followed him. "The car is still at the impound yard, and it's staying there until I see a change in y'all, boy."

"Daddy, I need stuff in that car."

"Y'all will have to do without whatever it is. I'm sure it's nothing good." He quickly pinned his son up against the wall. "Boy, y'all better straighten yourself out mighty quick. Do y'all have any idea the serious trouble it would cause if King Machmud found out his son was put in jail because of y'all? Y'all realize what's at stake here, right? If y'all do one thing to endanger this deal, I swear, Harold, I'll kill y'all with my own hands. And the state of Louisiana would give me a medal for it. I've worked too hard to put all of this in place and I'll see y'all dead before I let y'all fuck it up. You understand me, boy? Nod your head because I don't want to hear the sound of your voice!" Butch nodded and his father let him go.

They rode in silence to the airport and Ali refused to be anywhere near Butch once they got there and asked the ticket agent for a seat change. He couldn't wait to see Taraysa.

Khalid readied himself for the long trip back to America. The royal jet was equipped with all the comforts of home, so he tucked himself in for what would be a night in the Pacific Time Zone. He tried as much as he could to minimize the effects on the body going through time zones. After all, he was not a young man, and these zone changes put him out of sorts and fuzzy for a few days. He needed to make sure he was at the top of his game for what was to come. He settled in the bedroom cabin of the plane.

He was quite pleased with himself and with the meeting with the King. He didn't have to exaggerate the implications and threat of discovery by the American public of the oil shortage plan if he was right in his suspicions. The King agreed that if the American Embassy insisted on her return, it was quite reasonable that King Machmud wanted to personally thank the young lady who helped his son with his studies and befriended him while in a foreign land. If she were a spy or if no one from the Embassy claimed her, they'd know her motives for being friends with Ali were far from noble.

It'll be easy to nab the two young coeds. King Machmud was quite taken with the girl Athena. He ordered Khalid to make sure she was included in the "package" returned along with Ali. Once they knew for sure there'd be no diplomatic situations with the American government, they would, through their methods, find out who ordered them to spy on Ali, and then the dark-haired girl could be discarded or passed around, but the green-eyed girl was to go directly to the King.

Khalid spent most of the trip home trying to devise a plan to bring the two girls back with them. He opened his briefcase and made sure he had the pistol and ammunition to help make his plan an actuality.

All was in order, and as an extra treat to himself, he took a few more of the Cohiba cigars to enjoy during his celebration of success when he had the two girls in his possession, and they were off to the airport, headed to their possible perilous existence in Zatari.

# CHAPTER 39

Sunday came, and everyone was back from the Thanksgiving holiday. Sarah had rehearsal as soon as she got back and there was notable tension between Butch and Ali. It also seemed Ali had found a voice and didn't seem as afraid of Butch as he was before he left. He also eyed Adam and Christina as if he knew something was going on between them. They acted the same as they had before Thanksgiving break, so as not to give away their budding relationship. Neither wanted to hurt Ali. Besides, there was no time for it because they had to hunker down and get ready for exams.

Adam, Ali, and Christina studied together as they shared many of the same classes. Adam and Christina kept things cool except for their secret meeting at the clock tower at ten for their goodnight kiss. Any time they could sneak in an unnoticed display of affection, they took advantage of it, making sure they'd cool it around Ali, even though they felt dishonest about it.

They all took a break from studying for finals to support Sarah, and the five of them went to see *"Bye, Bye Birdie"* a couple of times, loudly cheering her on. They made sure to make Ali feel like he was not a fifth wheel. The guys all sat together, and Zoe and Christina sat next to each other. Sarah was so good in the part and was told by the head of the theater department that she had the role of Sheila in *"Hair"*. Her talent was evident, and one could see why she would become an award-winning actress.

Over the next few days, Adam agonized over those three names. He couldn't believe his insensitivity. He kept beating himself up over those three names. Why did he say them? The look on her face when he did haunted him. It was supposed to be a game, something fun, and he turned it into something that caused her anguish. Did he think she was going to tell him who they were? What could he possibly have gained from it?

They only had a few days left to be together before they had to head back home. He wondered exactly where that was for her. They were going to have to pack the lifetime he wanted to share with her into these final, precious days. Did he ruin the time they had left with that question hanging over them? He wished he could somehow take it back.

He'd make it up to her somehow. He finished the song for her, finding it easy to come up with the lyrics. He let his feelings roll off his heart onto the page and then to the strings of the guitar. It's going to be the first song he'll play for Mr. Martin. He knew once it got into the hands of a producer, it was going to be a huge hit. It was really that good. He was going to save it for their last night together and then sing it to her. She already knew how he felt about her, so the lyrics would come as no surprise.

He looked at the pictures they had taken at the photo booth, and he could feel his heart swell, especially when he looked at the picture where she told him she loved him. Every love song he'll write will be to her. No one will ever take her place in his heart. That thought put a lump in his throat that would lead to tears if he allowed it.

He got up and grabbed his helmet. He had a few things he needed to do before he left for England, before he left Berkeley, and before she walked out of his life forever. He was a man on a mission, and within minutes, he was off on his Harley, taking care of what he had to do.

On the last day of classes at noon, the Sather Tower played its song, *"They're Hanging Danny Deever in the Morning"* and then went silent. Christina stood rapt with Ali, listening to her obsession playing its tune, giving her chills. Stan told her the schedule to make sure she didn't miss it and was on campus for it. It didn't disappoint and she got a little emotional.

The time leading up to exams went by so quickly. Once exams were over, Ali was going to head home and asked if he and Christina could spend an evening alone together. Adam wasn't happy about it, but Christina told Ali she'd love to. It may be one of the last times she'll spend with him. She cared about him but wasn't in love with him.

They spent an evening walking around Berkeley, talking, enjoying the company of one another, having coffee together. He asked her again if she would consider visiting his country, to which she gave him the same answer she always did.

"Taraysa, you've meant so much to me this year. I don't know if I could've found this semester bearable without you. I apologize for being the cause of Butch's attack on you."

"You weren't the cause. He's an evil person."

"No, he was trying to ruin you because of me. He knew I admired you and that you managed to remain chaste in this atmosphere of free love. But that's what he does. He's not happy unless he's spreading misery."

"Ali, what happened during Thanksgiving? You seem so changed towards him. Do you want to talk about it?"

"If there was ever anyone I could talk about all of this, it would be you. But I can't. Butch Morgan has done nothing but disgrace me. If my country or family ever found out what happened, it would be impossible for me to ever recover from it. I'd be doomed. It's too shameful."

"Ali, sometimes talking about things can make it better. If you need to get it off your chest, I hope you know you can trust me with whatever it is. I'd never betray your trust."

"You'd think much less of me and that I could never bear."

"Ali, my opinion of you was formed by what I've learned from knowing you, which is all good. I could never think less of you. You've shown me that you're a good person, who's going to be a good man, one who's a kind, fair, compassionate, loving, and giving human being." She let her words sink in before continuing. "Meeting you and sharing this time we've spent together this semester has been such a great experience for me. You've introduced me to a completely different culture. You helped me step outside myself and my limited worldly experiences and learn more about Middle Eastern religion, traditions, and culture. I'm so enriched by knowing you, and I'll never ever forget you."

He smiled that winning smile that was genuine and not forced. "You always know what to say to make me feel better. I wish I could put you in my pocket and keep you with me always. Then when I'm troubled, I could lift you out to work your magic and help me solve my problems, especially with Butch."

She took his hand from across the table. "Ali, if you don't want to tell me, I understand. I don't like to see you so tortured over anything Butch has done. He's not worth it."

"Thank you for being my friend."

"And I want to thank you again for saving me from Butch and buying the tickets to '*Jesus Christ Superstar*'. You've no idea how touched I was that you did that. If you didn't come back to the dorm when you did, Butch would've been able to carry out his plan. I'm very much in your debt."

"Can we write to each other, Taraysa?"

"I'm sure when you're in Paris or wherever you decide to go next semester, you'll find some sweet girl who will totally erase me from your memory. Then you'll be thinking, 'What girl? Terry, who?'"

"That will never happen, Taraysa. I'll always remember you. Always."

They walked back to the dorm and as they got to the door of their building Ali stopped her. "Khalid has told me we're leaving tomorrow afternoon."

"Why so soon?"

"He's anxious to get me back home, and I need to report to my father and have time to work out what school I'll be attending after the first of the year. Hopefully, my grades will be satisfactory enough for him so that I may continue. Khalid seems to think that because I did as he asked of me, I'll be rewarded with his blessing to continue my studies in art."

"Gee, Ali, I didn't realize you were leaving so soon. Well, I'm glad we had this time together this evening."

"Are you in love with Adam?"

"What?" The question seemed to come out of nowhere and caught her by surprise.

"I can tell there's something between you. I don't want to leave tomorrow and know that I've lost you to him."

"Ali, you haven't lost me to anyone. In a few days, I'm going home, and I can guarantee I won't be seeing Adam after that. He's told you he's going back to England to further his music career, and I'll be on the East Coast. There's no possible way for anything to come of any relationship for me with anyone I've met here at Berkeley."

"May I kiss you, please?" They shared a kiss, and he held her very tightly. She felt guilty and like a cheat but couldn't refuse. It was the last night he was going to be here and one of their last moments together. They shared a lot in the short time they knew one another, and she was honestly going to miss him.

They walked back into the dorm and everyone except Butch was there. Adam was giving Christina the eye, and René asked to speak to her privately. They went into her room.

"Where is the lighter?" His question had a sharp edge to his voice.

"What lighter? Oh, I forgot!" She could tell he was pissed.

"Christina, what did I tell you when I gave it to you? You're to keep it with you at all times! I'm very serious about this. You don't seem to realize the dangers surrounding us with every passing day we spend here. We should have gone back in November! If I had known you left without it, I'd have followed you. From this moment on, you're to carry it with you at all times!

"Sorry."

"No, you're not, but you will be if you're in a position where danger presents itself and you have no way out. You're smarter than this, Christina! Don't be foolish, don't be trusting. If I have to, I'll shadow you wherever you go, and even that is no guarantee of your safety. You have three children whose lives depend on you getting back safely. If I have to glue it to your hand, I will!"

"Okay, René. I understand. I'll keep it with me, I promise."

"I want you to get it right now and put it in your pocket." She went over to her desk and took it out of the drawer. "This stays with you until we enter the chamber to go back. Is that clear?"

She wanted to say, "Yes, daddy," but didn't dare. She could tell he wasn't in the mood for jokes. Instead, she promised she would. They left the room, and Adam looked puzzled at the two of them. Christina felt he knew a lot more than he was letting on.

René saw only one foreseeable problem. Ali was scheduled to leave the same time Zoe would be finishing her English final. He didn't know which girl he should be watching. He preferred being with Zoe but then there would be no one who knew the situation with Christina. He'll talk that over with Glenn and see if he would be able to make sure Zoe gets back to the dorm safely after her final.

Butch was leaving the day after Ali so it would give them three days to remove the devices from their room, get them back into Theodore Edward, gather up all they needed to bring back and be ready on the 14th. Adam was also leaving on the 14th. Overall, René felt they had accomplished exactly what they were sent here to do. Now they had to get home safely.

Butch had been in a pissy mood since they returned from Louisiana. He was ostracized by his dorm mates, whom he knew despised him, and the feelings were mutual. He had no friends and without his stash of drugs to sell, no one wanted anything to do with him. "They'll all be sorry someday," he thought. And who did Ali think he was, that he could ignore him? He didn't like his new attitude. He didn't know what happened while he was rotting in jail for Thanksgiving, but for some reason Ali had a renewed sense of self-worth and now Butch felt he was losing his upper hand.

Another thing that pissed him off was Little Miss Priss got away with everything she did to him. He hoped the kick in the balls she gave him wasn't going to give him permanent damage. His genitals were still very tender and sore. If that bitch has done anything that fucks up his sex life, he'll hunt her down like a dog and make her pay. They'll all pay! Someday, he'll have the power to ruin them all, especially because he's going to be as rich as a king. He's going to get millions from this oil deal, and then he'll have the money Ali will be giving him. Of course, Ali didn't know it yet, but whatever scheme or money-making plan he comes up with, Ali will finance it. He'll have no choice. He'll get notice of it in the mail…blackmail, that is. That thought made Butch chuckle that sickening laugh.

He strolled over to the main office where the mailboxes were and opened his. He took a large envelope he had deposited there, opened it up and looked through its contents. He snickered his devious laugh and took one photo out of the large pile and put the rest back into the envelope and replaced it in his mailbox. This should remind Ali exactly who is in control.

"We'll see who's got balls now, Princey," he said to himself aloud. "This here's my ace in the hole." He laughed to himself at the pun he'd made. "Now Princey will see that y'all never fuck over Butch Morgan."

Butch noticed Ali in their room packing his things. This would be the perfect time to remind him exactly why Butch was still and will always be in control of their "friendship". He walked into the room and shut the door behind him.

"So, Princey, leaving tomorrow?"

"Why is it your worry?" Ali was not in the mood for anything Butch had to say. He was thinking more about how he would most likely never see Taraysa again, which made him sad.

"Got a going-away present for y'all, enough of them to last a lifetime, so I thought I could spare one for my buddy." He took the photo out of his pocket and threw it on the bed. Ali picked it up, looked at it and ripped it into tiny pieces.

"You're a loathsome person, and I wish I had never laid eyes on you. You shame the good family you come from, and you shame everything you touch." Ali's voice rose with every word he spoke.

"Well, Princey, I wanted to remind y'all of our friendship and that I'll be in touch. Maybe not in the way you'd like if you get my drift." He snickered his horrible laugh, especially when he knew he was being cruel.

The next day, they were all glum because the reality of the fact that they were all going their separate ways started to sink in. They spent time together in the dorm and Ali had his suitcases packed, ready to go. Khalid's driver came to the dorm announcing the car had arrived. Ali said his goodbyes to his dorm mates, hugging and thanking them for their friendship. Butch wasn't there and Zoe wasn't back yet from her English final. Ali was concerned that he was unable to say goodbye to her. He asked the driver for more time but was told their plane had to take off from the private airfield within the hour.

"Taraysa, would you please walk with me to the car?"

"Sure."

René immediately piped in, "Why don't we all walk you down?" Adam quickly agreed.

"Adam, Jean-René, thank you, but I'd like to spend my last moments alone with Taraysa. I hope you don't mind."

René gave Christina a look of panic and made a motion of a lighter. She nodded her head slightly to let him know she had it with her.

They walked to the waiting limousine and the driver put the bags in the trunk. Ali held both her hands and they looked into each other's tear-filled eyes. "Well, Taraysa, this is good-bye."

"Let's not say goodbye. Let's say see you later."

He laughed and said, "Very well. See you later."

"See you later, Ali. Best of luck in whatever you do." They hugged each other, and the driver opened the door to the back seat, and Ali reluctantly got in. She could see Khalid sitting there and thought she'd be polite. She leaned down and said to him, "It was very nice meeting you, sir."

In the flash of a second, she felt herself being pushed into the back seat by the driver, landing on the floor, the door being slammed behind her and then the car taking off. Ali seemed stunned and started yelling for the driver to stop, saying she needed to be let out. He helped her up to the seat and turned to Khalid and ordered him to stop the car and let her out.

"Your father has ordered this young lady and her pretty little friend to be our guests at the palace for an indefinite period. I take commands from my king, not a lowly prince such as you." He laughed an evil snicker. "Is this not what you wanted, Ali, your little lying, cheating American girlfriend to accompany you home?"

"Cheating? What do you mean, Khalid?"

"She has been carrying on with that English boy, right under your nose. I've proof if you'd like to see it."

Christina started to panic. "You have to let me out! I'm an American citizen! You can't take me to your country!"

"Ah, now that is where you're wrong, my dear. I can and will. I ask you, who will look for you? You don't exist! I've done extensive investigations, and there's no record of you or your friends anywhere. You've been sent to spy on Ali, a royal prince of a Middle Eastern country. For that, you'll be answering to his father, the king. We'll find out what you and your friends have been up to and why you've been spying on Ali."

"Is this true, Taraysa?"

"Ali, I have not been spying on you. He's wrong. It's not true! Please, I beg of you, you have to let me go!"

"You can plead your case to the king." He laughed again. "I can guarantee no one will inquire about either you or your friend, to whom the king has taken a shine. He's most anxious to add her to his bed chamber. You'll both at least find our plane quite comfortable."

"Khalid, you must let her go."

"She's a spy, and so is her friend! Are they really who they say they are? Do you even know her real name? Ali, you're such a fool! You fell right into the trap they laid out for you. But no need to worry. We'll find out the truth soon enough. There are people at the palace who will get it out of them."

"Please, Khalid, don't do this. She's been a friend to me and helped me. I care about her. I can't let you do this to her."

"Ali, you're so weak it sickens me. She's used you. They both have used you. Now you need to understand that your country comes first. We have ways of dealing with traitors and spies. Your friend here will answer to the ways of our country. Everything you think you know about them is nothing but lies. No one will look for either of them. They're spies, and their government won't care for the loss of two insignificant teenage girls. Ah, here comes the king's prize. Well, my dear, at least you won't be alone."

Khalid knocked on the divider. "There's the other girl, walking this way. Pull over and get her into the car but lock the windows before you do."

Christina looked out the window and Zoe was walking as though she was pissed about something. She tried to bang on the window to tell her to run when she felt herself being pulled away from the window with a hand over her mouth and a gun to her head. Ali started to try to help her when Khalid told him that one move and he was going to shoot.

Christina watched as the driver got out of the car and walked over to Zoe. He said something to her and pointed to the car they were in. She gave him the brush off and started to walk away. He grabbed her arm, which she recoiled from. He took hold of her arm and started to drag her towards the car with his hand over her mouth. She wasn't making it easy for him. Right before they got to the car, Glenn O'Connell came out of nowhere and knocked them both over, kicking the driver in the gut. He quickly pulled Zoe to her feet, and the two of them took off running.

Once the driver got up, he ran to the limo. Khalid told him to forget about the girl, they need to move quickly now because she'll tell the others. Ali kept trying to reason with Khalid to let Christina go and to put the gun away, continuously apologizing to her for putting her in this situation.

The driver got in and they sped off to the airport and it looked like Christina's fate was no longer in her own hands.

# CHAPTER 40

While Zoe was walking back to the dorm, she thought about her literature exam, knowing she aced it with her final essay on the works of Victor Hugo. She read all his novels and visited some of the very places he wrote about while in Paris. She knew his works like she wrote them herself. She was disappointed because now she'll never find out her mark. She was lost in those thoughts when this mountain of a man approached her and said Ali wanted to say goodbye to her, and his car was right there, pointing to the limousine.

Although he caught her off guard, this scenario immediately put her on high alert. There was no way she was going anywhere near that car. He'd have to drag her kicking and screaming. "I'm sorry, but I'm in a rush to get to my next final. Give Ali my love and tell him I said goodbye."

As soon as she started to walk away, he grabbed her arm, from which she quickly disengaged herself using some of the defensive moves René taught her. He grabbed her again, and this time she elbowed him in the ribs. He barely flinched. He immobilized her arms and covered her mouth with his hand and started to bring her towards the limo. She was stomping on the tops of his feet with her heel, knowing it had to hurt, but this goliath seemed impervious to pain.

She didn't have enough physical strength to fight him off and he kept her in a position where she was unable to use any of the moves she learned. She opened her mouth and chomped down on one of his fingers which only made him tighten his grip on her arms. All she could think of was her life and the future happiness she was looking forward to with René was not going to happen. That thought made her fight more, but her efforts were useless against his brute strength.

All at once, the two of them were being pushed to the ground by something. She was shocked to see that "something" was none other than Glenn O'Connell. He quickly grabbed her from her assailant's loosened grip, kicked him in the gut for any harm he may have done to her, and off they ran, hand in hand, not even hesitating long enough to turn around and see if he was coming after them.

They finally stopped outside the Science Building. They turned and saw the limo take off. "Are you alright? Did he hurt you?"

"I think I'm okay, a little shaken up…I think. What the hell was that? He was like a freaking giant!" She had been looking down at herself, brushing off the dirt on her jeans, when what happened settled in. Her knees buckled out from under her, and O'Connell caught her. She fell into his arms and kept thanking him for being there and saving her.

"You're safe now, Zoe. Did you think I'd let anything bad happen to you?" They went into the building, and he sat her on a windowsill. He walked to a water cooler and got her a cup of water. "Here, drink this. Try to keep an eye out to see if they come back. If necessary, I can get your backup."

"Oh my God, Glenn, was Tee in that car? I hope not! Do you think she's safe? This is the exact thing we were worried about! She has to be ok. Please tell me she's not in that car."

"Not sure where she is right now, but don't worry. We'll take care of it. Please try to calm down." He wanted to comfort her, but being socially inept, he wasn't sure how to accomplish that. He turned away from her but still kept her in his sights. He pulled something out of his back pocket. He pushed a button on the side and said, "Batman and Robin, Tesla here, do you read me? Over?"

"Read you loud and clear, Tesla. Status?"

Angel is safe. Repeat, Angel is safe. Operation 21 is a go. Do you copy? Over."

"Copy that. We're in place. We'll keep you informed. Is Cupid in vehicle? Over."

"Couldn't tell, windows were up. In any case, proceed as planned. Keep me informed. Over."

"We're on it. We'll get Cupid back to Rome. Operation 21 is a go. Over and out."

"What was that all about, Glenn? What is Operation 21? Who were you talking to? No one is supposed to know about us."

"We all have our little secrets. It's your backup. You'll find out everything eventually, but for now, rest assured that a plan is in place to keep you two girls out of harm's way and to get all three of you safely back to the 21st century with the information you came for. Part one of the plan worked perfectly; you're here with me and not in the limo. Now we have to find a way to get Christina out of there. We can only hope part two of the plan works."

They stayed in the Science Building for a few minutes, making sure the limo didn't return. Zoe was staring out the window, immersed in her thoughts, not sure what she was looking at or for. She heard a familiar rumble, which caught her attention, and saw the unmistakable blue Harley-Davidson whiz by. She knew at once it was Adam, chasing after the car. She wondered if he saw anything that happened. "There goes Adam! He's going after her!"

"Are you sure it's him?"

"Positive. No one has that color Harley but him. He'd move heaven and earth for her."

Glenn got back on the walkie-talkie. "Batman and Robin, do you read me? Over."

"Loud and clear. Over."

"Do you have the Candy Man vehicle in sight? Over."

"That's affirmative. They're on the freeway, most likely heading toward the private airport where they keep the big guy's plane. We're keeping back a few cars so as not to call attention to our van. Over."

"Player One is peddling in hot pursuit. Do not, repeat, do not impede. Use him if you have to. We need all the help we can get. Over."

"Copy that. What about Frogman? Over."

"No sign of him yet. Not with Player One. Over."

"Copy that. We'll keep an eye out for him. Can see Candy Man up ahead. We'll keep a comfortable distance until we turn off. Time to rock and roll. Proceeding as planned. Over and out."

Zoe looked puzzled. "Is Frogman your code name for René?" There was no response. She walked up close to him and linked her arm with his. "Am I Angel?"

He looked at her and once again the closeness of her to him jumbled his thoughts. "Um, what? That's classified information that I'm not at liberty to disclose."

"You really are a sweet man, Glenn."

"Yeah, too bad you keep filling up on French pastries."

She smiled, shrugged, and put her head on his shoulder momentarily. "What do we do next?"

"I think we should head back to your dorm and see what's happening there. Come with me. I have to get something first."

They walked to a door, which Glenn unlocked. He took out a baseball bat, then closed and locked the door.

"If anyone should come after us now, at least I have something to defend us with. I'll make sure you're safe."

They headed towards the dorm and saw René running towards them. He could hardly speak because he was out of breath but managed to get out what he needed to say. "Zoe! I'm so relieved to see you! They have Christina! Adam and I were watching from a few feet away and were unable to stop it. Adam looked away when they hugged each other, but I saw everything. It looked like nothing was going to happen when, all at once, their driver pushed her into the back seat. Adam moved like lightning to get his helmets and took off in hot pursuit. I hope he knows where they are going."

"They tried to grab me, too, but Glenn saved me. René, their driver is enormous! I tried the moves you taught me and was able to get out of his grasp at first, but he's like a Mack truck! And nothing I did to him had any effect. He's like, not human!"

"How did you escape?"

"Glenn came plowing into us, knocking us down. He grabbed my hand, kicked him in the gut, and off we went."

"I'm so relieved to see you, *Chérie*. I thought the worst. Thank you, Glenn, for being there for Zoe. Now, what do we do about Christina? She does have something with her to hopefully give her enough time to escape their grasp. We must contact the airport and stop the plane from taking off."

"We can't get the airport or any authorities involved in this. You both know that. We have another plan in place. If that doesn't work, then contacting the airport will be our last resort. I'm in communication with those who are helping, so we'll find out soon enough if we need to stop the plane."

They heard a crackling sound coming from Glenn's back pocket. "Batman and Robin calling Tesla. Do you read me, Tesla? Over." Glenn took the small walkie-talkie out of his back pocket.

"Affirmative, Batman. Report?"

"Off freeway heading to private airport. Ready to commence Operation 21. No sign of Player One yet. Proceeding as planned. Over and out."

"Glenn, who are you working with? No one should know about us."

"It's your backup, and we have a plan. And we may have bigger problems if this plan doesn't work. You all should have gone back on Thanksgiving as ordered."

"So, what do we do now, *mon ami*?"

"Pray."

Khalid had everything planned out to the exact minute. Everything was very calculated and timed. He used his connections to find out the time and usual duration of the final exam for the Christos girl to coincide with the departure of Ali. Everything was going exactly as planned.

He was certain the whoring spy would walk Ali to the car to say goodbye. She has to keep up the appearance that she cares about him. Ali will discover the truth about her once she's questioned by King Machmud's men. They'll all discover the truth.

He hired one of their most muscular bodyguards to act as a driver. There was no way a teenage girl or a teenage boy, for that matter, would have the strength to impede anything this man set his mind to. He was eager to please the King and eager to do whatever he could for his country. Khalid assured him that as long as he was with him, he would have diplomatic immunity and be safe from any sort of prosecution in the United States. He didn't see any glitches in his plan.

The taking of the girl was easier than he thought it was going to be. He had instructed his driver that if she did not offer to walk Ali to the car, then she was to be told that Ali's father had a gift of thanks for her and he was to give it to her. None of that was necessary because she came willingly, like a lamb to the slaughter.

Once she was in the car, she and Ali were begging for her release. It sickened him to see such weakness from a son of King Machmud. He hoped it wasn't necessary but had to bring out the revolver when they spotted the other girl to make sure neither of them warned her. He held the gun to her head and would've gladly pulled the trigger, but that would spoil the intentions of the King.

He couldn't believe the Christos girl escaped from his driver. He wasn't sure who knocked them over, but they didn't have time to run after her. She was not vital to the plan. They already had the prize.

He motioned the driver to get back into the car and leave immediately and watch for anyone who may follow them. He put the gun into its holster, took one of his Cohiba cigars, snipped the tip, and pushed in the cigarette lighter to light it. Both passengers asked him not to light it in the car, but what did he care? They're insignificant; a lying, spying whore and a weak, pussy-whipped prince. Maybe he'll have a taste of this fine young girl on the plane ride. He could even let Ali watch. Or better yet, lock him out and let him listen as he has his way with her.

He rolled down his window, enough to let the smoke out, and gloated over the success of his plan, thoroughly enjoying his cigar. Ali and the spy were huddled together, with him telling her he would protect her and get her back home. Khalid smiled when Ali said that because he had no power as an irrelevant son of an irrelevant wife. Khalid listened to her wails and tears and felt more powerful by the minute.

They were soon off the freeway, heading towards the private airport. She would have to be forcibly carried to the plane because it was certain she wouldn't go quietly. Khalid started to breathe easier, especially after looking in the rear window and seeing no one behind them. He sat back, took a few more puffs on his cigar, and reveled over the success of his brilliant plan.

He never could have imagined what would happen next.

# CHAPTER 41

Christina couldn't believe the predicament she was in and knew it was her own fault. If she'd gone back on Thanksgiving as instructed, she'd be sitting in her own home, with her children safe and sound. Instead, she's in this limousine with no hope in sight. She was terrified, seeing no way of getting out of this and could think of nothing to get her out of a moving car with a giant for a driver, a man with a gun, and a prince of a guy who was, like her, helpless.

She begged, cried, and pleaded with Khalid, but he would barely look at her. And when he lit the nasty cigar, she and Ali were hit with a coughing jag, so he cracked open the window a couple of inches. She looked out of that crack into the freedom that lay beyond and felt sick. How was she going to get out of this mess?

Ali kept telling her he'd protect her, but he had no power over either of these men. The more he ordered Khalid to let her go, the more Khalid laughed. When they turned off the main road, she looked behind to see if anyone was coming to help and saw no one. Khalid did the same and gave her a sick smile, as though he knew he'd won. If she ended up on that plane to Zatari, she'd be dead within three months, if she lasts that long. What will happen to her counterpart now living on the East Coast? And her children, will they perish? Will they disappear? Will they suffer? How could she have been so stubborn and stupid to think she could escape any intrigue planned against her?

"If you're planning on hijacking me to your country, you won't get away with it. I don't know what makes you think no one will look for me, but they will. My parents will do everything it takes to get me back. And you'll have to explain to the United States government why you thought it necessary to kidnap a teenager. How will your king feel when he's thrown into an international incident?"

Khalid blew thick cigar smoke in her face and laughed. Her temper flared, and she lunged at him, putting a nice scratch on his face. The cigar went flying and started smoldering on the floor of the limo. Khalid grabbed her wrists, and she started fighting against him. He pulled her closer to his face, stared into her eyes, and laughed. Then he did the unspeakable…he licked the side of her face from the bottom of her chin up to her hairline, which completely grossed her out. He licked his lips and laughed.

"Sweet, very sweet. Please, keep fighting. I like to see the spirit first before it's crushed. You're doing exactly as I desire. Tire yourself out before we get to the airport. Then it'll be much easier to get you onto the plane." He laughed, and Christina could smell the hideous cigar breath from his mouth that was now on her cheek. Ali kept yelling for him to let go of her as he picked up the cigar, which had lost its fiery head, and put out the fire beginning on the rug.

"Khalid, I order you to turn this car around and bring her back to Berkeley. That is a direct order from a member of the royal family. You must obey."

"I find it most amusing, Ali, that you believe you have the power to order me to do anything."

"You're making a big mistake, and going through with this plan of yours is only going to strain the relationship between our country and the United States. I'm sure my father won't be pleased when the United States government comes crashing into the palace, demanding an explanation and the return of its citizen. You must know the United States never leaves its civilians in hostile situations."

No matter what Ali said, Khalid wouldn't respond. He let go of Christina, pushing her into Ali. He touched the place where she scratched him, looked at his hand and noticed he was bleeding.

"Well, I see our little pussycat has sharp claws. You'll pay for this, you know, in time. I'd have thought a spy would have more defensive moves than a small scratch on the face."

"Why do you keep saying that? I'm not a spy!"

"We'll see."

Right then, the voice of the driver came through a speaker. "Honorable sir, a vehicle is coming up quickly. It doesn't look official, but you wanted to know if anyone came up from behind."

The three of them simultaneously turned around and looked out the rear window. Sure enough, an old VW van was coming up quickly. Christina said a silent prayer that it was the cavalry coming to save the damsel in distress. They were beeping their horn with smoke billowing from their windows. When they passed the limo, her hopes were dashed. It was a hippie van with psychedelic paintings on the sides. As they passed, the guy in the passenger seat, looking quite high and very much the hippie, flashed them the peace sign with a good-sized joint in his hand, smoke coming out of his mouth, and a huge smile on his face. Christina pounded on the window, yelling for help, but didn't know if he could see or hear her. The van sped off ahead of them.

"Did you think it was someone who could help you?" and Khalid laughed again. Up ahead, the van was barely visible. A loud popping noise came from ahead, and they could see the van veering out of control. It skidded to a stop, but not before it did an almost 180-degree turn. It finally came to a stop, ending up sideways on the road, making it impassable. Thank you, God! Christina thought. At least it will delay them for a little while and give her time to think of how to get out of this jam.

When they came up on the van, Khalid knocked on the window divider for the driver. "Go see if you can help them or move their vehicle out of the way. We need to get on that plane as soon as possible. Shut off the car so there's no hope of escape for our two passengers." The driver did as instructed and went to help. A few seconds later, he came back, opened the trunk, and got the jack and tire iron. He walked by the side of the car where Khalid was seated and informed him that it was a blowout, and he would help change the tire so they could be on their way.

Khalid picked up the cigar Ali had put in the ashtray and pushed in the lighter. He waited, but it didn't pop. He pulled it out and it was stone cold. He told Ali to try the lighter on his side of the car. That one didn't work either.

"I think because the car is turned off, none of the equipment will work. Isn't that why you wanted it turned off?" Christina felt a tiny bit smug that not everything was going his way.

"Ali, look in the compartments back here and see if there are any matches. No sense in wasting a good Cohiba." Ali sat defiantly, not doing as instructed. It forced Khalid to look around on his own, but there were no matches in the car.

"I don't suppose either of you has any matches."

"Khalid, you know I don't smoke, and neither does Taraysa."

"How about you, little girl, do you have any matches?"

The lighter! Oh my God! She put her hand in her pocket and there it was! This was her chance!

"I have a lighter, but I don't think it works."

"Give it to me."

"No! I won't give it to you. It was given to me by my brother, who fought and died for this country, and you can't have it. I carry it with me because it's the last thing he gave to me." She slipped into that lie so easily and hoped she could pull it off.

"Well then, little girl, light my cigar."

"No." She didn't want to seem too eager.

"I said, light my cigar."

"No!"

He grabbed her arm and twisted it. "Either you light it or I find the lighter and do it myself. If I'm forced to do that, you won't get it back."

"You're such a hateful man." She reached into her pocket and pulled out the lighter. She held it in her hand in the exact way René showed her. She flicked it, and the flame came up. He grabbed her arm and pulled it towards him to light his cigar. She let the flame go out, aimed it at his face, and pushed the button. The lighter popped, and projectiles came out and landed in Khalid's face. One was visible in the scratch she gave him. Khalid showed a look of surprise, and then he slumped to the side. He was out cold.

"Holy shit! It worked! I don't believe it!"

"Taraysa, what have you done? What happened?"

"I don't know! My brother gave me this before he went back to Vietnam. He told me it was a trick lighter. If you knew my brothers, you'd understand. They were jokesters, always playing practical jokes. He told me to always carry this lighter with me and if I was ever in a jam, all I needed to do was push this button. I didn't think it was real and never tried it out! Geez, Ali, I hope I didn't kill him."

She knew she didn't kill him, but that gave her a chance to act like she was listening to his heart and remove the gun from its holster using the excuse that it was in the way and put it on the floor at Ali's feet. She pretended to put her ear to his chest, listening for a heartbeat. "He's alive, thank God! Oh, Ali, he's going to be so mad at me when he wakes up! Now I've only made things worse! How am I going to get out of here?"

They tried the doors, but everything was locked, including the divider between the driver and the passengers and all the windows. It did her no good to knock Khalid out because there was no way to escape out of this car.

"Taraysa, where did you get such a thing? Did you really get it from your brother, or are you a spy, as Khalid has said? It certainly looks like something a spy would have."

"Me, a spy? Ali, I think you know me better than that. Of course, I'm…," and then she heard it…the rumble of a Harley-Davidson motorcycle. She looked out the back window and could see it heading towards them.

"It's Adam!" she exclaimed. "Oh, thank God!" He pulled up right next to them. "Adam, thank God you're here. Help me get out of here!"

"Ali, I hope you're not in on this whole business. I suggest you open the door, mate. I'm taking Terry back with me."

Christina didn't give Ali a chance to answer. "We're locked in. I don't know how to get out!"

Adam got off the bike, and as he did, the driver came out from behind the van to see what was going on. He had the tire iron in his hand and started yelling at Adam.

"Get away from that car. There is a royal prince in that car, under my protection. If you don't get back on your motorbike and get out of here, I'll be forced to take action against you." He menacingly held up the tire iron.

"Throw me the keys, mate, so I can open the door, and we'll be gone. Then you can all be on your way, but you're not leaving with this girl in the car."

Christina watched as the driver started to come towards Adam, with the tire iron still in his hand. One of the hippie guys yelled for him to come back; they needed the tire iron to change the tire, but the driver kept moving towards Adam, threatening him with every step. Adam stood his ground, looking as if he was ready to take on this massive giant. The two men from the van started coming up from behind the driver. He was almost up to the car when they both descended on him, somehow knocking him out, which sent the tire iron from his hand. Adam ran over and picked it up. The two men started going through his pockets. Christina wasn't sure if they were looking for the keys or mugging him.

Adam ran over to the side of the car where the window was cracked open. He looked in and saw Khalid passed out.

"What happened here? Never mind, there's no time for that now. We've got to get you out of there, Terry. Okay, you two, huddle up because I'm going to smash this window and I don't want either of you hurt by the glass."

It took him a few tries, but eventually they heard the smashing of glass. He couldn't get it all out, but there was enough room for Christina to be pulled out.

"Ali, mate, give me your jacket so Terry doesn't get cut." Ali took off his jacket and it was placed over the jagged edges.

"Come on, luv, it's time to go."

She turned and gave Ali a hug and a kiss. "Thank you, Ali. Don't ever forget that you're truly a prince among men: honorable, kind, brave, and humble. Hold on to these traits, especially if you ever get a chance to rule. You'd make a great king."

"Terry, hurry, please. Our window of opportunity may be shrinking."

One of the guys from the van came over and asked if they needed help.

"I need to get this girl out of the car. It's a bloody good thing you got that flat. If you chaps keep an eye on the bodyguard, I can get her out and home safely. Keep him away from the car and my motorbike if you would, and I'll get her out."

Christina climbed over Khalid, who was covered in glass from the broken window. A few shards were sticking up, so she needed to be careful on how she got out. Adam grabbed her arms and started to guide her safely around the sharp edges. When she thought she was home free, she felt a hand on her leg, pulling her back into the car. Then she saw a hand on Adam's arm, trying to inch it closer to a jagged piece of glass that was still in the window.

Khalid had awakened and was now trying to pull her back into the car, and at the same time, slice Adam's wrist on the glass. Adam seemed to be winning against Khalid, but he was not letting go of Christina's leg. She and Adam were both yelling at him to let go. One of the hippie guys came over to help, but there was nothing he could do because of the small space she was trying to be freed from. She couldn't do much fighting because of all the jagged glass she was suspended over. If he didn't let go, Christina was going to get some serious cuts down the front of her body. Maybe that's what he's trying to achieve.

Then they all heard it…the cocking of a revolver which made all of them freeze momentarily. Ali had picked up the gun and now had it ready to fire, pointed at Khalid's head.

"Let go of them, Khalid. She's not coming with us. I'd have thought you'd know better than to disobey a member of the royal family."

Khalid laughed. "What, are you going to shoot me?"

"Yes, Khalid, that's the plan if you don't let go of them right now."

Khalid ignored Ali and continued fighting to cut Adam's wrist and bring Christina back into the car.

"Very well, Khalid, you've made your decision." The next sound they heard was the gun going off and the screams of an injured man who was shot in the foot.

"My next shot will be your knee. I'm sparing your head because I don't want to get your brains all over Taraysa and Adam." The grip on the two of them was released as Khalid writhed in pain. Adam quickly pulled her out of the car.

Ali kept his eyes and gun pointed at Khalid. "Adam, get her out of here, *now*! Taraysa, I'm so deeply sorry all this has happened to you because of me. So many terrible things have happened to you since you met me. I'm sorry."

"Oh, Ali! You've saved me again! I can't thank you enough. I'll never forget you, ever!"

"You have no coat. Take my jacket. Hurry! Get out of here and find somewhere safe!"

"Thanks, mate." She and Adam ran to the bike. Adam shook out the jacket in case there was any glass lingering on it. They threw on their helmets, thanked the guys from the van, and took off.

"Hold on, Pook, we're going to make a run for it in case they decide to come after us."

They zigzagged through the streets of San Francisco, making sure they weren't being followed. Christina held on tightly, still incredulous as to the events that had taken place. She looked at Adam's back, the curls coming out from the bottom of the helmet and noticed a bright red mark on his neck. Was it from the broken window? That thought made her hold him closer. What would she have done without him today?

After tearing up and down some different streets, making sure they would've lost anyone behind them, they pulled up to a house. Adam pulled the bike around the back and parked. "I think you'll be safe here, Pookie. It's not a good idea to go back to the dorm tonight. One never knows if the shit is going to hit the fan. Do you have any cuts from the glass?"

"I don't know. I don't think so. I'll check later. Where are we?"

"My apartment."

"Your apartment? But you live in the dorm."

"Yes, well, I got the apartment last year when I was here. I was rarely at the university, you know, sex, drugs, rock and roll, and all that. It was my private haven."

"For girls?"

"Well, yes, that among other things. Please forgive me for being so naughty. I worked on my music here, which was fantastic. I also needed someplace to live this past summer. I've not been here in a while, so I'm sure it's a frightful mess. No one knows of it, so it's most likely quite safe."

He unlocked the door, and they went in. As soon as he closed the door, she grabbed him and held him close, burying her head in his chest, and felt the wave of tears which came from pure relief. He put his arms around her and kept telling her she was safe. Through her sobs, she was able to get a few words out.

"Oh my God, Adam, I've never been so scared in my life! What would I have done without you! They were going to kidnap me!"

"There now, it's over and you're safe." He was cradling her and kissing her head, holding her close, making her feel protected. "Try not to cry, Pookie. It hurts me so to see your tears. Well, I must say we've certainly foiled their plans, didn't we? I'd like to know how those two hippie chaps knocked out that gigantic ogre. They both actually seemed rather slight. It was bloody brilliant, they got that flat tire."

"I was so scared when he was coming at you with the tire iron. I could never forgive myself if you were ever hurt because of me. I think you may have some cuts on the back of your neck, and it's my fault. I noticed some redness when we were riding."

He rubbed the back of his neck and said, "No, that's the Wallingford birthmark. All the males of the family have it. Come to think of it, I don't think any of the girls have ever survived. There aren't too many of us, that's for certain; usually only one survives per generation. A doomed legacy. Well, anyway, we all have it. That's why I keep my hair long. It's feeling prickly at the moment."

He looked at her straight in the eyes and said very seriously, "Terry, I'd have stood up to ten like him if I had to in order to keep you out of harm's way." He held her face up to his, moved her hair out of the way, and kissed her. "Please, Pookie, no more tears. Have a seat, and I'll fix some tea for us. Sound good?"

"Yes, thanks." She took off Ali's jacket and held it up to her face. It smelled of him, which warmed her heart. She was lucky to have met these two extraordinary men. "Can you believe Ali actually shot his guardian? Scared the shit out of me when I heard that gun go off. You two are my knights in shining armor. Again! I hope he doesn't get in trouble for it."

"I didn't know the chap had it in him, either. The things you do for love, right? I'm sure being a prince will help him stay out of trouble."

"I hope so, for his sake, but you never know. They live by a different set of rules and values." She walked into the living room, and it was definitely a bachelor pad. It was untidy with papers all over the place, a couple of guitars on the couch with bottles, glasses, and ashtrays full of half-smoked joints and roaches on the tables. She picked up the stuff on the tables and brought it to the sink in the kitchen.

She started to fill the sink to wash the dirty dishes, but Adam shut off the water, took her hands, and told her to go into the other room and sit down while he put on a kettle of water for some tea. She slumped into a chair, and once again, the harrowing events she experienced came crashing down, and the floodgate of tears opened. She knew she was safe, but man, was that ever a close call! Adam came over and held her, telling her everything was okay and they were safe.

"This is not the first time you've come between me and disaster. What would I have done without you today?"

The tea kettle whistled, and he got up and prepared the tea. He came back with a tray with beautiful china teacups and the fixings for tea.

"Here you go, the English band-aid for everything: a cup of tea. Sorry, there's no milk. Hopefully, the non-dairy creamer will do."

"Whoa! Fancy-shmancy! Are these Royal Albert?"

"Now, how does an American teenager know about Royal Albert china? You're quite a mysterious enigma. Maybe that's one of the reasons I love you so."

They sat together, drinking tea, each with their own thoughts. Finally, Adam broke the silence. "So, Pookie, do you care to tell me exactly what all this was about today? And seriously, how did the two of you knock out the vicious man in the back seat? This whole kidnapping thing wasn't Ali's idea, was it?"

"No, it wasn't Ali's idea. He kept trying to get his guardian to let me go."

"Are you sure, Pook? Because I know Ali would've loved for you to come home with him. He's said it many times to me, and I'm sure to you. What makes you think he wasn't the one calling the shots here?"

"Ali wouldn't do that."

"Then why would they have taken you? It's totally bonkers. It doesn't make any sense. What other reason could there be? They must have said something to you to indicate the reason."

"I…uh,… I… don't know."

"Terry, I know you have this cloud of mystery about you. There is so much that you're not being honest with me about, and because I'm completely and totally bonkers in love, I'm willing to accept that, but only to a point. Today went well beyond anything I could overlook. I demand an explanation for what happened here today. I think the authorities should be notified about this attempted kidnapping. I care not if it causes an international incident."

"We can't report it, Adam. I don't want to get you involved in all this."

"Can you believe what you just bloody well said? Don't want me involved? In case you hadn't noticed, *luv*, I'm in this up to my ears. Who do you think broke the window of that limousine to get you out? And I want to know…how did you knock out Ali's guardian?"

"I…um…I…oh, I wish it wasn't so complicated."

"I've never asked anything from you. Well, I am now. I want answers, but not only that, I want the bloody truth! Don't hand me bullshit, Terry because I don't deserve that. It's hard enough knowing we will part in a few days, with me going home and you going wherever it is you're going, and that will be the end of us. I can't bear that all you're giving me are lies. It's killing me, Terry or whoever you are! It hurts so very deeply, because you're the first person I love with all my heart and soul, and I don't think I know one bloody thing about you that is real."

He was right. But what could she say? "I'm so sorry, Adam. Please don't be mad at me."

"I'm not mad, just totally frustrated. Please, what happened today? Jean-René insisted on watching you when you said goodbye to Ali. Did you know this was going to happen?"

"Of course not! I'd have never gone anywhere near that car if I thought I was going to be pushed into it."

"Did Jean-René know?"

"I don't know."

"Don't bloody lie to me, Terry! You do know!" His voice was getting louder with each question.

"I don't know what he knew, only what he thought. There was a rumor that I was being watched and investigated because of Ali."

"A rumor? Investigated by whom?

"Khalid, Ali's guardian."

"Why in God's name would anyone be interested in a teenager to the extent of what happened today? There's more to this. Tell me!"

"Probably because Ali took an interest in me, and Khalid didn't approve of me from the second he laid eyes on me. I guess I didn't make a good first impression."

"I can relate to that. Did you slam a door in his face, too?" She looked down at the floor because she couldn't bear to look at him. She wanted to scream the truth to him, but could she? It was destroying her to continue to lie to him, especially in light of what he said about everything being a lie.

"What did he find out about you?"

"I don't know."

"What did he find out about you?"

"Nothing, okay? He didn't find out anything at all! No Terry Brendes anywhere, no parents, no family, he found out nothing which raised his suspicions."

"In what way? Why would that make him suspicious?"

"He thought I was a spy, okay? That I was spying on Ali. He was bringing me back to his country so they could question me and find out what I knew about Ali."

Adam sat back in the chair and ran his fingers through his hair, looking at her. "So that's it then. The three of you are spies. I thought as much. Makes perfect sense now, looking back. But using teenagers? That makes it quite puzzling, actually." He sat there, and Christina could see the wheels turning in his head. "Was I part of the plan? Make the roommate fall in love with you so that he'll become added protection?"

"Adam, that was a low blow. You're the only wonderful, exciting, unexpected, life-changing part of this semester for me. No, that was definitely not part of the plan."

"So, there *was* a plan."

"Oh God." She stood up and walked over to the window, looking off into the distance. She couldn't keep lying to him. It wasn't right. She heaved a couple of very heavy sighs and walked over to him and sat next to him on the couch. He kept searching her face, and she could see he was hurting and couldn't bear it one more second. He'd done so much for her these past few months: saved her, protected her, loved her, and made her feel alive again. It was time to come clean.

"Adam, swear to me that nothing I say leaves this room. I mean it! You have to keep everything I'm going to tell you to yourself. If you care about me, you won't breathe a word of this to anyone."

"Go on."

"Swear to me."

"I swear, Terry. And please don't lie."

"I'll be as honest as I can. I can't tell you everything, but yes, we were sent here to gather information about one of our dorm mates. It wasn't Ali, and it wasn't you. It's someone who has some very powerful enemies. I'm sure you can figure out who the intended target was. I need you to know that I'm not a spy. I'm someone who fit the bill and was strong-armed with threats to my family to go along with it. The person who set this whole thing up would stop at nothing to get the people he wanted to recruit to do his dirty work, and that included murder."

He looked into her eyes, which were brimming with tears, searching them for the truth. He took her hand and interlocked their fingers, brought it to his lips, and kissed it. "My poor love. I believe you, Terry, and your secret is safe with me. So, I would suppose all this has something to do with the contracts on the oil rigs?"

"What?"

"You know, the contracts Ali brought back the night of all the excitement. I said I didn't read them, but of course I did."

"Adam, you have to promise me you'll keep all that to yourself. It could be extremely dangerous for you if any of this gets out. Things need to play out the way they're supposed to. No one can know what was in those contracts. I'm profoundly serious about this! No one! Hopefully if everything goes right, in time these contracts will come back to bite the ass of the correct person. I need your solemn promise that you'll never divulge to anyone any of what you read in those contracts. It's more important than you can realize."

"How can that be allowed? There are worldwide consequences in what they're planning. So, we let the world be manipulated by a Middle Eastern king and a corrupt senator who are controlling the oil market?"

"I have to say yes to that right now. These people are dangerous. It's not worth it for you to be killed over oil! Too many people are going to lose their lives over it, and one of them cannot be you! Please! They won't get away with it forever, and it'll become known at the right moment. It may take decades, but it will happen, and it will happen to the right person at the right time. You have to trust me on this. Please! I've stuck my neck out by telling you this. You absolutely must let it ride out its course so that what's meant to happen will happen. And more importantly, what's not meant to happen, doesn't."

"The guardian, what happened there?"

"I…um,…" How does she answer this? She took the lighter out of her pocket and handed it to him. "Jean-René gave me this when he heard about Khalid's investigation and that it was getting dangerous for the three of us. It's a lighter but also a weapon of sorts. Holding it a certain way and pressing a certain button releases these minute ball bearings, knocking the person out for a few minutes, giving one time to get away. I'm not sure how it happens, only that it worked."

"I'm bloody sure Ali must have asked you about that. What fantastic story did he get?"

"That it was the last thing my practical joking brother gave me before he went back to Vietnam. I was to use it to get myself out of an unwanted situation."

"And he believed you?"

"I'm not sure. I think so."

There was a long pause, and he ran his fingers through his hair and rubbed the back of his neck. "Are you married, Terry?"

"Not anymore. Please don't hate me."

"Hate you? Jesus, Terry, can't you tell? I adore you, and my feelings can't change. Do you think I'd stand up to that monstrosity of a man today if I weren't completely and utterly madly in love with you? How could you even think that? I'll tell you what I bloody do hate. I hate that all we have left are a few days. I'm not going to let you out of my sight until I leave Berkeley. We're going to spend every second together."

He walked over to the telephone, took a piece of paper from his wallet, and dialed.

"Who are you calling?"

"The dorm. I want to let them know you're with me and not to worry. I thought Jean-René was going to have a heart attack when you got shoved into the car. I didn't see it happen because I couldn't bear to see you kiss Ali goodbye." There was an answer on the other end.

"Hello, Sarah? Adam, here. Could you do me a favor please, and let everyone at the dorm know that Terry is safe and with me? We're going to hang out together for a day or two. Tell them we'll see them soon, okay? Thanks! Goodbye." He hung up the phone and turned to her. "Are you hungry? There's a family-run deli a couple of blocks away. Would you like to catch a bite? They have fantastic soup."

"Sure, sounds good. If you can show me where the bathroom is, I need to wash the stench of Khalid off my face. Ugh! I can still smell him." He gave her a puzzled look which prompted her to tell him how he licked her face. "He was very creepy and very scary. I can't believe I put myself in such a stupid and dangerous situation." She went into the bathroom and washed her face and hands.

She found a comb and brush and combed her hair over the sink, where bits of glass were brushed out. She checked herself out and noticed a few small cuts on her stomach, arms, and legs. It's funny, she didn't feel them. In the bright lighting of his bathroom, she noticed she was still sporting color on her face from Butch. Subtle, but still there. She needed a shower. Not to wash off, but to get her head on straight under the flow of water.

She came out and Adam was straightening out his apartment. She put her arms around him and didn't want to let go. "Every second I get to spend with you is worth everything that's happened here in Berkeley. I don't know how I could've thought a few hours ago when I was captive in that limo that I should've left on Thanksgiving as we were supposed to."

"You were scheduled to leave on Thanksgiving? But then you would've missed exams. You didn't tell me that. Why would you leave that early?"

Shit! Another cat let out of the bag. Her brain was off today. "Because of the danger from Khalid, we were instructed to leave on Thanksgiving."

"But you didn't. Why?"

"I couldn't. In fact, I not only refused, but I had a hissy fit and took off. I hid until I knew it was too late to leave. I got myself a room and spent the day and night alone. I'm sure I'm in hot water because of it, but I don't care. I wasn't leaving. I couldn't give up the rest of the time we could have together, not to mention leaving like a thief in the night with no explanation would be unfair to you." She held him close, hugging him tightly. "I didn't care about any danger; my only concern was seeing you. I needed more time with you. I love you."

"You put yourself in harm's way for me? I'm right glad you didn't leave then, but Terry, you should have."

"How could I leave without saying goodbye, especially when your mom was sick? How would you've felt if you came back and the three of us were gone? Adam, you've become everything to me. I'd have regretted it for the rest of my life."

"Thank you, Pookie, for doing that for me. I believe that you do love me."

"Did you doubt it?"

"Well, yes, of course. Lonely little chubby lads are always insecure, even when they grow up." He walked over to a drawer and pulled out a framed photograph and handed it to her. It was a photograph of his mother and father with two graduates. One was a very round young man, and the other was very flamboyant looking.

"That's me and my cousin and best mate Wills upon our graduation from Eton. I'm not the one wearing the outrageous socks. God, how I do love Wills. He loves to shock." He let out a chuckle. "I wish you could meet him. Always a jokester. So, do you recognize me?"

"No, not really? It doesn't look anything like you. I mean, even your face is different."

"Rest assured, Pookie, that fat young man with his fat little boy psyche is me. My cousin Wills and I were constantly badgered and teased by everyone – the fag and the hog, that was us. Self-esteem with girls or anything other than music was never something I had. Girls were always bored with my constant talking about music and obviously repelled by my rotundness and teenage acne. Coming to Berkeley last year, I started fresh. I crawled out of the pigeonhole I was put in and found myself and this great music scene. Along the way, I found pot, hash, and speed, which helped me shed the pounds and get the girls.

"When I saw the look on Mum's face last year when they came to visit, I swore I'd stop with the drugs, and for the most part I have, with only some smoke on occasion. The weight loss was drastic, and they both worried and threatened to bring me home. I wasn't ready yet. I bargained away the rest of my life to get this semester here in the heart of the hippie movement.

"I never had girls at my feet in England, ever. I mean ever. I'm sure if anyone from my past were to see me now, there would be no hint of recognition. In other words, I was an insignificant, chubby lad who could hardly believe a girl as fabulous as you could possibly ever love him. So yes, I definitely doubted it."

She looked down at the photo and said, "Well," she looked up into those eyes, "truer words never crossed these lips." She handed him back the photo. "Come on, Chubby. Let's get some grub." She put on Ali's jacket, and he interlocked their hands, and off they went.

They walked to the deli and the proprietors were overjoyed to see Adam. He must've been a regular while living at his apartment and treated him like a member of the family. They were making a fuss over him and scolding him for staying away so long. Watching him interact with this family was very heartwarming. Adam truly is such a special human being.

After eating they walked around and stopped at a store to pick up a few staples. When they got back to the apartment, Christina made coffee and they watched something mindless on television. He lit up a joint and they toked up, enjoying the mellowness of its effects.

"Do these guitars work? It's been ages since I heard you play. Would you play the first song I ever heard you play?"

"Whatever you like, luv. What song was that?" He grabbed his guitar and tuned it up.

"*'Coming Back to Me'* by Jefferson Airplane."

"When did I play that? I don't recall."

"The first day you were on campus. You got off your bike, ran your fingers through your hair, threw me a kiss or two, and started to strut like a peacock, asking every female you encountered, '*Who are you and where have you been all my life?'* Then you sat down and started playing that song. I was sitting with Ali, and you gave us quite a show. Will you play it for me?"

"I must have been quite obnoxious. I do apologize. No wonder you slammed the door in my face. How completely boorish of me."

"Nah! To know you is to love you, and I do. Serenade me, please?"

"Whatever you desire, I'm at your service." He started playing it, singing the words, which were somehow hitting too close to home. They started tearing up, so he stopped playing.

"If you don't mind, I find this song too heartbreaking in light of what lies ahead of us." He looked at her and wiped a tear from her face. "We can't have any more tears today, okay? I know! I'll play some fun songs. Do you like Herman's Hermits?" He played some familiar notes which were the beginning of *"Can't You Hear My Heartbeat?"* and they sang the song together, laughing their asses off. Then he went into *"Henry the Eighth,"* and they went on for a while with the "second verse same as the first."

After ending that song, Adam went into his "performance mode" and said, "Okay, ladies and gents, we're going to slow things down for all you lovers out there. This is dedicated to my special lady. This one's for you, Pookie." He sang *"I Only Have Eyes For You"*. She sat back on the couch listening to the beautiful words of that song, feeling on top of the world. After he finished, he leaned over and kissed her.

"Any other requests?"

"Yes, play *'Misty'* for me," in her best Jessica Walters imitation.

"That is one song I won't play for you. When I hear our song, I need you in my arms, holding you close, slow dancing as we did on our first date." She made a little frowning face, and he leaned over and kissed her. He started strumming the guitar.

She leaned back and closed her eyes, feeling very mellow, taking in and enjoying being in his company. Then his strumming started to take shape. What the hell? Is this…? How could it? It can't be. That would be too crazy. He started to sing the words:

*"When I looked up and saw her standing there,*
*With the wind dancing playfully through her long brown hair."*

She immediately sat up. He continued singing.
*"A chill went up and down my spine,*
*I knew that I had to make her mine.*
*With just one look, she stole my heart from me.*

*I have never felt this way before.*
*Her eyes reach down into my very core.*
*How can I get her to feel the same?*
*When I don't even know her name*
*I ask Cupid to please hear my plea.*

*Point your arrows at her heart,*
*Guide her love my way.*
*Make it so we will never part,*
*And by my side she'll always stay.*

*Please bring her love to me,*
*I ask all the stars above,*
*Please bring her love to me*
*I ask all the stars above,*
*Please bring her love to me*
*From her love, I never want to be free.*

*I'm in love, there's no denying,*
*When she looks at me, my soul starts flying.*

*I need her to feel the same,*
*Because my love burns like the hottest flame*

*Please bring her love to me,*
*I ask all the stars above*
*Please bring her love to me*
*I ask all the stars above,*
*Please bring her love to me*
*From her love, I never want to be free."*

"It's the song I wrote for you, Pookie. I was going to save this for our last day together, but since we're here and I've got my guitar in hand, I wanted to give it to you now. In the middle, before the bridge, I imagine violins playing," and then he hums the melody for the violins.

"Wait! Wait a minute. Are you telling me you wrote this song *for me? For me?"* She was thrown for a loop. Her brain went into a tailspin with a million thoughts jamming at once. That song! It's their song, hers and John's! From the first time he heard it on the radio, John declared it their song, that it fit them perfectly. It was the song they danced to on their wedding day, the song he sang to her every night when he was away. How? Who recorded it? Oh my God! It was "The Time Travelers"! Holy Shit! But she would've remembered the name of Adam Wallingford, right? But Adam said he wrote it *for her*. The thought kept swirling through her head: Adam wrote that song for me! It was written *for me*. At this moment, her heart was bursting with love for Adam.

He stopped playing and pulled her out of her thoughts.

"Adam calling Pookie. Come in, Pookie."

"I'm sorry. I'm astounded, Adam, and so honored. What did you say?"

"I'm speaking about your song. Of course, I wrote it for you and only you. Who else could it be for? Every love song I write from this day forward will be for you. But this is the one that is especially for you, and my heart desires that every time you hear this song, you'll know there's someone out there who loves you very, very much."

"You wrote this song *for me*?" Her heart was about to bust out of her chest. This was her song! It has had a special meaning for her from the minute it was released. She felt it was the song of her life. And he wrote it *for me*!

"Do you hate it?"

"Adam, it means more to me than you'll ever know. I'm speechless! Please, sing it again from the beginning. I want to memorize every note. It's not every day a girl gets this sort of honor."

He sang the song to her while she sat there, incredulous at what was happening, feeling so much love for him. He sang those words, looking into her eyes, and she could feel their truth. She was flabbergasted on so many levels. He finished singing and looked at her. "Are you well, Terry? You look like you've seen a ghost. Was it horrid?"

"It's the most beautiful song I've ever heard, and I can't thank you enough. This is unbelievable! I'm moved beyond words. I can guarantee that every time I hear it, I'll know I'm loved, truly and deeply." She took the guitar out of his hands and set it on a chair. She straddled him, held his face, and looked into those gorgeous blue eyes, and kissed him with her tongue searching for his, kissing full of passion and desire.

"Make love to me, Adam."

"Terry, what?"

"Make love to me. I need you to make love to me, please."

"Terry, that isn't why I wrote this song and played it for you tonight." She started kissing his neck, using her tongue around his ear, kissing his birthmark on his neck. "Pookie, no. I won't do that to you. I'd feel like I'm taking advantage of the situation. Please stop."

She whispered in his ear, "Make love to me, Adam." She took off her shirt.

"No! Pookie, please, you're making this bloody difficult. I know your feelings about this. I cannot!"

She continued to kiss him, unbuttoning his shirt and feeling the flesh of his chest, licking his neck, using her lips and tongue to seduce him.

"Terry, please, I can't. I can't take that from you."

"You aren't taking anything from me. I'm giving it to you. I love you, Adam. I love you more than you could ever know. And I need you. So badly. Make love to me. Don't make me beg because I will." She kissed him again, grinding up against his growing bulge. "Please. We can't waste any more time. I need you to make love to me. I need it and want it so very badly, Adam. Please. If you love me, you'll do as I ask."

"Isn't that usually the line used by the bloke in these situations? Terry, please! You're driving me totally bonkers. It's bloody hard to resist."

"Then don't! Make love to me. Make love to me now! I need to explore every part of you to keep with me for the rest of my life." She started to unbuckle his belt. When she did that, he picked her up and carried her into his bedroom. They lay on his bed, and he slowly finished undressing her, and she stripped his clothes from his body. They took their time caressing, kissing, and using their tongues to probe and learn about every part of each other's bodies. His body was extraordinary, and he felt the same about hers. She felt ready to explode.

"Please, Adam, I can't take any more."

"I don't want to hurt you. Are you quite sure? Because once it's done, it can never be undone, and I have no protection."

"I've never been more sure of anything. Love me, please!"

He mounted her, and after a few thrusts against the virginal wall, he was in. Christina thought she was going to burst. She immediately achieved an orgasm. He slowed down, and they went into a gentle motion. With every thrust, they both felt the thrill of making love to someone they adored. The momentum picked up, and they reached their fevered peak at the same time, with both making almost the same loud moaning sounds.

As they lay totally spent with him still inside her, she held him close, her hands trying to memorize the hollow of his back, his buttocks, and everything her hands could reach. She could feel tears of joy and sexual release slide down the sides of her face into her ears. She didn't want him to see her crying because she thought he might get the impression she regretted what happened. It was very much the opposite.

He raised himself up on his elbows, pushed the hair out of her face and looked into her eyes. She could see there were tears in his eyes too. His tears kept rolling down his cheeks, falling onto her neck.

"Thank you so much for this, Terry. I've never felt so bloody fantastic in my life. All this means so much more when one is in love with the person you're making love to. I hope with all my heart I didn't hurt you. I didn't think I could love you any more than I already do, but right now, my heart could burst because of the fullness of love I have for you."

"Thank *you*, Adam. We have to pack all we can into these next few days, a lifetime's worth. I only wish things could be different."

They lay there in the exact same position, his head buried in her neck, thinking of what will never be.

"Oh my God, Terry, I love you so very much."

"I love you too. More than I could ever express. And Adam?"

"Yes?"

"My name is Christina." He stared into her eyes, tears brimming up.

"Christina, oh my darling! I love you!"

They made love again and fell asleep in each other's arms. They both felt they were catching a glimpse of heaven.

# CHAPTER 42

Stewart Needham and Jeffrey Holbrook, the 21st century back up, had been perfecting a few scenarios of different rescues since they arrived in 1971 in case things didn't go the way they were supposed to or if any of the three coeds were put in danger. Their van was equipped with many items they put together with their expertise and knowledge to get a jump on the technology of 1971. Nothing in the van was from the 21st century. It was all put together on their training and know-how. They were experts, both like MacGyver.

For their most successful rescue scenario, they would simulate a flat tire. Needham was the driver, and this maneuver had been used many times by him in the past. He had been recruited by the CIA right out of college and trained for things of this nature. He had been driving since he was seven years old, growing up on a farm. He could drive anything and could look at an engine and be able to troubleshoot any problems with the knowledge to fix whatever was wrong. He became invaluable for quick getaways and extractions of persons from hostile countries or situations. He was a perfect fit for this operation.

The two men worked together on many occasions and were a great team, with each having different strengths. Holbrook was the techno geek, and Needham was the mechanical mind, along with the skills of a race car driver. They outfitted the van with the equipment they would need to pull off a flat tire and thereby block the road so the target vehicle wouldn't be able to pass until the tire was "fixed," and those needing to be rescued were safely in their hands.

Their main assignment of late was tracking Khalid whose code name was "Candy Man". They knew every move he made and had his home and telephone bugged. The listening devices were located outside of a few key windows and the phone was bugged from the pole. These devices could easily be removed when necessary.

Everything they needed for this mission had to be acquired in 1971. Their van housed the equipment necessary to listen to what was being said. They could park up to three blocks away to listen in on what was going on. They were staying in an apartment procured by O'Connell and in contact with the present day regularly. They were instructed to have no contact with the other three.

"Batman and Robin," as they called themselves, were the ones who found out about the investigations of the three coeds and the plot to bring the two girls back to Zatari. They were able to hear the report on the trio given by the private investigator, Pete See. When Khalid made the phone call to his king, they surmised the plot to bring at least Christina back with him was beginning to take shape. It was then that they made their recommendation that the three return on Thanksgiving.

They had been watching "Cupid", which was the code name for Christina, ever since they noticed her face looked bruised. They recommended the mission be scrapped at that time because she was obviously in danger. Martin Cater wouldn't hear of it. In fact, he seemed to enjoy that she was bruised. They were ready to step in and find out what happened but were told it was under control.

They watched and followed her when she was off on the motorcycle with "Player One", their code name for Adam. She wasn't supposed to be their focus, but the horrible bruising of her face caused them concern. Eventually, they'd find out what happened. Until they all were safely back in their present time, they'd keep an eye on her. They were told not to approach, just observe, only stepping in if the danger escalated. The only time they lost her was the day before Thanksgiving. They had no idea how she was able to give them the slip, even though they were using high-powered binoculars to keep an eye on all the involved players.

They spent much of their time in 1971 outfitting the van and going through the motions, and by coincidence, on the exact same road the actual event took place. All their equipment was disguised to look like regular junk found in a hippie van in case something happened that would cause the van to be under scrutiny.

They mapped out the whole thing and balanced the van so it would be controllable once the flat tire was initiated. Every move was calculated and measured so the van would land in a way that no vehicle could pass on either side of it. They also had equipment and filled syringes to knock out anyone who stood in the way of their success in any rescue.

They were watching from afar when "Cupid" was saying goodbye to "Abu", their code name for Ali. They saw her being shoved into the limo and immediately made contact with O'Connell through high-powered walkie-talkies. "Tesla, this is Batman. Do you read me? Over."

"Loud and clear. Status? Over."

"Cupid's wings have been clipped. Operation 21 commencing. Over."

"Shit! I knew it! Keep me up to date on everything. This rescue can't fail. Over."

"Roger that. Looks like they're heading to where 'Angel' will be walking by the English building. Recommend interception on your part. We'll be watching if you need help. Over."

"Roger. Keep me informed. Over and out."

Glenn raced out of his office and headed towards the English Building, which was not far from his office. As he rounded the corner of the building, he noticed a partially visible limousine. As he came to the top of a mound, he saw Zoe being manhandled by an enormous giant who looked as though he was trying to drag her. That set off Glenn's adrenaline, and with no thought of consequences, he ran right into the two of them, knocking them both over. He grabbed Zoe's hand and kicked the giant in the gut because of what he saw him doing to Zoe.

They took off running, not stopping until they were outside the Science Building. Glenn contacted "Batman and Robin" letting them know "Angel" was safe and told them "Player One" was in hot pursuit and to not intercept him. It would be better for all concerned if Needham and Holbrook were not looked at as being part of this rescue of Christina.

The two agents kept their distance from the limousine, staying behind several cars so as not to garner any attention from those in the following vehicle. Besides, they knew exactly where the limo was going. They had followed Khalid to this airport before, plus a call had been made from his home to the airport notifying them of their imminent departure.

They had weapons of all sorts hidden in the van but would rather use other means of getting the job done. While Needham was driving, Holbrook was preparing a small syringe with a drug that would knock out someone for five to ten minutes, enough time to get "Cupid" out of the vehicle and to safety. Although they'd only admit it to themselves, they were quite pleased the trio didn't make it home on Thanksgiving. They worked hard on different types of rescues, and now that they had the chance, they wanted to be able to see it through.

The limo turned onto the airport road, and the van slowed down to let the target get a little further ahead. Holbrook lit up what looked like a huge doobie but was regular tobacco. Not that they didn't partake of pot, they didn't while on an active mission. They wanted those in the limousine to think they were a couple of stoners who in no way were out to foil their kidnapping plan. They gunned the gas, and the van took off like lightning. Needham had rigged this engine to be as fast as a race car. One would never expect such speed from what looked like a rundown old VW hippie van.

When they passed the limo, they saw "Cupid" pleading for help. At least now they knew she was in the car, alive and conscious. When they got a safe distance ahead, they set the flat tire plan in motion. Needham expertly handled the vehicle, and it landed squarely in the middle of the road, with no room on either side for it to be passed, successfully blocking the passage of the limo.

When the limo caught up to them, their driver got out of his vehicle and walked to the van as the two were looking at the tire. He offered to push them out of the way, but without answering his offer, they asked if they could borrow a jack and a tire iron. The driver went back to the limo and retrieved the necessary items, leaving the keys in the trunk keyhole. He figured they would be safe there while he helped change the tire and be readily available when he returned to put the tools back into the trunk.

He walked back to help the two hippies and started to jack up the van when he heard a motorcycle approach and stop. He leaned over to see what was happening and noticed the driver of the motorcycle was stopped at the limo. There would be dire consequences for him and his family if anything went wrong and this girl didn't get on the plane. His king would be furious, according to Honorable Khalid, if all did not go as planned. He was quite upset with himself that he let the other girl get away, and he would do all in his power to ensure this girl got on the plane.

With the tire iron in his hand, he menacingly approached this guy who was nosy enough to get involved. Too bad for him. Khalid told him they had diplomatic immunity, and this kidnapping was at the order of their king. He must show his loyalty at all costs. He heard the two hippies running up behind him, and that was the last thing he remembered. When he awoke, Prince Ali was gone, and Khalid was in the back seat bleeding, shot in the foot. The hippies were also gone, and Khalid was screaming at him out of a broken window to get up. What the hell happened here?

He felt groggy at first, but after a minute or so he began to feel more himself. Khalid continued barking orders at him in their native tongue to get him to the airport immediately. The driver went to retrieve the keys, and they were gone. Khalid was screaming to him that Ali had thrown them in the grass somewhere and to find them. He looked in the general direction of where Khalid was pointing and found it difficult to see anything because the grass was so high. After about ten or fifteen minutes, he found the keys and got into the car. He started to ask what happened, but Khalid was screaming that they had to get to the plane now!

He drove at high speed towards the airport hangar where the private jet was housed. When they arrived, the plane was gone. Khalid told the driver to inquire as to when and who ordered the takeoff. When he came back, he told Khalid the plane left approximately fifteen minutes ago under the orders of Prince Ali. He was the only passenger. The driver then handed Khalid a taped-up bag with a note on it. He ripped the bag, and inside was his revolver, with all the ammunition removed. There was a note which said, *"You should have known better than to defy a member of the royal family. How unfortunate for you that when we swerved to avoid the van, your pistol discharged into your foot. How inconvenient and troublesome for you. A most fitting punishment for your disobedience."*

Khalid was furious and ordered his driver to take him home. Once there, he'll call his personal physician and have him look at his foot. From what he can figure, he may have lost a few toes and quite a bit of blood. Ali will pay for this. His father will punish him for this heinous act of defiance and treason against his country.

Once Adam and Christina were safely gone, the two hippie men came over and asked Khalid and Ali if they could help in any way. Khalid lied to them and told them Ali had kidnapped the girl and forced him to bring her home with them. With the gun now aimed at his head, Khalid recanted his story and told the truth. Ali asked them if they could find the keys and let him out of the limo. The hippies looked around and found the keys in the trunk and unlocked Ali's side of the car. Needham handed Ali the keys, which he used to relock the car, and then threw them into the grass.

"Would you gentlemen be good enough to give me a ride to the airport?"

"Hey man, we shouldn't get involved. Please don't shoot us!"

"You've no reason to fear me, gentlemen. I'm a prince of Zatari, and this man is my disobedient servant. I need to get to the airport."

"What about this guy? He looks like he needs a doctor." Holbrook was playing along with their charade.

"It was the only way for the girl to be saved. He is an evil man who got exactly what he deserved. Please, I'll pay you."

They looked at each other and did a funny handshake. "Yeah? American dollars? Now you're talkin'! You got it, buddy! Grab your stuff while we finish up the tire."

Needham and Holbrook walked to the van and pushed a button on the tire which made it immediately inflated. They never had the chance to loosen any of the bolts, so the van was ready to go as soon as they lowered the jack. The three of them got into the van with Khalid screaming at them that they'll be severely punished for this.

"Hey, man, are you sure you wanna leave him here? You gonna get in trouble for this? It sure sounded like he got shot."

"Yes, an unlucky accident occurred when we tried to avoid hitting your van. It was most unfortunate. I've warned him about carrying loaded weapons." The two men exchanged knowing glances, for they knew the shot was fired long after the limo was stopped.

Ali could not believe his own ears that these words were coming from his mouth, and his demeanor was so calm. He felt like a man, no longer a scared little boy. By standing up to Khalid and pulling the trigger of his revolver, he felt empowered. He had heard his father say many times that those who do not obey the royal family do not deserve their protection. Devotion and obedience are expected from subjects and servants.

Ali understood that his newfound feeling of power had come because he knew exactly what was going to happen to his beautiful Taraysa and had to save her from that fate. The vision of Butch standing over her was nothing compared to what would happen to her in his country, especially if there was even an inkling that she was a spy. She was right; his country at this time was no place for her. He was forced to become a man, defending and protecting his friends and demanding the respect his birthright gave him. He'll never be walked on again, for now he felt what it was like to have power and control.

He thanked the two men when they dropped him off at the airport and gave them each a couple of hundred dollars for their assistance. He ordered the plane to take off immediately. He removed the bullets from the gun and put them in his pocket as a reminder of this day. He hastily wrote the note, wiped his fingerprints off the revolver, and put it in a bag. He taped it up with the instructions to give it to Khalid when he arrived. When the pilot balked at leaving without Khalid, saying that he was to take orders only from him, Ali stared at the pilot with a look that could have killed.

"I'm Prince Ali. You do not take the orders of a servant over a prince. We leave immediately, and we leave without Khalid." The pilot bowed to the prince and had no choice but to obey the command. The plane took off for home with only one passenger. Ali noticed the plane was set up for four of them. He smiled to himself that he was able to prevent any further harm to the girl he loved and who changed his life.

During the long ride home, Ali was able to think about his future and his plan when he was face-to-face with his father. Ali assumed he'd be furious with his son for what happened, but after much thought, he was able to figure out a plausible argument for his actions.

When Ali arrived home, he wasn't sure what to expect, but he wasn't going to act like a scared little boy awaiting punishment. His father met him as he walked into the palace and was shocked when he embraced him. They went into the king's office for a private conversation.

"Ali, my son, back from the United States. You've done well, very well indeed. But you're alone? As I'm sure you know, I've heard from Khalid, and he quite angrily detailed what happened on your way to the airport. Where's the girl? Would you care to explain?"

"She's where she belongs. I would not let her accompany me here. I know what happens to women here, and I wouldn't allow it to happen to her."

"Khalid was acting upon my orders. Why did you think it was unacceptable for her to accompany you and to defy Khalid and my orders?"

"Father, I wasn't made aware of your desires personally, so how was I to know Khalid was acting upon your wishes and not his own? With all due respect, sir, if you had relayed to me what your arrangement was, I may have been more agreeable to Khalid's plan, but I highly doubt it. Bringing her here would've only caused an international incident with the United States, and what if it was on the whim of a servant? I thought it best to err on the side of caution and not burden our country or its king with a charge of bringing an underage young woman with no travel papers to a foreign country under mysterious circumstances."

King Machmud was deep in thought, letting what his son said sink in. He had never seen him in this light. His wisdom in assessing the situation was unexpected and insightful, to say the least. He thought carefully before speaking. "I see. And the fact that you had feelings for this girl had nothing to do with this decision? Khalid worried she was a spy and was there to find out the plan with Morgan. Have you given any thought that this could be the truth?"

"Yes, Father, I have, and I don't think she was spying on me. And it's true, I do have feelings for her. I'd have enjoyed showing her our country and our culture, but not in the way that was planned. She was more a friend to me than any I've had. She endured much because of our friendship. Causing trouble between our two countries could only bring scrutiny on whatever you and Senator Morgan are planning. I didn't think it would benefit your impending business. Besides, as I was a stranger in a foreign country, she was good company, a loyal friend, and an excellent study partner. I owe much of my success in my studies to her. I didn't think it was a fitting way to behave toward a friend."

"Speaking of which, did you shoot Khalid in the foot?"

Without hesitation, he answered, "Yes, Father, I did."

"You do realize Khalid had been looking after you in the United States."

"Yes."

The king eyed his son. When the young man spoke to his king, he looked him straight in the eye. This was not the same boy who left only a few short months ago. The change in him was unmistakable. A little mouse left only to return as a fierce lion. "Why did you feel it necessary to shoot him?"

"Father, you've always told me that members of the royal family were above all others. While Khalid has been a loyal subject in the past, he's not royalty, and I was being treated as the lowest servant of our household. He seemed to have forgotten that I'm the son of the illustrious King Machmud, ruler of the great country of Zatari, and he was a commoner. When he would not do as I ordered, I warned him first, and then I shot him in the foot. My next shot was to be his knee. I'd have shot him in the head, but then his brains would've ruined my clothes."

The king was bursting with pride for Ali because he never suspected this particular son of his could ever act as he did. He showed his father that he is a man to be respected. He never looked at his son in the same way again. Now they were more equals and that pleased his father immensely.

"Very good, Ali. You've been most helpful to me and your country and you'll be rewarded for your service. It seems this excursion to America was fruitful for all of us. Now, I'm sure your mother is anxious to see you. Within the next few days, we'll discuss your options for other learning establishments. I'm immensely proud of your accomplishments these past few months."

"Thank you, Father. I'll take my leave and seek out my mother and sister. There will be no need to discuss what university I'll attend next. I'm planning on studying at the Sorbonne in Paris. I hope our staff can make these arrangements in time for me to get in for the next semester. I bid you good evening, Father. It's good to be home."

He bowed deeply, only not as deeply as he had always done. He no longer felt fear being in his father's presence. He left the office and went to the living quarters where he was welcomed back by his mother and sister with much love and curiosity of his adventure in America.

Butch Morgan heard nothing of the excitement of what happened with the coeds on his dorm. After Ali left, he went to his room and packed his things. He couldn't wait to get out of Berkeley. He had all the items from his mailbox and packed everything that was there in a very secure location. He knew these photos were his key to further success and had no intention of them getting into the wrong hands. He only wished he had a photo of that bitch's face after he beat the crap out of her.

He checked his own face in the mirror and hated to admit it, but she did a pretty good job on his. His eyes were still blackened, and his nose looked crooked, but the worst part of it all was that his genitals still ached. Once he gets home and gets established, he may use part of the profits from this semester to hire a private detective and find that bitching whore.

After he packed all of his things, he called a cab and went to the airport. His flight was leaving early in the morning, and he decided to stay at the airport hotel instead of rushing in the morning. There were no sad goodbyes from anyone on his floor. In fact, there were no goodbyes at all. Not one person acknowledged him when he left. It never crossed his mind that it might be his fault that he had no friends here or anywhere else.

Because he had none of his drug stash with him, he spent the night at the bar getting drunk. He took advantage of one of the hookers there and paid for a blow job. He didn't get much pleasure out of it because it was painful. It took a long time for him to orgasm, and as soon as he did, he kicked her out of his room. He never knew that she told of this experience many times to countless ladies of the night about the teenager with the crooked penis who took forever to climax.

Needham and Holbrook went directly to the Science building after dropping off Ali at the airport. Once there, they relayed all the details of the rescue to O'Connell, Zoe, and René. René was not at all pleased that Christina was not with them. He had no way of knowing if she was hurt, where she was, or how to get in touch with her.

They were all shocked to hear that Ali shot his guardian. O'Connell was worried this would be something the authorities would find out about, and it would bring to light the time traveler's involvement and haul them in for questioning. The last thing they needed was a report on the day's events. They all needed to lie low for a while. René insisted that the two of them return to the dorm and act as if nothing had happened. Before they went back to the dorm, O'Connell asked them to come to his office to discuss their departure.

"The three of you are scheduled to leave on Tuesday, December 14th, at exactly 2:00 PM. Don't be late! Needham and

Holbrook, your departure back is Wednesday, December 15th, also at 2:00 PM. The regulations on bringing things back with you are not as strict as you can surmise. In fact, I suggest all of you bring some clothing with you as you'll find it's going to take your anatomy some time to adjust back to your previous physical composition."

That perked Zoe up. "Oh goodie! How long do I get to keep this tight young body?"

"For a while. The re-aging will happen slowly, probably eight to twelve months. We've never had women go through before so it will be interesting to see. All of you will be thoroughly examined by our physicians when you get back to your present time."

Zoe's one-track mind was in full force. "Will it be very noticeable? I don't want people to think I was off getting a facelift instead of working."

"You can explain it by saying you're well rested. Now, back to the return agenda. As soon as you arrive back, you'll be examined, and bloodwork will be taken for a full battery of testing. We'll need to make sure all of your bodily functions are working properly, heart, lungs, nervous system, digestive system, and endocrine systems. You'll be monitored for 24 hours and then you three will fly back to the east coast on Wednesday, the 15th around the time that Needham and Holbrook will be coming back through the chamber to the 21st century. The same holds true for the two of you. You return to the east coast on Thursday, the 16th. The lead team is scheduled to meet on Monday, December 20th, 10:00 AM at Langley with Chief Metzger. As the three of you will fly into New York City, you're to report to the New York office and go over your materials so the report you give to Chief Metzger is prepared and succinct. You say you have the proof you need. I suggest it be organized and precise."

They discussed a few things before Zoe and René returned to the dorm. They were worried about Christina and hoped she'd be safely back in the dorm. Zoe couldn't stop talking about how they got to keep their younger selves for a while after their return. René felt uneasy about everything. He wouldn't feel right until he saw Christina with his own eyes.

As soon as they entered the dorm, Sarah gave them the message from Adam and went back to her room to finish packing. She was also leaving that day; however, she was the only person in the dorm who was coming back, so her packing was rather light. Her father arrived in the late afternoon, and they said their goodbyes with promises to keep in touch that obviously would be broken.

René was not pleased that Adam had taken Christina somewhere and didn't leave an address or phone number. It frustrated him to the point of distraction. Zoe kept telling him to stop acting like an old lady and relax. He could not.

"What if Adam tries the same thing as Ali?"

"Tee knows she can't stay, and I hate to say it, but I think Adam knows there's more to the three of us than we're letting on. Besides, haven't you learned by now that Tee is capable of taking care of herself? We can handle what needs to be done here without her."

After Sarah left, it was just the two of them. The door to Ali and Butch's room was open so they went in. All Butch's things were gone so they assumed he also left for home. René closed and locked the door and the two of them removed the surveillance devices they had planted there.

"Do we need to put them back in the Teddy Bear? I don't dare touch him if we do. Tee would kill me. If we don't know when she's getting back, we may not have time for her to sew them back into the bear."

"I think I can slip them back in with me. Since we won't be scrutinized as we were when coming here, I believe I can safely keep them in my possession. And you're correct, who knows when Christina and Adam will return? I don't like the fact that I don't know where they are."

"Don't be such a worrywart! Things will be fine! I know! Let's see if there's anything I can do to take your mind off your worries." She walked into her room and within minutes she was standing in front of him completely naked.

In French, she whispered in his ear, *"S'il te plait viens mon amour. Il est temps de me faire un amour fabuleux. Vous savez que je ne prends pas non pour une réponse."* Which translates to: "Come, my love. It's time for you to make fabulous love to me. You know I don't take no for an answer."

"We have things to do, my desirable tiger."

"Yes, we do. First things first. We need to get you out of those jeans. Then you need to use your amazing body to make me scream with passion. End of story. Let's go. We only have a few more days here."

"Madame Zoe, you're such a bad influence on me."

"Good. Now let's see you use that bad influence."

They spent the rest of the day in the world of passion, enjoying their years of sexual experience in the bodies of their teenage incarnation.

# CHAPTER 43

When Christina opened her eyes the morning after the first night in Adam's apartment, she was momentarily confused. Upon seeing Adam sleeping so peacefully next to her, the events of the previous day and night came back. She relived the thrill at the memory of their first sexual experience together. It had been so long since she felt the tender closeness of lovemaking, and once she got home, she surmised it would be an equally long time before she felt it again, if ever.

She gazed at him for a few minutes, listening to his steady breathing, watching his body expand and contract with each breath. He looked like a little boy, sleeping so soundly on his stomach, hugging the pillow. She couldn't help but look at his uncovered backside. She wanted so badly to run her fingers down his back and re-explore this body, which gave her so much pleasure. She felt stirrings looking at him. "There's time for that later," she thought to herself. She planned on using her sexual knowledge to give him as much pleasure as he had given her. She and John had a great sex life, and she wanted to share her knowledge of lovemaking with Adam.

She carefully got out of bed and threw on one of his shirts. She went into the kitchen and made coffee, scrambled eggs, and toast. She found a tray and brought it in to serve Adam breakfast in bed. As she walked in, he opened his eyes and she was greeted with a huge smile.

"Good morning, my love. What a wonderful sight to see you first thing. What have you got there? Breakfast in bed? My, aren't you the sweet little Fanny Cradock? How bloody fantastic. I haven't had breakfast in bed in years. Thanks, Pookie."

"Who's Fanny Cradock?"

"Probably like your Betty Crocker, only she's a real person."

They sat on the bed with the tray between them, having their morning meal together. They were both quiet. Christina was basking in the glow of a glorious night and couldn't keep her eyes off him. He looked so cute in the morning, with his hair disheveled and a body that would make Adonis jealous.

"I want to thank you once again for the most fantastic night of my life. It wasn't a dream, was it? It was real, wasn't it? Because truth be told, the entire experience can never be topped. I've never felt so much in love and found out how much more it means to make love to someone you love. The mere memory of it gives me chills. I didn't hurt you, did I?"

"No, you didn't. The pleasure was all mine. Now I need to ask, did I hurt you?"

"Pookie, how could you hurt me?"

"Well, I need to make sure. Lay back so I can inspect you."

"What? Inspect for what?"

"I have to make sure you weren't cut?"

"Cut? How would I be cut? Did you find more glass on yourself from the broken window? You aren't hurt, are you?"

"No, I don't think so, but there may have been some diamonds forming up there, and I need to make sure you didn't get cut from any of them."

He gave her a little shove. "Go on! You're so wicked! Such a lovely little imp. I bloody well hope you aren't still angry with me over that remark. That was so unlike me. I think I was upset that I was unable to charm you. Forgive me, how caddish of me."

"Of course, I forgive you. I couldn't resist. In case you haven't figured it out, I'm quite the ball buster."

"Yes, you are, and I love you for it." He leaned over and kissed her. "So, luv, what would you like to do today?"

"Honestly, I wouldn't mind staying here. I'm sure we could find something to do together to pass the time. Don't you think so?"

"Are you being naughty? Oh, I do hope so. I must say, you've certainly awakened our little friend, and we both want to possess you, body and soul."

"First off, I'd never call him your 'little' friend. There's nothing little about him. Secondly, you already possess my body and soul. I'm yours, completely and totally. Thirdly, I am very naughty! Hopefully, we can spend some of our time together with me showing you exactly how naughty I can be."

He moved the tray onto the floor and unbuttoned the one button holding the shirt together that she was wearing. He started kissing her neck, her breasts, and started moving downward, kissing every part of her body.

They made love and for the rest of the morning they lay in bed holding each other, cuddling together, exploring, probing, kissing, and caressing. It was Saturday, and they were both leaving Berkeley on Tuesday.

"So, Pookie, when do you want to head back to the dorm?"

"Can we stay here until Monday? I don't know how much you have to pack, but my packing shouldn't take very long. Besides, here in this apartment, I feel like the world can't touch us. It's you and me."

"Should we let our roommates in on our plan? I'm quite sure they are bloody worried about you. Shall I give them a ring and let them know?"

"No. Not until tomorrow. I don't want to hear any bullshit or demands from either of them. This is our time, and no one is going to ruin it or shorten it. It's already short enough."

As midafternoon rolled around, Adam suggested they get dressed and go watch the sunset at their usual spot and then decide on dinner. They dressed, with Christina wearing Ali's jacket with one of Adam's sweaters underneath. She loved wearing Adam's clothes. She was enveloped by his smell, which to her was like being in heaven. They rode off to their spot and watched the sun set on the glimmering Pacific Ocean. They kissed with the brilliance of the setting sun directly opposite them on the horizon. His blue eyes looked at her with such love that it made her life feel complete.

As the evening darkness began to descend, they left their spot and headed back to the bike. "So, what shall we do for dinner, luv? I must say I've worked up quite an appetite."

"Let's stop at a store and we can pick up some steaks, potatoes, and a few other things and I'll cook."

"Really? You cook?"

"I have so many hidden talents it would boggle your mind."

"I look forward to being boggled. Sounds like a lovely idea. Let's go."

They hopped on the bike, stopped at a grocery store and picked up what was needed for dinner. As soon as they got back to his apartment Christina started cooking. She was making some things she knew could be made without any extra ingredients besides what they bought that day. She wasn't sure what he had in his pantry so she was keeping it simple.

While she cooked, Adam played the guitar and sang her song again. Now, whenever she hears that song, she'll be reminded of the two great loves of her life. Looking at him put butterflies in her stomach, the wonder of new love, one being fulfilled with tenderness and passion. She didn't want this feeling to end, all the while knowing it was doomed.

She set the table and put a candle in the middle, and they ate by candlelight. After dinner, they did the dishes together, had a cup of coffee, and turned on the television, mostly for white noise. Neither was attentive to what was on.

"What do you say we head to a nearby pub? There's one within walking distance from here and they have a fantastic juke box with loads of brilliant songs. Sound okay?"

"Sure! Except I have no make-up with me, no clean clothes, and no clean undies. As long as you don't mind being seen with a stinky, plain Jane with funny hair, I'm game."

"I love you no matter what, and you look bloody fantastic with or without make-up."

"I think you may be prejudiced, but I still appreciate it. Remind me to kiss you all over later."

"Gladly, Pook, and I'll do the same."

"We'll see. I may have a plan for later."

"How intriguing! Now I'll be thinking of nothing else until we get back."

She leaned over and whispered in his ear, "That's the point." Then she gently put his earlobe in her mouth and used her tongue to play with it. It had the desired effect on him. He pulled her close and they pressed their bodies together, holding her tightly. "If we're going to head off to the pub, we should get moving because if we stay like this much longer, I won't be able to walk, if you catch my drift."

Christina got up and brushed his genitals as she did and went into the bathroom to try fixing herself up as much as possible. She wished she had eyeliner and mascara because she cried most of it off yesterday. Her hair was completely unruly, mostly because of the hot-sweaty lovemaking of the last twenty-four hours. She used his comb and tried to tame her locks, but they were in free curl.

At the pub, they sat in a booth and Adam got some change for the jukebox located at their booth. He put his money in and said, "May I have this dance?"

He stood up and held out his hand for her. When the first few notes of "*Misty*" started to play he grabbed her waist with one arm and interlocked their fingers with his other hand and said during the musical intro, "*Come into these arms that yearn to hold you forever. You're in possession of my heart. Can you tell how much I adore you? It's so obvious if only you would...*" and then Johnny Mathis took over with the first three words of the song. They held each other and danced with Adam whispering the words of the song in her ear. When the music changed and got more dramatic, so did he. He swirled her around, sweeping her across the floor, and when the music went back to the original melody, he held her close as they swayed.

At the end of the song, Johnny Mathis repeats the first three words, which Adam replaced with "*And so much in love with you, Pookie.*" Then he did the dip and finished off with a kiss. He told her to stay where she was and went back to the table and played the song again. From that moment on, every time they danced to "*Misty*", he would preface the song with his own intro whispered in her ear, and finish with his personal replacement, stating his love for his Pookie.

While they were dancing, she told him how much she loved his little intro and finish and she'll never listen to that song again without remembering this exact moment. He played the song over and over, and they held one another and moved their bodies in unison on the makeshift dance floor in this quaint little neighborhood pub. With every return to feed the juke box, the patrons would playfully (or maybe seriously) yell out, "Not again!" to which Adam would smile at them and whirl Christina into his arms and whisper his intro.

They kept dancing for about an hour, non-stop. They were ready to head back to the apartment as the movement of their bodies together made them both long for the intimate touch of the other. After their last dip and kiss at the end of their song, Christina whispered in his ear, "Let's get back to your apartment. I want to play a game."

He looked at her with a confused look on his face. "A game? What sort of game?"

"A naughty one."

"What sort of naughty?"

"You'll see."

It didn't take long to walk to his apartment. When they got to the door, he put the key in and opened it. Christina immediately closed it and blocked his way in.

"Before we enter into *my* domain, there are a few rules you *must* obey. Are you ready for my rules?

"Terry, you're killing me."

"Hopefully in a good way. Ok. Rule number one, it's Christina. You may call me Tina, Tee, or, of course, Pookie. But if you're going to play with me, I demand you address me properly. I will *not* be addressed by another woman's name. Is that clear?"

"It's going to be hard because you've always been Terry, but I'll bloody well try. Probably should stick to Pookie."

"Good idea. Rule number two: I'm the boss. You have to do exactly as I say. There are consequences for disobedience. Understand?"

"Oh dear. Sounds intriguing so far."

She looked at him and smiled, turned to open the door, and then turned back to him. "Oh, and I almost forgot. Rule number three: You cannot touch me. Is that clear? I'm the only one who can do the touching. You're not allowed until I say so and only if I say so. If you play by my rules and are a good, obedient young man, I'll reward you with three questions answered truthfully, among other things. Think about what you want to ask carefully because you only get three. Are you ready to play?"

"Let's go, luv! We're wasting time out here."

"When we go inside, you're to go directly to the bedroom and sit on the bed and wait for instructions. Are you ready?"

"I'm more than ready, Te…Christina." When he said her name, a brilliant smile crossed his face.

"If you say so." She slyly looked at him out of the corner of her eye. "I wonder if you are." She opened the door, and he took off his coat and went into the bedroom. She watched him as he started to take off his shirt. "Um…excuse me, young man. I don't recall telling you to take anything off. Put your shirt back on and sit on the bed."

"May I visit the loo first?"

"Yes, you may."

He went into the bathroom, which gave her enough time to go into his room and get the shirt she was wearing earlier. She was in the kitchen by the time he came out. Once in the kitchen, she opened the freezer, took out some ice cubes, and put them in a bowl. Ice is always a good sex toy. It's been years since she played this game.

She put the bowl of cubes on the table and when the bathroom was clear, went in, disrobed and put on the shirt, buttoning only the middle button. When she came out of the bathroom, she picked up the ice, walked into the room, and turned on a small bedside lamp which gave the room a soft glow.

"Oh my God, Terr…ina. What are you doing? What's the ice for?"

"You almost made a boo-boo, my love. It's a good thing you caught yourself. You could have been in trouble. All things considered, I think you're going to be a good playmate." She walked up to him and opened up the shirt, exposing her naked body. He lifted his hands to caress her, but she bent over him and whispered in his ear, "No touching. For now, all you can do is caress me with your eyes. I want to feel your eyes on me."

"This is torture! You do know that don't you?" She put her index finger on his lips.

"Shhh." She removed his shirt and then kissed him with their tongues mingling in passion. Instinctively, he raised his arms to embrace her and then lowered them without touching her.

She started to use her hands to explore his chest. She took her time with every movement she made. She slowly lay him down on his back and began to kiss and use her tongue to probe his torso, starting with his nipples, and then went from his Adam's apple in a straight line to the top of his jeans. She grabbed an ice cube, put it in her mouth, and repeated what she had done. She turned him around and did the same thing down his back, first using her tongue and then the ice cube.

While he was lying on his stomach, she gave him a back massage, straddling him, then lay on top of him, rubbing her breasts into his bare back, snaking her arms through his underarms, holding him close. She alternated kisses and ice cubes on his neck and shoulders and ran her fingers through his soft curls, kissing his birthmark, using her lips, tongue, and ice to seduce him. His moans were telling her that it was pleasurable for him, which is what she wanted. She needed to make love to him, slowly, sweetly, and completely. While she was lying on his back, she kept whispering, "I love you". She needed to show him how much she loved him.

She caressed his birthmark and then turned him over. He tried to talk again, and she put her finger up to his mouth. "No talking, no touching. It's my turn to make love to you. Remember, I'm the boss."

She very slowly undid his belt and removed it from his jeans. "I'm going to keep your belt close by, in case I need it."

"Why would you need it?"

"Keep talking and you'll find out." She unbuttoned his button-down jeans so she was able to straddle him and slowly unbutton them one at a time, rubbing his genitals with each button. She probed his navel with her tongue and the exposed area above his growing penis, repeating the process with the ice cube. She pulled off his boots, massaging his feet, and gently pulled his jeans from his body, using her tongue to taste every part of his legs as they became exposed. She removed his boxers and kissed the scar on his hip from his childhood surgery.

She massaged his genitals and lightly brushed her lips and tongue over the most sensitive areas, kissing his upper thighs, massaging his pelvic area. A few times, he would reach out to touch her, and she reminded him of the "no touching" rule. "It's my turn to make love to you," she whispered in his ear, to which he replied with a groan.

When it was obvious he could take no more, she straddled his penis and lowered herself onto him, very slowly, then tightening her vaginal muscles with every upward motion. It wasn't long before they reached their climax together. Every time they made love, it got better and better.

They lay together in the afterglow of fulfillment, holding each other close, almost as if they were trying to blend their two bodies into one. The only words spoken were the declarations of love they had for each other. Both of them and the sheets were soaked in melted ice and sweat, but neither wanted to move.

Adam rolled over onto his side, leaned in, and kissed her. She'd forgotten so many of the feelings of intimacy when making love to someone, but even more importantly, the closeness afterwards. He ran his hands down her body and started kissing her neck and shoulders, moving to her breasts.

"I'm allowed to touch now, right? I don't want to break the rules. That was quite torturous, very erotic, and completely unfair. What a little minx you are."

"I needed to make love to you. Did you like my naughty game?"

"Very much so. I'm bloody glad you didn't have to use the belt. I got nervous about that."

"I'd never hurt you. I love you and everything about you."

"So, have I passed the test? Do I get my three questions?"

"Yup. But there may be things I can't divulge. Are you ready to ask, or do you need some time to think about it?"

"I'm ready if you are. Actually, I'd love to ask where you learned those fabulous moves!" He smiled, changed his position to lying on his stomach, and hugged the pillow. While talking, he was rubbing her stomach. "I know you're from the future, so I won't be asking that. When you go home on Tuesday, when will you go home to?"

"What?"

"Well, Pook, it's bloody hard to figure out how to ask that one. Ok, what year will you be returning to?"

"I can't answer that one, and don't ask my age. I don't want you figuring out anything. When we part, you need to forget about me."

"You should know that's impossible. Especially after this latest naughty lovemaking game we played. I'll never be able to bloody forget it, or you, so that's completely out of the question. You're forever etched in my heart and mind. I'll wait for you. I'll search everywhere until I find you."

"Adam, you can't for many reasons. Right now, you're young, and maybe I'm your first love. Believe me, there'll be lots of girls who'll adore you, and throw themselves at you, and why not? You're the complete hunk package, not to mention you're like British royalty. If you become a famous musician, groupies will be all over you."

"I'll find you."

"No, you need to find your destiny, not me. My part in your life ends when we leave Berkeley. You need to live your life, find a worthy woman, get married, and have children because honestly, that's what life's about."

"You don't understand, Pookie. I'll have to find you."

"Adam, you can't. Besides, I won't know you. If you found me, I'd have no recollection of any of the wonderful times we're sharing because they won't have happened for me yet. We can't change my past. That's so important. Every day of my life so far has led me to this moment. If things don't fall into place as they already have, I won't ever meet you."

"How can that be? How will you not know me?"

"I'll be part of your past, and you'll be part of my future. Promise me you'll live your life and not think of waiting around for the future. And besides, who knows if the three of us are going to get back to our present safely? Time travel can be tricky, and I don't know enough about it to assure I'll make it back alive, whole, or even healthy. Who knows what this sort of thing can do to one's body? You can't wait for me. Is that clear? That's why I won't tell you what year I've come from. Ask something else, please."

"Are you married?"

"No. I'm a widow. John was killed in order for me to be in a vulnerable place so I'd agree to this insane mission."

"Your husband was murdered? Who killed him?"

"Is that your second question?"

"No, luv, it's not. Shall I ask my second question? Will there be no embellishing on details?"

"We'll see. Ask the next one."

He hesitated before asking. "Why were the three of you selected for this time travel business, especially if you're not a spy, as you say?"

"Well, I was selected because I look like the wife of Prince Ali. I've only seen one picture of her, and it's really kind of spooky, the resemblance we have. It was assumed by the agent in charge of setting up this team that there would be an attraction towards me from Ali. We were assigned the same classes, and with my knowledge of art and living on the same floor, it was presumed we'd be able to form a friendship, which in turn would be helpful when trying to get the necessary information about his vile roommate who I'm sure you've guessed was our target. That's why we couldn't report his attack on me because there's no record of that, and if there was, it may have changed his life and the reason we three are here, and that couldn't happen."

"Well, luv, I think they got that a tad all to cock."

"What?"

"Mixed up, ass backwards."

"Not sure what you mean."

"I don't think you look like his wife at all. She looks like you. Not that I've ever seen her, mind you, but knowing how Ali feels about you, I'd say he was attracted to anyone who resembled you, not the other way around."

"I never thought of it that way. I really hope he finds happiness. Poor Ali."

"Yes, poor Ali, as you say. What about the other two members of your team?"

"Zoe has worked for the CIA in simpler things like taking photos or exchanging information. Because she's a fashion magazine editor, she travels all over the world and is fluent in many languages, so it wouldn't be questioned why she's taking photos of certain things. Our friendship goes back to kindergarten. She was brought on before me and was instrumental in recruiting me, as was René."

"Another piece of the puzzle I believe you have backwards. You were brought on first only you didn't know it and they were brought in to complete the team."

"I don't think so. René was probably first. He was retired with a wife and young daughter. They were killed, but it was made to look like an accident. We think it was for the same reason John was killed. The person in charge of this mission stopped at nothing to get this team. We've no proof but believe that's what happened to our loved ones. Hopefully, when we get back, we'll find the evidence needed to avenge their deaths."

"If you both knew this, why would either of you agree to help such a git! Will you be in danger when you return?"

"Is that the third question?"

"No, but I'll want an answer to it at some point. I don't want to think of you being in danger. After what you've said about possibly not making it back alive, I'm going to worry for the rest of my life that something happened to you on your return."

She kissed his cheek. "I'll be fine. Question number three?"

"Why can't you bloody stay here with me? Please explain that because I don't want to say goodbye to you."

"I can't stay here because I'll die, and not only 'Terry', but 'Christina' on the other side of the country. Two lives cannot be sustained in one time period for more than six months. If I don't go back, I'll be dead within a couple of months, which will endanger my children. That's why I panicked in that limo. I can't risk the lives of my kids for my own selfish reasons. They have lives, loves, careers, dreams, and aspirations. They're the three most important people in my life. I'd sooner chop my head off than let harm come to them, especially for only two months of selfish pleasure. It would only give us an additional two months together, and wouldn't it be harder to say goodbye in death? One way or another, this can't last."

He looked away, his head buried in the pillow. He looked at her and asked, "Mackenzie, Roxie, and Johnny are your children?"

"Yes, they're my life's greatest achievement. You'll see once you have children. When you hold the life that love created in your arms, nothing can match it."

"And what of the love we've created? That means nothing? I mean nothing?"

"You mean everything, Adam. There's no alternative but to say goodbye on Tuesday. Until then, let's live a lifetime with the time we have left."

He moved a curl from her face. "I'll miss your curls and their heavenly smell. This may sound odd, but may I have one, please?"

"One what?"

"One of your lovely curls. I'll keep it with me always. It's an old English tradition, I'm told, that when a suitor was serious about a girl, he would ask for a lock of hair."

She agreed, and he got a pair of scissors, moved the hair from her neck, kissed it, picked a curl from the underside, and cut it. He coiled it on his finger, then put it in his wallet.

"Thank you, Pookie. Now I'll always have part of you with me."

"Can I have one of yours?" He cut some from the back of his neck and found an envelope to put it in. They held each other through the night. The next day, they showered together, which led to another session of intense lovemaking. They spent part of Sunday in a sexual spin, taking advantage of their last day in his apartment, with her helping him pack.

They both jumped when the phone rang. It was his father telling him what time they're picking him up on Tuesday. Adam wanted to leave from the dorm, but they agreed it would be easier to leave from his apartment. The landlord would ship the motorcycle and whatever possessions couldn't fit into a suitcase. They agreed on a time so they could leave for the airport from there. All his belongings from the dorm should be with him.

He spoke with his mother and the connection between the two of them was obvious by his body language and his softer, sweeter tone of voice. He ended the conversation telling her he loved her.

"Mum says to say hello when I see you. She's disappointed she won't get to see you before we leave, but she's given you an open invitation to visit our estate, Grace Point, and see our artwork for yourself."

"How kind of her. Please thank her for me."

"I will. We should call the dorm and let them know you're alive and we'll be back tomorrow."

He gave her the number, and she called the dorm. René answered the phone and started yelling about her irresponsibility. She held the phone away from her ear, giving the mouthpiece the finger. After he was done bitching, she put the phone back to her ear.

"Are you done?"

"Answer me, Christina!"

"Sorry, didn't hear the question. If you think I was listening while you were bitching, you're mistaken. That's the reason I didn't call sooner. You're not going to ruin my last days here. I've done everything I was supposed to, we've gotten what we need, so there's no reason for me to come back until tomorrow."

He started yelling again, so she hung up on him. Adam called right back, and the two of them spoke in French, probably because René usually reverts to French when upset. Adam hung up the phone.

"All's well. I've smoothed all the ruffled feathers and assured him we'll be back tomorrow. I know! I've got a bloody fantastic idea! Let's put all this packing aside and head to our spot."

They jumped on the bike and headed to their spot on the Bay, kissing with the reflected sun shimmering on their faces, making his eyes a luminous shade of blue.

They stopped at a deli for some sandwiches to bring back to the apartment. After they ate, they went back to the pub for the last time and replayed what they did the night before, holding each other close while slow dancing to their song, with him singing the special intro and ending.

When they got back to the apartment, they finished packing up his things into boxes, leaving the rest for the landlord to finish. They were both sullen that night. Their time together was getting short, and they felt it. Needless to say, they hardly slept that night, taking advantage of every second they're able to share.

Monday morning, after coffee and toast, Adam made a phone call and was very secretive about who he was speaking to, bringing the phone into the bathroom for privacy.

"Are you saying goodbye to one of your old girlfriends?"

"I have no old girlfriends. I only have you, Christina."

"I love hearing you say my name."

"I wish I knew your full name."

"Why, so you can find me? If you have to think I'm dead, which in a way I am, or that we broke up and parted ways, that's fine. You need to move forward and live your life. And it has to be without me."

He looked down at the floor and shrugged his shoulders. "Well, I suppose we should get back to the dorm. We have to pack, and I need to make a stop on the way, if that's okay."

"You're the driver. I go where you lead." They cleaned up the apartment, and Christina walked around before they left, taking mental snapshots to carry with her. She could feel tears welling up and tried blinking them away. Adam came up beside her and hooked their hands together as he always does. He turned her face towards his and kissed her.

"Are you ready, Pookie?"

She heaved a heavy sigh. "As ready as I'm ever going to be." She grabbed the helmet and Ali's jacket, and they were off.

They rode through the streets of San Francisco, going up and down the hills, taking in the beautiful scenery. They pulled up to a familiar spot, and Adam parked the bike and got off.

"Would you come with me, please?" Christina got off the bike and he took her hand.

"Isn't this where we got the chain for my key?"

"Yes. I need to stop in and finish my business with them."

They entered the jewelry store and recognized him immediately.

"Hello, Adam. We've got it right here. One moment."

A young woman came out from the back with a small envelope and grabbed the black felt square. While they were talking, Christina was looking at the different jewelry cases.

"I hope you like it. I think they did a superb job on your design. I have to say, it's exquisite." The salesgirl opened the box and took out the piece, and put it on the black felt, holding it on with a long pin.

"Bloody fantastic! Well done! It's exactly what I wanted. Come here, Pookie. I want to know what you think."

She walked over to where they were and saw a beautiful ruby heart with two silver hands holding it. The heart looked broken, with what looked like small diamonds filling the jagged line going through the heart. At the bottom of the heart, at the place where the jagged line ended and the palms of the hands met, there was a ruby teardrop.

"Adam, it's beautiful. Is it for your mom?"

"No. It's for you." He turned her around, moved her hair, and removed the chain holding her key. He handed it to the salesgirl, and she carefully put the heart on the chain. The heart lay perfectly in front of the key.

"Oh, Adam! You shouldn't have. You've already given me so much. I can't accept this! It must have cost a fortune."

As he fastened the chain around her neck, he said, "I've told you before, I'm their only heir, and I have to spend it somehow. I designed this for you. So you will always remember every time you look at it, that you hold my broken heart in your hands. And the teardrop represents all those we've shed over our goodbyes. I hope you like it."

She looked into the mirror and was overwhelmed with emotion. "I'll cherish it forever. Thank you, Adam. Thank you so much." She hugged him tightly.

They thanked those in the shop and headed back to the dorm. When they got there, they got the cold shoulder from René. Zoe ran up to greet them. She immediately noticed the necklace and commented on it.

"We've been really worried about you, Tee. You should have called us."

"Why, so I could be yelled at? I needed to decompress from that whole kidnapping ordeal, and Adam took wonderful care of me. I gotta tell ya, it was scary as all hell."

They told them the story of the rescue and Ali shooting his guardian. Christina was surprised when Zoe said they already knew most of what happened.

"Who told you?"

"O'Connell."

"How'd he find out about it?"

"I'll tell you later, Tee. Right now, you need to start packing your stuff. We leave tomorrow at two o'clock. Do you need me to help?" She was giving Christina signals that she wanted to speak to her alone, so Christina agreed. They went into their room and left Adam and René in the Common Room.

In their room, she told Christina what happened after O'Connell rescued her. Christina was surprised the hippie guys were in on it.

"Tee, they've been watching all of us, including the guardian, since we got here. They're the backup that we never saw. They've been working on plans in case anything like this occurred. The flat tire was part of their plan. They didn't count on your knight in shining armor to come to the rescue, but it worked out for the best because then they were able to give Ali a ride to the airport, giving no hint that they were involved. We thought we might be visited by the cops over the shooting or because the guardian was such a dick. Because of the kidnapping attempt, there's a strong possibility we wouldn't enter the equation, but you never know."

Christina looked around the room and opened the drawers to her dresser. "Zee, what're we supposed to do with our stuff? Leave it here?"

"No, we can take stuff with us. So, did you fuck him?"

Christina started to laugh. "You know, there's no one on earth like you! You crack me up."

"Well? Did you? Come on…tell me!"

"Oh my God! Zee! It was amazing. We've had the most romantic few days together. I didn't think it was possible to fall in love again, especially this hard."

"Is he big?"

"Zee! Stop it!"

"Well, you know me. I've gotta ask, right? Tee, you're turning all red! I guess he is!"

"Stop it!" Christina changed the subject. "Why can we take stuff back with us?"

"Oh, that's the best part. It's going to take our bodies about a year to catch up with our true age. People are going to think we went for plastic surgery. O'Connell said to bring most of our stuff, so we have clothes that fit us. I guess everything gets put in the chamber with us."

"Do I have to sew the bugs back into Theodore Edward?"

"No, René and I have retrieved the devices, and he has them all, including the peace sign pin. Theodore is off the active-duty roster. It'll be interesting to see what's recorded. Maybe we'll find out what Butch was using against Ali."

"You know, Zee, maybe I was naïve, but I never encountered people that were evil before meeting Butch and Marty. I guess I've been sheltered most of my life. I don't look forward to our return. Marty despises me, and for the first time in four months, I'm more worried for my safety than when I was in that limo. Once he has what he wanted from us, I'm afraid I'll be his next target."

"Don't worry about that, Tee. Once he has this mission wrapped up, he'll be too busy basking in the glory of success to think of revenge."

"Whatever. I'm not convinced." She packed all the things she was going to bring with her and looked around the room. Zoe had gone back into the Common Room with René, and Adam knocked on the open door and came up behind her, wrapped his arms around her waist, and rested his head on her shoulder. She put her hand up to his cheek and turned her head and gave him a peck on the cheek. They stood there together in that position, looking around the room.

"Have you finished packing, Pook?"

"Pretty much."

"Today is our last sunset. Let's go and then pick up some Chinese food and bring it back for a farewell dinner. Sounds bloody fantastic, doesn't it?"

"It does."

So off they went. Their last sunset was bittersweet. Neither could stop the tears. Only love can break a heart, and theirs were shattered into tiny shards.

They brought dinner back and shared their last meal. After dinner, they sat with coffee, smoked their last joint, and after a while, headed into their rooms. Zoe and René were in his room, and Adam and Christina were in hers.

Their last night was not wasted. They took advantage of every second. The next morning, the mood was sullen. They stayed in bed until late morning, followed by a final shower together. Back in her room, Christina insisted on drying him off, which led to their last time making love. Their lips were frantically searching for each other. She looked at the clock, and time was running out.

They held one another after making love with neither speaking. What was left to say but goodbye. Tears are contagious and when Christina saw tears in Adam's eyes, she couldn't hold hers back. They lay in an embrace with tears flowing down their faces. This was it. This was the end. They parted today, and the ballad of Adam and Pookie is over.

They dressed and sat on the bed, holding one another. Christina got up and walked over to the bag holding her possessions and opened it. She took some things out and sat back down next to Adam.

"There are a few things I want you to have." She took most of the scarves she bought and handed them to him. "I want you to take these, something to remember me by." Then she opened a pouch, held out his hand and emptied it. All the fake diamonds she bought were now in his hands. "These are yours, especially created for you." They giggled. He handed her the envelope with his lock of hair, which she put in the pouch.

Then she held Theodore Edward. "This is, as you know, Theodore Edward Bear. I was given him when I was a baby, and he's the oldest and dearest possession I have. I've shared all my joys, sorrows, and secrets with him. I want you to have him. Promise me you'll take good care of him because he's the closest thing to my heart, and hopefully he'll remind you of how much I love you."

"Oh, Christina, are you quite sure? You have my word, no harm will come to him, ever. I'll treasure all of these forever." They sat holding each other in silence. He tipped her head up and kissed her nose and said, "Oh, Christina!"

"I love hearing you say my name."

"Speaking of names, would you like to hear my new name?" He had an impish smile on his face.

"New name?"

"Yes, for my music. You know, the solicitors?"

"Oh, right! I remember you saying you can't sully the Wallingford name."

"Yes, so they say. Well, I've decided what it's going to be."

"What is it?"

"If you tell me yours, I'll tell you mine."

"Adam, you know I can't."

"Can't or won't?

"Please, Adam. Right now, our hearts are sad, and our relationship is ending. You may feel you'll never love like this again, but you will. I *can't* give you my full name, and I shouldn't have given you my first name because of protocol. I *won't* because you need to follow where your life will lead and not think about waiting for your life to begin. Don't make this harder than it already is. I'd love it if I arrived home and you were there to greet me, but we'll soon be separated by time and space. If you're going to be a rock star, girls will be throwing themselves and their underwear at you, and why not? You need to taste the fruits of life while you're young. Promise me you'll move forward and live your life. Find someone who'll make you happy, give you children, and a family to love and cherish. I can wish you nothing greater. So I won't tell you my last name."

"Why? Because you think I'll look for you until I find you?"

"Yes. And besides, I've told you before, one must have a hint of mystery about them." She thought he would laugh, but it only caused him to sigh deeply.

"Okay, Pookie. I won't argue with you because our time is gone. I shan't waste it with unhappy words. You know I'm a great fan of symbolism, so my stage name will reflect that. Hopefully, when you get back to 'whenever,' I'm successful, and you'll recognize it immediately. Sadly, I know it won't cause any spark of memory should you hear it beforehand. It is an homage to our Berkeley adventure."

Before she could respond, René knocked on the door. "I hate to say this, but it's time we left. Adam, you said your parents were meeting you at your apartment at two. It's almost half past one now. We all need to say goodbye."

Adam gathered his belongings, and they all went down to see him off. He hooked his backpack and guitar on the bike with bungee cords. René whispered something to Adam, shook hands and they hugged. Zoe gave him a kiss and told him how great it was to meet him. Their final goodbye was heart wrenching. Neither wanted to let go of the other. René was the one who broke it up. "We all need to leave. I'm sorry, you two."

Their hands were clasped as they always were, and every time René tried to pull Christina away, Adam pulled her back.

"Adam, kiss me like it was the first and the last." With one final kiss to last a lifetime, they said their final tear-filled goodbye. He kick-started the bike, put his helmet on, and rode out of her life. As he rode off, he thought, "I'll find you, Christina, come hell or high water."

They went back to their rooms, gathered their things, and headed to the science building. O'Connell was waiting very impatiently. "Glad you finally decided to join us, Christina."

"Please, I'm in no mood for sarcasm. I want to thank you and the backup team for helping with my rescue. I appreciate everything done for me while I was here. I know I'm not the easiest person, and these were extraordinary circumstances. It was a pleasure to meet you. Thanks for everything."

"You're welcome. Now, as I've mentioned, the changes back to your true age will take about a year or so, which is why you're being allowed to take possessions such as clothing back with you. We don't want you to look like paupers upon your return. You'll all be checked out by our physicians for a complete physical with complete blood work to be sure your bodies have 'traveled' home safely. We've never had any problems, but as you two are the first women to time travel, we want to make sure all is well. Right this way."

They followed him to the room with the chambers, each placed in their compartment. O'Connell closed the chambers and started the sequence to send them back. Before Christina drifted off to sleep, she said, "Please, God, get me home safely and help Adam find me." Within minutes they were asleep and headed towards home.

## *Ten months later*

Adam checked the address given by his father. Ali sent a message through Edward Wallingford's office for Adam to give him a call and stop by his apartment in Paris whenever he got a chance. Adam was playing a gig in Paris, so Ali invited him to stop by.

Adam found the apartment on Rue Saint-Sulpice, knocked on the door, and was greeted with a bear hug from Ali. "Adam! So good to see you! I'm sorry I had to reach you through your father's office. We didn't have a chance to exchange contact information when we last saw one another. Please, come in."

"How've you been, mate? You're looking well! I was happy to hear from you. As you can imagine, I've thought of you quite often since last December."

They did some catching up with one another, and what was going on in their lives. Adam told Ali about the progress with his music and Ali relayed all that was going on with him and his studies at the Sorbonne. It wasn't long before the elephant in the room was addressed.

Adam spoke first. "I hope there weren't any repercussions after what happened in the limo."

"Surprisingly, everything worked out well for me. My father was impressed I stood up to Khalid, actually proud I shot him in the foot. Our relationship is no longer strained, and I'm comfortable in his presence. I walked into the palace and told him I'd be going to the Sorbonne. I think he was shocked to find me so changed. I became a man at Berkeley, and I owe it all to Taraysa and you." He paused a moment. "Do you ever think of her?"

Adam turned his face away and said, "Always. I know I promised to keep my distance, but the heart will go where it needs to. I'm sorry I betrayed you." He turned to Ali and asked, "You?"

"The same. She's one in a million, and we're lucky to have crossed paths with her. No need to apologize, Adam. I understand how you feel. I'm thankful I didn't see the two of you together. It would've torn me apart. Everyone knew how I felt about her. She taught me so much and changed my life."

"Mine, too." Adam was quiet for a moment and then said, "It's against my better judgment and I'm breaking a promise, but I'm going to tell you something you'll find unbelievable, but I swear it's true and it came straight from the horse's mouth." Adam started to pace. "I know you loved her too, which is why I'm telling you this, and you mustn't tell a soul. Terry, Athena, and Jean-René were from the future. I don't know how it was achieved, only that it's true.

"I overheard them talking about Professor O'Connell, that he's somehow involved. I know they went to the Science Building when they were ready to leave. After the limousine adventure I confronted her about everything, and when she said your guardian thought she was spying on you, she admitted to me they were sent back in time to Berkeley to get information about Butch.

"She said she wasn't a spy, just a housewife strong-armed by the CIA to accept their mission, with threats to her family if she refused. The other two were the agents. I forced the truth from her because I couldn't take the lies anymore. But it makes sense, doesn't it? I thought you should know."

"You loved her too."

"With all my heart, except now I don't have it anymore because she stole it from me. No, that's not true, I gave it willingly."

"I knew there was something between the two of you. With Butch forcing me to accompany him on his misadventures, I knew it was pulling the two of you closer together, especially after that horrible night. And now we've both lost her." Ali got up, went into another room, and came back with a package, handing it to Adam.

"What's this, mate?"

"A little something for you, in thanks for all you did for me and Taraysa. You saved her twice when both times she was put in danger because of me. Don't try to tell me no. I've had months to think about nothing else. So, this is for you."

Adam took the package and opened it. As soon as he saw what Ali had given him, he burst into tears.

"When I was sent my artwork from the Inspiration assignment, I was told you wanted to buy one of them, this one, in fact. I've put color into it, to make her more alive, and I think I was able to capture the colors in her curls and her olive complexion."

"Do you know, mate, this is the exact moment when I first set eyes on her, the day I came to Berkeley. I looked up and saw this vision, and something struck my heart. I loved her from that moment."

"And I loved her from the moment she knocked me over when I first arrived at Berkeley."

"I wrote a song for her. Would you like to hear it?" Adam sang the song for Ali, which made them argue playfully about which one loved her more.

Adam stared at the portrait and smiled. "I'd give anything to find her."

"I would, too, Adam, anything."

"Maybe between the two of us, we could find her. She told me not to look, and she wouldn't know me if I found her before 'her Berkeley adventure'. I don't even know her real name. Thank you, Ali, for this. You're a good lad."

They discussed more on the time travel aspect among other things and the evening flew by. As Adam was leaving and they were saying their goodbyes, Ali said, "Let's make a pact. If either of us finds her, we promise to tell the other who and where she is."

Adam held out his hand and said, "It's a deal, mate," and they shook on it. He almost told Ali her name but selfishly kept that one piece of her to himself.

As soon as Ali was alone his mind was swirling with the information Adam had given him. It all made sense now. He went into his bedroom, and there were the other two portraits of her from his Inspiration assignment. He sat on his bed and stared at her face.

"I'll find you, Taraysa. And I'll find your beloved art collection for you, too. I need you to know how you've changed my life, and I'll move heaven and earth to see you standing in front of me again."

*COMING SOON: SNEAK PEEK:*

# *AFTERMATH*

## C H A P T E R  1

*December 2003*

Martin Cater sat in his very comfortable private room at an elite Washington, DC rehab center where he was convalescing from hip surgery. In the week before Thanksgiving, he was called to Washington by CIA Chief Thomas Metzger because of the dangers brought to light regarding the safety of the three time-travelers. During that time, the infection of his hip worsened caused by the bullet from the night he and John Pucci had their shootout where John was killed and Martin injured. Much to the displeasure of Chief Metzger, who Martin angered when he overstepped the chain of command to okay the Back to Berkeley mission with the blessing of the United States president, emergency surgery was necessary. Martin was rushed to Walter Reed Hospital where the best surgeons in Washington performed a hip replacement on the Deputy Chief.

For the entire time the three time-travelers were in 1971, Martin was required to be at the Washington office, at his own expense, every Friday for the updates, which were followed by a short meeting on the findings or reports. After every meeting, Chief Metzger reminded Martin that if anything happened to these three, especially Mrs. Pucci, he'll be held personally responsible.

When the reports came in telling of the bruising of Christina Pucci after Halloween it made them all take stock of the dangers and reassess the timeline for the travelers. The smile that showed itself on Martin's face after the report didn't escape the watchful eye of Chief Metzger. He didn't think it was possible, but it made him all the more suspicious of Martin, his motives and methods.

As Martin heard the report, he secretly wished he could've witnessed the beating she'd taken, seemingly at the hands of Harold Morgan. He had no doubt he'd soon get his chance to do the same and looked forward to the moment when he could land the first blow to that smug face of hers. His fists opened and closed just at the thought of it. She had gotten off on the wrong foot with him right from the beginning and thwarted every move he made to get the upper hand. He was quite anxious to exact his revenge on her.

All others involved were concerned and wanted to bring them back in the weeks following Halloween, but Martin argued that this was a complicated mission with hand-picked personnel and with all that's currently invested, it wasn't wise to cut it short. They argued back and forth, and it was decided they would rescind the order for them to be called home early. Then the kidnapping plot became known and it was deemed too risky for them to stay any longer.

With Martin in the hospital, there was no resistance for them to be called home early. They were ordered to abort the mission, gather what they had so far and come back on Thanksgiving Day while much of the campus population was away celebrating the holiday. The direct orders were disobeyed and the three of them did not return on Thanksgiving as instructed. They stated there wouldn't be enough time to compile all the evidence needed to bring back in the allotted time if they left when directed. It put all the agents involved in this mission in both centuries on high alert.

Chief Metzger made sure some safeguards were put into place for the protection of the three of them and could only hope it was enough to keep them all safe and Mrs. Pucci out of the hands of her would-be kidnappers.

Martin was insistent he be kept in the informational loop on this mission while convalescing. He wished Charles, his much-abused assistant was here in Washington to do his bidding. He missed having his little lap dog around to bark orders to and watch him jump through hoops in order to please his boss. He did request Charles be flown in to assist him but was turned down by Metzger, which came as no surprise to Martin. Fucking asshole! One of the first things Martin was going to do once he got his Cabinet post was bring Tommy Metzger down. But for now, he had other fish to fry, mainly Christina Pucci.

His hatred of her and desire for revenge didn't diminish even though all the reports that have come in so far were leaning toward complete success. It didn't matter in the least to Martin. His plan for revenge didn't wane in light of the fact that she obeyed orders and succeeded in the mission Martin had headed. He had the memory of an elephant when it came to anything that even hinted at disrespect directed towards him. She'll pay, and as the time of their return got closer, it became his obsession.

While in his room, Martin was formulating his next steps which included Caveman, the man he recruited at the recommendation of his associate code named Jack the Ripper, who had been reassigned to Europe and unable to finish the job he had begun for Martin. He contacted Caveman immediately after his surgery in the way that was agreed upon by the two men using the secure email for them both. Caveman was put on retainer long before Martin was rushed to the hospital. One thousand dollars a week was the agreed upon rate to keep Caveman available for the whims and duties to be assigned by Martin.

Martin needed Caveman to have access to Christina Pucci before the meeting that was to take place in Washington. Somehow, he had to get her away from the other two so that she would be unprotected to ensure his plan could be carried out. Most importantly, she must not make it to the scheduled meeting on December 20th. Now that he's in rehab, this made his plan even sweeter. What better alibi could he have than being stuck in a rehab center with his doctors and all the staff as witnesses as to his whereabouts at the time of her "disappearance"?

Now he just needs to figure out a way for her to be isolated. He had thought of little else since he began his recovery and rehab. They would be flying back in a couple of days, so he had to concoct a plan rather quickly. And then it came to him! It was brilliant and he was disappointed in himself that he hadn't thought of it sooner. He could have had it all arranged in advance. He needed to act immediately.

He picked up his cell phone and called Professor O'Connell, hoping the arrangements would still be able to be made.

"Professor O'Connell speaking."

"Glenn, Deputy Chief Martin Cater here. Have our time travelers arrived back yet?"

"It's in progress as we speak. I expect them to arrive within the next hour. I'd be happy to let you know when they're back safely."

"Thank you, but that won't be necessary. I trust all will go as planned. However, I do have a favor to ask if I may."

Glenn O'Connell immediately became uneasy. He didn't want to do any favors for this man, but he most definitely didn't want to refuse his request. "What can I do for you, Deputy Chief?"

Martin put on his most sympathetic voice. "As you probably can surmise, Mrs. Pucci and I didn't get off to a good start, which I find to be most unfortunate. She's been vital to this mission, and it's appreciated that she put her life on hold and has undertaken this assignment that was most unconventional, to say the least. I'm sure she'll be very anxious to see her family so I'd like you to arrange for her to be dropped off at the Air Force base located near her hometown of Cheetaqua, rather than having her fly to New York City with the other two. She missed Thanksgiving with her family, and I think it would be good for her to reunite with them before the big meeting in D.C. on the 20th. It could be an early Christmas present for her service to her country. I'd like you to also make arrangements for her to get to Washington in time for the meeting with a car service to get her to the airport. It's the least we can do for her in appreciation for her assistance on this mission."

Glenn could scarcely believe his ears. "I have to admit this comes as a bit of a surprise. I was under the impression that she was mostly an annoyance to you."

Martin let out a fake chuckle he hoped sounded sincere. "You're grossly mistaken, Glenn. You know how it is when one is in constant pain. It's not easy to be pleasant when every movement causes agony. It brings out the worst in people, which I hate to admit, is what happened with me. While I'm certainly no saint, I am also no Scrooge. I'm so pleased with how she has handled herself during this mission, especially as she's had no training. I'd like to make up for the troubles she's experienced. I want to do something nice for her but given our history she may not want to accept my kindness. This is the perfect opportunity to repay her for everything." He chuckled to himself over that last statement.

When there was no response, Martin continued. "Please tell her that it is the wish of the CIA to reunite her with her children as soon as possible, to relieve her mind as she's probably worried about them. You know how mothers are when it comes to their children. Do you think it's possible?"

"Yes, I think that can be arranged. I must say, Chief Cater, I never thought you had a soft side. I'm impressed! I'll be more than happy to make those arrangements."

"Thank you, Glenn. I appreciate your help with this. Please don't mention it was my idea. I don't want her to refuse because she may not want to accept any kindness from me. I've learned she can be very stubborn, and I want her homecoming to be joyful."

They exchanged a few pleasantries of conversation, mostly regarding Martin's recent surgery and convalescence. Glenn was wary of the request, wondering if he was sincere, but pleased to see a different side to this very unpleasant man.

After they ended their conversation, Glenn made the appropriate call to add the stop to the current flight plan. Because they'll be flying home in a government airplane, there wouldn't be any problem making a stop at the Air Force base. It was actually quite simple and the flight plan was adjusted adding the stop at the base. It will be a nice surprise for her that was sure to make her happy.

He made the arrangements for her to fly out to Washington on Sunday afternoon, December 19th with car service to get her to the airport closest to her home and to the hotel when landing in Washington. Hotel arrangements were already made for the three of them at Hotel George in D.C. and along with flights to fly home late afternoon on December 21st along with car service for the three of them to get them to their respective residences from their point of landing.

After Glenn finishted the travel arrangements, he checked his watch and noticed the red light went on which signaled the imminent return of the three agents. He went into the chamber control room, checked the gauges, and adjusted the oxygen levels for each chamber. The travelers should be returning within the next few minutes. He was going to awaken Zoe first because he wanted to speak to her alone without the other two. He had so much he wanted to tell her when they first met in August, but because she had no idea of the circumstances they would share or the effect she had on his life, he decided to wait until her return from 1971. He increased her oxygen level and started the process of awakening her.

At the same time Zoe was being awakened, Martin was emailing confirmation of the instructions given to Caveman, with the address of Christina Pucci and a timeline that was to be followed. By Saturday night on the 18th, she and Caveman were to be in his secret apartment in New York City that was used by him for his sexual escapades with his hookers.

He let Caveman know where the key was, where the handcuffs were and instructions on what he could and couldn't do to her. Basically, he could do whatever he wanted except end her life. That will be the pleasure of Martin Cater. Caveman will be tasked with getting rid of the body so that it's never found. All of this was agreed upon by the two men using code words so none of what was planned was said outright.

Martin figured he could be back in New York by Monday night. He was hopeful he would be mobile enough to fuck her brains out before he beat the life out of her. He would relish the moment when he saw the life fade from her eyes. He has waited for four months to exact his revenge on this bitch and it will be so very sweet. He may even let Caveman hold her down while he finishes her off.

After all is said and done, he will have to let JTR know how everything turned out with his recommended assassin. If things don't go as planned and Caveman doesn't meet Martin's expectations or lacks discretion regarding the fate of Christina Pucci, he will take care of Caveman himself. Nothing is going to stand in his way of a Cabinet post, nothing and no one. He already had formulated a plan if Caveman decides to fuck him on this. He may even take him out anyway. It all depends on how well he performs the tasks at hand. As far as he can tell, all is going as planned. He will certainly sleep well tonight.

As he was about to settle in for the night, an elderly gentleman entered his room. Martin recognized him immediately by his distinctive walk.

"What are you doing here? I thought we agreed to meet in my office in New York."

"No, Mr. Cater. Our agreement was that I would get payment on the day of the return of the so-called travelers, which was today. I called your office and was told you were convalescing in Washington. As it so happens, I was already in this fair city so I am here to collect. I believe this is the date we agreed upon."

"Yes, it is but under the circumstances…"

His visitor did not give Martin the chance to finish his sentence. "I hope you're not reneging on our deal. My client would be most displeased and that could end up being most unfortunate for you."

Martin became instantly angered by this veiled threat. "It would be very unwise for you to start this conversation by threatening me. I can have you thrown out on your ear. I think it best that you get out of my room. We'll finish our conversation when I get back to the New York office."

"Mr. Cater, I see no reason for either of us to be bandying about. My sources have told me that your mission was a success, which was what we all wanted. My client gave you what you needed and is now asking for what was agreed upon. In light of the current affairs of our tremulous existence, it would be wise of you to keep your part of the agreement. I'm here to assure that you do as agreed and at the time you agreed. May I remind you that you don't want to make an enemy of my client? After all, without his intelligence and knowledge of your network's capabilities and resources, you certainly wouldn't be sitting in the position you're currently in with the promise of a cabinet post."

"How do you know about the Cabinet post? Who the hell are you, anyway?"

"Who I am matters not. All my client is concerned with is what was originally agreed upon. Give me that now and it will be the last you'll see of me. Refuse and the information will eventually come my way, but unfortunately you won't be around to see it. Understand?"

Now Martin was pissed. He wanted to tell this asshole to go fuck himself and have him removed but thought it best to give him what was agreed upon. He hated idle threats, but he thought whoever this guy is, his client means what he says. In all the excitement, he forgot about the man whose client was aware of programs and resources, such as the set up at Berkeley College for time travel.

Martin had been unaware that time travel was being used in the world of espionage and that it was one of the CIA's best kept secrets. It was well over a year ago when this man came to his office with eyewitness accounts of treasonous activity of Harold Morgan while at UC Berkeley.

His client had also attended Berkeley and during one of Morgan's drug induced stupors, he bragged that he was involved in some "serious shit with the A-rabs and was going to make a fortune scamming the gas guzzling pigs of America". With the potential of being the Republican nominee to the presidency, his client, who was to remain anonymous, insisted proof needed to be found and the only way would be to go back and get it. It was implied that it was imperative to the integrity of the office of President of the United States for this information to be secured. Harold Morgan cannot run for the presidency and his client, being a patriotic American, will do whatever it takes to see to that end. Proving treason would permanently end Harold Morgan's political career.

Martin asked for the name of the client, but his request was refused. He used all his resources and investigative information to find out the identity of the mysterious client but to no avail. Not being receptive to threats, he tried to lie his way out of giving in to this intruder.

"I don't have the agreed upon settlement with me at the moment. I'll have to meet you in my New York office when I return."

"I can assure you, Mr. Cater, if I walk out of here empty handed, you'll be carried out in a box and much sooner than you think. I will ask one more time. Give me what you owe my client and I'll be gone."

Martin stared his most intimidating gaze on this man, but he was unmoved. He hated to give in because it showed weakness. He thought about it for a few minutes and decided as they already agreed upon a date and payment, it wouldn't be a show of weakness on his part, just business as usual.

Martin asked the man to retrieve the briefcase from his closet, which the man obliged. He used the combination lock and then the key to open it. He pulled some papers out, went through them, looking for what the man had come for.

He took some papers out and after rechecking to make sure they were what was agreed upon, handed them over to the man. "Get out of here now that you have what you came for. I don't ever want to see your face again."

The man looked over the materials, folded them neatly and put them in the inside breast pocket of his suit jacket and walked out of the room without another word spoken.

Caveman heard the sound of his laptop alerting him to an email from Martin. This laptop was used exclusively for the purpose of his communications with the CIA Deputy Chief. He read the instructions and replied that he would not disappoint and was looking forward to finishing this job. In addition to his one thousand dollar a week retainer, he's to be paid half a million dollars, non-negotiable, with one-half paid up front and put in his account immediately. Martin knew getting her to the appointed place in New York would take some expertise and was willing to pay handsomely for it. Martin made it clear she could be roughed up as much as desired, sexually abused in any manner, but the final blow (pardon the pun) would come from him. Caveman was told to use restraint so she would be alive and conscious when Martin arrived. He was sure he could manage that.

He got his backpack out from the closet and started to pack what he would need. He looked through his various passports and IDs and selected an alias to use for this job if needed. He grabbed his binoculars, lock picking instruments, glass cutter, a 9mm Beretta and a small 22 caliber pistol with an ankle holster along with enough rounds of ammunition for this particular job. He didn't think he would have to fire either gun but needed to be prepared just in case he did. He packed a sack along with rope, handcuffs, bungee cords and a little something to keep things quiet. He packed his extra charger so his blackberry with the built-in camera will be charged when he needs it. Cater wanted proof of her capture before wiring the second half of the money to his account. That could be arranged very easily.

He had a car at his disposal and would drive to her hometown. According to Cater, she should get home sometime Wednesday night so he would need to be there by Friday morning. That should give him a chance to familiarize himself with her comings and goings and give her a chance to catch up with her children and get the family visits out of the way. He was not to deviate from his direct orders and go rogue as was his purported reputation.

He was to watch the house for as long as it takes to enable him to apprehend her when she was alone. Her children may be around because she would just be getting back so he'll need to be patient. There were to be no witnesses. The last thing he wanted was to have a confrontation with her State Trooper son-in-law. Orders are that no one gets hurt, there can be no witnesses and no event that will cause law enforcement to enter the picture. She is to just disappear. That's the easiest part.

It was vitally important that he pull this off without a hitch. Not only on a personal level but success with this will heighten his credibility with the world's spy network, which is something that would be to his advantage. Martin Cater is a powerful man in global intelligence and if Caveman can do what he was assigned, the sky is the limit in his future. He was banking on the fact that if this assignment is triumphant, it will lead to bigger and better things for himself. Martin Cater is just a steppingstone in his bid for reaching new heights in the world of espionage. Hopefully, when all is said and done, he'll be able to use his expertise to remove the shadow that has been hanging over him and show his experience and talents are needed in the big picture of the world spy game.

He was currently in his New York City residence, so he decided to take the subway to the address given by Cater where he was to bring Christina Pucci. He wanted to familiarize himself with the surroundings, the building, the layout, the neighborhood's atmosphere, and type of residents. While there he was going to locate the key and check out the apartment. He needed to acquaint himself to the rooms and use his memory to be able to make future plans. He threw a few things he may need into a small backpack and headed out.

When he got to the address given by Cater, he was quickly able to find the key in its secure hiding place. He put on latex gloves, entered the apartment, and started taking photos with the blackberry. Everything was very neat, which was surprising. He expected the apartment to be in a state of disarray, which was not the case. Looking around he found a bill for a cleaning service marked "paid in full". He took of photo of it so he could investigate the cleaning company. Always pays to find out as much as you can about a client, especially one as distasteful as Martin Cater. Kindred spirits, that's what Martin called the two of them. He chuckled to himself.

As he continued his search of the apartment, he found the handcuffs, brass knuckles, and some nasty looking dildos. There were no dishes, pans, or silverware with the exception of some carving knives, filleting knives, and a couple of chef knives. He sprayed some luminol to see if there were any traces of blood in any of the sinks and found minute traces. There were also traces around the bed.

There was very little furniture with the bedroom being the only room with any furnishings. Caveman surmised this was Cater's sick sexual hideaway. It was also the planned place of the demise of Christina Pucci. He took an instrument out of his backpack and began scanning the apartment for surveillance devices, which he found there were none. That was a relief. He didn't want Cater to know he had made a preliminary visit to the apartment that is to become the scene of the crime. He had no intention of giving Cater the upper hand in any way, shape, or form. He took photos of all the rooms, the bed, and the drawer with the "toys" in it.

When he felt he covered all the bases in his groundwork research for the events of the next week, he locked the apartment and put the key back in its secure location. He exited the building and walked around the neighborhood, scouting out businesses that may be open when his scheduled return occurs and noted their hours of operation. He made mental snapshots of his surroundings so he would be able to pull out information as it was needed regarding the area around the apartment building.

The cold December wind started to blow a freezing blast against the man. He put his collar up, tightened his scarf around his neck, took a knit cap out of his jacket pocket, and walked to the nearest subway entrance. Overall, it had been a very productive day. Now it's on to Central New York and his chance to show his worth to Martin Cater.

The package was delivered to Chief Metzger approximately 2 weeks after Martin Cater was rushed to Walter Reed for hip replacement. Right before the surgeon entered the operating room, Metzger took him aside and informed him that as a matter of global security, all foreign particles found in the hip of Martin Cater were to be sent to the Washington CIA office to his attention for analysis.

When the doctor informed the Director that he was not at liberty to do that without the consent of the patient who was now under anesthesia, Metzger stated that according to Cater, he received the injury from a detonated IED and it was of the utmost importance that the CIA have access to the fragments in order to try to pin down who was responsible and if it was a terrorist cell. He made a most convincing argument and the doctor reluctantly acquiesced.

Metzger opened the safe in his office and retrieved the envelope that held the items that were taken from Martin Cater's hip. The analysis of the materials stated that all metal removed during the surgery were particles of ammunition from a 38 caliber pistol. None of the analyzed materials seemed to be from an IED. One piece in particular was a partial bullet fragment that he was sure could be matched to a gun, but he had to find the gun and the circumstances of the injury to Martin.

He was certain if the gun was found, the owner was most likely dead, probably killed by Martin. He had some hunches on who the gun had belonged to and who the person was who put those fragments in Cater's hip. The CIA Chief had looked into the communications of Martin Cater before his injury, but he had covered his tracks very well. Nothing seemed to fit the explanation given by Cater as to the chain of events that let up to his injury and there was no documentation or report of any IEDs detonated by an agent either here or abroad.

He rolled the bullet fragment in his hand, possibly hoping for some revelation from the piece of metal, but it was not forthcoming. At least he was one step closer to getting to the bottom of the pile of bullshit Cater had laid at their feet. His sixth sense kept telling him that Operation Berkeley was tied into this piece of metal in his hands and he was not going to stop investigating until he got the answers he was looking for.

He pulled out the dossiers of the three time-travelers once again and laid the three files on his desk. He knew the puzzle began and ended with these three. Why these three? Why was Cater so hell bent on these three for this assignment? Martin's assistant Charles had been instructed to send copies of the files that Martin had on them. Metzger has been going over their files and two things were evident. Christina Pucci and René Barrineau's lives were thrown into turmoil with the deaths of her husband and his family, and these files did not possess what he was looking for. He knew Martin was much more thorough when picking out his teams and these are grossly incomplete.

His gut told him that Martin was responsible for the destruction of these two families, but there was no proof, at least not yet. He needed to find out if this bullet fragment came out of John Pucci's gun. It was a hunch that had been nagging at him. From what he knew of John Pucci from the FBI files he had been given; he would never have let his wife be a part of this dangerous undertaking. The only way would have been over his dead body, and he believed Martin knew that and acted accordingly. If the markings on the fragment match Pucci's gun then he'll have Martin dead to rights.

He contacted the FBI regarding the gun and was told it was given to his widow along with John Pucci's other possessions that were in his office. He needed to get that gun so that it could be tested. He thought about contacting O'Connell and having him reroute the plane so she could stop at her home before coming to Washington, but he thought that after the harrowing events Christina Pucci endured, he should wait until after they go over the findings. With security being what it is after 9/11, he thought it may be easier for her to not have to endure airport security questioning the gun in her suitcase. Even if he notified the airlines, protocol needed to be observed. They can discuss it when she's in Washington. Martin Cater is not going anywhere for the time being, especially if this mission is successful and a presidential assignment awaited him.

His private phone started to ring. There were only three people who had access to this number. He hoped it was the call he was expecting. He looked at the caller ID and flipped it open.

"Talk to me." The person on the other end spoke for about three minutes. "I see. Very good. You know what to do. We'll continue this discussion when you arrive back in Washington." He flipped the phone shut. He went back to his desk and resumed his perusal of the files and wondered how all of this was going to end.

## Acknowledgments

I would like to thank my husband Frank, my son Frank, my sister Pamela Fialkoff, and bestie Nina Haritos for the extra eyes that were needed to help with proofreading. Their input was greatly appreciated. Thank you to Mark Malatesta, who gave given me some excellent advice on what my manuscript needed, and a big thank you to Art Torsone who has guided me through the publishing process. And the chipmunk who inspired and delighted me with its antics.